READER'S DIGEST
SELECT EDITIONS

READER'S DIGEST

The condensations in this volume
are published with the consent of the authors
and the publishers © 2008 Reader's Digest.

www.readersdigest.co.uk

The Reader's Digest Association Limited
11 Westferry Circus Canary Wharf London E14 4HE

For information as to ownership of
copyright in the material of this book,
and acknowledgments, see last page.

Printed in Germany
ISBN 978 0 276 44288 9

SELECTED AND CONDENSED
BY READER'S DIGEST

THE READER'S DIGEST ASSOCIATION LIMITED, LONDON

CONTENTS

C.J. Box has a large following for his 'Joe Pickett' series in his native America and with this, his first stand-alone novel, is poised to win many UK fans. Set in an area of Idaho nick-named Blue Heaven, after the numerous LA police officers who retire there, the story begins when a ten-year-old girl and her brother witness a shooting in the woods. It's just the tip of an iceberg of crime and, having stumbled across the incident, the children are in mortal danger from the moment they go on the run.

If you haven't yet come across C. J. Sansom, start here—and enter a vivid recreation of Tudor times in which you can almost see, touch and smell the settings, both in and outside Henry VIII's court. While the king is preoccupied with wooing Catherine Parr, those who want a return to Catholicism are plotting against him. And, with religious feelings running high, Matthew Shardlake, lawyer and master of detection, is in pursuit of a serial killer who, bizarrely, is drawing his warped inspiration from the Book of Revelation . . .

NOTHING TO LOSE

LEE CHILD

325

Jack Reacher is on the road again, this time in Colorado, where he finds himself ousted from the town of Despair for no better reason than that the locals don't like the look of him. In Reacher's view, that's enough to justify some unofficial snooping around. First off, he wants to know what's inside the huge, high-walled compound on the edge of town. And why does a plane fly out and back every evening? Why, above all, are the local police so keen to send him away? What are they trying to hide?

Part love story, part moral tale, this debut novel is funny and touching by turns, reminding us that wealth doesn't always equate to happiness, or a high IQ to being smart. The thirty-one-year-old hero, Perry, may be a little slow but he's certainly not stupid. So, when he wins the state lottery and suddenly finds himself with a lot more money—and devoted relatives—than he could have dreamed possible, at least he's able to work out, with the help of his true friends, what's really important for a happy future.

LOTTERY

PATRICIA WOOD

461

Patricia Wood

BLUE HEAVEN

C. J. BOX

Two kids . . .

One murder that they should never
have seen . . .

For Annie and William Taylor, the
only safe place to be is well away
from anyone who might be a part
of what they've just witnessed . . .

But who can they trust?

Day One: Friday

If twelve-year-old Annie Taylor had not chosen to take her little brother William fishing on that particular Friday afternoon in April during the wet North Idaho spring, she never would have seen the execution or looked into the eyes of the executioners. But she was angry with her mother.

Before they witnessed the killing, they were pushing through the still-wet willows near Sand Creek, wearing plastic garbage bags to keep their clothes dry. Upturned alder leaves cupped pools of rainwater from that morning, and beaded spider webs sagged between branches. The ground was spongy in the forest and sloppy on the trail. Their shoes made sucking sounds as they slogged upstream.

Annie and William had left their home on the edge of town, hitched a ride for a few miles with Fiona, the mail lady, and had been hiking for nearly two hours, looking in vain for calm water.

'Maybe this wasn't such a good idea,' ten-year-old William said, raising his voice over the liquid roar of the creek.

Annie stopped and turned to her brother. A long fly rod poked out from beneath the plastic bag he wore. 'You said you wanted to go fishing, so I'm taking you fishing.'

'But you don't know anything about it,' William said, his eyes widening and his lower lip trembling.

'William, don't cry.'

He looked away. She knew he was trying to staunch it; she could tell by the way he set his mouth. He hated that he cried so easily, that his emotions were so close to the surface. Annie didn't have that problem.

'How many times did Tom tell you he was taking you fishing?' she asked.

William wouldn't meet her eyes. 'A bunch,' he said.

'How many times has he taken you?'

'You know,' he said sullenly. 'But I sort of like him.'

Annie said, 'I sort of don't.'

'You don't like anybody.'

Annie started to argue, but didn't, thinking: He may be right. 'I like *you* enough to take you fishing even though I don't know how to fish. Besides, how hard can it be if Tom can do it?'

An impudent smile tugged at his mouth. 'Yeah, I guess.'

'Look,' she said, raising her plastic bag to show him she was wearing Tom's fishing vest. She had taken it without asking. 'This thing's filled with lures and flies and whatever. We'll just tie 'em to your line and throw 'em out there. The fish can't be much smarter than Tom, so how hard can it be?'

That was when they heard a motor rev and die, the sound muffled by the roar of the foamy water.

THE BETRAYAL OCCURRED that morning when Tom came downstairs and asked, 'What's for breakfast?' Annie and William were at the table dressed for school, eating cereal. Tom asked his question as if it were the most natural thing in the world, but it wasn't. Tom had never been in their home for breakfast before, had never stayed over. He was wearing the same wrinkled clothes from the night before, when he'd shown up after dinner to see their mom. This was new territory for Annie and she didn't want to explore it.

'Where's your mom keep the coffee?' Tom asked.

'On the counter, in that canister thing,' William said, his eyes wide.

Tom repeated 'canister thing' to himself with good humour and set about making a pot of coffee.

Annie bored holes into the back of his shirt with her eyes. Tom was big, buff, always fake-friendly, she thought. She'd never seen him like this— dishevelled, sloppy, talking to the two of them like they were real people.

'What are you doing here?' she asked.

He turned his head. His eyes were unfocused, bleary. 'Making coffee.'

'No. I mean in my house.'

'Your house? I thought it was your mother's house,' Tom said. 'Is this *it* for breakfast?' He held up the cereal boxes.

'There's toast,' William said, his mouth full. 'Mom makes eggs sometimes. And pancakes.'

Annie glared at her brother with snake eyes.

'Maybe I'll ask Monica to make me some eggs,' Tom mumbled. He poured a cup of coffee before it filled the carafe. Errant drips sizzled on the hot plate. He came to the table and sat down.

'That's Mom's chair,' Annie said.

'She won't mind,' he said, flashing his false, condescending smile. He turned to William. 'School, eh?' He reached out and tousled the boy's hair. 'Too bad you can't take the day off and go fishing with me. I got into some nice ones last night before I came over. Fifteen-, sixteen-inch trout. I brought a few to your mom for you guys to have for dinner.'

'I want to go,' William said, swelling out his chest. 'I've never gone fishing, but I think I could do it.'

'You bet you could, little man.' Tom gestured towards the cluttered mudroom off the kitchen where he'd stored his fishing vest and fly rod. 'I've got another rod in my truck you could use.'

Suddenly, William was squirming in his chair, excited. 'Hey, we get out of school early today! Maybe we could go then?'

Tom looked to Annie for clarification.

'Early release,' she said. 'We're out at noon.'

Tom pursed his lips and nodded, his eyes dancing, now totally in control of William. 'Maybe I'll pick you up and take you after school, then. I'll ask your mom. D'you want to go, too, Annie?'

She shook her head quickly. '*No*.'

'You need to ease up a little,' Tom told her, smiling with his mouth only.

'You need to go home,' she replied.

Tom was about to speak when her mother came downstairs, her head turned away from the kitchen and towards the front door. Annie watched her walk through the living room and part the curtains, expecting, Annie thought, to confirm that Tom's vehicle was gone. When it wasn't, she turned in horror and took it all in: Tom, Annie and William at the kitchen table.

'*Tom*,' her mother said. 'Don't you need to get to work?'

Tom was a UPS driver. Annie was used to seeing him in his brown uniform after work. His shirt and shorts were extra tight.

'Yup.' Tom stood quickly. 'I better get going, kids. I'll be late.'

Annie watched him and her mother exchange glances as he picked up his shoes and hurried to the door. She thanked God there was no goodbye kiss.

'Mom,' William said, 'Tom's taking me fishing after school!'

'That's nice, honey,' his mom said vacantly.

'Go brush your teeth,' Annie said to William. 'We've got to go.'

William bounded upstairs.

Annie glared at her mother, who said, 'Annie . . .'

'Are you going to marry him?'

Her mother sighed, seemed to search for words. She raised her hands slowly, then dropped them to her sides as if the strings had been snipped.

That answered Annie's question. 'You told me . . .'

'I *know*,' her mother said impatiently, tears in her eyes. 'It's hard for you to understand. Someday you'll see, maybe.'

Annie got up from the table and took her bowl and William's to the sink. 'Oh, I understand,' she said as she rinsed them out. 'But William doesn't. He thinks he's got a new dad.'

Her mother took a sharp breath as if Annie had slapped her. But Annie didn't care.

'We'll talk later,' her mother said.

Annie avoided her, and went out through the mudroom to wait for William in the yard. She knew her mom would be heartbroken because she hadn't kissed her goodbye. Too bad, Annie thought. She's been kissed enough lately.

AT NOON, Annie waited with William at the front of the school. They looked for Tom's pick-up and didn't see it. When a UPS truck came down the block, William pumped his fist and growled, '*Yes!*'

But Tom wasn't driving the truck, and it didn't slow down.

After they got home, and after taking Tom's fishing rod and vest, they walked along the damp shoulder of the state highway out of town. Annie knew there was a creek up there somewhere. A woman driving a little yellow pick-up pulled over in front of them.

'Where are you two headed with such dogged determination?' she asked in a high-pitched, little-girl voice. Annie disliked her immediately. She was one of those wide, squat older women who thought they were young and pert.

'Fishing,' Annie said. 'Up ahead, on the creek.'

The woman said her name was Fiona, and she delivered rural mail, and was going that direction if they needed a ride. William shook his head no, but Annie said, 'Thank you.'

While they drove deep into the forest and began to see glimpses of a stream through the trees, Fiona never stopped talking. She seemed determined to convince them that delivering mail was a very important job and not just anybody could do it. Her perfume was overpowering. Annie threw an elbow at William, who was pinching his nose shut.

'Can you let us off here?' Annie asked at no particular landmark except that she could see the creek.

'Are you sure this is OK with your folks?' Fiona asked, well after the time she should have.

'Sure,' Annie lied.

They thanked her and got out. William was concerned that the fish would be able to smell the perfume on him now, but Annie convinced him fish couldn't smell. Not that she knew anything about fish.

MAYBE, ANNIE THOUGHT, the men didn't notice William and her because the dark green plastic they wore over their clothes blended in so well with the heavy brush. Maybe the men had seen no other vehicle and assumed no one else was there. But Annie could certainly see *them*: four men parked in a white SUV in a campsite space.

Everything was wet and dark under the dripping canopy of trees. Other than the white car, the campsite looked empty. There was a picnic table next to the SUV, and a low black fire pit.

Annie watched as the driver got out, looked around the campsite, then turned back to the vehicle. He was middle-aged or older, lean, fit and athletic in his movements. He had short white hair and a tanned, thin face. Three more doors opened and three more men climbed out. They wore casual rain jackets; one wore a baseball cap. The man in the ball cap put a six-pack of beer on the table, twisted the tops off four bottles and offered them around. The men nodded and smiled and talked. Annie couldn't hear what they said because of the sound of the creek behind her.

She felt William tugging on her arm through the plastic. He gestured back to the path and she gave him a *just-a-minute* nod.

What happened next was terrifying.

The Driver circled the group of men, as if returning to the car, then he suddenly wheeled and jabbed a finger into the chest of a wavy-haired man and said something harsh. The wavy-haired man stumbled back, obviously surprised. As if a signal had been given, both the Ball Cap Man and a tall, dark man stepped back to stand shoulder to shoulder with the Driver, facing down the wavy-haired man, who pitched his beer bottle aside and held his hands out, palms up, in an innocent gesture.

'Annie . . .' William pleaded.

She saw the Dark Man pull a pistol from behind his back, point it at the Wavy-Haired Man and fire three times, *pop-pop-pop*. The Wavy-Haired

Man staggered back, until he tripped over the fire pit and fell into the mud.

Annie caught her breath and her heart seemed to rush up her throat. She felt a sharp pain in her arm, and for a second she thought that a stray bullet had struck her, but when she glanced down she saw it was William's two-handed grip. He had seen what happened, too.

'*Annie, let's get out of here!*' William cried.

She started to back-pedal blindly, towards the creek. At the water's edge, she looked over her shoulder, realising they had lost the path. 'No,' she yelled at William. 'Not this way. Let's get back on the trail!'

He turned to her, panicked, his face drained of colour. Annie reached for his hand and tugged him along, crashing through the brush. When they reached the path, she looked back towards the campsite. All three men stood over the Wavy-Haired Man, firing pistols into his body. *Pop-pop-pop-pop.*

Suddenly, as if Annie's own gaze had drawn him, the Driver looked up. Their eyes locked and Annie felt something like ice-cold electricity shoot through her. It burned the tips of her fingers and toes and momentarily froze her shoes to the ground.

William screamed, '*He sees us!*'

SHE RAN LIKE she had never run before, pulling her brother along behind her, yelling, 'Stay with me!'

They kept to the trail, which paralleled the lazy curves of Sand Creek. The stream was on their left, the dark forest on their right. Wet branches raked her face and tugged at her clothing as she ran. She could hear her own screams as if someone else was making them.

Pop-pop. A thin tree in front of them shook from an impact. The men were shooting at them.

William was crying, but he was keeping up. He gripped her hand so tightly she could no longer feel her fingers. Somewhere, she had lost a shoe in the mud, and her left foot was freezing. How far were they from the road? She couldn't guess.

William jerked to a stop so suddenly that Annie was pulled backwards, falling. Had one of the men grabbed him?

No, she saw. His fly rod had been caught between the trunks of two trees. He was trying to pull it free.

'Drop it, William!' she cried. 'Just drop it!'

He continued to struggle, his face twisted with determination.

'LET GO!' she screamed, and he did.

As she got back to her feet she saw a shadow pass in the trees on their right. It was the Ball Cap Man, and he had apparently found a parallel trail that might allow him to get ahead and cut them off.

'Wait, William,' she said. 'We can't keep going this way. Follow me.'

She pushed herself through heavy, wet undergrowth, straight at the path she had seen the man running on. She plunged across it between two gnarled wild rosebushes, pulling William behind her.

They were now travelling directly away from the river. Annie let go of her brother's hand, and the two of them scrambled over downed logs and through masses of dead and living brush further into the shadows. It got quieter, and at one point they heard a shout below them, somewhere in the trees. '*Where did they go, goddammit?*'

She stopped and leaned back against a massive pine. William collapsed next to her, and for a few minutes the only sound was the steady dripping of the trees and their winded breath.

Annie looked down at her brother. His clothes were wet and torn. His face was pale, streaked with dirt. 'I'm sorry I brought you here,' she said. 'I didn't know what I was doing.'

'They killed that man,' William said. 'They shot him and shot him again.'

She didn't say, *They'll do the same to us*. Instead: 'If we keep going in this direction, we should find the road.'

'What if they're already up there?'

She shrugged, sighed. 'I don't know.'

'They just kept shooting him,' he said. 'I wonder what he did to make them so mad?'

THEY DIDN'T SEE the road so much as sense an opening in the canopy ahead. Annie made William squat down in the wet brush and they remained still. Then she thought she heard a motor. She pushed through the brush into the grass near the edge of the road and felt a twinge of relief.

William crawled up next to her. 'What are we doing?'

'We're going to wait until we hear a car. When it gets close, we're going to jump up and try to get a ride to town.'

'What if it's the white car?' he asked.

'Then we keep hiding,' she said.

'I thought you heard something.'

'I thought I did. Maybe not.'

'Hold it,' he said, raising his head. 'I hear it, too.'

The sound slowly rose, the baritone hum of a motor spiced by the crunch of gravel beneath tyres. Annie inched forward, parting the grass. She saw an antenna, then the top of a cab, then a windshield. She raised her head. It was a new-model red pick-up with a single occupant. She scrambled to her feet and pulled William along with her, and they stood in the road.

At first, she wasn't sure the driver saw her. He was going slowly, staring out into the trees at the side of the road. But the pick-up slowed more and she recognised the driver. Mr Swann had once dated their mother and, although he was much older and it didn't work out, he had not been unkind to them.

As Swann stopped and leaned over and opened the passenger door, Annie Taylor wept with relief, hot tears streaming down her face.

'Whoa,' Mr Swann said, looking them over. 'Are you two all right? Did you get lost out here?'

'Will you please take us home?' Annie said through her tears.

'What happened?'

'Please take us home,' William said. 'We saw a man get killed.'

'*What?*'

As William climbed into the truck, Annie heard another motor. She looked up the road where it curved to the right and could see a vehicle coming, glimpses of it flashing between the trees. It was the white SUV.

'Get on the floor,' she yelled to her brother. 'It's *them*!'

'Annie, what's going on here?' Swann asked, frowning.

'They want to kill us!' Annie said, hurtling inside and shutting the door behind her. She cowered with William on the floor of the pick-up.

'Oh, come on now,' Swann said.

'Please, just drive,' Annie said. 'Please just drive ahead.'

Swann slid the truck back into gear, and she looked up at him as he drove, saw the confusion on his face. What if the men in the SUV waved Swann down to talk? It wasn't unusual on these back roads to see two vehicles stopped side by side as the drivers exchanged information and pleasantries. 'Please don't stop,' she said.

'I don't know what's going on,' Swann said, 'but it has you two scared to death, that's for sure.' He pursed his lips and looked ahead.

Wishing she could see what the men in the white SUV were doing, Annie wrapped her arms round William and watched Swann.

'They want me to stop,' he said, not looking down.

'Don't, please.'

'If I don't stop, they'll wonder why.'

Annie stifled a cry. The pick-up slowed. She tried to push William down even further into the floor, and herself as well, then she closed her eyes.

'Afternoon, Mr Singer,' Swann said as he rolled his window down.

'Afternoon,' Singer said. Singer was the Driver, Annie guessed. Mr Swann *knew* him.

Singer said, 'Hey, did you see some kids along the road?'

'They yours?' Swann asked.

'No, mine are grown, you know that. Me and my two compadres here were horsing around down on the river, target shooting, and we scared a couple of kids. We didn't know they were there. We think they might have thought they saw something they didn't.'

'Target shooting?'

'Yeah, we try to get out every couple of months to stay sharp. Anyway, we want those poor kids to know we meant no harm.'

Annie cracked an eye to look at Swann. *Don't do it*, she wanted to shout.

'Scared 'em pretty good, eh?' Swann said.

'I'm afraid so. We want to let 'em know everything's OK.'

'Is everything OK?' Swann asked.

'It will be when we find those kids,' another man said with a trace of a Mexican accent. The Dark Man, Annie guessed.

'So you haven't seen them?' Singer asked again.

Swann hesitated.

Annie closed her eyes again. She didn't hear the bulk of the conversation that followed because it was drowned out by the roar of blood in her ears, although she did hear Swann say that someone had come up behind him and he'd better go.

She couldn't believe her luck—their luck—when she realised the truck was moving again.

'I think you kids should stay down,' Swann said.

Annie asked, 'Where are you taking us?'

'My place is just up the road, and I need to make a call.'

'Why aren't you taking us home?'

'Because I don't want to run into those boys again,' Swann said. 'I know them from back on the force, and that story they just told me doesn't make a lot of sense.'

'That's because we're telling you the truth,' Annie said, feeling the tears well up in her eyes.

'Maybe,' Swann said. 'Keep your heads down.'

JESS RAWLINS was doing groundwork with his new horse, Chile, in the round pen near the corral when a new-model Lexus emerged from the timber on the southern hill and drove down the access road towards his ranch house. It caught him by surprise because he was concentrating so fully on the three-year-old red dun trotting in a circle at the end of the rope he held loosely in his left hand. A short, stout, heavily muscled little mare with a kind eye and two white socks, she moved in a nice smooth stride, and Jess was mesmerised by the rhythmic cadence of her hoofbeats. People who thought horses should be aquiline and sleek would have found Chile ugly. Jess didn't. She was a classic foundation quarter horse, a cow horse.

As he watched her, in his peripheral vision he noted the slow progress of the Lexus. It crawled down the access road, the only way into the Rawlins Ranch from the state highway, the afternoon sun gleaming off the windshield and the chrome grille.

Jess Rawlins was tall, stiff, all sharp angles: bony elbows and knees, prominent hawklike nose, pronounced cheekbones. The only thing soft about him, his wife, Karen, told him once, were his eyes and his heart, but not in a good way.

When the Lexus parked between his house and the barn and the driver's side door opened, Jess shot his first glance over. The man who climbed out was slim, well built, with thick blond hair and a bristly moustache. He was wearing khakis and a purple polo shirt. He looked like a golfer, Jess thought. No, worse. A real estate agent.

Jess brought Chile to a stop, and waited for the man to approach the round pen. The man—his name was Brian Ballard; Jess recognised him from his photo in the real-estate pages of the newspaper—stopped on the other side of the railing. Jess's eyes slid to the Lexus and saw the passenger inside for the first time. It was her, all right.

'How's it going, Mr Rawlins?' Ballard asked with false good cheer. 'I see you're training a horse there.'

'Groundwork.' Jess looked at Ballard. 'What do you want?'

Ballard smiled and his eyebrows arched. He was uncomfortable, despite the smile. 'I'm Brian Ballard, but I guess you know that.'

'I do.'

'I'm pleased to meet you, finally. This is a pretty place, all right.'

Jess didn't move.

'I saw Herbert Cooper in town this morning. He said you had to lay him off at the ranch.'

Herbert Cooper had worked for Jess for thirteen years. The day before, Jess had to tell his long-time foreman that he couldn't pay his wages any more, that there wasn't enough income for both bank-loan payments and an employee. It was one of the hardest things Jess had ever had to do and he hadn't slept well. Plus, it was calving season and he was now on his own.

Jess noticed Ballard looking at Chile. Jess could tell what he was thinking, and it made him angry.

'This horse came to me as payment for leasing out a quarter section for grazing.' Jess wished he hadn't said it. There was no need to justify himself, certainly not to this man. He nodded towards the Lexus. 'I see Karen in there. She put you up to this?'

'Let's leave her out of this, if you don't mind. There's no reason you and I can't be gentlemen about this.'

Jess said, 'There are plenty of reasons. So why don't you get back in your car and get the hell off my ranch? Remember to close the gate.'

'Look,' Ballard said. 'Everybody knows the situation out here. It's a real hard struggle. You had to let Herbert go, and everybody else is'—he searched for the right word and came up with a wrong one—'*gone*. I've been sending you offers for months now, and they're more than generous. I was hoping we could have a discussion man-to-man, feelings aside.'

Jess felt his chest tighten. 'To have a man-to-man discussion, you need two men. So we're out of luck in your department. I've asked you to leave. If I have to say it again, it'll be from behind the sights of my Winchester.'

Ballard's mouth opened, but nothing came out. Jess glared at him, then he took a step forward to tie Chile up to the rail. Ballard flinched.

'You don't need to threaten me. I can buy this place from you or I can wait and buy it from the bank.'

'Git,' Jess said.

Ballard backed up, then turned. He said over his shoulder, 'You're making a mistake, Jess. I'll be more than fair.'

Jess watched him walk towards his Lexus. He saw Karen turn in her seat towards Ballard as he opened the door. Then Ballard swung into the vehicle and made a U-turn, and Jess watched the car drive away. It took him a few minutes before he stopped trembling.

So that was Brian Ballard, the man Karen left him for. The man she married after him.

Jess had not fought back when she announced that she was leaving, said that she'd outgrown him. Said that just being on the ranch with him made her claustrophobic. That he had to get past what had happened to their son. That he was an anachronism. How could he fight that?

Karen got their savings and the feed store in town, which she promptly sold. And she got the Lincoln and his horse. Sold them too.

Jess kept the ranch.

THE TREK UP THE HILL through the timber to the mailbox seemed longer than it ever had, he thought. For years, Jess never got the mail. Herbert did it, or another ranch hand, or Karen.

To make matters worse, more often than not he ran into Fiona Pritzle, the woman who had the rural mail route, at his mailbox. She was a vicious gossip, the woman who had spread the word when his wife left. Fiona would feign concern for his well-being, and try to pump him for information. Had he heard from his ex-wife? Did he know she had moved back to town? Was it true the ranch was in trouble? So when he heard a vehicle coming up the road, he stopped in the wet foliage.

There had been a time, in Pend Oreille County, when everybody knew Jess Rawlins and Jess knew everyone else. That was when the lumber mills were running and the silver mines were hiring. It was rough, isolated, fiercely rugged country then. The Rawlinses had come from poor stock but managed to build an enterprise, rather than simply remove commodities to be shipped elsewhere. By doing so they moved up in status and respectability, and established a heritage that was shared and celebrated.

Jess grew up feeling like a local hero. His grandfather and father had bequeathed the mantle of exceptionalism: that he had a special *something* because his name was Rawlins—a legacy of hard work, honest but tough business dealings and high moral character.

The Rawlins Ranch was all the more admirable because North Idaho was not optimal cattle country. There were too many trees, not enough pasture. It rained too much. But the quality of Rawlins beef became widely praised, and the ranch prospered.

Jess, like his father and grandfather, felt proprietary towards the valley, the community and the ranch. After serving in the army, he had no doubt, ever, that he would return. Which he did.

Jess often wondered if he had made the right choice. He also wondered if he'd been the catalyst for the things to come, for the decline. Had the spark of exceptionalism died in him?

Maybe, he thought, it had just played out.

FIONA PRITZLE, behind the wheel of her little yellow Datsun pick-up, stopped at his mailbox and grinned. How did she know when he would be there? he wondered. *He* didn't even know from day to day. Fiona had a wide, pockmarked face obscured by heavy make-up. A cloud of perfume was released into the air when she climbed out, and she leaned over the top of the hood, fanning his mail across it as if laying down a hand of cards.

'Catalogues,' she said, 'three of 'em today. Two for women's clothing, so you're still on their list, even though . . .'

He looked at her grimly.

'And a property tax notice, again,' she said in her little-girl voice. 'Jess, I saw Herbert in town. He waved but didn't stop. Is something wrong?'

Damn, he thought. 'He just moved to town,' he said.

She looked at him suspiciously, then gathered up his mail and handed it to him. 'This road is getting busy. I almost rear-ended a vehicle back there when I came around the corner. A Cadillac Escalade with three men in it. They were barely crawling down the road, looking into the trees.'

He shrugged, hoping his lack of response would signal her to go away.

'Brand-new Idaho plates. Probably more transplants.'

'There's a lot of them moving up here,' he said.

'Most of them are retired cops from LA. I've heard that there's more than two hundred up here, and about a dozen on my route alone.'

'How do you know that?'

She puffed up. 'I put the pension cheques in their mailboxes, and police newsletters. Some are real nice guys, but some are like hermits. If it wasn't for their mail, I don't know if they'd ever come out of their houses. They call North Idaho "Blue Heaven" at the LAPD. Did you know that?'

Herbert had told him that. Jess didn't object to the idea of retired policemen moving into the valley. In fact, it seemed to him that ex-cops were similar to the original settlers, working men with blue-collar backgrounds like his grandfather. After years in crowded cities, dealing with the dark underbelly of society, they had opted to move to fresh, green country where they could be left alone. Better ex-cops than actors or dot-com heirs, Jess thought.

'It sort of makes you feel safer, doesn't it?' Fiona said. 'But some of them, you'd think they'd want to be friendlier. Why did they move here if they just wanted to keep to themselves? I mean: *Here I am!*' She did a clumsy little twirl. 'One of them might steal me away from you, Jess Rawlins!'

Enough, he thought. 'I better get back,' he said, gesturing towards his mail as if he couldn't wait to read it.

'You wouldn't believe how many LAPD newsletters I deliver these days,' she said, repeating herself. 'They're all up and down this road.'

'Then you better get after it,' he said cheerfully.

She reacted as if he'd slapped her. 'Just being neighbourly,' she huffed. 'I guess I caught you in one of your moods, Jess.'

He didn't like it when she used his first name, or that she studied his mail before she gave it to him. She should be more professional, he thought.

Her back tyres spat gravel as she roared away. Maybe if I pick up my mail at night? he wondered.

EDUARDO VILLATORO pressed his nose against the window of the Southwest Airlines flight to Spokane from Los Angeles. Below him was an ocean of green broken up only by lozenge-shaped lakes that reflected the sky. Snow-capped mountains rose in the distance, the tops of the peaks at eye level as the 737 descended. He had seen so much green only once before in his life, when he flew to El Salvador to bring back his mother. But that was jungle and this was not, and El Salvador had silvery roads slicing through the green and an ocean holding it in, and he could see no roads here. His anxiety lifted, slightly, when squares of farmland finally appeared and the flight attendant asked the passengers to put their tray tables in the upright position.

He had been keenly aware as he boarded the flight that he was the only passenger wearing a suit, even though it was his old, lightweight brown one. The other passengers seemed to pay no attention to him, but in a deliberate way, and it took him a while to realise why. He was the only person on the plane who wasn't Anglo. This phenomenon was new to him. A big part of his success in his career had always been that he didn't stand out, allowing him to study people without being observed himself.

Villatoro raised his arm and shot his cuff to look at his new gold watch. He was grateful he didn't need to reset the time, since he didn't yet know how the watch worked. His former coworkers had all contributed to buy the retirement gift, and his long-time partner, Celeste, had taken it to a jeweller to have the back inscribed: *For 30 Years of Service*.

In the airport, he retrieved his two bags from the carousel. At the car-rental counter, a boy with moussed hair told him the company could upgrade his reservation from a compact to a midsize for only five dollars more a day.

'No, thank you.'

'But it looks like you'll be in the area for a week,' the boy said, looking at the reservation on his computer monitor. 'You might be more comfortable in a larger car. I'm sure that your company would understand.'

'No,' Villatoro said. 'There is no company. I'm retired, as of two days ago. The compact, please.'

'Arcadia, California,' the boy said as he keyed in Villatoro's licence number and address. 'Never heard of it. Is it near LA?'

'It's a small town, fifty thousand people.' Villatoro smiled bitterly. 'It was swallowed by LA like a snack.'

'You wouldn't believe how many folks from LA we rent to,' the boy said, pushing the button to print out the contract. 'Have you been here before?'

'Spokane?' Villatoro said.

'It's "Spoke-Ann", Mr Villatoro, not "Spoke-Cain".'

'And it's "Vee-Ah-Toro", not "Villa-toro",' Villatoro said, smiling. 'May I please get a map to Kootenai Bay?'

'I'm sorry.' The boy tore one off a pad and used a highlighter to mark the route. 'You just take a right out of the airport and follow the signs to I-90 East.' He handed Villatoro the map and a thick, four-colour real-estate booklet. 'I assume you're looking for property?'

'No,' Villatoro said, taking the booklet anyway. 'I'm here on business.'

'Really?' The boy looked puzzled. 'I thought you said you were retired.'

'I am,' Villatoro said, and as he walked out onto the sunbaked lot he chastised himself for saying too much.

Villatoro pointed his little red Ford Focus towards the mountains to the east and eased onto the interstate. He passed a sign that read: WELCOME TO THE INLAND NORTHWEST. Spokane itself seemed old and industrial, and he drove into Idaho past acres of strip malls that looked just like the strip malls in LA. But when he turned north at Coeur d'Alene, the strip malls thinned and the forest seemed to shoulder its way to the road, as if to intimidate the drivers. Forty miles later, he was on a long bridge crossing a huge lake. On the other side of the lake, twinkling through a pine forest, was the town of Kootenai Bay, and beyond that, thirty-five miles north, was Canada.

DOWNTOWN KOOTENAI BAY was small, the vestige of another era, when it was more of a railroad outpost than what it had become. Old brick buildings sported signs for snowboards, espresso, bicycling, fishing, real estate. Villatoro turned right, dipped under a railroad trestle and emerged on the lakefront near the Best Western, where he had a reservation.

He pulled up under a slumping verandah, uncoiled from the small car and stretched. The boy at the car-rental counter had been right, he thought as he entered the small lobby. A larger car would have been better for his back.

He looked over the rack of real-estate brochures near the door and took several because they contained maps of the area. When he stepped up to the counter and gave his name, the check-in clerk nodded at the brochures.

'A girlfriend of mine sold her house for a hundred eighty-nine thousand dollars last week,' she said, 'and the guy who bought it resold it the next day, *the next day*, for two hundred fifty thousand.'

'Goodness,' Villatoro said.

'Damn right,' she said, finding his reservation card. 'Makes me wonder what my place is worth.' She looked up at him. 'Business or pleasure?'

'Business,' he said.

'What kind of business?' she asked pleasantly.

'Unfinished business,' he said, a little amused at how it sounded.

'Sounds interesting and mysterious.' She laughed.

He felt his face flush. 'I'm retired,' he said. He was still having trouble saying it without being self-conscious. It reminded him of the weeks after his wedding thirty-two years ago, when he stumbled as he introduced Donna as 'my wife'. It just didn't sound natural.

'How long?'

'Two days. I was a police detective in Arcadia, California.' As soon as he said it he didn't know why he had volunteered the information.

'Do you have a real-estate agent? I can recommend a good one.'

'Excuse me?'

She looked at him. 'I assume you're looking for a house here.'

'I'm not interested in retiring here,' he said, somewhat defensively.

'Hmm.' She clearly wasn't sure she believed him. 'OK, Mr Mysterious, how about I cut you a deal, then?' she said, almost whispering. 'I'll give you the AAA rate instead of the rack rate. Saves you twenty dollars a night.'

He couldn't refuse. 'Thank you,' he said.

'You bet, Mr Villatoro.'

She pronounced it 'Villa-torro'.

IN HIS ROOM, which was on the lower of two floors, Villatoro opened his curtains and looked out. While the hotel itself was tired and dowdy, the view was magnificent. Through a sliding glass door was a lawn that led to a beach. The lake was smooth as a tabletop all the way to the mountains, which were white with snow. He expected an orchestra to swell at the sight.

He dug in his pocket for his cellphone and powered it up to check for messages. There was no signal. He had not even considered this possibility. He turned and looked around his room—a television, two double beds with worn bedspreads, a telephone on the desk with a small phone book beside it.

Sitting on one of the too-soft beds, he opened his briefcase. After placing the photos of his wife and daughter on the nightstand, he pulled out a thick manila file, labelled SANTA ANITA RACETRACK: CASE FILE 90813A.

This was what had brought him to Kootenai Bay. This was the unfinished business. It had imposed such a strain on his marriage and family and his last few years in the department. It was a black cloud that loomed over him, blocking sunshine, preventing him from truly retiring and starting a new life.

'THEY SHOULD BE home by now,' Monica Taylor said to Tom, who had just come into the kitchen from the living room, where he had been watching an NBA game. He was wearing his brown UPS uniform shirt untucked over dark shorts, and his muscular legs were already tanned.

Tom looked at the clock on the stove. It said 5.30. He shrugged, opened the refrigerator. 'What, no beer? Do I have to go get some?'

'It's going to be dark in two hours,' she said, wiping her hands on a paper towel. 'I wonder if I should call somebody.'

Three place settings were on the table. Lasagne—Annie's favourite—was baking in the oven. The kitchen smelt of garlic, oregano and cheese.

Against her better judgment, she'd let Tom in when he showed up after work to apologise for not leaving early that morning. He said when he got up he didn't want to leave. He was trying to flatter her.

He was good at flattering her. That was part of the problem—she liked being flattered, even when she knew better. She'd first heard about Tom when she started work as manager of women's casual apparel at the store. The three women at the registers said his arrival was the highlight of their afternoon, and Monica learned why. He was tall, well built and single, and as he carried the shipments in the back door he made a point of flirting with each of them. Monica was onto his act instantly, but she admired his endless good cheer and undeniable charm, which he soon turned on her. She didn't object when he lingered after his delivery, engaging her in small talk, offering to help stack boxes or move displays. When the employees started gossiping about the amount of time he spent in the store, Monica asked him to stick to business. He would, he told her, if he just wasn't so darned attracted to her. When she said she had kids at home, he said he liked kids, and hey, how about dinner sometime? That was four months and a dozen dinners ago.

Tom shut the refrigerator door and turned to her with his arms crossed. His forearms were massive. 'I wouldn't worry so much,' he said. 'When I was growing up here people didn't worry. I remember staying out after school fishing, shooting hoops until all hours. Now, it's a federal case if kids get out of sight for a minute.'

'Are you talking about me?' she asked.

He started to say yes, she could tell, but he caught himself. 'No, I just mean people in general. It pisses me off, is all. She's probably just staying away to make a point. She's a prickly little number.'

'Tom,' Monica said, measuring her words, 'Annie and William had early release today. They should have been home at two if they weren't going fishing with you.'

Something washed over him, the look of a guilty man.

'What?' she asked. 'You showed up at the school, didn't you? I assumed they weren't there.'

Tom closed his eyes. 'We had two guys out sick today. I guess I forgot.'

Monica's face tightened.

'Things happen, Monica,' he pleaded.

Monica had spent the day in a kind of stupor. All day, her throat felt constricted, and at work she'd gone to the back room to cry. She'd thought about calling the school, asking for Annie. She would explain what had happened with Tom, but how could she possibly put it? Your mom screwed up. Your mom drank too much wine with Tom after you and William went to bed and invited him up to her bedroom.

But Monica had sworn she'd never let a man into the family unless it meant they'd really have a father. Annie didn't ask for the vow; Monica had volunteered it. Now she'd betrayed her own children. How could she have let herself do it? Tom was an idiot, and it would be easy to blame him, but she was the one who'd brought him into their home.

'I need to be alone and wait for my children,' she said. 'They are probably the only thing I've ever done right.'

He responded by visibly softening, and approached her, wrapping his arms round her. She remained stiff, refusing to give in to his physicality. 'I'm sorry, honey,' he said, pushing her blonde head onto his hard shoulder. 'They're your kids. Of course you're worried about them.'

'I'm sorry, too, Tom,' she said. Sorry she'd ever met him. She wanted to pull away and run somewhere. How could he not read her in the slightest?

'I'd like to think you consider me one thing you've done right,' Tom said.

She didn't respond, hoped he wouldn't press her for an answer. He didn't. 'It's not often we're alone without your kids here, honey,' he said. 'We could, you know, use this time just for *us*.'

She couldn't believe he'd said it. She looked at the clock—5.45. 'Tom,' she said, pushing away, alarmed at the revulsion she felt for him, 'why don't you go home? You shouldn't be here. You've done enough for today.'

A shadow passed over his face. 'OK,' he said. 'I'll get out of your sight.'

She didn't correct him.

'This is all about not taking Willie fishing?' he asked, his eyes hard. 'Is that what this is about?'

What had she ever seen in him? she wondered. How could she have ever let his looks cloud the glaring fact that he was a self-absorbed ass?

'Go,' she said.

Tom rolled his eyes. 'Later, then,' he said, heading towards the mudroom.

'Don't come back,' Monica said. 'It's over. It's so very over.'

He shook his head in disbelief. 'And I came here to apologise.'

Opening the door of the stove to check the lasagne, she said, 'No, I don't think so.' The cheese was bubbling and turning brown. She reduced the heat.

'Hey,' Tom yelled from the mudroom. 'That little bitch took my fishing rod and vest!' He filled the door frame, his face red.

'What?'

'That's a six-hundred-dollar Sage fly rod. I've got hundreds of dollars of flies in my vest. And the little bitch *took* it.'

She thought she had never seen such an ugly man before. 'Leave,' she said, her voice rising, 'and don't you *ever come back in my house!*'

'Oh, I'm coming back,' he shouted. 'I'm coming back for my rod and vest, goddammit.'

'GET OUT!' she screamed.

He shook his head, glaring, and went out, slamming the door behind him.

She put her face in her hands and sobbed, calling him every name she could think of, feeling her heart break, terrified by the fact that she didn't know where her children were. Knowing it was her fault they were gone.

WHAT ANNIE had noticed first, as they drove up the private two-track drive to Mr Swann's house, was the smell. Something ripe and bold coursed through the pine-scented air, and it got stronger as they neared his home in the thick trees. He had allowed them to get off the floor once he'd turned off from the road, and Annie saw what it was that made the odour: hogs.

'There's *my* family,' Swann said. 'They know Daddy's home.'

'Look at the pigs.' William leaned over Annie towards the open window of the pick-up. 'Man, they're excited.'

When the hogs saw the red truck coming, they squealed and ran about in their pen, splashing through puddles. Annie counted at least twenty hogs. One was tan and bristly, and looked to be the size of a small truck. She didn't know hogs could get that huge.

'The big one's name is King,' Swann said. 'He won me a blue ribbon at the Pend Oreille County Fair this summer.'

'He's *awesome*,' William said. 'I bet he can eat a lot.'

Annie had stopped trembling, although she still felt numb. She couldn't wrap her mind round what she and William had seen at the campsite. The image would never leave her.

'Are you OK?' William asked, feeling her shiver.

'Yes,' she said, not interested in the hogs the way he was. How could he be interested in hogs after what had just happened? Boys were different, all right. Even William.

Swann thumbed a remote control, and one of three garage doors opened. Slowing to a crawl, he parked inside. The children waited in the pick-up until the garage door was shut, then followed Swann into the house.

It was clean and light, with one big room after another. It was as unlike her mother's house as could be, Annie thought. Except for the kitchen and the den, the house seemed not to be lived in at all. There were photos of Mr Swann in his police uniform above the fireplace, and a framed set of medals and ribbons. Other than that, the walls were bare.

Swann opened a bag of cookies and set two glasses of milk on the table, saying, 'Eat up. I need to go make a couple of calls. There's more milk in the fridge if you want it.'

'Are you going to call our mother?' Annie asked, while William fished three cookies out of the bag.

Swann's expression darkened. 'Not immediately. If those men figure out who you are, the first thing they'll do is go to your house. If your mother knows you're here, she'll probably tell them, or they'll make her tell them. Do you understand what I'm saying?'

Annie felt herself nod yes, felt a ball of fear knotting in her stomach.

'I need to make a couple of calls,' he said again. 'There are two guys who might have an idea what is going on.'

'Are you going to call the sheriff?' Annie asked.

'After I get a little more information, I'll call the proper authorities,' Swann said, then padded down the hallway to, she presumed, his office.

Annie heard the door close and the sound of a lock being thrown. Why did he do that? she wondered.

She turned back to her brother. 'How can you eat?'

'I'm hungry,' he said, spewing crumbs across the tabletop.

AFTER A FEW MINUTES, Annie left the table and washed her hands and face in the kitchen sink. As she dried her face with a dish towel, she looked out of the window and watched the sun drop from beneath the clouds and plunge into the treetops. It would be dark soon. The house was still and quiet.

'Mr Swann is nice,' William said. 'I'm happy he picked us up.'

'He's a policeman, too.'

'He probably has a few guns around here,' William said. 'I wonder if he'll show them to me.'

'Why do you want to see his guns? Didn't you see what guns did today? To that poor man?'

'That's why *we* need 'em. So that won't happen to us.'

'Oh, brother.' She didn't want to argue about this.

'I'm ready to go home, though,' William said, sitting back. 'When do you think he'll take us home?'

Annie looked down the hall at the closed door. 'I don't know.'

'Maybe we should knock,' William suggested.

Annie shook her head. 'I need to find the bathroom,' she said.

She paused at the closed office door as she went down the hall. She could hear Swann's voice inside, but she couldn't make out any words.

The bathroom was at the end of the hallway. She turned on the light and shut the door. She looked at herself in the mirror and was shocked at how pale and wild she looked. Her blonde hair was tangled, with bits of leaves in it. Her clothes were crusted with dried mud. There was a scratch across her cheek she didn't remember getting, and only now did it begin to sting.

When she was through, Annie left the bathroom quietly and peeked into Mr Swann's bedroom. Even though she knew she shouldn't, she stepped into the room and looked around. The walls were bare except for several framed photos over a dresser. A phone was on a nightstand next to the bed, and she stared at it. Who was he talking to? The sheriff? Her mother?

She knew it was wrong, but she wanted to know. As slowly as she could, she lifted the receiver and covered the mouthpiece with her hand.

'You've got him with you now?' Swann asked someone.

'Wrapped up tight,' the man said. 'Leakproof packaging.'

Swann chuckled nervously. 'Everybody's with you?' he asked.

'Almost,' the man said. 'I'm waiting on Gonzo to get back.'

'I hope it's soon. I don't know how long I can keep them entertained.'

Annie's eyes shot open wide. *Keep them entertained.*

'Wait, I think I see his car now. Yeah, it's him. We're ready.'

'Good. Let's get this over with, then,' Swann said. 'This is bad, you know?'

'I know. Newkirk is wavering on us.'

'I don't blame him.'

'That was a good move, taking them home with you. God help us if some citizen saw us on the road with them.'

Annie eased the phone down and hung it up, which was difficult because her hand was trembling.

By the time she looked up, her eyes had adjusted to the dark of the room. She could see the photos above the dresser and she approached them. More shots of Mr Swann in his police uniform, and another of a group of men, fellow police officers. As she looked at it, her heart began to race.

Mr Swann stood in the middle of a group of five men. They had their arms round each other and several had big grins. But not the Dark Man, who scowled. Singer, the Driver, stared at the camera with the same ice-blue intensity she had seen in his eyes at the campsite. The Ball Cap Man grinned. And the Wavy-Haired Man who had been killed that afternoon looked to be laughing so hard his face was blurred in the photo.

As she ran down the hallway she heard the office door being unlocked.

William saw her coming. Luckily, he had left the table and was standing next to the door. He was obviously surprised to see her running so fast.

'Let's go,' she hissed at him. '*Run!*'

He didn't argue but threw open the door to the garage. Annie heard Mr Swann holler 'HEY! Where are you going?' from down the hallway.

The garage was dark except for the blue squares of the garage door windows. She didn't know where the button was for the door opener but saw a faint glow next to the doorjamb and pushed it. A light came on and the door began to rise. 'Go!' she yelled, and the two of them rolled under it.

'Stop! Get back here, now!' Swann yelled after them.

It was raining again. Annie had William's hand and they ran past the hog pens. A huge mass hurled itself against the fence and squealed—King—causing them to veer away into the dark brush.

'Stop running from me!' Swann was shouting. 'You'll get lost out there! I talked to your mother. Everything's OK. *She's coming to get you!*'

'Annie . . .' William gasped, winded.

'He's lying,' she answered, not stopping. 'He's friends with those men we saw today.'

William said something she couldn't understand. It sounded more like an animal noise. He was crying. She stopped, and reached out and grabbed him, holding his thin shoulders in her hands, thrusting her face into his.

'William, I heard him talking to them. They're on their way here to find us because we saw them kill that man. We can't trust *anybody*, you understand?'

He looked away. 'I just want to go home,' he said.

'We can't go home yet. That's where they'll look first. That's the one thing Mr Swann told us that wasn't a lie.'

'Where do we go, then?'

She pulled him close, wrapping her arms round him, speaking into his ear. 'As far away from here as we can get.'

'OK,' Ex-Lieutenant Eric Singer said to Dennis Gonzalez and Jim Newkirk at the rear table in the Sand Creek Bar. 'At least we know who they are.'

Their names were Annie and William Taylor. Newkirk would rather he didn't know their names because it made what they were trying to do so much more personal.

The Sand Creek Bar was a dark, run-down place just out of Kootenai Bay on the old highway, the kind miners and loggers used to stop at on their way home. Now, at just past ten thirty, there were only a few vehicles in the parking lot, two pick-ups and a UPS truck. Newkirk had been told that the credo of the Sand Creek was 'Drink hard and fast because you never know when you might die'. He'd been there a couple of times with his softball team, but Singer and Gonzalez had not. Those two never went anywhere.

They'd spent the last three and a half hours patrolling the state highway and old logging roads near Oscar Swann's house, looking for a sign of Annie and William Taylor. They'd found nothing. Singer had a police scanner in his SUV, and as they patrolled the forest they'd listened to the sheriff's dispatcher. Monica Taylor had called repeatedly, saying her children weren't home yet from school. The calls were treated as routine.

Newkirk felt numb, as if he weren't really there. He was tired, hungry, dirty. He hadn't been home all day. The first glass of beer affected him on an empty stomach. He poured another from the pitcher. It tasted crisp and good.

'This is a critical time,' Singer said. 'If those kids show up . . .'

'We're fucked,' Gonzalez said, finishing the sentence for his former boss.

'Where could they be?' Newkirk asked.

Singer and Gonzalez simply stared at him, as they did whenever he asked an unanswerable question.

'The sheriff probably won't take it seriously until tomorrow,' Singer said. 'It's obvious he thinks those kids will show up at home tonight.'

That was why Singer had ordered Swann to go and stake out the Taylor house. Swann knew where they lived and could contact Singer via cellphone if the kids showed up. So far, there had been no call.

'I think they're hunkered down in the woods,' Gonzalez said. 'There's a lot of country out there to get lost in. Nothing but trees all the way to Canada.'

While they'd patrolled, Gonzalez had kept remarking on the absence of houses, the lack of lights back in the forest. It struck Newkirk as an odd observation, but Gonzalez and Singer rarely ventured out of their trophy homes—woodland fortresses with satellite television and Internet, back-up power generators at the ready. They hadn't tried to get to know their neighbours and went to town only to transact necessary business. Newkirk was different. He was married and had three kids at school. He and Maggie had met other parents, other families. They travelled to soccer and basketball games with locals, had got to know and like some of them. Newkirk felt he was the only one of the ex-officers who actually *lived* here.

'So what do we do?' Gonzalez asked Singer.

'Just let me think,' Singer said.

Newkirk watched him. The lieutenant was the most icily efficient commander he had ever served under, even in the army. But despite his calm façade there was a palpable feeling of something tightly coiled up just beneath the skin, like a high-tension spring. Singer was the kind of guy who got quieter and colder the worse things got, as if his concentration alone would cut a swath of reason through chaos. He processed the situation, then flicked out commands. But a deep-seated bitterness had grown in him, and Newkirk had been there, on the LAPD, as it happened.

There had been a minor scandal, one of many, within the department, and Singer was assigned the investigation. He determined that no officers were at fault, but an on-the-make television news reporter edited Singer's comments in such a way that he sounded not only incompetent but also complicit. The lieutenant was furious and asked the department to take action. The outgoing police chief, who later wound up being hired as an expert commentator for the television station, bunkered down. Singer felt betrayed, and the dedication and passion he had felt towards the department took a 180-degree turn, and the quiet and effective hatred he had once focused on criminals and spineless politicians pointed inwards towards his employers. Only those close to him knew of the sea change.

Although Newkirk was physically outmatched by big, malevolent Ex-Sergeant Gonzalez, it was Singer, a head shorter than Newkirk, whom he feared the most.

Singer had barely touched his beer. Newkirk and Gonzalez had emptied the pitcher, and Gonzo tried to get the attention of the bartender by lifting it whenever he thought the man looked over.

'What we've got to do is steer things in our favour,' Singer said softly. 'We can't wait for things to happen.'

'Like waiting for that scumbag to get us a pitcher,' Gonzalez said.

Newkirk sighed. 'I'll get it.' He got up and approached the bar.

There were only two other drinkers, a skeletal man in stained working clothes who looked like an old miner, and a much younger man in a UPS uniform. Newkirk perched between them and put the pitcher on the bar.

'What was it? Coors?' the bartender asked, rousing himself.

'Yes,' Newkirk said, and glanced at the miner.

The old man nodded at him, then went back to watching *SportsCenter* on the television mounted to the ceiling. The UPS man seemed to be waiting for Newkirk to say something. Oh no, he thought, a talker.

'Don't get too close to me,' the UPS man slurred. 'I'm radioactive, and I might rub off on you.'

Newkirk shifted to look him over. He was heavy built: solid, thick thighs, but a broad friendly face. Newkirk guessed six two, two twenty pounds. A brass-coloured name tag read TOM BOYD. It was unusual to see a package-delivery employee in uniform so long after the workday was over.

'Don't you turn your truck in at night?' Newkirk asked.

Tom snorted. 'S'posed to. But I pitched camp here on this stool, right, Marty?' he said to the bartender.

'Yes, Tom,' Marty said wearily, as he filled the empty pitcher from the tap.

'I'll take care of that pitcher,' Tom said, fishing a wad of bills out of his pocket. 'And another double Jack for me.'

'You sure you need another one?' Marty asked.

'What are you, a bartender or my counsellor? Pour 'em!'

Marty shrugged, and Tom shook his head in drunken exaggeration.

'I'm poison,' he said. 'Everything I touch turns to crap.'

Tom Boyd was one of those guys, Newkirk thought, who was begging to be asked what was wrong and wouldn't give up until he was.

'Women problems, eh?' Newkirk asked, not really interested.

'Is there any other kind? I mean really?'

'Just call her. Let her talk it out and keep your mouth shut while she does.'

Boyd said, 'I *tried* to call a while ago, and she hung up on me. She was waiting for the sheriff to call back. It's bull. That kid's just getting back at her by not coming home.'

Newkirk felt a thrill race down his spine. 'Why is she waiting for the sheriff to call her?'

'Her kids didn't come home from school,' Boyd said, rolling his eyes, smiling ruefully. 'Somehow, that's *my* fault.'

'What did you say her name was?' Newkirk asked, knowing that Boyd hadn't said it yet.

'Monica.'

'Monica Treblehorn? I know her.'

'No, Monica Taylor.'

'Don't know her. What did you do?' Newkirk asked conversationally.

'I forgot to take her little mama's boy fishing, so she threw me out. And that little bitch daughter of hers. Took my six-hundred-dollar Sage rod, too!'

'That sucks, doesn't it?'

'Don't go out with a woman who has kids,' Boyd said. 'They'll all conspire against you.'

Marty handed the pitcher to Newkirk, and said, 'Keep it on the tab?'

'Yes, and buy my new friend here another.'

Newkirk returned to the table. 'You won't believe who I just met,' he said. 'Monica Taylor's boyfriend. And we have a problem. Things might be moving faster than we thought. He says she's waiting for the sheriff to call her back. He just talked with her. Says she threw him out of her house tonight.'

Singer looked at Newkirk, his face expressionless. Then, oddly, a tight, faint smile. 'That isn't a problem,' he said. 'It's an opportunity.'

THEY WAITED until Marty cut Boyd off. While the UPS man pleaded for a last drink, Gonzalez and Singer slipped outside. Newkirk settled the tab while Boyd stumbled his way to the door.

When he got to the parking lot, Newkirk saw Singer and Gonzo standing under the pole light. Tom Boyd was leaning against the UPS truck.

Gonzo said, 'You sure you should be driving, mister?'

'I'm fine,' Boyd slurred. 'Besides, I ain't going home. I'm going to Monica's. We got some things to straighten out.'

Newkirk approached them. He could see something square and long protruding from Gonzalez's back pocket. It was called a 'Stun Monster', 650,000 volts. The department had banned them after some guy died.

Boyd said, 'I gotta go. Where you fellows from, anyway?' He cracked a smile. 'I'd guess LA, like half the new guys up here.'

'Right you are,' Gonzalez said, stepping towards Boyd as if to assist him into the truck. Newkirk caught a glint of metal electrodes winking in the lamp's light. Gonzo plunged the stun gun into Boyd's neck, and the electricity arced and snapped like furious lightning. Boyd dropped like a sack of rocks, half in and half out of his driver's door. His muscles twitched violently as they pushed him into the truck and dragged him between the rows of parcels in the back. Newkirk could smell the awful stench of burnt flesh.

Gonzo rolled the body over and cuffed Boyd.

'You drive,' Singer said, handing Gonzo the keys. 'Follow me.'

In his white SUV, with the headlights of the UPS truck filling the rearview mirror, Singer turned to Newkirk.

'This was a gift,' he said. 'Now we can control the situation.'

Day Two: Saturday

After pulling two calves during the night, feeding his cattle at 5 a.m., and a big breakfast of steak, eggs and coffee, Jess Rawlins showered and put on a jacket and tie and his best grey Stetson Rancher and went out to start his pick-up. The sky was clear of clouds, but mist from the rain the night before sharpened the smell of alfalfa and cow manure from the hayfield. He put a boot box full of documents on the passenger seat.

Jim Hearne was waiting for him in the lobby of the bank, wearing a sports jacket, tie, slacks and boots. Jess still wasn't used to the new building, even though it had been there for five years. It was impressive, with its big windows and modern furniture, but he preferred the old one, the elegant, two-storey redbrick structure on Main. It had once been called the North Idaho Stockman's Bank. That was three name changes ago, before it became First Interstate and started opening on Saturdays. The Rawlins family had banked there since 1933.

Jim Hearne was in his late forties, stocky, broad-faced, with thinning brown hair and sincere blue eyes. He had once been the agriculture loan officer, but his duties and titles had multiplied. A bareback rider who had qualified twice for the national finals, he still had a bow-legged hitch in his walk. The Rawlins Ranch had been his college rodeo sponsor. Jess had known him for thirty years, had watched him become a community leader.

Hearne led Jess to his office and shut the door behind them. Jess sat in one of the two chairs facing Hearne's desk and put his box of documents in the other. He removed his hat and placed it crown-down on the floor.

'Plenty of moisture lately,' Hearne said, sitting down. 'That's got to help.' Despite the fact that he was now president of the bank, he still handled his old customers personally, and lapsed easily into the old banter.

Jess nodded. He wasn't good at small talk, and they both knew why he was here. Jess owned and operated a 3,000-acre ranch. He ran 350 Herefords in a cow/calf operation and when the grass was good took in fifty to a hundred feeder cattle on a lease. It was the second-largest private holding remaining in the county.

'Jess, I'm just not sure where to start,' Hearne said.

Jess shrugged. 'There's not much to say. I can't make my payments and I don't see how that's going to change, Jim. I'm broke. I laid off Herbert Cooper the day before yesterday. Calving's going well, alfalfa's doing great, folks want to pasture their cows, but even with that . . .'

Hearne pursed his lips. Silence hung in the air.

'Everyone I know, practically,' Hearne said, 'is on that low-carb meat diet. You'd think beef prices would rise.'

This was a conversation they'd had before. Meat-processing conglomerates controlled prices and had long-term options on supply. Jess had agreed to those prices years in advance, before the increase in meat consumption.

'No one held a gun to my head to make me sign those futures contracts,' Jess said. 'I'm not here to whine.'

'I know you're not.'

'I'm not here to tell you everything's going to get better, either. But I run a good outfit and I don't waste your money or mine.'

This was as close as Jess would come to asking for a favour, and it made him uncomfortable. It had made Hearne uncomfortable, too, Jess could tell.

'No one ever said that,' Hearne said. 'I sure as hell didn't. It's just that the day of the pure cattle outfit in northern Idaho may have passed us by. You're land-rich and cash-poor. Your place is worth millions, if developed properly,' he said morosely, delivering news neither one of them wanted to hear. 'There are ways to get out from under this debt, Jess.'

Jess sighed. 'I'm no developer.'

'You don't have to be,' Hearne said. 'There are probably a half-dozen developers who would work with you. I've had some calls on it, in fact.'

Jess bristled. 'I've had some calls, too, and offers in the mail. Karen even came out yesterday with her new husband.'

Hearne sat back. 'None of us who grew up here wants to see you lose that ranch. If all the old ranches are replaced by those five-acre ranchettes, the county won't be the same. But I can't let sentiment run my bank. Is there any way you'd consider selling some of it? That would buy you some time.'

It was a bitter pill for Jess to swallow. He had been left a legacy and he had screwed it up. The ranch was all that defined the Rawlins name.

'I'm a rancher,' he said. 'I don't know anything else.'

Hearne rubbed his face with his hands. 'We've got to figure something out,' he said. 'We can't extend the loans any more. I've got directors and auditors who want to know what the hell I'm doing with these bad loans.'

'I'm sorry, Jim.'

'Don't say that. I can't stand for you to say that.'

The intercom chirped and Hearne picked up the handset. 'I'm in a meeting.' Jess could hear a muffled voice. 'Oh, I hate to hear that. Of course they can put it up.' Hearne continued to listen, then glanced over Jess's shoulder into the lobby. 'Yeah, I see him. He'll have to wait.' He cradled the handset. 'Sorry,' he said, his face drained of colour.

'No problem. What's the matter?'

'Do you know the Taylor family? Monica Taylor?'

'I've heard the name,' Jess said, trying to remember the context.

'She's got two kids, a girl and a boy. They're missing, been gone since yesterday. Some women want to put a poster up in the lobby.'

Jess shook his head. 'They'll probably turn up.'

'Things like this never used to happen,' Hearne said. Then, remembering why they were there, he said, 'Jess, give me a couple of weeks to come up with some options for you. You don't have to take any of them, of course. But we both know you're in default. If I can come up with something to get us out of this mess, I will.'

Jess sat back, overwhelmed. 'You don't have to do that, Jim.'

'I know I don't,' Hearne said. 'But we've known each other for a long time. I don't want to see your ranch turned into more starter castles for California transplants, either.'

Jess stood, clamped on his hat, and extended his hand. 'Jim—'

'Don't say it,' Hearne interrupted. 'It's good for business, is all.'

AS HE OPENED the office door, Jess recognised Fiona Pritzle as one of the women putting up the posters in the lobby. Before he could slink away, she came rushing over.

'Jess,' she said, taking both of his hands in hers, standing too close and blocking him in the doorway, 'did you hear about the Taylor children?'

'Just did. It's terrible.'

'I was the one who gave them a ride along Sand Creek yesterday,' she said, her eyes shining. 'They were going fishing.'

'They'll probably show today,' he said.

'Oh, they could have been drowned in the creek! Or who knows who could have taken them. There are people here now we don't know anything about. Who knows how many sexual predators have moved up here?'

Jess winced. 'Is there a search team?'

'Thank God, yes. The sheriff has his deputies out and people are lining up to volunteer to look for them.'

'That's good.' Jess wished he had more confidence in the new sheriff, who seemed more a public relations type than a lawman. As he thought this, he realised he was trapping Hearne in his office. Gently he broke Fiona's grip.

'It is good,' she said. 'I heard that a bunch of those retired police officers have volunteered to head up the investigation. They showed up this morning. Isn't that great?'

'Excuse me,' Hearne said, sliding past Jess.

Jess watched as Hearne strode across the lobby and greeted a portly Hispanic man in a light brown suit.

'Well,' Jess said, extricating himself and nodding at the poster Fiona had mounted on the wall, 'that's a good thing you're doing. I'll keep an eye out myself since I'm upstream of Sand Creek.'

Hearne and the portly man went into Hearne's office, and before the door shut, the banker said, 'Take it easy, Jess. I'll call you.'

'Thank you, Jim.'

Fiona watched the exchange and Jess could see the wheels spinning in her head. 'Does that mean you get to keep your ranch?' she asked eagerly.

ON HIS WAY OUT through the lobby doors, Jess paused to look at the poster. MISSING, it said. ANNIE AND WILLIAM TAYLOR. LAST SEEN AT 3.35 P.M. FRIDAY NEAR SAND CREEK. It said Annie had been wearing a yellow sweatshirt, jeans and black sneakers and William was dressed in a black T-shirt, jeans and red tennis shoes. One of them might be wearing an adult's fly-fishing vest.

The school photos of the children tugged at his heart. Jess thought about how you could see the future personalities of adults in children's photos if you cared to look hard. Even now, when he stared at the photos of his own son, in his home, he could see what he would become. The clues were there, the blueprint. If only he had known.

William smiled broadly, his chin slightly cocked, his hair a comma over his forehead. He looked happy-go-lucky and tragic at the same time. It was Annie who most affected Jess. She was blonde, open-faced, and looked to be challenging the photographer. But there was something in her clear eyes. He liked her immediately, and felt an affinity he couldn't explain. Had he met her before? He searched his memory and came up with nothing.

MONICA TAYLOR was beside herself. Annie and William had been missing for over twenty hours. She hadn't slept, eaten, showered or changed clothes since Tom had walked out the evening before. It had been a long night, made worse when smoke rolled out of the oven—she had forgotten about the lasagne—and set off the alarms. She had stood weeping on her front lawn, being comforted by a volunteer fireman, while the rest of the crew charged through her front door with extinguishers and hoses, to emerge a few minutes later with a smoking pan of black goo. The neighbours who had been outside in their bathrobes went back inside their houses.

Before the lasagne burned, sheriff's deputies had been to her home twice, once to hear her initial concerns and again near midnight to obtain photos and descriptions of the children. The sheriff eventually tired of her hourly calls and sent over a doctor, who prescribed Valium.

She had developed a routine, of sorts, which consisted of walking through the house and out of the back door into the yard, circling left and re-entering through the front, all the while clutching the cordless telephone as if to squeeze it into juice. When the phone rang, and it rang often, she would gasp and ask God that it please be one of her children. It never was. Over and over, she replayed the morning before, each time revising the situation so Tom left the house before breakfast or, better yet, that he'd never come at all. She asked God, over and over, for a second chance to make it right.

There would be no more Tom, she vowed. No more *Toms*, period.

Monica had never been blessed with a road map. Her own parents had not provided one, certainly not for a situation like this. She always envied those who seemed to have a plan, a destination. In times of confusion, she had little to fall back on and no one to call for support. Certainly not her mother. And who knew where her father was?

It was tough raising two children alone. The men she met were either divorced themselves and loaded with baggage, married and looking for a fling or an easy out, or immature like Tom. None of them had the potential to be a good father to her children. There had been too many years wasted hoping, too many years of listlessness and paralysis, treading water, hoping some man would throw a lifeline.

Now, for the first time she could remember, her life was absolutely focused: she needed her children back.

She was sitting at her kitchen table, staring at the digital time display on the microwave, when Sheriff Ed Carey rapped on the screen door of the mudroom. It was 9:15 a.m.

'May I come in, Miz Taylor?'

She looked up and nodded, not having the energy to speak.

Sheriff Carey was tall and wore his uniform well, but there wasn't much he could do to disguise the pot-belly that strained the buttons on his khaki shirt. He gestured towards a chair.

'Do you have anything to tell me?' she asked.

He sat down. 'I wish I had better news, but one of my deputies found some things up by Sand Creek. A fly rod and a shoe stuck in the mud. I was hoping you could identify them.'

Her mind raced. Of course she could identify a shoe if it was Annie's or William's. But what was the brand of the fly rod Tom said was missing?

'I could do that,' she said. 'But I might have to call someone to identify the rod.'

'That would be Tom Boyd, I presume?'

'Yes.'

Carey shifted in his chair. He had been barely elected just a few months ago in a close contest. His background was in real estate. She wondered how much he really knew about his job.

'My deputies think this may be more than the kids getting lost.'

Monica wished the Valium would wear off so she could concentrate. 'What are you saying to me?'

'Well, we've decided to treat this matter as a criminal investigation, not a missing persons case. The rod was found hung up in some brush a hundred yards from the river. The shoe was easy to see in a mudhole further up the path. That leads my deputies to believe that whoever lost the shoe—and we think it might have been Annie—could have easily pulled it out. But she didn't. That indicates she might have been in a hurry. You know, like she was running from something or somebody.'

Monica felt her eyes widen. Carey produced a quart-size Ziploc bag. Inside was a muddy shoe. The sight of it welded her to her chair.

'It's Annie's,' she said, scarcely raising her voice. 'Who were they running from?'

Carey put the shoe on the table. 'That, we don't know. My men found some prints up there, but the rain last night fouled up anything definitive. My guys are combing the area inch by inch.'

The world had suddenly made a hard turn and darkened. Throughout the sleepless night, she had envisioned her children lost in the forest, huddled together in the rain. She had hoped they'd found shelter of some kind and were smart enough to stay put. She had even thought of the creek, thought of them falling into it and being swept away. It was awful, that thought. But she hadn't considered what the sheriff was now telling her. That her children were prey to someone.

'Oh, no . . .' She stared at the shoe, the mud, the broken laces.

Carey narrowed his eyes. 'Miz Taylor, are you OK?'

She shook her head slightly. 'No, I'm not. You're telling me that someone was after my children.'

'We don't know that. It's speculation based on very little evidence. They could turn up any minute. Maybe they stayed at a friend's.'

She continued to shake her head. She had given a deputy the names and numbers of all Annie's and William's friends and had called their parents herself. None of them had seen her children.

'Miz Taylor, I need to ask you if you know of anyone who may have something against you or your kids.'

'What?'

'Has anyone threatened you? Stalked you? Do you know if your children had any trouble with anyone who might try to scare or hurt them? They each have a different father, right?'

'Right,' she said, wincing at how it sounded. 'But neither is around.'

William's father, Billy, had been killed in a prison riot in Boise. She had divorced him three years before, while he was on trial for operating four methamphetamine labs, which apparently generated a lot more income than his struggling construction business. The marriage had been dead eighteen months after the ceremony, but went on for two more years. Billy had been proud that he fathered a son, but didn't particularly like William and, like Tom, called him a mama's boy. William barely remembered his father, but sometimes talked about him as a mythical being, a legendary Western outlaw. Annie knew Billy for what he was, and up until a year ago had assumed he was her father, too. Then she did the maths. That had been a bad day for Monica, when Annie asked. Monica simply said, 'He's watching over you.' Annie didn't really accept the answer. Monica knew there would be more questions as time went by, and she had dreaded them. Now, she hoped Annie would be back so she could answer them.

'Dead?' the sheriff asked.

'Something like that.'

The sheriff eyed her closely, withholding judgment. 'We need to explore every possibility so we can rule things out,' he said. 'Anyone you can think of at your place of work?'

'No.'

Carey glanced at his notes. 'You're the manager of women's casual apparel at the outlet store, correct?'

She nodded. 'It provides a steady income and decent health benefits.'

'Any problem with the neighbours?'

She shook her head.

'What about extended family? Is there money there? Would a kidnapper have a reason to hold your children for ransom?'

'My mother tends bar in Spokane,' Monica said evenly. 'My father's been gone for years. We have nothing.'

'This Tom Boyd,' the sheriff said. 'A neighbour reported that she saw him leaving your house last night, and she heard him yell and slam your door. She heard you yelling, too. Was there some kind of disagreement?'

Monica swallowed. 'We had an argument.'

'What about?'

'Tom found out his fishing rod and vest were missing. He thought Annie had taken them. I told him to leave, but I'm sure he had nothing to do with it. The kids were already gone a long time when it happened.'

The sheriff asked her for the time of the argument.

'It was around six,' she said. 'I waited two more hours before I called you.'

She could see Carey calculating it in his head. Tom would have had enough time, and enough light, to track down Annie and William.

'Tom called me last night,' she said. 'It was after ten, maybe ten thirty. He asked whether my kids had come home.'

'How did he sound?'

She swallowed again. 'He was drunk. He was at some bar.'

Carey nodded. 'The Sand Creek Bar. The bartender said he was inebriated and distraught. They refused to give him more drinks, and he got angry and left. He's a body builder, right? Maybe some steroid use? Would you say he has a violent temper, Miz Taylor?'

SHERIFF CAREY asked questions for another half-hour. She could see how he was building a case against Tom. No, she didn't know he'd been arrested twice for assault. No, she didn't know Tom's ex-wife had accused him of beating one of his children. She felt stupid, duped. Again.

But she still didn't think it was Tom. 'I just can't believe it,' she said.

Carey stood. 'Tom didn't show up for work this morning,' he said. 'He's not at his house, and no one saw him come home last night. His truck is missing. He was supposed to turn it in last night, but he didn't.'

'His UPS truck?' she said incredulously.

For the first time, the sheriff almost smiled. 'You'd think we'd find a vehicle that distinctive easy enough, wouldn't you? I hope we can find him soon. If we can tie Tom Boyd to your kids, we can issue an Amber Alert, but first law enforcement must confirm that an abduction has taken place. We don't know that to be true. Luckily, though, I have an ace in the hole.'

'What do you mean?'

Now he grinned outright. 'Four experienced, seasoned investigators showed up this morning and volunteered to help. After I talked with 'em, I gave them the authority to run with it, and already things are happening.'

She was confused. 'Who are they?'

'LAPD's finest,' he said. 'Retired cops who've worked dozens of situations like this. They want to serve their new community. They helped me establish a command centre, and they're the ones who figured out Tom Boyd. We're glad to have them here.'

She nodded. For the first time, she felt a lift of encouragement.

'I know you want to stay by the phone,' he said, looking round the sooty kitchen. 'But you need some help around here. Some support. Is there anyone we can call to stay with you?'

'That woman, Fiona Pritzle, keeps offering to stay,' Monica said. 'But I don't think I want her help.'

'I'll ask one of the volunteer investigators to come over, if you don't mind. If someone contacts you about your kids, we'll want to screen the call. His name is Swann. Ex-sergeant Swann.'

'I know him,' Monica said dully. She thought of Swann, kind but obscure, and so set in his ways. 'He's a clean freak. Very organised. He'll probably help me out with all this.'

The sheriff smiled and reached out his hand. 'Miz Taylor, we'll do our best to find your kids.'

'SORRY TO KEEP you waiting,' Jim Hearne said to Eduardo Villatoro as he slipped back behind his desk.

Villatoro settled into a chair, his briefcase on his knees. He dug in his breast pocket for a card, then handed it to Hearne.

Hearne read it, a glimmer of recognition in his clear blue eyes. 'Detective Villatoro of the Arcadia, California, police department. You called and asked for a meeting a few weeks ago. All the way from Southern California.'

'Thank you for meeting me. I've retired from the department since then.'

'Congratulations,' Hearne said, his face showing what he was thinking, that the meeting wasn't official after all but of a personal nature. And maybe a waste of his time. 'Have you ever been to North Idaho before?'

'No. It's very green,' Villatoro said, thinking: It's very *white*.

'Yeah, it's our little piece of heaven,' Hearne said.

Villatoro smiled. 'It's a very pretty place. Very peaceful, it seems.'

'It usually is. We've got a problem this morning. You probably saw the poster out there. A couple of kids are missing.'

Villatoro had observed it all: the women who arrived with the poster, the conversation between the loud one with the little-girl voice and the rancher who had left Hearne's office. 'I hope the children are OK,' he said. 'I've been struck by how the town thinks *their* children are missing. It warms my heart to witness such an attitude.'

'We do tend to take care of our own.' Hearne looked at Villatoro's card again. 'So, if you're no longer with your police department, what can I do for you? Are you looking to retire here?'

Villatoro held up his hand. 'No, no. I want to complete an investigation I worked on for years. It led me here.'

Hearne sat back. 'What are you still investigating?'

Villatoro snapped open the locks on his briefcase, slipped five sheets of paper out of his file and handed them across the desk. They were back and front photocopies of hundred-dollar bills.

The serial numbers for the bills were typed on each one, followed by a series of bank routing numbers highlighted by a yellow marker.

'These came through my bank,' Hearne said. 'Are they counterfeit?'

'No, they're real. As you know, there are authorities who electronically scan currency as it flows through the system to check for marked or counterfeit bills. It isn't a perfect system, but when it registers a hit, they increase the frequency of scanning. Several hits from a single bank may be significant.'

Hearne raised his eyebrows. 'Meaning?'

'I'll start at the beginning. Eight years ago, there was an armed robbery at a horse-racing track in my town, which is—or was—outside of Los Angeles. Millions in cash was taken, and a man died during the commission of the crime, one of the guards. As you can guess, it was an inside job, and the employees were convicted and sent to prison. My chief turned the investigation over to the LAPD and I served as the liaison.'

'Hold it. Was this *the* Santa Anita robbery? I read about that.'

'Santa Anita Racetrack.' Villatoro nodded. 'One of the largest employers in Arcadia. Yes—thirteen and a half million dollars in cash was stolen. One employee gave up the others and testified against them all. But none of the cash was ever recovered and not one of the people convicted has yet to come forward. I've talked to them and they're desperate to get out of jail, but they swear they have nothing to tell us. It doesn't seem like they know.'

Hearne frowned. 'What about the guy who testified against them?'

Villatoro sighed. 'He is no longer with us. He was the victim of a convenience store robbery less than a year after the trial. He was there buying milk and was caught in crossfire between the store owner and the robber.'

'Interesting,' Hearne said. 'So what does that all have to do with me and my bank?'

Villatoro gestured towards the photocopies of the hundred-dollar bills. 'The cashiers and accountants at the racetrack had an efficient procedure for counting the money, but an incomplete method for recording the cash. The racetrack didn't have marked bills, like your bank surely does, or dye packs. You can imagine the sea of cash that washes in during a big day, every twenty minutes or so when betters come to the windows. It's all computerised, of course, but the cash still needs to match the computer at the end of the day, so it's hand-counted in the back. Once the cash matches the computer, armoured cars take it to the bank. In the kind of rush they are in, there was no way to mark the money in any comprehensive way. The best they could do at the time was to randomly record serial numbers—in this case, the serial number of every fiftieth hundred-dollar bill.'

Hearne was listening closely and urged Villatoro on.

'In the end, we had the serial numbers for one thousand, three hundred and seventy-seven hundred-dollar bills. For three years, not a single bill with a recorded serial number was reported. Then one came in that had been routed through four different banks, but the bank of origin was yours. Two others surfaced over the years, one from California, then Nevada, the other from Nebraska. There appeared to be no link at all.

'Two months ago, though, four more turned up, all from your bank. I took this information to my liaison contacts in the LAPD, but as far as they were concerned the case was closed. They'd moved on. My department was small, my mandatory retirement date approaching. But these bills bothered me, and they bother me still. You see, Mr Hearne, Arcadia is a peaceful place, or it used to be. The only unsolved murder on our books was assigned to me. I can't leave without trying to solve it, even if it is on my own time.'

Hearne studied the bills, waiting for more.

'I think someone who has access to at least some of the Santa Anita money lives in this area and banks with you,' Villatoro said. 'I would like to look at accounts that were opened with you four years ago and that are still active. I may find a name that will jump out at me. Especially if I can trace the name back to California.'

Hearne made a face. 'You know we can't just turn over a list of our customers to you. That's illegal.'

Villatoro nodded. 'But if I can get the proper authorities to request access, I hope you will be cooperative. That's all I ask.'

Shaking his head, Hearne handed back the photocopies. 'We have hundreds of new accounts and I'd bet a quarter of them came from California. Talk to the sheriff. His name is Carey. If you make your case to him, he might escort you to a judge who can request an order to see the accounts. Otherwise, there's no more I can do.'

An uncomfortable silence hung in the office. Finally, Villatoro shut his briefcase and stood up. 'Thank you, Mr Hearne,' he said.

Hearne shook his hand. 'Well, good luck. And welcome to Kootenai Bay.'

'Thank you. I trust everything we've discussed is confidential?'

'Of course,' Hearne said, showing Villatoro to the door. 'Of course it is.'

AFTER VILLATORO LEFT, Jim Hearne shut the door of his office and leaned with his back to it. This, he knew, was the only place in his office where no one could see him through the windows.

He closed his eyes tightly and breathed deeply. Villatoro had taken him by surprise. There was a time a few years ago when Hearne thought about what he'd done, or, more accurately, what he *hadn't* done, and the thought kept him awake at night. But like everything, it gradually went away. He thought he'd got away with it, since there had been no repercussions. Sure, he'd known better, deep down.

He should have known this day would come.

OSCAR SWANN parked his pick-up behind a white Fox News van and got out quickly. He could see plainly what was happening and was there to stop it. Monica Taylor stood on her front lawn looking aimless and haggard. A young man was fitting a video camera on a tripod in front of her. Near the van, a slim blonde held a mirror to her face and was adjusting her hair.

He was nearly too late. He should never have taken the time to shower, shave and put on fresh clothes before he left his house. But he still had a thing for Monica. She was the best-looking woman he'd run across in Kootenai Bay. Unlike Singer and Gonzalez, Swann couldn't stand endless hours at his own place with only himself and his hogs for company. He had to get out, liked to roam the town. He had needs, after all.

Swann strode towards the van. 'No, no,' he said to the newswoman. 'There'll be no interview.'

The reporter glared at him. 'What do you mean, there'll be no interview? I asked her, and she agreed. She wants to put out a plea for her children.'

'Sorry, that won't happen. I'm with the task force for the sheriff's department.' He showed her a laminated graphic of a badge on a lanyard they'd made just that morning. 'If you want an interview, you need permission from Sheriff Carey. In fact, he's going to hold a press conference in a few hours. But we need you to leave Mrs Taylor alone for now.'

'Hey . . .' the reporter called after him, but he was already gone.

He positioned himself between the camera and Monica, who had watched the whole thing.

'Oscar,' Monica asked, 'what's going on?'

He kept his voice low. 'Monica, this isn't a good idea.' He told her how the task force had decided to funnel all requests for interviews through the sheriff's department so they could keep some control of the information.

'But why?' she asked, her eyes big. She was tired, pale, worn out, and she wore no make-up. Still, he thought she was lovely.

'We don't want things to turn into a circus side show,' he said. 'We've got to keep a lid on the information we put out. Look, the person who has your kids will be watching the news. We don't want him to know what leads we're pursuing. You might inadvertently say something that will help keep him from us. If he decides to contact you, we don't want to scare him.' Swann pointed to the reporter. 'All she wants is a story. Trust us, Monica. We've got only your best interests and your kids' welfare in mind.'

She looked at him as if she wasn't sure about that, but she called, 'Later, maybe,' to the reporter, and turned back towards her house. Swann followed her in through the front door and closed and locked it behind them.

What he didn't say was what he was thinking: And we don't want your children to see you crying on television.

JESS RAWLINS PULLED off the road near his mailbox, got his mail and tossed it on the seat next to him. Fiona had placed a Post-it note on an envelope from the county tax assessor with the words *BETTER OPEN THIS!!!* on it.

After changing into his work clothes and replacing his new Stetson with his sweat-stained old one, Jess stuck a pair of fencing pliers in his back pocket and saddled Chile. There was a cold, heavy stone in his belly as he rode up a slate-rock ridge that overlooked the ranch on the northern side of the near meadow.

Growing up, Jess had explored every inch of the ranch within riding distance of the house. The slate ridge was 150 yards away. Its teeth could be seen against the horizon from his porch and from the road, but the slope behind it was obscured from view. It was the perfect place to see but not be seen.

As a boy, Jess had created scenarios where he went into action and saved his family from outside threats—Indians, escaped criminals, communists. From his perch behind the slate rocks, he aimed down the length of a broom handle and picked off his targets as they moved out of the trees into the open ranch yard below. He would see his mother in her kitchen, but she couldn't see him. She had no idea he was up there saving her, saving the ranch. Sometimes, when the situation got desperate, he would rise to his feet, holler a war cry and charge down the hill, bobbing and weaving as his enemies shot at him. By the time he made it to the house he had dispatched the last of the bad guys, despite his massive, fatal wounds.

Years later, he had shown this place to his son, Jess Junior. Not that he wanted the boy to create scenarios of his own, but he hoped his son would simply appreciate the view the ridge afforded of the ranch, the land, the open vista. His son had looked around, then turned to Jess with a shrug and asked how long it was until dinner.

Now Jess picked his way down the slate-rock ridge, looking out at the newborn calves and their mothers in the fenced-off meadow. He rode through them to the other side of the corral and followed the fence to the top of the hill. The barbed wires had sagged between two posts, leaving enough of a gap that the calves could escape. He dismounted, tightened the wire and pounded new staples into the posts. After finishing, he walked along the fence thumping each post, making sure the bottoms hadn't rotted away.

That's when he saw the strip of colour hanging from a barb on the second strand from the top.

Jess bent over and looked at it. The yellow strip was about a half-inch wide and an inch long. It wasn't frayed or bleached out, which meant it was new. Maybe a member of the search team had brushed too close to his fence. But he remembered the description of the Taylor girl from the poster, that she was last seen wearing a yellow sweatshirt.

Then, in the mud near his boots, he noticed two footprints. One was from a small sneaker. The other, slightly larger, was made by a bare foot.

He stood up and looked out over his ranch in the direction the footprints were aimed. They were headed for his barn.

'I HEAR SOMEONE coming,' Annie said, clapping her hand over William's mouth and muzzling a long complaint about how hungry he was. William squirmed in protest and reached up to prise her hand away, but he heard it too: crunching footfalls in loose gravel outside the barn.

It had been Annie's idea to hide in the barn the night before, after they had shimmied through a barbed-wire fence. They had seen the barn roof glowing in the cloud-muted blue moonlight in a clearing at the foot of the slope. There was a house down there, too, but she didn't want to knock on any doors. After what had happened at Mr Swann's, she didn't trust anyone.

They had held hands as they crossed the ranch yard, stepping as lightly as they could through the gravel. Luckily, the barn was empty except for a fat cow that stood still and silent in a stall. Half the barn was filled with pungent hay stacked up to the rafters. Annie and William climbed the stair-stepped bales until they were on the top of the hay. From there, Annie could look down on the floor of the barn and see all the doors.

'We need to build a nest,' she told William.

'Let's call it a fort,' he said. 'A fort sounds better.'

'OK, a fort.'

The bales were heavy, but not so heavy that the two of them couldn't lift six out of the top row and stack them round the hole they had formed. Their fort was two bales deep into the stack.

Even though William was literally falling asleep as he stood, Annie coaxed him back down to the ground, where they found a tack room. They carried saddle blankets and a canvas tarp up to their fort, and William was asleep before Annie could adjust the tarp to cover him. She made one more trip to the tack room and found a long, scythe-shaped hay hook and a pitchfork, which she took up to their fort. The pitchfork was now within reach on the top of the bales. The hay hook was stuck in the hay at eye level.

Annie had slept fitfully. Every sound scared her. Events of the previous day kept replaying in her head. The last thing she remembered, until now, was the muted glow from the rising sun through gaps in the side of the barn.

Someone was coming.

It was much warmer in the barn now, and heat beat down on them from the roof just a few feet over the top of their hay wall. Annie guessed it was afternoon. She threw the tarp back and found herself drenched in sweat. Her mouth was so dry her lips stuck to her teeth as she tried to speak.

'Here they come,' she said thickly.

A LARGE SLIDING DOOR opened, flooding the barn with light. The sound of it was like a roll of distant thunder. William's eyes widened and Annie withdrew her hand from his mouth.

Who is it? he mouthed.

She shrugged. She didn't dare peek over the hay bales.

'Hello, is someone in here?' a man called. 'I saw some tracks outside. If you're in here, speak up.'

Annie and William exchanged looks. Annie narrowed her eyes and gestured towards the hay hook and the pitchfork. William saw them for the first time and looked back at her with admiration.

For a moment, there was no sound at all from below. What was he doing? Annie wondered. Had he left?

'Annie and Willie, are you in here?' the man asked softly.

Annie's heart raced: *He knew their names!*

She looked at William, who was scowling. He didn't like to be called

Willie. He reached up and drew the hay hook out of the bale, and ran his finger along its sharpened tip.

The man below was walking through the barn, and she heard the tack room door open, then close. The man called out even more softly than before.

'Annie and Willie, you can come out. You're probably pretty hungry and thirsty, and I'd guess your family's worried about you. I see I'm missing some blankets and a tarp. That was smart thinking. But I bet a shower and something cool to drink would sound even better right now.'

William looked to Annie and made a face indicating, *It sure would!* Annie scolded him with her eyes.

'I imagine you two are scared,' the man said. 'But I'm not going to do you any harm. My name's Jess Rawlins. I own this ranch.'

Suddenly, Annie had doubts. The man's voice seemed kind and caring. But how could she know he was telling the truth? Or that he wasn't friends with people like Mr Swann or the executioners?

'I'm coming up there on the top of my hay,' Rawlins said, 'because if I was a kid your age, that's where I'd go. Plus, it looks like my stack is one row higher today.'

William clutched the handle of the hay hook with both hands. Annie grabbed the pitchfork and pointed the rusty tines at the top of the hay bales.

They could hear him breathing hard as he climbed the stack, and felt a slight vibration in the closely packed hay from his weight.

'Don't get scared,' Rawlins said. 'It's going to be OK.'

When the long, brown hand reached over the top bale, William swung the hook, striking flesh. The man responded with a sharp intake of breath. The point cut through the webbing between his thumb and index finger. Blood spurted from the wound.

Annie's first, instinctive reaction was revulsion. She wanted to run away, but there was nowhere to run. So she swallowed hard, stood with the pitchfork ready and leaned forward, following the arm down towards a shoulder, then a battered cowboy hat and a lean, weathered face. She pointed the tines towards his face and tried to scowl.

Rawlins looked back at her, obviously in pain, but his eyes didn't seem to threaten her. 'Damn,' he said. 'Why'd you go and do that to my hand? It really hurts.'

Annie wasn't sure what to do. The rancher's hand was pinned with the hook to the bale of hay, but it was held there by just a quarter-inch of skin. The rancher could pull away and keep climbing. She glanced back at

William and saw the terror in his eyes. She turned back to Rawlins. His other hand was now on the top bale as well.

'I need to pull that hook out,' Rawlins said. 'I don't want you jabbing me with that fork, though.'

Annie knew she had him. So why did she feel so awful?

'You're Annie, right?'

She nodded.

'And Willie?'

'William,' her brother corrected.

'Well, Annie and William, I'm glad you're all right. The whole county's looking for you. Mind if I pull this hook out of my hand?'

'We're hungry,' Annie said. 'You can pull it out if you'll get us something to eat and drink.'

Jess Rawlins looked at her with something like amusement. 'I was going to offer that anyway,' he said.

THE BANKER, Jim Hearne, shouldered his way through the knot of men in jackets and ties and women in cocktail dresses and ordered another Scotch and water at the makeshift bar. It was his fourth in barely an hour.

It was the opening night reception for the Kootenai Bay Recreation Center, financed through his bank. He had been the principal officer for the project and was on the board of directors. The centre had a full-size gymnasium, an Olympic-size pool, tennis courts, weight rooms, a climbing wall, sauna rooms, Jacuzzis. Enough charter memberships had been sold—primarily to newcomers to the valley—that first-year projections would be exceeded. Over 200 people were touring the facility, drinks in hand, talking excitedly, slapping him on the back.

Two of the bars were located in the gym, one under the rim of each basketball hoop on opposite ends of the floor. Hearne alternated bars each time he ordered a drink so the guests wouldn't notice how much he was drinking. As The Banker, he was always being watched, observed, talked about. It came with the territory, and he accepted it. But tonight there was too much on his mind.

He circulated through the building, exchanging pleasantries, welcoming new residents. He tried not to be drawn into any conversations, most of which were about either the new facility or the missing Taylor children.

The sheriff had held a press conference in the afternoon that was televised on the local affiliates and excerpted nationally. Hearne had not supported

Carey in the election, thinking him pompous and unqualified. But he was pleasantly surprised how well the new sheriff presented himself. Carey stressed to the media that at this point it was a missing persons investigation, not kidnapping or worse. Photos of the Taylor children were flashed on the screen along with a hot-line number. Carey explained that he'd tapped the resources of a team of retired big-city police officials to assist him. He seemed competent, in charge. Hearne wondered who had coached him.

As the banker, Hearne was sort of a host at this reception, but he was having trouble mingling. The fact was, he couldn't think of much else other than the missing Taylor children and the meetings he'd had that morning with Jess Rawlins and Eduardo Villatoro. He approached a bar in the alcove to the swimming pool and ordered a fifth Scotch. As he sipped it, he looked out on the pool. The black lines painted on the bottom wavered in the water more than they should. He would have to slow down.

'What's wrong with you?'

It was his wife, Laura. He hadn't seen her approach.

'What do you mean?'

'I've been watching you,' she said. 'You've been running around like a chicken with its head cut off. The only places you stop are the bars.'

He felt himself flush. Caught.

Laura was a plain-speaking, handsome woman, with strong features and all-seeing eyes. Her skin was dark from being outside so much, riding her horses, working at her stables. She was a horsewoman, a former barrel racer at rodeo events from a third-generation Idaho family. Despite their status within the community, Laura chose to dress in Western shirts, jeans, sometimes a broomstick skirt and boots, like tonight. Hearne appreciated her sense of tradition, but sometimes he wished she would dress up a little.

'Are you OK?' she asked. 'You seem just a tad distracted.'

'I keep thinking about those Taylor kids,' he said, which was true but only part of the reason. 'That isn't the kind of thing that happens here.'

'Maybe it didn't used to'—she gestured towards the crowd—'before the immigration and all your new friends.'

He smiled sourly. 'My "new friends", as you call them, helped buy your last three horses and the new barn.'

'I know. Boy, you are testy tonight.' She nodded towards his glass. 'You'd better slow down. And, Mr Jim Hearne, don't play coy with me.' She leaned into him, staring up into his eyes. 'I know you. You drink when you're fretting about something. It never helps, but it's what you do.'

'I said—'

'Right, the Taylors. Which Taylor are you most worried about? The kids or Monica?'

Hearne felt his neck get hot. Laura had never liked Monica Taylor and harboured suspicions about her, even though he'd explained that Monica thought of him as a father figure because of his friendship with her father.

When Jim Hearne was riding saddle broncs on the college rodeo team, and later when he was sponsored by Rawlins Ranch, Ty Taylor had been his closest friend and travelling companion. Monica's father was handsome and enigmatic, a star performer, a man who attracted women like a magnet, despite the fact that he was married with a young daughter at home. Early on, that was one of the reasons Hearne partnered with Ty—where Ty went, women appeared. When Hearne injured his knee and returned home, his on-again off-again courtship of Laura got serious, and they married. He finished up his degree in finance while he recovered, but the rodeo was in his blood. Laura didn't like it when he went back to rodeoing, and liked it even less when he hooked up again with Ty. Although he was faithful to Laura and tried to rein Ty in, he wasn't successful. On a warm May day, Ty left his family without a word and never came back.

Hearne was no psychologist, but it was easy for him to see how Ty's abandonment affected Monica and her mother. Monica's mother became an alcoholic and moved to Spokane, supposedly looking for a permanent job before sending for her daughter. Monica bounced around from place to place, growing wilder and more beautiful by the year. Boys were as attracted to her as women had been to her father. And she looked for men who were dazzling, dangerous and charismatic, like Ty had been.

Hearne had done what he could, from a distance. He approved a home loan after the loan committee turned her down due to insufficient assets. He quietly dismissed overdraft charges on her bank account. When she was overdrawn, he would call her and, on occasion, lend her a few hundred. She'd always thanked him for his help very sincerely and never acted as if she was entitled to it.

He liked her, in spite of the poor choices she had made. Was he attracted to her? Sure. Every man was. But it wasn't that. She was a casualty and he had been there when the damage was done. Looking back, he felt responsibility for the way things turned out with the Taylors. He should have knocked Ty down, sat on him, and told him to straighten up. Instead, he had stood by, shaking his head, watching Ty wreck his own family.

'They'll find those kids,' Laura said, breaking into his reverie. 'I'm sure they'll turn up at somebody's house.'

'I hope so,' Hearne said.

But, of course, it wasn't only the missing children. He thought of Jess Rawlins, how he could see no way to save him. Jess had been the conscience of the valley as Hearne was growing up. He was stubborn, independent, but intrinsically fair. That his own family had failed the way it did was a tragedy, Hearne thought, and he blamed Karen, Jess's ex-wife. Hearne knew things about Karen, about her personal bank account and growing balance while the ranch accounts went dry, about her many dinners with men other than Jess. After Karen finally left and Jess was devastated, Hearne felt immensely guilty for not softening the blow by telling what he knew. It would have been an ethical breach, but it would have been the right thing to do, he saw in retrospect. Jess had not recovered from the financial or emotional loss, and now his ranch was literally on the block.

And it wasn't that Jim Hearne was immune to ethical breaches, and that's what troubled him most. His own actions—or lack of them—had brought Eduardo Villatoro to North Idaho.

Hearne recalled his first meeting with Eric Singer, who had flown up from Los Angeles to make him an offer just days after the board of directors decided that the only way to keep the bank viable was to change from low-return, high-maintenance agricultural loans to commercial finance. The bank needed to increase its cash deposits exponentially. So when Singer walked into Hearne's office, it was as if fate had sent a messenger.

Singer told Hearne that he sought isolation, cheap land and a live-and-let-live attitude. He was not the first retired LAPD officer to find his way to North Idaho, nor the last. But unlike the others Hearne had met, Singer promised to bring up a small but well-heeled group of colleagues with him if Hearne was willing to make the conditions right.

Hearne made the conditions right. Singer delivered. Hearne was promoted personally by the chairman of the board. But it haunted him still.

Despite the disapproving look Laura was giving him, Hearne put the empty glass on the bar and ordered another.

THE COMMAND CENTRE for the disappearance of the Taylor children had been established in a conference room off the Kootenai Bay City Council chambers, down the hall from Sheriff Carey's office. Off-duty dispatchers had been called in to set it up with telephones, computers and a fax machine, along with a coffeemaker and mini-refrigerator. Ex-Lieutenant Eric Singer stood at the whiteboard with a fistful of coloured pens.

Ex-Officer Newkirk was slumped at the foot of the long table, looking vacantly through a window. He felt ill, his skin gritty. His stomach was acting up. The scenario that was playing out in front of him was the last thing he wanted to be involved in. This was the situation that had kept him awake at night for years. This, right here, was the reason he had ulcers.

'Are we ready?' Singer asked, pulling the cap from a green pen.

'Ready,' Gonzalez said, adjusting a legal pad filled with scribbles. He began to read and Singer started writing on the whiteboard.

'When we're done, I want Newkirk to go get the sheriff,' Singer said, pausing and looking over his shoulder. 'Newkirk?'

Gonzalez leaned over and whopped Newkirk on the arm with the back of his hand, saying, 'Wake the fuck up.'

Newkirk wheeled in his chair, startled. 'What?'

'I asked if you'd go down and get the sheriff when I'm done here,' Singer said quietly, with exaggerated enunciation. 'We need his approval to proceed.'

'OK.'

'Are you OK, Newkirk?' Singer asked, his ice-blue eyes unblinking. 'You with us here?'

Newkirk nodded, then looked to Gonzalez and nodded again.

'You better be,' Gonzalez said.

As NEWKIRK ENTERED the Pend Oreille County Sheriff's office, he noticed a paunchy man in a brown suit waiting in reception. Newkirk nodded at the man, then told the receptionist that Singer was ready in the command centre.

'The command centre, Officer Newkirk?' the receptionist asked.

'The conference room,' Newkirk said, an edge to his voice. 'We're calling it the command centre now, until we get those kids back.'

The receptionist flushed and walked back towards the sheriff's office.

'It's a good thing you are doing,' the man in the brown suit said to Newkirk. 'Very community-minded.'

'What?' Newkirk turned, adjusted his ball cap and studied the man. A man wearing a suit in the sheriff's office on a Saturday evening. He looked out of place, enough so that Newkirk's antennae went up.

'I heard your name. You are among the volunteers who have come forward. You used to be with the LAPD,' Villatoro said pleasantly.

'You have some kind of interest in this case?'

The man shook his head. 'I'm here on another matter.' He stood and extended his hand. 'Eduardo Villatoro.'

Newkirk didn't reach out immediately. It grated on him when Latins gave their names with Spanish pronunciation, playing up the accents. He felt his street cop dead-eye stare take over. Usually, when he did that, the other person would reveal himself, talk too much.

'I'm here to see the sheriff as well,' Villatoro said. 'But it's after six. I was wondering how long you might be with him before I can talk with him.'

'About what?'

'Another matter.'

'Fine, don't tell me. I doubt it's as important as this one.'

Villatoro smiled. 'You are right. I was just wondering if I should wait or come back tomorrow. That's why I was asking.'

This dark guy made Newkirk uncomfortable, and he wasn't sure he knew why. 'Come back tomorrow,' he said.

The receptionist came out of the sheriff's office and said to Newkirk, 'He's finishing up a call and will be with you shortly.'

'I'll wait.'

He watched Villatoro dig for his wallet and approach the receptionist.

'I would like to leave this card,' Villatoro said. 'I'll be in early tomorrow morning to see the sheriff.'

The receptionist took the card without looking at it and placed it on her desk. She watched the light blink out on her handset. 'He's through,' she said.

Sheriff Carey came out of his office a moment later, looking haggard. 'That was the FBI in Boise,' he said. 'They want to know if we're ready to call them in. I told them to give us a day or two. We should have things wrapped up by then. I hope.'

Newkirk nodded. Singer had advised the sheriff to keep the Feds at bay.

'So you're ready for me?' Carey asked.

'Yes, we are. In the command centre.'

Newkirk noticed that Villatoro had slipped out during the exchange.

'OK, then.' Carey heaved a weight-of-the-world sigh.

'Sheriff . . .' the receptionist called after him.

'Yes, you can go home now, Marlene.'

Newkirk waited a moment while Marlene cleared her desk and the sheriff strode down the hall towards the conference room. When she turned round, he reached over, plucked the business card from her desk and slipped it into his back pocket.

ON THE WHITEBOARD, in green, Singer had written TIMELINE. Under the heading, each fact of the case was bulleted next to the military time it had occurred. The children had left school the previous day, Friday, at noon on early release. Between noon and 15:35, when the mailwoman Fiona Pritzle had picked them up on the road and dropped them near Sand Creek, they had presumably gone home, taken the fishing rod and vest, and set out on foot. Monica Taylor became concerned about their absence at 17:30. Her fight with Tom Boyd had occurred around 18:00. She called the sheriff's department two hours later at 20:00. Boyd staggered from the Sand Creek Bar at 23:30 and hadn't been seen since.

Singer ran his finger down the list. 'Our last timeline entry was oh-eight ten this morning,' he said, looking pained. 'These kids have been missing for twenty-seven hours. Our experience is that once we pass twenty-four, we've got a problem.'

'I *know* we've got a problem,' Carey said.

'Word is out,' Singer said. 'Everyone's looking for them. But there have been no solid leads since we found that shoe and the fishing rod. There are three teams of ten volunteers out there now, combing through the woods on a grid from where that shoe was found. So far, we've got nothing.'

Carey swallowed. 'I know.'

'Sheriff, how long would it take for a body to surface on Sand Creek? Assuming the person drowned?'

The sheriff shook his head. 'It's not very deep, but it's fast with run-off. The creek completely shallows out before the lake, so there's no chance any bodies floated all that way. It's only eighteen inches deep at the mouth. So all we're talking about is four miles of creek before it empties into the lake.'

Singer looked thoughtful. He rubbed his chin with his hand. Then: 'Let's continue.'

Singer had written SUSPECTS in red. Under it were Tom Boyd, Monica Taylor, Fiona Pritzle, 'transient unknown', and 'area paedophile'.

'Can you think of any others?' he asked.

'I'd scratch the mother and the mail lady off the list,' Carey said. 'The mother's just too upset. And that mail lady was the one who called us. If she had something to do with it, she could have just kept her mouth shut.'

Singer gestured to Gonzalez. 'Gonzo?'

Gonzalez cleared his throat. 'I had a guy once who came into the station and said he'd seen a man lure a kid, a young white male, into his car in East LA. Turned out the witness had tortured and killed a half-dozen boys. He reported the first one just for the thrill of it, to see how we worked.'

Carey shivered. 'Still, I can't imagine Fiona Pritzle . . .'

'Let's not scratch her off just yet,' Singer said. He pointed to TRANSIENT UNKNOWN. 'This is the hardest one. It could be a guy passing through, or maybe on a sales route. I'd have your guys start interviewing owners of motels and bed and breakfasts, asking owners if they've got—or had—anybody suspicious staying with them. We should assume they checked out today, probably first thing this morning, so I'd get a list on that.'

Carey pulled a notebook from his pocket and wrote that down.

'Area paedophile,' Singer said. 'A little easier. I'm sure you've got a list of registrations, right?'

Carey nodded. 'There are a couple of names on it, last time I looked. I think one of them moved away, though.'

'I'd key on the other name,' Singer said casually. 'Then we've got Tom Boyd.' He drew a star by the name. 'He's got priors. He's probably on steroids. He had a fight with the kids' mother. He never turned in his truck last night, and now he's missing. When he left the Taylor house, he likely had an idea where kids might go fishing. M, M and O.'

Carey looked up. Newkirk could tell he was trying not to reveal that he didn't know what the initials meant.

'Motive, method and opportunity.'

Carey nodded, visibly grateful that Singer had let him off the hook.

Next to the list of suspects was another list, headed ASSIGNMENTS.

'This is only a recommendation,' Singer said softly, 'based on a cumulative seventy-six years of experience in this room. But you're the sheriff, and we're just volunteers trying to help out. You need to make the call.'

Carey didn't hesitate. 'Looks good to me.'

'Then we should go to work,' Singer said.

AFTER THE SHERIFF left the room, Singer looked to Gonzalez.

'Hook, line, sinker,' Gonzalez said. 'He reminds me that democracy works, though. A county full of idiots elects an idiot to be their chief law enforcement officer.'

Newkirk turned away, thinking: I'm going to throw up.

Singer said, 'Take it easy on the sheriff. He's our media strategy. He comes across great on camera. Doesn't he look like he might burst into tears any second?' A beat of silence. 'You don't look so good, Officer Newkirk.'

'I'm fine,' Newkirk lied, and thought: This is the nightmare, all right. The one where something happens that could reveal them, and lead to something worse, another crime. And the only way to keep ahead of the situation, to circumvent discovery, was to think and become truly evil, to become the antithesis of everything he believed in, all the reasons he had become a cop.

'The fuck is the matter with you, Newkirk?' Gonzalez said. 'In for a penny, in for a pound. That was the deal.'

'What are the odds on a couple of kids being there?' Newkirk asked. 'Ten minutes either way and we wouldn't be here now.' If his own kids were missing . . . he couldn't even imagine how he'd feel.

Singer shrugged. 'Forget that odds business. We can't play that game.'

You saw her face, Newkirk wanted to say. She had seen something no child should ever have to see. She would be forever tainted. They had poisoned her, and the little boy. Ruined them.

'How many kids did you save?' Singer asked suddenly. 'Did you ever tally the kids you saved when you busted some scumbag father or live-in?'

Newkirk thought back. 'Hundreds,' he said.

'Hundreds,' Singer repeated solemnly. 'Don't worry. I'm not going to suggest that because you saved so many kids these two don't mean anything. But if they talk, we go down. Between you, me, Gonzo and Swann, we've saved thousands of citizens. We did *good*, Newkirk.'

Newkirk said nothing.

'We earned what we've got now,' Singer continued, his voice a whisper. 'We can't let anyone take that away from us.'

Newkirk nodded weakly.

Gonzalez suddenly leaned forward and placed a huge hand on Newkirk's knee and squeezed with surprising force. His black eyes burned. 'You know what happened to Rodale when he forgot the deal we all made.'

Newkirk nodded again.

'You in?' Singer asked. Everything rode on the answer.

'I'm in.'

Then he remembered the business card in his back pocket.

'ARCADIA POLICE DEPARTMENT,' Singer said, fingering the card. 'Eduardo Villatoro, Detective. Then he handwrote "Retired" under it. From our old stomping grounds.'

Gonzalez asked, 'You know him?'

'I know *of* him. He's that pain-in-the-ass local who kept asking questions. He couldn't recognise a stone wall if he drove into it.'

Newkirk said, 'What if he's here because of, you know?'

'Then we'll handle him.' Singer handed the card back.

'*Eduardo Villatoro!*' Gonzalez said in heavily accented English, rolling his tongue just like Villatoro had done. 'Maybe he wants to retire here. He's probably worn out from getting kittens out of trees and shit like that. It means zilch. Let's not get paranoid.'

Something banged the door, and the three ex-cops exchanged glances. Singer signalled Newkirk to check out the sound. Newkirk approached the door silently, then grabbed the doorknob and threw it back.

A janitor stood in the hallway, pulling a mop back from where he had hit the bottom of the door. There were arcs of soapy water on the linoleum floor. The man looked to be in his mid-thirties—a trusty, judging by his orange jailbird jumpsuit. Stringy brown hair coursed to his thin shoulders. Unfocused—and alarmed—eyes moved from Newkirk to Singer to Gonzalez.

'What do you want?' Gonzalez asked, folding his arms.

'Nothin',' the janitor said. 'Jes' cleanin'.'

'You hear anything?' Singer asked conversationally. 'What's your name, anyway?'

'J.J. I'm jes' cleanin'. I didn't hear nothin'.'

'Not that there was anything to hear,' Singer said. 'We're assisting with the investigation into those two missing kids.'

The janitor nodded. His hair bobbed up and down.

'Take it easy, J.J.,' Singer said. Newkirk closed the door.

'You boys are paranoid, all right,' Gonzalez said.

NEWKIRK NEVER TIRED of driving his car up the long, heavily wooded road to his home and seeing it emerge through the trees. It was a mansion, his mansion, even though it was neocolonial and looked out of place among the huge log structures that were being built throughout the county. The only thing he liked better than seeing it in the daylight was seeing it lit up at night. After three and a half years, he still couldn't believe he lived there.

Three cars were in the circular driveway: his wife's Land Rover, his sons' Taurus and the old pick-up he used for cargo. The Taurus was parked in the place Newkirk reserved for himself, so he entered his home peeved. Sometimes he thought his family didn't appreciate what they had now. They had no idea what kind of sacrifices he'd made to create this new life. Singer and the others just wanted to get out from careers that had become intolerable. Newkirk got out for his family. He wished they knew that.

The boys and his daughter were at the kitchen table, already eating dinner. His wife, Maggie, looked up and glared at him.

It was only then that he remembered Maggie telling him to be home early to have a family dinner with his kids since getting everyone together was so rare these days, with spring baseball practice and ten-year-old Lindsey's soccer and all.

'Ah, jeez . . .' Newkirk moaned. 'I totally forgot.'

'I guess you did,' Maggie said. She was slight, pale, with red hair and green eyes that could flash like jewellery when she was angry.

He eased the door closed behind him. Most of all, he felt bad for his kids. His sons, Josh and Jason, could take it—they were in their teens and totally absorbed in sports, girls, iPods. Lindsey, though, she could break his heart. Lindsey worshipped her dad.

Maggie pushed her chair back and approached him. She was livid. 'The one night I ask you to be home at a certain time, you can't bring yourself to do it. The one night!'

Newkirk stepped back. 'Look, I'm sorry. But there are some kids missing and I volunteered to help find them.'

'So are you home now?' she asked.

He paused. 'No, I'm here long enough to get a change of clothes. I'm likely to be down there all night.'

Maggie's face tightened. She turned on her heel and walked straight to the cloakroom off the living room. The slam of the door echoed in the house.

Newkirk stood there, his face red. 'I'll see you kids tomorrow,' he said as he went up the stairs to his bedroom for his clothes. 'Tell your mother I had to go.'

JESS RAWLINS CLEANED the wound again in the sink and looked clinically at the hole in his hand. He flexed his fingers, cringed at how much it hurt, and stuck his hand back under the running water.

Annie and William Taylor sat at the dining-room table, watching him, looking guilty. They looked smaller at the table than they had in the barn. Annie's feet—one with a shoe and the other dirty and bare—hardly touched the floor. William swung his legs, filled with nervous energy. William looked at him furtively, Jess noticed, not full on, like Annie. He was probably afraid he would be in trouble.

'Let me get this bandaged, and I'll get some food going,' Jess said. 'Then we'll call the sheriff and let him know I found his strays.'

'Sorry about your hand,' Annie said.

'I'll live. You're pretty good with a hay hook. Ever consider stacking hay?'

'No. Besides, William did it.'

Jess looked at William, who reacted with a mixture of fear and pride.

Annie shot him a glance. 'You should apologise.'

'I said I was sorry,' he said. To Jess, he said, 'My dad was an outlaw. Maybe that's why I did it.'

Jess thought that over. 'I'm not sure you want to be too proud of that.'

William looked hurt, and Annie looked vindicated.

'I'm cooking pancakes, steak and eggs,' Jess said quickly. 'OK with you?'

'It's almost dark out,' Annie said. 'Why are you going to cook breakfast?'

Her eyes were fixed on him. He thought he noted a kernel of hardness in them, like she'd seen a lot in her brief life and was used to being disappointed. Jess felt a pang. There was something about her, all right. He recalled how he felt when he saw her photo on the poster. He didn't want to disappoint her.

'Because,' he said, 'I know how to cook breakfast for kids. I used to do it. That's why.'

'Where are your kids?' William asked.

'Only one son,' Jess said. 'Gone. Grown up.' He winced as he rubbed the wound with salve, applied a square of thick gauze and wrapped white medical tape round his hand. When he had a good, tight wrap, he tore the tape off with his teeth. He could hear Annie admonish William in a whisper, saying the rancher was pretty old, so of course his son was gone.

'OK, I'm calling now,' Jess said, gingerly taking the handset from the wall with his bandaged hand. 'You kids created quite an uproar in town. They've got posters up, and even some volunteers, ex-policemen, looking for you. Your mother must be worried sick about you.'

Annie and William exchanged looks.

He thumbed through the directory. As he punched the number for the sheriff's department, he saw Annie, who had left the table, reach up and pull the phone cradle down, ending the connection. He looked at her, puzzled.

'Mister, is Mr Swann with them? The police, I mean?'

'I don't know him,' Jess said. 'Could be.'

'Tell him, Annie,' William urged from the table.

'Tell me what?'

She said, 'We saw some men kill another man. Down by the river. We saw their faces, and they saw ours.'

Jess looked at her, hard.

While she talked—the words rushed out, and William interjected things to abet her story—she never took her hand down from the cradle of the telephone. Jess still held the handset, but listened. A cold-blooded murder, followed by a chase, a close call with a Mr Swann, the biggest pigs she'd ever seen, fleeing through the dark to the barn.

'But, Annie,' Jess said gently, 'I haven't heard anything about a man being shot to death. If that had happened here, I'd have heard about it.'

Annie shook her head from side to side, pleading, 'That's what we saw. Me and William. We saw them shoot that man over and over, then they saw us and chased us. They *shot* at us!'

'But how do you know Mr Swann wanted to hurt you?'

'I heard him talking on the telephone. I told you that.'

'But you might have thought he was saying one thing when he was talking about something else.'

'What if you call the sheriff and those men come after us? They know we can recognise them,' she said, her eyes misting.

He started to say he would explain directly to the sheriff, get things sorted out. But her face showed such raw desperation, such fear, that he couldn't make himself say it. She was so sure of what she'd seen. But a murder in Pend Oreille County would be big news. Somebody surely would have reported a missing man. It didn't make sense. He wasn't sure what to do. Should he feed the kids, clean them up, wait until they fell asleep and call?

But wasn't that what Swann had done to them, if Annie's story was true? He didn't want to give them a reason to run again. People could be trusted, he wanted to show them. This was a good place, after all.

'How about I call your mother?' Jess said finally. 'I'll let her know you're OK. I'm sure she'll know what to do.'

'We're mad at her,' Annie said.

'You may be, but I'm sure she loves you and misses you. You know how moms are.'

Annie wanted to argue, Jess could tell. But she didn't. She let her fingers slide off the cradle, and Jess heard the dial tone.

'What's your phone number?'

THE CORDLESS PHONE burred in Monica Taylor's hand, and she looked at it as if it were a snake. Swann entered from the kitchen at the sound.

Every time the telephone rang, panic rose from her belly and momentarily paralysed her. It could be good news, or the worst possible news.

'Monica,' Swann asked, 'are you going to give me that?'

'Why do you have to answer my calls?'

'We've been over that. In case it's kidnappers . . . or a crank call. Sickos like to prey on people in your situation.'

Reluctantly, she handed him the phone.

'Monica Taylor's,' he said.

She watched his face for some kind of reaction. She could tell from the low range of the voice on the other end that it was a man.

'Yes, she's here,' Swann said. 'Who's calling? . . . Hello?'

The caller spoke, and she recognised it as a question by the way his voice rose at the end.

'This is Sergeant Oscar Swann, LAPD, retired. I'm assisting Miz Taylor. Who is calling?' Swann said 'yes' a few times. Then: 'I'm afraid I can't help you with that. I'd suggest you call the sheriff.'

Swann punched the telephone off.

'Nothing?' Monica asked, already knowing the answer.

He shook his head and put the phone down. 'Some rancher. I didn't get his name. First, he wanted to tell you he hopes your kids get found real soon. But what he was really calling about was that one of the search crews knocked down part of his fence and some cows got out. He's wondering who will pay for the damage. Jesus, you'd think with all that's going on he'd wait a bit before bitching about a fence.'

'YOU LIED,' Annie said.

'Yes, I did.' Jess's face had flushed red.

'Why?'

'Because Swann answered the telephone.'

'He's at our house? So now do you believe us?'

Jess rubbed his eyes with his left hand. 'I've got to think about it.'

'Is my mother all right?' William asked.

'I don't know. I didn't talk with her.'

Jess was trying to think, trying to put things together. Swann could be what he claimed to be: a volunteer with big-city police experience helping out a bereaved mother. He could have an entirely different take on what Annie claimed had happened in his house. Maybe Jess was buying into a child's delusion when he should be the adult, notifying the authorities so the whole county could breathe a collective sigh of relief. Not to mention the mother. He was glad he hadn't given his name.

'You two go get cleaned up,' he said finally. 'There are towels in the hall closet. In the back bedroom are some boxes of old clothes, from when my son lived here. There might even be some shoes that fit, Annie. I'm going to cook while you clean up, then we'll figure out our next move.'

The children nodded and went down the hallway. He pulled a package of steaks from the freezer to thaw in the microwave.

He heard the shower turn on, then a brief argument over who went first. Annie won, as he thought she might.

JESS WASHED THE DISHES after dinner, still amazed how much the children had eaten. He had found himself simply watching them at the table, enjoying the way they dug into their food with unabashed enthusiasm.

Now, as he put the plates into the drying rack, he said, 'You kids must have been starving.' When no response came, he turned and found them both asleep in their chairs. Annie was slumped forward on the table, her head in her arms. William was splayed out as if shot, his hands limp at his sides, his head tilted back, his mouth open.

Jess carried them one by one into a spare bedroom. Years ago, it had been his son's room. How small the kids were, he thought, how frail. But he'd forgotten how heavy a deeply sleeping child could be. Calves, which weighed twice as much, were easier to lift and carry.

Leaning against the doorjamb, he looked at them while they slept. It had been a long time since there had been children in the house. They brought a fresh smell with them, something else he had forgotten.

What in the hell was he doing? he asked himself.

VILLATORO SAT on one of his two beds and ate his dinner from a paper bag between his knees. Two McDonald's hamburgers, fries and the second beer of a six-pack. He ate voraciously, wishing he had ordered more since it was late and he had skipped lunch. A freight train rattled through town to the south, shaking the walls.

The television was on with the news out of Spokane. The disappearance of the Taylor children led the broadcast, but the anchor and the reporters knew nothing more than Villatoro did simply from being in the bank and the sheriff's department that day. He leaned forward, though, when a reporter interviewed Sheriff Ed Carey.

'I've heard it said that you've assembled what amounts to a Dream Team to help locate the children,' the reporter said.

Villatoro noticed a hint of a smile on the sheriff's mouth, a whisper of relief, as if this was the only good news he could convey.

'That's right,' Carey said. 'We're blessed in our community to have plenty of retired police officers with years of experience, who have volunteered their services, and they're working tirelessly, without compensation. We've greatly expanded the scope of our investigation.'

The anchor closed the story: 'The retired officers are reportedly from the Los Angeles Police Department . . .'

Villatoro paused, a hamburger poised in the air. Besides Newkirk, he wondered, who were the other ex-cops who had volunteered?

After dinner, he called his wife, Donna. She picked up quickly, and he visualised her in bed with a book.

'Where are you again?' she asked. 'Ohio? Iowa?'

'Idaho,' he said gently. 'Almost in Canada.'

'Isn't that where potatoes come from?'

'I think so, yes. But not this far north. Here there are mountains and lakes. It's very beautiful, and very . . . isolated.'

'Would I like it?'

'For a while, I think. There's not much shopping, not many places to eat.'

He told her about the missing children, and she said she thought she'd seen something on the news about it.

Donna was Anglo. In the last ten years she had put on a great deal of weight and was constantly fighting to slim down. Villatoro had told her, repeatedly, truthfully, that it didn't matter to him.

'Have you heard from Carrie?' he asked, inadvertently glancing at the framed photo he had brought. Their daughter was going to college, majoring in cinematography.

'An email. She needs money for some kind of film club.'

'Then send it to her,' he said automatically.

He listened while Donna replayed her day: breakfast with his mother, grocery shopping, fighting with the dry-cleaner. Too late he realised she had asked him a question while his mind was elsewhere.

'What?'

'I asked you when you thought you'd be back.'

'I don't know,' he said. 'A few more days. I have a feeling I'm getting close. It's more than a feeling, in fact.'

'You've said that before.' She sighed. 'This obsession, it's not healthy. You need to find out what it's like to be retired. You haven't even tried.'

'I'm not ready.'

'I talked to the Chows down the street,' she said. 'Mr Chow retired a month ago and they just bought a big RV. They're going to tour the country. They're like a couple of kids, they're so excited.'

'Is that what you think we should do?'

Hesitation. 'No, not really.'

He faked a laugh, hoping to defuse the topic. He had explained it to her before. She had said she understood, but it didn't stop her bringing it up.

For eight years since the robbery, he had lived with the case. It was the only open murder investigation within the department, and it had been his responsibility. Retirement didn't change that. Villatoro had always taken good police work seriously and considered it a calling, like the priesthood. He knew most of his fellow officers didn't think that way.

He had been shocked when his chief agreed to turn over the investigation to the LAPD and assigned Villatoro a peripheral liaison role in it. The LA detectives were used to messy, unfinished cases. To them it was about putting in their time, filing a few reports to grow the file. And it bothered Villatoro that these men were the vanguard of a sprawling, dirty, indefinable city that continued to expand, overwhelming small communities like Arcadia.

Villatoro was a proud man, despite his humble nature. No one—not the prosecutors, not the judges, not the LA detectives—had met the widow of the slain guard, as he had. She was young, with a toddler, and eight months pregnant at the time. She deserved justice, and only he could deliver it.

He told his wife good night and that he loved her.

HE SAT BACK on his bed with the television on but the volume turned down, and thought of Santa Anita Racetrack. He had always loved the place. The old, stately stadium, blue and massive, had the look and feel of lost elegance, of a 1950s Los Angeles bursting with energy, pride and money.

Once again he ran through the events of that day in May, eight years earlier. The cash had been counted by a dozen employees in a windowless office. Two armoured bank cars idled outside, on a gated service road manned by armed guards. The cash was banded and placed in fourteen heavy canvas bags, each holding $900,000 to $1 million in cash as well as computer-generated bank deposit slips. On a signal, the office doors were opened by the guards and bonded staff from the bank cars picked up the bags, which were secured with steel cable and clasp locks. Eight were placed in the first armoured car and six in the second. The driver of the second car was a man named Steve Nichols, a young father of two children.

As always, the armoured cars waited until the last race of the day commenced. They timed it that way so the cars could slip away from the facility before the races were completed and thousands of customers left for their cars. When the roar went up from the packed house, guards opened the front gate and the armoured cars rumbled away, taking an employee-only road obscured by trees, then proceeding east along Huntington Drive.

The vehicles stopped for the red light at Huntington and Santa Anita Boulevard. From there, they planned to turn left for the westbound I-210. But at that intersection, something happened.

A man walking his dog along Huntington testified later that he could see thick rolls of yellow-brown smoke pour out of the shooting ports of the armoured cars, followed by the rear doors opening. The police investigation said that canisters of tear gas hidden in the bags of cash were triggered by remote control. The guards rolled in agony on the road, the gas now so thick in the air that the witness couldn't see. What he heard, though, was squealing tyres and, a moment later, the sharp crack of gunshots. The speculation was that the robbers had been parked in the parking lot of a building on the other side of the intersection, and that two cars converged on the armoured vehicles. The robbers probably wore gas masks, or they couldn't have entered the smoking vehicles to remove the cash bags or kill Nichols.

The only witness to the crime, the dog walker, had turned his back to run and couldn't see the cars tear away. No vehicles were ever recovered that could be tied to the robbery, since no reliable description of the cars was ever made.

Because of the placement of the tear-gas bombs, the counting-room staff were immediately questioned. The police determined that several employees were involved, and a witness came forth to name names. Despite protestations of innocence, three people were convicted and jailed. But no one ever came forward with the names of the men in the two cars who had taken the money, killed Steve Nichols and escaped. Those imprisoned either refused, or, as Villatoro now suspected, *did not know* the identities of those men.

DESPITE THE HOUR, and even though it was the weekend, Villatoro called his former partner and left a message on her cellphone.

'Celeste, I'm sorry about the time and the day, but will you please go into the office on Sunday and pull all the Santa Anita files? I need you to see if you can find the name Newkirk.' He spelled it out. 'I don't know his first name, but he was an officer with the LAPD. And the name is familiar, somehow.'

He paused. 'If you find it, call me immediately. I realise what I'm asking is beyond what I should, now that I've retired. You don't have to help me, and there are no hard feelings if you don't. But I don't know where else to turn.' He paused again. 'Thank you, Celeste.'

GONZALEZ LIVED on a hilltop, in a home that perched over a cliff and afforded a vast, breathtaking view of a dark forest valley and the moonlit mountains eighty miles away. From the deck, Newkirk could see a kidney-shaped lake far below that mirrored the stars and moon. Like all of them, Gonzalez lived in a home that would have been unattainable ten years before, something beyond their dreams. The house would have cost $7 or $8 million in LA, and that didn't include the eighty acres that went with it.

Singer stepped out through the open sliding glass door and handed Newkirk a beer as he joined him at the rail. 'You know the deal when we go downstairs,' he said. 'You and I don't talk, no matter what happens. We don't want him to hear our voices again, or he'll put things together.'

'And Gonzo is OK with that?'

'Sure he is.'

Newkirk took a deep breath, looked away.

'Yes,' Singer said, 'we're taking a calculated risk here. We need to get the search teams out of the woods before they find something. With the sheriff's attention on Tom Boyd, the odds go way down that the Taylor kids will be found by law enforcement and put into protective custody. And we can use the time doing good, solid, professional police work, chasing up every lead, using our training to locate those kids. It always works, Newkirk, it always works. This way, we'll find them before some idiot deputy does.'

'What if a citizen finds them?' Newkirk asked.

'We're the first responders,' Singer said. 'We'll deal with it.'

Newkirk felt a chill. 'But Boyd . . .'

'Don't worry. We'll keep him alive. We might need him again.'

THEY WENT DOWNSTAIRS, Gonzalez clomping loudly, Newkirk replicating Singer's gentle steps. The man in the basement would probably sense there was more than one of them but wouldn't know how many for sure. As he followed the others, the dread Newkirk felt grew stronger.

Gonzalez snapped on a light, a bare bulb in a fixture attached to the upper floor joists. The basement was unfinished, the floor concrete.

Tom Boyd shouted, 'Who's there?' His voice was muffled because of the cloth sack tied over his head. Burn marks from a Taser stun gun could be seen just under the collar of his light brown uniform shirt. Newkirk was glad he couldn't see the man's face.

'Remember me?' Gonzalez said in a fake voice. 'You probably thought I had forgotten about you down here, Mr UPS man.'

'I know who you are,' Boyd said. 'You're those cops.'

Singer and Newkirk exchanged glances.

Boyd was in a stout wooden chair, his hands triple flex-cuffed behind his back. His thick torso was tied to the chair with tight bands of climbing rope, his bare ankles flex-cuffed to the chair legs. Newkirk could see where the cuffs dug deeply into Boyd's skin. Gonzalez had removed Boyd's shoes. When Newkirk saw why, he almost retched.

Gonzalez had glued Boyd's feet to the floor with construction adhesive.

'Please,' Boyd pleaded, his head slumping forward. 'I don't know what you think I did, or why you're doing this to me . . .'

There was a workbench attached to the basement wall. On the bench were a video-camera bag, Boyd's shoes, a half-empty box of department flex-cuffs, a glue gun and an open toolbox.

Gonzalez took a stool from the workbench, moved it near Boyd and perched on it. 'We're going to start where we left off this morning. You know those kids pretty well. I want to know where they would go if they were trying to hide. Where would they run?'

A sob came from inside the cloth sack. 'I told you, I don't know . . . I don't know. If I knew, I'd tell you. I thought they'd run to their mother's house, I told you that. I don't know of any relatives, I don't know their friends. I never paid any attention to them.'

Gonzalez turned and looked at Singer. Singer nodded.

'Look, I'll be straight with you,' Gonzalez said, leaving his stool for the workbench. 'I kind of believe you don't know where those kids went. But I'm not a hundred per cent. You're not giving me a hundred per cent.'

Boyd moaned and thrashed his head. 'What do you want?'

Gonzalez rattled through the toolbox. He removed a pair of needle-nosed pliers. 'I want you to confess.'

'WHAT?'

'I want you to confess you killed those kids. Because you were pissed off at their mother and your brain was fucked up with steroids at the time.'

Boyd moaned again, and the moan turned into a sob.

'You can say it was an accident,' Gonzalez said. 'That you didn't intend to hurt them. You sort of blacked out, and when you came to they were dead.'

'I can't . . . You'll kill me after I say it.'

'No,' Gonzalez said, shaking his head. 'That's not going to happen if you confess, but it sure as hell will if you don't. If you cooperate, I'll put you in a car and you'll be driven to Las Vegas, where you can start a whole new life. I'm not going to give you money, or a new name, nothing. You're on your own. A guy like you should be able to find a job pretty easy. Big muscles and little lizard brains look good on a résumé in Vegas. And you can't ever come back here, you understand?'

Newkirk looked away, afraid he would get sick.

'I can't confess to that,' Boyd said.

Gonzalez sighed theatrically. Then he snapped the pliers together in the air a few times, *clack-clack-clack* and bent down to Boyd's naked feet. 'How many toenails does a guy really need?'

Newkirk didn't care if Singer saw him close his eyes and cover his ears with his hands to drown out the scream.

Day Three: Sunday

If anything, the second night was even harder than the first for Monica Taylor. The sedatives helped, but beneath the blanket the pills pulled over her was the relentless fact that her children were still missing.

She lay fully clothed on the bed in her darkened bedroom, trying not to roll her head over and look at the time on the digital clock radio. She ached for sleep. But it was more soothing to stare into darkness with her eyes open than to close them and enter horrific nightmares involving every possible scenario of what could have happened to Annie and William.

Replaying the last argument with Tom, she still couldn't believe he had anything to do with the disappearance of her children. How could she have not seen that in him if it was true?

She knew, somehow, they were still alive. She just knew it.

She sat up, wide awake. She needed desperately to talk to someone.

Monica padded through the living room past Swann, who was sleeping under a light blanket on the couch. The phone was on the stand next to him, and she plucked it out of the cradle as quietly as she could, took it back into the bedroom and dialled.

As she expected, it was picked up on the first ring. Her mother would have just got home from the bar she worked at near the airport.

'Mom, it's Monica.' She talked softly, hoping not to wake Swann.

Hesitation. A long breathy draw on a cigarette. 'I'm not surprised you're calling at this hour.'

Monica pictured her mother in her apartment bedroom, lying on her bed in a housecoat with a Scotch and water on the nightstand and the television at the foot of the bed flashing washed-out colours on the close walls.

'Mom,' she said, 'Annie and William are missing.'

'I heard. It's all over the news. I seen their pictures on the TV in the bar. It's a damn shame. I didn't even recognise them at first. That reporter who bought me drinks asked me if I was related to you, since my name is Taylor. I told him "She used to be my daughter, but she ain't no more."'

Monica closed her eyes. 'Mom, you didn't talk to a reporter, did you?'

The long suck of the cigarette. 'Not at first, anyhow. Then I told him I lost track of you years ago, or more precisely that you shut me out. That I hadn't seen my grandbabies in four years.'

Monica remembered the last time her mother showed up to see her 'grandbabies'. She was drunk, and had been driven to Kootenai Bay by a seedy barfly in a porkpie hat. Her mother asked Monica right in front of Annie and William for a loan to get her through the month. The barfly leered at eight-year-old Annie, and Monica threw them both out.

Her mother said, 'I told him things like this don't just happen in a vacuum. You probably brought it on somehow with your damned attitude, that sense of entitlement you always have. Your daddy always thought you were a little queenie. He'd bring you presents and pile them high in your room. But what did he bring me? Nothing but a bucketful of trouble.'

'This has nothing to do with him, Mom. This is about William and Annie. They're innocent. They did nothing wrong.'

'Not what I heard on the news.'

'*They did nothing wrong*,' Monica said through clenched teeth.

'Someone is at fault and it ain't me.'

'Please don't,' Monica said. 'I feel so alone and you aren't helping. I wish you hadn't talked to that reporter,' she added in a whisper.

'I got bills, girlie.'

'He paid you?'

'That and the drinks.'

Monica lowered the phone to her lap and shook her head.

She could hear her mother say, 'I'm tired. I can't talk no more.'

'Mom,' Monica said, raising the phone, 'this is about my children.'

'I don't even know 'em,' her mother said.

Monica pushed the OFF button.

She sat on her bed with the phone in her hand, hot tears streaming down her face. She wiped them away with the back of her hand.

Suddenly, she wanted Swann out of the house. She was becoming more and more uncomfortable around him. Maybe it was the way he looked at her with what she thought was a mixture of malevolence and predation. Where there should be pity there was, she thought, overfamiliarity. As if he knew more than he let on.

But who kept calling him on his cellphone? Why did he immediately leave the room after seeing who was calling? And why, when she asked him who had called, were his explanations so lame?

And, she realised with a sudden shudder, why was he standing in the doorway to her bedroom *right now*?

'What are you doing?' she said.

'I thought I heard something. I wanted to make sure you were all right.'

'I was talking to my mother.'

'I wondered where the phone went. Here, give it to me.'

Meekly, she handed it to him. But he didn't leave her bedroom.

'Is that all you wanted?' she asked.

He paused.

'Get out of my room.'

Swann didn't respond, but simply withdrew.

Groggy, she climbed out of bed, closed her door. This time she locked it.

THE PREGNANT COW stood with her legs braced in the stall, her muscles quivering, her eyes wide, her breath heavy and rhythmic. It took effort for her to turn her head and look back at Jess, who sat on an upturned bucket just out of kicking range.

'Just relax, sweetie,' Jess said. 'It'll be all right.'

The only sound in the barn, besides the laboured breathing, was the *grumble-mumble* sound of grass hay being chewed. There were two more pregnant cows in the barn, and Jess noticed that they would look over at the labouring cow, stare with impassive eyes, then go back to eating.

The sliding door squeaked as it opened a few inches. Jess slitted his eyes at the sound. He saw a shock of blonde hair and Annie's face peering in.

'What are you doing?' she asked.

'What are *you* doing? You should be sleeping.'

Annie pushed the door open a few more inches and stepped in. She wore oversized sweatpants and a hooded sweatshirt several sizes too big. Seeing the familiar clothes tripped something in Jess.

'I woke and couldn't find you,' she said. 'I was afraid you'd left us. Then I looked out and saw the light shining here.'

'Why do you think I'd leave?'

She shrugged.

'I've got a cow here about to calve any minute,' Jess said.

'What time is it?'

He looked at his wristwatch. 'It's after three in the morning,' he said.

She shivered. Jess stood up and found another bucket and an old army blanket in the tack room.

'Come and sit over here, Annie. You can wrap yourself in this blanket.'

Annie nodded and joined him.

'Have you ever seen a calf being born?'

'No. A boy down the street had a dog who had puppies.'

'This can get pretty, um, basic,' Jess said. 'You'll have to decide how long you want to stay.'

She paused for a time. He could see how exhausted she was. Her eyelids were at half-mast. 'I'll stay for a while.'

'It's nice to have some company,' he said.

'You told Mr Swann something about a fence. I didn't understand. Was my mother there when you called?'

'We covered that. I assume she was there, but I don't know for sure. In fact, I'm not sure I did the right thing at all.'

'What are you going to do tomorrow?'

He rubbed the stubble on his chin. 'I guess I'll drive into town, see if I can find out what's going on without showing my hand. I need to find out why nobody has said anything about a man who got shot.'

'We saw him.'

'I know you think you did.'

'No, we *saw* it. I could take you to the exact place it happened. I could draw you a picture of the men who did it.'

'You could? Tomorrow, after breakfast, I'd like you to do that.'

'OK.'

After a few minutes of silence, she asked, 'Do you do this every night?'

'I do this time of year. It's calving season. The rest of the year I can pretty much sleep like a normal person. Unless the cows knock down a fence, or one of 'em gets sick or injured.'

Another long silence. Jess watched the cow. A wet stream ran down one of her legs. 'Won't be long now,' he said.

'Where is your wife?' Annie asked in a matter-of-fact way.

Jess snorted. 'She left me.' He didn't like saying the words. In fact, it was the first time he had ever said them. 'I guess she figured there wasn't much of a future on this place. She's an ambitious woman, and when our son was gone, she didn't have much to do.'

'Where's your son?'

'Jess Junior? He's around. He's sick, though. Spent some time in rehab, spent some time in jail. Got mixed up with drugs. He's not all there any more. It's not a good story.'

Jeez, he thought. Why am I telling all this to a little girl?

'Why didn't you have more kids?'

'I wanted more,' Jess said. 'A couple more, at least. Maybe a little girl or two. She said she didn't want to bring another child into this world. But she meant the ranch, I know now. She meant *me*.'

He realised he had said too much and turned his head away.

'You do all this ranch stuff by yourself?'

'I do now,' Jess said. 'I had to let my foreman go a couple of days ago.'

'What if you get sick or something?'

'Then things don't get done.'

She paused, something else on her mind. 'I'm pretty sure Billy wasn't my father. He's William's father, not mine. Someday, I want to find out where I come from. I know I come from somewhere.'

Jess had no clue how to respond to that.

Her probing eyes finally slipped from his face back to the cow.

'What's that?'

'That's the first sign of a little one trying to get out.'

A gush of liquid burst forth and hit the packed dirt with a splash.

'Here we go,' Jess said, grunting to his feet and pulling on latex gloves. 'Help me welcome a brand-new cow to the world, Annie.'

'Wow,' she said. 'A brand-new cow. It's pretty gross.'

'Life is messy,' Jess said.

WHEN THE SUN BROKE over the mountains, Villatoro was in his compact on a two-lane highway headed west, trying to get a sense of what this place was about. He'd been awake since five, spent an hour drinking the entire pot of bad weak coffee from the motel room coffeemaker. Now, he skirted the lakeshore, plunged into shadow and emerged on a straight road over the inlet.

He got a better read on the area as he distanced himself from Kootenai Bay. It was a community in transition, with a new population and culture superimposing itself over another. Older, smaller homes were near the road. Many of them had lawn decorations made of massive old circular saw blades with alpine scenes painted on them. These homes were quaint but tired, and had a sense of humility about them. Then there were the huge new glass-and-log homes with sweeping grounds and signs out front with names like 'Elkhorn Estate' and 'Spruce Casa'. And HOMESITE FOR SALE signs were everywhere. A whole new community was forming around the skeleton of the old one. Golf courses were being constructed. An espresso bar occupied an old storefront that still had a fading GENERAL STORE sign.

Within sight of the Montana border, he turned round and drove back. As he re-entered town, he checked his watch. It was still too early for Celeste to have come to work if she got the message from him the night before. He drove downtown and swung into a space behind a battered pick-up across from an old-fashioned diner called the Panhandle Café.

As he killed the engine, he looked through the windshield and gasped. The massive round face of a bear stared straight at him from six feet away.

It took a moment for his heart to stop whumping. It was a bear, all right, in the bed of the pick-up in front of him. Despite open eyes and a grey tongue that lolled out, the bear was dead, its head propped up over the tailgate, its front paws arranged on either side.

Once his breathing returned to normal, Villatoro opened his car door and slid out, never taking his eyes off the dead bear.

'Spring bear hunt,' someone said behind him, and Villatoro jumped.

'Sorry,' the man said. 'Didn't mean to scare you.'

It was a mature man in early sixties, thin, wearing a stained cowboy hat and light denim jacket. One of his hands was bandaged. Villatoro recognised him as the rancher who had preceded him with Jim Hearne at the bank.

'I'm fine now,' Villatoro said. 'I just looked up and there was that bear . . .'

'I know,' the man said. 'I wish they wouldn't do that, but it's a tradition. When a hunter gets a bear, he's obligated to drive it into town and buy a round for the house.'

Villatoro nodded towards the Panhandle Café across the street. 'Is that a good place to get breakfast?'

'Yup. Not as good as it used to be, but still the sort of place where old-timers like me gather in the morning.'

'Well, thanks,' Villatoro said, and crossed the street to the restaurant. Before entering, he dropped two quarters into a newspaper machine and took the last copy of the *Kootenai Bay Chronicle*. As he did so, he glanced over his shoulder. The man in the cowboy hat was still across the street, examining the bear. His truck had the name RAWLINS RANCH on the door.

THERE WAS A TIME, years ago, when the big round table in the corner of the Panhandle was reserved most mornings for ranchers. Jess had first taken a place there as a boy, with his father. He could still remember his elation when his father motioned him over from where he sat at the counter. It meant something to be invited to sit with the adults, and they all knew it, and grumbled good-naturedly when they shifted along the half-moon-shaped vinyl seat, making a place for him. They teased him about his hot chocolate and offered to fill his mug with strong coffee. He let them. He knew enough to sit silently, to defer, to listen. The talk was of cattle prices, noxious weeds, predators, politics, cattle buyers. But that was a long time ago. How different it had been when Jess had duplicated the gesture with his own son. Jess Junior had refused to come over, rolling his eyes and turning his back to the table. It was the first of many humiliations involving his son.

The table was now occupied by a large family of hikers. Jess took a stool at the counter and put his hat crown-down on the bar. A knot of men talked loudly at the end, surrounding a young man with a beard. The bear hunter.

'What can I get you?' the hunter asked Jess.

'Coffee's fine,' Jess said.

'Nothing stronger? I got a bear out there.'

'I saw it,' Jess said. 'Congratulations, but coffee's fine.' Not saying: I already cooked and ate breakfast a while ago with a couple of missing kids.

VILLATORO WATCHED the exchange from a booth while he waited for his coffee. There was something about Rawlins he admired: a quiet dignity, something solid and old-fashioned. He wished he had introduced himself.

The former detective ordered and spread the newspaper in front of him. The Taylor children's photos were on the front page. A photo of the woman he'd seen clutching at Rawlins in the bank—she was identified as Rural

Postal Contractor Fiona Pritzle—was featured under the headline THE LAST
TO SEE THE CHILDREN. He read a little of the interview. Pritzle said she'd 'had
a feeling something wasn't right' when she'd dropped off the siblings to go
fishing. 'I should have gone with my best instincts and taken those kids
home,' she said. 'But I figured there was no way they would have just taken
off like that without their mother's approval.'

That poor mother, Villatoro thought. That's all she needs. He found a
photo of Monica Taylor on the next page. She'd refused to be interviewed by
the *Chronicle*. Instead, a volunteer named Oscar Swann, who identified himself as her spokesman, said she was too distraught to make a statement.

The name Swann was familiar to Villatoro. He felt himself take several
quick, shallow breaths. Could it be that two of them were up here?

JESS WAS READING the same article, after deliberately covering up Fiona
Pritzle's face with his coffee cup.

Swann was Monica Taylor's spokesman? What did *that* mean? If what
Annie and William told him was true, Swann had ingratiated himself with
their mother so he could head off or prevent any contact with her by them.
He would be there if one of them called, probably answering the telephone.

Jesus, Jess thought.

On the television in the corner, the now-familiar photos of Annie and
William Taylor were shown, followed by a graphic with a map of the state
of Idaho. The room hushed as everyone turned towards the screen. A live
shot followed: a reporter standing in the middle of a street in Kootenai Bay
holding a microphone. Over his shoulder was the sign for the restaurant.

'That son of a bitch is right outside,' the bear hunter said. 'If I walked out
the door, you guys could see me on Fox News!'

'We've seen enough of you already,' his buddy said.

Seeing Annie's and William's faces on national news, Jess realised he had
a momentous decision to make. Whether he believed those kids or not, he
was harbouring them, telling no one, while the entire nation worried and
searched for them. By not reporting their presence immediately, he had
crossed a line. Every minute he kept his secret, he was guiltier.

'SHERIFF,' the waitress behind the counter said. 'What can I get you?'

Like every set of eyes in the place, Villatoro's watched the sheriff enter
the restaurant, walk wearily to the counter and take a stool. As the rancher
next to him had done, Carey took off his hat and placed it on the bar.

'A coffee, please. And I guess I should eat, even though I ain't hungry,' Carey said. 'Eggs over easy, ham, wheat toast.'

The waitress poured coffee into a mug, then took the order to the kitchen.

The sheriff sat with his shoulders slumped, his uniform shirt wrinkled, his face unshaven. His eyes were dark and hollowed. He held his coffee mug with both hands and sipped it cautiously.

'Any news, Sheriff?' the bear hunter asked.

Carey sighed. 'Nope.' Then, as if he realised how hopeless he had sounded, he added, 'We're working on it, though.'

JESS TRIED TO KEEP his own voice calm. He spoke softly. 'What's the deal with the volunteers? Are they really ex-cops?'

Carey eyed him with cool eyes. 'And you'd be . . .?'

'Jess Rawlins. I've got a ranch north of town.'

'That's right,' the sheriff said, pretending he remembered. 'Yes, they're LAPD retirees, but not all that long in the tooth.'

'How many of them are there?'

'Four working with me directly, another couple dozen on search teams.'

Jess nodded. Annie had made the drawing he had asked for. It was folded in his pocket. The caricatures were rudimentary: a thin man with white hair and blue eyes, another wearing a ball cap, the third bigger, darker, with a black moustache. Three, not four. Then Jess remembered Swann.

'Did they all know each other before this?' he asked.

'I think so,' Carey said. 'They seem familiar with each other. They all pretty much agree who the leader is, anyway.'

'Who is that?'

'A man named Singer. Used to be a lieutenant.'

'This guy Swann'—Jess tapped the newspaper with his finger—'the paper says he's the spokesman for Monica Taylor. How'd that come to be?'

'Do you know him?' Carey asked.

'I've heard his name,' Jess said truthfully.

'Well, apparently he's friends with the mother. He volunteered to stay with her in case someone calls.'

Jess nodded. 'This is kind of a crazy question, but is this the only big case you're working on right now? I heard a wild rumour about a possible murder in the county.'

Carey's eyebrows shot up. 'Where in the hell did you hear *that*?'

'You know how people talk.'

Carey shook his head. A vein had enlarged in his temple. 'I wish they'd stick to real life, goddammit.' He reached over and tapped Jess's newspaper, his eyes angry and pleading. 'Isn't this enough right now?'

The waitress emerged from the kitchen with Carey's breakfast and topped up their coffee.

'If you'll excuse me . . .' Carey said, turning to his plate and stabbing egg yolks with points of toast.

Jess leaned back. Another man had entered the restaurant and was walking straight towards the sheriff. The man threw an arm over the sheriff's back, clearly so he could tell him something private. The man wore a ball cap.

Jess kept his eyes averted but listened carefully. The man whispered something about a videotape.

'How'd we get it, Newkirk?' Carey asked, his toast poised in the air between his plate and his mouth.

'Somebody dropped it by this morning. We found it in a grocery sack near the front door of the station. Nobody saw who left it.'

'Have you looked at it?'

Newkirk nodded. 'It's something you need to see, Sheriff.'

Carey called for the waitress to box up his breakfast. 'Who's on it? Are the kids on it?'

Newkirk looked quickly around the room before answering. He seemed suddenly agitated, and Jess followed his line of sight. Newkirk was looking at the dark man eating his breakfast in the booth, the man who had been startled by the bear across the street.

AFTER NEWKIRK had ushered the sheriff out, Jess withdrew Annie's sketch. There he was, the one in the ball cap. Jess stood, threw down two dollars and slid off his stool. He was clamping his hat on his head when the man in the booth intercepted him.

'I didn't introduce myself earlier. I'm Eduardo Villatoro.'

'Jess Rawlins.'

'May I buy you a cup of coffee?' Villatoro asked, gesturing to the empty seat in his booth.

'I'm kind of coffeed out, thanks.'

'May I ask you a question?'

'Shoot.'

'I overheard you talking with the sheriff. He mentioned a man he's working with, an ex-lieutenant. What was the name?'

'He said it was Singer.'

Villatoro's eyes narrowed. *Singer.* Now there were three.

'You know him?'

'Yes. This name I know for sure.'

Jess tried to read Villatoro's face, wondering what he meant by that.

'I guess I will have that cup of coffee,' he said.

THE FIRST THIRTY SECONDS of the videotape was of a Seattle Seahawks football play-off game from the previous season. As the quarterback pulled back to pass, the screen faded into snowy static, then was filled with a starkly lit head-and-shoulders shot of a man in an otherwise dark room.

'My name is Tom Boyd . . .'

They were in the command centre with the door closed. Newkirk stood at the back, his belly on fire and his eyes watering from the acid taste in his throat. He hadn't seen the video before because he'd refused to watch it being filmed the previous night. Instead, he had stayed upstairs on the deck drinking Wild Turkey and looking at the reflections of stars on the faraway lake. It had taken nine tries before they got it right, Gonzalez said later. Newkirk had rolled home at 4.30 a.m. His bedroom door was locked, blankets and a pillow on the couch in the den. Even his dog avoided him.

'I work for United Parcel Service in Kootenai Bay. I got to get something off my chest before I split the country for good . . .'

Boyd looked terrible, Newkirk thought. His face was white and drawn, his eyes gleamed and looked vacant at the same time.

'I didn't mean to hurt those kids. I don't even remember how it happened. It was like I was there one minute, and I didn't wake up until after it happened. Like I blacked out, or something. I feel real bad about it . . .'

The sheriff moaned, 'Aw, shit.'

Newkirk looked at him. It was as if Carey were collapsing into himself. His shoulders slumped and his hands hung limply at his sides.

'I ain't saying where the bodies are at, only that you won't likely ever find them. All I can say is they didn't suffer nearly as much as I am now.' Boyd paused, swallowed as if it hurt, then continued. 'Don't bother looking for me, either. By the time you see this, I'll be so far away you'll never find me. But it'll never happen again. I'm through with drugs and alcohol.'

For the first time, Boyd glanced away from the camera lens, then returned to it. To Newkirk, the reason was obvious: he was looking for approval. Would anyone else see it that way?

'That's it. I'm gone.'

You sure are, Newkirk thought. He felt a hot surge in his throat.

The tape once again faded into snow before the game returned. No one spoke for several minutes. Finally, Singer walked to the VCR and paused it.

'Do you want to see it again?' he asked the sheriff.

'Jesus,' Carey said. 'No, I don't want to see it again right now.'

'Looks like we've got our guy,' Singer said. 'Whether we'll be able to find him is another thing.'

'Those poor kids. My God.'

'The tape belonged to Boyd, no doubt about it,' Singer said. 'He kept a library of Seahawks games from last year: eighteen tapes, lined up on his bookshelf. The last one was missing, which is the one we just looked at.'

'Maybe we should get some dogs,' Gonzalez said. 'We could get the scent from clothes at the mother's house and send the dogs out near the river. I'm guessing that's where we'll find the bodies.'

Carey stared at the frozen screen. 'The mother needs to know,' he said. 'I don't look forward to that conversation.'

Singer screwed up his face in sympathy. 'We could call Swann,' he said. 'He could break the news.'

The sheriff looked troubled. 'No. That's something I should do.'

'Swann knows her. It might be better coming from him.'

Carey considered it. 'You're probably right.'

Coward, Newkirk thought.

'Time to issue an Amber Alert and call in the FBI,' Carey said. 'This is beyond us. Boyd's probably halfway across Nevada or in Canada by now.'

'No FBI,' Singer said. 'Do you know how they come in and completely take over a case? I've been there, believe me. The most dangerous place on earth is between an FBI spokesman and a television camera. They make the locals come off as incompetent and lame. There's nothing the Feds can do that we've not already thought of.'

Carey shook his head. 'We need somebody to analyse the tape. Maybe they can figure out where it was shot, or see something in it we can't.'

'Why does it matter where he took it?' Singer asked. 'What matters is what he said. He confessed, Sheriff. We've got our man.'

Carey cleared his throat. 'It doesn't feel right to me that Boyd would confess on a tape and, in effect, dare us to come find him. He doesn't seem proud of what he did. He's no hardened criminal. He's just a local boy gone bad.'

'Sheriff . . .'

Carey looked at Singer. 'That's right. Last I looked, I was still the sheriff around here. It makes sense to bring in some expertise.'

Singer's face was calm, impassive. 'OK,' he said. 'You're the sheriff. But please realise that when the FBI comes in, it will no longer be your show. The Feds will look at everything. The way the investigation was run, how you manage your office, everything. If they don't find Boyd or those bodies, they'll say the investigation was botched in the early stages. You've worked hard, Sheriff Carey. But there'll be people out there, voters, who'll think you waited until the case was botched before you called in the cavalry.'

Carey listened in silence, never taking his eyes off Singer. Finally, he looked at Gonzalez, who was sitting back in his chair, arms crossed, obviously disappointed with him.

'Twelve hours,' Carey said, standing up. 'You've got that time to clear things up. There's a guy down in Coeur d'Alene with bloodhounds we contract with. And we'll need to reissue the APB for Boyd along with the Amber Alert. We'll say we suspect him to be armed and dangerous. But if we don't have Boyd or those bodies in twelve hours, I'm calling in the FBI.'

'Fair enough,' Singer said.

SINGER WAITED until the sheriff was back in his office down the hall before addressing Gonzalez and Newkirk.

'That means we've got today to find those kids.'

'Son of a bitch,' Gonzalez said. He looked at the map of the county push-pinned to the wall. 'Maybe they *are* dead by now. How long could a couple of kids survive out there in those woods and not be seen by anybody?'

Singer's voice dropped to a whisper. 'It could be that somebody is hiding them. If so, we've got to find out who. We've got to deal with this *now*.'

Gonzalez agreed. Newkirk said nothing.

'Gentlemen, make sure your cellphones are charged up. After we take care of the package, I want you both out in the field. I've kept the volunteer search teams concentrating on the river. So start at Swann's place. Go house to house and start checking buildings. They could be hiding in some old shack.'

Newkirk suddenly remembered he was supposed to pick up his sons after baseball practice that evening. Jeez . . .

Singer was on his cell. He gestured to Gonzalez. 'Swann can meet you at his place in forty-five minutes. Can you deliver the package by then?'

Gonzalez nodded. 'Same as before?'

'Yes.'

'How much can they eat, for Christ's sake?'

Singer smiled. 'They can eat a lot, Gonzo.'

'Isn't it inhumane to feed them meat laced with steroids?' Gonzalez laughed. 'It won't be organic pork any more.'

'Hold it,' Newkirk said. 'What aren't you telling me?'

Singer said, 'Mr Boyd expired on us.'

'He died of fright or something. I found him dead this morning.' Gonzalez put his palms out, in a what-can-you-do? gesture.

'You were too rough,' Newkirk said to him. To Singer, he said, 'You were going to keep him alive.'

'We'll deal with it,' Singer said dismissively. 'Go fill in for Swann at the mother's house. He'll be back soon enough to relieve you.'

Newkirk nodded his head.

'Oh,' Singer said to Swann on the cell, 'tell her Tom Boyd confessed. That ought to keep her in her room for a while.' He snapped the phone closed, then asked suddenly, 'Newkirk, you're not wavering, are you?'

'It's just I had things to do tonight.'

Gonzalez snorted.

'This is a little more important, don't you think?' Singer threw an arm over Newkirk's shoulder. Despite the gesture, Newkirk could feel Singer's fingers digging hard into his neck. 'I'll get us through this, then everything will be like it was. Trust me.' His fingers stopped digging.

Suddenly a thought came to Newkirk, something he'd meant to tell Singer earlier. 'I saw that ex-cop from Arcadia again this morning, at the restaurant.'

'Villatoro?'

'He was sitting there watching everything. The guy makes me nervous, Lieutenant. There's something about him.'

'I'm running a check on him,' Singer said. 'He'll likely turn out to be trouble.'

Gonzalez actually laughed. 'More trouble. The hits just keep coming.'

MONICA TAYLOR took the news with a calmness that surprised her, and told Swann, simply, 'I don't believe it.'

'What do you mean you don't believe it?' Swann said, closing his cell-phone. 'He confessed on *videotape*.'

Monica shook her head. 'No.'

Swann's eyes were unblinking. 'Why would he lie about something like this? What could possess *you* not to believe it?'

She didn't know, and she didn't care. And it wasn't about Tom Boyd at all, she thought. It was about the feeling she had when she'd woken that morning. She couldn't explain it, but it was as if, for the first time, she had recognised an invisible cord that connected her to Annie and William, and was sure it hadn't been severed. They were still out there. Probably scared, probably alone. Possibly hurt. But they were still out there.

'Do you want to see the tape?' Swann asked. 'We can go to the station—'

'I don't want to see it.'

Swann sighed angrily. Monica sipped her coffee. She had refused to take the medication that morning. Her head was clearing. She could see Swann thinking, see him thinking while holding his phone. Was he weighing whether to call someone back?

'Denial is a natural first reaction,' he said. 'At some point, though, you need to accept the truth, Monica, as hard as that may be.'

'I don't have to accept anything, Oscar.'

His eyes bulged and he turned away. It seemed odd, she thought. He was dealing with her intransigence not with sympathy or pity but with anger.

'Is it Boyd?' Swann asked. 'Is that your problem? Do you still love the guy, or what?'

'I never loved him,' she said.

Swann started to speak, then drew back. He simply stared at her, as if she were a mutant, devoid of appropriate human emotion.

'What was the name of that rancher you talked to yesterday? Do you remember?' she asked.

'What does that have to do with anything?' Swann said. 'Besides, he didn't give me a name.'

'Why did you open my door last night?'

The question derailed him. 'What?'

'Why were you standing in my room?'

'I was making sure you were all right.'

She smiled. 'You weren't hoping I would invite you into my bed?'

His neck flushed. 'You're nuts, lady,' he said, but he couldn't meet her eyes.

The doorbell rang in the front room and Swann moved towards it. Monica waited, hearing the murmur of a brief conversation on the threshold.

Swann ushered a man younger than himself into the kitchen. 'This is Officer Newkirk,' he said. 'He'll be staying for a couple of hours while I attend to some business. He knows the situation and he's here to help you.'

She looked Newkirk over. He was shorter than Swann, with a shock of dirty blond hair sticking out from beneath his baseball cap. He looked strained and pale, but his eyes had the same hardness Swann's did. Another ex-cop.

'You're my new jailer?' she asked.

Newkirk looked quickly to Swann for an explanation.

Swann shook his head sadly. 'She just found out about the videotape,' he said. 'She's shaken up by it.'

Newkirk nodded as if he understood. 'I'm here to do anything I can.'

'Who exactly are you helping?' Monica asked.

Again, Newkirk looked to Swann.

Swann sighed. 'See if you can get her to take her meds. If you can't, call the doctor and ask him to come over.' He zipped up his jacket and left.

JESS RAWLINS and Eduardo Villatoro left the restaurant together after Villatoro had insisted on paying the tab. Jess was aware of the ex-cop behind him as he walked across the street towards his pick-up.

'Nice morning,' Jess said, stopping on the centre line and looking around at the mountains on all sides. There was no traffic. The sky was clear of clouds and endlessly blue.

'Very nice,' Villatoro answered. He could see the crew from Fox News packing their equipment into their van down the street.

During the last half-hour, Jess had learned why Villatoro was in Kootenai Bay and had listened patiently to the details of the robbery at Santa Anita. Trying not to let his mind wander to his ranch, where the children were, he had waited until the story looped back to the present, to hear what Villatoro had to say about the ex-cops who were helping the sheriff.

When it came to Singer, Villatoro had not provided as much information as Jess had hoped. Lieutenant Singer was a familiar name to Villatoro because he'd been one of the prime administrative hurdles in the investigation of the Santa Anita robbery. Villatoro was pretty sure that Newkirk was one of the team assigned to the case as well. There were others, he said. He was waiting for names.

'It's simply too much coincidence,' Villatoro had said, 'that two of the names involved in Santa Anita are now here, of all places. Don't you think?'

Jess had said he didn't know. And he didn't. 'I don't like the idea of bad cops up here,' he said. 'I don't like the idea of bad cops, period.'

Villatoro agreed. 'I've worked with police officers all my life. For the most part, they've been dedicated and honest. Sure, there were some lazy ones. But truly bad cops—no. The idea disturbs me and I hope it's wrong.'

Jess liked this Eduardo Villatoro. Approaching his pick-up, he decided that this might be a man he could trust, an outside resource if nothing else. He slipped his hand into his pocket to make sure Villatoro's card was there. The man had written down the number of his motel and his room. In turn, Jess had given Villatoro the number for his ranch.

'I hope I can talk to you from time to time,' Villatoro said. 'It's good to have a local expert who knows how things work. I hope you don't mind. This is a foreign place to me.'

Jess turned. 'I don't mind. Just don't ask me to gossip about my neighbours. I won't do that.'

'I wouldn't dream of asking,' Villatoro said, flashing a smile. 'It's just that I see this place as, I don't know, a million trees with a few people walking around in them. I can't see the whole picture; it is too strange.'

Jess reached for his door handle, then thought better of it. He could walk where he needed to go. 'You're an interesting man, Mr Villatoro.'

'I'm a fish out of water, is what I am. But I'm a determined fish.'

'That you are,' Jess said. 'I kinda feel that way myself.'

They shook hands.

BECAUSE THE COUNTY building was only two blocks away, Jess decided to walk. He needed a few minutes to think, to put his plan together. He was overwhelmed and confused. Everything he had learned that morning seemed to lean towards Annie and William's version of events. But without a body, what the children had told him could be dismissed as the result of overactive imaginations. It all hinged on a murder that apparently hadn't happened, on a dead man who wasn't missed by anyone.

He needed more information. What was on the videotape Newkirk had whispered about to the sheriff?

He had to find out. Then, he would make his decision.

LEAVING HIS POCKETKNIFE and change with the woman running the security check, Jess entered the sheriff's office and stood behind the counter.

The receptionist told him the sheriff was in, but not available. Before Jess could ask, she said, 'He's sleeping at his desk. The poor man's exhausted. He just held a press conference to announce the Amber Alert. Now everybody in the country is looking for Tom Boyd and those poor children.'

Tom Boyd. He'd heard the name. 'The UPS guy?' Jess asked.

'That's him,' she said.

Across the room Jess recognised Buddy Millen, a sheriff's deputy who had once worked on a hay crew on the Rawlins Ranch. Buddy waved, and Jess waved back, then went through the batwing doors on the side of the counter and took a seat at the deputy's desk.

'I was just thinking about you,' Buddy said. 'I've been on a search team not far from your ranch, looking for those little kids.'

Buddy looked tired, and Jess noted that his uniform was dirty.

'No luck, huh?'

Buddy shook his head sadly, then leaned forward. 'I shouldn't be telling you this, but things are moving fast. A local guy confessed on camera.'

Jess sat back. 'Really? The UPS guy?' The videotape.

Buddy nodded. 'Unfortunately, we're changing our mission from looking for lost kids to looking for bodies. It's awful.'

Jess staunched his impulse to say, *They're OK, Buddy.* But what did this mean that Tom Boyd had confessed? To what?

OK, Jess thought. Buddy is a good guy. Maybe he can help sort things out. 'Buddy . . .'

The telephone rang on the desk. Buddy held up one hand and snatched the receiver with the other. Jess waited, trying to form his words.

Buddy made reassuring sounds to the caller and jotted down an address on a pad. 'OK, ma'am. Does he have a cellphone? Have you tried his hotel?' He looked over at Jess and wiggled his eyebrows while the caller talked.

'We can't file a missing person's case until he's been gone twenty-four hours,' Buddy said. 'I'm sorry. In ninety-nine point nine per cent of these situations, everything turns out all right. I'll give the information to the sheriff and follow up with you first thing tomorrow. But when he shows up, please call us and let us know right away, OK?'

Buddy cradled the phone. 'A wife says her husband was supposed to be back from a fishing trip last night, but he hasn't shown up. He probably got stuck in the mud or broke down, or had too much fun in some strip club.'

The words hit Jess like a hammer blow. A man was missing.

Buddy scribbled some more on his pad. 'She said he's a retired police officer,' he said, 'and he'd never be late without calling.'

'One of those LA cops?' Jess asked, his mouth suddenly dry.

'That's what she said. Why?'

Jess couldn't think of a lie. He wasn't good at them. Instead, he glanced at the pad Buddy had scribbled on and memorised the name on it.

'No matter,' he said.

JESS FOUND the men's room and splashed cold water on his face. He felt weak; his legs were rubbery and his wounded hand throbbed.

As he dried off with a paper towel, he heard the splashing of a mop in a bucket and saw the janitor behind him. Jess closed his eyes for a moment. He hadn't thought of this. It was too much for him right now.

The janitor swirled his mop, keeping his head down with his long hair covering his face and his shoulders hunched.

'J.J.?'

The mop stopped. Slowly, the janitor looked up. Eyes looked out through the strings of hair. Jess thought of how he had observed earlier that you could see the future adult in the photograph of a child. Not that he'd recognised it at the time, but when he looked at old grade-school photos he could see it now. The boy was disconnected early, already on a destructive path. His sickness was always there, lurking, but didn't show itself until he was in his late teens. The doctors said it was paranoid schizophrenia. The boy had had quirks—talking to himself, refusing to be touched. Then it got worse: hallucinations, rages. He used chemicals to try to bring the world around him into line with what he perceived it to be, and he had succeeded, to some extent. J.J. had never been meant to join the ranchers at the breakfast table.

'Jess Junior, do you recognise me?'

His son stared at him dully. The medication that allowed him to work while incarcerated rendered him emotionless. 'Dad.'

'How are you doing, son?'

A slight, simple smile. 'Not good.'

'You're working hard, it looks like.'

J.J. nodded. 'Jes' moppin'.'

Jess tried to sound encouraging. 'Things going all right?'

J.J. swept his head from side to side. Jess stepped forward, but J.J. held the mop out. 'Don' you touch me.'

'I won't, son. I remember how you hate that. What's wrong?'

Jess waited a full minute. J.J.'s struggle to answer broke Jess's heart.

'There's some bad men here, Dad.'

'In the jail, sure.'

'No,' J.J. said, making his eyes big.

'Do you mean the ex-cops?' Jess said. He withdrew the sketch Annie had made and unfolded it. 'Is this them?'

J.J. nodded, a look of alarm in his face. 'They're really bad.'

'Son,' Jess said, feeling his eyes mist, 'I believe you.'

JESS FOUND a payphone in the lobby of the county building and dug Villatoro's card out of his pocket. He dialled, and was transferred to the motel room. The line was busy, so he left a message.

'Mr Villatoro, this is Jess Rawlins. I don't know what it means yet, but maybe you should check on another name . . .'

As he spoke, Jess thought things had become much clearer, and much, much worse. He knew for sure now which side he was on.

NEWKIRK ROOTED through Monica Taylor's refrigerator, not because he was hungry but because he knew he should eat. His body was starved for something besides Wild Turkey. His hands shook as he pushed a carton of milk aside on the shelf and looked for something he could warm up. He checked the freezer. There was only a large, foil-covered pan, frozen solid.

He was unsettled from a telephone conversation he had just had with his wife. She was furious with him when he told her he probably wouldn't be home for a while. She reminded him of their son's baseball practice, and of plans to prepare her vegetable garden. It all sounded so trivial, he thought, given the situation right now.

Monica Taylor was in the living room, sitting on the couch, staring at who-knows-what. She seemed frustratingly serene. There was something wrong with her, he thought, to be that way, given the circumstances. She was also more attractive than he thought she would be. Now that she was sure her children were alive, she was intolerable. It was almost as if she knew what they were up to, but there was no way she could.

He slammed the freezer shut. 'Don't you have anything to eat?'

'Excuse me?'

He charged into the living room. 'I haven't had a normal meal in two days. All you've got in the refrigerator is milk, salad and eggs.'

She said, distracted, 'I think there's soup in the pantry.'

'What's that in the freezer? In a casserole dish?'

She turned and looked at him. 'Leave that alone. It's lasagne I made yesterday and froze. It's Annie's favourite, and I'm saving it for when they're back. The first one got burned up Friday night.'

Newkirk snorted. His cellphone burred and he drew it out. Singer calling. He went into the kitchen and closed the door.

'How is it going there?' Singer asked.

Newkirk sighed. 'OK. She's nuts, though. She insists that her kids are coming back.'

A pause. 'They aren't.'

Newkirk felt a flutter of both terror and relief. 'Did something happen?'

'No, not yet. But we're in control. I just heard from Gonzo. The package was delivered to Swann and Swann is overseeing disposal. He should be heading back to the house within an hour to relieve you.'

Newkirk tried not to think of what Swann was disposing of.

'I told Gonzo to start on the house-to-house. He's got good maps from the sheriff's office. He's going to start visiting people one by one, working out from Sand Creek. When Swann returns, I want you to recon with Gonzo and do the same.'

Newkirk cracked the door to check on Monica Taylor. She was still sitting there, hands in her lap. 'I'm kind of looking forward to getting out of here,' he said. 'This lady is creeping me out.'

Singer laughed softly. 'Oh, I nearly forgot. I heard information about your guy Villatoro. We may have more trouble than I thought. He was the lead investigator for the Arcadia PD on the Santa Anita robbery. That's where I'd heard his name. He used to give our guys headaches.'

'*Fuck.*'

'Our former friend's indiscretions brought him here, no doubt.'

'What are we going to do?' Newkirk asked.

'I'm not sure yet.' A note of hesitation, which was unusual in Singer. 'He's retired, so he's got no juice. But before you join Gonzo, take a look around town at motel registers. If anybody asks, just tell them you're doing follow-up for the sheriff's sexual predator list. See when he plans to check out. Be discreet. Then go help Gonzo. Let's wrap this thing up.'

VILLATORO'S HEART leapt when the receptionist at the motel handed him a sheaf of documents that Celeste had faxed from his old office.

But disappointment set in as he read over them. There were duty rosters, lists of security personnel at Santa Anita, copies of *Los Angeles Times* clippings, police reports he'd already read a dozen times.

Newkirk had been at Santa Anita Racetrack that day, all right. Along with three other off-duty policemen, he'd been hired to provide security in the counting room. It was common for the track to hire off-duty cops, and Newkirk was one of the regulars on race days. Officer Newkirk's affidavit stated he had not seen any irregularities during the counting by track personnel. He had recognised the men in the armoured car crew, and stood outside while the truck rumbled away during the final race.

That Newkirk was at the track and also now living in Kootenai Bay was interesting, but evidence of nothing, really. Villatoro read the names of the other three off-duty cops: Anthony Rodale, Pam Gosink, Maureen Droz. None of them connected to anything else he could find.

Lieutenant Singer's name showed up in several documents. As the liaison between the LAPD and the California Department of Criminal Investigation on the case, he had been quoted in the *Times*. It was Singer who announced before a press conference that one of the track employees had come forward and arrests had been made. Singer had also announced the untimely murder of the star witness. Villatoro had never met Singer. The lieutenant had been remote, unapproachable, always too busy to accompany his officers to Arcadia. And, Villatoro remembered, the LAPD detectives, who would joke about anything and anybody, never joked about him.

So, Singer and Newkirk were both connected to Santa Anita, Villatoro thought, and both now lived in North Idaho. But how many police officers were involved in the Santa Anita investigation in some way? Hundreds. How many ex-cops had retired and moved to Blue Heaven? Hundreds. And Swann's name had yet to appear on the documents.

Villatoro sat back in his chair and stared at the motel room ceiling. So far, he didn't have enough information to go to the sheriff to ask for a subpoena. Ex-cops would know immediately to get lawyers to delay or prevent interviews. They knew how the game was played.

The telephone rang and startled him. It was Celeste. He thanked her sincerely for giving up her Sunday to come into the office.

'Are we getting closer?' she asked.

'Closer,' he said. 'But we don't have enough yet to do anything. Officer Newkirk and Lieutenant Singer are up here. An officer named Swann is involved with them, but I don't see any connection between him and either the crime or the investigation.'

'Is there anything else I can send you?' she asked.

'I don't even know what to ask for.'

'There's one more thing,' she said, 'but it doesn't come from the files. I just did a simple Google search, typing in both their names. I found something called the SoCal Retired Peace Officers Foundation. According to the public filing, it's a non-profit group, a 501(c)3 that provides scholarships to officers' children, grants to widows, things like that. Both Singer and Newkirk are on the board.'

Villatoro thought about it. 'Where is it incorporated?'

'Let's see,' Celeste said, obviously scrolling down her screen. 'Burbank,' she said. 'And . . .' She hesitated. 'And Pend Oreille County, Idaho.'

That made him sit up. 'When was it formed?'

She gave him the date of the filing with the secretary of state's office, two months prior to the Santa Anita robbery.

'How is the organisation funded? Does it say?'

Her fingers tapped the keyboard. 'Voluntary contributions. It doesn't look like they've got a membership set up.'

His mind was spinning. 'Voluntary contributions from, I assume, other police officers. Contributions that would come in cash. Officers throwing bills into a hat passed round the squad room. Is there a list of contributors?'

'Not here,' she said. 'I don't know where I'd find that without contacting the organisation.'

'Who would likely not provide it, because there are no contributors. It's a perfect way to launder a lot of money in small bills.'

Celeste was quiet for a moment. 'I don't follow.'

'Banks notice when all-cash deposits are made. They have to report them if they're over a certain amount. But if the money is deposited over a long period, a few thousand dollars at a time, the bad guys cover themselves. Especially if it's understood that the cash came from contributors to a charity. It's perfect.'

Celeste was getting it. She said, 'My God, Eduardo . . .'

'But the plan wouldn't work if someone didn't deposit the money as he was supposed to, and spent some of it. Especially if the bills were marked. '

While he talked, Villatoro thumbed through his file for the copies of the marked hundred-dollar bills. 'We may have something,' he said, trying to keep the excitement out of his voice. 'Who are the other officers?'

She read him the list.

Eric Singer, President. Oscar Swann and Dennis Gonzalez, Vice-Presidents. James Newkirk, Secretary. Anthony Rodale, Treasurer.

Bells went off in his head. 'Newkirk, Singer and Swann are all up here. I need to find out about the other two.'

He could hear her shuffling through papers. 'I'm looking at the LAPD duty rosters for that day,' she said. 'Swann was on duty. Newkirk, Singer, Gonzalez and Rodale were off duty. We know Rodale and Newkirk were working security in the counting room.'

Villatoro slapped the side of his chair with his open palm. 'Good work, Celeste,' he said. 'Good work. Tell the chief we may be close.'

VILLATORO STOOD, and his knees popped and his back crackled. His mind spun with possibilities. Finally, things were connecting. Or were they? What had he overlooked? He needed time to sort it all through, connect all the dots that were growing bigger and closer to one another on the page.

Then he realised something. He'd heard there were four ex-cops helping out the Taylor investigation. What about the fifth?

The phone book, he thought. He would simply look up Gonzalez and Rodale in the telephone book. But he'd left it in his car that morning, when he'd used it for the maps inside as he was driving.

Villatoro threw open his door and bounded down the hallway and out through the glass door to the parking lot. He saw Newkirk pull in before the ex-cop could open his door.

There you are, Villatoro thought, checking up on me.

'Hello, Mr Newkirk. What can I help you with?'

'Hey.' Newkirk was obviously trying to come up with a good excuse why he was there. 'How do you know my name?'

'I recognise it from my investigation.'

Seeing Newkirk flinch, Villatoro recognised this as an opportunity. Surprised by his presence, Newkirk might give something away if pressed.

Newkirk stepped forward, his eyes hard. 'What are you saying?'

'What I am saying, Mr Newkirk, is that it's not too late for you to save yourself. I'm no longer an officer of the law. I can't arrest you, and I don't necessarily want to arrest you. I was the lead investigator for the Arcadia police and spent eight years looking into this crime. I'd like to find the killers, and the money, or at least as much as there is left.'

'*What?*'

Keep going, Villatoro thought. 'When I first saw you I thought I saw a man with a conscience, Mr Newkirk. Work with me to solve this crime. If you do, I'll do everything I can to keep you out of the trouble to come.'

'I don't know what you're talking about,' Newkirk sputtered.

'Ah, I think you do. You were a police officer, and a good one. You know as well as anyone that deals can be struck that benefit all parties. But the chance to help voluntarily lasts only so long. If you don't take your single opportunity, well, who knows what will happen?'

Villatoro could see the veins throb in Newkirk's temple.

'I noticed the wedding band on your finger. You've got a family, a good life here. Are there things you can tell me that would help preserve that?'

To Villatoro's mild surprise, Newkirk appeared to be listening.

'It's Sunday. Tomorrow, I will make a call to my contact at the FBI,' Villatoro said. 'So you need to make your decision tonight. Think hard, Mr Newkirk. Go see your family. Then decide.'

'I've got something to say right now.'

'Yes?' Villatoro said softly.

'Fuck off, mister.'

Newkirk slid into his car and drove away.

When he was out of sight, Villatoro breathed in deeply. His knees felt weak. It wasn't what Newkirk said that struck him. It was what he *didn't* say. He didn't ask Villatoro what specific case he was investigating. And he didn't ask why the FBI was going to be called.

IN HIS ROOM, Villatoro opened the phone book on his knees. The two names he was looking for didn't have listings. He thumbed through the book for Singer, Newkirk and Swann as well. All unlisted. As he searched, he saw his message light blinking. The message had been left an hour before, when he'd been on the phone with Celeste.

'Mr Villatoro, this is Jess Rawlins. I don't know what it means yet, but maybe you should check on another name. It's another ex-cop, Tony Rodale. R-O-D-A-L-E. His wife called the sheriff and reported him missing. I've got an address.'

THE OLD TELEVISION in Jess Rawlins's home received only three channels, and only one of those came in clearly. An older satellite dish was outside on a concrete pad and an electronic box sat on top of the set. Annie watched William try to manipulate the blocky old remote control to access the satellite. He wanted to watch cartoons.

'This is driving me *crazy*,' William said, pushing button after button.

'Keep trying,' Annie said. 'You'll figure it out.'

'I wonder if all the wires are connected from that dish out there? Maybe something is busted?'

'Stay inside,' she said. 'You heard what he said before he left. Keep the curtains closed and the lights off. We're not supposed to go outside.'

William made a face. 'If I can't get this to work, I'm going out.'

She took the remote and looked at it. There was a button marked SAT, and she pushed it. The snow cleared on the screen to reveal a Spanish soap opera.

'What did you do?' William cried. 'Give me that!'

She handed it over.

'He's not as big a hick as I thought he was,' William said as he scrolled through the channels.

Annie got up off the couch and went into the kitchen. Before he left, the rancher had locked the doors and windows. Annie was surprised to hear him say that it was the first time he had ever locked the front door.

She looked through the kitchen cabinets. Crackers, spices, oatmeal, tea and coffee. Ground beef and steaks in the freezer. She'd never seen so many tins of chilli powder in her life. Mr Rawlins had said he would bring groceries back from town, and he had asked what Annie and William liked to eat. Annie had scribbled a list and given it to him. He had read it and smiled.

'When will you be back?' she had asked.

'Early afternoon, I reckon,' he said. 'And remember, keep the doors locked and everything shut off.'

'You told me that three times already.'

Jess had looked at her. 'Well, I hope one of 'em took.'

Suddenly William yelled from the living room, 'Annie, come look at this!'

He had found the Fox News channel, and on the screen was a photo. She hardly recognised him, he looked so bad.

'Why is Tom on TV?' William asked, trying to find the volume button. 'Why are our pictures on TV?' he asked, as their school photos filled the screen over a scrolling graphic that read AMBER ALERT.

MORE THAN ONCE, Annie had considered calling her mother. She had gone as far as lifting the receiver and hearing the dial tone before talking herself out of it. With their pictures on television, Annie considered it again now.

What would it hurt to call? To hear her voice? To say, 'We're all right, and we love you, Mom.' But Mr Rawlins had said Swann was there, in their home, and she couldn't bear to think of him answering the phone.

'Hey, Annie, come look at *this*!' William yelled again.

'What now?' she said. She found him poised in front of an opened dark wood cabinet.

'This is awesome.' He stepped aside so she could look.

Rifles and shotguns, seven of them altogether, stood in a rack. Boxes of bullets and shells were stacked near their butts. William reached for a rifle.

'Leave them alone,' Annie said, pushing his hand down.

'But they're cool. I wonder why he has so many?'

'He's a rancher. Ranchers have lots of guns.'

'Yeah, for bears and stuff,' he said, his eyes wide.

She wished Mr Rawlins had a lock of some kind on the guns. She didn't trust her brother not to take them out and play with them.

'Look at this one,' William said. He reached in and snatched a rifle with a lever action. It was obviously old, its barrel rubbed silver, scratches in the wood of the stock. 'This looks like something a cowboy would use.'

Annie read the stamping on the barrel. 'Manufactured by the Winchester Repeating Arms Company. Patented August 21, 1884.'

'Wow, I wonder if it's too old to shoot?'

'I don't know,' she said. 'Put it away.'

'Annie . . .'

'Put it away, *now*.'

He did, taking his time. She closed the cabinet.

'There's something else,' William said, walking across the living room to an old roll-top desk. 'Wait until you see this.'

'You shouldn't be snooping,' she said as she followed.

He pulled open one of the desk drawers. In it was a framed photo of a much younger Mr Rawlins, wearing an army uniform and a peaked cap. Inside the drawer were hinged boxes containing war medals.

William opened them. 'He was an army sharpshooter.' He showed her the medal. 'He also got this silver star thing and a couple of other ones.'

She touched the silver star medal with her fingertips.

When they heard the sound of a motor, they looked at each other, then furiously returned the medals and shut the drawer. William went to the window and inched the curtain aside before she could tell him not to.

'Someone's coming down the road,' he said. 'But it isn't Mr Rawlins.'

THEY HID under the desk with their arms wrapped round their shins, looking out. 'Could you see anything?' Annie whispered.

'Just a black truck.'

'Next time, just look through the slit between the curtains, OK?'

William started to argue, then stopped himself. 'OK,' he said.

The motor grew louder, then stopped. A car door slammed shut.

'They're right outside.' Then Annie realised: 'The TV! You left it on!'

William scrambled out and found the remote on the coffee table. He pointed it at the set and started pushing buttons. Before he found the power button, he inadvertently hit the volume, and the sound of a cartoon roared through the empty house, then went silent. Annie sucked in her breath.

'Sorry,' William whispered as he rejoined her.

As she glared at him, there was a heavy knock on the front door that rattled dishes in the kitchen.

'Hello, hello!'

They looked at each other. A man with a deep voice.

'Hello. Open up. It's the Kootenai Bay police. Hey, I heard the TV. I need to ask you some questions.'

She recognised the slight Mexican accent. It was the man who had spoken to Mr Swann while they cowered on the floor of his truck.

William dropped his face in his hands. Annie patted his back.

'Helloooo in there.' The pounding on the door was brutal.

Next, she heard the doorknob rattle. He was trying to get in.

A form passed by one of the curtained windows, and Annie could see the silhouette clearly. She recognised him as one of the killers, the dark one. He was a stocky man, with a big head and a moustache.

The man passed by a second window, then came back, filling it. He pressed his face against the glass, trying to look through the slit between the curtains, using his hands to frame his eyes. It took a few seconds of terror to realise he couldn't see her.

At last he moved on. His heavy shoes clumped on the porch, then gravel crunched on the side of the house. He was going to try the back door.

Again, a heavy pounding. 'Wake up in there. It's the police!'

She wondered how easy it would be to break down the door. Pretty easy, she thought. It didn't seem very thick.

Then he was gone. There was no sound.

Had he left? No, she thought. She hadn't heard the engine start up.

His shadow again filled the window. There was a squeak, a cracking of paint. He was trying to open it. After a few moments of pushing he moved to the next window. The man couldn't open that, either. She saw him turn. Then, the chirp of a phone.

'Newkirk,' the man said, 'where the fuck are you?'

FOR TWENTY MINUTES, clutching Annie's shopping list, Jess pushed his cart down unfamiliar grocery aisles. Twice he had to ask a stocker where to find items on the list. Frosted Flakes, juice boxes, frozen pizza rolls, string cheese. Things he had never eaten or purchased. As he rolled into the check-out line, the only thing he recognised in his cart was the can of Copenhagen chewing tobacco. That was for him.

He found himself looking forward to seeing the children again. He had always wanted grandchildren and he had once looked forward to it. This was kind of like that, he thought. There was no reason why he couldn't spoil them a little, figure out how to cook frozen pizza rolls—whatever they were—if that's what they wanted.

Someone bumped him gently in the back with a cart and he looked over his shoulder to see a beaming Fiona Pritzle.

'Hey, good-lookin',' she said in her little-girl voice.

He nodded a greeting as his heart sank.

'Did you see the newspaper today, Jess? They interviewed me about the Taylor kids. There's a picture, too.' He saw a dozen copies of the paper in her cart. 'Would you like one?'

'I've seen it,' he said, wishing that the woman in front of him would quit fishing in her bag and find her chequebook.

'It's a pretty good story,' Fiona said. 'Amazingly accurate. I've got an interview tomorrow with CNN, and a request from Fox News. They all want to talk to the last person who saw the kids alive.'

'So you don't think the kids will be found?' Jess asked.

Fiona's eyes got huge, and she squeezed round her cart so she could whisper in his ear. 'I don't want to say much,' she said, 'but I think a sexual predator has them. Or had them. It's just a matter of time before the bodies show up, and I wouldn't be surprised if those kids have been . . . violated.'

Jess leaned away and squinted at her. 'A sexual predator?'

'Don't talk so loud,' she said. 'Somebody will overhear us.'

'Sir?' The check-out clerk was ready for him.

Jess gratefully pushed his cart forward. As he unloaded it onto the belt, he could feel Fiona Pritzle studying him.

'String cheese? Juice boxes? What are you doing with those?'

Jess felt his face flush. 'Wanted to try some new things,' he said.

He paid in cash and left her standing there, staring at him.

AS HE DROVE out of Kootenai Bay, Jess surveyed the northwestern sky and saw the thunderheads nosing over the mountains. It had been clear and warm all day, but rain was coming again. The barometric pressure would change, and it was likely that two of the cows would calve tonight. He hoped he could get some sleep before they came. And he prayed the children would be at his house, where they should be, and that everything was OK.

He stopped at his gate as he always did before realising that someone had left it open. He drove quickly over the cattle grid, and shut the gate behind him. Who had come onto his ranch? When he topped the hill and cleared the trees, he could see his home below and felt a rush of ice-cold fear. A vehicle he didn't recognise, a black pick-up, was parked at a rakish angle on the circular drive. A dark man he had never seen before stood on his porch, talking on a cellphone. Jess recognised him from Annie's drawing. It was the big one with the moustache.

The rancher accelerated. The house looked to be as he left it: locked up tight. The children must still be inside, he thought, probably scared out of their minds. Who was this man, this trespasser, who strode along his porch with such contempt and familiarity?

Jess parked behind the pick-up. The man on the porch had seen him and was closing his phone and glowering. The man stopped, his arms folded across his massive chest, waiting for Jess.

He spoke before Jess could. 'Is this your place?'

Jess shut his door, leaving the groceries inside. The man exuded menace. He outweighed Jess by at least forty pounds, and he was younger.

'This is my ranch,' Jess said. 'The question is what *you're* doing on it.'

'I'm with the sheriff's department. If you haven't heard, there are a couple of local kids missing.'

'I've never seen you before.'

'I'm a volunteer. Several of us are assisting Sheriff Carey.'

As he spoke, Jess could see the man's reflection in the window. The butt of a pistol poked out from his belt behind his back.

'You're one of the cops, then,' Jess said. 'Do you have a name?'

'Dennis Gonzalez. Sergeant Dennis Gonzalez. LAPD.'

'Not any more.'

Gonzalez smirked and rolled his eyes. 'No. But that don't matter.'

'So what are you doing trespassing here?'

'Trespassing? You need to watch that language, mister. We're going house to house looking for any sign of those kids. This place is on my list.'

To Jess's horror, he saw the curtain part behind Gonzalez and William's blue eyes in the window.

Jess sighed. 'All right, then. I'm back. You can go now.'

'Not so fast. I heard activity inside when I drove up. I'd like to look around.'

'It's just me here,' Jess said. 'My foreman left a few days ago.'

'So why not invite me in for a cup of coffee or something?'

'I've got work to do. Couple of cows about to calve.'

Gonzalez studied his face. 'I'd really like to take a look around this place so I can scratch it off my list. I'd like to take a look in your barn. I want to make sure I wasn't hearing things when I drove up.'

'You were,' Jess said.

A tense silence hung in the air. Jess shot a glance at the window. Gonzalez noticed it and looked behind him. Thank God, William was gone.

'Let me get this straight,' Gonzalez said, turning back round. 'Are you denying me the opportunity to clear you off my list as a kidnapper?'

Jess tried not to flinch. 'That's what I'm saying. You're trespassing without a warrant. Now get off, and don't come back without a piece of paper.'

'You're a piece of work, *compadre*.'

Something flashed in the man's eyes, and for a second Jess expected him to bolt off the porch and jam the gun into his face. But the moment passed.

'I'll be back here,' Gonzalez said, stepping off the porch and walking slowly to his pick-up. 'You and me are going to tangle. You could have avoided it, but you had to get all fucking cowboy on me.'

Jess kept his palms firmly on the hood of his truck so they wouldn't shake. 'Don't threaten me,' he said, his voice firm and low.

Gonzalez opened his door and looked back. 'I don't threaten. I advise.'

Jess watched the pick-up drive up the road and into the trees. Slowly, he withdrew his hands from the hood, leaving long wet streaks.

'HE WAS ONE of them, wasn't he?' Jess asked.

He was unpacking the groceries in the kitchen. Annie and William stood in the doorway to the living room, their faces pale white.

'Yes,' Annie said. 'We thought he was going to come in and find us.'

Jess swung round and pointed a trembling finger at William. 'You nearly got yourself hurt and your sister hurt along with you by looking out that window like that. When I tell you to stay inside and not look out, I mean it!'

William stood still, but mist filled his eyes. 'I'm sorry,' he said, his mouth curling down, even though he was fighting it.

'Ah, man,' Jess said, walking across the kitchen and pulling them both into his legs. 'I'm just glad you're all right. It's OK, Willie. It's OK.'

'William,' the boy said, his voice muffled by the hug.

'Is he coming back?' Annie asked.

Jess released them and squatted so he could look both children in the eye. 'I think so, yes.'

'What are we going to do?'

'I don't know yet,' he said. 'I'm thinking it over.'

'You could show me how to shoot one of those guns in there,' William said. 'You could show me and Annie.'

Jess looked at him, about to argue. Then he didn't.

'For now, let's get you something to eat,' he said instead.

JIM HEARNE SAT in a recliner with the newspaper on his lap and a Seattle Mariners game droning on in front of him. He didn't know the inning, the score, or who they were playing. His mind was filled with thoughts of his meeting with Eduardo Villatoro and what he had read in the newspaper about the effort to find the missing Taylor children. About the ex-cops from LA who were heading up the task force. About his own role in everything.

As if seeing things for the first time, Hearne looked around the room he was in. It was a magnificent living room, with high ceilings and slate floors covered with expensive rugs. Through the huge picture window was a long, sloping lawn that led to a small, tree-bordered lake. He could hear Laura in the kitchen, cooking and talking to her mother on the telephone. She was frying chicken, his favourite, the old-fashioned Southern way. He wished he could get excited about it, but eating was the last thing on his mind.

Hearne felt like an impostor in his own home. A real businessman should live there, he thought. Not a piss-poor rodeo cowboy who'd made a pact with the devil. But he needed to stop fretting and do something about what was happening in the valley. He stood up and stretched, then tucked the paper under his arm, grabbed his phone and went outside. Afternoon rain clouds were moving across the sky and he could sense the moisture coming.

The article in the newspaper listed a telephone number to report any information regarding the Taylor children. Hearne punched the number into his phone and the call was answered by a receptionist.

'I'd like to speak to Lieutenant Singer, please.'

Hearne was placed on hold for a moment, then: 'This is Singer.' The man's voice was flat and businesslike.

'Lieutenant Singer, this is Jim Hearne,' he said.

No response.

'Your banker,' he reminded, after a beat.

'I know who you are.' Deadpan, slightly annoyed.

'I was hoping we could have a few minutes to talk.'

'Why? I'm busy right now, as you can imagine.'

'It's about a retired detective from California who was in my office asking about cash deposits and certain marked bills that were traced back to my bank. I think we should get together and talk about this situation.'

'Why?' Singer said quickly, his voice dropping.

'It won't take him long to identify certain accounts.'

'Listen to me carefully, Mr Banker,' Singer said. 'Do not say a thing to that man. Not a thing. As far as you're concerned, you don't have any idea what he's talking about. He can't hang around here for ever. He'll go away. When this is over, we'll get everything straightened out. Is that a deal?'

Hearne looked at his cellphone as if it had switched sides and turned against him. Then he closed it, ending the call. When he turned back to the house, Laura was standing in the doorway.

'Since when do you make calls out on the lawn?' she asked.

He shrugged and tried to shoulder past her, but she stepped in his way. 'Jim?'

Enough, he thought. Enough holding things in. He reached up and grasped her shoulders, looked straight into her eyes. He could see that she was prepared for anything but scared at the same time.

'I've put us in a situation,' he said. 'At the bank. Now it's coming back to kick me in the ass. I may be in a lot of trouble.'

She searched his face for more. 'What did you do?'

'It's not what I did,' he said. 'It's what I didn't do. I looked the other way when I knew better, which is just as bad. I let something happen without stopping it, because I knew it would lead to a lot more business, and that's what happened. But I knew something wasn't right.'

She slowly shook her head. 'Jim, that's not like you.' It hurt more than anything else she could have said.

He dropped his head, couldn't look into her eyes. 'Laura, I need your permission to try to square this, knowing that I might not be able to do it. What's at risk is my job and our reputation.'

She sighed. 'You've always cared a lot more about our status than I have. It doesn't matter how nice our house is. I'd be just as happy in our old one.'

He slowly raised his head, amazed at her, in love with her.

'Do what you need to do to make things right,' she said.

'Then I'm going to miss dinner,' he said.

WHILE ANNIE AND WILLIAM ate at the table, Jess thumbed through the phone book in the Federal Government listings and found the number for the FBI office in Boise. He looked at his watch. Five fifteen on Sunday night. Would anyone even be there?

Turning his back on the kids, he dialled and got a recording to leave a message. When he heard the beep, Jess hesitated for a moment. Then, in a hushed voice, he gave his name and number and said he knew something about the missing Taylor children.

He hung up, not at all sure he had done the right thing. Would the agent call him back directly, or contact the sheriff first? He stared at the receiver, wishing he could erase the message somehow. He should have waited until tomorrow, when he could talk to a real person. This wasn't like him, being impulsive. But Gonzalez on his own porch had unnerved him. They would suspect him now, and he was sure they'd come back.

THE CHILDREN seemed to be as comfortable as they'd been since they arrived, Jess thought. They sat in the living room, surfing through television channels. He found himself staring at them from the kitchen, wishing he could be as carefree. Annie looked over and smiled at him, then turned back.

Something had happened, he thought. Because they had overheard the exchange with Gonzalez, they trusted him completely now. They thought he could take care of them. Jess wasn't so sure. He needed help, and a plan.

He thought of the man he'd had breakfast with, Villatoro. Perhaps the ex-detective could put him in contact with a friendly FBI agent who could circumvent a call to the sheriff. Jess dug the card out of his pocket, called the motel and again got voicemail. He cursed to himself and left a message asking Villatoro to call him back.

Jess paced his kitchen, washed and dried the dishes, stared at his watch and the telephone that didn't ring.

Maybe, he thought, Sheriff Carey would believe him if he could talk to the man without the ex-cops around. Maybe. He would need to try, and he couldn't chance waiting until morning. As he looked at the children sprawled on his couch, he thought: Don't let them down. You've already overseen the destruction of one family. Don't let it happen again.

'I'm going to be gone for a while,' he told them, muting the volume on the television. 'I need to go to town.'

'Tonight?' Annie asked. 'Are you going to leave us here?'

He nodded. 'I have to.'

'What if that man comes back?'

Jess paused. 'Annie, I'm going to show you how to operate a shotgun. If anybody besides me comes into this house tonight, I want you to know how to use it.'

Annie nodded. William looked at her with obvious jealousy.

Jess opened his gun cabinet, withdrew his twenty-gauge over and under, and broke it open. 'Just remember it's not a toy. Come here, and I'll show you how it works . . .'

'WHAT DO YOU THINK you're doing?' Swann asked Monica sharply.

She was packing, throwing clothes into a small suitcase on her bed. Her clothes, Annie's clothes, William's clothes. They would surely need a change of clothing. She was startled, hadn't realised Swann was in the hallway.

'I've got to get out.'

'You're not going anywhere. What if they call?'

'What if who calls, Oscar? I thought you were all convinced Tom took them? Since when is Tom a *they*?'

'Monica, sit the fuck down.'

His command froze her. She could tell by his face that, if necessary, he would cross the room and make her stay.

'This is for the best,' he said. 'Trust me on this.'

She weighed his words against the crazy look in his eye, his clenched fists.

'I don't trust you at all,' she said.

He raised one of his fists, opened his hand. Her car keys were in it. 'You're not going anywhere,' he said.

THE HOME of Anthony and Julie Rodale was magnificent, Villatoro thought. A huge new log home built with lots of windows, soft underground lights marking the pathway, thick Indian rugs on the hardwood floor, and a cathedral ceiling in the great room that made him feel insignificant. Mounted heads of deer and elk flanked the fireplace, and a half-dozen colourful lacquered fish glowed in the light from the chandelier.

Julie Rodale had been watching *60 Minutes* when he arrived, sitting in an overstuffed chair in front of the wide-screen TV, eating a large bowl of macaroni and cheese. She was tall, blonde and heavy, with a round face. She was not hesitant to talk with him.

'You said you were a detective?' she asked. 'I thought you were with the sheriff's office when you drove up. I'm waiting to hear something on my husband, Tony.'

Villatoro took notes on a small pad. 'You said he went steelhead fishing.'

'Yeah.' She rolled her eyes. 'He lives for it. Every weekend, at least. All winter he buys equipment and reads fishing magazines, and all spring, summer and fall he goes fishing. I tried it with him a couple of times, but I thought it was boring, boring, boring.'

'Does he often go alone?'

She shovelled in a mouthful of macaroni. 'Not all the time,' she said, chewing. 'Jim Newkirk goes along sometimes, but he's got kids at home and can't get away as much as Tony. Nobody can, it's ridiculous.'

His tone was soft. 'He was supposed to be back this morning?'

'If not last night. He said he had something to do on Monday, so I'd have expected him back by now. I'm starting to get pretty pissed off.'

'Are you worried about him?'

'Not really. He's a tough guy. He always takes his service weapon with him. I just think he got his truck stuck somewhere, or he got lost. I tell him to take his cellphone, but he claims he goes too far to get a signal.'

Villatoro shifted in his chair. 'So you've been here four years?' he asked.

'Yeah, we moved here just after Tony took early retirement from the force.'

'I heard several retired officers were helping your county sheriff with the Taylor case. But obviously, Tony isn't involved in that.'

She laughed. 'Believe me, if he wasn't fishing, he'd be with them. Tony likes hanging out with all of his old cop buddies. You'd think he'd be sick of them after all of those years, but that's not the case.'

'Have you called any of them to see if they know anything about where Tony went?'

'Sure I did. But all they knew is that he was going fishing.'

Villatoro changed the subject. 'This is quite a place you've got here. I bet it would cost a few million back home.'

'More than that,' she said, grinning. 'Tony did really well. All those years, I had no idea he was buying stocks and stuff. But when he told me he wanted to take early retirement, he said he's been building up this . . . fortune . . . in the stock market. He got out before the bubble burst.'

Villatoro watched her carefully. She spoke without guile.

'My wife Donna would kill for a home like this,' he said.

She smiled. 'The man really shocked me. I didn't know he had any interest at all in stocks or anything. I didn't even know about this fishing thing until we moved up here. Just goes to show you can live with somebody for twenty years and not really know them, you know?'

Villatoro stood up and closed his pad. He felt sorry for her. She seemed like a nice, normal woman, someone his wife would be friends with.

'I know,' he said.

THE SKY FLASHED and there was a rumble of thunder as Villatoro approached his car. The storm clouds had shut a curtain over the dusk sun.

Tony Rodale, who had been working security at Santa Anita with Jim Newkirk on the day of the robbery, who sought early retirement, who was the treasurer for the SoCal Retired Peace Officers Foundation and therefore in charge of making cash deposits into their account, was missing.

There had to be a reason why only four of the five ex-cops had volunteered to help the sheriff, and the fifth went on his way. Maybe an argument between them, maybe, Villatoro conceded, Rodale just wanted to go fishing.

A flash of lightning and a thunderclap seemed to sway the trees. The rain came furiously. He switched his wipers to high. As he drove, he was so consumed with his thoughts and the rain that when his headlights swept over a parked car nearly blocking the road to Rodale's home he almost sideswiped it. He braked a few feet beyond it and glanced into his rearview mirror.

The driver's door opened and Newkirk got out, lit in the glow of Villatoro's taillights. The ex-cop tapped on the passenger-side window. Villatoro found the switch and the window whirred down.

Newkirk leaned in. There was a smell of whisky on his breath. 'I've been thinking about what you told me,' he said. 'I think we need to talk.'

'Do you want to meet somewhere?' Villatoro asked.

Newkirk shook his head. 'No place is safe. And too many people know my car. Let's go in yours.'

Villatoro found himself gripping the wheel. 'I'm not sure . . .'

'Do you want to talk or not? Make up your mind. I don't like standing out here where someone could see me.'

Villatoro was scared. But he realised what an opportunity this could be. He gathered up the maps and papers on the passenger seat and tossed them over the headrest. 'Where are we going?'

Newkirk swung in heavily and closed the door. 'Just drive. I'm going to show you where the bodies are buried, so to speak.'

JESS ENTERED Kootenai Bay under a hard, steady rain. A close flash of lightning lit the cab of his pick-up, leaving the afterimage of his Winchester, muzzle-down, on the seat.

Sheriff Ed Carey lived in a modest ranch house in an older neighbourhood not far from downtown. Carey's county Blazer was parked in his drive. A white SUV was in front of the house. A white SUV? Like the one Annie and William had seen?

Behind Carey's Blazer was a small yellow pick-up. Jess frowned. What in hell was Fiona Pritzle doing at the sheriff's home this time of night?

He drove by slowly, and saw that the curtains were open and the lights on. He parked down the block under a canopy of old cottonwood trees.

Leaving the Winchester in the truck, he walked to Carey's house, a thin stream of water pouring from his hat brim. There was a picture window in front of the house and a smaller window on the side that was open except for a storm screen. Jess stood in the shadows to the side of the open window. The sound of Fiona's sharp, high-pitched voice cut through the rain like a razor through fabric.

'There's always been something odd about him, don't you think?' Fiona was saying. 'I've really noticed it lately. Like he's got a secret life and he doesn't want anybody to know it.'

Jess took a chance and looked in the window. He hoped he wouldn't be entering anyone's view.

Fiona sat in the middle of the room, perched on a chair. Carey sat on his couch in a T-shirt and sweatpants, his hair uncombed, looking troubled or irritated. Since it was Fiona sitting there talking, Jess figured both were likely. A man sat listening in an overstuffed chair. He was trim and compact, with close-cropped silver hair, his face a mask of world-weariness except for his eyes, which studied Fiona with a kind of manic fascination. Jess identified him from Annie's drawing. It was Singer.

'He seems evasive,' Fiona said. 'I try to be friendly and sweet as pie, but he always seems somewhere else, you know?'

Singer turned to Carey. 'Do you know him, Sheriff? Gonzo had a problem this afternoon with him. He wouldn't let him search his property.'

'I know him,' Carey said. 'In fact, I sat next to him at breakfast at the Panhandle just this morning.'

Jesus, Jess thought, they're talking about me.

Fiona said, 'You know as well as me what's happened out there over the past few years. First, his wife left him. His son's a tragedy.'

Carey said to Singer, 'He's the trusty who mops the floor at the station. You've probably seen him around.'

Jess couldn't believe what he was hearing.

Fiona continued, 'Why else would an old single man be buying food that only little kids eat? He shows no interest in the opposite sex. I mean, single lonely man, available woman, and he doesn't do anything? At first I thought it was me, but maybe he has other interests, you know? He's completely by himself out there. Maybe he's holding those kids prisoner!'

'Fiona . . .' The sheriff was sceptical. He turned to Singer. 'What's this do to our theory about Tom Boyd?'

'Not much. We've got the tape. Boyd's missing. That still holds.'

'I've read magazine articles about sexual predators,' Fiona interjected. 'It *grows* in them until they get the opportunity to gratify it. I've never thought before how much he fits the profile.'

Fiona suddenly got an idea and nearly shot out of her seat. 'Hold it! UPS delivers out there. Maybe the two of them struck up a friendship based on a common interest—*paedophilia*. I've read those people seek each other out.'

Jess didn't know what to do. Burst in, set the record straight? But how would he explain the groceries? And what if the sheriff arrested him on the spot? Singer could send Gonzalez back to his house to find the children.

'You do something,' Fiona threatened, 'or I'll call my contacts at the networks. I'm sure they'd find this new development very interesting.'

Jess walked away, the rain pounding on his hat. He swung into his pickup and roared down the street, not caring if anyone could hear him leave.

JESS COULD SEE J.J. through the locked doors of the county courthouse. In his orange jumpsuit, as usual, J.J. was cleaning, spraying banisters with disinfectant. Jess rapped hard on the glass. Inside, J.J. looked up and his eyes narrowed. There was something canine in the way he looked at Jess.

'J.J., I need to talk with you,' Jess shouted over the pounding rain.

J.J. shrugged, couldn't hear him. But he let the cloth fall and walked to the doors. Jess could see his mouth. 'Locked.'

Who had a key? Jess wondered. He pulled futilely, rattling the doors. J.J. watched as if he expected alarms to go off.

'Hold on.' Jess raised his hand and turned for his pick-up.

He returned with the rifle. J.J. backed away, his eyes wide.

Jess used the butt to break through a panel of glass. No alarm sounded. He reached through the hole and opened the door.

'I don't mean to scare you,' he told J.J. as he stepped inside.

'I could get in trouble,' J.J. said.

Jess noticed that J.J.'s voice was clearer, deeper than usual. Jess knew what that indicated. That was when sometimes a window opened—a window of illumination. It didn't last long.

'J.J., I need your help,' Jess said.

'You broke the door. Man, I'm going to get in trouble.'

'Tell them I did it. You seem OK. Are you OK?'

'Not really, no,' J.J. said. 'I gotta go back for my meds. What time is it?'

Jess looked at his wristwatch. 'Nearly seven.'

'I'm late. They're gonna come looking for me.'

Jess tried to calm himself. If he was calm, J.J. was more likely to respond. He stepped closer. J.J. recoiled.

'Don't worry,' Jess said, 'I won't touch you.' He breathed deeply. 'J.J., tell me about the ex-cops. There are four of them. You've been around them here. Are they good? Are they honest?'

'No.' Emphatic, spittle flying.

'What have you heard?'

'They want to hurt those kids,' J. J. said. 'And they called Monica a *bitch*.'

'Monica Taylor?' Jess asked. 'You know her?'

J.J. smiled a dark and secret smile. It reminded Jess of the way J.J. used to be, before all this happened. 'She's a pretty woman. She was wild.'

This startled Jess. 'What do you mean? How'd you know her?'

'Some things I remember like they happened yesterday. I remember Monica that way.'

'J.J., about the ex-cops. Why don't you tell the sheriff?'

'He won't believe me. I don't want to get in trouble. I like this job, cleaning. I can't stay in my cell. The nightmares . . .' J.J. looked away.

'J.J., stay with me,' Jess admonished gently. 'I know you can leave here whenever you want. You've done your time.'

'Man, I need my meds, Dad.'

Dad. He called him Dad. Jess felt his chest well up.

'Come with me,' Jess said suddenly. 'Let's get you out of here.'

A slight smile. 'I want to see the ranch. And Mom.'

Jess didn't want to explain. He just wanted to get J.J. away from there. With what he knew, his son was in danger from the ex-cops and possibly the sheriff. He felt a tumble of emotions. This was the first real conversation he'd had with his son in over ten years. He wondered if J.J. had been in there all along, waiting to come out. And Jess had neglected to try.

He backed up and opened the door. 'Come on, son,' he said gently.

J.J. stiffened. 'No. I can't go out there. No, Dad! I can't.'

Jess stood at the door, his heart breaking. J.J. had retrieved his cleaning cloth. He rubbed a desktop violently.

'I'll come back for you, son,' Jess said.

J.J. didn't look up. He was gone again. Jess turned and walked away.

MONICA LOOKED UP when the doorbell rang, and Swann scrambled to his feet from the couch. He had been on his cellphone. They had not spoken since he'd showed her that he had her keys.

'You expecting someone?' he asked as he neared the door.

'Of course not,' she said.

Swann bent and looked out through the peephole. 'Some man,' he said, then opened the front door.

Monica didn't recognise the wet cowboy on the porch. He looked angry, though, the way he squinted inside like the sun was in his eyes.

'What can we do for you?' Swann asked.

'Are you Monica Taylor?' the man asked, not acknowledging Swann. Intuitively, she knew it was about her children. She nodded.

'Then you must be Swann,' the man said, reaching back for something that was out of sight. Then he strode into the house holding a rifle in both hands. Before Swann could reach for the pistol in his belt, the man clubbed him in the face with the butt of the rifle. Swann staggered back, blood gushing from his nose. He fell against the wall and slid down. The man straddled him, and, to Monica's horror, clubbed Swann again in the head. Swann went limp.

The cowboy bent over and came up with Swann's pistol, which he shoved into a pocket of his Wranglers. Then he looked up, caught his breath.

Monica had drawn back into her chair, her fists at her mouth.

'He'll live,' the man said, nodding his hat brim towards Swann. He looked right at her. 'I'm Jess Rawlins. I'm here to take you to your kids.'

JIM HEARNE felt panic growing as the rain receded into a cold mist and his tyres sluiced through the standing puddles on the streets. Something was going on in his town tonight, but he couldn't figure out exactly what it was.

He swung his Suburban into the county building lot, parked it next to the sheriff's Blazer and got out. He was grateful for locating Sheriff Carey, since the two other men he had tried to find earlier had been gone. Lieutenant Singer was not at the task-force room in the county building, or at his home. And Eduardo Villatoro had not been back to his hotel room since late afternoon. For all his running around, Hearne had accomplished exactly nothing.

Three network satellite trucks took up most of the parking lot, and technicians were unfurling thick cables across the asphalt. A reporter, brightly lit by a portable bank of lights, seemed to be waiting for somebody to tell him something in his earpiece. Avoiding the news crews at the front of the building, Hearne walked round to the back, where the dispatcher let him in.

Sheriff Carey's office blazed with lights, even though the rest of the department was dark. When Hearne stepped into the doorway, the sheriff was hanging up his telephone. His looked up slowly, without expression. His eyes seemed moist, oily, with dark circles surrounding them.

'Hello, Mr Hearne.'

Hearne reached across the sheriff's desk to greet him. Carey's hand was without strength.

'Sheriff, you look like hell.'

Carey smiled sadly. 'I'm real tired, Mr Hearne. Take a seat.'

'Call me Jim,' Hearne said, sitting down. 'I won't keep you. I'm just trying to figure a couple of things out, and I hoped you could help me.'

'Pretty late for that.'

'I know,' Hearne said, not knowing if the sheriff meant the time of night or the situation in general.

'When I ran for sheriff, I really didn't think there would be nights like this,' Carey said softly. 'I don't think I'm . . . *equipped* for this sort of thing. I'm in over my head, Jim.' He gestured outside. 'Those people out there want a statement from me. Now, it's big-time.'

Carey began to tell Hearne about what had been happening for the last three days, right up to the call he had just received reporting Oscar Swann severely beaten and Monica Taylor taken by a man who fitted the description of Jess Rawlins. 'Fiona Pritzle suspects Rawlins as well,' Carey said.

Hearne was stunned by it all. 'How could this all be happening?' he asked. 'It's like I don't know this place any more.'

Carey shook his head. 'Me neither.'

Hearne thought about it for a minute, his mind whirling. 'Sheriff, do you know where Singer is right now? Or the rest of the task force, for that matter?'

Carey shook his head no. Like everything, he seemed to be saying, the task force was out of his control.

'What about Eduardo Villatoro? Do you know where he is?'

Carey shrugged again.

Hearne sat forward in his chair, angry. 'Look, Sheriff, I realise it's tough but you can't just sit here. And what you told me about Jess Rawlins. I don't believe it. I've known Jess all my life. There is no way—NO WAY—he's involved in the disappearance of those kids. Fiona Pritzle is a common gossip, the worst kind. Do you think Singer and the others believed her?'

The sheriff looked away. 'Maybe,' he conceded.

Hearne stood up. 'You've got to get hold of them, set them right! And tell those reporters out there before they broadcast these allegations to the whole country. It's time to show some leadership.' He heard himself yelling, something he rarely did. 'That's why the people elected you *sheriff*!'

Instead of getting through to Carey, Hearne's shouting had the opposite effect. Carey seemed to withdraw further, saying nothing.

Hearne calmed his voice. 'So you don't know where anyone is?'

Carey shook his head. 'Singer might be at the hospital, with Swann.'

'OK, then,' Hearne said, standing. 'Please, get in touch with Singer. Tell him Jess Rawlins is a good guy. Don't let the press run with this.' He turned towards the doorway.

'Jim,' Carey said. Hearne looked over his shoulder. 'I'm turning the whole thing over to the Feds. They'll be here by morning. I know it's only been two days, but this is too damned big for me.'

HEARNE TRIED to contact Jess Rawlins on his cellphone as he drove away from the county building. No one picked up and Jess didn't have voicemail. He decided to stop by the hospital on his way out of town in case Singer was there. Hearne felt a compelling need to tell Singer their business relationship was over, that it was time to let the chips fall where they may. It would be his first step back to respectability.

He parked his car at the back of the hospital and left it running while he called Laura to tell her he would be even later than he thought. As he told her what he knew, a man with a heavily bandaged head staggered past his car.

'My God,' Hearne said to Laura. 'You won't believe who just walked by the car. That ex-cop I told you about. The one who was beaten. Oscar Swann.'

'You're kidding.'

'I'm not,' he said distractedly, watching Swann lurch from car to car, bending, looking inside. For what?

Hearne knew the answer when Swann opened the door of a red compact and painfully bent himself into the driver's seat.

'He's stealing a car,' he said. 'I'm following him.'

SWANN DROVE the stolen car beyond the city limits onto the wooded state highway. After half an hour, the banker saw Swann's brake lights flash before he turned off the highway onto a track. Hearne pulled to the side of the road and cut his headlights. He waited until Swann's car had vanished into the trees before turning his lights back on and following. He had no intention of confronting Swann. All he wanted was to find out where the road took him.

When he could see a dull glow through the trees, Hearne cut his lights again, pulled over and killed the engine. He slid outside, careful not to slam the door, and walked through the trees, his eyes adjusting to the darkness.

Seventy-five yards up the hill, Swann's house was bright with lights. In addition to the red car Swann had stolen, Hearne recognised Singer's white SUV. There was also a shiny black pick-up with chrome wheels. He immediately guessed the whole task force was there, at Swann's house.

Fear gripped him, seemed to make his legs heavy. As he walked close to a large pen, a massive hog false-charged him, grunting. Hearne jumped back, tripped over a tree root and broke his fall with his elbows. While he lay in the mud he could hear the shallow, staccato breathing of the hog.

He scrambled to his feet and, as he did so, his cellphone fell out of his shirt pocket, bounced off his knee and landed a few feet in front of him, in a pool of light from the house that slipped through the panels on the fence. He stepped out of the shadows to retrieve the phone, at the same time that the front door of Swann's house was thrown open. Hearne froze and watched as three men—he recognised the profiles of Singer, Swann and Gonzalez—stepped onto the front porch. Could they possibly see him?

The men looked in his direction. Then Singer turned to Swann and said something he couldn't hear. Hearne realised that they were looking down the dark road and not at him. Like they were waiting for someone.

Hearne backed up further into the shadows, then felt his way through the trees towards his car. He prayed he wouldn't step on a dry branch or trip again in the mud. He would leave the phone. He had no choice. The Rawlins ranch was just a few miles away. He had to warn Jess.

SINCE JESS AND MONICA cleared Kootenai Bay, heading north, the rain had been sporadic. He had filled her in. How her children had shown up in his barn, defended themselves, told him their story. Where things now stood.

She was calm and seemed to trust him. He wondered why. He stole glances at her as he drove. She was obviously exhausted. In the passing lights, the hollows of her eyes and cheeks were shadowed. Her voice was soft when she said, 'I knew they were alive. I don't know how, but I knew it.'

It made him feel good to know he was bringing her together with her children. She seemed to want nothing more than to be with them.

'You're familiar to me,' she said. 'I've always thought of you as what was old, tough and good about this valley, before everything changed.'

He looked at her, puzzled, and said, 'You got the "old" part right, anyway.'

JESS STAYED OUT of the middle of the reunion. He went to the kitchen to make coffee after Monica sank to her knees, crying, and took her children into her arms. He heard William and Annie talking over each other, retelling the story about the murder they had witnessed and Mr Swann, about the dark man who had come to the house. How Jess Rawlins had taken care of them.

Halfway into measuring coffee for the pot, he remembered the shotgun in the living room and went to get it. The Taylors had now settled on the couch, with William clinging to his mother, his head in her lap, Annie next to her, talking a mile a minute. Monica looked as if she were glowing from within. This scene, Jess thought, made what he had done to Swann worth it.

Jess put the shotgun next to the Winchester on the kitchen table. As the talking subsided in the living room, he noticed that the rain had stopped.

He felt a presence next to him, his waist being squeezed, and he looked down and saw Annie, her wide-open face turned up to him. He couldn't speak, so he reached down and mussed her hair gently.

'I'm so glad she's here,' Annie said. 'Thank you for bringing her. I'm so happy it's all over.'

Jess, feeling his eyes sting, thought, It's not over, Annie. Not even close.

THE SMELL INSIDE the car was of bourbon, rain and burning dust from the heater, which hadn't been used in a while. Villatoro tried to adjust the level of the fan. Newkirk, damp, drunk and agitated, had fogged the glass.

After leaving Rodale's driveway, Newkirk pointed the way with the mouth of the open pint of Wild Turkey he'd produced from his jacket. Villatoro wasn't sure what road they were on. Everything looked the same: dark wet trees bordering the road, wet asphalt, no lights.

Newkirk drank from the bottle. 'Harsh stuff, man,' he said, wiping his mouth with his sleeve.

Villatoro said, 'So, you want to talk?'

'No. I just didn't want to drink alone. Don't be a dumb fuck.'

Villatoro clamped his jaws. *Just let the man talk. Don't prompt him.*

Moments passed as they drove. Newkirk drank again, then settled back into his seat. Villatoro kept his eyes on the road.

'I wanted to be the best on the force,' Newkirk said. 'I didn't have notions like I was gonna change the world or anything, but I wanted to do my job the best I could and take care of my family. I wanted to look in the mirror and say, "Man, you are a *good* policeman." '

Villatoro nodded as he scaled back the fan of the heater.

'I tried too hard at first. When I saw a crack baby or human beings who treated other human beings like crap, I thought I could show 'em somebody cared. But you know what? I learned that the best thing you could do, overall, was to arrest as many of 'em as you could and follow through. Just fill the prisons, keep those scumbags away from the good people. And I did a damned good job of it. But you have no idea what it was like.'

'No, I don't.'

'You can't talk about this stuff with anybody except other cops. You can't come home and say, "Gee, how was your day, dear? Did you go shopping? I had an interesting day today. I found the corpse of an eleven-month-old baby in a Dumpster with cigarette burns all over her body."'

Villatoro shot him a look. Newkirk was staring straight ahead, talking as much to himself as to Villatoro.

'You know what it's like trying to raise a family with kids on a cop's salary. So I discovered the world of off-duty security. I could just about double my income if I was willing to be a rent-a-cop.'

'At Santa Anita,' Villatoro said.

'Among other places. But yeah, Santa Anita was the most steady.' Newkirk took a long drink, then said, 'It was a pretty good gig. We didn't even open the doors until the security truck got there. Then we just guarded the perimeter while they loaded the trucks. We stuck around until all the paying customers cleared out, then went home. Me and Rodale, we worked it all the time together. They liked us, we liked them.

'Gonzalez was our sergeant,' Newkirk said. 'Everybody respected and feared the guy. Singer was our commanding officer, over Gonzo. He defended his officers to the death, went to the mat for them. There wasn't a guy in our division who wouldn't take a bullet for Lieutenant Singer or Gonzo. They were, like, *mythical*.

'So when Gonzo invited me and Rodale for beers at a cop bar one night, we thought that was pretty cool. Swann was there, too—it was the first time we'd met him. After a few cocktails, Gonzo started asking us how we'd rob Santa Anita if we were bad guys.'

Villatoro found himself looking over.

Newkirk curled his lip. 'It's not like that, man. It was just a conversation. You know how cops do it all the time, try to figure out how bad guys would do a job, so they can *prevent* it. Turn here.'

'Where are we going?' Villatoro asked, taking another dark two-lane highway. He was beginning to get a bad feeling.

'Just driving. I told you that.' Newkirk drank. Then: 'Nobody was supposed to get hurt. That wasn't the plan.'

At last, Villatoro thought. He had worked years to hear this.

'We planned the robbery for a year and a half. We had meetings, tried to shoot parts down, did a couple of run-throughs at night so we could time everything. Once we had the perfect plan, it was still another four or five months before we decided to do it. Singer had to figure out how to launder the money. Also, we had to wait until all the stars lined up perfectly. A big cash day at the track, me and Rodale on security, Singer and Gonzo off duty so they could trigger the gas and rush the truck, Swann on patrol so he could escort the getaway vehicle to the salvage yard, where it was crushed. Remember, no one ever found a car?'

Villatoro wished he was wearing a wire. 'I remember.'

Newkirk chuckled. 'Swann drove Singer and Gonzo and thirteen and a half million dollars in cash back to LA in a police van and dropped them off at their houses. Imagine that.'

Villatoro whistled. 'But a security guard got killed.'

Newkirk seemed to darken. 'That wasn't supposed to happen. Some yahoo tried to be a cowboy. Gonzo had to take him out.'

'His name was Steve Nichols. He had a wife and two young children.'

Newkirk didn't respond at first, just stared out of the windshield. 'That wasn't supposed to happen,' he said again. Then he fell silent.

Finally, Villatoro asked, 'What about the guy who fingered the other employees in the counting room? Why did he do that if he wasn't involved?'

Newkirk shrugged. 'Singer's boy,' he said. 'The lieutenant had something incriminating on the guy—unrelated to the track. I never knew what.'

'But the employee died before he had a chance to testify.'

'Yeah, wasn't that convenient?' Newkirk said darkly. 'He gets caught in a crossfire buying cigarettes at a 7-Eleven. The clerk gets popped, the witness gets popped and the robber empties the cash drawer. All they can see on the security tape is a big masked guy in black walking in and blasting away.'

Villatoro let it sink in. 'Gonzalez?' he asked.

Newkirk nodded. 'And Swann was the investigating officer.'

Jesus, Villatoro thought. It's worse than I imagined.

'Creating the charity was the master stroke,' Villatoro said. 'Making small deposits in a bank in northern Idaho never attracted any attention at all for years. The only problem was, you must not have realised that some of the hundred-dollar bills could be traced to the robbery.'

Newkirk's face screwed up in contempt. '*Of course* we knew about the serial numbers. That's where Tony Rodale screwed the pooch,' he said, his eyes flashing. 'His job was to drive all around the country to break the hundred-dollar bills in restaurants, gas stations, bars, or wherever. He told his wife he was going fishing. All he had to do was cash the hundreds and deposit the change later. But he got greedy. Singer noticed that some of the deposits were off, and figured Tony was skimming, which he was. The idiot was using some of the hundreds to bet on football with some bookie in Coeur d'Alene. Singer found the bookie and shook him down.' Newkirk leaned across the car so his face was inches from Villatoro. 'Tony risked *everything*. Singer knew it would be a matter of time before someone like you came up here.'

'And here I am,' Villatoro said, not sure why he'd spoken.

'Here you are,' Newkirk said, as if in pain.

'But where is Tony Rodale?'

Newkirk started to speak, then looked away. Beads of sweat sparkled on his forehead. 'That's what I'm going to show you.'

'Oh no,' Villatoro whispered. 'You killed him.'

'Not just me. All of us. The agreement was we all put a couple into him, so we were all equally responsible. All of us except for Swann, who was late.'

Another murder, Villatoro thought. It was too overwhelming to process.

'It might have worked,' Newkirk was saying, 'but those two kids saw us.'

'The Taylor children. Oh my God.'

'It keeps getting worse,' Newkirk said. 'One perfectly planned crime. We were set for life. Then Tony fucked up, and those kids saw us take him out. Then the UPS guy.' His voice cracked. 'I feel like I'm already in hell.'

Villatoro realised that his hands were shaking. What UPS man?

'This is so much bigger than I imagined,' he said.

The ex-cop laughed bitterly, then wiped tears from his face with his sleeve before reaching behind him to withdraw his black semiautomatic. He shoved the muzzle into Villatoro's neck. 'It's about to get bigger. I'm sorry I've got to do this, man. Especially since you were a cop yourself.' He nodded towards a wet black mailbox marking a dirt road. 'Slow down and turn here.'

'What are you doing?' Villatoro asked, his voice stronger than he expected.

'Turn here,' Newkirk said, with more force.

The road was a two-lane dirt track pooled with rainwater that inclined into trees. As Villatoro floored it up the hill, the rear tyres fishtailing in mud, he recalled the name on the mailbox: SWANN.

With a strange kind of calm, Villatoro thought, I'm going to die.

JESS WAS PICKING UP the phone to try to reach Villatoro when he saw the lights of a car blink through trees on his road. He hung up and glanced into the living room, where Monica, Annie and William were huddled up on the couch, talking softly.

He leaned in. 'Turn off the lights and don't open the door unless it's me,' he said calmly. 'Someone's coming down the hill.' He reprimanded himself for not taking a chain up to the gate and locking it closed.

Monica turned her face to him. It drained of colour.

'There's only one car,' Jess said. 'Please, turn off the lights.'

Annie disentangled from her mother and bounded across the room to flip the light switch. On the way back, she turned off the table lamp.

'It may not be anything,' Jess said, trying to reassure them.

'Where are you going?' William asked. 'Are you coming back?'

'Sure,' Jess said, picking up the Winchester. He turned off the kitchen lights and felt his way to the back door.

His boots crunched in the gravel as he walked across the ranch yard to the side of the barn. The car approached quickly and there was a flash of brake lights before the engine was shut off. Jess timed the sound of working the lever action on the rifle to the car door's opening. He saw a wink of brass as the cartridge slid into the chamber. Jess raised the rifle but didn't aim.

As the door opened, the interior lights showed one occupant, not three or four. That occupant was Jim Hearne. Jess frowned in the dark, puzzled.

Jim stepped out and called, 'Jess? Jess Rawlins? Are you in there?'

'Behind you,' Jess said from the shadow.

Hearne spun and ducked. 'You scared me,' he said.

'What do you need?' Jess asked.

'Jess, you didn't answer when I called earlier. You've got to hear what's going on.'

Jess lowered the Winchester and approached.

Hearne's eyes shifted to the rifle. 'My God, were you going to shoot me?'

'Maybe. Let's go inside.'

'SO ALL OF 'EM are up at Swann's place now,' Jess said, shaking his head and sipping from the mug of coffee he had just brewed.

'All except for Newkirk—I didn't see him. But it was obvious they were waiting for someone.' Hearne turned in his chair and looked through the doorway into the living room. 'I still can't believe they're here,' he said softly. 'What a relief.'

Jess nodded. He was rehashing what Hearne had told him about the sheriff giving up, about the FBI coming, about Fiona Pritzle and her gossip. About the conclave of ex-cops at Swann's house.

'Maybe we should gather everyone up,' Hearne said, gesturing towards the Taylors, 'and make a run to town. If the sheriff saw everyone together . . .'

Jess shook his head. 'What if he calls in Singer? No, I feel safer here until we know what's going on. All we have to do is wait until morning. We can explain it all to the Feds when they get here.'

Hearne said, 'Maybe we could go to my house?'

'Either way, we'd need to drive down the highway in front of Swann's place. What if they have a couple of men in the trees waiting for us?'

'I hadn't thought of that,' Hearne said sullenly.

'I know one thing,' Jess said, standing and tossing the rest of his coffee into the sink. 'I don't like speculation. We'll just drive ourselves crazy with it.'

'So what are you going to do?'

'I'm going to see what those boys are up to,' Jess said.

'You're going to Swann's house? What if they see you coming?'

Jess grinned. 'I'm not going to drive.'

It took Hearne a few beats to understand. Then: 'I'll help you saddle up.'

IN THE BARN, Jess shoved his rifle into the saddle scabbard and swung up on Chile. Hearne stepped aside, nearly backing into the pregnant cow in the stall.

'I can get there quicker overland,' Jess said, turning his horse towards the open stall door. 'Straight across my meadows and up into the timber on the side of Swann's place. They'll be looking for headlights, not a rider.'

'If you aren't back in an hour,' Hearne said, 'I'm going to pile the Taylors into my car and go to town.'

'That sounds like a plan,' Jess said over his shoulder as he walked the red dun out of the barn. 'Hand me that length of chain there so I can lock the gate on my way. Keep that shotgun handy while I'm gone. And keep an eye on that cow. She's ready to pop.'

AFTER LOOPING the chain round the gate and snapping two big locks through the links, Jess nudged Chile into the trees until they emerged in a meadow, where he let her settle into a slow lope. The rain had begun to drizzle again. When they climbed up into the dripping pines, he glanced down at his house, picturing the Taylors on the couch in the dark and Hearne sitting on the porch with the shotgun across his lap, looking nothing like a banker.

THE LITTLE CAR made it up the hill and the road levelled out. Villatoro could see a lone porch light blinking through the trees. He could no longer feel his fingers. A sense of utter calm sedated him.

'Stop here,' Newkirk said.

When he did, Newkirk leaned over him and pulled out the keys. 'Get out.'

Villatoro opened the door. There was some kind of pen in front of him, and huge, dark forms scuttled behind the slats of a fence. He heard a grunting noise, then a squeal. Pigs.

A big man, Gonzalez, stepped out from a shed, pointed a pistol at him. 'Good job, Newkirk.'

'I've got a wife and a daughter,' Villatoro said. His voice seemed to be coming from someone else.

Gonzalez levelled his gun with both hands.

Villatoro heard Newkirk say, 'Sorry, man.'

He heard Gonzalez say, 'You going to do this or am I?'

He heard Newkirk say, with a choke in his voice, 'You do it.'

'You never should have come out here, old man,' Gonzalez said.

Villatoro looked up and saw a silver ring hanging in the dark inches from his eye. It was the mouth of the muzzle. He wondered if he should strike out, try to hit someone, try to run. But he had never been a fighter. In thirty years, he'd never drawn his weapon.

'Fuck this,' Gonzalez said, and the ring dropped away. 'You need to finish the job you started. That's what the lieutenant told you, right?'

'I guess,' Newkirk said.

Villatoro hoped he wouldn't get sick.

'Take care of this fake cop.' Gonzalez walked away, laughing softly.

Villatoro was humiliated and angry. But most of all, he was terrified. He felt Newkirk's gun in the small of his back, pushing him forward.

'Walk down to the end of the pen along the rails,' Newkirk said, his voice weak. 'And don't look back at me.'

He's going to shoot me in the back of the head, Villatoro thought. Better than in the face. As he stumbled forward, he sensed one of the hogs walking along with him on the other side of the fence, grunting with each breath.

Newkirk pushed him ahead until they were under a canopy of trees at the corner of the corral. He gripped Villatoro's shirt collar, guiding him.

Any second now. He could barely hear the drip of the trees because of the roar in his ears. And something else . . .

'Mister, I'm ready to shoot your eyes out of the back of your head.'

It was not Newkirk who spoke. It was a voice from the trees, from the dark. The voice was deep and familiar, but Villatoro couldn't place it.

The gun twitched on his back. Newkirk said, 'Who is it?'

'The guy who's about to blow your head off.'

Newkirk kept his grip on Villatoro's collar, but the gun left his back. There really was someone out there! And the voice, it was that rancher, Rawlins.

The gun returned, this time pressed to Villatoro's temple. 'I don't know who you are,' Newkirk said, 'but if you don't back off, he's a dead man.'

'He's a dead man anyway from the look of things,' the rancher said. 'So fire away. There'll be two dead.'

Villatoro expected to feel an explosion at any moment, to experience a flash of orange lights and his body dropping away.

'Who are you?' Newkirk asked, his voice weak.

'Tell you what,' Rawlins said. 'Let the guy go and I'll let you walk away.'

'I can't just go back,' Newkirk said, sounding like a little boy.

'Let him go and I'll let you fire your gun in the dirt,' Rawlins said. 'They'll think you did your job, and I'll never tell. Neither will Mr Villatoro.'

He pronounced my name correctly, Villatoro thought.

'It will never work,' Newkirk said.

'I don't think there's a choice in the matter.'

Villatoro felt the grip on his collar loosen, felt the absence of the gun on the side of his head. He chanced a step forward, and nothing happened.

'Keep walking, Eduardo,' Rawlins said. 'Don't stop.'

Villatoro did as he was told. From the dark, a hand gripped his arm, pulled him into the warm flank of a damp horse.

'Go ahead, shoot,' Rawlins said to Newkirk, 'but don't even think about raising the weapon again.'

The explosion was sharp but muffled, and Villatoro felt his knees tremble at the sound of it. But there were no more shots.

NEWKIRK WATCHED the red end of Gonzo's cigar, watched it brighten as the ex-sergeant sucked on it, the glow bright enough to light up his eyes.

They were on the deck of Swann's house, sitting on metal lawn furniture. Newkirk was still shaking. He could hear the pigs grunting and squealing, hungry. Those damn pigs were going to give him away. If Gonzo walked down there and couldn't find the body . . .

'That guy from Arcadia must taste good,' Gonzo said, mistaking the sound. 'Did he give you any trouble?'

Newkirk felt a wave of relief. 'No.'

'One shot to the brain, right?'

'Yeah,' Newkirk grunted.

He was drunk but not drunk enough. Violent shivers coursed through him. He tried not to think about what had happened. It wasn't him who gained Villatoro's confidence, told him everything for the purpose of getting the man to Swann's place. It was someone *playing* him, acting out a role, reading a script he'd been handed. He wasn't evil. He had a wife and kids.

'What's Singer planning in there?' he asked, taking a long pull from the bottle he'd brought with him.

'He's figuring things out,' Gonzalez said, irritated. 'You asked me the same question five minutes ago.'

Newkirk was glad that Gonzalez couldn't see the mixture of hate and self-revulsion he was sure was on his face.

'You better cool it with the boozing, too,' his old boss said. 'We might have to go into action. You need to be sharp.'

'I thought I'd just let you do the killing.'

'What the fuck does that mean?'

'Nothing.' Newkirk was surprised he'd actually said that.

Gonzalez put his huge forearms on the table between them. 'You think I like it? Is that what you think?'

'No, I don't think that. Forget I said anything.'

'But you said it, asshole,' Gonzalez said, his voice rising.

Newkirk shook his head hard. 'No, really, I . . .'

Gonzalez was across the table and his hand shot out. Before Newkirk could pull back, a thumb jammed between his teeth and cheek, fingers clamped and twisted as if trying to tear his face off. Newkirk groaned and gagged, his head driven into the tabletop.

Gonzalez bent over him, his mouth inches from Newkirk's ear. 'Don't you dare get sanctimonious on me. I had nothing against that guy . . . except he wanted to put me into prison, take my new life away. I like my life, Newkirk. I'll do anything to keep it. And if that means shooting a prick like *you* in the head, I'll do that, too.'

Newkirk blinked away tears and tried not to make a sound, to give Gonzalez a moment to cool down.

Gonzalez relieved the pressure and Newkirk sat back up.

'I'm sorry,' he said. 'It was the bourbon talking.'

'Yeah,' Gonzalez said. 'But the bourbon used your mouth.'

They heard a chair being pushed back inside. Singer stepped out onto the porch. 'Did you solve our problem?' he asked Newkirk, all business.

'Solved,' Gonzalez said, standing. 'The pigs are happy.'

'What did you do with his car?'

Gonzalez said, 'It's in the garage for now. We can take it to the chop shop in Spokane later.'

Singer narrowed his eyes at Newkirk. 'What happened to your face?'

Before Newkirk could reply, Gonzalez threw an arm round him, crushing him into his hard barrel chest. 'Emotions were running a little high, Lieutenant. We had a little scrap, but everything's cool now, isn't it, Newkirk?'

Newkirk nodded and said, 'Yup. We're cool.'

Singer moved his eyes from Newkirk to Gonzalez, back to Newkirk. 'OK, let's meet inside,' he said.

THEY SAT at the kitchen table. Swann looked bad. Cuts on his face were stitched closed and dark bruises were forming under his eyes. Newkirk thought the sight of him was sickening.

Singer said, 'He's got a broken nose and cheekbone and a busted jaw. Somebody worked him over and took Monica Taylor.'

Newkirk thought he knew who had done it.

'The sheriff's in a panic,' Singer continued, his voice calm. 'He's contacted the state DCI and the Feds. He thinks he's got a double kidnapping on his hands. The Feds will be here first thing tomorrow in a chopper.'

'Who did it?' Gonzalez asked Swann.

Swann's face was half again its normal size. He had trouble talking but said, 'Tall, thin old guy, maybe sixty, sixty-five, wearing a cowboy hat. He had a lever-action rifle with him.'

Yes, sounds like him, Newkirk thought.

'Why'd he take the woman?' he asked.

'I don't know why he took the woman,' Singer said, giving him a laser-beam stare. 'But I can guess. Have you been drinking, Newkirk?'

Newkirk felt his face get hot. 'Some,' he said.

'Are you OK to work?'

'Yes,' Newkirk said, his voice thick.

'You remember Fiona Pritzle?' Singer asked. 'She's the one who gave the Taylor kids a ride to go fishing. She's a gossip, a local busybody, but she showed up at the sheriff's house tonight with an interesting story. She said she saw a local rancher in the store buying food that only kids eat, but the guy doesn't have any kids. She says he lives up the valley, about eight miles from the Sand Creek campsite. The sheriff knows the citizen: Jeff Rawlins. Anyway, Pritzle thinks Rawlins may have the kids. Says he's an old pervert.'

'Rawlins,' Gonzo said. 'The guy who threw me off his ranch.'

Newkirk kept quiet.

'He's got them,' Singer said. 'The kids and Monica Taylor. Obviously, we've got to force a confrontation. What happens is the rancher gets killed and the Taylors go down in the crossfire. The dead rancher gets pinned with kidnapping, sex crimes, murder. We use the rancher's gun to shoot them.'

Newkirk couldn't say anything. He was too busy trying to stop the surge of sour whisky from coming back up.

'We've got a hostage situation,' Singer said. 'Newkirk, what do we do when we've got a hostage situation?'

Newkirk gagged, then stumbled to the sink and threw up. He felt their eyes on his back but didn't turn until he'd gulped down two glasses of water. Finally, he said, 'Cut off power and electricity. Force them into the open.'

'Right,' Singer said, satisfied.

'I THOUGHT for a minute you were going to let Newkirk shoot me.'

'Nope,' Jess told Villatoro. 'It was a bluff.'

'It was a good bluff,' Villatoro said emphatically. 'I believed you.'

'Mr Villatoro, you need to keep your voice down a little. Sound carries out here. We don't want them to hear us.'

'I'm sorry,' Villatoro whispered. 'My nerves are jangling. And I never rode a horse before.'

They were deep in the woods, the mare picking her way over downed logs and between crowded trees. They were on the ranch now, Jess could feel it. His passenger clutched him tightly. The Winchester lay across the pommel of the saddle. Although the moon was still behind clouds, the sky was clearing and muted shafts of moonlight shone through the branches.

'Will your horse carry both of us all the way back?' Villatoro whispered.

'Hope so.'

'I hope I don't fall off.' Villatoro sighed, as if suddenly exhausted. 'What a night. I feel foolish for not fighting back, but what could I have done?'

'Not much,' Jess said. 'I've been thinking. Hearne's right. As soon as we get back let's pack everybody into his car and my truck and get to Kootenai Bay. We'll go straight to the sheriff and the media and try to make our case. I'd rather those kids were there than here tonight.'

Villatoro took a cautious breath before asking, 'What kids?'

Jess explained.

All Villatoro could say was, 'My God.'

After a while, Chile slowed down, getting tired. They dismounted, and Jess led her by the reins so that she could catch her breath and cool down.

Above them, in the trees, was a sweep of light.

'What was that?' Villatoro asked.

Jess put a gloved finger against his lips. 'Headlights.'

They stopped and listened. Far above them and to the east, they could hear a motor and the crunching of gravel. There was the squeak of brakes, a surge of the engine, then another squeak before the motor was killed.

'They blocked the gate,' Jess said.

VILLATORO AND HEARNE sat at the kitchen table drinking coffee. The shotgun was on the table as well, along with a box of shells. In hushed tones, Villatoro was telling Hearne about the encounter in the trees at Swann's place. Hearne kept shooting glances at Jess, who sipped his coffee with his back to the counter and half listened.

Annie and William were asleep on the couch under a blanket. Monica rifled through Jess's refrigerator and cupboards looking for ingredients so she could make lasagne, but she gave up. She said she wanted to cook something. She settled on a cake mix, and Jess could tell she was doing something just to be doing it. Who would want to eat cake?

Villatoro looked at his wristwatch. It was nearly midnight. 'I wish there was someone we could call,' he said.

Hearne said, 'I'm going to call my wife, let her know I'm safe.'

'That's a good idea,' Villatoro said. 'You call, then I'll call my wife.' He said it with a tone that barely disguised what he meant, which was, *in case we never see them again.*

Hearne held the receiver in his hand. 'There's no dial tone.'

Villatoro said, 'They've cut the line.'

Jess said to Hearne, 'Try your cellphone.'

'It's gone,' Hearne said, gesturing with empty hands. 'I lost it at Swann's.'

'What about you?' Jess asked Villatoro.

He shrugged. 'Mine never worked up here. Wrong company.'

'So we're blocked in and we can't communicate,' Jess said flatly.

In midsentence, the lights went out. From the living room, Jess heard Annie scream.

Day Four: Monday

Carrying two hissing camping lanterns, Jess entered the house from the barn. He put one lantern on the table and held the other up at shoulder height, so he could see the faces shining back at him.

To Hearne, he said, 'Can you still ride?'

'I haven't forgotten how.'

Jess nodded outside. 'Then take Chile into town. That way you can avoid the road. You might be able to get to Sheriff Carey before daylight, convince him to get his men out here.'

Hearne nodded, went to the gun cabinet and pulled out another shotgun. 'Should I take this?'

'Yup.' Jess turned to Villatoro and the Taylors. 'I'm not running. I know every inch of this ranch. We're going to hold our ground. Don't worry, I've been preparing for it all my life.'

'But you're old, Jess.' Annie sounded concerned.

'*Annie!*' Monica said.

'Hell, let her be.' Jess laughed. 'She may be right.'

AS JESS PULLED Chile's flank strap tight and adjusted the stirrups for Hearne, the banker said, 'Jess, let's make a pact.'

Jess finished, turned.

Hearne said, 'If I don't make it, promise me you'll take care of Annie and see her through. William and Monica, too. I'll do the same if something happens here to you.'

Jess tried to read Hearne's face, but couldn't get past the resolve in it. 'You trying to tell me something?' he asked.

Hearne simply looked at him. 'I mean it, Jess.'

'OK,' Jess said after a beat. He held out his hand and Hearne shook it. 'Remember,' he added, 'trust your horse to find the way in the dark.'

MONICA FOUND JESS in the barn, sitting on an upturned bucket, the Winchester across his knees, a lantern throwing out warm yellow light. In the stall in front of him was a hugely pregnant cow, legs splayed, tail twitching with pain. She could hear the cow's shallow breathing.

'I was wondering where you went,' she said. 'I got the kids down again and realised you weren't in the kitchen. Then I saw the light out here.'

Jess looked over at her. 'These cows, they just keep having little ones no matter what else I have to do.'

'I don't know how you can concentrate right now.'

Jess shrugged. 'Doing something normal helps me think.'

Monica stepped inside the barn. 'How close is she?'

'Any minute,' he said. Then he nodded at a bucket near him. 'You can sit down, if you'd like. Annie used that bucket last night to watch the same thing.'

'Annie watched a cow being born? How'd she take it?'

'She's pretty tough,' the rancher said. 'She's a good kid, if you don't mind me saying that.'

Monica smiled and sat down. 'Of course I don't mind. She really likes you. So does William. He told me when I tucked him in.'

Jess looked down at his boots. She couldn't tell what he was thinking.

'Jess,' she said, 'I've known a lot of men in my life. I can't think of one of them who would have done what you did.'

He wouldn't look over at her and she noticed how his ears turned red. 'There's a couple more,' he mumbled. 'One inside the house and the other on horseback right now.'

'I can't tell you how much I appreciate it. But I don't mean to make you uncomfortable.' It took her a few moments to summon the courage for what would come next. 'Jess, I know there've been rumours about me and I want to clear them up.'

He glanced at her but didn't stare, making it easier for her.

'Thirteen years ago,' she said, 'I was seventeen and I thought I was a pretty hot little number. I wanted to grow up fast. So, along with three friends, I went to Spokane on a Friday night, to a university frat party. Not long after we arrived, my friends and I got separated. I was a little scared because there were so many people, and a lot of drinking. I'd had way too much myself. Luckily, there was a boy I recognised from around here. He was very friendly, very handsome. Smart, too. He said if we couldn't find my friends at the frat house, we'd go from party to party on campus until we did.'

She saw Jess shake his head, probably not even realising he was doing it.

'I was head over heels,' she continued. 'He was the most charismatic man I'd met other than my dad. We spent the next two days together locked up in his room. It was magical. You could just look at him and know something big was going to happen—like he was on the verge of something. Finally, my friends found me and practically dragged me back to Kootenai Bay.

'I still wanted to see him, but when I called the frat house they said he wasn't there any more, and wouldn't tell me how to reach him. I started to get worried. So I called the one friend who'd always been there to help me out and told him the situation. We drove to Spokane, and that's when I found out he'd had some kind of severe breakdown and got arrested.'

When she looked at Jess, he was staring at her with an intensity she hadn't seen before.

'Jess, the boy was Jess Junior.'

'He told me he knew you.'

'Was that all he said?'

Jess swallowed. 'He said you were wild. You aren't going to tell me Annie is my granddaughter, are you?'

She hesitated. 'No, I'm not. Annie is Jim Hearne's daughter.'

Jess was speechless.

'He was the friend I called to take me to Spokane. He was my father's best friend, and I think he felt he owed something to me and to you. But one thing led to another, and afterwards Jim felt horrible. But he didn't take advantage of me. He gave in to *me*. I was like that then. But I didn't want to ruin a good man. I never told him I was pregnant. I let him think Annie was J.J.'s. But J.J. and I never completed the act, so I know for sure. In a way, I think Jim knows, too, but he's been too frightened all these years to ask. If you're wondering why the local banker is on that horse right now, I think you've got your answer.'

'My God,' Jess said. 'Now I know what he was trying to tell me.' He smiled sadly. 'I was kind of hoping you were going to tell me I had a grandchild.'

'I'm sorry she isn't.'

'It doesn't matter,' he said. 'I like 'em just the same.'

'Jess, I've made a vow to myself during all this that I'm going to keep: my kids come first. I've learned that lesson. No more Tom Boyds, no more J.J.s, no more Jim Hearnes, no more anyone. Annie and William come first.'

He nodded. 'I think that's good.'

'Yes, it is. I need to make my own way in the world without relying on any man to make things happen for me. I think that's possible, don't you?'

'Sure,' Jess said. He looked at her full on. 'But however things work out, I'd like to keep up with Annie and William. We can pretend they're my grandkids. My own family got pretty screwed up. I'd like to help your kids if I can, maybe make up for the damage I've caused.'

Now it was Monica's turn to be speechless.

'This place,' he said, gesturing towards the open barn door but meaning the ranch, 'is the only thing I've got that connects me to my father and mother, and to my granddad. They said to work hard and pass it on to my own kids. That'll never happen. Developers want it, and it belongs more to the bank than it does to me. So there'll be nothing for me to pass on. But if I can help out Annie and William, maybe help them get a leg up, well, that'll be fine. It means I've got something to live for. I've got someone to defend. That means . . . everything.'

He turned away, and she leaned over and hugged him, buried her face into his neck, said, 'You're a good man, Jess,' and meant it.

JIM HEARNE THOUGHT, It feels good to sit a horse again.

He had slowed Chile to a walk once they entered the woods on the other side of the meadow. She could see much better than he could in the dark beneath the tree branches, so he gave her her head and let her go.

The rain had stopped, and the sounds of the forest returned. Chattering squirrels warned of their arrival as the horse picked her way through gnarled undergrowth. He knew there was a barbed-wire fence ahead somewhere, the fence that separated the Rawlins place from forest service land.

Chile was purposeful; he liked that. She was the kind of horse that was best if she had a job: cutting cattle, herding, or delivering him to Kootenai Bay. He was glad he had a purpose, too, that he was finally doing something right, for Monica and Annie. This was his ride of redemption. When he thought about that, he smiled.

He could feel Chile hesitate, feel her muscles bunch beneath his thighs, and in a moment he could see the four thin ribbons of barbed wire coursing through the trees ahead. At the fence he turned her uphill, parallel to the fence. If he couldn't find a gate, he'd do the old cowboy trick of detaching the wire from the posts to stand on while leading the horse over.

Hearne was studying the fence line with such intensity that he almost didn't realise that the forest sounds had stopped. Chile was looking ahead, her eyes wide, her nostrils flared.

Above, in the black woodlands, a twig snapped.

Hearne signalled Chile to stop with a tug on her reins, and he sat the saddle, trying to make his eyes pierce the darkness. The fence line goes all the way to the road, he thought. If someone were to walk the perimeter of the ranch, they would likely use the fence line as their guide.

The voice came from the trees. 'You need some help, mister?'

It was deep and had a Mexican inflection. Hearne froze.

The shotgun was deep in the saddle scabbard under his right leg. Hearne leaned back. He felt the metal butt plate and slid his fingers round the stock.

Chile crow-hopped as a form emerged from the dark trees. Hearne scrambled for balance as a light from a flashlight blinded him. There was a metallic click, and he never heard the shot.

AS THE CLOUDS parted to reveal a wash of hard, white stars, Newkirk felt a hangover of epic proportions forming in the back of his brain. His mouth was dry and tasted of whisky, and his eyes burned for sleep. He looked at his wristwatch. It was 4.08 a.m. Gonzalez had been gone for hours.

Newkirk and Singer were in the white Escalade, backed up into a stand of trees, pointed at the locked gate to the Rawlins Ranch. Before leaving to scout the ranch house below, Gonzalez had parked his pick-up beside them. Swann was inside it, slumped against the door, sleeping and useless.

Gonzalez had taken a handheld radio and his scoped .308 Winchester rifle with him. Above them, resting on pine branches, were the power and phone lines Gonzalez had cut away from the utility pole earlier. Singer and Newkirk thought they had heard a muffled gunshot in the distance, and Singer had tried to raise Gonzalez on the handheld, but there was no response. Singer assumed Gonzo had squelched the receiver. They had no choice but to sit and wait.

Singer had a police scanner and radio under his dashboard. It had been silent for most of the night, other than cops calling in the ends of their shifts. On the bench seat between Singer and Newkirk was a map of the area, with a handheld and Singer's cellphone resting on it.

Newkirk couldn't figure out what Singer was thinking. The plan had been simple: cut the power and phone, set up at the gate, wait for Rawlins to come to them. But he never came. And Newkirk knew the rancher had Villatoro, so that might complicate things. But Singer didn't know that.

When the handheld chirped, Newkirk jumped.

Singer snatched the receiver, whispered, 'Gonzo? Is that you?'

A beat. 'It's me. I'm approaching the gate.'

A moment later, Newkirk saw a glint of a rifle barrel in the starlight as Gonzalez climbed through the barbed wire of the fence. Then the sergeant was at the driver's side window.

He said, 'I walked the fence line and ran into your banker. I thought it was that cowboy trying to get away on horseback. One shot and he went down.'

'We heard it,' Singer said, distracted. Then: 'I didn't think Hearne would be around. How did *that* happen?'

Gonzalez shrugged. 'Who knows? I went down the road, looked through the scope. The house is dark and nobody's moving. The rancher's pick-up is parked in front. Another car is there, too. I'd guess the banker's.'

'Maybe they're sleeping,' Newkirk said, his voice a croak. 'Maybe they don't even know they don't have power.'

Singer and Gonzalez looked at him, dismissing him. Newkirk closed his eyes, tried to tone down the pounding in his head.

The radio came to life. 'This is USGID-4 in Boise for Sheriff Ed Carey. Come in, Sheriff Carey.'

'The chopper pilot,' Singer said, looking at the radio.

'This is Sheriff Carey.'

'The chopper's fuelled and we've got clearance. Everybody's on board. ETA is 0600.'

'About an hour then you'll be here,' Carey said.

'Roger that.'

'An hour,' Singer repeated. Snatching the mike, he keyed it and spoke. 'Sheriff, this is Singer. Do you read me?'

'Yes, Lieutenant. I didn't realise you were on the frequency.'

'I've been monitoring communications, Sheriff,' Singer said. 'Right now, our position is directly across from the Rawlins ranch. We think he has them in his house. We've cut off power and communications and are waiting for him to come out.'

'For God's sake, Lieutenant,' Carey sputtered, 'who authorised you to do that? Who do you have there with you?'

Newkirk saw the faint smile form on Singer's lips. 'Sergeant Gonzalez and Officer Newkirk. Officer Swann is here too. He checked himself out of the hospital so he could be of service. As for authorisation, no one, sir. We took it upon ourselves as deputised officers. We want to make sure the subject doesn't escape before you and the FBI arrive.'

'I don't know, Lieutenant . . .'

'We can withdraw, sir, but we risk the possibility of the subject escaping, or hurting those kids and the mother.'

Newkirk marvelled at Singer's ability to turn Carey any way he wanted. The sheriff couldn't risk making another mistake.

'We don't know if we've got the right guy,' Carey said. 'You shouldn't have gone there without talking with me.'

'Sir, it was a decision we made after we saw Mr Swann in the hospital, beaten within an inch of his life by the subject.'

Gonzalez turned away. Newkirk heard him snort with laughter.

The radio remained silent for a few moments. Then: 'OK, Lieutenant. But stay put. Do not engage the subject until we get there.'

'Roger that, Sheriff. We will remain in place without engagement unless the subject confronts us.'

'Hey, I didn't say anything about . . .'

'Roger that, Sheriff,' Singer said, talking over him, then hanging up the mike and reducing the volume to zero. He looked at his watch. 'OK, we've got about an hour before dawn and we've been given our hunting licence.'

JESS LAY ON TOP of the slate-rock ridge, the dampness of the grass long since soaked into his jeans and ranch coat. His scoped .270 hunting rifle was next to him, as was the Winchester and a box of bullets. He watched the sky lighten, felt the dawn breeze move along the ground with an icy pulse.

His heart hardened when he saw the riderless horse cantering across the meadow towards the barn. He could see that the saddle had slipped upside down and the stirrups were flapping. He knew how unlikely it was that Jim Hearne, ex-rodeo cowboy, had been bucked off.

Jess knew what it meant. He thought about Annie, and Monica. Jim Hearne had been a good man. But now they were on their own.

Up in the woods, in the direction of the road, there was a ping of metal, faint but distinct. And familiar. It was the sound of a link of chain being cut. A moment later came the throaty sound of engines starting. Jess looked towards his dark house, wondering if Monica and Villatoro could hear them.

There was no way to stop it now.

NEWKIRK RUBBED his thumb nervously along the handgrip of his shotgun. The M-16, a fully automatic rifle with a banana clip, was on the seat next to Singer. It was still too dark to make out the road, and the trees on either side were so tall that it felt like he was moving through a tunnel. They were creeping down the hill, the Escalade in four-wheel-drive low. How could Singer see where he was going?

Almost imperceptibly, the terrain opened up before them. They'd cleared the trees. Singer brought the vehicle to a gentle stop. Newkirk hoped Gonzo had seen the flash of brake lights and wouldn't drive right into them.

'We'll wait here until we can see better,' Singer whispered.

JESS WATCHED the two vehicles emerge from the woods and stop, saw a blink of brake lights. Even though they were there, as expected, a part of him couldn't believe it was actually happening.

Nosing the .270 over a piece of slate, he looked at the vehicles through his rifle scope. Minutes went by before he thought he could make out two forms in the white car, two in the pick-up behind it.

The cross hairs rested on the driver's side window of the white SUV. It was too far for an accurate shot. Nevertheless, he worked the bolt of the rifle and chambered a round.

After a long while, the cross hairs trembled. He realised his legs and arms were cramping up. He tried to steady himself, flatten out his aim.

Again, he glanced down at his house. No movement, no light. Good. In the barn, the calf he had delivered the night before bawled for its mother.

Then the vehicles were moving forward, down the switchback. The white SUV was picking up speed. The black pick-up, the same vehicle Jess had seen the day before in front of his house, was right behind it.

There was a curve in the road about 250 yards from him, close enough for a decent shot. Jess pulled the stock tight to his shoulder, eased his eye to the scope, saw the cross hairs bounce on Singer's face. He pulled the trigger and nothing happened.

'Shit!' he said, remembering to thumb the safety off, but by the time he sighted through the scope again, the trucks were barrelling away from the curve. He was furious with himself for making such an amateur mistake.

SINGER UPSHIFTED and the engine roared as they reached the bottom of the hill. Gonzalez and Swann shot past them in the pick-up. Both vehicles slid to a stop in the gravel, facing the front door of the house.

Training took over now, and Newkirk bailed out of the Escalade, keeping the open passenger door between him and the structure, aiming at the front door of the house over the lip of the open window. In his peripheral vision, he saw Singer do the same after arming the M-16.

Gonzalez was out of his pick-up, racking a shell into the chamber of his shotgun. While Newkirk and Singer covered him, he jogged up the porch steps and flattened himself against the wall. Holding the shotgun diagonally across his body, he spun round and used the butt to pound the door.

'Jess Rawlins! This is the sheriff's department. Come out right now!'

Newkirk racked the pump on his own shotgun, aimed again.

Gonzalez shot a glance to Singer. Singer nodded.

This time, Gonzalez pounded the door so hard Newkirk expected the panes of glass to fall out of the picture window. He saw Swann open the truck door and slide out, stand unsteadily on the lawn with a pistol in his hand.

'Jess Rawlins!' Gonzalez yelled. 'Come out RIGHT NOW!'

Nothing. The pounding echoed back from the wall of timber to the north. Swann limped across the lawn, climbed the steps to the porch and struggled to the corner of the house.

They're not there, Newton thought. No one's inside. The chopper's on the way. Thank God it's over. But no . . .

Gonzalez stepped away from the front of the house, and for a second Newkirk expected the sergeant to try to kick the door down. But he must have decided against it, because he turned, took a step towards the picture window and leaned over, trying to see through a slit in the curtains.

JESS WATCHED IT ALL through the scope on his rifle. He had not taken a breath since Gonzalez had pounded on the door. Gonzalez was in front of the window, leading with his head, trying to see in.

Jess whispered, 'Now.'

INSIDE THE FRONT ROOM, Eduardo Villatoro sighted down the barrel of the shotgun at the shadow on the other side of the curtain, put the front bead on the bridge of Gonzalez's nose through the glass, and fired.

NEWKIRK HEARD the boom, saw Gonzalez's head snap back and come apart at the same time, shards of glass cascading through the air, the shotgun clattering on the porch. The sergeant took two steps straight back, and fell onto the grass. He lay with his arms outstretched, his boots still up on the porch.

Swann cried out and flung himself against the wall of the house. He held his pistol with both hands, muzzle pointed down, ready to react.

'Goddammit!' Singer said, raising the M-16, and the morning was filled with a long, furious ripping sound as he raked the house on both sides of the window from right to left, then back again.

ANNIE HAD PEERED out from behind the cast-iron stove in time to see Villatoro raise the shotgun and fire. Her mother pulled her back down. After the blast, which was much louder than anything Annie had anticipated, her mother gathered her and William closer as bullets ripped through the walls, a few clanging off the stove behind which they hid.

PLACING THE CROSS HAIRS between Singer's shoulder blades, Jess squeezed the trigger. The rifle bucked, the scope jerked upwards. He quickly worked the bolt and peered back down the scope, saw Singer arch his back, slowly turning, holding his weapon out away from his body.

Did I miss? No—Jess could see a bloom of dark red blood on Singer's jacket and a spray of it across the hood of the white SUV.

Jess quickly found Newkirk in the scope. The man was crouched, looking up, searching the ridge for the source of the shot. Jess shot him, saw him fall back, then roll away, under the car.

When Jess swung the rifle back to Singer, Singer was gone, probably hiding under the SUV.

And where was Swann? Jess couldn't see him on the porch.

NEWKIRK FELT as though someone had kicked him in the stomach so hard it took his breath away. Slowly, the feeling receded, and something burned like a red-hot poker. He knew he'd been shot.

Under the car, he rolled his head back, looked around.

Gonzalez's body was in the grass ten feet away. Newkirk flopped his head the other way. Singer had pulled himself up. His boots were there, near the front of the car.

'Newkirk, goddammit,' Singer was saying, his voice filling with liquid, 'I'm hit. Where are you? I need cover fire.'

Newkirk kept his mouth shut, for once. He wondered where his shotgun was. Instead, he drew his service weapon, racked the slide, held it tight.

Monday morning, Newkirk thought. The boys and Lindsey should be getting ready to go to school. Wouldn't they be ashamed to know where their father was right now?

The car rocked, and another shot boomed down from the ridge. Then another. This time he heard breaking glass, and it cascaded down around him.

A long rip from Singer's M-16 made his ears ring.

Where had Swann disappeared to?

JESS SWITCHED to the Winchester when he was out of cartridges for the .270. As he levered in the first shell, an angry burst of bullets ricocheted off the plates of slate. Something stung his face. He rolled to his side, then pushed the barrel of the gun through a V in the rock.

Without the scope, he could barely see Singer's jacket through the broken windows of the SUV. But he aimed, and he fired.

ANNIE HEARD the back door smash in but didn't see Swann until he jerked her out from behind the stove by her hair. She screamed and struggled, kicking at the floor, heard William shout 'NO!', saw her mother wheel and both of her hands go up, pleading. Villatoro had been crouching behind a desk, but he rose when he heard the scream.

'Drop that shotgun or everybody dies,' Swann said.

Villatoro hesitated, but dropped the shotgun.

'You were supposed to be dead. That fucking Newkirk . . .' He shot twice and the retired detective collapsed in a heap on the floor.

'Oscar, don't hurt her,' her mother pleaded. 'Take me if you need to take someone. Don't hurt Annie.'

Swann pressed the muzzle of the hot pistol into Annie's neck. 'Shut up,' he said. 'I've got to use her to get that rancher.'

Monica glanced at the shotgun on the floor, and Annie saw Swann's pistol rise over her shoulder and aim at her mother.

Swann said, 'Back off now into that room through there and take your boy. I'm going to lock you in because I may need you for later. If you try to get out, she dies—you all die.'

NEWKIRK HEARD another bullet hit Singer, a punching sound, heard it go *thump*. Saw Singer suddenly drop back into view, on the ground with him again, squirming like he had ants in his clothes. Inside the house there had been two quick gunshots. Newkirk thought, Hell has broken loose.

Singer's jacket was drenched with red. Blood foamed from his mouth and nostrils, but his eyes were blue and sharp.

'You hid,' Singer said, spitting blood. 'You fucking hid.'

'It never should have gone this far,' Newkirk said.

'We deserved it, we *earned* it!' Singer said in a rage. He sounded like he was drowning inside and he probably was.

'It wasn't worth it,' Newkirk said. He raised his weapon and shot Singer in the forehead.

Singer stopped squirming.

'There,' Newkirk said. 'Enough.'

Then he heard the sound of a car coming down the road, and the faraway beating of a helicopter.

But the front door to the ranch house burst open, and there stood Swann, holding the little girl with his gun to her head.

'HEY, RANCHER!' Swann yelled towards the ridge, his voice cutting through the sudden morning stillness. 'I've got the little girl here. Stand up and throw down your weapon. We can work this out so nobody else gets hurt.'

As he yelled, Annie could feel his arm tighten round her neck and the muzzle of the pistol press hard through her hair, biting into her temple.

She thought, If Jess goes for it, he's a dead man. Look what happened when Mr Villatoro listened to Swann.

'You need to answer me!' Swann shouted, his voice cracking. Annie craned her neck to see that blood streamed down his face and dripped onto his shirt.

Be tough, she thought. No crying.

Swann took a sudden gasping breath of alarm. She turned back round and couldn't believe what she saw.

Jess Rawlins was running down the hill towards them, holding his rifle.

'Stop right now, old man. Drop the weapon,' Swann yelled. 'STOP!'

He jerked the pistol from her head, pointed it unsteadily at Jess and fired off three quick shots. Jess jerked and stumbled, but didn't stop.

The old rancher was close enough now that Annie could hear the sound of his boots crunching in the gravel.

Swann suddenly threw her aside so he could aim with two hands. He fired again, four shots. There were blotches of blood on the front of Jess's jacket, but the man's look of pure determination hadn't changed a bit.

When the rancher finally stopped it was to raise his rifle from twenty yards away, aim calmly, and shoot Oscar Swann squarely between the eyes. Swann dropped straight back into the doorway, his pistol thumping on the porch. Annie rolled away, unhurt.

MONICA RAMMED the dressing-table drawer as hard as she could into the locked door of the bedroom, and it swung open, the lock broken. She stepped over Villatoro's body and grabbed William's hand, pulling him through the living room behind her. She saw Swann in the doorway, flat on his back, blood pouring from his ears, pooling on the floorboards. Annie was scrambling to her feet and running off the porch towards the yard.

Monica heard it. The sound of a helicopter approaching, blades thumping bass. She stepped over Swann's body and saw everything at once.

Singer, dead on the grass in front of his car. Gonzalez splayed out, most of his head gone. The helicopter slipping over the southern hill, flying so low it was kicking up dirt and branches. The sheriff's SUV, siren suddenly whooping, speeding towards the ranch, followed by two other departmental vehicles and an ambulance. Jess slumped in the yard, his head bowed as if he were sleeping. Annie running towards him, her arms outstretched.

THE LAST THING Newkirk saw before he turned the pistol on himself was Monica Taylor and her two kids down on the ground with the rancher, hugging him, wailing, keeping him still as the sheriff bore down on them.

May

Jess Rawlins almost died three times in the helicopter before he finally stabilised, although there were periods when he wasn't sure which side of that line he was on. That was a month ago.

Now, he seemed to be emerging from his trauma, if only for a while. There were things he just knew had happened, without recalling the details. The EMTs in flight suits prising his eyes open, asking him questions. Villatoro lying next to him on one side, Hearne on the other. Both either asleep or gone. Jess's world going black and white twice while in the air, once while landing. But turning back each time, thanks to the electric shocks that restarted his heart. Then surgery, doctors, bright lights, more surgery, the prick of needles on his arms, the sharp smells of antiseptic and his own blood, the tinny sound of bullets being dropped into metal trays.

In the midst of the surgeries, there had been a long parade of faces, some he knew, some he didn't. He would try to sit up to greet people, but his legs wouldn't cooperate. He would be able to speak sometimes, and smile. There were instances when he couldn't will his lips to move. He hated that.

But there were things he could recall clearly.

Monica telling him to get well, pull through, she needed him to live, it was important. Sheriff Carey, hat in hand, apologising as much to himself as to Jess, saying, 'They're mounting a recall petition to get rid of me. The whole damned valley. I'll resign before they throw me out, though.' Karen, shaking her head as if she just *knew* this would happen. J.J., escorted by Buddy, reaching out and touching his hand through the sheets before recoiling, making Jess's heart soar when he said he was feeling better, that he'd like to re-enter the world to see how it worked out, that he missed the ranch and his father more than he realised.

Doctors showing other doctors where the five bullets had hit, re-enacting the trajectory of the bullet that had really done the damage when it broke his collarbone and angled down, nicked a lung, exiting through his spine. The others, two in the thigh, one that passed straight through his neck, and a really painful one in his butt.

Two surprising visits, although they didn't seem surprising at the time.

Jim Hearne, in jeans and cowboy boots instead of his banker's suit, apologising for not making it into town. Saying, 'It wasn't the first time I didn't finish a ride, I guess.'

'I'm proud of you,' Jess said. 'You tried.'

'There's nothing I wanted more than to be the hero.'

'You're a hero.'

'No,' Hearne said, looking away, moisture in his eyes. 'I betrayed Laura. I wish I could tell Laura one more time that I love her.' He collected himself. 'I betrayed people who looked up to me, and I betrayed myself. And in the end, I didn't come through for Annie and Monica.'

'They know you did your best. You gave your life for them.'

'Doesn't seem like enough,' Hearne said.

'What more is there?' Jess asked.

Jim Newkirk came into his room after dark, wearing a ball cap. He stood at the foot of the bed and wouldn't meet Jess's eyes.

'I thought you were dead,' Jess said.

Newkirk looked out of the window. 'I am. I just wanted to see how you were doing.'

'Not very damned good.'

'Better than me.' Newkirk had haunted eyes. 'If a man does what he knows is right, at least he can live with himself.'

Jess fell asleep and never saw Newkirk again. But he had a feeling he'd see Hearne.

EDUARDO VILLATORO, on crutches, wearing his brown suit, introduced Jess to his wife, Donna, and his mother. They had flown up from Southern California, he said, and were staying at Julie Rodale's house, keeping Julie company.

'Julie has convinced Donna to consider moving here,' Villatoro said, raising his eyebrows in disbelief. 'We might even do it.'

'Great,' Jess said, smiling. 'Another ex-cop moving here.'

After Donna and his mother left, Villatoro told Jess that the wrongfully convicted Santa Anita employees were being released. He also said that the

FBI had figured out everything, even how the ex-cops used the pigs to dispose of the bodies. Thanking Jess again for saving him from that.

Laura Hearne, Jim's wife, came. She said she knew that the situation with Jess's ranch had troubled Jim greatly, and felt she owed it to her husband's memory to do some research. Her idea was to donate the ranch to the State of Idaho on the condition it be kept intact.

'Poor Jim,' Jess said. 'I miss him.'

Tears flooded her eyes. 'I miss him, too,' she said. 'I always knew about Monica, even though he never told me. He didn't have to. I forgave him years ago, but I never told him that. I wish now I had told him.'

Jess nodded, hoping Hearne knew it now.

He told her to forget about the donation. He had a better idea. When he told her, she responded with a devilish look, said she'd help with the details because Jim would have wanted her to.

'He loved you,' Jess assured her. 'He told me.'

JESS WOKE, his head clearer than it had been since he'd arrived in the hospital. The pain was gone. Everything, gone. No feeling below his chest. Sun streamed through the window and warmed his face. The room was filled with flowers, which was probably why he kept dreaming he was in a garden.

Annie sat in a chair at the side of the bed.

'Shouldn't you be in school?' Jess asked.

Annie looked up. She seemed older, more serious. 'Is this really you?' she asked. 'It's hard to tell. Sometimes you're there, and sometimes you're not.'

'I'm here,' he said. 'I think.' He could feel the sun, and it felt real. The lack of pain was certainly real.

'We've been coming here every day for two weeks,' Annie said. 'My mom brings us after school.'

'Two weeks? I had no idea,' he said. 'It's May, then.'

'I guess so.'

He tried to recall the days, the weeks. It was impossible to sort out. He knew what he knew: the faces, the visits, the explanations from people living and dead. Maybe, when he was strong again, he could sort it all out.

Annie glanced towards the door, then rose and leaned to Jess. 'Mrs Hearne told us what you did.'

Jess worked his arm out from beneath the covers. He was shocked at how spindly it looked, how gnarled his fingers had become. But she took his hand. He felt a twitch of a smile. 'What does your mom think about that?'

'She can't believe it.'

He snorted, anticipating pain. Astonished, he said, 'It used to hurt to laugh. Now it doesn't.'

'Why did you do it?' Annie asked, demanding an answer.

Jess said, 'Because you're tough. You can handle it. You'll do well.'

She nodded. No point in arguing that.

'Annie.' It was Monica, entering the room, her face flushed. 'Jess, I'm sorry,' she said. 'You know Annie.' She glared at her daughter, who smiled.

Jess looked up at her. 'She's a pistol,' he said, his voice thick.

'Jess, we need to talk about what you're doing. Laura Hearne explained how it works. She says she'll help us every way she can, just like Jim would have done. She's a remarkable woman.'

'I agree,' Jess said.

'But I still don't understand why.'

Jess nodded. 'Annie knows,' he said, looking at Annie, who nodded, as if they were sharing a secret.

'You might want to rethink this when you're well,' Monica said.

Jess lowered his eyes, looked at the contours of his body under the blanket. He wanted to see a fitter version of himself, but it was not to be.

Annie was still squeezing his hand.

'Like Laura told you, Annie, I don't care what you do with it as long as you benefit from it. You can sell it to developers, or divide it up. Jim had some good ideas on how to keep most of it intact. He was a smart man and Laura's just as smart. You and your mom should listen to what she has to say.'

Annie flushed and rolled her eyes, saying, 'Jeez.'

Monica put her hands on Annie's shoulders. 'This is a lot for Annie to understand right now. I can't believe it myself. You'll likely want to change your mind when you get better.' She chuckled softly.

Jess reached up and brushed a strand of hair out of Annie's face. She had tears in her eyes. She knew.

He felt suddenly exhausted and happy, as if he'd just had a huge meal in the middle of the day. He felt sleep reaching up and pulling him back to somewhere dark, shadowed and peaceful, and when he opened his eyes it was light again, and he was riding Chile, his legs firm and strong, the sun high, the sky cloudless, and the air smelt of pine and cattle.

C. J. BOX

Home: Wyoming, USA
Date of birth: November 9, 1958
Website: www.cjbox.net

RD: After seven novels starring your popular character, Joe Pickett, you've created a stand-alone novel, *Blue Heaven*, and it's gathering extraordinary amounts of praise. Does that encourage you on to the next book, or make it more daunting?

CJB: The success of *Blue Heaven* is validation in every regard, and it is a fresh wind in my sails both for future Joe Pickett books and additional stand-alones. I especially appreciate new readers giving it—and me—a shot.

RD: For UK readers who may not yet have come across Joe Pickett, can you sum the character up in a few words?

CJB: Joe Pickett is a Wyoming game warden who loves his family, his low-paying job, and his frontier code of right and wrong. He finds himself constantly in the middle of contentious environmental issues and vicious criminality and tries to put things right.

RD: Is it true that before your first book, *Open Season*, was published you wrote secretly for some twenty years, afraid of failure as a writer?

CJB: Yes. I didn't want my daughters to think, 'My dad—the failed novelist.' I didn't reveal what I'd been working on all those years until I had a book contract in 2001.

RD: Your first job was as a reporter on a newspaper in Saratoga, Wyoming. But you've also worked as a ranch hand and fishing guide, which suggest that you love the great outdoors and the American West. Is that so? And could you imagine living anywhere else?

CJB: I grew up in a state—Wyoming—with a population density of two people per square mile. The environment dominates everyday life and the history of the American West is still very fresh. There are more pronghorn antelope than people. Although I've travelled throughout the world, I would never want to return to anywhere else.

RD: What is it you love about Wyoming and Idaho, where *Blue Heaven* is set?

CJB: Although both states are rural, scenic and isolated, they also play host to extreme things: weather, issues, events. It is as if the lack of crowds makes those who live there step up and become more powerful characters. People are close to the earth and have very strong opinions about it. Plus, there's great trout fishing.

RD: I think many in the UK think of those big-sky places as special, both because of the Western culture that still prevails, and because of the beautiful, pristine scenery. But is the ranching way of life disappearing to some extent, as you suggest in *Blue Heaven*?

CJB: Yes. It has been a trend in the last twenty years for the wealthy to buy their little piece of heaven and pretend that they're lords or ranchers. It has changed the economics and culture of the Mountain West.

RD: It's interesting that because so many LAPD officers have retired to Idaho there's now an area of the state called 'Blue Heaven'. Did you meet any of them during the writing of the book?

CJB: Yes, a few. And a few more during the book tour for the novel. All of them were friendly and interested in the novel. They know it's only fiction.

RD: Hunting, shooting and fishing all seem to be part of your way of life. Do you love one of them above the others and, if so, why?

CJB: In order: fishing, hiking, skiing, riding, hunting—but only for game meat, not trophies.

RD: You serve on the board of directors of the Cheyenne Frontier Days Rodeo. Is that fun, and do you take part yourself?

CJB: I love it. The rodeo culture has roots in the earliest days of Western expansion and the people involved are earthy, tough and passionate about what they do. I've been a volunteer in the rodeo itself for over twenty-five years now.

RD: Have you ever been to the UK? And are there any areas of our tiny country that you'd like to visit?

CJB: Because my wife and I own a tourism marketing company that promotes the Rockies on behalf of five states, I've visited the UK twenty-five or thirty times, I suppose. Nearly always to London. Someday, I would love to explore more of the countryside as well as spend time in the Midlands and the Highlands of Scotland.

RD: Do you have any particular ambitions you'd still like to fulfil?

CJB: I want each book to be better than the last, and I hope some of them resonate with readers in ways far beyond the crime-fiction plots. I also want to spend more time catching fish on flies.

RD: What are your greatest loves, apart from fly-fishing and novel-writing?

CJB: My family: wife Laurie and three daughters, Molly, Becky and Roxanne.

RD: And what riles you most?

CJB: Blind extremism; arrogant and stupid bureaucrats and public officials; and political correctness.

RD: How would friends and family describe you?

CJB: I hope they would describe me as very busy but always available.

C. J. SANSOM

revelation

It is 1543 and England is in
a state of flux as various
factions, Protestant and Catholic,
vie for power.
At the court of Henry VIII,
political intrigue and rivalry are
rife. It's a world that lawyer
Matthew Shardlake is familiar with,
but has no desire to be drawn into.
However, when his best friend is
murdered, he has no choice.

Chapter 1

The high chandeliers in the Great Hall of Lincoln's Inn were ablaze with candles, for it was late afternoon when the play began. Most members of Lincoln's Inn were present, the barristers in their robes and their wives in their best costumes. After an hour standing, my back was starting to ache, and I envied the elderly and infirm members who had brought stools.

The play was new, *The Trial of Treasure*, a heavy-handed moral fable, with the gorgeously robed actors portraying the vices and virtues of mankind. As Virtue, in a long white false beard, lectured Dissimulation on his deceitful ways—appropriately, perhaps, to an audience of lawyers—my attention wandered and I cast my eyes over the shadowed faces of the audience. Treasurer Rowland, a thin-faced, acerbic old man, was eyeing the actors as though wondering whether it might have been better hiring a troupe with less expensive costumes. Across from me I saw my old enemy Stephen Bealknap, perhaps the crookedest lawyer I had ever come across, his greedy pale blue eyes studying his fellow lawyers. As he saw me looking at him, his gaze slid away. It struck me that he seemed tired, ill.

Some distance away my friend Roger Elliard, to whose house I was invited to dinner afterwards, held his wife's hand. A new scene had begun; Lust had made a pact with Inclination to Evil. He was suddenly seized with pain and fell to his knees, struck down by divine judgment. Roger turned away. I knew why; I would talk to him later.

At last the play ended; the players bowed, the audience clapped, and we stepped out into Gatehouse Court. The setting sun illuminated the redbrick buildings and the melting snow in the courtyard with an umber light. As I waited in the doorway for the Elliards, I looked across to their lodgings. All the windows were lit and servants could be seen bustling within. Dorothy's dinners were well known around the Inn, and even at the end of Lent I knew that she would have good belly cheer for the group they had invited.

Despite the cold I felt relaxed, more peaceful than I had for a long time. Next Sunday, March 25, was Easter Day, the official start of the New Year of 1543. In recent years I had wondered at this time what grim events the coming year might bring. But I reflected that now I had only interesting work and times with good friends to look forward to. That morning while dressing I had paused to study my face in the steel mirror in my bedroom, something I seldom did because the sight of my hunched back still distressed me. I saw streaks of grey in my hair, deepening lines on my face. Yet I thought perhaps they gave me something of a distinguished look. I had passed forty the previous year, and could no longer expect to look young.

Standing in the doorway of the Great Hall, I suddenly shivered, despite my fur-lined coat. I jumped slightly as someone clapped me on the shoulder. It was Roger, his slim form swathed in a heavy coat. Beside him his wife, Dorothy, her plump cheeks red with cold, smiled at me.

'You were in a brown study, Matthew,' Roger said. 'Reflecting on the high moral sentiments of the play?'

'High as a house but heavy as a horse,' Dorothy said.

'That they were,' I agreed. 'Who chose it?'

'The treasurer.' Roger looked to where Rowland was talking to an ancient judge. Roger lowered his voice. 'He wisely wanted something that wasn't politically contentious. But an Italian comedy would have been better.'

We walked across the courtyard together. I noticed that the snow on the Gatehouse Court fountain, which had been frozen this last three months, was almost gone, revealing patches of grey ice.

Roger's steward, an old man called Elias, greeted us at the door and took me upstairs to wash my hands. Then I went into the parlour, where candles cast a warm, buttery light on the chairs and cushions. A dozen guests, all barristers and their wives, sat or lounged, served with wine by a boy. A roaring fire warmed the room, bringing sweet smells from the herbs on the wooden floor, its light glinting on the silver knives and spoons on the table. Above the fireplace stood Roger's pride and joy: a large, carved wooden frieze of intricate design, the branches of trees in full leaf interlaced with flowers and fruits, the heads of animals peering through, deer and boar and even a unicorn. Roger stood beside it, talking to Ambrose Loder from my chambers. Dorothy stood with him, wearing an expression of good-natured amusement, her colourful clothes a contrast to the black robes of the two lawyers. She wore a green damask dress with a high collar open at the throat; it suited her well. Seeing me, she excused herself and came across.

I had known Dorothy near twenty years. She was the daughter of a serjeant in my first chambers, and I had at once been attracted to Dorothy's elegance, wit and kind nature—a rare combination. She seemed to like my company too, never seemed to mind my bent back, and we became good friends. After a while I dared to think of trying to turn friendship into something more. I had given no signs of my real feelings, though, and therefore had only myself to blame when I learned that my friend Roger had already proposed marriage and been accepted. He later said—and I believed him—that he had not realised my feelings for Dorothy.

Dorothy was, like me, past forty now, though apart from little wrinkles visible around her eyes she looked a good deal younger.

I bent and kissed her cheeks. 'A merry Palm Sunday to you, Dorothy.'

'And to you, Matthew.' She squeezed my hand. 'How is your health?'

'Good these days.' My back had often given me trouble, but these last months I had been conscientious in the exercises my physician friend Guy had prescribed, and had felt much better.

'You look well.'

'And you look younger each New Year, Dorothy. May this one bring peace and prosperity.'

'I hope so. Though there has been a strange portent, have you heard? Two huge fish washed up by the Thames. Great grey things half the size of a house. They must have been under the ice.' The twinkle in her eyes told me she found the story delightfully absurd.

'Were they alive?'

'No. They lie on the mud banks over at Greenwich. People have been crossing London Bridge in hundreds to see them. Everyone says that coming the day before Palm Sunday it portends some terrible happening.'

'People are always finding portents these days. It is a passion now among the busy Bible-men of London.'

'True.' She gave me a searching look, catching a bitter note in my reply.

Twenty years ago, Dorothy, Roger and I had all been reformers, hoping for a new Christian fellowship in the world. They still did. But though many of their guests had also been reformers in the early days, most, like me, had retreated to a quiet professional life, frightened and disillusioned by the rising tides of religious conflict and repression since the King's break with Rome. I wondered if Dorothy guessed that, for me, faith was almost gone.

She changed the subject. 'For us at least the news has been good. A letter from Samuel came today, and reading between the lines, I think he has a girl.'

Samuel was Roger and Dorothy's only child. Some years before, the family had moved to Bristol, where Roger had obtained the post of city recorder. He had returned to practise at Lincoln's Inn a year ago, but Samuel, now eighteen and apprenticed to a cloth merchant, had decided to stay behind.

I smiled. 'Are you sure you are not reading your wishes into his letter?'

'No, he mentions a name. Elizabeth. A merchant's daughter.' Dorothy smiled roguishly. 'Perhaps your assistant Barak would travel to Bristol to spy on her for me. I hear he is good at such jobs.'

I laughed. 'Barak is busy with my work. You must find another spy.'

'I like that sharp humour of his. Does he well?'

'He and his wife lost a child last year. It hit him hard.'

'And she?'

'I have not seen Tamasin. I keep meaning to call on them at home.'

'The Court of Requests keeps you busy, then. And a serjeant. I always knew you would reach that eminence one day.'

'Aye.' I smiled. 'And it is good work.' A year ago Archbishop Cranmer had nominated me as one of the two barristers appointed to plead before the Court of Requests, where poor men's pleas were heard. A serjeancy, the status of a senior barrister, had come with the post.

'I have never enjoyed my work so much.' I paused. 'I have a new case, a boy who has been put in the Bedlam. I meet with his parents tomorrow.'

'A mad client.'

'Whether he is truly mad is the issue. He was put there on the Privy Council's orders. It is one of the strangest matters I have ever come across.'

'You will see justice done, I have no doubt.'

'Matthew!' Roger had appeared beside me. He shook my hand vigorously. He was small and wiry, with a thin but well-favoured face and black hair. He was as full of energy as ever. Despite his winning of Dorothy all those years before, I still had the strongest affection for him.

'I must go to the kitchen,' Dorothy said. 'I will see you shortly, Matthew. Talk to Roger. He has had an interesting idea.'

I bowed as she left. 'How have you been?' I asked Roger quietly.

He lowered his voice. 'It has not come on me again. But I will be glad when I have seen your doctor friend.'

'I saw you look away when Lust was struck down during the play.'

'Aye. It frightens me, Matthew.'

In recent weeks, Roger had several times lost his balance and fallen over, for no apparent reason. He feared he was developing the falling sickness, that terrible affliction where a man or woman, healthy in other ways, would periodically collapse on the ground, out of their senses, writhing and grunting. The illness was untreatable and was regarded as a kind of temporary madness. It would mean the end of his career.

'Guy will find the truth of it. And remember, you have had no seizures.'

'I know. 'Tis true.'

'Dorothy tells me you have had some new idea,' I said, to distract him.

'Yes.' He smiled wryly. 'I have been reading Roderick Mors's book, the *Lamentation of a Christian against the City of London*.'

'You should be careful. Some call it seditious.'

'The truth affrights them.' Roger's tones were quiet but intense. 'By Jesu, Mors's book is an indictment of our city. It shows how all the wealth of the monasteries has gone to the King or his courtiers. The monastic schools and hospitals closed down, the sick left to fend for themselves. I saw a boy in a doorway in Cheapside yesterday, his bare feet half rotted away with frostbite. I gave him sixpence, but it was a hospital he needed, Matthew.'

'But as you say, most have been closed.'

'Which is why I am going to canvass for a hospital funded by subscriptions and bequests from the lawyers of the Inns of Court. Will you help?'

'I will help if I can.' If anyone could accomplish this task it was Roger.

'I knew you would help me. I will organise a committee—'

'Another committee?' Dorothy had returned, red-faced from the heat of the kitchen.

Roger put his arm round his wife's waist. 'For the hospital, sweetheart.'

'People will be hard to persuade. Their purses smart from the King's taxes.'

'And may suffer more,' I said. 'They say this new Parliament will be asked to grant yet more money for the King to go to war with France.'

'The waste,' Roger muttered. 'Think of how the money could be used.'

'I have heard that the King is after a new wife,' Dorothy said.

'They have been saying that since Catherine Howard was executed,' Roger said. 'Who is it now?'

'Lady Catherine Parr,' Dorothy replied. 'Her husband, Lord Latimer, died last week. 'Tis said the King has had a fancy for her for some years.'

'Poor woman,' I said. I lowered my voice. 'She needs fear for her head.'

'Yes.' Dorothy nodded, then raised her voice and clapped her hands. 'Dinner is ready, my friends.'

We all walked through to the dining room, where servants were laying out dishes of food under Elias's supervision. Pride of place went to four large chickens; as it was still Lent the law would normally have allowed only fish to be eaten at this time, but the freezing of the river had made fish so expensive that the King had given permission for people to eat white meat.

I took my place between Loder, with whom Roger had been speaking earlier, and James Ryprose, an elderly barrister with bristly whiskers. Opposite us sat Dorothy and Roger and Mrs Loder, who was as plump as her husband.

Roger began talking to old Ryprose about his hospital. 'Think of the sick and helpless people we could take from the streets, maybe cure.'

'Aye, that would be a worthwhile thing,' the old man agreed. 'But what of all the fit, sturdy beggars that infest the streets, pestering one for money. What is to be done with them? I sometimes fear to walk out alone.'

'Very true.' Brother Loder leaned across me to voice his agreement. 'The city council should appoint some strong men to whip them out of the city.'

'But, Ambrose,' his wife said quietly, 'why be so harsh? You used to argue the workless poor had a right to be given employment, that the city should pay them to do useful things like pave the streets.'

Loder frowned. 'So what are we supposed to do? Take ten thousand scabby beggars into the Inn and feed them at High Table?'

'No,' Roger answered gently. 'Merely use our status as wealthy men to help a few. Till better times come, perhaps.'

'It's not just the beggars that make walking the streets a misery,' old Ryprose added gloomily. 'There's all these ranting Bible-men springing up, barking and railing that the Apocalypse is coming.'

There were murmurs of agreement up and down the table, and I nodded myself. In the years since Thomas Cromwell's fall, the King's patronage of the reformers who had encouraged him to break with Rome had ended. He was moving back to the old forms of religion, a sort of Catholicism without the Pope, with increasingly repressive measures against dissentients.

'There'll be another purge,' someone said darkly. 'I've heard rumours Bishop Bonner is going to crack down hard.'

'Not more burnings,' Dorothy said quietly.

'The city wouldn't stand for that,' Loder said. 'People don't like the radicals, but they like burnings less. Bonner won't go that far.'

'Won't he?' Roger said. 'Isn't he a fanatic too?'

'Fanatics on both sides,' old Ryprose said sombrely. 'And all we poor folk are in the middle. Sometimes I fear they will bring death to us all.'

THE COMPANY broke up late, and I was one of the last to leave. I stepped out into a night that had grown colder, my mood less cheerful after the conversation round the dinner table. It was true that London was full of beggars and fanatics now, an unhappy city. And a purge would make things worse.

I paused. A quiet footstep, crunching on the slush behind me. I turned, frowning. The precincts of Lincoln's Inn were supposed to be secure, but there were places where entry could be gained.

'Who's that?' I called.

There was no reply, but I heard the slush crackling again as someone walked rapidly away. Frowning, I followed. The sound came from the far end of the building, where the Elliards lived. I put my hand to my dagger. The outer wall of Lincoln's Inn was ahead of me. Whoever was there was trapped in a little square of ground between the buildings and the twelve-foot-high rear wall. But no one was there. A shiver trickled down my spine.

Then I saw that the snow on top of the wall had been disturbed. Whoever it was had climbed over. I stood and stared; to scale that wall would require a good deal of strength and agility. I frowned and turned away.

NEXT MORNING I set out in heavy rain for my chambers. It was the first rain after two months of snow and when I reached my chambers I was soaked.

The parents of the boy who had been put in the Bedlam were due at nine. The details the Court of Requests had sent me were sketchy; the Privy Council itself had put him there, 'for blaspheming true religion in his madcap frenzy'. The matter was therefore political and dangerous, and I cursed the luck that had sent this case to me.

The papers described the boy, Adam Kite, as the son of a master stonemason and a communicant at St Martin's Church, Greek Lane. I had got my clerk Barak to investigate and he had reported back that the vicar was, as he put it, a 'great railer and thunderer'.

This was unwelcome news. In the dealings I had had with the godly men, I had found them difficult, crude, hard men who drove at you with biblical verses like a carpenter hammering in nails.

To my surprise, Barak was already in the outer office when I arrived. He had lit the fire and sat at the table, getting papers in order. His handsome, impish features looked tired, his eyes bloodshot and his face stubbly.

'You need to get a shave, or the judge will call you out for a disrespectful demeanour.' Though I spoke roughly, Barak and I had a fast friendship. We had originally come together on an assignment for Barak's late master, the

King's minister Thomas Cromwell. After Cromwell's execution three years before, Barak had come to work for me.

'All right,' he said grumpily. 'I've prepared everything for this afternoon's hearings. And the madwag's parents are due soon.'

'Don't call him that,' I said, as I looked through the papers. Everything was in order. 'In on Sunday? You are neglecting your wife.'

'Tamasin's all right.' Barak rose and began filing away papers.

I looked at his broad back, wondering what was wrong between him and his wife that he should thus drag out his time at work. Tamasin was a pretty, spirited girl, and he had been happy to marry her last year, even though they had been forced into a speedy wedding by her pregnancy. Their son had died the day he was born and in the months since, though Barak had been as cheerfully irreverent as ever, there was often something forced about his banter.

'You saw Adam Kite's parents yesterday when they called to make their appointment,' I said. 'What are they like?'

'Working people. He's a stonemason. He started on about God's mercy in allowing them to take their case to Requests, how He doesn't abandon the true faithful.' He wrinkled his nose. 'They look like busy Bible folk to me.'

I looked down at the papers. 'The boy is seventeen. Brought before the Privy Council on March the 3rd for frantic and lewd behaviour at the Preaching Cross in St Paul's churchyard. Committed to the Bedlam in the hope of a cure. No further order. No examination by a doctor or jury of his state of health. That's improper.'

Barak looked at me seriously. 'He's lucky they didn't arraign him for a heretic. Remember what happened to Richard Mekins.'

I nodded. Mekins had been a fifteen-year-old apprentice who eighteen months before was burned alive at Smithfield for denying the presence of Jesus in the Eucharist. The cruelty of cases such as this had turned the populace against Bishop Bonner's harsh religious rule of the city.

'They say Bonner's after the radicals again,' Barak said.

'So I heard at dinner last night. What do you think's going on, Jack?' Barak still had friends on the shadier fringes of the King's court.

'The word in Whitehall is that the King will try to get a law through this Parliament banning women and common folk from reading the Bible, giving Bishop Bonner encouragement to crack down on the London Bible-men.'

'I see. Thank you,' I said. This only made matters more delicate. 'Well, I've got the case now, so I'll just have to handle it with care. Send the Kites in directly when they arrive.'

I went to my inner office and closed the door. The Bedlam, I thought. The very name aroused fear and disgust in London. For a long time the Bethlehem Hospital had been the only hospital in London that treated the insane, and although mad folk were a common enough sight begging in the streets, people avoided the mad, fearing they were dangerous or even possessed.

Shortly after, there was a knock on the door and Barak ushered in a middle-aged couple. The woman was small and thin, her husband tall and broad with a craggy face. I was disconcerted to see that a clergyman accompanied them. The couple were dressed in sober black; both looked deeply dejected. The man bowed, and his wife curtsied deeply.

'I am Serjeant Shardlake. You must be Master and Mistress Kite.' I smiled at the nervous couple to put them at their ease.

'Daniel Kite, at your service,' the craggy-faced man said, bowing. 'This is my wife, Minnie.'

The small, birdlike woman curtsied, and smiled uncertainly.

'It is good of you to see us on a Sunday,' Daniel Kite added.

'Palm Sunday,' the clergyman said with distaste. 'I am Samuel Meaphon. This afflicted family are of my congregation.'

'Please sit,' I said.

They sat in a row on a bench, Meaphon in the middle.

'I have seen the papers the court forwarded,' I told them, 'but they tell only a bare story. I would like you to tell me what happened to your son.'

Daniel Kite cast a nervous look at Meaphon, before beginning in a sad, heavy voice. 'Our son Adam was a good boy until six months ago. A lively, strapping lad. I had him as apprentice in my workshop, out by Billingsgate.'

'You are a stonemason?'

'Master stonemason, sir.' Despite his distress, there was a note of pride in his voice. 'I hoped Adam might follow me into the business. He's our only child. He was a hard worker and a faithful attender at our church.'

'That he was.' Reverend Meaphon nodded emphatically.

'We are true Bible folk, sir.' A note of challenge crept into Kite's voice.

'Whatever you tell me of your beliefs will be held in confidence,' I said.

'You do not believe as we do, I see,' Daniel Kite said sorrowfully.

'It is not my beliefs that are at issue,' I replied with a strained smile.

Meaphon's eyes swept over me. 'I see that God has seen fit to afflict you, sir. But He has done so only that you may turn to Him for succour.'

I felt myself flush with anger that this stranger should take it on himself to refer thus to my hunched back.

Minnie Kite interrupted hastily. 'We only want you to help our poor boy, sir, to tell us if the law may help us.'

'Then tell me what happened, from the beginning, straight and simple.' Minnie quailed at the sharp note in my voice.

Her husband continued his story. 'About six months ago, Adam became very quiet, withdrawn into himself. One day I had to leave him in the shop; I came back and found him crouched on his knees in a corner. He was praying, begging the Lord to forgive him for his sins. I said, "How now, Adam. God has ordained a time for prayer and a time for work." He obeyed me then, though he rose to his feet with a great sigh like I'd never heard. From then on he . . . he wouldn't stop praying.' Kite's voice broke, and I sensed the fear in him. 'Any time of day, in the workshop or even in company, he'd just drop to his knees and start praying, frantically, for God to forgive his sins.' Kite looked at me. 'He is certain that he is damned, sir.'

I did not know how to reply. I knew that the radicals believed that God had divided humanity into the saved and the damned, that only those who came to him through the Bible would be saved at the Day of Judgment. The rest of humanity was condemned to burn in Hell for ever.

'These good people brought their son to me,' Meaphon said. 'I spoke with Adam, tried to reassure him he was saved, told him God sometimes sends doubt to those He loves most, to try their spirits. For two whole days I prayed with him, but I could not break through.' He shook his head.

Minnie looked up at me. Her face was bleak, bereft. 'By then, Adam was naught but skin and bone. He will not eat.'

'What sins does Adam believe he has committed?' I asked quietly.

'He does not say. Before this he was just an ordinary cheerful boy. He has never done anything wicked,' Minnie said.

'Then ten days ago he disappeared,' Daniel continued. 'We searched up and down but could not find him. That afternoon an official from the archbishop came to see us. He said Adam had been found on his knees in the snow before the Preaching Cross in St Paul's churchyard, screaming that the end of the world was coming, and begging God and Jesus not to take him down to Hell at the Last Judgment.'

Minnie began to cry, and her husband stopped and bowed his head.

'So then Adam was brought before the Privy Council,' I prompted gently.

'Yes. I was summoned to appear at Whitehall Palace. I was shown into a great room where four men all dressed in rich robes sat at a table. One of the men was Archbishop Cranmer; I've seen him preach at St Paul's.' Daniel's voice shook at the memory. 'Adam was there, chained and with a gaoler.'

'What did they say to you?'

'They asked me how Adam had got into the state he was and I answered them honestly. One of the men said it sounded like heresy and the boy should be burned. But the archbishop said Adam was clearly out of his wits and he should be sent to the Bedlam to see if they could find a cure.'

'I see.' Archbishop Cranmer, as well as being naturally merciful, would not want to further inflame London. Shutting Adam away in the Bedlam would dispose of the problem, for a while at least. I nodded slowly. 'That raises the crucial issue.' I looked at them. 'Is Adam in fact mad?'

'If he is not mad, sir,' Daniel said, 'we fear it may be something worse.'

'Worse?' I asked.

'Possession,' Meaphon said starkly. 'That is my fear. That a demon has hold of him and is urging him to mock God's mercy in public.'

'Is that what you would believe?' I asked the stonemason.

He buried his head in his big hands. 'I do not know, sir.'

'I think Adam is only in great confusion and fear.' Minnie looked up and met Meaphon's eye, and I realised then that she was the stronger of the pair. She turned to me. 'But whatever the truth, being in the Bedlam will kill him. Adam lies locked in his cold chamber. He just crouches there, praying.They ask us for three shillings a month in fees, more than we can afford, yet they will not make him eat, nor take care of himself. If he stays there he will die.'

'He should be released to my care,' Meaphon said. 'But they will not do that. Not the backsliders and papists on the Council.'

'Then you are all agreed that he should not be in the Bedlam,' I said.

'Aye, aye.' The boy's father nodded, relieved to find common ground.

I thought hard a moment. 'If he were released and there was a repeat of what happened at St Paul's, he might find himself accused of heresy after all. But if we could get his conditions improved, the Bedlam may be the safest place for him, unless he can be brought to his right mind.'

'He must be released,' Meaphon said. 'The only cure is for Adam to understand that God has sent him this trial, and he must not doubt His Grace.'

Daniel Kite said, 'Amen,' but Minnie looked down at her lap.

'His release will not happen unless the Council become convinced that he is sane,' I said. 'But there is one thing we can do. I know a physician who would be able to assess Adam, might even be able to help him.'

Kite looked dubious, but Minnie grasped eagerly at the straw. 'Bring him in, sir; we will try anything. But we have no money to pay him . . .'

'I am sure some arrangement can be made. I have no doubt it is the sensible thing to do, and in Adam's best interests. In the meantime, I will apply to have Adam's care monitored, and the fees remitted.'

'Thank you, sir,' Minnie said.

'And I think I ought to visit the Bedlam, perhaps put some fear into this keeper. And see Adam.'

'We are going to see him tomorrow, at nine, sir,' Minnie said. 'Could you come then?'

'Yes, I will be there.' I smiled at her and stood up. 'I will do what I can. But this is a most difficult matter.'

EARLY NEXT MORNING I set out from my house in Chancery Lane for the Bedlam. Under my coat I wore my best robe, and I also put on my serjeant's coif. It would do no harm to impress the warden. During the night there had been another dusting of snow, which glittered in the cold sunlight. I rode out on my good horse Genesis, for the streets were too slippery to make for easy walking and the Bedlam was on the other side of the city.

I passed under London Wall at Newgate and rode along Newgate Street to the market. Traders were setting up their stalls under the looming bulk of the abandoned church of the dissolved St Martin's Friary, a few white-coifed goodwives already looking over the produce as it was laid out. As I rode past the market I saw a young ranter standing on an empty box, shouting and waving a large black Testament at the passers-by.

The butchers in the slaughterhouses behind the Shambles had already started work. Lent would be over on Thursday and already they were killing sheep and cattle. Trails of blood were trickling from the yards to the sewer channel in the centre of the frosty street.

At Bishopsgate I passed through London Wall again, and soon came to a pair of large wooden gates in a high wall. They were open, and riding through I found myself in a wide courtyard, a chapel at its centre. The backs of houses formed three sides of the yard; a long, two-storeyed building of grey stone, which looked very old, made up the fourth. People were passing to and fro across the yard, and I saw a couple of narrow lanes running between the houses. The Bedlam was not, then, a closed prison.

I rode to a large door at one end. My knock was answered by a thickset man with a hard, sardonic face, who wore a dirty grey smock.

'I am Master Shardlake,' I said. 'I have an appointment to see Adam Kite. Are you Keeper Shawms?'

'No, sir. I'm one of the keepers, Hob Gebons. Keeper Shawms is with young Kite's parents in the parlour.' He stood aside to let me enter. 'Welcome to the chamber of the mad,' he said as he closed the door. 'You think you can get Adam Kite released?'

'I hope so.'

'We'd be glad to see him go; he makes the other lunatics nervous. We keep him shut away. Some think him possessed,' he added in a low voice.

'What do you think, Gebons?'

He shrugged. 'Not for me to think.'

Gebons led me along a whitewashed corridor running the length of the building, windows on one side and a row of green-painted wooden doors on the other. It was cold and there was a faint smell of ordure.

'How many patients do you have?'

'Thirty, sir. They're a mixed lot.'

He showed me into a small room with cheap stools set around, a table and a fire in the grate. Minnie Kite sat on a stool, looking utterly dejected, while her husband argued with a plump, surly-faced man in a black jerkin.

'You could try to make him eat!' Daniel was shouting.

'Oh, aye. Get one of my keepers to force him to his feet, then another to force the food into his mouth. They haven't the time.'

'Is there a problem?' I asked quietly. 'You must be Keeper Shawms,' I added as the fat man turned. 'I am Master Shardlake, the Kites' lawyer.'

Shawms looked between me and the Kites. 'How come you can afford a lawyer, when you can't afford my fees?' he said in a bullying voice.

'I have been appointed by the Court of Requests,' I said.

'Oh,' he sneered. 'Poor man's lawyer, then, for all your fancy rig.'

'Who can apply to the court to have your fees waived, and any question of mistreatment considered,' I replied sharply.

Shawms fixed me with his piggy eyes. 'That boy's hard to take care of.'

'He only needs feeding,' Minnie said. She turned to me. 'It's so cold in there, and this wretch won't lay a fire—'

'Fires cost money!'

'Perhaps I could see Adam,' I said.

'We were about to go in.'

'See him if you want to,' Shawms said. 'You'll get no sense from him.'

The keeper led us to one of the green doors. It was locked; Shawms unlocked it and glanced in. 'He's all yours,' he said, and walked away.

I followed Minnie Kite into the room. It was light, whitewashed, the shutters partly open, and there was a dreadful stench. The place was furnished with only a truckle bed and a stool. A tall youth with filthy black hair knelt in a corner, his face to the wall, whispering to himself, the words coming so fast they were hard to follow.

'I repent my sins I repent please listen in Jesu's name . . .'

He was dressed in a food-stained shirt and leather jerkin. A large dark stain on his hose showed he had soiled himself. There was a fetter round his ankle, a chain running from there to an iron ring in the floor. Minnie knelt by her son, putting an arm round his shoulders. Daniel Kite did not approach Adam, merely stood beside him with his head bowed.

I took a deep breath and went over to the boy, noticing he was a broad-shouldered lad, though reduced now to skin and bone. I bent to look at Adam's face. It was a pitiful sight. He might once have been handsome, but now his brows were contorted into an agonised frown; his wide, terrified eyes stared unseeingly at the wall, strings of spittle dripping on his chin.

'Tell me I am saved,' he went on. 'Let me feel your grace. Jesu! Please!'

'Adam,' his mother said in a pleading voice. 'You are dirty. I have brought you new clothes.' She tried to pull him to his feet, but he resisted.

'Leave me! I must pray!' he cried, squeezing himself into the corner.

'Is he like this all the time?' I asked Minnie.

'Always, now.' She relinquished her hold, and we both stood up.

'I will get my physician friend to call,' I said quietly. 'Though, in truth, if I can make sure he is cared for he may be better off here.'

'If you would leave us, sir, I will try and clean him a little.'

'I will speak to the keeper now,' I said. 'I will do all I can to make sure Adam's better cared for. You must tell me if his care does not improve.'

'I will. We visit every day. Thank you, sir.' She curtsied, and gave me a trembling smile.

Her husband was still avoiding my eye. I left them and went in search of Shawms. The horror of what the boy's broken mind was experiencing was beyond my understanding, but lazy, venal officials I could deal with.

SHAWMS WAS in a little room of his own, sitting drinking beer and looking into a large fire. He stared at me truculently.

'I want that boy fed,' I snapped. 'By force if need be. His mother is changing his clothes and I want to see he is kept clean. I shall be applying to the court for an order that his welfare be properly attended to, and that the Council be responsible for his fees.'

'And who's to pay for all this work my keepers will be put to with him?'

'The Bedlam's own funds. Do you have a doctor in attendance?'

'Aye. Dr Frith comes once a fortnight.'

I looked into his fat red face, and felt angry at the thought of the helpless mad being left to such as he. 'I want a fire made up in that room,' I said.

'You go too far now, sir,' Shawms protested. 'I won't pay for fires out of the Bedlam funds. Warden Metwys would have my job.'

'Then I'll apply for the fees to be waived altogether.'

Shawms glowered at me. 'You take liberties, crouchback.'

'Fewer than you. Well?'

'I'll order a fire set.'

'See you do.' I turned and left him without another word.

As I walked back to the entrance, one of the green doors opened. A white-haired woman was led out by a younger woman in a keeper's grey smock. I was surprised to see a woman keeper, but guessed they would be needed if the female patients were to preserve any modesty. Seeing me, the woman keeper curtsied. She had an arresting face, with keen, dark blue eyes. The hair round the sides of her white coif was dark brown. She looked to be somewhere in her thirties.

'You have been visiting a patient, sir?' she asked.

'Aye, young Adam Kite.'

'His poor parents.' She hesitated. 'Many here are afraid of Adam, fear he is possessed. And Keeper Shawms hopes that without care he will waste away and die.' She frowned. 'He is a bad man.'

'I have just given Keeper Shawms a warning. He will find himself in trouble with the courts if he does not give Adam proper care. Thank you for your information.' I smiled at her. 'What is your name?'

'Ellen Fettiplace, sir.' She paused, then added. 'What ails poor young Adam, sir? I have never heard of a case like his.'

'Nor I. I am having a doctor come to look at him. I am glad to see at least one keeper here cares for her patients,' I added.

She blushed. 'You are kind, sir.'

'How did you come to work here, Ellen?'

She looked at me, then smiled sadly. 'I used to be a patient here, and when I was . . . was better they offered me a position as an under-keeper.'

'You did not want to leave?'

The sad smile again. 'I can never leave here, sir,' she said. 'I have not been outside in ten years. Although I am sane, I will die in the Bedlam.'

Chapter 2

I was busy in court over the next two days, but Thursday afternoon was free and I had arranged to take Roger to see Guy. It was Maundy Thursday, the day before Easter, and as I walked back from the court at Westminster to Lincoln's Inn I saw that the churches were full. Tomorrow the great veil that shrouded the chancels during Lent would be removed, and those who cleaved to the old traditions would creep to the cross on their knees. After Mass the King would wash the feet of twelve poor men at Whitehall. I felt sad at how little any of it meant to me now. At least when Lent was over Joan, my housekeeper, had promised me roast saddle of beef.

The weather was still cold, although there had been no more snow. I called in at my chambers before going to fetch Roger, and was pleased to see that a large fire had been lit. Barak and my junior clerk, Skelly, were both busy at their desks. Barak looked up as I took off my fur-edged coat and warmed my hands before the fire.

'I called at the court office,' he said. 'They're going to hear Adam Kite's application next Tuesday.'

'Good.' I looked through a couple of new briefs that had come in, then donned my coat again. 'I am going to take Master Elliard to Guy,' I said.

Barak had risen and was looking out of the window. 'What's the matter with that old rogue Bealknap?' he said curiously.

'Bealknap?' I rose and joined him.

'Looks like he's about to peg out,' Barak said.

Through the window I saw my old rival sitting on a bench next to the still-frozen fountain. His lean face looked an unhealthy white.

'They say he's been faint and ill for weeks,' Skelly said from his table.

'Let's hope it's nothing minor,' Barak said.

ROGER WAS in his outer office when I arrived at his rooms. He smiled nervously. 'I see you have your riding boots, Matthew. Sensible. I will get mine.'

He collected his boots, and we walked to the stables.

'No more sudden falls?' I asked him quietly.

'No, thank God.' He sighed deeply; I could see he was still worried.

The sun was setting as we rode into the narrow alley in Bucklersbury, where Guy lived and worked. It was full of apothecaries' shops, and Roger's face became uneasy as he saw the stuffed alligators and other strange wonders displayed in most of the windows.

As we dismounted and tied our horses to a rail, Roger said, 'Why does he practise in this godforsaken place if he is a physician?'

'Guy was only admitted to the College of Physicians last year, after saving a rich alderman's leg. Before that, his dark skin and his being an ex-monk kept him out, despite his French medical degree. He could only practise as an apothecary.'

I knocked at Guy's door. It was opened almost at once by a boy in an apprentice's blue coat. Piers Hubberdyne was an apprentice apothecary whom Guy had taken on the year before. He was a tall, dark-haired lad of about eighteen, with features of such unusual comeliness that he turned women's heads in the streets. Guy said he was hard-working and conscientious, a rarity among London's notoriously unruly apprentices.

He bowed. 'Good evening, Master Shardlake. And Master Elliard?'

'Yes.'

Piers ushered us into the shop. 'I will fetch Dr Malton,' he said, and left us.

I inhaled the sweet, musky scent of herbs that pervaded Guy's consulting room. Roger looked up at the neatly labelled jars on the shelves.

'Good day, Matthew,' Guy said, as he entered the room. 'And you must be Master Elliard.' His dark eyes studied Roger closely.

'Aye.' Roger shuffled nervously.

Guy was sixty, and his curly hair, black when first I knew him, was white now, making the dark brown hue of his lean face even more striking by contrast. When we became friends six years before, Guy had been a monastic infirmarian; the monasteries had housed many foreigners and Guy came originally from Granada in Spain, where his forebears had been Muslims. Having abandoned a Benedictine habit for an apothecary's robe, he had now in turn exchanged that for the black high-collared gown of a physician.

'Come through to my examination room,' Guy said to Roger. 'Let us see what the problem is. Can you wait here a while, Matthew?'

'Of course.'

They left me. I sat on a stool by the window. The light was growing dim, the jars and bottles casting long shadows on the floor. The door opened and Piers entered, carrying a large book under his arm. He put the book down, then lit the candles in a tall sconce. Yellow light flickered around the room.

He turned to me. 'Do you mind if I continue my work, sir?' he asked.

'Please do.'

He sat at the table, took a handful of herbs and began grinding them.

'How long have you been with Dr Malton now?' I asked.

'Just a year, sir.' He turned and smiled. 'Dr Malton took me on when my old master died. I am lucky; he is a man of rare knowledge. And kind.'

'That he is,' I agreed.

Piers turned back to his work. How different he was from most apprentices—noisy, lewd lads forever looking for trouble. His self-possessed, confident manner was that of a man, not a boy.

IT WAS AN HOUR before Guy and Roger returned. It had grown dark, and Piers had to bend closely to his work.

Guy put a hand on his shoulder. 'Enough for tonight, lad. Go and get some supper, but first bring us some beer.'

'Yes, sir.' Piers bowed to us and left.

I looked at Roger, delighted to see an expression of relief on his face.

'I do not have the falling sickness,' he said, and beamed.

Guy smiled gently. 'The strangest matters may have a simple resolution. I always like to start by looking for the simplest possible explanation, which is most likely to be the true one. So I began with Master Elliard's feet.'

'He had me standing barefoot,' Roger said, 'then measured my legs, lay me on his couch and bent my feet to and fro.'

Guy smiled triumphantly. 'I found the right foot turns markedly to the right, the cause being that Master Elliard's left leg is very slightly longer. It is a problem that has been building up for years. The remedy is a shoe with a wooden insert that will correct the gait. I will get young Piers to make it.'

'I am more grateful than I can say, sir.'

There was a knock, and Piers returned with three pewter goblets.

'Let us have a drink to celebrate Master Elliard's liberation from falling over.' Guy took a stool and passed another to Roger.

'Roger is thinking of starting a subscription for a hospital,' I told Guy.

Guy shook his head sadly. 'Hospitals are sorely needed in this city. That would be a good and Christian thing. Perhaps I could help, advise.'

'That would be kind, sir,' Roger said.

Roger talked a little longer about his plans for a hospital; then I turned to Guy and said, 'I have a case I wanted to ask your advice about, Guy. A case of religious madness, perhaps.' I told him Adam's story. 'So the Privy Council have put him in the Bedlam to get him out of the way,' I concluded. 'His parents want me to get him released, but I am not sure that is a good idea.'

'I have known of obsessive lovers,' Roger said, 'but obsessive praying—I have never heard of such a thing.'

'I have,' Guy said gravely. 'It is a new form of brain-sickness, something Martin Luther has added to human misery.'

'What do you mean?' I asked.

'There have always been some people who torture themselves with guilt for real or imagined offences. I saw such cases sometimes as an infirmarian. Then we could tell people that God promises salvation to any who repent their sins, because He places no one outside His mercy and charity.' He looked up, a rare anger in His face. 'But now the Lutherans tell us that God has decided to save some and damn others to perpetual torment. Most of us are content with the hope of salvation and leave matters in God's hands. But now there are some who crave the certainty of salvation yet are convinced they are unworthy, and that can end in the piteous condition of this young man. I have heard it called salvation panic.' He paused. 'The question perhaps is why the boy became consumed with guilt in the first place.'

'Maybe he has committed some great sin,' I said.

Guy shook his head. 'No, usually in such cases their sins are small. It is something in the workings of their minds that brings them to this pass.'

'Will you help me try to find what it is, Guy? Some in the Bedlam think Adam is possessed, and I fear they may do him harm.'

'I will come and see him, Matthew,' Guy said.

'Thank you,' I said. 'And now we must be getting back to Lincoln's Inn.'

Guy brought our coats, and Roger left his fee of a mark. Guy promised the inserts for Roger's shoes would be ready in a couple of weeks. We left, Roger thanking Guy again profusely for his help.

When the door was closed Roger clasped my arm. 'I cannot tell you how grateful I am for your guiding me to Dr Malton. I will ever be in your debt.'

'There are no debts between friends,' I said. 'I am glad to have helped.'

WE RODE ON, up Bucklersbury. We passed the ancient mansion from Henry III's time, the Old Barge, long converted into a warren of crumbling tenements. Barak and Tamasin, I knew, lived there.

'Roger, do you mind if I leave you to go on?' I asked. 'There is a visit I would like to pay. To my clerk and his wife.'

'And I should go and see my new client.'

'What is the case?'

'I do not know yet. A solicitor has sent me a letter about a client of his, who has some property dispute over in Southwark. His client is too poor to pay for a barrister, but he says the case is a worthy one and asked if I will act pro bono. It is all a bit vague, but I agreed to go and meet the client.'

'Who's the solicitor?'

'A man called Nantwich. I've never heard of him. But there are so many jobbing solicitors looking for work around the Inns these days.' He drew his coat round him. 'It is cold for riding; I would rather go home and quietly celebrate the end of my fears.' He waved a hand and rode off into the night.

THE STAIRS of the old mansion creaked loudly in the darkness. I had visited Barak's tenement in the days before he married Tamasin, and remembered it as a typical young man's lodging: dirty plates piled on the table, clothes strewn about the floor and mouse droppings in the corner. It was no place for a young girl, especially one as fond of domesticity as Tamasin.

On the second floor I knocked on their door. After a minute it opened a fraction, and I saw a coifed head outlined against the candlelight within.

'Who is it?' a female voice asked nervously.

''Tis I. Master Shardlake. I was passing on my way back from Dr Malton's.'

'Ah, sir. Come in.' Tamasin opened the door and I followed her inside.

The big room served as dining room, bedroom and parlour. She had been at work here; everything was clean, the plates stacked in an old dresser, the bed tidily made. But the place stank of damp.

'Will you sit, sir?' Tamasin indicated a chair at the table. 'May I take your coat? I am afraid Jack is out.'

'I will keep it. I . . . er . . . will not be long.' In truth it was so cold in the fireless apartment that I did not want to remove it.

I sat and took a proper look at Tamasin. She was a very pretty young woman in her early twenties. Before her marriage she had taken pride in dressing as well as her purse would allow. But now she wore a shapeless grey dress and her blonde hair was swept under a large, white housewife coif. She smiled at me cheerfully, but her shoulders were slumped, her eyes dull.

'It has been a long time since I saw you, sir,' she said.

'Near six months. How are you faring, Tamasin?'

'Oh, well enough. Would you like a cup of beer, sir?'

'I would, Tamasin. But perhaps I should go . . .' I was breaking the proprieties in being with her alone.

'No, sir, stay,' she said. 'I should like a little company.' She went and poured some beer from a jug on the dresser and brought it over, taking a stool opposite me. 'Dr Malton is a good man. I believe he saved you when you had that fever the winter before last.'

'Yes. I think he did.'

'But he could not help my poor little Georgie.'

'I know. I am sorry I did not come to see you after the baby died, Tamasin. I wanted to, but Jack said you were both better alone.'

'I used to get upset a lot. Jack would not want you to see.' She sighed. 'He looks up to you, sir. Always has.'

'Does he?' I laughed. 'Sometimes I feel he thinks I am a noddle.'

'That is just his way.'

'Yes.' I smiled at her. When we first met two years before, on the King's Great Progress to York, I had been suspicious of Tamasin's confidence and liveliness. But I had since developed an almost fatherly affection for her. Looking at her now, I wondered where all that spirit had gone.

Something of my thoughts must have shown in my face, for her mouth trembled, then two tears rolled down her cheeks. She lowered her head.

'Tamasin,' I said, half rising. 'What is the matter? What ails you?'

She took a shuddering breath and wiped her eyes on her sleeve before turning her tear-stained face to me. 'It all began with the child,' she said quietly. 'His death was a shock to Jack as well as me. He is so *angry*.'

'With you?'

'With everything. With God Himself for taking his child.' She set her lips. 'It comes out when he is drunk.'

'Is he drunk often?' I remembered his dishevelled look the other morning.

'More and more. He goes out with his old friends and sometimes does not come back all night. I think he goes with other women too.'

I was shocked. 'Can you be sure?'

She gave me a direct look. 'From the smell of him some mornings, yes.'

I sighed. 'Is there no sign of . . . another child?'

'No. Perhaps I am like old Queen Catherine of Aragon, and cannot produce healthy children.'

'But it is only six months since your baby died. That is no time.'

'Time enough for Jack to turn away. Sometimes when he is drunk he says that I would rule him, make him into some weak domesticated creature.' She looked around the room. 'As if you could domesticate anyone in this place.'

'Sometimes Jack can be insensitive. Even cruel.'

'Well, at least he does not beat me. Many husbands do.'

'Tamasin—'

'Oh, he apologises when he is sober again. He is loving then, calls me his chick, says he did not mean his words; it is his fury that God took our child. That I can share. Why does God *do* such cruel things?' she asked angrily.

I shook my head. 'I am not the man to answer that. It puzzles me too.'

'Sir,' she said, sitting up and looking at me, 'can you speak to Jack, find out what is in his mind? You have a way of making people talk.'

'I will try, Tamasin. But I will have to pick my time carefully.'

She nodded gratefully. 'Thank you.'

I stood up. 'And now I should go.' I laid a hand on hers. 'But if things become too much, a note to my house will bring me.'

'You are kind, sir.'

I left her. As I descended the dark staircase, I remembered when Barak and Tamasin had married, on a fine spring day the year before. I had felt envious; a single man can easily assume that all marriages are blissful. But tonight I had seen the sad things that could lurk beneath the surface.

'Damn Barak!' I said aloud as I stepped out onto the road, startling a gentleman going into the Old Barge.

I SPENT MOST of Good Friday and Easter Saturday at home, working on papers. On Saturday I went to bed early but could not sleep. I lay thinking how I might broach the subject of Tamasin to Barak without making matters worse. Then when I did get to sleep, I dreamed of poor mad Adam Kite, crouching in his wretched room at the Bedlam, praying desperately.

It was still dark when I awoke, but dawn was not far off and I thought I might as well go into chambers, even though it was Easter Sunday. My housekeeper was already up, chivvying the kitchen boy, Peter, to light the fire. I breakfasted, then wrapped myself in my coat to walk to Lincoln's Inn.

There had been a light fall of snow. I passed under the Great Gate and walked across the yard. To my surprise I saw a light in my chambers; Barak must have come straight here from wherever he had been last night.

Then I jumped at the sound of a cry. A man's voice, yelling out in terror. I made out two figures standing by the fountain. 'Oh God!' one cried.

I turned and crossed to them. I saw the ice was broken into pieces. The water under the ice was red, bright red. My heart began thumping.

By their short black robes, I saw that the two young men staring into the fountain were students. One was short and thickset, the other tall and thin.

'What is it?' I asked sharply. 'What is happening?'

The thickset student turned to me. 'There's . . . there's a man in the fountain,' he said in a trembling voice.

As I stepped close, I saw in the growing light that a man's booted leg was sticking out between the chunks of ice. I felt a moment's giddiness, then pulled myself together. 'Help me get him out,' I said abruptly.

The tall student approached. Together we hauled out the body and laid it on the slushy ground. It was wrapped in a long dark robe, which had ridden up over the head, hiding the face. I looked at the body: a small, thin man. I crouched down, and pulled the robe away from the face.

'Oh Christ Jesus!' one of the students cried, and I heard a retching sound.

But for me it was a double horror. The first was the great gaping wound in the man's throat. The second was the face. It was Roger's.

FOR A FEW MOMENTS I stood transfixed, staring at that awful corpse, the terrible wound in the throat, red against the dead-white skin. Roger's eyes were closed; the alabaster face looked peaceful. I thought, Surely his face should be contorted with horror as he suffered that appalling death?

'Please, sir, cover him!' the stocky student called in a shrill voice.

I removed my coat and bent down to cover the body. Suddenly I was overcome by emotion. 'Oh, my poor friend!' I cried out, letting the tears come.

A hand on my shoulder made me jump. I looked up at the anxious face of the tall student. 'Please, sir,' he asked tremulously, 'what shall we do?'

I rose shakily to my feet. 'Go and tell the gatekeeper to rouse the constable, who must fetch the coroner. Can you do that, lad?'

'Yes, sir.' The boy nodded and ran off towards the lodge.

I turned to the other boy, who was shivering violently. 'You, will you run across the court to my chambers—see, there where there is already a light? My assistant is there; tell him to come at once.'

The boy gulped, nodded and staggered away. I looked up at the windows of the Elliards' quarters. There were no lights; I prayed Dorothy was still abed. I realised with sinking heart that I would have to tell her that Roger was dead. I could not leave that task to some stranger. Moments later, I saw Barak running towards me. His mouth fell open when he saw the body.

'Judas's bowels! What's happened here?' He looked red-eyed and smelt of drink, but there was no one I would rather have by me now.

'Roger Elliard is dead,' I said, my voice shaking. 'He has been murdered.'

'Here?' Barak asked disbelievingly.

'During the night. Someone cut his throat and put him in the fountain.'

'Jesu.' Barak bent gently, twitched back the corner of my coat, then quickly replaced it. He looked at the fountain. 'His throat must have been cut in there. There's no blood on the ground.' He frowned, and thought for a moment. 'If those students hadn't come by he wouldn't have been found till the resident barristers left chambers to go to the Easter services.'

I looked again at the body. I clenched my fists. 'Who could do such a monstrous thing to a good and peaceful man? On Easter Day? Why?'

I heard a murmur of voices. Some barristers had emerged from their quarters and were approaching. One of them was the treasurer, Rowland.

'Brother Shardlake?' he asked. 'What is going on? The porter roused me—' He broke off, his eyes bulging in horror at the red fountain.

I told him what I knew. He took a deep breath, then bent and uncovered Roger's face again. There was a murmur of horror from the onlookers.

Barak spoke quietly at my elbow. 'There is something you should see.'

'Could you excuse me for a moment?' I said to Rowland.

Barak led me to a point twenty feet away. 'See these footprints?'

I looked down. Around the fountain the students and I had churned the snow to slush. But Barak was pointing to a separate double trail, one approaching and another leading away from the fountain, that went round the side of the building where the Elliards lived.

'Look how deep the ones leading to the fountain are,' he said. 'Deeper than the ones returning. Like he was carrying something heavy.'

'I heard someone there at New Year,' I said. 'He got over the wall . . .'

'Let's follow the trails before they melt in the morning sun.'

I hesitated, then followed Barak round the side of the building. The footprints ended at a heavy wooden gate.

'He got through here,' Barak said. He tried the gate. 'It's locked.'

'I've got a key, but it's in chambers,' I said.

'Help me up,' Barak said. I made a stirrup of my hands and he climbed up, resting his elbows on top of the wall. 'The footsteps go on into the orchard,' he said. He jumped down. 'I'll run and get the key.'

I hesitated. 'I should go back. It should be me that tells Dorothy—'

'I'll go by myself. But I must go now, before the footprints melt.'

'You don't know what you may find at the other end,' I cautioned.

'He's long gone. But I'll follow the footsteps as far as they go. We need to find out all we can. You know as well as I that if a murderer is not taken quickly, he is often never found.' Barak took a deep breath. 'And this is no normal killing, done for money or lust. The killer knocked him unconscious, then carried him into Lincoln's Inn and put him in the fountain. He was still alive when his throat was cut or he wouldn't have bled. It looks like some sort of awful vengeance.'

'Roger hadn't an enemy in the world. And only a member of Lincoln's Inn would have a key to that door.'

'We should go now, sir, if you are to tell the lady.'

I nodded, biting my lip. Barak began running back to Gatehouse Court. I followed more slowly. As I rounded the corner, I heard a woman's scream. I felt a violent shiver down my spine as I started to run.

I was too late. In the middle of the growing crowd around the fountain, Dorothy, dressed in a nightgown, was kneeling on the wet ground by her husband's body, wailing piteously, a howl of utter desolation. My coat had been removed from Roger's head; she had seen that awful face. She wailed again. I ran to her and grasped her by the shoulders.

She lifted her face to me; she looked utterly stricken, her eyes wide, her mouth open, her brown hair wildly disordered. 'Matthew?' she choked.

'Yes, Dorothy. Oh, you should not have come out, they should not have let you see . . .' I looked accusingly at the crowd.

'I could not stop her,' Treasurer Rowland said stiffly.

'You could have tried!' I snapped, and turned to lift Dorothy up.

As soon as she stood she began trembling. 'Who . . . killed him?'

'We will find out. Now come inside.'

Dorothy allowed me to lead her inside, where Roger's clerk, Bartlett, stood in his office doorway, looking shocked.

'Sir?' he whispered. 'They say the master is murdered. Is it true?'

'I fear so.'

Dorothy was staring at Bartlett as though she had never seen him before. I led her gently up the wide staircase to their rooms.

A young maid in a white apron and coif stood in the open doorway. 'Oh, my lady,' the maid said in an Irish accent. She turned her tearful face to me. 'She must have looked out of the window and—'

'All right,' I said gently. 'What is your name?'

'Margaret, sir.'

'Fetch your mistress some aqua vita, Margaret, and a thicker gown.'

I led Dorothy into the parlour and sat her in a chair before the fire.

The maid returned, draped a warm gown round Dorothy's shoulders and passed her a glass of aqua vita, but Dorothy's hand trembled so much I took it from her fingers.

'Stay,' I said to Margaret. 'In case she needs anything.'

'The poor master . . .' Margaret brought a stool to her mistress's side and sat on it heavily, shocked herself.

'Come,' I said gently to Dorothy. 'Drink this, it will help you.'

She did not resist as I held the glass to her lips and helped her. Her face grew pink from the spirit and she seemed to come slowly back to herself.

'Matthew,' she said. 'Who did this cruel, wicked thing? And why?'

'I do not know. Dorothy, where was Roger yesterday evening?'

'He . . . he was out. His new pro bono client.'

'The same client he went to see on Thursday? After we saw Dr Malton?'

'Yes, yes.' She gulped. 'A letter came on Tuesday, from some solicitor. A man called Nantwich.'

'Did Roger say where he was writing from?'

'Somewhere by Newgate, I think. He asked if Roger could meet his client at a tavern in Wych Street on Thursday evening, as the man worked during the day. But the man never turned up. Then another letter arrived on Good Friday, apologising that the client had not been able to get to the tavern and asking Roger to meet him yesterday night, at the same place.'

'And Roger went, of course.' I smiled sadly. 'I would not have done.'

Dorothy was silent for a moment, then went on. 'I was surprised when it got to ten o'clock and he had not returned. I was tired so I went to bed and drifted off to sleep. I woke in the small hours, and when he wasn't beside me I thought he had bedded down in the other bedroom, as he does if he comes in late. And all the time . . .' She broke down then, sobbing loudly.

I tried to think. Nantwich had asked Roger to meet the client at Wych Street, on the other side of Lincoln's Inn Fields. The easiest way to get there was through the orchard. But why had the man not turned up on Thursday?

I looked at Dorothy, my heart full of pity. Her sobs ceased. She glanced at me and I saw an anger in her eyes that reflected my own.

'Who did this?' she asked quietly. 'Roger had not an enemy in the world.'

'I will see him caught, Dorothy. I promise you.'

Her face crumpled. 'Oh, Roger!' And then the tears came again.

Margaret put an arm round her sobbing mistress, while I held her hand. We were still there, like some pitiful tableau, when Elias came in to say that the coroner was below and must see me at once.

Archibald Browne, the Middlesex coroner, was a sour old man, bald and squat. When I came out he was standing beside Treasurer Rowland, looking down at Roger's body. I wondered wearily where Barak was.

Rowland gestured to me. 'This is Brother Matthew Shardlake,' he told Browne. 'He had the constable roused.'

'I hope I'll get more sense out of him than those two lads,' Coroner Browne grunted. 'Now, tell me what in Jesu's name has happened.'

I told him about finding Roger's body, about Barak following the footprints and what Dorothy had told me about the strange client.

'Nantwich?' Treasurer Rowland frowned. 'I've never heard of him.'

'This is a strange business,' Browne said. 'A fountain turned to blood.' He addressed the Treasurer. 'You should get that drained.'

I frowned. *A fountain of blood.* I had heard the phrase before somewhere.

'Where's the man who went to follow the prints?' Browne asked.

'I don't know. He set off half an hour ago.'

'Well, have him report to me when he comes back. I shall have to visit the King's coroner before empanelling a jury.' I recalled that the King was at Whitehall now, and cursed the fact. Any murder within twelve miles of the royal residence and outside the City of London came under the authority of the King's coroner. That would cause delay.

'We need to hunt this solicitor Nantwich,' I said. 'Could you do that, sir— just a general query under the Treasurer's authority?'

'Yes. That must be done,' Browne said.

'And if I may suggest something. The manner of his death is so strange, it might be good to have the body opened.' It was a grim thought, but Guy might find something that would help us. 'Dr Malton does that duty for the London coroner. I could send for him.'

'Oh, that old Moor,' Browne grunted. 'And who's to pay?'

'I will, if need be. Roger Elliard was my friend.'

'All right.' The coroner rubbed his pudgy hands together. 'I'll see the widow now. Master Treasurer, have a cart take that body to my shed.'

DOROTHY HAD somewhat recovered her composure when old Elias led us to her parlour. She sat by the fire, holding Margaret's hand.

'Dorothy,' I said gently, 'this is Coroner Browne. He would ask you some questions, if you feel able.'

The coroner looked at the frieze above the fireplace, the carved animals peering through the branches. 'My, that is a fine thing,' he said.

Dorothy stared at it. 'A piece got broken off when we moved back here,' she said dully. 'Roger got it replaced but it was badly done.' I noticed that a corner of the frieze was rather poorly executed, a slightly different colour.

'It is still fine,' Browne said, clumsily trying to put Dorothy at her ease. 'May I sit?' Dorothy waved him to a chair. He repeated the questions about the pro bono client, and asked about Roger's recent movements. 'Had your husband any enemies?' Browne asked finally.

'None. He had barristers he did not like particularly. But that is true of every barrister in London, and they do not murder their fellows in'—her voice faltered—'this ghastly, wicked way.'

Browne rose from his chair. 'Very well,' he said. 'That will do for now. I must go to the palace, see the King's coroner.'

He bowed to us stiffly, and I accompanied him out. To my relief, I saw Barak in the courtyard watching as Roger's body was loaded onto a cart. I saw he was carrying a dark coat that I recognised as Roger's.

'I found this in the orchard.'

'Did you follow the prints?'

'As far as I could. They led through the orchard into Lincoln's Inn Fields, but the snow there was pretty well gone.'

'Was there anything in the pockets?'

'A set of house keys. The killer must have kept the key to the orchard. And his purse—he left his purse, with near two pounds in it.'

'Were there any papers? Any notes?'

'Nothing.'

'He went to meet a new client at an inn in Wych Street last night.'

'Taken somewhere in Lincoln's Inn Fields, then. That's a hell of a way to haul a body.' Barak looked at me, frowning. 'What on earth is going on?'

Chapter 3

Two days later, on the Tuesday after Easter, Barak and I walked down to the river to catch a boat to Westminster. I had a busy day ahead, five poor men's pleas to be heard before the Master of Requests.

The ice had quite gone from the river now, which was high, the grey water flowing rapidly. The man at the oars of the boat we took at Temple Stairs had a pinched, hungry look. It had been a hard winter for the wherrymen. I told him to make for Westminster.

'The stairs there are broken, sir. The ice has crushed the supports.'

'Whitehall Stairs, then,' I said, not relishing a walk through the crowds.

The man pulled out. I sat staring over the river. I had spent the previous day studying Roger's cases and giving instructions to his clerk, Bartlett.

''Eard about those great fish?' the man asked, interrupting my thoughts. 'Almost as big as houses they are.' He nodded and smiled. 'I've seen 'em.'

'What are they like?' Barak asked curiously.

'Grey, with huge heads full of strange teeth. They're starting to stink, and they're cutting them open to get the fish oil. Some say they're cursed.'

'Maybe they're whales,' I said. 'A kind of giant fish.'

'They're bigger than any fish could be. Giant heads they've got.'

The boat pulled up at Whitehall Stairs. We walked under the Holbein Gate and down into King Street. I kept a hand on my purse, for Westminster was as disorderly a place as could be found in England. Pedlars, hucksters and prostitutes thronged the streets. Ahead of us loomed the vast bulk of Westminster Abbey, dwarfing even its neighbour, Westminster Hall, where most of the courts sat. We jostled our way down to Palace Yard.

'The inquest is tomorrow,' I told Barak. 'I had a message first thing. I am sorry, I forgot to tell you.'

'Will I need to be there?'

'Yes. Dorothy too, poor woman.' I bit my lip. 'I hope the pamphleteers do not get hold of the story and start spreading it round the city.'

'They would love it.'

'I know. God's death, that coroner Browne is useless. The inquest should have been yesterday. The killer could be in another county by now.'

'Tammy says you called in a few nights ago,' Barak said. 'Came to visit.'

So she had told him. Was that to pressure me into speaking to him? This was not the time. I made my voice light. 'I passed the Old Barge on the way home from Guy's. That tenement of yours is very damp.'

He shrugged. 'I'd have moved if the baby lived. But it didn't.'

'Tamasin seemed a little . . . downcast.'

'She should get over the baby. I've had to.' His voice went hard. 'I don't know where her old spirit's gone.' He did not meet my eyes as he spoke.

We entered White Hall, a small chamber opposite the Painted Hall, where the House of Commons sat. A crowded little entrance hall was set with benches along the walls. There plaintiffs sat huddled, watching the lawyers talking in the body of the hall. Poor folk from all over the country came to have their suits pleaded here, by me and my fellow state-funded barrister. I saw my first client sitting there: Gib Rooke, a stocky man in his thirties with a square, sunburnt face. He wore a red surcoat, far too gaudy for court. He was frowning at two men who stood talking in the body of the hall. One was a tall, expensively dressed man; the other, to my surprise, was Bealknap.

'How now, Gib,' Barak said, sitting beside Rooke.

Rooke nodded to Barak, then looked up at me. 'Good day, Master Shardlake. Ready for the fight?'

I gave him a stern look. Having their own barrister went to some of my clients' heads, and they would take the chance to strut and mock. 'I am ready,' I said. 'We have a good case. If we lose, it may be because the court judges you insolent. Dressing like a peacock is a bad start.'

Gib reddened. He was one of the many cottars who had set up market gardens on the Lambeth marshes over the last fifteen years; the growth of London meant an endless demand for food in the city. The cottars had drained patches of bog land, and squatted there. Recently, however, the landlords had realised there were profits to be made, and sought to turn the cottars out and reap the benefits of their work. Gib had applied to Requests against eviction, citing ancient laws that said that if a man occupied land under two acres in extent for a dozen years unchallenged, he could remain.

Gib nodded at Bealknap. 'Sir Geoffrey seems unhappy with his lawyer.'

'I know Bealknap,' I said. 'Don't underestimate him.' And in truth, he was a clever lawyer. Today, though, he seemed to have a problem with his papers; he was searching frantically through his bag.

I sat on the other side of Gib. He looked at me, eyes greedy with curiosity. 'They say there's been a terrible murder at Lincoln's Inn,' he said. 'A lawyer found in the fountain with his throat cut. On Easter Sunday.'

It was as I had feared. The story was spreading. 'The killer will be rooted out,' I said.

Gib shrugged. 'There have been some nasty killings lately. One of the marsh cottars was found murdered horribly in January. I wouldn't be surprised if his landlord killed him,' he added loudly. People turned to look.

'If you don't control your mouth, you'll lose this case,' I snapped at him.

'Here's trouble,' Barak whispered. Bealknap was coming over to us.

'May I speak with you, Brother Shardlake?' he asked.

I stood. 'Very well.'

We stepped away a few paces. Bealknap bit his lip. 'There is a problem, Brother Shardlake. I have not filed my client's title to the land.'

I stared at him, astonished. The most routine piece of a lawyer's work was to ensure the paperwork was properly filed in court.

I saw panic in Bealknap's eyes. 'Assist me, Brother Shardlake,' he whispered desperately. 'Get the case adjourned. I can file the deeds then.'

'If you file them now, the judge might hear you.'

'I have *lost* them,' Bealknap said, a sudden frantic blurt. 'I appeal to you, Shardlake. I thought they were in my bag. I have been ill! Dr Archer has purged me again and all last night my arse was in a bloody sweat . . .'

Many lawyers would have helped him for the sake of the fellowship of the bar, but I had set my face against such arrangements at a client's expense.

'I am sorry, Bealknap,' I said quietly. 'My duty is to my client.'

Bealknap leaned forward, almost hissing. 'I knew you would not help me, you . . . you bent-backed toad. I won't forget this!'

SIR STEPHEN AINSWORTH, Judge of Requests, was fair but sharp-tongued. As soon as he came to our case he saw the court record was incomplete. As I had expected, Bealknap rose and said he had filed the deeds but the court clerk must have lost them, asking quickly for an adjournment.

'Where is your receipt for the deeds?' Ainsworth asked.

'I left it with my clerk, but he has the key to the office and has not arrived. I had to leave early to get here, the Westminster Stairs being down . . .'

I had to give Bealknap credit for quick thinking. But Ainsworth asked for the Clerk of Requests to be brought into court. The clerk confirmed the deeds had never been lodged.

'I suspect you lied to me there, Brother Bealknap,' Ainsworth said coldly. 'Your client's claim against Gilbert Rooke is dismissed for lack of title. Goodman Rooke, you may remain on your land. You have been lucky.'

Gib grinned from ear to ear. Bealknap sat down, his face grey. His client leaned close and began whispering fiercely, his face furious.

'Brother Shardlake,' Ainsworth continued. 'I am told you have filed an application in the case of a boy sent to the Bedlam by the Privy Council.'

'Yes, Your Honour.'

He frowned thoughtfully. 'Do I have the jurisdiction to hear this?'

'The issue, Your Honour, is that no enquiry has been made into the boy's state of mental health. That should be done before a person is deprived of their freedom.' I took a deep breath. 'I propose to get a doctor to examine him, sir. But in the meantime, there is also the issue of who should pay the fees they charge in the Bedlam. The boy's parents are poor.'

'That I can deal with,' Ainsworth said. 'Very well, the court will set an early date for a hearing.'

GIB WAS DELIGHTED at the result; his arrogance had gone and he was tearful with relief. He promised me undying gratitude and almost danced from the courtroom. The cases continued; it was a good day for me—all the cases I had listed won. The court rose at four thirty, and I went directly to Guy's.

It was dark by the time I arrived. Guy's shop was closed, but he answered my knock. He invited me to sit with him in the consulting room. The candlelight emphasised the lines in his dark face.

'How is poor Mistress Elliard?' he asked.

'Distraught. And we are no further forward in investigating Roger's murderer. What do you have to tell me of your examination of his body?'

'So far as I could see, Elliard's health at the time of his death was good.'

'It always was. Till someone knocked him out and cut his throat.'

'There *was* a lump on the back of his head. So I think his killer did knock him out. But . . .' Guy paused. 'Have you ever heard of *dwale*?'

I shook my head.

'There is no reason you should. It is a liquid compound of opium and certain other elements, such as vinegar and pig's bile, which induces deep relaxation and unconsciousness. It has been used on and off for hundreds of years to render people unconscious before surgery.'

'Then why have I never heard of it? That would save terrible pain.'

He shook his head. 'There is a severe problem with it. The correct dose is very hard to determine. It is easy to give the patient too much and then the physician is left with a corpse. For that reason very few use it now. But I think Master Elliard's killer did. The taste and smell of dwale is distinctive, and I found some on one of Elliard's boots.' He looked at me. 'The first stage after it is taken is nearly always a sense of euphoria, then unconsciousness. That explains your poor friend's peaceful look.'

'You said it is out of use now. So who *would* use it?'

'Very few physicians or surgeons, some unlicensed healers.' He hesitated. 'And there was a tradition of its use in certain monasteries.'

There was a moment's silence. Then I said, 'You used it, didn't you?'

'Yes. When I thought the shock of surgery might kill a patient.'

'But it needs great skill to administer.'

He nodded. 'When Master Elliard came round from the knock on the head, his killer forced him to drink enough dwale so he would not wake even when his throat was cut. But he would not have wanted to give a fatal dose. He meant to make that terrible display in the fountain.'

I nodded. 'And when Roger passed out, the killer brought him to Lincoln's

Inn. Across the fields and through the orchard gate.' I told him about the footprints. 'Roger was a small man, but this brute must be very strong.'

'And determined. And vicious.'

I shook my head. 'And from what you say he has knowledge of the medical profession. And perhaps the legal world too, if he could fake a letter from a solicitor well enough to take Roger in. But why? Why kill a man who has harmed no one, and leave that terrible spectacle?'

'He had no enemies?'

'None. Will you be giving evidence at the inquest tomorrow?' I asked.

'Yes. Of course.'

'And Adam Kite? Do you know when you may be able to visit him? I ought to come too. The court is not sitting on Friday morning, if that would be convenient for you.'

'Yes, Friday at noon?'

'Good. Then I will leave you,' I said, rising from my stool. I shook Guy's hand. 'Thank you for taking on Adam. His parents will be relieved.'

NEXT MORNING I accompanied Dorothy to the inquest at the Guildhall. Unusually, a pair of constables in city livery was posted by the door. Within, council and guild officials scuttled to and fro. A large group of black-robed lawyers was gathered in a corner. I recognised the stern face of Treasurer Rowland; the others were all Lincoln's Inn barristers—the jury. The two students who had found Roger's body stood on the fringe of the group, looking distinctly uneasy. Guy stood a little apart, talking to Barak.

Dorothy looked at the crowd, hesitated, then moved to a bench by the wall. She sat, signalling Margaret to join her. 'I cannot face talking to anyone,' she said. 'I will come into court when we are called.'

'Very well.' I crossed to Barak and Guy.

'Good day, Matthew,' Guy said. 'Jack here has noticed something strange.'

'What?' I asked.

'A spectacular death like this,' Barak said, 'you'd think the public gallery would be full. But those constables are turning folk away.'

'Really?' The coroner's court was supposed to be public.

A black-robed usher called from a doorway. I went back to Dorothy.

She rose to her feet. 'Take my hand, Margaret,' she said quietly.

The jurors parted to let her enter the courtroom. The usher guided us to the front row of benches, and the jurors took the two rows behind. I studied the two coroners sitting at the table facing us. Browne slouched with his plump hands folded across his ample stomach. Next to him sat a very different man: in his early forties, short but strongly made. He met my look; the gaze from his bright blue eyes was sharp, appraising.

'That's Sir Gregory Harsnet,' Barak whispered. 'The King's assistant coroner. He used to be in Lord Cromwell's camp; he's one of the few reformers who's kept his place.'

'We will come to order, please.' Harsnet spoke in a clear, quiet voice with a West Country accent. 'We are here today to adjudicate on the sudden and dreadful death of Roger Elliard, barrister of Lincoln's Inn.'

The jury was sworn in, then Harsnet addressed us again.

'I call Dr Guy Malton, who has been charged with examining the body, to tell us what he found.'

Guy stood and recited his impressive medical qualifications, then spoke of how he believed Roger had been rendered unconscious using the drug called dwale, and carried to the fountain where his throat had been cut.

'He was alive when he went in. He died from a massive loss of blood.'

'How long before he was found?'

'Some hours. Rigor mortis would be delayed by the cold, but I understand a skin of ice had reformed on the fountain.'

Harsnet frowned at Guy. 'What object could anyone have in creating such a terrible spectacle? A man dead in a fountain of blood.'

Guy spread his hands. 'I cannot say.'

Again I thought that the phrase seemed familiar. *A fountain of blood.* But from where?

'A ghastly thing.' Harsnet shook his head; he looked troubled. 'What we have to determine today is how Roger Elliard died. Murder, clearly, but by whom? I would like to call Jack Barak.'

He asked Barak about the footprints he had followed.

'The footsteps led to the fountain, then went back in the opposite direction,' Barak said. 'He was carrying something on the way in, not on the way back. The snow was melting fast but the impressions were clear.'

Harsnet looked at him. 'No ordinary man, surely, could carry an unconscious body as far as you have suggested, and over a wall.'

'A very strong and determined man could.'

Other witnesses were called: the two students, then I, then Treasurer Rowland. Asked about Roger's state of mind, Rowland replied that he was a happy, cheerful man, respected in the profession, with no known enemies.

'He had one enemy,' Harsnet said. 'A vicious and clever one. This killing was planned, with patience and cunning.' I looked at him. He was no fool. He turned to Rowland. 'What of this solicitor who wrote to Master Elliard?'

'Fictitious, sir. No one knows anything of a solicitor with the unusual name of Nantwich. I have made enquiries at all the Inns of Court.'

'In a case of savage vengeance such as this,' Harsnet said, 'I would expect there to be an obvious culprit, yet there seems to be none. We must be realistic,' he went on. 'I foresee a verdict of murder by person or persons unknown, and I fear that they may remain unknown.'

I was astonished. This was blatant leading of the jury. Yet none of the men who had been selected dared speak up.

Then I heard a swish of skirts. Dorothy had risen to her feet.

'I have not been asked to speak, sir, but if anyone has that right it is me. I will see my husband's murderer caught. With the help of faithful friends, I will.' Her voice, though quiet, cut the air like a knife. She sat down.

I expected some sort of explosion from Harsnet, but he merely sat with his lips pressed into a narrow line. His face had reddened. Browne was grinning at his discomfiture. At length, Harsnet spoke.

'I can make allowances for Mistress Elliard's state of mind; I will not censure her. But it seems to me we need more evidence before the jury can deliver a verdict. Therefore I will not ask it to deliver a verdict now; the matter will be left open while I undertake an investigation myself—'

I rose to my feet. 'With the help of the jury, sir, I take it. As is normal?'

'A coroner may investigate without a jury if he feels it appropriate, as I do here. Now sit down, sir.'

I sat, but glared at him.

'Now all of you note something, and note it well.' Harsnet looked over the room. 'I will not have the details of this case hawked around London. There is a royal order going out today banning the printing of any pamphlets on the subject. I order everyone here to keep these matters secret. Anyone who disobeys will be punished.' Then he rose, Browne heaving himself to his feet beside him. 'This inquest is adjourned *sine die*. It will be recalled when I have more evidence. Good morning, gentlemen.'

The usher opened the door, and the coroners left. There was an immediate babble of talk.

Margaret turned to me. 'We should get my mistress out of here.'

And indeed Dorothy looked as though she might faint. I rose and helped Margaret steer her out of the room. We led her to a bench and sat her down. Barak and Guy followed. Dorothy looked at each of us in turn.

'They want it buried,' she said bitterly. 'Don't they? They think the killer has got away, and it will be too much trouble to investigate.'

'Well . . . '

'Come, Matthew, I was not married to Roger near twenty years without learning a good deal about the law. They want this dropped and forgotten.'

'It looks like it.' I shook my head.

'Please help me, Matthew. I am a woman—they will take no notice of me.'

'I give you my word. I will start by talking to Coroner Harsnet. Jack, will you take Dorothy back to Lincoln's Inn?'

Barak nodded and I hurried outside.

In the paved square I saw the black-robed figure of Harsnet. He was talking to a tall man in his thirties with a copper-coloured beard, dressed in a green jerkin with gold piping and a red cap with a white feather. Normally I would have hesitated to challenge a royal official in public, but I was as fired by anger as seldom before in my life.

As I approached, the bearded man turned to Harsnet with a smile. 'He was right,' he said. 'Here he is.'

I looked from one to the other. 'What do you mean, sir?' I asked.

Harsnet took a deep breath. Close to, he looked strained, burdened. 'I was told you might be unhappy with the verdict, Brother Shardlake.'

'Told? By whom.'

'I dare say you have come to ask why I adjourned the hearing.'

'Yes. It seems you do not want the killer discovered.'

The tall man laughed bitterly. 'Oh, you mistake us there, lawyer.' He spoke in a deep, musical voice. 'There is nothing we want more.'

'Then why . . . ?'

'Because this matter has political implications,' Harsnet said. He glanced round to ensure nobody was in earshot. 'You asked who told me you would contest the verdict. It was Archbishop Cranmer.'

'What?' A chill ran down my back at Cranmer's name.

Harsnet fixed those hard blue eyes at me. 'Do you truly seek to find Master Elliard's killer, above all else?'

'Yes,' I said.

The richly dressed man laughed. 'There, he has courage after all.'

'Who are you, sir?' I asked boldly, and he frowned at my insolence.

'This is Sir Thomas Seymour, brother of the late Queen Jane.'

'So watch your manners, churl,' Seymour growled.

I was lost for words for a moment.

'If you questioned the verdict,' Harsnet continued, almost apologetic, 'my instructions were to bring you to Archbishop Cranmer.'

'What is this about?'

'Much more than the death of Master Elliard.' He looked me in the eye. 'Something truly dark and terrible. But come, we have a wherry waiting to go to Lambeth Palace.'

ONE OF ARCHBISHOP CRANMER'S own boats was waiting for us at Three Cranes Stairs, four oarsmen in the archbishop's white livery in their places. Harsnet told the men to row fast for Lambeth Palace.

After the thaw the river was thronged with white sails as wherries carried customers to and fro. Behind us I saw London Bridge with its crowds of houses and shops. Atop the arch at the south end of the bridge long stakes thrust into the sky, the heads of those who had defied or angered the King set atop them mercifully indistinct. I shuddered at the thought that I was now sailing back into the world of the King's court.

'Aye, 'tis still cold,' Seymour said, mistaking my tremor. He had wrapped his heavy coat round him.

I studied him covertly. I knew he was the younger brother of Henry's third queen, Jane Seymour, who had died giving birth to his heir, Prince Edward. Seymour's older brother, Edward, Lord Hertford, held high office at court, but Sir Thomas was known as something of an adventurer and a ladies' man. I wondered fearfully what he could have to do with poor Roger.

We reached the far bank in silence and sculled quickly down to Lambeth Palace. We were taken directly to Cranmer's study.

The Archbishop of Canterbury sat behind a large desk, wearing a white robe with a black stole, his head with its greying dark hair bare. He looked strained and worried. He was far from an extreme reformer, but was always under threat from the conservatives at court. The King's long affection for him was all that kept him safe.

Another man stood beside him, wearing a plain dark robe. His prominent nose, long face and athletic frame were so like Thomas Seymour's that it could only be his brother. Yet where Thomas was handsome, the same elements, slightly recast, made Edward, Lord Hertford an ugly man.

'Well, Matthew Shardlake,' Cranmer began, 'we meet once again on strange business. Serjeant Shardlake,' he added, reminding me I had gained that post through his patronage, following a mission I had performed for him in York. He turned to Harsnet. 'Is it as we feared?'

Harsnet nodded. 'Yes, my lord. Exactly the same as the other.'

Cranmer exchanged a look with Edward Seymour, then stared for a moment into the dancing flames of the wood fire burning in the grate.

Sir Thomas broke the silence. 'Well, can we trust the hunchback?'

'Do not call him that!' Cranmer looked genuinely angry. 'I am sorry, Matthew.' He turned to Sir Thomas. 'Yes, I believe we can.' Cranmer looked at me intently. 'Matthew, you were a close friend of Lawyer Elliard, I believe. How deep are you in this?'

'I promised Mistress Elliard to find her husband's killer,' I said. 'It is a debt of honour.'

'And would you still work to redeem that debt, even if it turned out to be a matter of politics?' Cranmer asked.

I took a deep breath. For a second I seemed to see Roger's face before me, smiling, animated, full of life. I faced the archbishop. 'If I can help you in this, my lord, I am yours.'

Cranmer looked at the other three. Harsnet and Edward Seymour nodded; Thomas Seymour shrugged. Cranmer frowned at him.

'You are only here, Thomas, because of your association with . . . her.'

Seymour reddened with anger but nodded.

Cranmer turned to me. 'You will wonder, Matthew, what the political link is to your friend's murder.'

'Yes, my lord.'

He took a long breath, then said, 'Your friend was not the first to be killed in that terrible manner. It was kept secret because of who the victim was.' The archbishop nodded to Harsnet. 'Tell him, Gregory.'

Harsnet looked at me. 'One morning a month ago, in late February, a labourer was walking to work along the river here on the Lambeth shore. There was snow on the banks then, and the river was frozen a yard deep, but the tide still ebbed and flowed underneath into the tidal pools. That morning the labourer saw that one of the pools was red, with something floating in it.' My eyes widened. Harsnet nodded seriously. 'Yes. He found a man lying there with his throat cut. Exactly as Elliard was in that fountain.'

'Dear God.'

'Our labourer went to the constable, who fetched the coroner. When my colleague, the Surrey coroner, realised who the man was, he came to me, as he knew of my connection with the archbishop.'

'Has there been an inquest?' I asked.

'No. The dead man was a physician, Dr Paul Gurney, an eminent man.'

Harsnet paused. 'Dr Gurney had attended Lord Latimer, late husband of Lady Catherine Parr, since he sickened last autumn.'

So that was the connection. 'They say the King is courting Lady Latimer,' I ventured.

'They say right,' Cranmer agreed.

'We can't tell him all,' Thomas Seymour burst in. 'If this leaks out, it could be to the peril of that good lady.'

'Matthew will not break a confidence,' Cranmer said. He turned to me. 'Do you swear, Matthew, to say nothing of this matter, even if it means you may not be able to tell your friend's widow the circumstances should the killer be found?'

I hesitated, then said, 'May I tell her the killer is caught and dealt with?'

'Yes. And he will be,' Edward Seymour said grimly.

'Then I swear, my lord.'

Cranmer leaned back, satisfied. 'Then continue, Gregory. Tell him all.'

'I investigated, quietly,' Harsnet said. 'But I found no clues as to who killed him, or why. As with Master Elliard, Dr Gurney was a man respected in his profession, with many friends and no enemies. He was a childless widower, and we had his friends told he had died suddenly in his sleep. According to discreet enquiries, he had left Lord Latimer's house late the evening before, telling the steward he had an urgent "errand of mercy".'

'Was a note delivered to him? As with Roger?'

'Not that we know of, though there may have been.'

Cranmer spoke again. 'The King has long had an eye on Catherine Parr. When it became known in January that Lord Latimer would die soon, the King let his interest be known. He has now proposed marriage.'

'Another older husband.' Thomas Seymour spoke with bitterness in his voice. 'Latimer was past forty.'

'This would be a sensible, safe marriage and God knows we have had few of those,' Cranmer said. He looked at me. 'The Lady Catherine has also an interest in religious reform, which she kept quiet, for Lord Latimer was a conservative. And we need an ally now. Bishop Bonner's campaign against the London Bible-men is soon to escalate. A bill will be laid before Parliament shortly, restricting reading of the Bible to nobles and gentlemen only.'

He hesitated, frowning. 'I am told they seek also to attack me. There have already been arrests of radicals among my staff at Canterbury, and among some of the junior courtiers at Windsor. They will be charged with heresy.' His cheek twitched uncontrollably, and I saw the archbishop was afraid.

Lord Hertford spoke, quietly and seriously. 'What protects us more than anything is that the King still has moderate reformers in his household, men he trusts. His physician, Dr Butts. His new secretary, William Paget. A queen of reformist sympathies could help us more than anyone.'

'But would this marriage be safe for *her*?' Thomas Seymour interjected. 'Anne Boleyn pressed the King too far on religion and was executed.'

Cranmer nodded. 'Yes, it is no wonder Lady Catherine has not yet accepted. But she has placed her decision in God's hands. The situation could not be more delicate. An extraordinarily brutal murder close to her, still more now there has been a second, would worry the King, for he is a superstitious man. That is why we wished to send Master Elliard's death officially to sleep. *Unofficially* I will leave no stone unturned to find the killer. Catherine Parr, like the rest, thinks Dr Gurney had a sudden seizure.'

Now I understood the strain in their faces. The King did not look kindly on those who kept secrets from him. I realised I was involved in something that could get me in bad odour with the King. Something dangerous. Yet I had sworn, and there was nothing to do but go on.

'Well, Matthew,' Cranmer said. 'You come fresh to this matter, and you knew poor Elliard well. Where do you think we should go next?'

I squared my shoulders. 'I suggest we find out whether Roger and Dr Gurney had any acquaintances or clients in common.'

'I have a list of all Dr Gurney's patients and friends,' Harsnet said.

'And I can do the same for Roger. With his widow's help.'

'Very well.' Cranmer nodded. 'But she is to know nothing of Gurney.' I hated the thought of not being frank with Dorothy, but saw it must be so.

'What were Dr Gurney's views on religion?' I asked.

'He was a reformer.'

'As was Roger Elliard. Though a safely moderate one, these days.'

'Which encourages the view that this has been done by the papists to scotch the King's marriage,' Harsnet said. 'Jesu, they are capable of anything.'

'And you, Master Shardlake,' Hertford asked quietly. 'What are your religious views? They say you are a man of little faith.'

'Matthew would not harm our cause,' Cranmer interposed. 'So long as he thought our methods just, eh?' That sad smile of his again.

'Who is he to tell us what is just?' Thomas Seymour scoffed. 'A crook-back lawyer.'

His brother turned on him with sudden anger. 'God's wounds, Thomas, I will have you kept out of this if you say another word!'

Cranmer turned to me. 'Matthew, I apologise again for Sir Thomas.'

'It does not matter, my lord.' Though it did. Why was this foolish boor involved? 'If I may,' I went on, 'I would like to talk to the labourer who found the body, and visit the scene. These correspondences with Roger's death are so close they may help us.'

Harsnet answered. 'I'll have the man sent for.'

'Thank you, Coroner.'

'I want you and Gregory to work together on this,' Cranmer said.

'Might I bring in my man Barak? He could be of much use.'

Cranmer smiled. 'Ah, yes, him. Yes, I know Lord Cromwell trusted him. But no one else. And keep me closely informed. Contact me here and only through my secretary, Ralph Morice.'

'Yes, my lord.'

Cranmer stood up. Harsnet and I followed, bowing low.

'Gregory, Matthew, I pray you may be able to resolve this.'

'Amen, my lord,' Harsnet answered feelingly.

I CAUGHT A WHERRY back to Temple Stairs, and walked up to Lincoln's Inn. The anger I felt after the inquest had been replaced by fear; as I thought of the mighty men in that room, my stomach twisted with anxiety.

It was a relief to find Barak in chambers, working at his desk. I told him all that had transpired at Lambeth Palace. I had expected him to show pleasure at the prospect of some excitement, but he heard me in silence, frowning.

'That Thomas Seymour's a dangerous character,' he said. 'Lord Cromwell distrusted him, though he respected his brother.'

'I don't understand his involvement in this,' I confessed.

'I've heard that he wished to marry Catherine Parr, and that she was in love with him. He had to step aside for the King. Perhaps he made his brother involve him in this so he could protect her interests. But he's known as an indiscreet woman-chaser. And it sounds like an indiscreet man is the last thing this business needs, if Cranmer's keeping it from the King.'

'I know. But I am bound to assist them; I promised Dorothy.' I looked at him. 'But you do not need to be involved if you do not wish,' I said.

'No,' he said. 'I'll help. Though I don't understand any of it. One man killed as your friend was is strange enough, but *two*?'

'Could the killer be mad? Someone who conceived a wild hatred for Roger and that doctor, perhaps developed a belief they had wronged him?'

'A mad person couldn't have planned and carried through these murders.'

Barak frowned. 'That time you disturbed an intruder near the Elliards' lodgings, maybe he was looking over Gatehouse Court? Preparing the way.'

'Perhaps,' I said, 'but we do not know enough yet to speculate. We must think of practical steps.'

'All right. Where do we start?'

'First I shall prepare a list of Roger's clients and acquaintances, to see if he had any in common with Dr Gurney. I shall go across now and speak to Roger's clerk, and to Dorothy.' I sighed. 'I must be careful how much I tell her. I should like you to come with me to meet the man who found the doctor's body, out by the river. Harsnet is arranging it.'

'What's Harsnet like on closer acquaintance?'

'A pure Bible-man, I think. But his feet are on the ground. Clever, efficient.' Something struck me. 'I think Harsnet should check there have been no other killings like this in neighbouring jurisdictions. I'll suggest it.'

'Gib Rooke said a cottar had been killed horribly.'

'Not in the same way as Roger, or he would have said. But it might be worth talking to him. Good idea, Barak.'

I walked across Gatehouse Court, and entered Roger's chambers.

'Good day, Bartlett,' I said to his clerk. 'How are things here?'

'We're coping, sir,' he replied in his Bristol burr. 'Mistress Elliard told me the inquest was adjourned. If I may ask, what is to happen now?'

'All I can say is that there is to be an investigation, and I am part of it. To that end, can you make me a list of all the clients and lawyers Master Elliard had professional dealings with since he came back from Bristol?'

'I'll set to it, sir.'

'What will you do now, Bartlett? Go back to the West Country?'

'I'd as soon stay in London. All my family are with me here.'

'Then I'll see if I can get you a job in another chambers when Roger's work is wound up.'

His face lit up. 'Thank you. You . . . you are a good man, sir.'

'I hope so, Bartlett. Though not all would agree.'

I mounted the stairs to the rooms above. Old Elias answered my knock, and led me to the parlour, where Dorothy was sitting in her chair by the fire.

She looked up and ventured a smile, but her white face was tight with anger. 'What happened?' she asked. 'Why did you go off with that coroner?'

'To discuss the investigation. There will be one, I promise you.'

'If they know he was murdered, why that . . . performance?'

'Politics. I may not say more. I wish I could.'

Her eyes widened. 'Roger had naught to do with politics.'

'I know. But there must be some link to . . . this other matter. I have undertaken to help find it privately.'

'Undertaken to whom, Matthew?'

'Cranmer. And I have already told you more than I should.'

'But you hate politics as much as Roger did. You have said so often.'

'But working with these people is the only way I can ensure Roger's killer is found. They and I want the same thing.'

She looked at me with sad, exhausted eyes. 'I am become a burden,' she said flatly. 'As a middle-aged woman alone will always be.'

I leaned forward and ventured to take her hand. 'No, Dorothy. You are a strong woman. Just now it is all too much to bear, I know, but you will regain your strength. You need time to grieve.'

'I have years of empty time now.'

I felt my heart clench at her suffering. 'Dorothy,' I said, gently, 'this is not the best time, but I must ask you. We need to see if Roger and . . . this other man who died knew anyone in common. Bartlett is preparing a list of professional contacts. Can you make me a list of anyone else he knew? Any non-lawyer friends. And tradesmen, his barber, his tailor, former servants.'

'I will prepare it now,' she said. 'Anything else?'

'The body will be released tomorrow. You can arrange the funeral.'

'That must wait till next week. Samuel will be here from Bristol. And afterwards, Matthew, come and eat with us. Let us sit and remember Roger then, in peace.'

'I shall be glad to.'

Chapter 4

The following day a letter arrived from Harsnet asking me to meet him by the Southwark bear pits at eight the next morning.

I set off early on Friday, and rode through the city to London Bridge. Barak was waiting for me there, as arranged, looking bright and alert, with no sign of a hangover. He had put on his sword, I saw.

Barak greeted me cheerfully. 'Well, let's see what awaits us over the river,' he said with a touch of his old swagger.

'Some answers, I hope.'

We walked across the bridge to the Southwark waterfront, where Harsnet was to meet us. He was already there, wearing a coat lined with marten fur over his lawyer's robe, looking every inch the royal official.

'Good day, Master Shardlake. And you are Barak, yes?'

Barak bowed to him.

'Did you bring the list of those known to Master Elliard?' Harsnet asked.

I produced the list from my coat. 'Master Elliard's wife and clerk helped me. They knew of none who wished him harm.'

'Dr Gurney had no enemies either. I have his list.' He produced a paper from his coat and we stood together to read. It was as comprehensive a list as mine, but there were no names that matched.

'Nothing.' Harsnet frowned. 'If I may keep your list?'

'Of course.'

He rolled both documents up, putting them in his coat.

'I wondered if there might have been any other killings,' I said. 'We are on the borders of Kent and Surrey here. The coroners do not always liaise.'

Harsnet nodded agreement. 'You are right, sir, thank you.' He gave me an approving look. 'I will speak to the other coroners.'

'I know of at least one strange killing this side of the river recently. One of my clients told me. I thought I might ask him for details.'

'Yes. Good idea. Thank you.' He raised his eyebrows, took a long deep breath. 'And now we must meet the man who found the body.'

We walked along the south bank. Soon the houses inland gave way to wide marshes, with tall green reeds waving in the breeze. Here and there patches of higher ground were cultivated, fields of vegetables laid out beside little cottars' houses. At length we came to where the river turned south to Westminster. Ahead of us, standing in the mud by a small pool left by the tide, we saw a lonely figure outlined against the sky: an elderly labouring man in a grey smock and wide leathern hat. Harsnet stepped down from the path into the mud. It quivered as his boots sank in six inches.

'Careful, sir!' Barak called. 'That mud can suck you in!'

We followed Harsnet carefully to where the old man stood.

'How now, Wheelows,' the coroner said. 'I want you to tell these gentlemen exactly what happened when you found Dr Gurney's body.'

A look of irritation crossed the man's face. 'I've told it so many times—'

'Then tell it once more,' Harsnet said, smiling but firmly.

'It was three weeks back, when the snow was still thick on the ground. I was coming along the path to Southwark at first light. The river was frozen but the tide still ran and would seep out under the ice and make tidal pools as usual. I was walking along and something caught my eye. One of the pools was a strange colour. I looked and saw it was red, bright red. Then I saw a dark shape floating in it, and I went down to look.'

'Were there footprints?' Barak asked.

'Aye. Quite large ones, I'd say.' Wheelows shook his head. 'That red pool, standing out against the snow, it was like something from a nightmare. It turned my stomach.' He swallowed. 'There was a place beside the pool where all the snow was churned up. There was blood there too.'

Where he cut the doctor's throat, I thought. 'What did you do next?' I asked the old labourer gently.

'I went into the pool, turned the body over. I saw it was a gentleman by his clothes. His face was white as bone, was no blood left in him. I saw what had been done to his throat.'

'What was the expression on his face?'

'It was strange. He looked peaceful, as if he was asleep.'

Dwale, I thought. 'So, what did you do then?'

'I ran to Southwark, to find the coroner. Then ever since I've had gentlemen questioning me, pressing me to keep it all a secret.' He looked scared.

'So make sure you do as you're told.' Harsnet took a shilling from his pocket and passed it to Wheelows. 'All right, you can go.'

The old man bowed quickly to us, cast a last frightened look over at the marshes, then clambered grunting through the mud to the path.

'It's just like Roger,' I said. 'The doctor was lured to a meeting with someone, drugged, then carried out here. His throat was slit and he was dumped in the pool. People walk along this path every day. If the old man hadn't come on the body early, it would have made another spectacle.'

Harsnet looked down the path. 'But how could he drag the body out here? Dr Gurney wouldn't have met anyone on this path at night, surely.'

I nodded at the river. 'People were walking across the ice then. It was very thick. I would guess the killer met Dr Gurney on the far bank, drugged him there and hauled him over here.'

'He must have timed it right at low tide,' Barak said. 'Like now. When the sea tide rose under the ice, the bloodied water would have leaked out underneath and covered the shore and the pool.'

Sea tide. Water turned to blood. The phrases snagged at my mind, as had the treasurer's about a fountain turned to blood. I knew them. But from where?

Then Barak leaned in close to us. 'Don't look round, but there's someone watching. On a patch of higher ground behind us I saw a head outlined against the sky, just for a second.'

'Are you sure?' I asked.

'I'm going after him.' The light of excitement was back in his eyes.

I put a hand on his arm. 'You don't know how deep the marsh is.'

'I'll risk that.' Barak turned, ran across the path and plunged into the reeds. There was a great splashing and the water came up to his thighs, but he ploughed on towards a green knoll about fifty yards away.

'I'm going to follow,' Harsnet said, and leapt into the reeds after Barak.

I followed in their wake, gasping at the chill of the muddy water.

Ahead, we saw Barak step onto dry land. 'Hell's teeth!' he said loudly.

I followed Harsnet up onto the knoll.

Barak was looking out over the marshes. 'I thought if I got up here and he ran, I could see where he went,' he said. 'But he's vanished.'

'But where to?' Harsnet stared out across the wide empty landscape. 'It's not been a few minutes. We should see him running.'

'I'd guess he's lain down somewhere in those reeds,' I said.

'Then we wait,' Harsnet said. 'No man could stand lying out among those reeds for long. The water's freezing. He has to move sooner or later.'

The three of us watched the marshland below. Occasionally a water bird started up, but otherwise we saw no movement, even when a heavy shower came and soaked us all. I was becoming uncomfortable and my back hurt.

Harsnet looked at me, probably thinking I would be of little use in a tussle. 'You go,' he said. 'Barak and I can deal with this.'

I left them to their vigil. Reaching the path, I looked back at the little knoll, where Harsnet stood outlined against the sky, a waiting, avenging angel.

AN HOUR LATER I walked through the Bedlam gates and approached the long building. I did not want to enter. A monstrous killer and a deranged boy—it seemed as though this past fortnight I had left the normal world behind and entered a strange, terrifying new country. On the doorstep of the madhouse I took a deep breath, then knocked. Keeper Shawms answered.

'Oh, you're here, then,' he said grimly. 'I've had notification of a hearing at the Court of Requests, about my care of Adam Kite. It's next week.'

'Good,' I said. 'They've let you know. Now, I have to see my client.'

'There's a man who says he's a doctor waiting for you,' Shawms said. 'Skin as dark as coal. As if it's not enough having that madwag boy upsetting everyone, now you have to bring a blackamoor here to affright Christian folk. I put him in the parlour, so the patients could have a gawp at him. The ones in there are not violent.'

I followed him to the parlour. An old woman sat in the corner sewing, while a man and two women sat playing cards at a table. The keeper Ellen was not there. I was disappointed, for she had intrigued me. Guy sat on a stool by the fire, ignoring the curious looks he was getting.

'Guy,' I said. 'Thank you for coming. Have I kept you waiting?'

He stood up. 'I got here early.' He smiled gently. 'The residents seem to find me interesting.'

'Let us go and see Adam,' I said, keen to get him away.

As we stepped outside, Ellen emerged from a nearby room.

'Are you here to see Adam Kite, sir? I'll let you in; then I must go to the parlour.' She led us to Adam's cell and unlocked the door. 'He's as usual, sir,' she said. Then with a quick curtsy, she turned and left.

'I warn you, Guy, this is . . . bad,' I said.

'I am ready,' he answered quietly.

I led the way in. The notice from the court had had an effect: the room smelt better, there were fresh rushes on the floor and Adam wore clean clothes. But he was as before, a creature of skin and bone crouched in a corner, praying, 'God, please tell me I am *saved*, *saved* by Your grace . . .'

Guy looked at Adam for a second, then crouched down beside him and looked into his face. Adam gave him a quick sidelong look. His eyes widened a little as he registered Guy's unusual colour; then he turned his head away and began praying again.

Guy waited till Adam paused for breath, and asked softly, 'Adam, why do you believe God has abandoned you?'

Something flickered in Adam's eyes; some connection had been made. 'No,' he whispered fiercely. 'If I pray to Him, He will show me I am *saved*!'

'You pray so hard,' Guy said, 'would you hear God if He answered?'

Adam frowned, looked at Guy suspiciously. 'How could I not hear Him?'

'Because your fear is so strong it drowns everything. Is it Hell you fear?'

'The eternal burning,' Adam whispered.

'Why do you think God visits this suffering upon you, Adam? Do you think He has singled you out?'

'No.' Adam shook his head vigorously. 'All should fear the pains of Hell as I do. Burning, in agony, for ever and ever. In our church we know the truth; that is what awaits those who are not *saved*, who sin.'

'The others in Reverend Meaphon's congregation, are they sinners too?'

'Yes, but they have all received God's assurance that they are saved.'

'But not you?'

'No.' He turned full-face to Guy. 'I know I am not saved. Reverend Meaphon says it is a devil inside me. I must ask God to release me. Save me. Now leave me. *Leave me!*' His sudden shriek made me jump. Adam began his dreadful intoning again. 'God, hear my prayer I beseech You . . .'

Guy rose and inclined his head to me. I followed him outside.

His expression was very angry. 'Will you fetch the keeper here?' he asked me. 'The woman, not that oaf who is in charge.'

'Very well.' I went up the corridor to the parlour. 'Mistress Ellen, Dr Malton would like a word,' I said awkwardly.

The keeper rose, keys jangling at her waist, and led me outside.

Guy was waiting in the corridor, looking through the viewing hatch. He turned to Ellen with a smile. 'My friend says you have been kind to Adam.'

Ellen reddened. 'I try to be.'

'He is very ill. It is vital he is kept locked up so he cannot make another exhibition of himself. But it is important that he is made to take food, even if he struggles. And try, but only very gently, to distract him with practicalities, the need to eat, keep warm and so forth.'

'As though he were mopish or melancholy, and needed to be lifted from his dumps? But it is much worse than that with Adam, sir.'

'I know. But can you do that? Will the other keepers help you?'

'Some will and some won't. But I'll tell Keeper Shawms those are your instructions.' She smiled sardonically. 'He is afraid of Serjeant Shardlake.'

'Good. Thank you.' Guy clapped me on the shoulder. 'Now come, Matthew, let us find somewhere to talk. I feel in need of strong drink.'

WE FOUND A TAVERN nearby. I went to the bar and returned with a bottle of wine and two mugs. Guy was sitting frowning, preoccupied.

'The boy is suffering as much as anyone I have ever seen,' he said. 'How did his parents say his illness started?'

I told him what the Kites had related to me, that Adam had been a happy, outgoing child, until a while ago he became increasingly preoccupied, and thus descended to his present state. 'They are good folk,' I concluded. 'They are under the sway of their minister, a canting dogmatist, but concern for their son is leading them towards an independent stand.'

'I should like to meet them.' Guy stroked his chin. 'Something happened, something specific brought this on, I am sure. If I can only find out what . . .'

I looked at him curiously. 'Have you worked with the mad before?'

'It was part of an infirmarian's duties. And diseases of the mind have always interested me.'

'I wonder,' I said, 'whether Roger's killer may be suffering some form of madness. To kill so brutally, so pointlessly.' Twice, I thought, but did not say, remembering Cranmer's injunction not to tell anyone about Dr Gurney.

'It is possible,' Guy said. 'Unless Master Elliard gave someone cause to take such a terrible revenge, which having met him, I doubt.'

'That is impossible.' There *was* something I could ask him about, I realised. 'Guy, you said some of the monastic infirmarians used dwale. Do you know of any infirmarians in London who might have?'

'The use of dwale was mainly restricted to the Benedictines,' he replied. 'And the only Benedictine foundation in London was Westminster Abbey. But there may be many healers who still use it.'

'Its basis is opium, is it not? Poppies would need to be grown and cultivated. Whoever it is would need to have a garden.'

'True. Though many grow poppies in their gardens for their bright colour. And I myself grow them in my herb garden, to make opium.'

I drained my wine. 'I have to go,' I said. 'Thank you, Guy, for seeing Adam. Will you come to the court hearing next week, give evidence as to his state of mind, ask that he be kept in the Bedlam for now?'

'Yes, of course.'

I bade him farewell and hurried home through the busy streets. Barak was waiting for me in chambers. He was towelling his hair, which like his clothes was soaking wet. Skelly had gone home.

'No luck?' I asked.

'We waited till it got dark, then came away.' Barak frowned. 'That bastard's got away now. Harsnet's furious with himself, said he should have left us two there to watch, and roused some constables to flush him out. He hadn't believed anyone could have sat it out in those cold marshes all day.'

'We know how determined this creature is,' I said. 'But how did he know we would be there to look at this man's body; that is what worries me.'

'And me,' Barak said with feeling. 'Well, I've some news at least. I sent word to Gib Rooke, and he sent a reply, at once. He'll meet us at his house tomorrow, tell us about that killing in Lambeth last winter.'

The news lifted me. It was something positive after a day of horrors. 'Thank you, Jack. Get off home now. Tamasin will be worried about you.'

NEXT MORNING, Barak and I set out once again for the marshes. We took the horses; it was bright and sunny, a truly springlike day, and crocuses and snowdrops were springing up everywhere. We rode across London Bridge and took the path on the far side of Southwark village to where a Norman church stood on the edge of the marshes. We passed a group of cottars shoring up a muddy, sunken stretch of path with cinders and branches. Cottages began to appear beside the path, surrounded by little market gardens. Gib's was the fifth along, a mud-and-daub cottage like the rest. Gib was working in his patch, loosening the heavy soil with a spade. A woman and several small children were also at work digging and sowing. Barak called out Gib's name and he came across, his wife and children following.

Gib introduced me proudly. 'My barrister,' he said. 'He seeks my help on a certain matter.'

His wife, a thin, tired-looking woman, curtsied, then smiled at me warmly. 'We are so grateful, sir, for what you did. We won't ever forget.'

'Thank you.' Like all lawyers, I was delighted by gratitude. It was rare.

Gib clapped his hands. 'Come on. Maisie, children, back to work! Master Shardlake and I have confidential matters to discuss.'

The family returned to their labours.

'I don't want them to hear about this bad business,' Gib said, suddenly serious. 'Tie your horses to this post, sir, and come inside.'

We followed him into the cottage, which smelt of damp and smoke. A fire burning in the hearth in the middle of the floor provided some warmth.

Gib brought some weak beer and sat on a stool opposite us. 'Now then,' he said. 'You've questions about poor Wilf Tupholme?'

'He was the man who was murdered?'

'Yes.' He paused, remembering. 'He was found in January. They are after Welsh Elizabeth. A Bankside whore.' He spat in the fire. Barak and I looked at each other. This sounded as though we were on the wrong track.

'Are they sure she did it?' I asked.

'Sure enough to issue a warrant against her. She and Wilf had been living together a few months, but they were always fighting. He turfed her out in December; then he was found dead a month later, murdered horribly. The coroner's trying to trace her but the other whores say she's gone back to Wales. She'll go to earth there; they won't find her.'

'At Westminster you said his landlord probably killed him.'

Gib grinned. 'That was just to annoy Sir Geoffrey.'

'So what happened?' Barak asked. 'You said he was killed horribly.'

'So he was. I'll tell you on the way to his house.'

I glanced at Barak, who shrugged slightly. 'Very well,' I said, 'let us go.'

We followed Gib outside, and he led us eastward along the path. The cottages became fewer as the ground became marshier.

'Wilf was a strange man,' Gib said, 'always bad-tempered and surly. A couple of years ago he became a hot-gospeller, telling everyone the end-time was nigh. Plagues, earthquakes and Jesus coming to judge us all. But last autumn he took up with Welsh Elizabeth and she moved in. They'd get drunk and argue, like I said, and he booted her out. Then he disappeared, and his neighbour saw his cottage was locked up. After a while his neighbour thought, If he's gone, I'll take the land over before it goes back to marsh. He broke open a shutter and looked inside. Said the smell nearly felled him.'

Gib looked sombre. 'Wilf was on the floor, dead. He was gagged. Someone had cut him all over, then tied him up. His thigh had this great sore on it, all black and crawling with maggots. Whether his diseased leg got him, or cold and hunger, nobody knows, but they said his face was terrible.'

We were silent. This death was even worse than Roger's. This man would have died in slow agony.

Gib led us up a side path to where an isolated cottage stood. The door had a heavy padlock. He stared at the house, then crossed himself.

'Pete Lammas has given me the key; the coroner left him responsible for the house. He doesn't want to go in again, though.' He paused. 'Look, sir,' he said. 'I'd rather not go in either. Can I leave you to bring me back the key?'

'All right,' I agreed.

Gib handed the key to Barak, bowed to us and left.

'I'll be the one to open the door, then, shall I?' Barak asked with heavy sarcasm. He unlocked the padlock and pushed open the door.

We both stepped back at the smell that hit us, a great butcher's shop stink overlaid with the stench of sweat and dirt. Carefully we moved into the dark interior. Despite the season, blowflies were everywhere, buzzing around the room. We batted them away from our faces. Barak went to the shutters and opened them. We saw the place was filthy, stinking old rushes on the floor, a full chamber pot in a corner, rags everywhere. The flies began to settle again.

'Let's get out of here,' Barak said. 'There's nothing but filth and rags.'

'Not yet,' I said. 'This is a lonely spot and he was unpopular. If Wilf Tupholme's killer knew him, he would know that in winter if he was tied up and left to die it might be weeks before anyone opened the place up.'

'Why do you say he? Surely it was his woman.'

'I wonder.' I looked at the dark bloodstain on the floor. 'Surely a drunken whore he'd kicked out would be more likely to knock him on the head.'

'This has nothing in common with those others,' Barak said impatiently. He stirred the rags on the floor with his foot. 'Hello, what's this?' He bent and felt among the scraps of clothing. He came up with a large tin badge .

I took it from Barak's hand. 'A pilgrim badge. From St Edward the Confessor's shrine at Westminster. That's an odd thing for a hot-gospeller to have in his house, is it not? Don't they see shrines as papist images?'

'Maybe one of the constables dropped it while they were clearing the body out,' Barak suggested.

'Unlikely,' I said. 'People don't wear pilgrim badges these days, in case they're taken for papists. But see what else you can find, Jack.'

Barak turned over all the filthy clothes and other rubbish. 'There's nothing else here,' he said at length. 'Poor bastard. I wonder if he repented him of his fornication as he lay watching the maggots eat his leg.'

I gave a start. 'What did you say?'

'I said I wondered if he regretted his time with the whore—'

'No, no, you said "repented him of his fornication". Why did you use that phrase?'

He looked at me as though I had lost my senses. 'I don't know, it just came into my head. It's from the Bible, isn't it?'

I clapped him on the shoulder. 'Yes, it is. Oh Jesu,' I said quietly. 'I hope I am wrong. Come.'

'Wrong about what? You talk in riddles—'

'We must get to a church. That one on the edge of the marshes will do.'

I led the way out of the cottage and unhitched the horses, leaving Barak to lock up and hand over the key to Gib.

'What's the hurry?' Gib called as Barak ran after me. 'What did you find?'

'Nothing!' Barak called back as he swung into Sukey's saddle. 'He has to go to church, that's all!'

THE DOOR of the church was open, and we stepped into the cool interior. It was, I saw, still decorated in the old style, the walls painted in bright colours, worn patterned tiles on the floor. On a lectern beside the richly decorated altar lay a Bible, fixed to it by a chain. The English Bible, ordered by Lord Cromwell to be set in every church.

'Why are we here?' Barak asked, following me down the aisle.

'I want to look at that Bible. Sit down in a pew while I seek what I want.'

'But what *do* you want?'

I turned to face him. 'We've been talking about the hot-gospellers who say Armageddon will soon be here. They preach their message everywhere. But where do they get their message from, which part of the Bible?'

'The Book of Revelation, isn't it?'

'Yes, the Apocalypse of St John the Divine. That's where most of their quotes come from. The last book of the Bible, full of wild, fiery language.' I mounted the lectern, opened the great blue-bound book and turned the heavy pages till I came to Revelation. I found the part I was seeking.

'Look,' I said, 'this is the part of the Book of Revelation where St John is shown the seven angels who pour the seven vials of wrath upon the earth.' I read from Chapter 2: '*And I gave her space to repent of her fornication; and she repented not.* When you used that phrase, or a version of it, I realised where all these other gobbets that had stuck in my mind came from. Here.' I turned several pages, until I came to Chapter 16: 'Now, listen to this,' I said. '*And I heard a great voice out of the temple saying to the seven angels, Go your ways, pour out your vials of wrath upon the earth. And the first went, and poured out his vial upon the earth; and there fell a noisome and grievous sore upon the men which had the mark of the beast, and upon them which worshipped his image.* A noisome and grievous sore. Gib said "a great sore". Poor Wilf Tupholme was murdered in the manner of the victims of the first vial. And he was a believer who had lapsed into fornication. Many would say he had the mark of the beast on him.'

Barak frowned. 'Aren't you making what happened to the cottar fit what's in here?' he asked dubiously.

'If it was only the one reference I would agree with you. But listen to this: *And the second angel poured out his vial upon the sea; and it turned as it were into the blood of a dead man: and every living thing died in the sea.* If Wilf Tupholme was the first to die, that means Dr Gurney was the second. He died in salt water, a tidal pool, turned to blood.'

Barak frowned again, and read the passage for himself.

'And it continues,' I went on quietly. '*And the third angel shed out his vial upon the rivers and fountains of waters; and they turned to blood.* Roger Elliard died in a fountain of blood.' Suddenly overcome with emotion, I gripped the sides of the lectern. 'Poor Roger. This is a blasphemy.'

'Dr Gurney and Master Elliard were good people, though,' Barak said.

'Yes, they were. It looks as if they did something sinful, or the brute that killed them thought they had.' I took a long deep breath. 'And Roger, like

Tupholme, had once been a radical but abandoned that path. I wonder if Dr Gurney did too.' I looked at Barak. 'Well, do you agree with me? Someone is killing people in accordance with the prophecy of the vials of wrath?'

'To fulfil the prophecy,' Barak said slowly. He looked truly shocked. 'That means four more murders.'

'Yes. I do not think this is to do with Catherine Parr,' I said. 'This is not politics after all, Barak; it is religion. Mad, debased religion.'

'What happens after the seven vials have been spilled? Where does it end?'

I laughed, heard the half-hysterical sound echo round the old church. 'What do you think? This is the Book of Revelation, Barak. It ends with the destruction of the whole world.'

Chapter 5

We rode to Lambeth Palace, where I asked at once for Cranmer's secretary, Ralph Morice. He quickly appeared, a little pale-faced man in a black robe. I told him who I was and that I had urgent news, and he scuttled away, returning a few minutes later to tell us that the archbishop had sent across to Whitehall for the others involved in the matter. He showed us into a comfortable little room to await their arrival.

'Could you please fetch me a copy of the New Testament in English?'

'I will have one brought.' He bowed himself out.

'Are you sure about this notion?' Barak asked when the door was closed. 'It seems fantastic. I don't know what Cranmer will make of it.'

'You saw the chapter. It speaks for itself, surely.'

'But it talked of thousands being killed by each vial of wrath, not just one man each time.'

'I think this is some sort of devilish, perverted symbolism—' I broke off as a servant appeared bearing a copy of the Testament. I laid it on the table and again I pored over the text of Revelation, only too well aware that if I had misread something, my reception from the great men now being gathered from Whitehall was likely to be unpleasant.

We both started when the door opened to reveal Cranmer's secretary once again. He bowed. 'His Grace will see you now, Master Shardlake,' he said. 'Only you. Your man is to stay here.'

CRANMER SAT behind his desk. Lord Hertford, Thomas Seymour and Coroner Harsnet stood round him. All looked at me seriously, expectantly.

'What have you found, Matthew?' the archbishop asked quietly.

I took a deep breath. 'My lord, I believe I know why Dr Gurney and my friend were killed. And a third who was killed in December.'

Cranmer leaned forward. 'A third?' His voice was horrified.

'Yes. And if I am right, there are four more deaths to come.'

Sir Thomas Seymour spoke. 'Come on then, man, spit out your tale.'

I told as concisely as I could how I had learned of Tupholme's death, how the manner of it had led me to the connection with Revelation. My auditors heard me in silence. 'If you will check Chapter Sixteen, my lord—'

'I know the New Testament by heart, Matthew.' He frowned, thinking hard.

Thomas Seymour laughed, a rich, booming sound. 'I have never heard such a tale. The crookback's mind is addled by too much reading.'

Sir Edward gave his brother a stern look. 'Watch your language, Thomas.'

Cranmer's eyes were full of sorrow. 'I think Matthew could be right,' he said. 'These deaths do fit exactly with Revelation Sixteen, even to their sequence. And yes, a man who was mad and vicious enough could believe he was inspired to fulfil the prophecy—for Revelation is, above all, a prophecy of what must come to pass.' He gave a sigh that was almost a groan.

Hertford had pulled a Testament from Cranmer's shelf and was reading it. 'He *is* right, my lord. These murders fit the pattern of the vials of wrath too closely to be coincidence. But we may take a little comfort from this.'

'Comfort? How?' Cranmer asked incredulously.

'If the killer's purpose is to fulfil these prophecies, the fact that the second victim was Lord Latimer's doctor surely has no significance.' Hertford looked at Cranmer. 'This is not aimed at the proposed marriage.'

Cranmer nodded slowly. 'Yes, that follows. But the King is very superstitious; he still might see the killer as inspired by the devil, and turn away from any possible involvement with Lady Latimer.'

'Would His Majesty necessarily be wrong to think this was inspired by the devil?' Harsnet asked. 'Does it not speak to you of a man possessed?'

'Why are you gospel men always so ready to cry possession?' Thomas Seymour snapped irritably. 'We should be catching this man, not wasting time on these speculations. We cannot know what he is until then.'

For once I agreed with Seymour. 'Sir Thomas speaks true, my lord,' I said.

Cranmer looked to me. 'Well, Matthew, where would you go from here?'

'Tupholme and Roger had both held radical reformist views, though in different ways both had abandoned them. Was that also true of Dr Gurney?'

'Yes,' Cranmer said. 'He had once been very radical, but recently he had become . . . disillusioned.' He frowned. 'You think the killer may be seeking men who were religious radicals but have now abandoned that position?'

'I fear so.'

Archbishop Cranmer buried his face in his hands. Everyone fell silent. When he lowered his hands again, his face was set hard.

'Matthew, the danger to me, to everyone in this room, grows by the hour. Some of my staff are still being questioned for heresy, though they will find nothing, for they are not heretics. Butchers are being arrested for selling meat during Lent. Now there is talk of a purge of booksellers. We are hanging on by our fingertips. Can you imagine what a gift to Bonner this would be, someone murdering radicals who have backslid in London? This horrid blasphemy would be meat and drink for his cause.'

'I found one clue at the scene of Tupholme's murder,' I said. I produced the badge from my pocket and laid it on Cranmer's table.

Lord Hertford bent to study it closely. 'A pilgrim badge from St Edward the Confessor's shrine in Westminster Abbey. I saw enough of them on people's coats before the shrines were done away with.'

'It can't have come from Tupholme, if he was a reformer,' Harsnet said.

'And I never heard of a whore that wore one,' Thomas Seymour added.

'So the killer dropped it,' said Cranmer. 'Perhaps it was torn from his coat as he struggled to tie that poor wretched cottar—'

'Or it could have been dropped deliberately,' Edward Seymour said.

'Yes, my lord,' I agreed. 'That is possible. But there may be another connection to the old religion.' I took a deep breath. 'According to my friend Dr Malton, the only certain place dwale has been used in recent years is in the infirmaries of Benedictine monasteries. I wanted to ask you, my lord, whether I might make search among the Court of Augmentations records, to see what became of London's Benedictine infirmarians.'

'Could that be the explanation?' Cranmer asked eagerly. 'An ex-monk. A crazed papist making an example of men who were radicals once—'

'But is it not the radical godly men, not papists, who claim they understand the secrets of Revelation?' Sir Thomas's perceptiveness surprised me.

'And perhaps these killings are to make an evil mockery of those very views,' Cranmer said. He looked at us in turn. 'Master Harsnet, I want you to investigate whether the cottar had any links with the first two victims, especially through their religious affiliations. Matthew, look into the Court of

Augmentations records. Edward'—he turned to Hertford—'you are close to the King these days, I leave it to you to ensure no word of this comes near him.'

Hertford nodded. 'So long as no one here talks, I can do that. But what of the future? If the lawyer is right, there will be a fourth killing.' He opened his Testament and read aloud: '*And the fourth angel poured out his vial upon the sun; and power was given unto him to burn men with heat of fire.*'

'What of the final three vials of wrath?' Sir Thomas asked.

Cranmer took a deep breath. 'The pouring of the fifth vial brings death to the sinful by darkness and great pain. The sixth vial dries up the waters of the Euphrates, and when the seventh angel pours out his vial there are thunders and lightnings and a great earthquake.'

'My lord,' I said, 'there is one more thing I would ask. Dr Malton told me some of the old monastic infirmarians used dwale. He may know of them, even if he did not know them himself. I would like to take him into my confidence, if I may? He helped us over the dwale.'

'He's an ex-monk, isn't he?' Hertford asked sharply.

'Yes, but if Matthew says he will keep his confidence'—Cranmer gave me a long considering look—'I will accept that. You may tell him.'

There was silence for a moment, then Sir Thomas laughed. 'By Jesu, this killer would need devilish powers indeed to bring about an earthquake.'

'I am sick of your mockery, Thomas!' Cranmer turned on him with sudden fierceness. 'We all know the devil may indeed be moving in this. But we must investigate this matter with reason.' The archbishop turned back to us. 'Each of you knows what to do,' he said. 'Do it, with dispatch.'

THE NEXT DAY, I rode down to Guy's. It was Sunday, April 1, All Fools' Day, when people will play tricks on each other, but mercifully nobody shouted out that my horse's tail was on fire or suchlike.

Barak and I had spent the previous day at the Court of Augmentations office, searching for the records of infirmarians at the London Benedictine houses. All the records of monks receiving pensions were being reorganised and the result was chaos. It was evening before we emerged, a good deal dustier, with three names, although the addresses were now held in a separate file and it would be Monday morning before that office opened.

As I turned into Guy's street I felt an unease, as though I were being followed. I turned quickly in the saddle, but could see no one in the narrow street. Telling myself that the hunt for Roger's killer was making me overanxious, I tied Genesis up outside Guy's shop, and knocked on his door.

He let me in, and called out to Piers to fetch us some wine. 'Sit down,' he said and took a seat at his consulting table. 'How can I help you, Matthew? I see by your face this is no social call.'

I paused before answering. Close to, I saw he looked tired, drained, and I felt reluctant to draw him again into the terrible affair of the murders; yet I needed his counsel. I told him about Tupholme and Dr Gurney, the link to the Book of Revelation, the possibility that the killer was seeking out apostates from radical religion. Guy's dark features seemed to sag as I told him.

'I knew Paul Gurney,' he said, when I had ended my narrative and sworn him to secrecy. 'Not well, but we met at a few functions.'

There was a knock at the door, and Piers entered with a tray of wine. His handsome face was again impassive, but there was an intentness in those large blue eyes that made me wonder if he had been listening at the door.

'This was found at the site of Tupholme's murder,' I said when Piers had gone. I produced the badge.

Guy turned it over in his fingers. 'So you think the killer is a Benedictine infirmarian? Because of this, and the dwale?'

'I think it possible. Barak and I spent yesterday tracing Benedictine infirmarians in London at the time of the Dissolution of the Monasteries. The Westminster infirmarian and his two assistants are still in London. We won't have the addresses until Monday, but we have names. The infirmarian is Goddard, Lancelot Goddard; his assistants are Charles Cantrell, a monk, and Francis Lockley, a lay brother. Guy, have you heard those names?'

He shook his head. 'Remember, I came to London from Sussex when my old monastery was dissolved. I was no longer a monk. And, Matthew, many ex-Benedictine monks came to London after the Dissolution. What was done to the monks was enough to drive men mad,' he added with sudden bitterness. 'Torn from their homes and lives. Thrown into a different world, where the Bible is interpreted as literal fact, its symbols and metaphors forgotten, and fanatics react with equanimity to the blood and cruelty of Revelation. Have you ever thought what a god would be like who actually ordained and executed the cruelty that is in that book? A holocaust of mankind. Yet so many of these Bible-men accept the idea without a second thought.'

'Bishop Bonner would destroy them just as cruelly.'

'Do you think I do not know that?' he answered angrily. 'I, whose family were made to leave Spain by the Inquisition, loyal Catholics though we were, because we had the taint of an Islamic past?'

'I know. I am sorry.'

'So am I. Sorry for what the world has come to.' He shook his head. 'I am sorry, Matthew,' he said wearily. 'You came here for my help.'

'No, I spoke insensitively. It is this matter—Guy, Harsnet thinks the killer is possessed, thinks a madman could not organise these murders so carefully. I do not know what to think. I have never heard of anything like it.'

'I have,' he said quietly.

I stared at him.

'Obsession,' he said. 'It is a type of madness. A man may have a strange, bizarre obsession in one part of his life and yet seem normal, or pass for normal, in others. Obsessions can take many forms. Love is the commonest. Someone convinces themselves that they must have the beloved, even if that person is utterly unsuitable, does not care for the lover at all.'

'Everyone has heard of cases like that.'

'And if a life can be dominated by fierce, twisted love, may it not equally be ruled by fierce, twisted hate? When I was studying in Paris, people still spoke of the Marshal Gilles de Rais when they wanted to curdle their blood.'

'Who?'

'He was a French knight who served with Joan of Arc, to all appearances a normal man. But when he retired to his estates in Brittany he began abducting and murdering children in the most terrible manner. The local people knew what he did but he was a powerful man, beyond the law.' Guy fixed me with a bleak gaze. 'He would get the local barber to come and style the hair on the heads of murdered boys that he had placed on stakes in his hall, and invite him to judge which looked the best.'

'Jesu.'

'Eventually, he annoyed the Church in some dispute, and the local bishop stepped in at last. De Rais was tried and hanged for the murders. At his trial he said he had committed his crimes purely because they pleased him.'

'Dear God.' I felt my skin crawl, as though some insect were on it.

'I think there have been more monsters like this creature than we know,' Guy said. 'You know how difficult the detection of crime is, Matthew. Each city and parish enforcing the law through Justices of the Peace and coroners who are often corrupt, with the aid of constables who are usually stupid.'

'And who investigate killings with little or no reference to what is happening in neighbouring districts. I have been talking about this with Harsnet and Barak. And how most killers who are caught are impulsive and stupid . . .'

'Whereas this one plans, is careful, meticulous, patient. He puts his whole self into his terrible work—the expression perhaps of a limitless rage. Obsession,' Guy said quietly. 'It is a wicked, wicked thing.'

'The killer is mad, then?'

'He cannot be sane as we understand the word. But his cleverness may mean he is able to pass himself off as normal, although I would have thought there must be signs . . .' He shook his head again, then fixed me with intense brown eyes full of pain. 'From the study of those past cases, Matthew, there is one thing I am sure of. This man will not stop at seven. Revelation is a whole sequence of violent stories, one after another, layers of them. When this cycle is finished, he has many more to choose from.'

'Jesu.' I sat there feeling utterly drained, staring at Guy. Then my eyes widened, for I saw that behind Guy the door to his inner chambers was open, just a crack. Something glinted in the crack, and now I saw it was another eye, staring back at me. Filled with terror, I pointed at the door.

Guy turned, then before I could stop him he jumped up and threw it open. The boy Piers stood there, a large bowl in his hands.

'Piers,' Guy's voice was sorrowful as he stood over the boy, 'what are you doing? Were you listening to our talk?'

'I am sorry, master,' the boy replied humbly. 'I was bringing you the powdered henbane I had prepared.' He gestured at the bowl. 'I knew you wanted it urgently. I heard you talking, was uncertain whether to knock.'

I knew he was lying, and Guy was not fooled either.

'Is this how you repay me after I took you in?' His voice rose, a note of pain in it; then suddenly he broke off and sighed. 'You must learn to curb your curiosity,' he said gently. 'The keeping of confidences is part of our trade.'

'I am sorry, master.' The boy cast down his eyes.

Guy took the bowl of henbane. 'Thank you, that was well done.'

Piers turned to go, but I called him back sternly. 'Your master and I were discussing a matter of state. If you breathe one word of what you have heard outside these walls, I will make sure you will end in the Tower.'

'I promise to say nothing, sir,' Piers answered.

'Go, Piers,' Guy said wearily. The boy closed the door behind him.

'You give that boy too much latitude, Guy.'

'That is my business,' he answered sharply, then shook his head. 'Don't worry, I will make sure he keeps quiet.'

'You must, Guy.'

He fell silent. I frowned. When he had criticised Piers I had seen that the boy met his gaze, not with humility but a sort of cold challenge. It seemed to me that, in some way I could not fathom, Guy was frightened of him.

I RODE BACK to Lincoln's Inn, the sun warm on my face, the breeze gentle for the first time that year. The horrors I was labouring with seemed to make the brightness a mockery. I passed under the Great Gate, left Genesis with the ostler, then went to my chambers and worked for a while. I jumped when the door opened and Barak came in. He looked tired and smelt of sweat, but was smiling.

'I have the addresses,' he said. 'And some news.'

I threw down my quill. 'On a Sunday?'

'I went down to Augmentations this morning. A lot of clerks were there, trying to sort out the mess. I managed to chivvy them into getting the Westminster records. I got the addresses and a register of payments with them.'

'Well done.'

He sat down opposite me. 'The infirmarian has not been in to collect his pension since December. Just before the first murder, of the cottar. His name is Lancelot Goddard, and he lives near the steelyard. I went down there, asked around the neighbours. They said an ex-monk had rented a house there since Westminster Abbey went down three years ago. He left in January, saying he had inherited a house from his mother. I went to see the landlord, who said the monk was a good tenant, quiet and always paid on time.'

'What did this Goddard look like?'

'A man nearing forty. Distinctive. High cheekbones and a big mole on the side of his nose. Tall and well set up, dark hair.'

'What about his assistants?'

'I got their addresses. One, Cantrell, lives in Westminster still, the other out near the old Charterhouse. At a tavern, called the Green Man.'

'A tavern.' I raised my eyebrows.

'So it seems. That's Lockley, the lay brother.'

I nodded. As he was not a monk, he would not have got a pension. But a tavern was a far cry from a monastery.

'It is strange Goddard vanished in January. Do you think . . .?'

'That he could be the killer? Hold on, Jack, there could be another reason he disappeared.' I looked at him seriously. 'He could be another victim.'

Barak shook his head. 'Sounds like he deliberately vanished.'

'I must send a note to Harsnet. You did well,' I added. 'You should go home now. You look as if you have had enough for one day.'

'Aye.' He looked guilty. 'I told Tamasin I'd be back for lunch. I'd best go.'

After he had gone, I penned a long note to Harsnet and took it to the porter's lodge, telling him to have it delivered urgently. Then I walked back across Gatehouse Court, to Dorothy's, where I was invited for dinner.

The maid, Margaret, let me in. Dorothy was sitting in her usual place before the fire, embroidering a dress with little flowers. She looked up with a smile, and I was glad to see a little colour in her cheeks.

'How are you?' I asked gently.

'Life must go on, must it not?'

'Yes, it must.'

'Samuel is coming tomorrow. And I have arranged Roger's funeral for Tuesday.' She looked at me. 'A week today since he died.'

'I know.'

'I am trying to keep occupied. And I have supervised the preparation of a fine repast. To thank you, for all you have done.'

'It is little enough, Dorothy. I am sorry I cannot myself take on Roger's cases. But Bartlett has brought me a list of honest lawyers who can.'

'Good. I shall need the money. The treasurer is hinting they will be appointing a new Inn member soon and he will want these rooms.'

'Have you enough to take a house? If not, I can—'

She raised a hand. 'No. Thank you, Matthew, but Roger was a prudent man. There is enough saved for me to live carefully. But I do not know where I shall go. Samuel suggested in his letter that I return to Bristol.'

'Will you go?' I found my heart sinking at the thought.

She hesitated. 'I do not know, yet. Is there any news?'

'We are making progress. I'm afraid that is all I can say.'

'Do you know yet why Roger was killed?' Her voice was a whisper.

'No. But, Dorothy . . .' I paused. 'We know of three men this man has killed now. While he is at large, I think you should not go out alone.'

'You think I might be in danger,' she said quietly.

'No. Only . . . it's as well to be safe.'

Dorothy looked at me intently for a moment, then nodded.

A serving man appeared, bearing a large tray of meat with sweet-smelling sauces. I followed Dorothy to the table.

'There,' she said. 'A saddle of lamb. I am glad Lent is over.'

We ate in silence for a while, enjoying the meal. She dabbed her lips with a napkin, then gave me a doubtful look. 'I have been thinking on Roger's idea for a hospital for the poor. Would you take up the plan? It was something he wished to do so much; it would honour his memory—'

Suddenly she broke off and began to sob gently. I rose and went round the table to her. Hesitantly, I took her shoulders.

'There now,' I said.

She reached out and took my hand, a smile coming to her tear-stained face. 'You have been so good, Matthew. What would I do without you?'

Her words and her touch sent a wave of feeling through me. I had to prevent myself from embracing her fully, kissing her. Something must have showed in my face, for she released my hand. I stepped away.

'I am not myself,' she said quietly. 'I am suddenly tired; today has been too much. Would you mind if I went to bed now?'

'Of course not.'

'Come and dine again after the funeral. Samuel will be here. You have not seen him since he was a boy.'

'Yes. I will.' I was suddenly tongue-tied. 'I . . . I should go.'

'Very well.' She wiped her face. 'There. All over now. But still I find it hard to compose myself.' She looked at me seriously. 'I need time.'

OUTSIDE I LEANED against the stone wall, breathing deeply. I realised now what I had been hiding from myself: the fact that Dorothy was single again had kindled old fires. I thought again of her hand on mine. Then I thought of Roger, dead in the snow. 'God forgive me,' I whispered to myself.

And then I saw, across the courtyard, a figure standing by the door of my chambers. It was a woman and I realised with shock that it was Tamasin. As I ran across the yard, I saw to my horror that her face was puffy and swollen, her dress torn and her coif askew. She stared at me, trembling.

'Tamasin,' I said. 'Dear Jesu, who has done this to you? Was it . . .?' For an awful moment I thought it might have been Barak.

'I came to find Jack.' Her voice came thickly through swollen lips. 'We had an argument; he went out again. I could not stand being in that house alone: I kept feeling someone was outside, kept fancying I heard breathing at the door. I had to leave. I was going to your house if Jack was not here. All the way here, I thought someone was behind me.'

'Tamasin . . .'

She looked at me, a stare of pure fear. 'Then as I was about to turn in here, someone leapt at me, pulled me into a corner and began beating me—' She broke off, breathing heavily, though she did not cry.

'Who?' I asked. 'Who?'

'His voice was . . . strange. He said he knows you and Jack are hunting him, but you would not stop his mission. Master Shardlake, he knows your name, and Jack's. He knows where we live. Who is he?'

Chapter 6

I unlocked the door to my chambers and helped Tamasin to a seat in my room. I returned to the outer office and locked the door. I lit a taper from the embers of the fire and took it through to light the candles in my room. Tamasin was sitting where I had left her, head sunk on her chest. I poured a goblet of strong wine and held it to her lips. She took a couple of sips. I felt fury towards whoever had ravaged her pretty face, and horror, as well, for an even worse fate might have befallen her.

'Tamasin, do you know where Jack is?'

She sighed. 'His usual haunts, I expect. The Turk's Head tavern by Newgate or the Red Dog near the Old Barge. We had an argument. He stormed out.'

Damn him, I thought. 'I am going to get the gatekeeper to send someone to find him, and Guy too. You need attention.'

'My face hurts so much. Do you know who attacked me?'

'I fear it may be the man we are seeking. Thank God I was here tonight. Listen, Tamasin, I am going now, to rouse the gatekeeper. I will lock the door.'

'Be careful, sir. He may be out there still.'

I took the dagger I kept in my desk, took a deep breath and stepped outside, locking the door behind me.

I crossed the yard rapidly. Ahead, the gatekeeper's lodge was dark. I banged on the door as loudly as I could. After a minute, the gatekeeper opened up, his breath stinking of beer. I quickly told him a woman had been attacked and ordered him to send his assistant in search of Barak and Guy.

Back in chambers I did what I could to help Tamasin, fetching water and a cloth for her to wash her poor ravaged face.

Barak arrived half an hour later, rousted from the Newgate tavern by the gatekeeper's assistant. He rushed in, wide-eyed. 'What's happened? They said Tammy's been hurt!' He hurried over to his wife, but halted as she lifted her head and turned her ravaged, angry face to him.

'Yes, Jack,' she said. 'By that imaginary fellow outside our door.'

He turned to me. It was one of the few times I had seen him at a loss. I gave him some wine, sat him down and told him what had happened. All the time he kept glancing at Tamasin, who still sat looking at him fiercely.

'I never thought he could know where we lived,' Barak said to Tamasin.

He turned back to me. 'And why do this? It's as if he was taunting us!'

'You know, I thought I too was being followed,' I said quietly. 'Tamasin, did you see nothing of him?'

'No. He hit me from behind. When I fell to the ground he kicked me and then said what I told you, that he knew you were hunting him, but you would not stop his mission. Who is it you are hunting? Who has he killed?'

Barak and I looked at each other. He nodded, and I told Tamasin the story of the three murders, the link to the Book of Revelation, the mission from Cranmer. I did not mention Guy's theory about obsessive killers.

'Oh my God,' she said when I finished. 'Why did he not finish me off?'

'I think you did not fit what he calls his mission. Revelation speaks of the fourth vial causing men to be scorched with fire.'

'So he wanted to threaten us?' Barak said. 'Warn us off?'

'I think so. You two should move to my house. Tonight. I will send a message to Harsnet asking him to send a man to keep watch.'

'That's a good idea, Tammy,' Barak said gently.

'Yes,' she answered bitterly. 'Leave it to your master to protect me.' She began to cry again, clearly at the end of her tether.

I nodded impatiently to Barak, and mouthed the words, 'Comfort her.'

But Barak was angry too now, at the insult to his manhood. 'That's not fair. If I'd known this man was real, but you've had so many fancies—'

It was the worst thing he could have said. She half rose and would have thrown herself at him, had a knock on the outer door not made us all start.

I went to open it. Guy stood there, his eyes wide. 'Matthew,' he said, 'a man came to call, with a message about a woman attacked here.'

'Come in, Guy.' I sighed. 'You have arrived at just the right moment.'

Guy attended to Tamasin. She had suffered bad bruising to her face, and a cracked rib, but there was no permanent damage apart from two broken teeth, fortunately at the side rather than the front of her mouth.

'I will fetch some stuff from the Barge,' Barak said, as Guy applied some soothing oils to Tamasin's face. 'Could you take Tammy to your house, sir?'

'I will.' I followed him out to the outer office. There I took his arm. 'If you do not comfort her,' I said in an angry whisper, 'and accept your part in what has gone wrong between you, you will lose her.'

He shook off my arm and glared at me. 'Leave my wife's affairs to me,' he said thickly. 'What do you know of married life?'

'Enough to know you have a rare pearl in Tamasin.'

'I'll keep her safe,' he said. He threw open the door and went out.

AFTER GUY LEFT, I led Tamasin home. Barak arrived with baggage from the Barge and I installed them both in a room upstairs. I told my housekeeper, Joan, that Tamasin had been attacked by someone we were investigating, and that I had sent the gatekeeper to ask Harsnet for some protection.

Harsnet responded to my message with commendable speed. Not long after first light the next day, a man arrived from him, a muscular fellow of around thirty. He told me he was Philip Orr, one of the Westminster constables, and had taken on the job of watching the house. Orr told me the coroner wished to question Dean Benson of Westminster Cathedral at once about his former infirmarian and his assistants. He asked Barak and me to accompany him, saying he would meet us by the abbey gatehouse at eight thirty.

The coroner was already standing by the ancient gate when Barak and I arrived. He nodded as we approached, and I began by thanking him for sending Orr to my house.

'The women must be protected. And if the rogue does try to gain entry, we have a chance to catch him. Orr is a good man. I hope your wife is not too badly hurt, Barak.' His face softened with what seemed genuine concern.

'A bit of rest and she'll be all right.'

'But what exactly happened?'

I told Harsnet about the attack on Tamasin. He set his lips. 'How can that have happened? We must talk further after we have seen the dean.'

'And you, sir?' I asked him. 'Have the neighbouring coroners reported any . . . any horrific murders like our three?'

'None. And we are still in the dark as to how our killer got to know those men, why he chose them.' He sighed. 'Well, let us see what Dean Benson has to say.' He led the way under the gate into the old monastic precinct.

It was ringed with a mixture of fine houses and poor tenements, home to criminals of all sorts, all paying profitable rents to the monks. We walked past St Margaret's Church and the huge old bell tower, then turned into the southern precinct, where there were more houses, mainly poor tenements for pedlars and jobbing workers. To our left a high wall separated off the inner precinct; the gates that had once sheltered the monks' comfortable lives from the world stood open, though a guard with a pike stood outside. Harsnet told him who he was and we were allowed through the gateway, into a yard full of monastic buildings in the course of demolition or conversion. We walked to a large attractive house that stood amid the ruination in a little crocus-filled garden of its own. Harsnet knocked at the door.

A servant answered and bade us enter. He asked Barak to wait in an anteroom, and ushered Harsnet and me into an office furnished with rich hangings and dominated by an enormous oak table strewn with papers.

The door opened, and a short man in white cleric's robes entered. We exchanged brief bows, and he took a seat behind the table.

'Please, gentlemen, be seated,' he said in mellifluous tones.

I studied William Benson, the last abbot of the monastery, a monk who went over to Cromwell and had been put in the abbot's place to hasten the Dissolution. The deanery of the new cathedral was his reward. A stocky man nearing fifty, he had an air of contentment, ambition achieved.

'What can I do to aid the archbishop?' he asked.

Harsnet spoke first. 'It is a most secret matter, sir. The archbishop charges that nothing be said outside these walls.'

'Nor will it be. My duty is to obey my superior,' Benson said, smiling.

'I fear it is a very disturbing story,' I added.

Benson gave a throaty chuckle. 'I have laboured in God's English vineyard for many years. Nothing disturbs me now.'

I watched to see whether his detached expression would change as Harsnet told of the murders and the prophecies in Revelation. It did not.

'And you think the man may be a former monk?' Benson shook his head. 'I think not. Most of the monks accepted the Dissolution quite happily.'

'How many monks were there at the Dissolution?' I asked.

'Twenty-four. Not all the older brethren were happy with what happened. But they were realists, mostly. All signed the surrender.'

'What of the infirmarian, Lancelot Goddard?' Harsnet asked. 'And his assistants? There were two listed at Augmentations.'

'And do you know if Dr Goddard used dwale?' I added.

'Used what?' I thought he answered a little too quickly; something sparked for a moment in his sleepy eyes.

I explained what the drug was, and he sat thinking.

At length he raised his eyes to meet our faces. 'I do not know whether Dr Goddard used dwale. I left the infirmary to him.' He paused. 'I will give you what help I can, gentlemen. But I think you are wrong. Whoever this . . . abomination is, I do not believe he is from here.'

'What of Dr Goddard's helpers?'

'Charles Cantrell worked in the monks' infirmary. Francis Lockley in the lay infirmary, for poor men of Westminster. Goddard trained them both.'

'Goddard has disappeared from his lodgings,' Harsnet told him. 'Have you any idea where he might have gone?'

Benson shook his head. 'I am afraid not. I do not remember who his family were. And most of our records were destroyed.'

'Yes.' I knew that was true; most of the monastic records had been burnt along with their illustrated books during the Dissolution.

'What sort of man was Dr Goddard to deal with?'

'Not difficult. Correct, self-contained.' He smiled. 'He had a disfigurement, a large mole on the side of his nose. I think he was conscious of it. He would seem angry if people looked at it. Some said he had no warmth towards the sick. But perhaps a doctor has to be detached.'

As you are, I thought. Benson hadn't cared about the monks; they were pawns in the game of Dissolution. He was hiding something, I felt sure.

He gave his thin smile again. 'I remember his assistant in the lay infirmary, Brother Lockley, used to mock Goddard's cold, precise speech.'

'And the other assistant?' I asked. 'Cantrell.'

'Ah, yes, young Brother Cantrell. Goddard trained him up, but he never seemed satisfied with him, I recall.'

'How strong were these men?' I asked. 'Our man is strong, and clever too.'

The dean laughed. 'I think you may discount both the assistants. Neither showed any great brains or muscle. Lockley is a small, round man in his fifties with a taste for the bottle. Young Cantrell was a tall and stringy fellow. He had trouble with his eyes. Goddard found he was short-sighted and got him some glasses so he could do his work.' He raised a finger. 'I remember now, Cantrell lives in the precinct outside here; his father was a carpenter. I saw him some time ago in the street and remember thinking he would have trouble carrying on his father's trade. Cut his fingers off likely as not.'

Harsnet looked at me. 'We should see those two men, Master Shardlake. Barak has the addresses?'

'He does.'

'Good. Then we will leave you, Dean. But we may call on you again.'

'Of course.' Benson gave a puzzled smile. 'You believe this man will commit seven murders? To fulfil the prophecy of the seven vials in Revelation?'

'Yes, sir,' I answered. 'He has only reached the third vial as yet.'

Benson shook his head. 'Then I pray you soon catch him.'

WE COLLECTED BARAK and went outside. 'It might be interesting to take a look around,' I suggested. 'At the chapter house, perhaps.'

Harsnet nodded. 'Very well. But let us first find somewhere to talk.'

We picked our way carefully over rubble, heading for the cloister.

'What did you think of Benson?' I asked Harsnet.

'A greedy careerist.' Harsnet frowned. 'It is sad that Lord Cromwell had to use such people in the cause of reform. It disillusioned many people.'

We entered the old cloister, and sat down on a bench.

'I think Dean Benson knows more than he allowed,' I said.

Harsnet nodded. 'I agree.' He shook his head, sighing deeply. 'Is Goddard the man we seek, or another victim, or neither?'

'It is over two months since he disappeared. I think if he had been a victim he would have been found by now.'

'But where has he gone?' Harsnet frowned. 'The dean should have known. Had he no care for the monks he led?'

'He was just a political appointment,' Barak ventured.

Harsnet looked at him and nodded. I was glad he seemed to respect Barak. 'Yes,' he agreed. 'That is true. But we must find him somehow.'

'Well, whoever the killer is, he has found us,' Barak added grimly. 'Found my wife.' He looked down and clenched his hands.

'I think he marked us that day out at the marshes,' I said.

Harsnet shook his head. 'What sort of man could lie out on there all day? Such patience, such endurance, it seems . . . not human.'

I knew he was thinking of possession. I hesitated for a long moment, then told them both of Guy's theory about obsessive madness, about the case he had mentioned. Harsnet listened carefully, then shook his head.

'That Frenchman sounds to me as though he *was* possessed. As this man does. I am sorry, Serjeant Shardlake, but I do not trust Dr Malton. I feel he still cleaves to his old loyalties. And with Bishop Bonner showing as much mercy to Protestants as a butcher shows to the poor lambs at Eastcheap, you must forgive me if I am still dubious about his involvement.'

Barak turned to us, his eyes suddenly fierce. 'Whether he's possessed or mad, that doesn't answer the question of why he's doing this.'

'I wonder if we should be looking for him among the radical Protestant sects,' I said, looking Harsnet firmly in the eye. 'This man seems to think he has a mission from God to kill lapsed radicals.'

'Or wants us to think that,' Harsnet answered.

'Either way, he knew the religious past of Dr Gurney and Tupholme and my poor friend Roger,' I insisted. 'The three had nothing else in common.'

Harsnet sighed, then nodded. 'Very well, I will see some gentle enquiries are made. Now, let us take a look at the chapter house. I expect it will be full of papist imagery.'

WE ASKED a clerk where the chapter house was located. He pointed us to a heavy oak door, which stood ajar. We passed inside down a short passage into one of the most extraordinary rooms I have ever seen. It was enormous, octagonal, and lit by huge stained-glass windows. Statues of the Virgin and St Peter stood guarding the entrance. But what transfixed all three of us were the panels beneath the windows, brightly painted and embossed with gold leaf, showing scenes from Revelation. There were scores of them, the whole story, in unsparing, vivid colour: St John, Christ in Judgment, the flaming pit of Hell, the beast with seven heads and ten horns, and the seven angels, pouring their vials of wrath upon a world red with torment.

We stood in silence, turning on our heels to survey the great panorama of destruction. The style of the paintings was that of two hundred years ago, the figures lacking the realistic fluidity we had achieved in these latter days. But it was vivid and terrifying nonetheless.

'The Westminster monks saw this,' I said quietly. 'Goddard, Lockley, Cantrell. Every day, in chapter. This could eat into a man's soul.' I looked at Harsnet. 'Is this what the dean was hiding from us? Did he remember this panorama, perhaps the effect it had on someone?'

Harsnet set his lips. 'That we shall discover. I shall see the dean again tomorrow. Can you talk to the other two ex-monks before then?'

'I will,' I said. 'After court today, if I may.'

He nodded agreement. 'And I shall send word to the Common Council of London; someone there may know of Goddard's family.'

Harsnet cast a last look of distaste round the chamber, then led the way out. I paused at a panel showing a grim-faced angel, winged and clad in white, pouring liquid onto an earth that was turned to fire.

'The fourth vial,' I murmured to Barak. 'Dear God, I hope we catch him before he butchers someone else.'

WE WALKED BACK with Harsnet to the main gate. The southern precinct had come to life now, the shops busy, people milling around. Seeing us, a couple of pedlars hurried over. One carried a tray full of old jars, the stink of their contents reaching us from yards away. 'Oil from the great fish, masters,' he called. 'Full of magical properties!' Barak waved him away.

As we headed into the gate leading out of the precinct, we saw there was a melee outside one of the shops. A middle-aged man and his wife, both looking frightened, stood outside between two parish constables. Two more constables were heaving battered chests from inside the shop. It seemed to contain a variety of outlandish costumes. The crowd that had gathered looked sour and hostile; among them were a couple of women with weather-beaten faces, passing a leather bottle between them and laughing.

'No books yet,' the constable searching through the chest said.

'We've no forbidden books,' the shopkeeper pleaded. 'All we do is supply costumes for plays. It's our livelihood. Please—'

'Aye,' the constable beside them said. 'For companies that perform John Bale's plays, and other heretical rubbish.'

'They're bringing the purge to Westminster too,' Harsnet muttered.

'I must get to court,' I said, shoving a way through the growing crowd. I did not want to get involved in what could turn into a nasty scene. A ragged youth stepped in front of me. 'Get out of my way!' I said irritably.

'Yah! Hunchbacked crow!' he shouted.

Just as we pushed through the edge of the crowd I felt a sharp pain on my upper left arm. At the same moment, I heard my name spoken, faintly, a whisper. 'Shardlake.' I cried out and put my other hand to my arm. It came away covered with blood. Harsnet and Barak turned as I cried out once more. I lifted the sleeve of my robe, which was torn, to reveal a long rip in my doublet. Blood was seeping through it.

'I've been stabbed,' I said, feeling suddenly faint.

'Take off your robe,' Barak said briskly. His eyes darted over the crowd, but it was impossible to see who had done this in the melee.

Passers-by looked on curiously as I did as I was bid.

Barak opened the rip in my upper hose wide, then whistled. 'That's some cut. Lucky he missed the artery.' He took his dagger and cut my ruined robe into strips. Then he wrapped the strips round my upper arm, making a tourniquet. 'Let's get you to the courthouse; then I'll send for Dr Malton.'

We staggered across Gatehouse Yard into Westminster Hall. Harsnet spoke to the guard and I was helped into a side room, where I sat on a bench.

'Go to the Clerk of Requests,' I said to Barak. 'Tell him I have been injured. Ask for today's cases to be adjourned. Then go to Guy. It's all right, the bleeding's much less,' I added. 'Hurry, now.'

'I will stay with him,' Harsnet said. Barak nodded and left.

'It was him.' I clenched my teeth at a sharp stab of pain from my arm. 'He went for Tamasin, and now he has gone for me. It is another warning.'

'But how could he know where you would be today?'

'You did not tell Cranmer you were meeting me? Or the Seymours?'

'No. There was not time last night.' He looked suddenly frightened.

'Dear God, what powers has the devil lent this creature?'

My tired brain could see no rational way to answer him, to account for this man's ability to hound us unseen. Suddenly I felt giddy. I closed my eyes, and I must have fainted, for the next thing I knew I opened my eyes to find the boy Piers standing over me. Guy and Barak were beside him.

'You passed out,' Guy said. 'It was the shock.' He took a pair of scissors and cut away my doublet and shirt. A deep gash, three inches long, ran below my shoulder. 'I am going to put an unguent on it that hinders infection,' he said. 'Then we must stitch you up. It will be painful, I am afraid.'

'Do what is needed,' I answered. 'Barak, have you been to the court?'

'I told the office you were taken ill. The judge has agreed to hand your cases over. The other Requests barrister will take some of them.'

'Good. I must attend Adam Kite's hearing on the fourth, though. That is too delicate a matter to hand to someone else.'

Guy patted my arm. 'Let's stitch you up. Piers will do it. Do not worry; he has done it many times now. I will supervise.'

The boy approached, holding a thin, sharp needle to which black thread was already attached. He smiled. 'I will be gentle, sir,' he said quietly, then brought the needle down to pierce my flesh.

Two HOURS LATER I was back home, lying on cushions in my parlour.

Barak sat beside me. 'How could the killer have known we were at Westminster today?' he wondered aloud.

I shook my head. 'Knew we were due at court, perhaps. But how would he know which court I worked at?' I bit the side of my finger. 'Unless someone is helping him, telling him our movements.'

'Thomas Seymour?' Barak asked, narrowing his eyes. 'I don't trust him.'

'No. Seymour wants him caught. But I believe someone may be helping him, with legal information and perhaps medical information too.' I sighed. 'I think he spends his whole life planning, waiting. Endlessly, obsessively, working toward the next time he will break free of all restraints and kill wildly. And make a spectacle, for that is what he likes.'

'He's taking a hell of a risk, attacking you in public. But in that crowd he could have killed you. He could have killed Tamasin too.' Barak's voice ended on a gulp and I saw how the whole thing had harrowed him to the core. 'Why didn't he?' he asked. 'It's as though he's taunting us.'

I sighed. 'Whoever he is, I pray we catch him before someone else dies horribly.' I frowned. 'Before he shows us again how clever he is, for—'

We were interrupted by a frantic knocking at the door, then urgent voices, Joan's and a man's. Barak and I looked at each other.

'He's struck again,' I breathed.

But when the door opened it was Daniel Kite who stood there.

'Sir!' he said. 'You must come! Adam has escaped. He's got himself on top of London Wall, out by Bishopsgate. He's calling on the crowds to repent, to forsake the priests and come to God! They'll burn him this time!'

IT WAS A MILE and a half to Bishopsgate, a painful walk through the London throng, my arm in its sling throbbing at every jolt. Daniel and Minnie strode on as fast as possible. I had sent Barak to fetch Guy, with a pang of conscience at disturbing him again.

As we walked up All Hallows Street we heard the murmur of a crowd and shouts of laughter. A moment later, Adam came into view. Dressed in his filthy rags, his hair matted and his eyes wild, he was standing on top of the crumbling city wall, shouting down at the crowd that had gathered thirty feet below. He was standing fifty yards out from Bishopsgate Tower; somehow he must have got to the top of the gatehouse and clambered out.

'You *must* come to Christ!' he bawled at the crowd. 'You *must*, you must ensure you are one of the elect! The end is coming, the Antichrist is here! Please, you must pray!'

I saw Reverend Meaphon in the crowd. We shouldered our way over to him. Another cleric stood beside him, a tall, thin fellow with white hair.

Minnie clasped Meaphon's arm. 'Oh, sir, you came! Thank you.'

Meaphon turned to me, clearly frightened. 'He has to be got down,' he said urgently. 'If he's taken I will be questioned, the whole congregation will!'

'And mine!' the other cleric said. 'I am William Yarington, rector of the next church to Reverend Meaphon's. That mad boy should have been kept locked away, someone praying with him all the time.' He glared at Meaphon.

'He manages enough prayers by himself,' I snapped. I turned to Meaphon. 'Have you tried speaking with him?' I asked.

'Yes, yes! I have ordered him down, told him to stop his shouting. I said he could put his parents in danger. But he won't listen.'

'It might be better for everyone if he fell and broke his neck,' the white-haired cleric muttered.

Minnie broke down and was sobbing on her husband's breast.

'Do something, sir,' Daniel implored me. 'Please!'

There was a fresh gust of laughter from the crowd. Some wretch had brought a dancing bear to entertain the crowd. Its keeper thwacked it on the nose, called 'Dance!' and the poor creature began to shift from leg to leg.

'Here!' someone called up to Adam. 'You dance too!'

Two middle-aged men in the robes of the Cutlers Guild were standing next to me. 'This is blasphemy,' one said angrily. 'The Common Council should be fetched. He should be imprisoned, punished for this display.'

'You are right, brother!' someone called out. 'You have the spirit in you!' The crowd saw this as a spectacle, a joke. But it could turn nasty.

I stepped to the front of the crowd, directly underneath Adam, and looked up at him. 'Adam,' I called. 'Please come down! Your mother is sore upset!'

He looked down at me, then shifted his gaze to the crowd. 'The world is ending!' he yelled. 'The Antichrist is here! If you do not deny Satan and come to Jesus, you will all burn! Burn!'

I felt an angry despair. I might as well try talking to a brick wall.

There was a murmur behind me. Some men were shouldering their way through the crowd. A moment later Bishop Bonner, surrounded by his guards, appeared. The crowd stepped away and he moved through, short and stocky and powerful, leaving only me, the Kites and Meaphon exposed.

Above us, Adam had started declaiming a garbled paraphrase of Revelation: '*The fearful, and unbelieving, and whoremongers and sorcerers, shall have their part in the lake that burneth with fire and brimstone . . .*'

'Cease that blasphemy!' Bonner's thunderous roar silenced the crowd and made even Adam pause. The bishop turned his furious eyes on me. 'Who are you, lawyer? And you . . .?' His gaze turned to Meaphon. 'Oh, I know you, sir. You are a leader of the mad, giddy company of schismatics.'

'It's not his fault, sir.' Daniel Kite spoke up bravely. 'He was trying to talk Adam down. Our son. He is mad, sir, stark mad—'

'*Jesus will come with sword in hand.*' Adam had begun again.

Bonner turned to the soldiers. 'You! Go up through the gatehouse, bring him down. If he falls, it'll be no loss.'

The soldiers approached the wall, then paused, as three figures stepped through an upper window of the gatehouse onto the wall. Guy, Barak and Piers. They moved slowly along the wall towards Adam. The crowd fell silent.

'Come, Adam,' Guy called. 'Remember me. Remember we talked?'

The boy stared at him foolishly. Barak and Piers were almost next to Adam. They looked at him dubiously, fear in their faces. If they tried to grasp Adam, he could bring all three down.

'Why are you doing this?' Guy asked.

To my surprise, Adam answered him. 'I thought if I could bring others to God, it would prove I was saved.'

'But not all who are saved can be messengers to the world.' Guy waved at the crowd. 'See, look at those people. You are not strong enough to convert that heathen crowd. It is no shame.'

Adam began to cry then, and sank slowly to his knees. Some lumps of old dislodged mortar pattered down on the crowd. Barak and Piers eased him carefully to his feet and with difficulty led him back along the wall and through the window of the gatehouse. Guy stepped in after them.

Bonner walked toward the gatehouse, the guard following. Daniel and Minnie stepped after him. Meaphon hesitated a moment, then disappeared into the crowd. Cowardice, or the realisation that his presence would only anger Bonner? Then I tensed. I felt someone watching me, caught the merest glimpse out of the corner of my eye. Someone with a beard. I whirled round. I saw a figure turn away into the crowd, a glimpse of a brown doublet. My heart thumped. Was it him, following again? I stood rooted to the spot.

'Master Shardlake, please, help us!' Minnie Kite's voice. I turned away.

Adam had emerged from the gatehouse onto the street. Guy and Barak each held one of his arms, for he was trying to drop to the ground again. His eyes were closed and his lips moved in silent prayer.

Bonner planted himself in front of Adam, arms akimbo. 'What did you think you were doing, boy?' he thundered.

Adam ignored him, praying even now.

Bonner reddened. 'Answer, boy, or you will find yourself in the fire.'

'Slave of the Roman harlot!' someone shouted out from the crowd. Bonner turned, frowning mightily. 'Traitor!' someone else called out. This time there was a murmur of approval from the crowd. The soldiers took a firm hold on their pikes. The mood was beginning to turn.

Minnie stepped forward. She fell on her knees before Bonner, grasped the hem of his robe. 'Please, sir,' she said. 'My son is mad. Sick in his mind. The Privy Council sent him to the Bedlam. He must have escaped.'

Bonner was quite unmoved. 'I heard of that decision. The Privy Council was wrong. This display shows your son to be a wild heretic.' He glared round at us. 'I will shortly make matters so hot for you people, you will wish yourselves gathered into God.'

I stepped forward. 'Sir, he *is* mad,' I said. I waved at Guy. 'This man is his doctor, he will certify it. I have been unhappy with the boy's security, his care at the Bedlam. The matter is before the Court of Requests.'

Bonner looked curiously at Guy. 'So you are Dr Malton,' he said. 'I have heard of you. The ex-monk. Why are you working with these heretics?'

Guy was at his diplomatic best. 'The Privy Council decided he was mad, my lord, not a heretic. I believe he is indeed mad and I hope he may be cured. Brought to his right thinking,' he added meaningfully.

One of the guards leaned over and whispered something to Bonner. He looked over at the crowd, then back at Guy and me. 'Very well,' he said. 'But I shall keep myself informed on his progress.' He turned to me. 'As for you, lawyer, make sure he is kept safely locked up. I might not be so accommodating next time.' He gave me a stern nod and walked away.

'Well done,' I breathed to Guy.

He gave me a sombre look. 'I think he realised that if he were to burn a boy a doctor had certified mad, London would be even more against him than it was with Mekins. But he will not forget. Adam *must* be kept secure.'

'Are we taking him back to the Bedlam?' Barak asked.

'Yes,' I said, 'though I fear Keeper Shawms allowed Adam to escape on purpose. But come on. It is a short walk.'

We set off, Daniel and Minnie following behind. The crowd stared after us, sorry to be deprived of their entertainment.

Chapter 7

It was late afternoon by the time I left the Bedlam. Adam was safe in his cell, but I was exhausted and I had not eaten since breakfast. Barak was waiting for me in the parlour; it was a moment before I remembered he and Tamasin had moved in.

'A message from Harsnet,' he said. 'He's still trying to trace Goddard. He wants us to meet him tomorrow night to report on those two ex-monks.'

'All right,' I said. 'We will go and visit them tomorrow, after court. There is a case I must attend myself in the morning, but the afternoon is free, until five, when Roger is buried. The funeral is at St Bride's Church, down by the river. It is to be quiet, only friends and relatives. Samuel will be home now.' I massaged my arm. 'We can see the ex-monk who lives at Westminster first, then ride out to the other one . . . Where is he?'

'Up at the Charterhouse, beyond Smithfield.'

'I am going to get something to eat before I go to bed. How is Tamasin?'

'She's sleeping. Her teeth have been hurting her. She's going to the tooth-drawer tomorrow.'

'Go up to her. I will see you in the morning.'

NEXT MORNING Barak and I rode down to Westminster. I felt safer riding, above the crowd and better able to watch it. My arm throbbed, but less than yesterday. I had to admit Piers had made a good job of his stitching. Barak had been quiet at breakfast and Tamasin had not made an appearance.

'It was brave of you to go out on London Wall yesterday,' I said.

'It was the old Moor. He just clambered out without a thought, the boy Piers going after him. He's got guts, I'll give him that. I felt I had to follow.'

I looked at him. 'He was there, you know. Our killer. I caught a glimpse of him, turning into the crowd, when you were in the gatehouse.'

'What did you see?'

'A glimpse of a brown doublet. He was tall, I think.'

'Might just have been someone in the crowd leaving.'

'I don't think so. I . . . I felt it. I feel he has me marked.'

I spent the morning at court; then we rode down into Westminster, moving slowly through the busy streets, and into the southern precinct.

Barak looked round the buildings. 'The record said he lived on the same street as the White Oak Inn. See, it's over there.' He pointed to a small, two-storey house in poor repair. There was a large door, locked and padlocked. *Adrian Cantrell, Carpenter* was painted above it in faded letters.

I knocked on the door. There was no answer, and I was about to knock again when I heard shuffling footsteps from within. The door opened to reveal a gaunt young man in his mid-twenties. He wore a scuffed leather jerkin over a shirt that was in sore need of a wash. His face was thin, framed by a shock of straw-coloured hair, and he wore wood-framed spectacles, the glass so thick his eyes were like blue watery pools.

'Are you Charles Cantrell?' I asked.

'Aye.'

I smiled to put him at ease. 'I have come on behalf of the King's assistant coroner. We hoped you might be able to help us. May we come in?'

'If you like.' The young man led us up a dim corridor into a parlour.

The room had only a table of rough planks and some hard stools for furniture. Through a dusty window we saw a yard, containing a small shed. Cantrell waved us to the stools, sat down on one himself and faced us.

'I understand you were an assistant in the monks' infirmary at Westminster,' I said. 'Before the Dissolution. We are seeking information on your master, Dr Goddard. Do you know where he is?'

Cantrell gave a short, bitter laugh. 'As though he'd keep in touch with me. He treated me like a louse. I was glad I'd never see him again.' He paused. 'Has he killed a patient? It wouldn't be the first time.'

'What?' I stared at him. 'What do you mean?'

Cantrell shrugged. 'There were one or two he sent to their rest before their time through bad treatment.'

'You know this for sure?' I asked.

He shrugged again. 'There was nothing I could do; Abbot Benson wouldn't have listened to me. Besides—you didn't cross Goddard.'

'You were frightened of him?' Barak asked.

'You didn't cross him.' The boy licked his lips nervously.

'We have spoken to Abbot Benson,' I said. 'He told us Goddard got you some glasses. You have problems in seeing?'

'Yes. He didn't want the trouble of training someone else up.' I caught a bitter note in Cantrell's voice. 'Not when the abbey was soon to go down.'

'How came you to work in the infirmary?'

He shrugged. 'Goddard wanted someone to train up and I was the only young monk there. I didn't mind; it was better than copying old texts, which is what I did before.'

'Tell me about Dr Goddard,' I said. 'What he did that killed his patients.'

Cantrell considered. 'Dr Goddard was an impatient man. He used to do all the operations himself—it cost money to bring in the barber-surgeon— and sometimes he gave patients a big dose of some stuff that sends you to sleep; they slept through the operation all right but some never woke up.'

'This medicine, was it called dwale?'

'Yes, sir.' He looked surprised that we knew.

'Surely if you thought the doctor was hastening people out of the world, you should have spoken.'

Cantrell shifted uncomfortably. 'I wasn't sure, sir. I'm no doctor. He would have talked his way out of it, and I'd just have got into trouble. And you don't know what he was like.' He hesitated. 'What has he done, sir?'

'I am afraid I cannot say. Your eyes, they are still weak?'

'Even with the glasses I can hardly see. When I left the monastery I went to work for my father, but I was no good. After he died I gave up the business.' He looked at an inner door. 'That was his workshop. Do you want to see?'

I looked at Barak. He shrugged. I stood up.

'Thank you for your help,' I said. 'If you think of anything that might help us, I can be reached at Lincoln's Inn.' I hesitated, then added, 'I am sorry for the trouble with your eyes. Have you ever seen a doctor?'

'I have little faith in doctors, sir.' His mouth twisted in a sardonic smile. 'After my time with Dr Goddard. You understand.'

OUTSIDE, I SHOOK my head. 'I don't think young Cantrell stirs much from that house,' I said.

'Shouldn't think there was ever much go in him,' said Barak, 'even if he could see properly.'

'No. But he damns Goddard, more than ever.'

'Now all we have to do is find him. Let's hope Lockley is more help.'

We rode up to Smithfield through a countryside coming to life after the winter, the cattle out in the meadows again after months indoors. We reached the great empty square—it was not a market day—and rode on, up Charterhouse Lane and under the stone arch leading into Charterhouse Square. A ragged little group of beggars sat huddled outside the old chapel that stood at its centre. To the north, beyond a low redbrick wall, lay the buildings of the Charterhouse, whose monks had defied the King over the break from Rome. Most had been brutally executed as a result. I had heard that the King's Italian musicians, whom he had recently brought over at great expense, were lodging in the buildings now.

As with all the monastic houses, the monks had rented out land in their precinct. On this side of the square the dwellings were small wooden affairs, but opposite was a row of fine stone and brick houses. I had heard that the best one, a large redbrick mansion with tall chimneys, belonged to Lord Latimer, and now therefore to his widow, Catherine Parr. As I watched, a horseman in red livery galloped into the drive, raising clouds of dust. More pressure from the King?

Barak brought me back to earth, pointing to a sign dangling over a ramshackle old building nearby. 'There's our place. The Green Man.'

We knocked on the tavern door and waited. A powerfully built woman opened it. She wore a stained apron over a creased dress and a white coif from which tendrils of black hair escaped. Her grey eyes were sharp and intelligent in a face that showed the remnants of past beauty.

'We're not open till five,' she said.

'We don't want a drink,' I said. 'We are looking for Francis Lockley.'

She gave us a sharp, suspicious look. 'What do you want with him?'

'Some private business.' I smiled. 'He is not in any trouble.'

She hesitated, then said, 'I suppose you'd better come in.'

We found ourselves in a medium-sized tavern, with whitewashed walls and tables and chairs scattered across a rush-strewn floor.

'Do you work here?' I asked.

'I own the place. Ethel Bunce, widow and licensee of this parish, at your service,' she added sardonically.

'Oh.'

'Francis!' she called loudly.

A serving hatch in the wall opened, and a short, fat man with a bald head peered out. 'Yes, chick?' He caught sight of us, and his eyes narrowed.

'These gents want a word. What have you been up to?' She laughed as she said this, but her look at us was as uneasy as the fat man's.

Lockley emerged through a side door. He was a little barrel of a man, a powerful physique run to seed, but still strong-looking.

'We have come from the King's assistant coroner. We seek the whereabouts of the former Brother Goddard of Westminster Abbey.'

Lockley pressed his lips together. 'That old shit Goddard?'

'You did not like him?'

'Treated me like dirt. Because my father was a potman. As I am now,' he added, glancing up at the widow with a look that was hard to read.

She laid a hand over his. 'You're more to me than that, sweet.'

'We are questioning those who worked with Goddard in the infirmary. We have spoken with young Master Cantrell, and with the dean.'

Lockley laughed nervously. 'Young Charlie, eh? He had a bad time with Goddard.'

'Have you any idea where Dr Goddard may be now?'

Lockley shook his head. 'Haven't seen him since the day we all left the abbey. Nor wanted to.' He hesitated. 'May I ask why you are seeking him?'

'We are investigating a death.'

'Whose?' he asked. His whole body seemed to tense again.

'I may not say. Tell me, did Dr Goddard use a drug called dwale?'

One of Lockley's hands clenched. 'I knew Dr Goddard used something to make his patients sleep if he had to operate on them in the monks' infirmary. But he wouldn't have wasted anything like that on the sick in the lay infirmary where I worked.' He shrugged. 'He wasn't much interested in what went on there. Mostly he left that to me.'

I nodded slowly. 'Tell me more about what you thought of Dr Goddard.'

'He had a high opinion of himself. Though I dare say all doctors are alike in that. He could be very sharp and rude.'

'What was your background?' Barak asked.

'I was an apprentice to a barber-surgeon for ten years before I went to Westminster. Then I worked with one again afterwards. But he was one of those hot-gospellers. They're even worse than the old papist bunch, puffed up because they think they have the keys to Hell and death.'

'So you came here, to me,' Mistress Bunce said, squeezing his hand. 'To find rest.'

Lockley did not respond to her gesture; instead he gave me an angry look. 'Maybe neither the radicals nor the papists have it right; maybe the heathen Turks do.' He laughed bitterly. He was not a man at ease in his mind.

'Now, chick,' Mistress Bunce said warningly, casting us a nervous glance. 'He says things without thinking. You don't mean it, do you?'

A sudden rumbling came from under the tavern, and I felt the stone flags tremble. From somewhere far below came the sound of rushing water.

'What's that?' Barak asked, startled, as I was.

Lockley smiled faintly. 'Like most of the buildings round the monastery, we're connected to the old sewer that was built to drain the Charterhouse. It runs under the cellar. Water flushes down from springs up at Islington Fields.'

'Yes.' The widow took the chance to move the conversation away from religion. 'All the tavern's waste goes through a cellar hatch into the sewer. The only thing is, the watchman of the Charterhouse is a drunkard and has to be reminded to open the lock gates, or the water builds up, then rushes through, like just now.'

Lockley got up. 'Well, sir, we must get back to work. I am sorry I could not help you more.'

I hesitated, then rose too. 'Thank you, sir. If you think of anything else, please contact me. Master Shardlake, at Lincoln's Inn.'

'I will.' He looked relieved the interview was over.

'I'll see you out.' Mistress Bunce accompanied us to the door. 'I'm sorry for his words about religion, sir,' she said quietly. 'Francis has found life outside the abbey hard. I knew that love and care and something to do could help him.' She looked at me, her bossy manner gone. 'He doesn't drink now, but he says bitter things.'

'Do not worry, goodwife,' I said gently. 'I have no interest in Goodman Lockley's beliefs.'

WE RODE AWAY from the tavern deep in thought. Barak broke the silence.

'He was hiding something, wasn't he?'

'I think he was. Something about Goddard.'

'I might have forced it out of him.'

'No. That's Harsnet's job. I'll tell him tonight.'

The sun was setting as we returned to my house. I was tired, my arm sore whenever I moved it. I could have done with an evening at home resting, but I was due at the chapel for the funeral.

Tamasin was lying on a pile of cushions in the parlour when we went in. Her eyes were less puffy, but her face was still bruised and her mouth swollen.

'How are you, chick?' Barak asked.

'Sore. My mouth hurts.' Her voice was a mumble, and when she opened her mouth I saw her cheeks were padded with bloodstained cotton.

'Could have been worse,' he said. 'The teeth were at the side. You'll still have your pretty smile.'

'Oh, that's all right, then,' she said sarcastically.

'I didn't mean—'

Tamasin looked at me. 'Do you know what the tooth-drawer said? He told me his fee would be five shillings, but that he'd waive it and give me ten shillings if I'd let him take out all my teeth. Said they'd make a good false set for rich folk.' She shuddered. 'Ugh. He was a vile man.'

'You should go to bed, Tamasin,' I said. 'Rest.'

'Are you going to Master Elliard's funeral, sir?' she asked.

'Yes. I am accompanying Dorothy. When I come back, Barak, we shall have a quick supper, then go to meet Harsnet at St Agatha's.' I glanced at Tamasin.

'I'll be all right,' she said pointedly. But she looked furious.

FOR THE FIRST TIME since Roger's death, Dorothy was dressed in her best. Beside her stood a slim, dark lad of eighteen, handsome in his black doublet, whose resemblance to his father was so close it took my breath away.

'Samuel,' Dorothy said, 'you will not remember Master Shardlake. You were but a child when we moved to Bristol.'

The boy bowed to me. 'I remember you, sir. You brought me a spinning top for my birthday. It was very brightly coloured. I thought it a marvel.'

'Yes,' I said with a laugh. 'I remember. You have a good memory.'

'I do for kindnesses, yes. I must thank you, for all you have done for my mother.' He laid a hand on Dorothy's.

'She has been very brave.'

'Is Samuel not the very image of Roger? It comforts me that Roger lives on in my son. But, Matthew, you hold your arm strangely. What's wrong?'

How observant she was. 'A careless accident. It is not serious. Will you stay in London long, Samuel?'

He shook his head. 'I must go back to Bristol next week. I am hoping that when matters are . . . settled, my mother may come and join me there.'

'Oh.' I had not thought she might go so soon. The news disconcerted me.

'My son is engaged, Matthew,' she said quietly. 'What do you think of that? To a Bristol merchant's daughter.'

'Congratulations,' I said.

Samuel blushed. 'Thank you, sir. We hope to marry next year.'

There was a knock at the door. Margaret came in. 'The coffin is here,' she said quietly to Dorothy.

'I will see them,' she said, and left the room.

There was an awkward silence for a moment, then Samuel asked, 'Is there any more news, sir? Of the investigation? It eats away at Mother, not knowing why my father was killed in that awful way.'

'We are making progress, Samuel. I cannot say much now, but if it helps I may tell you that we believe your father was not killed from malice against him. I think he attracted the attention of . . . let us say, of a madman.'

'But why is it so secret?' the boy burst out.

I hesitated, then spoke cautiously. 'There was another murder like your father's. The victim was a man of some importance. Though that was not why he was killed; it was just this madman chose him too.'

'A lunatic.' Samuel frowned. 'Yes, anyone who killed a man as good as my father would have to be mad.' Suddenly there were tears in his eyes. 'Take care of Mother, sir. She says you and Margaret are her only true friends.'

'I will,' I said. 'I will.'

Dorothy reappeared in the doorway, pale, holding herself tightly. 'The other mourners are gathering outside. We must go.'

I took a deep breath and followed Samuel from the room.

ROGER WAS BURIED, laid to earth in a peaceful corner of old St Bride's churchyard. All through the service, as the priest spoke of Roger being gathered to the Lord, all I could think was that he should not have been laid there for another twenty, thirty years.

Afterwards, I left Dorothy and Samuel to have some time alone together, picked up Barak from my house, and we rode south to meet with Harsnet.

St Agatha's Church stood in a lane leading down from Thames Street to the waterfront. It was a mixed area, ancient crumbling wood-framed tenements gradually being displaced by newer, modern houses of stone. The church itself was small and very old, though looking up I saw it had a new lead roof and steeple. It was dusk when we arrived, and the wherries on the river at the bottom of the lane were just lighting their lamps.

A number of horses were tied to a rail outside the lych gate, where a little group of men stood. The men turned as we approached.

'Can I help you, gentlemen?' asked a small man with a grizzled beard.

'We have been asked to meet Coroner Harsnet here,' I told him.

At once his expression changed and became friendly, almost servile. 'Ah, yes. He is here. With Sir Thomas Seymour and Lord Hertford too.' The man swelled with pride. 'They do us a great honour by attending the reopening of our church. I am Walter Finch, churchwarden, at your service.'

We followed him through the churchyard to where more people, men and women, stood round a fire. There were merchants and guildsmen, and a smattering of people from the labouring classes who stood against the wall, looking uncomfortable. There were several clerics there; I saw Meaphon talking earnestly to a merchant. He caught my eye and nodded.

A spit had been placed over the fire, and a small boar was roasting on it. The handle was being turned by two boys at each end, white aprons over their good clothes. Nearby stood Sir Thomas Seymour and his brother, Lord Hertford, who were talking with Harsnet. Sir Thomas raised his eyebrows when he saw us, and nudged his brother.

'Master Shardlake.' Lord Hertford nodded to us as we approached. 'And this must be Jack Barak.'

'Yes, my lord.' Barak bowed.

'I remember my poor friend Thomas Cromwell speaking highly of you,' he said, a sad note in his voice.

'Any news, Shardlake?' Harsnet asked.

I told him of my interviews with Cantrell and Lockley.

He nodded. 'It looks like Goddard is our man, doesn't it?'

'It is too early to say, I think.'

'Yes, perhaps. I have been unable to find any trace of Goddard's family as yet. I am still making enquiries.'

A serving man appeared at our side, offering us platters of roast pig. The fire still burnt merrily, throwing up yellow sparks as the boar fat sizzled.

'I can smell bad fish somewhere,' Barak said.

'So can I. It must be coming from the river.' And indeed the smell of roast meat was now unpleasantly mingled with a stray fishy smell.

'Where is Reverend Yarington?' someone asked. 'He should be here.'

I winced as Sir Thomas grasped me by my bad arm. 'Harsnet says one of those ex-monks you saw lives on Charterhouse Square.'

'The lay brother, Lockley, yes. In a tavern there.'

He frowned. 'Lady Catherine Parr lives in Charterhouse.'

'Easy, Thomas,' his brother said. 'It is surely clear now there is no connection between her and the murders.'

'I would not have her near any danger.' Sir Thomas looked anxious.

'Is there any more news of the projected marriage?' I asked.

Lord Hertford glanced at his brother, then said, 'The lady still refuses to give the King an answer. She says she needs more time.'

Sir Thomas smiled, a flash of white teeth against his dark beard. 'Lady Catherine refuses because she does not want to marry him. As who would?'

'Keep your voice down,' Hertford snapped.

'I would like to go,' I said to Harsnet in a low voice. 'My arm throbs. I need rest.'

He nodded. 'Of course. I will stay here.' He looked around. 'It is strange Reverend Yarington is not here yet. I am sorry you were hurt.'

'It is getting better.'

He smiled. 'That is good. Good night.'

I shook Harsnet's hand, and turned to leave.

Suddenly a woman screamed. 'The church! The church is on fire!'

Everyone stopped eating and talking. Through one of the windows a flickering light could be seen casting strange shadows on the churchyard.

Reverend Meaphon was the first to step forward and grab the handle of the church door. 'It's locked!' he shouted. 'Who has the key?'

'Reverend Yarington!' Everyone looked around, but there was still no sign of the white-haired minister.

The churchwarden Finch stepped forward. 'I've a key! I left it at home!'

'Then go and get it, you fool!' Harsnet said, giving him a push.

Lord Hertford appeared beside us. He bent and spoke quietly to Harsnet. 'I think I should leave. There is nothing I can do, and there is going to be a scene here if the church is on fire.'

Harsnet nodded agreement. 'Aye, my lord, that may be best.'

'I am staying,' Sir Thomas said. 'I want to see this.'

His brother frowned at him, then shrugged and walked swiftly away.

A minute or two later, Finch ran back into the churchyard, a large key in his hand. He unlocked the door and half a dozen people dashed in. They stopped just inside. Someone gave a yell of terror. Sir Thomas lunged his way through the crowd, Barak and I following. We were hit by an awful stench of burning flesh, and something more: a rotting fishy smell. Inside the doorway we all stopped dead at the horrific, extraordinary sight within.

A man in a white clerical robe was chained to a stone pillar in the nave and he was on fire, blazing like a human torch in the darkness, though there was no fuel stacked around him, no visible reason why he should be burning. In the doorway someone fainted, and others sank to their knees and called out to the Lord. The heat was so intense we had to stop seven or eight feet away. I shall never forget that dreadful sight. It was Reverend Yarington who was burning there, red seared flesh showing through, blood trickling into the flames with a sizzle. He stared at us in terrible agony, and I saw he was gagged, a cloth tied round his mouth with strings.

He watched with bulging eyes as his congregation stood horror-struck. Then someone shouted, 'Water! Get water!' and three men rushed out of the church. But it was too late. As we watched, the flames engulfed Yarington's head. I gazed with horror as that proud head of white hair caught light, becoming a yellow halo for a second, then vanishing with a hiss.

'No smoke,' Harsnet said in a shaking voice beside me. 'No smoke and no fuel. This is the devil's work.'

The men who had run out returned with buckets of water and torches. They threw the water over Yarington, and the flames went out.

Sir Thomas Seymour stepped forward and looked into the burnt face. 'He's dead,' he said. He stepped back. 'Ugh, he stinks.'

I looked at Yarington's body slumped in its chains, the white clothes melted into burnt flesh. Someone turned away to vomit. It was not just the sight, but the smell, roasted flesh mixed with that stink of rotten fish. I looked at the floor. There were spots of some thick liquid there. I bent and put my finger to one of them, sniffing hesitantly.

'Fish oil,' I said. 'He was covered in it, probably the oil from those great fish that is being sold everywhere.' I turned to Harsnet. 'That was the fuel.'

The coroner looked at the body of the vicar, and quoted from the book of Revelation: '*And the fourth angel poured out his vial upon the sun; and power was given unto him to burn men with heat of fire.*'

'The killer knew we would be here,' I said. 'How could he know that?'

'Jesu, he's right,' Harsnet said. 'This spectacle was meant for the church people to see. But it cannot be coincidence that we are here too. My vicar. My poor vicar.' Tears started to his eyes.

'Taunting us,' I said bitterly. 'Again. Playing with us.'

Meaphon took off his cassock and threw it over Yarington's ruined head.

Harsnet looked round at the shocked congregation. 'Listen to me, all of you!' he said. 'I will investigate this outrage; the murderer will be caught! But until then say nothing—nothing—of what has happened here tonight! It would only give comfort to our enemies.'

There were murmurs from the crowd.

'Finch, I make you responsible for people keeping silence until I return. Bring down the minister's poor body when the chains are cool enough.' Harsnet turned back to Sir Thomas and Barak and me. 'Come, let us go to Reverend Yarington's house to see what we can discover there.'

WE WALKED a little way down the lane until we found a fine rectory. Harsnet banged loudly on the door. Flickers of light appeared at a window as someone lit a candle. A man's voice called, 'Who is it?'

'We come on Archbishop Cranmer's business,' Harsnet answered.

There was the sound of bolts being drawn back, and the door opened to reveal a small, elderly fellow. His eyes widened with fear at the sight of us.

'Is it the master?' he asked. 'Oh God, he hasn't been arrested?'

'It's not that.' Harsnet walked past the old man, and I followed him into a little hallway, doors and a staircase leading off. 'Are you his servant?'

'His steward, sir. Toby White. What has . . .?'

'Why should he be arrested?' Harsnet asked sharply.

'They say Bonner will arrest all godly men,' he answered, a little too quickly I thought. I did not like the steward; he had a mean look.

'Who else lives here?'

The servant hesitated, then said, 'Only the boy, and he's abed in the stable.'

'I am afraid I have bad news, Goodman White,' Harsnet said. 'Your master died this evening.'

The old man's eyes widened. 'Died? I didn't know where he was, I was starting to worry, but . . . dead?' He stared at us incredulously.

'When did you last see him?'

'He had a message late yesterday. He said he had to go and see a fellow cleric. He didn't say where. I thought he must have stayed overnight.'

'You knew he was going to the reopening of the church tonight?'

'Yes, sir. I thought perhaps he'd gone straight there.'

I saw the servant glance quickly at the staircase, then away again.

'Perhaps we should look over the house,' I said.

'There's nobody here,' the servant said, too quickly. 'Just me.'

Harsnet looked at him suspiciously. 'Give me that candle,' he said firmly. The old man hesitated, then handed it over.

'Stay here,' Harsnet told him. 'Barak, keep an eye on him.' The coroner inclined his head to me, and I followed him up the stairs.

The first room we looked into was a study, well-thumbed books lying among papers and quills on a big desk.

Harsnet held up a hand. 'I heard something,' he whispered. He pointed across the corridor to another door, then marched across and threw it open. A shrill scream came from within.

It was a bedroom, dominated by a feather bed. A young woman lay there, naked. She grabbed the blankets and pulled them up to her neck.

'Help!' she shouted. 'Robbers!'

'Quiet!' Harsnet snapped. 'I am the King's assistant coroner. Who are you? Are you Yarington's whore?' There was anger in his voice.

'What is your name, girl?' I asked quietly.

'Abigail, sir, Abigail Day.'

'And are you the minister's woman? There is no point in lying.'

She reddened and nodded.

Harsnet's face twisted in disgust. 'You seduced a man of God.'

'It wasn't me did the seducing,' the girl said defiantly.

'Don't bandy words with me! Do you not fear for your soul?' Harsnet was shouting now, his face filled with anger. I had grown to respect the coroner these last few days, but the terrible events of the evening were bringing out another side of him: the hard, implacable man of faith.

The girl made a spirited reply. 'Keeping body and soul together's been all I've worried about since my father was hanged.' There was bitter contempt in her voice. 'For stealing a *gentleman*'s purse. It killed my mother.'

Harsnet was unaffected. 'How long have you been here?' he snapped.

'Four months.'

'Where did Yarington pick you up?'

She hesitated. 'I was in a house down in Southwark where he used to come. We get many ministers down there,' she added boldly.

'Your master is dead,' Harsnet said bluntly. 'He was murdered.'

Abigail's mouth opened wide. 'Murdered?'

He nodded. 'Get some clothes on. I'm taking you to the archbishop's prison. There will be some more questions. Hurry. We shall be downstairs.'

Outside, he shook his head sorrowfully. 'The snares the devil sets to pull us down,' he said.

'Men are men,' I answered impatiently. 'And always will be.'

'Do you realise, Matthew, if Yarington hadn't been keeping that whore he wouldn't have died tonight? He was killed for his hypocrisy, wasn't he?'

'Yes. I think he was. I wonder if the murderer got his information through a whorehouse. Tupholme's woman was a whore, too,' I added.

Harsnet's face set hard. 'I'll find out what house this one was at.'

'Be gentle with her, please. Nothing will be served by harshness here.'

He grunted. 'We'll see.'

THE STEWARD TOBY was sitting in the kitchen, together with a scared-looking boy of around ten, ragged and smelling of the stables, with dirty brown feet. He stared at us, wide-eyed, from under a mop of brown hair.

'Who is this?' Harsnet asked.

'Timothy, sir, the stable boy,' Toby said.

'Leave us, boy,' Harsnet said.

The child turned and scurried out.

'So much for there being nobody at home,' Harsnet said sarcastically.

'He paid me well for keeping her presence quiet,' Toby replied.

'People must have seen her coming in and out,' I said.

'He only let her go abroad after dark. It was easy enough in the winter, but I wondered how he'd keep her secret now the days were getting longer. He'd probably have kicked her out soon.' Toby smiled sardonically.

'So he found the girl in the stews?'

Toby shrugged. 'I think he went there often. Funny thing, since he brought Abigail here you'd think he'd be happier, but he only ranted against sin more and more. Bad conscience, I suppose.'

'What about the boy?' I asked. 'He must have known she was here.'

'I told him to keep his mouth shut or he'd lose his place. He's an orphan and he'd end on the streets if he was kicked out of here.'

'We have reason to believe whoever killed him knew he had the girl here.'

Toby sat up, alarmed. 'I told you, I said nothing to anybody—'

'Then who else could have known?' Harsnet asked. 'Who came here?'

'No one. If he had business to conduct, he met people in the church.'

Harsnet got to his feet. 'You are coming with me, sir. You and the girl can spend a night in the Lollards' Tower, see if you remember any more.'

I rose. 'I think I'll question the stable boy,' I said.

Harsnet nodded. 'Good idea.'

I went out to a yard at the side of the house. Candlelight winking through an open door led me to the stable. The boy sat on an upturned bucket beside a straw mattress, leaning against the side of a grey mare and stroking it.

'Are you Timothy?' I asked gently.

'Yes, sir,' he whispered. 'Sir, is the master dead? Did a bad man kill him?'

'I am afraid so.'

'What is happening to Master Toby?'

'He is going with the coroner. I would like to ask you some questions.'

'Yes, sir.' Soothingly as I had spoken he still looked frightened.

'You know about Abigail, the woman who lives here?' I asked.

He did not reply.

'Were you told to keep it a secret? It does not matter now.'

'Toby said Master would beat me if I ever mentioned her name. But I'd not have told, sir. She was kind to me, for all Toby said she was a great sinner.'

'You told no one about her? You will not be punished for telling the truth.'

'No. I swear I didn't. On the Bible, sir, if you wish. I liked Abby being here. She was kind.' His eyes filled with tears.

I sensed there was something more, something he was keeping back in his fear. But if I told Harsnet of my suspicions, the boy would be dragged with the others to prison. And something within me could not do that.

'I must go now, Timothy,' I said. 'But I shall come and see you tomorrow. You will be without a place now that your master is dead. You have no family?'

'No, sir.' He sniffed. 'I will have to go a-begging.'

'Well, I shall try to find you a place. I promise I will come again tomorrow and we will talk more. For now, close the stable door and go to sleep.'

WHEN WE REACHED home, I asked Barak to have me wakened no later than first light, and wearily mounted the stairs to bed. Exhausted as I was, I could not sleep. Lying in bed in the darkness, I kept turning Yarington's terrible death over in my mind, trying to fit it into the pattern of the others.

I was sure the killer had been there when we got Adam down from London Wall. Yarington had been there too. Was that when the killer had decided that Yarington would be his next victim? No, that spectacle had been planned a long time, and Yarington's fornication with that poor girl had been known to the killer. But how, when the cleric had kept it so secret? I would see that boy tomorrow, find out if he knew anything. But first I needed to sleep.

I WAS STILL deeply asleep when Joan knocked gently at the door. I rose slowly, my back stiff and sore, although my arm ached less. I decided to leave off the sling. For the first time in several days I did my back exercises, grunting as I twisted and stretched. Then I dressed and went downstairs.

In the parlour, Barak, dressed in his shirt and upper hose, was already breakfasting on bread and cheese. 'Is your arm better?' he asked.

'Yes, it is today.' I pulled the loaf towards me. 'Is Tamasin not up yet?'

'Just. Her bruises are going down, and her mouth, but she still doesn't like to be seen. She'll be all right in another day or two.'

'She could have been killed,' I said. 'All because of our work. My work.'

Barak was silent a moment, then said, 'I hate this job, chasing after this lunatic or devil-possessed man or whatever he is. I suppose I've been taking it out on Tamasin. When all this is over I've decided to leave the Old Barge and see if I can't find a decent little house for us to rent nearer to Lincoln's Inn. And I'm going to stay home more. Spend less time in the taverns.'

I smiled. 'That is marvellous news. Have you told her?' I asked.

'Nah. I'll wait till things have settled down a bit.'

'But you should tell her now.'

He frowned. I realised I had gone too far. 'I'll tell her when I think it's right,' he said brusquely. 'I'll get dressed; then I'll tell Peter to get Sukey and Genesis saddled and ready.' He got up and went out.

His mention of Peter reminded me of my promise to the boy Timothy. I paused to eat some bread and cheese, then went to the kitchen to find Joan.

WE RODE BACK through the city to Yarington's house, and tied the horses up outside. I feared for a moment the boy might have run off, but Timothy was in the stable, sitting on his bucket beside the horse. It was obvious he had been crying; there was a bubble of snot at one nostril.

'Good morning, Timothy,' I said gently. 'This is my assistant, Barak.'

He stared at us with frightened eyes.

'I have a position for you,' I told the child. 'Working in my house.' I had asked Joan this morning if she could use the help of another boy, and she had gratefully agreed. 'Kitchen and stable work. How would you like that?'

He brightened. 'Thank you, sir. I . . . I will do my best.'

I took a deep breath. 'There is a condition, though. You must tell me something. Yesterday you said that you told no one about Abigail?'

'No, sir. I didn't.' But he reddened, squirmed uneasily on the bucket.

'But there is something else, isn't there?'

He hesitated, looked between me and Barak.

'Tell us, lad,' Barak said. 'Master Shardlake's house is warm. You'll like it.'

'I watch people,' the boy blurted out suddenly. He pointed to a knot-hole in the stable door. 'Through there. I get tired of being in here all the time.'

'What did you see?' I asked quietly.

'Tradesmen who called. The egg-man. The chimney sweep, and the carpenter to repair the wooden screen when Toby knocked it over. And after Abigail came, a man used to come and see her sometimes. When the master was out and Toby had his day off.' He bowed his head.

'Who was he?' I asked.

'Don't know.' He shook his head. 'He was young.'

'How young?'

He thought for a moment. 'I don't know . . . maybe twenty.'

'What did he look like?'

'Taller than either of you. Strong-looking like him.' He pointed to Barak.

'Fair or dark?'

'Dark. He was handsome. Abigail used to say he had a handsome face.'

'She talked to you about him?' I tried to keep my voice steady.

'Not much, sir. I told her I'd seen him and she said the less I knew, the less I could tell. She didn't like me knowing.'

'Was he in the reverend's congregation?' I asked.

'Don't know, sir. I only saw him because he came round the back door.' He began to look upset. 'Please, sir, I've told you all I know.'

'All right,' I said. 'Thank you, Timothy. Now come, you are coming back with us. Barak, you go on to court. I will join you there after I have delivered Timothy home.' I leaned close to Barak. 'I want him kept safe at my house. He may be one of the few who has seen the killer and lived.'

Chapter 8

Barak was waiting for me in the crowded vestibule of the Court of Requests. I looked around the familiar scene: the parties sitting round the walls watching the lawyers negotiating in the centre of the room. Daniel and Minnie Kite stood huddled together in the doorway with Guy, who was dressed in his physician's robe and cap. Barak and I joined them.

'Adam's not here yet, sir,' Daniel said anxiously.

'We are a little early. They will bring him. Is Reverend Meaphon not with you today?'

'He's been detained at a neighbouring parish. The minister there is sick.'

So, I thought, Harsnet has prevented the news getting out again.

I was interrupted by a rattling sound that echoed round the crowded chamber. Everyone turned round. Keeper Shawms, assisted by two stout under-keepers, was dragging Adam into the vestibule. His legs were chained together, and the keepers held him up by his stick-like arms. He was trying to sink to the floor to pray. Daniel Kite bit his lip and his wife let out a sob. Somehow the spectacle of Adam's condition seemed more terrible in this— to me—ordinary environment than it had in the Bedlam. Minnie made a move towards him. Guy laid a restraining hand on her arm.

'Not now,' he whispered.

At last the usher appeared and called everybody into court. I went to the advocates' bench in the front. Barak, Guy and the Kites sat with Adam. Judge Ainsworth appeared from an inner door and sat down on his bench. As he cast his eyes over the court, Adam let out a groan.

Ainsworth looked at me. 'I think we will take the case of Adam Kite first,' he said. 'Brother Shardlake?'

I outlined my applications. Ainsworth nodded slowly, then cast a sharp look at Shawms. 'This poor creature looks to be at death's door,' he said. 'Are you feeding him?'

Shawms rose, looking red and uncomfortable. 'Sometimes he will not eat, Your Honour. Sometimes he spits it out over the keepers.'

'Then you must redouble your efforts, fellow.' He turned to a man dressed in an expensive fur-lined coat, who was sitting at the back of the court. 'Sir George Metwys, you are warden of the Bedlam. What say you to these applications?'

Metwys rose. 'I am willing to consent, Your Honour. But it is our rule that we only take people in the Bedlam who can be cured, and for a limited time.'

'But surely there are many who have been there for years?'

I thought of the keeper Ellen, who had said she could never leave.

'Only when their relatives cannot care for them themselves.'

'And are rich enough to pay to be rid of them.' Ainsworth tapped his quill on the desk. 'I am minded to grant this order, but I am concerned at how long this situation may last.' He turned to Guy. 'Dr Malton, you have been treating this boy. What do you say?'

Guy stood. 'Adam Kite is very sick, Your Honour. He has come to believe himself cast out of God's favour, for reasons I do not fully understand. Yet I believe that I can help him.' He paused. 'From the point of view of public order I believe he is best kept where he is. But I too would not want him to be left in the Bedlam indefinitely.'

'That would be a little unfair on Sir George Metwys's purse.' Ainsworth permitted himself a little smile, then looked again at Adam.

'Is there any point in my questioning him?'

'None, Your Honour. I doubt Master Kite is even clear where he is.'

'Yet you think he can be helped? How long do you think you will need?'

'I do not know,' Guy said. 'But I am willing to treat him without payment.'

'Then I will make the order. Reports to me every fourteen days. Payments to be made from the Bedlam funds subject to review by me. Review hearing in two months.' He looked again at Adam. 'This boy is too young to be left to rot indefinitely in the Bedlam because in his madness he says dangerous things. Make sure he is cared for, Serjeant Shardlake.'

'I will, Your Honour.'

Ainsworth looked down at his papers, and I nodded to Barak. He nudged Shawms. The keepers manhandled Adam into the passage.

I followed with Daniel and Minnie. Outside, they expressed their thanks. Guy offered to walk part of the way home with them. They nodded, turning sorrowful eyes to where Adam was being hauled through the door, followed by many curious looks. Barak and I left them on the courthouse steps.

'By God, the old Moor will need all his skills.' Barak's voice was angry. 'Sometimes these days I feel that everywhere I look there is madness.'

I watched the receding figures of Guy and the Kites. 'We are bound to find the killer, as we are to aid Adam Kite,' I said, to myself as much as to him.

'Aye, and here comes the man of sure and certain faith to tell us where to go next.' Barak nodded to where Harsnet was approaching, his coat swirling round him as he shoved through the crowds. He looked weary, exhausted.

'The girl's escaped,' he began without preliminary.

'Abigail?' I asked. 'How?'

'Asked to go to the jakes and slipped out through the window. It's on the first floor; she's lucky she didn't break her neck.'

'What about Yarington's steward?'

'Oh, he's safe in the Lollards' Tower. Whining creature. But there's no more to be got out of him.'

'I have some news at least.' I told him what the boy Timothy had said.

Harsnet thought hard for a moment, then shook his head. 'That might mean nothing. Abigail's visitor isn't necessarily the killer.'

'But who else would know Yarington was keeping a whore? Unless he had a history of it.'

'He didn't.' Harsnet shook his head. 'I've spoken to all the congregation. In their eyes, Yarington was a man devoted to celibacy. It was only in these last few months he started being cautious about people coming to his house.'

'Any progress in finding Goddard?'

'I've asked the London city council and the coroners and sheriffs of Kent, Surrey and Middlesex to seek out a well-to-do family of that name, whose son went for a monk. Nothing. And I've put the word out among all the radical churches and religious groups. So far, no one knows anything.' He looked at me. 'I am going to have to change our arrangements today. Bonner is extending his search for butchers and performers of forbidden plays down to Westminster, but it's not his jurisdiction. I am going to try and stop him. You will have to go to Lockley yourself, Serjeant Shardlake.'

'It might be worthwhile visiting young Cantrell again,' I suggested.

'Yes. Anything. Anything that may help us, Master Shardlake.' He gave me a desperate, harried look, then walked quickly away.

WE PASSED through a busy throng at Smithfield, for it was market day, and arrived at Charterhouse Square. There were a couple of other horses at the rail outside the Green Man tavern when we tied up Sukey and Genesis. Inside, Mistress Bunce and Lockley were busy, the latter moving among the tables and the former serving behind the bar hatch.

Lockley caught sight of us, and exchanged a glance with the widow.

'We would like another word, sir,' I said loudly to the potman.

'Come into the back.' His tone was low and fierce.

The clientele looked on with interest as I followed Lockley into a back room, where a moment later Mistress Bunce joined us.

'What do you want?' Lockley asked.

'We have not found Infirmarian Goddard yet. Are you sure you know nothing about him that could help us?'

'I told you all I knew last time. Goddard wasn't interested in the patients in the lay infirmary. So far as he was concerned they were just a nuisance.'

'I told you before that we are investigating a death. We think it possible that Goddard may have murdered someone.'

'How?'

'I may not say. Only that it was a violent attack.'

I would swear that Lockley seemed relieved. He laughed contemptuously. 'Goddard would never attack anyone. He was a cold man and a lazy devil. And he had plenty of money, I know that. Why should he kill someone?'

I nodded slowly. 'Yes, I can see you believe that,' I said quietly. Then I looked him in the eye. 'But I think you are hiding something. Something else to do with Goddard. I advise you to tell me what it is.'

Lockley clenched his fists harder on the table. His face grew red. 'Will you leave me alone!' His sudden exclamation startled me, and I saw Barak's hand go to the hilt of his sword. 'I know nothing! Leave me alone! All my life it's been nothing but pester, pester, pester. The patients, Goddard, that wretched barber-surgeon. And you!' He glared at Mistress Bunce. Then he put his head in his hands. 'I don't know whether I'm coming or going.'

Ethel Bunce's mouth set in a tight line, but I saw tears in her eyes.

'What are you hiding, Master Lockley?' I asked quietly. 'Tell us, and perhaps that will resolve your confusion. Otherwise I might have to have you arrested, and questioned in a hard place.'

He stood up suddenly and started walking to the door. 'Then do it, do it! I'm past caring! To hell with you all! I'm going back to my customers!'

Barak made to step in front of him, but I shook my head.

As Lockley left, Mistress Bunce looked at us beseechingly. 'Francis is not strong in his mind, sir,' she said. 'I have tried to help him, but I think it has ended by him seeing me as another . . . persecutor.' She looked at us bleakly.

'All right, madam, leave us,' I said.

When she had gone, Barak said, 'Could he be our man? Most people would be terrified at the prospect of arrest, but he seemed hardly to care.'

I shook my head. 'Running a tavern is a full-time job. He couldn't possibly have done what the killer has done without Mistress Bunce knowing. No, let Harsnet deal with him.'

MY HEART GREW heavier as we rode down into Westminster, with all its noise and smells and danger. We dismounted near Cantrell's house, and I knocked loudly on the door while Barak tied the horses to the rail.

Once again, footsteps approached slowly from within, but this time they stopped before reaching the door and Cantrell's voice called out in timorous, cracked tones. 'Who's there? I am armed!'

'It is Master Shardlake,' I called out. 'What is the matter?'

There was a brief pause; then the bolt was drawn back and the door opened a few inches. Cantrell's thin, bespectacled face peered out. 'Oh, sir,' he said with relief. 'It is you.' He opened the door wider.

I stared at a long piece of wood he held in his hand. On the end was a large smear of what looked like dried blood.

'Someone attacked me,' he said.

He allowed us in, and led us into the bare parlour. A wooden plate with the remains of a greasy meal lay on the table. I saw that the dirty window giving onto the yard was broken in one corner. There was glass on the floor.

Cantrell sat down on one of the hard chairs. He looked strained and miserable. We sat at the table, facing him. I avoided looking at the filthy plate.

'What did you want, sir?' he asked. 'Have you found Brother Goddard?'

'Not yet.'

'I told you all I know.'

'Only a few more questions. But what happened here?'

'It was two nights ago. I heard glass breaking. I always keep a piece of wood by the bed in case of burglars. I went downstairs. It was dark but I saw a figure standing by the open window, a man. I don't think he saw the piece of wood. When he said something, I knew where his head was and hit out.'

'You seem to have done some damage,' Barak said.

'Aye, I got him on the head. He groaned and staggered and I hit him again. Then he got out of the window again, stumbled away.'

'What did he say to you?'

Cantrell frowned. 'It was a strange thing for a burglar. He said, "It is your time now." Why would he say that?'

I looked at him, appalled. Had Charles Cantrell escaped becoming the killer's fifth victim? 'Did you tell the constable?' I asked.

He shrugged his thin shoulders. 'What's the point? There are always burglaries in Dean's Yard. He won't try here again, though. I hurt him hard.'

I chose my words carefully. 'Was there anything you recognised about the man? Anything familiar about his voice?'

'He was just a figure in the dark, a shape.' He thought a moment. 'There *was* something familiar about that voice. A sharp voice.'

'Could it have been your old master?' I asked quietly.

He stared at me in silence for a long moment. 'I . . . I suppose it could have been. But why . . . why would that old bastard attack me? What has he done, sir? You never told me last time.'

I hesitated. 'Could I see that piece of wood?'

'I won't get into trouble for this, sir? I was only defending myself.'

'I know. I just want to see it.'

Reluctantly he passed it over. I had noticed a few hairs among the blood. They were black. Like Goddard's, like Abigail's unknown visitor.

'You dealt him a couple of good blows, by the look of it. But scalp wounds bleed a lot. He may have been more shocked and hurt than damaged.' I passed the stick back to Cantrell and said, 'Have you ever had anything to do with the radical religious reformers? The godly men.'

He was silent for a moment. Then he bowed his head.

'It is important,' I said. 'It may explain why you were attacked.'

'When I was a monk,' he said in a quiet voice, 'my father became a reformist. He joined a group that used to meet together at an unlicensed preacher's house, in the Sanctuary. When I left the abbey and came home, it was all "You monks got what you deserve. You will go to Hell unless you follow the true path of the Word." I was losing belief in the old faith then. I let him drag me to some of the meetings. There were only half a dozen in the group. They were stupid; they only knew a few bits of the Bible that suited their arguments and didn't even understand those.'

'There are many such,' I said.

'I only went to keep Father quiet. He was already ill when I came home. He had a growth. After he passed away I stopped going.' Cantrell fell silent.

'What happened to this little group? Are they still active?' I asked.

He shook his head. 'The vicar of St Margaret's heard there was some radical preaching going on. He got their leader arrested and the others fled. Last year.' He gave a bitter laugh. 'They ran like rats.'

What had happened to them? I wondered. They had probably joined other groups, other churches. Perhaps, somewhere among them, the murderer heard Cantrell's name spoken of as a backslider. If the killer was Goddard, he would have recognised the name.

'Can you remember the names of the people in the group?' I asked.

He gave me half a dozen names. They meant nothing to me.

'But, sir,' Cantrell asked, 'what is all this to do with Master Goddard?'

'I am not sure, Master Cantrell. But I think you may be in need of protection. I might be able to arrange for a guard to stay here.'

Cantrell shook his head vigorously. 'No. I do not want anyone here. Criticising and saying the place is filthy.' He looked at me again with those wide swimming eyes. 'I care little if I live or die. What is death anyway? Afterwards it will be eternal bliss or eternal torment, one or the other, who may know which these days?' He gave a humourless cracked laugh.

WE LEFT THE HOUSE, returned to the stink and the noise of Dean's Yard.

'He's in a bad way,' Barak observed.

'A state of deep melancholy, I would say. Not surprising given what his life has become, and the condition of his eyes. When I see Harsnet, I will see if I can arrange a guard.' I did not think the killer would return to Cantrell now his victim had been alerted, but I could not be sure. 'There is one more piece of information we have,' I said. 'We are probably looking for a man with an injured head.'

We led the horses across the road to the gate in the wall of Westminster Abbey. Barak nodded to the guard. There was still an hour before Harsnet was due. I felt a need to be alone for a while.

'Barak,' I said, 'see if you can find somewhere to stable the horses. I am going to take a walk inside the precinct. I will meet you back here in an hour.'

'Are you sure that's safe?'

'I shall be within the precinct. It is guarded. I will see you soon.' To settle the argument I turned away from him, nodding to the guard.

Recognising me, he opened the door in the wall to let me into the precinct.

Inside, I picked my way through the maze of rubble to the old cloister. All was still and quiet. I walked the ancient flagstones, thinking. I had picked up clues, but they only seemed to deepen the mystery. Was it Goddard we were looking for, or the young man who had visited Abigail? And why had the killer chosen Cantrell to be the fifth victim, as it looked likely that he had? Cantrell, like Yarington, had a peripheral link to me. Was it foolish to imagine that the killer was somehow focused on me as an audience? I could not prevent a clutch of fear at my heart at the recollection that I fitted the pattern of a man who had turned away from radical religion.

I realised how weary I was. I decided to take a walk through the ancient Westminster Abbey Church, to calm myself. The nave was deserted except for black-robed attendants walking slowly to and fro. The great space, stripped now of all its images and ornaments, was lit dimly by a grey light from the high windows. There was only one monk in the church, by the door, and he was asleep. There was nothing of value left to steal; the King had it all.

I walked up to the sarcophagus of Edward the Confessor, naked stone now. I had seen it in the days before the Dissolution, magnificently framed by rich gold and silver statues and images reflecting the glow of a thousand candles. I became aware of a group of people nearby, grouped before a bare stone altar adorned only with a cross. Four stout men in livery, holding their caps in their hands, while their other hands rested on their sword-hilts. In

front of them a woman knelt in prayer on the stone floor. She was beauti-
fully dressed, in a red silk dress with black cuffs inlaid with gold leaf. Her
black hood was inlaid with pearls. One of the guards, seeing me looking,
shot me a warning glance that said I should not approach. Then the woman
lowered her hands with a sigh and I saw it was the Lady Catherine Parr. She
rose to her feet, her small mouth settled into a mild, gentle expression as
she smiled at her guards. She nodded, and they began walking away.

They were halfway to the door when there was a sudden disturbance. I saw
that a ragged little man was praying before one of the tombs, and no sooner
had I registered his presence than he got up and threw himself to his knees
in front of her. I started forward out of some instinct to protect her but her
guards got there first. One of them pointed a sword at the beggar's throat.

Then another figure stepped from the shadows with a drawn sword. It
was Sir Thomas Seymour, dressed in a blue doublet with jewels to match.

'Are you safe, Lady Catherine?' Seymour asked.

'Quite safe, Thomas,' Lady Catherine said. She frowned. 'Put down your
sword, you foolish man.' She looked down at the beggar.

'Good lady,' the wretched man burst out, 'I cannot find my teeth, I cannot
eat. Please, my lady, make them give them up to me!'

'You madwag,' the guard said, still holding his sword to the beggar's
throat. 'What do you think you're doing, accosting Lady Catherine?'

'My teeth—only my teeth . . .'

'Let him go,' Lady Catherine said. 'He is out of his wits. I know nothing
of your teeth, fellow. I see you have none. But if they are gone, they are
gone. Mine will go too one day.'

'No, good lady, you do not understand—'

'We should have him taken in charge, my lady,' the guard said.

'No,' she answered firmly. 'He cannot help himself.' She delved in her
purse and brought out a shilling. 'There, fellow, go and buy some pottage.'

The beggar looked from Lady Catherine to the hard faces of the guards,
then rose to his feet, bowed and scampered away. Sir Thomas was still
standing there, a faint look of amusement on his face.

She took a step towards him. 'Thomas,' she said, her voice quivering.

'I wanted merely to see you, watch you from a distance.' He looked serious. 'But when I saw you might be threatened, I had to draw my sword.'

'You know you must not try to see me. It is cruel of you, and dangerous.'
Lady Catherine cast a worried look around, her eyes resting on me, still
standing at some distance.

Sir Thomas laughed. 'The crookback will say nothing; I know him.'

Lady Catherine hesitated a moment, then gestured to her guards and walked away rapidly. Her men followed.

Thomas turned to me. 'You won't say anything, will you?' His tone was quiet, with a threatening undertone. 'Not to my brother, or Cranmer?'

'No. Why should I wish to be involved?'

Seymour smiled, white teeth flashing in his auburn beard. 'Well judged, crookback.' He turned and walked away, his steps loud and confident.

I REJOINED BARAK at the gate to Dean's Yard and I told him about my encounter with Catherine Parr and Thomas Seymour.

He raised his eyebrows. 'He's taking a risk meeting her in Westminster Abbey, if the King's told him to leave her alone.'

'I don't think Seymour intended to talk to her. I think he just wanted her to see him in the shadows, know that he had not forgotten her.'

'He doesn't strike me as the lovelorn type.'

'No. But I think she may be. Where he's concerned, at least.' I shook my head. 'What could she see in him? She struck me as an intelligent, good-hearted woman—you don't often see that in ladies of the court.'

'Nor anyone else there, for that matter—' Barak broke off. 'Watch out, here comes Harsnet. I take it we say nothing about this to him.'

'No. That's not our business. We know now these killings have nothing to do with Catherine Parr.'

I watched as Harsnet walked across Dean's Yard with his confident stride, looking neither right nor left. 'Good afternoon,' he said cheerfully.

'A good meeting?' I asked.

He nodded. 'We are going to be able to stop Bonner spreading his persecution down here. Westminster is well out of his jurisdiction.' He fixed me with his keen eyes. 'What news from Lockley?'

I told him of my suspicion that he was still keeping something back, and of the attack on Charles Cantrell.

'I'll have Lockley taken in for questioning after we've seen the dean,' he said. 'But why does Cantrell not want someone posted at his house?'

'He says he does not care if he is attacked again. I am not sure he is quite in his right mind. He has suffered much.'

'I'll have a guard posted there whether he likes it or not. The fact that he joined his father's group of reformers and then withdrew from it would be enough for our killer to believe he deserved death.' He sighed. 'But I'm running out of men. I'll have to speak to Sir Edward Seymour, see if he can supply anyone. What were those names that Cantrell gave you?'

I gave Harsnet the names of the men who had belonged to Cantrell's father's group.

He rubbed his chin. 'I've heard of one or two of these. I will ask my contacts. Now, let us see what we can get out of Dean Benson.'

THE DEAN was in his study again, in the fine house amidst the warren of half-demolished or half-converted monastic buildings, labouring over papers, his plump face irritable. When we were shown in, he gave us a look of hostile enquiry, bidding us sit down with a patrician wave of the hand.

'I see by your expressions this matter is not resolved,' he said.

'There has been another murder,' Harsnet replied, 'and we can find no trace of Goddard or his family.' He looked the dean squarely in the eye.

Benson frowned. 'And do you know of any direct connection between Goddard and these killings?' he asked smoothly. 'Beyond the suspected use of dwale, and the pilgrim badge? That's little enough to go on.'

'Maybe,' Harsnet said. 'But we need to find him.'

'I have told you all I know. I have no idea where he is.'

'Master Shardlake here has been talking to the lay brother who worked in the public infirmary, Francis Lockley. And he believes Lockley knows something about Goddard, and is hiding it.'

'What is that to do with me?' Benson's look did not change, but he picked up a quill and began fiddling with it. 'Be careful how you deal with me,' he went on. 'I have important contacts. I have the gratitude of the King himself for the way I brought Westminster Abbey to a peaceful surrender.'

'We are hunting a murderer,' Harsnet said. 'Someone who has brutally murdered four people and already tried to murder a fifth.'

'And I tell you again, it has nothing to do with the abbey.' Impatience entered his voice. 'God's bones, man, I knew Goddard. He was one of the few monks in this place with any intelligent conversation. But all he ever cared about was his comfort and his social status. The idea of him killing people to fulfil some prophecy is . . . ludicrous.'

'If a man is possessed,' Harsnet said, 'it does not matter what he was like before. He will be consumed by the desire to do the devil's bidding.'

Benson stopped playing with his quill. 'Possession.' He laughed cynically. 'Is that what you think? That idea will get you nowhere.'

'I saw the wall paintings telling the story of the Apocalypse in the chapter house,' I said. 'I do not think one could look at them day in, day out, as the monks once did, and not think about the story they portrayed.'

He shrugged. 'I used hardly to notice them, except to think what poor quality the paintings were.'

'They could still affect a certain type of man, perhaps.'

Benson stared at me fixedly for a moment, then stood up, indicating that the interview was over. I saw from Harsnet's expression that he would have liked nothing better than to take the dean in for questioning, but in the absence of any evidence he had to proceed cautiously.

OUTSIDE THE HOUSE, Harsnet turned to me. 'Did you believe him?' he asked.

'I think he is hiding something. But either he believes it is immaterial to our investigation, or he thinks himself safe because of his contacts.'

'His contacts wouldn't protect him if he were hiding information about a murderer four times over.'

'No.' I paused. 'At least, they shouldn't.'

Harsnet set his lips tight. 'Let's see if Lockley says something that will help us put Benson under a bit of pressure. Now I must find a couple of constables and pick him up.' He bowed and strode away.

IT WAS DARK when Barak and I rode back into Chancery Lane. The air was still mild but damp, and I saw the stars were hidden by cloud.

It began raining heavily as I prepared for bed, drops pattering the window the last thing I heard. I slept well and woke early; the sky was still cloudy, but the rain had stopped for now. The rest of the house was still quiet; Barak and Tamasin were not up yet and I wondered if they were managing to mend things between them. I hoped so.

Until some news came from Harsnet's enquiries there was plenty of work awaiting me at Chancery Lane. First, though, I would visit Dorothy. I wished I had some news of Roger's killer for her. I heard Joan's voice in the kitchen, talking to Constable Orr, but I did not feel like breakfast yet, so I left the house quietly and I walked the short distance to Lincoln's Inn. The road had turned to mud and I was glad I had put on my riding boots.

At Lincoln's Inn the working day had begun, black-robed lawyers stepping to and fro across Gatehouse Court with papers under their arms.

Margaret answered the door at Dorothy's rooms. She told me her mistress was in the parlour, going through papers.

'How is she?' I asked.

'Trying to get back to a normal life, I think, sir. But she finds it hard.'

Dorothy was in the parlour. She still looked wan and pale, but greeted me with a smile. 'You look tired,' she said.

'This hunt.' I paused. 'It's been nearly two weeks and he is still at large.'

'You are doing all you can.' She rose from the table. 'Come, will you take me for a walk in Coney Garth? I need some air.'

'Gladly. You will need boots; the ground is wet.'

'I will get them.'

She left me in the parlour. I stood by the fire, the animals peering at me from the undergrowth on the wooden frieze. Dorothy returned, dressed in a black cloak and high walking boots, and we went out and walked into the bare heathland of Lincoln's Inn Fields. Dorothy was silent, thoughtful-looking.

'Samuel will have arrived in Bristol by now,' I said.

'Yes. He wanted me to go back with him. But there is business I must finish here. Master Bartlett has kindly made a summary of monies due to Roger for his cases. And I am not lonely. Many kind people have visited.'

'Will you stay in London, do you think, or go to Bristol?'

She sighed. 'Samuel would like me to move back to Bristol permanently. But it is too early to decide on something like that.'

'Dorothy, the business you feel you must stay for. Is part of it waiting for the killer to be caught? Because I do not know when that will be.'

She came to a halt, turned and laid a hand on my arm. Her pale face was full of concern, 'Matthew,' she said, quietly, 'I can see this dreadful thing is burning you up. I am sorry it was me that set you on this hunt. I thought officialdom did not care. But now I know they are seeking this man, I want you to leave the matter to them. This is having a bad effect on you.'

I shook my head sadly. 'I am bound tightly into the hunt for him now, bound into those official chains. He . . . he has killed others.'

'Oh, no.'

'You are right, the horror eats into me, but I have to see it through. And I have involved others, too. Guy, Barak.' And even if I were willing to leave the killer alone, I thought but did not say, would he leave me? 'Do not be sorry,' I continued. 'We think we may know who the killer is. We will catch him. And one thing we are certain of now is that Roger was a chance victim.'

'That is little comfort, Matthew. Somehow it makes it worse. But it has happened, I must bear it. Nothing will bring Roger back.'

I smiled at her. 'You are so much calmer now, Dorothy.'

'Perhaps.'

We had reached the edge of the little escarpment and stood looking out over Lincoln's Inn Fields. Grey clouds raced across the sky.

'Do you remember when we first met?' Dorothy asked suddenly. 'That business of Master Thornley's paper?'

I smiled. 'I recall it as though it were yesterday.'

Thornley had been a fellow student who studied with Roger and me twenty years before. The three of us shared a little cubbyhole of an office at the Inn. I had been sitting working with Roger when Dorothy had called, with a message from her father, my principal, about a case the following day. Scarcely had she told me the message when Thornley had burst in, his face white as a sheet. He had been set a fiendishly complicated problem in land law, and had to present a paper on the morrow.

I laughed aloud at the memory. 'He told us he would be unable to present his paper because his dog had eaten it. And it was true.'

'Yes, the dog lived in his lodgings, did it not?'

'A great big lurcher he brought up from the country. It chewed all the furniture in his room, then started on his work. You helped us sort out all the chewed-up paper, as Thornley, Roger and I copied out the exercise again. Some of it was illegible and Thornley had to cudgel his brains to remember it. But the next day he presented it, and was praised for the precision of his answer.' I looked at her. 'Was that the first time you and Roger met?'

'Yes, it was. But it was you I came to see that day.'

'Me?'

She smiled gently. 'Do you not think my father could have got a servant to deliver his message? I offered to bring it round so that I could see you.'

'I did not realise,' I said. 'But I remember noting that you and Roger got on very well, and feeling jealous.'

'I thought you were not interested in me. So when I met Roger—'

'So you came to see me,' I said quietly. Something seemed to pull at my heart. 'How easy it is to make mistakes,' I said at length.

'Yes,' she agreed, with a sad smile.

I hesitated, full of confused emotion, then looked at her. 'I hope you do not go to Bristol, Dorothy. I will miss you. But you must decide.'

She lowered her eyes. 'I feel I am a burden to my friends.'

'Never to me.'

She stared out over the fields. There was an awkward moment of silence. 'We should go back,' she said quietly. She turned and led the way, her skirts rustling on the wet grass.

RECOGNITION of my feelings for Dorothy, which perhaps had never really gone away, and the thought that there might be some hope for me in the future, cheered me. Amidst all the danger and confusion it was something to hold on to. And then, going back to my chambers, I saw Bealknap. He was walking across Gatehouse Court, stooped and bent, and I saw that now he needed the aid of a stick. I could have avoided him, but I did not do so.

Bealknap looked up as I approached. His face, always thin, was skeletal now. He glared at me, an expression full of spite and malice.

'I am sorry to see you with a stick,' I said.

'Leave me, get out of my way.' Bealknap grasped the stick tighter. 'You will regret the way you have treated me.'

'At that Court of Requests? I had to do that. But believe it or not, I do not like to see anyone ill.'

He put a hand to his stomach and winced. 'My physician has given me a new purge to take. The lax comes on so quick it plucks my stomach away.'

'Have you thought of getting a second opinion?'

'What would going to a second doctor serve except . . . confusion? And expense. Dr Archer will get me right in the end.' He looked at me defiantly.

I took a deep breath, then said, 'Bealknap, why do you not go and see my friend Dr Malton? Get another opinion?'

'That brown Moor? He would want paying in advance, I imagine.'

'No,' I said evenly. But if Bealknap went to Guy, I would pay him myself rather than leave Guy to chase him for payment.

'Very well.' He spoke aggressively, as though accepting a challenge. 'I will go. I will hear what he has to say.'

'Good. You will find Dr Malton down at Bucklersbury. I am seeing him tomorrow. Shall I make an appointment for you?'

His eyes narrowed. 'Why are you doing this? To find profit for your friend?'

'I do not like to see anyone brought low by bad medical treatment. Even you, Bealknap.'

'How can laymen know what is good or bad treatment?' he muttered, then turned and walked away, leaving me to wonder why I had ever tried to help.

FOR THE REST of the day I worked steadily in my office. Towards evening a rider came from Cranmer summoning me to a conference at Lambeth the following afternoon. I reflected there could have been no dramatic developments, or he would have wanted to see me at once. Perhaps it was our lack of progress he wished to discuss.

Next morning was fine and sunny again, the warmest day so far. The spring was moving on. Sitting at breakfast I saw Tamasin walking on her own around the garden, pausing to look at the crocuses and the daffodils. She walked back towards the house and sat on the bench next to the kitchen door. I went outside to join her. Her bruises were quite gone now, her face strikingly pretty once again.

'Your garden is beautiful,' she said as I approached.

'I have had a lot of work done here over the years. How is Jack this morning? I think he did not go out again last night.'

'No. He is fine.' She took a deep breath. 'Last night he told me that when this business is over he will move us to a little house somewhere. Perhaps even with a garden. He said it would give me something to do.'

'Would it?' I was surprised that she was not more cheered by this.

'I would like a garden,' she replied. 'But I doubt we could afford that.'

'Perhaps it is time I reviewed his salary.' I took a deep breath. 'When all this is over, Tamasin, and you are settled somewhere, things will be better. You will see.'

She shook her head. 'It is our lost child that has driven us apart.'

'Give him time, Tamasin.' I looked at her seriously. 'For what it is worth I think you should remember that Jack is under other pressures now.'

'I used to admire his adventurousness, at the same time as I wanted him to settle down. After this I think he will be only too happy to live a quiet life. But will he want to live it with me?'

'I believe so. I am sorry; it was me that involved him in all this. Because my friend was killed.'

She looked at me. 'How is his widow?'

'She is strong. But the weight of grief still lies full on her.'

Tamasin gave me a searching look. I wondered if she had divined something of my feelings for Dorothy.

'I have to go,' I said, 'to Lambeth Palace.'

I took my leave and went round to the stables. I decided not to take Barak with me. Left alone together, perhaps he and Tamasin might talk more.

Young Timothy was in the stable, scraping dung-laden old straw into a pail. Genesis stood in his stall, looking on placidly.

'How are you faring, Timothy?' I asked.

'Well, sir.' He smiled, a flash of white teeth in his dirty face. 'Master Orr has been teaching me and Peter our letters.'

'Ah, yes, it is good to know them.'

'Yes, sir, only . . . Well, he talks about God all the time.'

And you will have little time for God after your experiences at Yarington's, I thought. 'You seem to have made friends with Genesis,' I said.

'He is an easy horse.' He hesitated. 'Do you know, sir, what became of Master Yarington's horse?'

'I am afraid not. Someone will buy him.' Timothy looked crestfallen. 'I do not need another horse,' I said. 'Now come, saddle Genesis for me.'

I rode out, thinking how sad it was that the child's only friends had been Yarington's horse and a prostitute. I pulled aside hastily to avoid a red-bearded pedlar pushing a cartload of clothes. Waifs and strays, I thought. And beggars and pedlars. Everywhere. The hospital—when this was over I must set to work on the hospital.

WHEN I ARRIVED in Cranmer's office at Lambeth Palace, the atmosphere was tense. Harsnet stood near the door, looking downcast. Lord Hertford stood opposite, stroking his long beard, anger in his eyes. His brother, Sir Thomas, stood next to him, arms folded, looking grim. Cranmer sat behind his desk in his white robe and stole, his face severe.

'I hope I am not late, my lord.'

'I cannot stay long,' he said. 'There are matters I must attend to. Among them trying to persuade the Privy Council to allow me to have Dean Benson in for questioning without saying why.' He laughed bitterly. 'When most of them would rather have me arrested than him.'

Hertford looked at me. 'We have been asking Coroner Harsnet how it is he cannot find this Goddard despite all the resources we have given him.'

'It is easy to disappear in London,' I said.

Harsnet gave me a brief, grateful nod.

'But this man must have antecedents,' Hertford said. 'Or did he spring from the earth like some demon from Hell?'

'I do not believe his family are from London,' Harsnet said. 'I am making enquiries with the officials of Middlesex, Surrey and Kent, but it takes time.'

'Time is what we do not have,' Cranmer said. 'There are three more vials to be poured out, three more murders to come. With each it is harder to conceal what is happening.' He looked at me sternly. 'Master Harsnet says you think there may be another suspect. Some young man who visited Yarington's whore. The whore who escaped.' He gave Harsnet a sidelong look.

'The fact he knew Yarington kept a girl in his house makes him a suspect,' I said carefully. 'But there is nothing to link him to the other murders.

Still, all the evidence against Goddard, too, is circumstantial. My lord, the man we seek is very clever. He seems to have made killing his life's mission.'

'Maybe we should leave this man to fulfil his prophecy,' Sir Thomas said. 'Concentrate on covering up the murders. When he has completed the seven, he will stop, surely.'

'I do not think someone so devoted to killing could stop,' I said quietly.

'I agree,' Cranmer said. 'And how can we allow these outrages to continue?' He turned to Harsnet. 'How many men at your disposal, Gregory?'

'Four.'

'And now we need to find Lockley as well as that girl Abigail.'

'He was gone by the time my men arrived there,' Harsnet explained to me. 'The Bunce woman was in a great state. Said he'd been jumpy all day.'

'You need more men, Gregory,' said Cranmer. 'I dare not take men from my household; there are spies there now.'

'I need to be careful too,' Lord Hertford agreed.

'Perhaps I can help,' Sir Thomas said. 'I have a household full of clever young men, and a good steward. I can lend you a dozen if you like.'

His brother and Cranmer exchanged glances. I could see that they were wondering how far he could be trusted. Hertford hesitated, then nodded.

'Very well, Thomas,' Cranmer said. 'If you could make some men quietly available that would help us greatly. But they must come under the direct supervision of Coroner Harsnet.'

'My men are to be placed under the orders of a clerk?'

'If you want to be involved, yes,' Lord Hertford told him bluntly.

Sir Thomas met his gaze for a moment, then shrugged.

'I will use them well,' Harsnet said. 'I can send them to the constables of all the villages round London—from Barnet and Enfield to Bromley and Surbiton—to find whether the name Goddard is known.'

The archbishop nodded. 'And you, Matthew. Keep thinking, keep puzzling it over. That is your role. What will he do, do you think, when he has poured out the seven vials?'

'Find a new theme for murder,' I replied. 'There are plenty in Revelation.'

Cranmer closed the meeting shortly after, asking the Seymour brothers to stay behind. Harsnet and I walked together along the dim passageways of Lambeth Palace.

'I feel I let the archbishop down,' Harsnet said, 'letting the whore escape, then losing Lockley.'

'We all make mistakes, Gregory.'

He shook his head. 'I should have served him better. Particularly with all the strain he is under now. You saw how troubled and afraid he is.'

'No evidence of heresy has been found among his associates?'

'No. He is too cautious to hire men the papists would call heretics.'

'Then perhaps he will be safe. His enemies cannot go to the King without evidence.'

'They will not give up easily.'

'What news on Catherine Parr?' I asked, to change the subject.

'Still she will not agree to marry the King. They say she thinks on the fate of Catherine Howard. Better to think on God's will.'

'How can we ever be sure what that is?'

He smiled. 'Oh, but one can, Matthew. If one prays. As one day you will understand, I am sure of it.'

Chapter 9

The following morning I rode down to Guy's shop. I tied Genesis up outside and knocked at his door. Guy himself opened it. I followed him inside. He had been sitting at his table. A big anatomical volume lay open there, revealing some gruesome illustrations.

'How is your arm?' Guy asked.

'The stitches pull. I would like to have them out.'

'It has only been five days,' he said doubtfully. 'But let me look.'

I removed my robe and doublet, and showed him my arm.

He smiled warmly. 'Piers did a good job there. He learns so fast. And it has healed well. Yes, I think those may come out. Piers!' he called out.

I told Guy about Bealknap. 'He has been complaining of weakness and nausea, and his physician, Dr Archer, has been purging and bleeding him so that there is little of him left. I fear he may die. He wants a second opinion.'

'Bealknap. He has done you harm in the past, has he not?'

'Yes. He is the greatest rogue in Lincoln's Inn. In fact, I will pay your fee, otherwise you will have to battle for it.'

'You would help an enemy?'

I smiled. 'Then he will owe me a moral debt. I would like to see how he deals with that. Do not think my motives are of unalloyed purity.'

'Whose are?' He looked sad, then smiled at me. 'I think also you do not like to see suffering.'

'Perhaps.'

The smile faded from my face as the door opened and Piers entered, the usual bland, respectful expression on his handsome face.

Guy stood and touched his arm. 'Piers, your patient is here. Take him through to the treatment room, would you?'

Piers bowed. 'Good morning, Master Shardlake.'

I rose reluctantly and followed him out. I had hoped Guy might come to supervise, but he stayed with his anatomy book.

Piers smiled and gestured to a stool set beside the table. 'Would you bare your arm, sir, then sit there?'

I rolled up my shirtsleeve again. Piers selected a small pair of scissors, then turned to me with a deferential smile. I watched apprehensively as he snipped the black stitches. He did it gently, though, and I sighed with relief when it was over, the constant pulling sensation of the last few days gone.

Piers looked at my arm. 'There. All is healed. It is wonderful how Dr Malton's poultices prevent wounds from becoming infected.'

'Yes, it is. You are learning a lot from Dr Malton?'

'Far more than from my old master.' Piers smiled. 'He was one of those apothecaries who believed in exotic herbs prepared in consultation with astrological charts.' He gave a cynical smile that made him look older than his years. 'It is good to be working with Dr Malton now. A man of reason.'

'Your old master died, I believe.'

'Yes.' Piers fetched down a jar, containing the ointment Guy had used before. He put some on the end of a spatula and spread it gently on my arm. 'It was the smallpox killed him. The strange thing was, he did not dose himself with any of his own remedies. He simply took to his bed and waited to see if the pox would kill him. Which it did. There, that is done, sir.'

I found Piers's unemotional tone in talking of his master's death distasteful. 'Had he family?' I asked.

'No. There was just him and me. Dr Malton came and did what he could for him, but the smallpox takes its own path, does it not? Sometimes it kills; sometimes it disfigures. My parents died of it when I was small.'

'I am sorry.'

'Dr Malton has been father and mother to me since I came here.'

'He said he is going to help you train to become a physician.'

Piers looked up sharply, perhaps wondering why I was asking so many questions. He hesitated, then said, 'Yes, he has shown me much kindness.'

'His kindness is of a rare sort,' I agreed, and stood up. 'Thank you for seeing to my arm.'

Piers bowed. 'I am glad it is better.'

I left the room. He did not follow me. I remembered him listening at the door when we were talking of the murders. I thought, Guy might be kind, but you are not. You are cold and calculating, like a predatory animal. You have some hold over my friend, and I will discover what it is.

NEXT DOOR, Guy was still reading his book. He offered me a glass of wine and asked to look at my arm. He nodded with satisfaction. 'Piers has done a good job. And the arm has healed well.'

'I do wonder if he possesses the human sympathy one would hope for in a physician.'

'He has had little chance to develop it. His parents died when he was young. And Apothecary Hebden worked him hard and taught him little.'

'He told me. He says you are a father and mother to him now.'

'Did he say that?' Guy smiled, then his expression turned sombre.

'What are you thinking?' I asked gently.

'Nothing.' He changed the subject. 'I have been to see Adam Kite again. You know, I think there is improvement. That woman keeper, Ellen, she works hard with him. She forces him to eat and clean himself. The other day he even talked of normal everyday things. But still I cannot get him to explain why he feels such a sense of sin. I wonder what brought it on?'

'What do his parents say? You left with them after the court hearing.'

'They say they have no idea. I believe them.'

'Thank you for doing this. Adam cannot be . . . easy to work with.'

Guy smiled sadly. 'He touches me, yet intrigues me too. So, like you with Bealknap, my motives are not all pure. I am going to see him again tomorrow morning. Would you like to come?'

'Very well. If I can.'

'You do not sound as if you want to.'

'I find it distressing. He is in such pain. And religious madness makes me think of the man we are hunting, and who has been hunting me.' I looked at Guy. 'He still has three murders to commit. And if he succeeds, I, like you, do not think he will stop. I told Cranmer that today.'

'No. Such a momentum would carry forward. Till he is caught, or dies.'

We both jumped violently at a loud hammering on the door to the street.

We exchanged glances. As Guy crossed to open it, the inner door opened and Piers came in. I wondered whether he had been listening outside again.

'Who is it?' Guy called out.

'It is I, Barak!'

Guy threw open the door and Barak stepped inside.

'There has been another killing,' he said, breathing hard. 'There's some strange mystery about this one. Dr Malton, sir, can you come with us?'

'Who is it?' I asked.

Barak glanced at Piers. Guy turned to the boy. 'Would you fetch my horse to the front of the house?' he asked.

Piers hesitated for a moment, then went out.

Barak looked between us. His face was set hard. 'It's Lockley's wife.'

'He has killed a woman?' Guy gasped.

'Sir Thomas sent a man round to the inn. He found Lockley's wife lying on the inn floor. She's been mutilated. We're to join Harsnet there at once.'

Through the window I saw Piers leading Guy's old white mare round to the front. We went outside.

'May I come too?' Piers asked Guy as we mounted.

'No, Piers, you have studying to do. You should have done it last night.'

The apprentice stepped back, a sulky expression crossing his face.

'How much does that boy know?' I asked Guy as we rode off.

'Only that there has been a series of murders. He could not fail to see that,' Guy added with a touch of asperity, 'as he has been helping me at the autopsies. He knows he must hold his tongue.'

'You know he listens at doors,' I said.

Guy did not reply.

WE RODE ON RAPIDLY, up to Smithfield and on to Charterhouse Square. The square was deserted except for two men standing at the door of the inn—Harsnet and a tall man who was coughing into a handkerchief. We tied the horses to the rail next to Harsnet's. Guy went over to the tall man.

'What ails you?' he asked quietly.

The man lowered his handkerchief. He was in his twenties, with a neat black beard. He stared for a moment at Guy's dark face, then said, 'I do not know. I came here two hours ago. I knocked but could get no answer. The shutters were all closed so I broke in. There is a woman lying on the floor. She's . . . mutilated.' He sputtered noisily. 'There's something in the air in there. It's poisonous; it burns at my throat.'

'Have you been inside?' I asked Harsnet.

'No. I looked in—one sniff was enough; it's like something trying to rip your throat out.' Harsnet looked at Guy. 'How do you come to be here, sir?'

'He was with me when the message came,' I interjected. 'Dr Malton may be able to help us. Guy, what can have happened to the air?'

'There is only one way to see.' He pulled a handkerchief from his pocket, held it to his nose and threw the door wide open. I took a step back as something sharp and stinging caught my nostrils. Guy went in and threw open the shutters. A body was lying under the open serving hatch.

It was Mistress Bunce, lying face down in a pool of colourless liquid. Her coif had been removed, revealing her long dark hair. Her dress had been pulled up to beneath her armpits, and her underskirt torn off. Her plump, pale body was half naked, her arms tied behind her with rope.

'God's wounds!' Barak breathed.

I saw red weals at her wrists where the poor woman had struggled to free herself, but the knots were tight. There was another piece of cloth lying beside her face, something dark red on top of it.

'Dear God, what has he done to her?' Harsnet breathed.

Guy crossed to the body and stood looking down at it. Quickly, he crossed himself. 'It is safe to come in,' Guy said quietly. 'The fumes are dispersing. But put handkerchiefs to your noses and mouths.'

Harsnet and Barak and I drew out our handkerchiefs and stepped cautiously inside. 'What was that stuff?' Barak asked.

'Vitriol,' Guy answered. 'It burns and dissolves everything it touches.'

We looked down at the body. The white flesh on the trunk and legs bore big red marks that looked like burns. To my horror, half the woman's posterior had been burnt away, leaving a huge, monstrous red wound. Yet there was no blood around her, only a pool of colourless liquid.

'Janley!' Harsnet called.

The guard entered, staring with horrified eyes at the mutilated corpse.

'Search the rest of the building.'

Reluctantly, his hand on his sword, Janley went upstairs.

'*And the fifth angel poured out his vial upon the seat of the beast,*' I quoted from the Book of Revelation. '*And his kingdom waxed dark; and they gnawed their tongues for pain, and blasphemed the God of Heaven for sorrow and pain of their sores, and repented not of their deeds.*'

Guy bent and, very carefully, turned the brutalised body over. He let out a groaning sigh. I made myself look at Mistress Bunce's face. The lower half was covered with blood. Guy took a spatula from his pocket and gently touched the piece of cloth beside her face, and the red thing on top of it.

'What . . .?' I asked.

'It is her tongue. He gagged her with this cloth while he tortured her. Then at the end he removed it. To fulfil the part of the verse that talks of gnawing tongues. He pulled out the tongue and snapped her jaw shut on it.'

'The cottar was cut up and left to die,' Barak said. 'But this is even worse.'

'When the Bible talks of the seat of the beast,' Harsnet said, 'it means the place ruled by the devil, not a human—a human rear. This is like some hideous blasphemous joke. A devil's jest.'

We all turned as Janley returned through the inner door.

'There's nothing,' he said. 'The rest of the house looks normal.'

Barak looked at me. 'Begins to seem like Lockley's the killer after all.'

'I still can't see it. I could see him having knowledge of dwale, but what about the legal knowledge that letter to Roger demonstrated? I wouldn't have said Lockley was someone who could write a proper letter.'

'Then where is he?' Harsnet burst out. The terrible scene had unnerved him deeply.

'I think we should give this house a full search,' I said. 'Come on, let's start with the living quarters.'

We walked up the narrow wooden staircase. There were two bedrooms. The one where Lockley and Mistress Bunce slept together had only a cheap truckle bed and a chest full of women's clothes.

'Poor bitch,' Barak said as he searched through them.

The second bedroom contained broken chairs and other odds and ends, and another chest, locked with a padlock. I set Barak to picking it, a skill he had learned in his days working for Cromwell. After a couple of minutes, he heaved the lid open to reveal men's clothes this time, but at the bottom there were a number of small wooden boxes.

Barak took out the boxes and began opening them. One contained coins, another some cheap jewellery. But the next contained something very different, a wooden block with a hinge, in the shape of a human jaw.

'What the hell is this?' Barak asked.

'A block to set dentures in,' I said quietly. I took it from him. 'They set teeth in those sockets and fix them in people's mouths.'

The remaining four boxes all contained denture blocks in different sizes.

'What's he got these for?' Barak asked incredulously. 'Lockley wasn't a barber-surgeon, was he? He worked for one, and left.'

I turned the ugly wooden things over in my hands. The blocks had never been used to house teeth; there were no traces of glue in the tooth-holes. Pictures in my mind came together, some pieces of the puzzle fitting at last.

'No,' I said quietly. 'He wasn't. I understand now what they were being so secretive about. Come, we must go to Dean Benson. Bring those boxes.'

I led the way downstairs. Guy and Harsnet had both sat down at a table. Harsnet looked up. 'Anything?' he asked.

'Yes,' I said. 'We need to go to the dean—'

I broke off as there was a sudden loud rumbling noise beneath our feet. Harsnet's eyes widened. 'What in God's name is that?'

'This place is connected to the old Charterhouse sewer system,' I said. 'They must have opened the sluice gate over there. It happened when we came here before. We ought to investigate that cellar.'

'I'll help Janley look,' Barak said, laying the boxes on the counter.

I glanced over at the body. 'What will you do with it?' I asked Harsnet.

'Store it in my cellars at Whitehall. With Yarington.' He gave me an anguished look. 'And keep quiet.'

I nodded.

'Why did you say we must go to the dean?'

'I think I know what he has been holding back.'

'We've found the cellar.' Barak called from inside the house. 'There's a metal hatch in the hallway.'

I went into the stone-flagged hallway, Harsnet following.

Barak stood looking down through the hatchway. There was a ladder. Janley appeared with a lamp, a lighted candle inside, and the two of them climbed down. But the candlelight showed only bare stone flags, barrels stacked against the walls. They found another hatch there, leading down. Janley opened it and we caught a whiff of the sewers.

'Should we go on down?' Janley asked.

'No,' Barak said. 'Listen.'

There was a sound of rushing water, faint then suddenly loud as someone up at the Charterhouse opened the sluice gates to flush excess water through. Barak and Janley climbed back up and we returned to the main room.

'What is Benson holding back?' Harsnet asked.

'I'll tell you on the way. We—'

There was a knock at the door, faint and hesitant. We looked at each other, and Harsnet covered the body. 'Come in!' he called, and the door opened. An elderly couple stepped nervously inside. Both were small and thin, grey-haired, poor folk. They looked at us and then at the thing on the floor, and the woman let out a little scream and clung to her husband.

'Who are you?' Harsnet asked roughly.

'We lodge next door,' the man said in a thin voice. He rubbed his hands together nervously. 'We wondered what was happening.'

'Mistress Bunce has been murdered. Master Lockley has disappeared. I am Master Harsnet, the King's assistant coroner. We wish to question you.'

'We think this happened last night,' I said. 'After the tavern closed. Did either of you hear anything?'

'There was a lot of noise at closing time, about twelve. We were in bed; the noise woke us. It sounded like tables going over. But you get rough people in this tavern now. We knew Francis had gone. Poor Ethel.' He looked down at the covered body. 'Did some drunk kill her?'

'Yes. You heard nothing later on in the night?'

'No,' the man said.

'How well did you know Mistress Bunce?'

'We've lived next to the tavern for ten years. We knew Master Bunce before he died. He kept a quiet house. He was a godly man.'

'What do you mean?' I asked.

The neighbour looked between us nervously. 'Only that he belonged to one of the radical congregations.'

'Yet he kept a tavern?' Harsnet sounded incredulous.

The old man shrugged. 'I think he was converted after he bought it.'

'And he kept it very orderly,' his wife added. 'No swearing or fighting.'

'When did Mistress Bunce take up with Lockley?'

'Francis? He came two years ago, as a potman. Then they got together.'

'She didn't try to bring Lockley into her husband's congregation?'

The woman shook her head. 'No, we never heard any more about Bible truth after Master Bunce died. She must have left the church.'

Harsnet and I exchanged glances. So Mistress Bunce was an apostate from a radical congregation, like the others.

The old man looked at us. 'Please, sir, what do you think happened? We only ask because we wonder if we are safe.'

'You are not in any danger,' Harsnet said. 'But that is all I can tell you till we investigate further. In the meantime, this is to be kept quiet. You tell no one Mistress Bunce is dead. It could hamper our investigation.'

'But how—'

'You *will* keep quiet. I order it in the King's name. A guard will remain here for now. Thank you for your help,' he concluded in a tone of dismissal.

Harsnet shook his head after the old man led his wife away. 'Poor old creatures,' he said. 'Come then, Matthew, let us go to see the dean now. I want to know what you have puzzled out. Janley, stay here, secure that door and keep enquirers away. I will arrange for the body to be removed.'

We all stepped outside, relieved to be out of that dreadful place. Harsnet unhitched his horse from the rail and I made to follow, but Barak touched me on the arm.

'What is next?' he asked. 'What happens when the sixth vial is poured?'

Guy answered. 'Great waters dry up. The Euphrates.'

'How's the killer going to symbolise *that*?' Barak asked.

'He'll find a way,' I answered grimly.

GUY RODE BACK to Smithfield with us. There he turned left into town, bidding us farewell. 'Shall I see you at the Bedlam tomorrow morning, Matthew? I am going at nine o'clock.'

I agreed to the rendezvous, and we rode down on to Westminster. It was a Saturday; Parliament and the courts were shut, and there were fewer people around. Shopkeepers and pedlars eyed us as we passed, and one or two called out, but we ignored them.

We turned into Dean's Yard, passed under the wall into the abbey courtyard and once again tied up the horses outside the pretty old house. Enquiries of the steward revealed that Dean Benson would be occupied in the cathedral all day. Harsnet sent a message asking him to attend us on a matter of urgency. In a short time we heard footsteps approaching up the garden path.

The dean entered. He was breathing heavily. 'What in the name of Heaven has happened now?' he demanded.

'May we speak in your office?' Harsnet asked.

'Very well.' The dean led us down the corridor. After a few steps he turned, staring at Barak, who was carrying Lockley's boxes. 'And you propose to bring your servant to an interview with me?' he asked haughtily.

'He has something to show you,' Harsnet replied firmly.

The dean shrugged, and walked on to his office.

Once inside, Harsnet told the dean of Ethel Bunce's murder, Lockley's disappearance and the attack on Cantrell, concluding, 'So the killer seems to be focusing his attention now on those associated with the infirmary.'

'Why should that endanger me?' The dean looked at the boxes on Barak's lap and took a sudden breath. I saw that he guessed what they might be.

'There was a connection between you and them,' I said. 'More, I think, than the mere fact that you had overall authority over the monks' infirmary and the lay hospital. I think that is what you have been hiding.'

Barak opened the boxes, revealing the dentures. From the way the dean's eyes widened and he sat back in his chair, I knew my suspicions were right.

'Let me tell you what I think happened,' I said quietly. 'Goddard used to administer dwale, a powerful and dangerous soporific, to render people unconscious for operations. Meanwhile a fashion came in among the rich for wearing false teeth set in wood. The teeth are usually obtained from healthy young people, preferably as a complete set.'

'Is there some meaning to this story?' the dean asked angrily.

'In the abbey church I encountered a beggar who was asking anyone who would listen if they knew where his teeth were—he had not a tooth in his head. He was mad, of course, but I wonder what drove him so. Something that was done to him here? Perhaps when he came here to have an illness treated, his teeth were removed, under dwale?'

The dean took a deep breath. 'I congratulate you, Serjeant Shardlake. Yes, you are right. Back in 1539, four years ago, I learned that Goddard was inviting patients in the lay hospital to sell their teeth. The fashion for false teeth was coming in then, and he had made an arrangement with a local barber-surgeon in Westminster. Lockley worked with Goddard. By then, everyone knew the monasteries had no future and many of the monks tried to protect their financial security in various ways.'

'How did you learn about this?'

'Young Cantrell told me, after overhearing Goddard and Lockley talking one day. He suspected that one or two of the people Goddard and Lockley anaesthetised for their teeth never woke up.'

'Cantrell,' I said. 'Did Goddard know Cantrell had informed on him?'

'No. I never told him I knew.'

'So more people could have died?' Harsnet said.

'Perhaps. I was under Lord Cromwell's orders to close the monastery quietly. As all of you know, one did not defy him lightly.' He leaned forward. 'And the King would not like to hear a scandal about Westminster. He knows nothing of this, does he? This killer you are seeking? I have been making soundings—oh, very discreetly, do not worry. The King would not be glad to hear Archbishop Cranmer had been keeping things from him.'

Harsnet turned to me, ignoring Benson. 'Where does this leave us? Is the killer some demented ex-patient of theirs?'

'I doubt it,' I said. 'They were poor, helpless folk. Yet there is some link, there has to be.'

'It's Goddard,' Harsnet said. 'He is choosing victims he knows.' He looked at the dean. 'You've told us everything?'

'All, now. On my oath as dean of Westminster.'

'I know how much that is worth, sir,' Harsnet replied contemptuously.

Benson glared at him, then turned to me. 'Am I safe?' he asked.

'I do not think you are at risk,' I replied. 'All five victims so far were associated with radical religion and moved away from it. But you, I think, were always a time-server,' I dared to say.

OUTSIDE THE HOUSE Harsnet shook his head. 'Why didn't Cantrell tell us about this?' he asked.

'Too afraid, I should think. We had better go and see what he says now. We can leave the horses here.' I pointed to the door in the wall, leading to Dean's Yard. 'There, that is where he lives.'

We crossed the road to the tumbledown shop. I knocked at the door.

After a moment Cantrell opened it. 'It is you, again, sir,' he said without enthusiasm. He peered at Harsnet through his glasses. 'Who is this?'

'I am the London assistant coroner,' Harsnet said, mildly enough. 'Master Shardlake is working with me. We hoped to see a guard at the house.'

'He is out the back.'

'May we come in?'

Cantrell's shoulders sagged wearily as we followed him down the musty corridor to the dirty little parlour. The window to the yard had been repaired. Outside, a burly man wearing a sword sat on an old box, eating bread and cheese. Cantrell gestured at him.

'How long will I have to have that man here guarding me?' he asked.

'He may be needed for some time yet,' Harsnet said. 'I have to tell you that Francis Lockley has disappeared and the woman he was living with has been killed. The man who broke in—could it have been Lockley?'

Cantrell stared at us in surprise. 'No, it wasn't Francis. He was short, and the man who broke in here was tall.'

'We have just been to see Dean Benson,' Harsnet said. 'He told us about the wretched scheme of Goddard and Lockley's, extracting patients' teeth under dwale. He told us you reported them to him.'

Cantrell sank down on a stool, a gesture of utter weariness. 'Is that why Dr Goddard is after me?' he asked. 'Because I told?'

'Dean Benson never told Goddard about that,' I said. 'But why did you not tell me?'

'Much good it did me when I told on him. Though he never said he knew, Dr Goddard's tongue seemed harsher than ever after that.' The young man sighed deeply. 'It wasn't just patients they took teeth from, you know. Word got around among the beggars and pedlars that there was money to be had with no pain for young folks with good teeth. I was always surprised nobody in authority found out; all the beggars knew. But no one takes notice of beggars, do they.' He relapsed into silence, staring at the floor.

'I will have a word with the guard.' Harsnet went out and spoke briefly with the guard, then returned. 'There's been nothing suspicious while he's been here,' he said. 'But he's unhappy at not being allowed into the house. Why will you not let him in, Goodman Cantrell?'

'I just want to be left alone,' Cantrell replied.

I feared he might burst into tears. I put a hand on Harsnet's arm, and he followed me out of the parlour. I said farewell to Cantrell. He did not reply, just sat looking at the floor.

Once we were outside, Harsnet shook his head. 'The smell of that place. Did you see how dirty his clothes were?'

'Yes, he is in a bad way. I hope that guard knows his business. I don't want to lose Cantrell too.'

'He's competent enough. And he is the last man I have.' He sighed heavily. 'In the end it will be as God wills.'

IT WAS LATE AFTERNOON when we turned into Chancery Lane. As soon as I opened my front door, Joan came hurrying down the stairs.

'Dorothy Elliard's maid has been round with a message,' she said.

'Has something happened to her?' My heart was suddenly in my mouth.

'No. She's all right. But Master Bealknap is at her lodgings. He collapsed on her doorstep. Margaret asked you to go over there when you returned.'

I hurried round to Lincoln's Inn. Margaret let me in, her face anxious.

'What is going on?' I asked.

'I heard a knocking at the door early this afternoon, sir, and I found this man in a barrister's robe collapsed on the doorstep. He said you knew him—'

I went into the parlour, where Dorothy was standing by the fire.

'Thank you for coming, Matthew,' she said.

'What has happened? Why is Bealknap here?'

'He was asking for help. What could I do? He said he was dying.'

'He knew a woman would not turn him away. I will deal with him.'

They had put Bealknap in Samuel's old room. He lay in the bed in his shirt. I was shocked by how bad he looked, his face against the pillows as pale as death. He was conscious, though; he stared at me with wild, terrified eyes.

'Why have you come here?' I asked quietly. 'You know what this household has suffered.'

'I knew . . . Mistress Elliard . . . was still here.' His voice was faint, his breath rasping. 'I knew she was kind. I have . . . no one else . . . to help me.'

'Anyone would help a fellow barrister in a state of collapse.'

'Not me. Everyone hates me.' He sighed, closed his eyes for a moment. 'I am finished, Shardlake. I cannot eat; the food just passes through me. Dr Archer said the last purge would wear off, but it has not.'

I sighed. 'I will arrange for Dr Malton to come and see you here.'

'I think it is too late. My vision blurs; I feel faint all the time.' With a great effort, he pulled a skinny hand from beneath the covers and grasped my wrist. I tried not to flinch. 'I do not believe in God,' he whispered, fixing me with his agonised gaze. 'But now I am frightened. The Catholics say if you confess your sins, God will receive you into Heaven. I need a priest.'

I took a deep breath. 'I will have Dr Malton fetched now, and he may know a priest who will confess you. But I think, Bealknap, with proper treatment you may come round.' I tried to rise, but he held me fast.

'The priest may not come in time. At least I can tell you about one sin, tell you what I did. Though I do not know why he asked—'

'What do you mean, Bealknap? You are making no sense.'

'The day after you lost me the case involving that marsh cottar, a solicitor called Colin Felday came to my chambers. He said he had a client who would pay good money for information I could give him about you.'

'What sort of information?'

'Anything I could give. About your work habits, where you lived. What sort of man you were. About your man, Barak. I told him you were a starchy prig. I said you were persistent. But no fool. Oh, no, never that.' He tried to laugh, but the crackling sound turned into a cough.

This was the killer, it must be. 'Who is Felday's client?' I asked sharply.

'He said he could not tell me that. Only that he wished you no good. That was enough for me.' His eyes were full of anger now. This might be a confession, but there was no real contrition. Only fear at the prospect of death.

'I think Felday's client has killed five people,' I said. 'I have been hunting him. And he has been hunting me. He hurt Barak's wife badly.'

Bealknap's eyes slid away. 'I didn't know that. No one can blame me for that.' I smiled wryly at the reappearance of the old Bealknap.

'Where does Felday live?' I asked.

'Some cheap lodgings by the cathedral. Addle Hill.'

'I will have Guy fetched here,' I said. 'And I will ask about a priest.'

Bealknap nodded weakly. I left him, closing the door quietly behind me.

DOROTHY WAS SITTING in her chair by the fire, Margaret on a stool opposite her. They both looked drained.

'Margaret,' I said, 'could you bear to go back to him? I think if he gets some liquid into him, that would be good.'

'Is he going to die?' Dorothy asked bluntly after Margaret left the room.

'I do not know. He thinks he is. He wants me to send for a priest.'

She gave a mirthless laugh. 'Bealknap never struck me as a believer in the old ways. Or in anything save lining his pockets.'

'I think for him it is a sort of insurance.' I shook my head. 'He is a strange man. He has no friends, only enemies. What drove him to be so?'

Dorothy shrugged. 'Who can say? Well, I hope he lives. I would not want another death here. Thank you for coming, Matthew.' She got up. 'At least let me give you some supper. I'll wager you have not had any.'

'No. There is something I must do urgently. There is a possible lead.'

She took my hand. 'You have been through so much.'

'I think we may be near the end of the trail.'

'Seeing that man Bealknap lying on the doorstep, so white, it brought everything back. When I first saw Roger's body.' She burst into tears, bringing her hands up to her face.

I forgot myself and took her in my arms. 'Oh, Dorothy, poor Dorothy . . .'

She looked up at me with her tear-streaked face. Looked into my eyes. And I felt if I kissed her now, she would respond. But then she blinked and took a step back. She smiled sadly. 'Poor Matthew,' she said quickly. 'Running from pillar to post to help me.'

'Whatever I can do, at any time.'

'I know,' she answered quietly.

I bowed and went out. On the front doorstep I paused, suddenly overcome with emotion. She did feel something for me, I knew that now. I took a deep breath, and began walking briskly homeward. I would send Peter to fetch Guy. Barak and I had another mission now. At last perhaps we had found our route to the killer.

BACK AT THE HOUSE, I climbed the stairs to Barak and Tamasin's room and knocked on the door. Barak's voice bade me enter.

They made a peaceful domestic scene. Tamasin was sitting at the table, sewing; Barak was lying on the bed, looking relaxed.

'Jack,' I said, 'I am afraid I need you for a while.'

'Not another,' he said, his eyes widening.

'No,' I said. Tamasin looked at us with anxious eyes. I smiled reassuringly. 'It is all right. We need to go on an errand.'

'What's happened?' Barak asked as we walked back down the stairs.

I told him about Bealknap's confession about the solicitor Felday. 'You go drinking with some of the jobbing solicitors,' I said. 'Do you know him?'

'I've had him pointed out to me,' Barak answered. 'Thin, sharp-faced fellow. My friends said he will do anything for money.'

I paused at the bottom of the stairs. 'We must go and see him now. If this client of his is the killer, we can identify him at last.'

I went to the kitchen. Philip Orr was seated at the table, a mug of beer in his hands. I hastily scribbled a note to Guy and gave it to him.

'Ask Peter to take this down to Dr Malton in Bucklersbury,' I said.

Orr hurried off to the stables.

'Right,' I said to Barak. 'Let us see what good Master Felday has to say for himself. Bring your sword.'

WE WALKED quickly along Fleet Street to the city wall. The guard there, seeing my lawyer's robes, let us through.

Addle Hill was a quiet street leading down towards the river. The houses were large old four-storey buildings that looked ready to topple over.

A group of figures was approaching up the street, conversing quietly.

'Excuse me,' I said, stepping into the path of the group. 'Do any of you know where a solicitor named Felday lives?'

A young man stepped forward. 'I know him.' He pointed down the hill. 'Half a dozen houses down, on the right, the house with the blue door.'

The house we had been directed to was less shabby than the rest; the blue door recently painted. I knocked several times before the door was opened.

A woman in her thirties smiled at us. 'Yes, sirs?'

'We are seeking Master Felday.'

The smile turned immediately to a scowl. 'He's not been in for days. I keep having to answer the door to people looking for him.'

'Perhaps we could go to his rooms. Where are they?'

'First floor, on the left. And tell him when you find him that if he goes away again to let people know. It's not a neighbour's duty to answer the door every five minutes.' She delivered her last words as we hurried up the stairs.

We reached a wide landing with two doors leading off it. We knocked hard on the left-hand door. There was no reply. Barak tried it. It was locked.

'Break it down,' I said. 'We have Cranmer behind us if anyone complains.'

'We should get some light first. I'll go and ask that woman for a candle.'

Barak went back down the stairs and returned carrying a candle. He took a step back, then kicked hard and expertly at the lock. The door flew open with a crash. Inside, darkness and an unexpected breath of cool air.

Barak drew his sword and we stepped carefully inside. Several doors led off the hallway. One was half open; that was where the draught of air was coming from. Barak gently pushed it fully open with the point of his sword.

Inside I made out a wall lined with shelves. Under the open window was a large desk, and my hand tightened on my dagger as I saw the figure of a man lying slumped across it. Barak prodded the prone figure lightly with his sword-tip. He did not stir. The man was young, no more than thirty, with thick brown hair and a thin, handsome face.

'It's Felday,' Barak said.

Something moved in the room. We both jumped round. Barak pointed his sword at a corner. Then he gave a tense bark of laughter as we realised the edge of a brightly coloured wall hanging had been caught by the breeze.

'Jesus, my heart was in my mouth there,' he said.

'Mine too.'

He went over to the window and closed it, then used the candle to light a lamp that stood on a table. Then he took the man gently by the shoulders and lifted him upright in his chair. His shirt front was a mass of blood, which had flowed onto the table and congealed there. Barak ripped the man's shirt open, revealing a large stab wound in his chest.

'At least he died quickly,' Barak said. 'Is this the sixth victim?'

'No,' I said quietly. 'I see no symbolic linking to waters drying up.'

'You mean someone else killed Felday?' Barak asked, astonished.

'No, I think it was our killer. But not as part of his sequence. I think Felday was killed in case we found our way to him, or in case he talked.' I began prowling round the room. 'Come,' I said. 'Let's see if there is any sort of clue. A note, a receipt, anything.'

For an hour we searched the solicitor's neat little dwelling. But among all the papers we found nothing. The trail had gone cold.

I RODE OUT early next morning to the Bedlam. I had passed a disturbed night, constantly waking to the sound of the rain, and was in a tired and worried frame of mind as I rode along. Felday's death preyed on me; if I had not become a focus of the killer's attention, he would not have died. But then if he had not been so crooked, he would not have died either.

The sight of the Bedlam gates ahead brought me back to the present. I tied Genesis up and knocked at the door. Keeper Shawms answered.

At the sight of me he forced a smile. 'Master Shardlake,' he muttered.

'Good day. I am meeting Dr Malton here.'

He stood aside for me to enter. 'He ain't here yet. But Ellen is with Kite. He is getting the best of care.' Shawms's voice was respectful, but there was a nasty look in his eyes.

'Good.'

'That black doctor and Ellen like to get him out of his chamber, but it upsets the other patients.'

'I am sure you cope.'

The door of Adam's room was open. The boy was still chained; there could be no repeat of what had happened at London Wall.

Ellen was seated on a stool opposite him. 'Come, Adam,' she was saying, 'take the spoon and feed yourself. I am not going to put it into your mouth like a little baby. Come on.' She put on a babyish voice. 'Goo-goo, ga-ga.'

To my surprise, Adam responded to her gentle mockery with a smile. He took the spoon and bowl, and started eating the pottage in the bowl.

'Well done, Ellen,' I said. 'I have never seen Adam smile before.'

She got to her feet and curtsied. 'I did not see you, sir.' She blushed.

'I am meeting Dr Malton here.'

'Yes, I knew he was coming.'

Adam was now eating as fast as he could. He ignored me.

'I hear the King has proposed legislation forbidding women to read the Bible,' Ellen said.

'Yes, that is right. And uneducated folk.'

She smiled sadly. 'Everything is going back to the old ways. Well, perhaps that has to be; it is the new ways that brought poor Adam to this pass.'

I looked at her, wondering whether it was because of some religious nonconformity that Ellen was not allowed to leave the Bedlam.

'Ellen,' I said quietly, 'I do not know why it is you may not leave the Bedlam, but if I can help you in any way, I would be pleased.'

'Thank you, sir. But I am happy enough.' Yet her expression was sad. I thought, How can such an intelligent woman bear to spend her whole life in this place, secondhand news her only knowledge of the world outside?

Adam, having bolted down his pottage, curled himself over and began to pray. 'Heavenly Father,' he whispered, 'forgive me, I have sinned . . .'

'I will let him pray a little now he's eaten,' Ellen said, 'until Dr Malton comes. That is another of his ideas, to bargain with Adam, allow him some time to pray but insist he does other things too. And Dr Malton says it is important for Adam to have other people around him. So I take him into the parlour to mix with other patients now.'

'Shawms says Adam still upsets the other patients.'

'Less than he did. They call on him to be quiet, to stop praying. That is no bad thing for him.' She smiled sadly. 'Everyone here can see everyone else's problems. But usually not their own.'

'No, indeed,' said a voice from the doorway. Guy came in. To my surprise, he had a copy of the New Testament under his arm.

'How is Bealknap?' I asked.

'Dr Archer should be arraigned for assault,' he said. 'Apparently Master Bealknap had gone to him with no more than a prolonged stomach ache. He was not eating and so had grown weak. All Archer's bleeding and purges have done is make him weaker yet. I have prescribed good food and bed rest for a week; then he can hopefully look after himself.'

'Good. Thank you, Guy. Come to dinner tonight after you have seen him. As a reward for all your trouble. And I will give you Bealknap's fee.'

Guy smiled. 'He is a strange man. He answered my questions about his symptoms readily enough, for he was in great fear. But after I told him he was not going to die he hardly said a word, nor gave me any thanks.'

'That is Bealknap. I will tell you later,' I added grimly, 'about something he has done.'

Guy raised his eyebrows. Turning to Ellen, he asked, 'How is Adam?'

'He has had some breakfast. Even gave me something like a smile.'

'Then we make progress. Thank you for all you are doing,' Guy said.

Ellen curtsied and left us. I watched her go, her long brown hair swinging round her shoulders under her coif. I turned back to Guy, who had the Bible open and was struggling to engage Adam in conversation.

'If you read the gospels, you will see that Jesus wants his followers to live together in harmony, not to cut themselves off as you have done.'

'But God *does* test His people, test their faith. Look at Job. He tested him and tested him.' Adam banged a skinny fist on the stone floor.

'Is that what you feel? That God is testing you?'

'I hope so. It is better than being cast out. To suffer in Hell for ever and ever.' Adam bent over and began to pray again, his lips moving soundlessly.

Guy sighed, then stood up. 'I will leave him be for a few minutes,' he said. 'That is our bargain.'

'Guy, your patience is as bottomless as the sea.'

'I am following the trail of a mystery. Trying to understand what started all this. It is often something terrible that has happened in the real world that causes mad people to withdraw into a world of their own.' He looked over at Adam's crouched figure, and sighed. 'Matthew, I should spend some time with Adam. We will talk more tonight.'

THAT NIGHT I had Joan prepare a rich chicken stew. Guy arrived at six, and we sat to our meal. Tamasin had told me Barak had gone out drinking with his friends again. She sounded weary and angry. It was not a good sign. As we ate I told Guy more about Felday.

'So you had to encounter yet another body.'

'Yes. It is affecting Barak hard.'

'How are he and his wife?' I had told Guy something of their problems.

'I tell myself once this nightmare is over, Barak will make it right with her again. God knows,' I burst out in sudden vehemence, 'it has taken over all our lives. I was going to take some time this afternoon to work up the subscription list for Roger's hospital, but I found it hard to concentrate.'

'You will do it.' He looked at me. 'That will please his widow.' He hesitated. 'She will need time to set herself in order, Matthew, strong though she is.'

'I know.' I smiled wryly; he had guessed my feelings. I looked at him. 'How long a wounded soul takes to mend. And Adam, can he ever mend?'

'I think so. With the help of Ellen, who is putting much effort into his care, I think he can be brought back to the world. I will untangle how he was set on this terrible path, I am determined.' He spoke with passion.

'That sounded heartfelt.'

He nodded, slowly and heavily. Then he looked at me and said, 'I am far from being as sure and certain of things as I might appear, Matthew.'

'You are troubled, Guy?'

'Yes. Yes, I am.' He paused, then sighed, a sigh that was half a sob. 'Not about God or His goodness, but about what I am.'

I took a deep breath. 'Has this got something to do with Piers?'

He gave me a piercing look, but did not answer.

'Has he some hold over you, Guy?'

'No. Or at least, not in the way you mean.' His face was suddenly anguished. 'He was so tractable when he came, did everything to help me. But now he goes out roistering in the evenings at will. And yes, you were right, he listens at doors when I am consulting with patients. And I thought—' He broke off, resting his head on a tightly clenched fist.

'Thought what?'

When Guy spoke again, it was in broken, fractured tones, head bowed. 'I have wondered if my feelings for him are honourable.'

So that was it. 'What do you think?' I asked gently.

He shook his head sadly. 'I am not sure. When I first met him, it was his intelligence that struck me. But I noted his fair form and face, and when he came to my home, I found I had feelings that were new to me.'

I could think of nothing to say. Selfishly, I thought, Guy is my rock. Do not let him crumble now.

'Oh, I have pondered on it deeply,' he said. 'And you know what I think? I think what I want, perhaps have always wanted, is a son. To educate, to exchange ideas with, to come and visit me when I am past working. In the cloister there was always company, but now I am so often alone.'

Guy's face was full of sadness. 'Piers . . . flirts with me. The way he smiles, the way he touches me gently sometimes, he is inviting me to something. And part of me, I fear, would follow. I fear he has raised something in me I did not know was there, something more than this urge to be a father to him.'

'Guy, in a way it does not matter what your feelings are. It matters more what Piers is. He is cold, calculating, exploitative. I have seen how he listens at doors, seen his wheedling and his arrogance when he is with you.'

Guy put his head in his hands. 'Something else has happened now,' he said. 'I have noticed that money has begun to go missing.'

'You must get rid of him,' I said quietly.

'Cast him out, I that took him in?'

'You took a viper to your bosom. He uses tricks to gain an advantage.'

'I cannot believe he is as bad as you think. He has a good mind.'

'And a bad heart.'

When Guy left, I sat thinking of the loneliness so many men carry in this divisive, fractured age, and the ruthless people who would exploit it.

And then another thought took shape, one that sent a chill down my spine. We had been talking of Piers as cold, intelligent and ruthless. He knew about our hunt for the killer. I shook my head. It was impossible; he worked for

Guy, and the killer had freedom to come and go as he pleased. No, Piers was no killer. And it could not be Piers who followed us. My mind was in a fever. I would be suspecting Joan or Tamasin next. But who was it, who was it?

Chapter 10

In the morning it was still raining. I found Barak sitting at the table in the parlour, looking dubiously at a plate of bread and cheese.

'I heard you come in late last night,' I said, sitting down opposite him.

'Went out drinking with some friends.'

'Again? Could you not take Tamasin out one night?'

He fixed me with a bleary-eyed look. 'I needed to get out. I'm fed up of hanging around waiting for some new horror to happen.'

I reached for some bread. 'Where is Tamasin?'

'Still in bed, snoring. She woke up when I came in last night and went on at me, so she's catching up on sleep.' His expression made it quite clear he was not going to talk about it further.

'Guy came to dinner last night,' I said. 'He told me money has been going missing. He thinks it is Piers but cannot quite bring himself to believe it.'

Barak gave me a penetrating look. 'When I saw the old Moor with Piers, he seemed to think the sun shone out of his arse.'

'He wanted someone to care for, to teach. But he is beginning to see what Piers is really like.'

'What if we pay a visit to young Piers, put a bit of pressure on him? We could see how he reacts and take it from there.' Barak smiled a hard smile.

'You mean when Guy is not there?'

'He's not going to let us do it when he is there, is he?'

I hesitated, then said, 'I know Guy is going to see Bealknap this evening.'

'We go to Bucklersbury then?'

I nodded agreement. 'We only talk to the boy, though, nothing rough.'

'Even if he's not a thief, he's an eavesdropper and a nasty bit of work. Won't do any harm if we put some salt on his tail.'

'All right.' I rose from the table. 'We must go to Whitehall,' I said. 'I had word last night. Harsnet has called a meeting to discuss latest developments.'

Barak got up. 'And I need something to do, or I will end up as mad as Kite.'

LORD HERTFORD and Sir Thomas Seymour were already in the coroner's office when we arrived. Barak was told to wait on a bench outside Harsnet's room.

Harsnet was sitting behind his desk. Lord Hertford stood by the wall. Both looked grave. Sir Thomas lounged against the wall, an angry look on his louche, handsome face. As always he was dressed like a peacock, a bright blue doublet today, a cap with a huge feather in his hand.

'Close the door, Matthew,' Harsnet said. 'I do not want us to be overheard.'

'Not more bad news?'

'Bonner is tightening the screw further on the London radicals,' said Lord Hertford. 'Early this morning the London constables arrested eight men for possession of unlawful books, together with three printers and a bunch of apprentices for acting unlawful plays. The archbishop needs to know if any of these men have associations with him.'

'Is there any danger of that?' Thomas Seymour asked.

'He thinks not. Yet if this were to come out now—that the archbishop has launched a secret hunt for a madman who is killing lapsed radicals because the Book of Revelation told him to—it would be very dangerous. Have you learned nothing more, Gregory?' he asked Harsnet with sudden passion.

'I wish I had. I have been working day and night but there is no trace of him in London or the neighbouring counties.'

Lord Hertford turned to me. 'And you found he had been using a lawyer as his agent, but now has killed the lawyer too.'

'He has.' I told him the story of Bealknap and Felday.

'So there have been five murders linked to the vials of wrath. And this poor lawyer killed along the way. We must catch him.' Hertford turned to his brother. 'Judging by your news, the King is determined to marry Catherine Parr, however long she keeps him waiting.'

'What news, my lord?' Harsnet's head jerked up.

'My brother has been appointed Ambassador to the Regent of the Netherlands.'

'Because the King fears Lady Catherine may still have a mind to marry me,' Sir Thomas said with a slight swagger.

'We cannot be sure that is why,' his brother said. 'And if it is, think yourself lucky the King is sending you abroad, not to the Tower.'

I jumped at the sound of a loud knock. A shiver of fear seemed to pass through the room, but Lord Hertford called out firmly, 'Come in.'

Barak entered. 'I am sorry to interrupt you, my lord, but the guard from Lockley's tavern is here. Janley. They have found Lockley.'

'Alive?' Hope came into Harsnet's face.

'No, sir. Dead.' Barak looked around the company. 'In the old Charterhouse water conduit. The manner of his death shows he is the sixth victim. His body was fixed to the lock gates somehow, blocking them.'

'Stopping the waters of the Euphrates,' I said quietly.

Lord Hertford seemed to slump. 'Who knows?'

'Nobody who matters, my lord. Yet.'

'He has made us all dance, has he not? And now again. Will we ever have him dancing as he should, at the end of a rope?'

THE RAIN CONTINUED during our long ride to the Charterhouse. I was constantly blinking water out of my eyes. Sir Thomas, Harsnet, Barak and I rode with the guard Janley, as he told us more about what had happened.

'The Charterhouse watchman came running over to the Green Man this morning,' Janley told us. 'The place is empty but for him and the Bassano family, the King's Italian musicians. The watchman's known as a hopeless drunk. One of his duties is to open and close the lock gates in the old conduit house. He would forget, and the locals had to go over and remind him.'

'Do the locals know about this?' Harsnet asked.

'No, sir. I've told everyone who called that it looks like Lockley came back, murdered Mistress Bunce and fled. I've hinted it was about money.'

'Good. Well done.'

We arrived at Charterhouse Square and followed the path between the trees covering the ancient plague pit. We rode past the chapel and drew up at the small gatehouse set in the long brick wall of the dissolved monastery. There was a rail for horses there and we tied our animals up.

Janley knocked loudly at the door. Shuffling footsteps sounded and a thin middle-aged man opened it and peered at us with frightened eyes.

'I've brought some people to see the body, Padge,' Janley said gently.

The watchman looked at us uncertainly. 'They'll have to climb down to the sewer. I don't know how you'll get him out. It's horrible.'

'Leave it to us, matey,' Barak said soothingly.

We followed the watchman through the gates, past the ruins of the old monastic church and into a large, square, grassed courtyard. In the centre stood an octagonal copper-roofed building, with taps on the sides. That had to be the old monastic conduit, fed by the streams from Islington, where the monks had drawn their water and which then went on to drain the sewers under the houses in the square. Round the sides of the yard stood the old monks' cells, little square two-roomed houses, and to our left was a larger building, the doors open. I saw figures within.

'I've put the Bassano family in there,' the watchman said. 'They came into the gatehouse earlier, gabbling away about being flooded out. I went to look at the conduit house where the lock gates are, and saw a body jammed in front of them. I leaned over the rail and saw his face, saw it was poor Francis.'

'Master Padge, did you hear anything last night?' I asked quietly.

'No. A man has to sleep,' he added in a truculent mumble.

'Not if he's a watchman,' Seymour said sharply. 'Where are the Italians?'

Padge led the way to the building with the open door. It had evidently been the monastic chapter house, a small, austere room with benches round the wall. A little group of people sat huddled together on the benches, looking scared: four men and three women with children on their laps. All were clutching musical instruments, lutes and tabors and even a harp.

'Does anyone speak English?' I asked.

One of the men stood up. 'I do,' he said in heavily accented tones.

'You are the Bassano family, the King's musicians?'

'Yes, sir.' He bowed. 'I am their servant, Signor Granzi.'

'What has happened?'

'We woke this morning to find the floors of our quarters in water above our feet,' the Italian said. 'We had to rescue our instruments. We called the watchman. What is it, sir? We heard the watchman cry out.'

'Nothing to worry you,' Sir Thomas said.

'Did any of you hear anything strange last night?' I asked.

Granzi consulted the others. 'No, sir,' he said. 'We were all asleep.'

Sir Thomas grunted. 'Come on, Padge. Take us to where you found the body.' He pushed the watchman out into the rain.

We crossed the courtyard. Padge went into the gatehouse, and returned carrying three lighted lamps. He passed them to Barak, Janley and then me.

'We'll need these, sir,' he said, and led the way back to the courtyard.

We followed him into a low, square building standing on its own. In the centre of the stone floor was a large square opening, protected by a low railing. An iron ladder led down into a brickwork shaft.

'I left the lock gates slightly open last night,' Padge said. 'After all the rain there is a lot of water coming through and it needs to drain. When I came this morning, I thought to open them fully with the wheel but they were stuck fast. I looked down the shaft and . . .' The lamp he held began to shake.

We all went to the rail and looked down, holding our lamps out over the shaft. It went down twenty feet. At the bottom, on one side, a pair of heavy wooden gates was set into the brick wall. My eyes widened as I made out the body of a naked man spread-eagled against the gates. His face looked upwards, and I could see that it was Lockley.

'We'd better go down to look,' Sir Thomas said. 'Barak, Harsnet, come with me. You too, Shardlake—if you can climb down ladders.'

'Of course I can,' I replied sharply, though I did not relish the prospect.

Sir Thomas swung easily over the railing and began his descent. Barak and Harsnet followed. I made up the rear, grasping the slippery rungs hard.

At the bottom we found ourselves standing on wet brickwork that sloped down to a central channel where the water ran off into darkness. We looked at the lock gates, rendered speechless by what we saw. The naked body of Francis Lockley had been nailed to the gates, in some terrible mockery of the Crucifixion. His hands were nailed to one gate and his feet to the other. Big, broad-headed nails, driven in to the hilt. The gates, slightly ajar, could not be opened without ripping them out. I saw a mass of dried blood on the back of his head, but little sign of blood flowing from the terrible wounds. At least Lockley had died quickly, though the savagery was unspeakable.

'How in hell did the killer get him down here?' Sir Thomas asked.

'Dropped him, I'd guess,' Barak said. 'Then climbed down the ladder.'

A loud creak from the gate made us start. 'There's water building up behind the gates,' Barak said. 'At some point those nails will give way.'

'You're right,' Sir Thomas agreed. 'Let's get out of here.'

We climbed the ladder again, and followed Harsnet outside, shocked and overwhelmed. The rain seemed to be easing off.

'It will be a hard job getting Lockley out,' Harsnet said quietly. 'We will have to block the gates in some way while we remove the body.'

'I will arrange that now,' Sir Thomas said. Even he appeared subdued.

'I do not understand how he got Lockley into the precinct, how he knew where the conduit house was,' Harsnet said.

I looked around. 'If he was hanging about the vicinity, he could pick up that the watchman was a drunk,' I said quietly. 'Easy enough to get in here at night and explore the buildings to see if they would suit his purpose.'

'If he talked to the watchman, the drunken old sot may remember him,' Sir Thomas said, his eyes lighting up with excitement.

'I doubt he did, because Padge is still alive. Remember the killer has already murdered one man who could have led us to his identity.'

Harsnet nodded. 'Then we must question the tavern customers again.

Ask them if a stranger has been asking about the Charterhouse.'

Sir Thomas looked at me. 'Do you think there is any significance in the last two murders being round the Charterhouse?' he asked. 'Because do not forget, Lady Catherine Parr lives on the other side of that green. And Dr Gurney was staying there when he was killed.'

'I do not think so. I think he chose Lockley and his wife because of their past. Dr Gurney's presence across the square is surely a coincidence.'

Just then three figures walked under the gatehouse arch. I recognised the leading figure as Dean Benson. He indicated to his two retainers to stay where they were, and came up to us, his plump face anxious.

Harsnet stepped forward. 'What are you doing here, sir?' he asked.

'I have ridden halfway across London in the rain looking for you, sir. We should go inside. What I have brought here should not get wet.'

Harsnet hesitated a moment, then led the way back into the conduit house. Janley and Padge bowed as the gentleman of the church entered.

The dean looked round him, puzzled. 'What is going on in here?'

'Never mind that now,' Harsnet said. 'Please, why have you come?'

Benson delved in his pocket and pulled out a piece of paper. 'This was pushed under my front door just before dawn. My steward brought it to me.'

He handed the paper to Harsnet. It was folded, Dean Benson's name and the words MOST URGENT written on it. Harsnet opened it. Inside was written: *Lancelot Goddard, Kinesworth Village, by Totteridge, Hertfordshire.*

We stared at the simple, stark message, the address.

'Hertfordshire,' Harsnet said. 'I did not think to make enquiry so far.'

'The killer knew we were about to find the sixth victim,' I said quietly.

'And now he is giving us his address? He is surrendering?'

'No. That would be to abandon his mission,' I replied. 'The killer may be inviting us to this village to show us the seventh killing. The last. The great earthquake that will signal the end of the world.'

There was silence for a moment. The dean looked between us, puzzled. 'There has been a sixth death? Who? Here?' He looked around, his eyes widening as he recognised Sir Thomas Seymour.

'Down there,' I said quietly. 'Your former lay brother, Francis Lockley.'

The dean looked at the hatch, then stepped away.

'Dean,' Harsnet said, 'go back to your house. Tell nobody. You have seen that the Seymour family is involved in this, how high this matter reaches.'

The dean looked round us again, then turned and went out.

'We should ride up to Totteridge now,' Harsnet said.

'I'm not sure we should do that,' I said urgently. 'It could be a trap.'

'The hunchback's right,' Seymour said. 'This creature's got something waiting for us up there. It would be better for me to send a couple of trusted men up to that village, to spy out the land, find out whether Goddard lives there, make contact with the local magistrate. They can report back tonight. Coroner Harsnet, tell the archbishop what has happened. I will report to him personally as soon as I have news. We can go in force tomorrow.' He looked at the coroner. 'But we shall need the archbishop's approval.'

Despite his insulting behaviour to me, I looked at Sir Thomas with a new respect. He was thinking strategically.

Harsnet looked at me. I nodded. 'Very well,' he said reluctantly.

Seymour glanced at Padge. 'You'd better keep him somewhere safe for a bit, ply him with drink. His big ears have been flapping all this time.'

The watchman gave him a bitter look, but said nothing.

Suddenly Seymour grinned. 'The chase is nearly over, gentlemen.'

WHEN SEYMOUR and Harsnet had left, Barak and I stepped outside, leaving Janley and the watchman in the conduit house. Mercifully the rain had ceased and a weak sun was trying to penetrate the clouds.

'Shall we see if we can find where he got in?' Barak asked.

I nodded. Barak led the way through the long grass around the trees. My shoes and netherhose were getting a further soaking from the grass.

'Can't see anything,' he said. 'No, wait, look there.' He pointed to a single long line running through the grass. It had left a heavy impression.

'What is it?' I asked.

'A wheelbarrow,' Barak said. 'Wherever he was hiding Lockley, he must have had some distance to bring him. This is how he did it.'

We followed the thin line to where it disappeared in the short grass of a pathway round a field. Then we walked back to where Sukey and Genesis stood, cropping the long grass growing against the outer wall.

'Where now?' Barak asked as we mounted.

'Let us go and visit Master Piers. See if he has been stealing. We may be called to Hertfordshire later.'

'What if the old Moor is there?'

'Then we make some excuse. And please stop calling him that.'

The apothecaries were working in their shops when we arrived at Bucklersbury; through the window next to Guy's a man in a long robe could be seen pouring powder into an apothecary's jar. We tied up the horses. I had agreed that Barak would take the lead in questioning Piers.

He knocked loudly on the door. Piers opened it, carrying a candle. He looked at us in surprise. 'Dr Malton has gone out, sir.'

'We know. It's you we've come to see, young cock,' Barak said cheerfully, shouldering his way into the consulting room.

I followed him in, giving Piers a thin smile.

'Cut anyone up today?' Barak asked.

'I was upstairs, studying. I do not understand.' Piers voice was quiet, his expression subservient, but there was anger in his eyes as he turned to me. 'Why do you allow your man to talk to me thus, sir?'

'I have some questions. Barak can ask them as one servant to another.'

'I hear Dr Malton has had some money go missing;' Barak said. 'Know anything about it?'

'I cannot believe Dr Malton has authorised you to question me like this,' Piers said coolly. 'If he has had money missing, he would talk to me himself.'

'Ah, but Master Shardlake here is his attorney. Remember, stealing is a capital offence.'

The boy's eyes narrowed. 'I have done nothing.'

'Where is your room?' Barak asked.

'Up the stairs. But you have no permission to go in there.'

'Tough.' Barak turned to me. 'Shall I go look in his room?'

'I will go. You stay here and keep an eye on him.'

Barak drew his sword and Piers watched as I passed through the inner door. I mounted the staircase. On the upper floor I saw a door was open.

I searched the room. Guy's anatomy book lay on a desk. Piers had been copying one of the drawings. There was a chest containing clothes, some of surprisingly good quality. I explored the bed, turning over the mattress, and there I found a small leather bag. Inside was a collection of silver coins, totalling over a pound: far more money than an apprentice was likely to have. I took it and returned down the narrow staircase.

As I entered the room, I held up the bag. 'Money,' I said.

'So, my pretty, you *are* a thief,' Barak said grimly.

Piers's face took on a hard, calculating look. The mask is gone, I thought.

'I could say some things about that old blackamoor if I chose,' he said. 'Like how he prostrates himself before a big old cross in his bedroom. How he is a pederast. How he makes me commit immoral acts with him.'

'That is a lie!' I shouted angrily.

'Perhaps. But part of him would like to, and he would look uneasy at such an accusation. If I lose all, he will lose as well.' He looked at me grimly.

'Nasty piece of work, isn't he?' Barak said.

Piers's next move took us unawares. He reached behind him to the table, grabbed a flask of liquid and threw the contents in Barak's face. Barak gave a yell and stumbled backwards, dropping his sword as he raised his hands to his face. Piers ran to the door and fled into the night.

I ran to Barak and gently pulled his hands from his face, dreading what I might find. His eyes were red and weeping but there were no other marks, and I caught the sharp, sweet smell of lemons.

'My eyes,' he groaned.

'I'll get some water from the kitchen. I think it's just lemon juice. You'll be all right.' I hurried out, coming back with a pail of water and a cloth.

After a thorough wash, the pain in Barak's eyes subsided. 'That little rat will be miles from here by now,' he said.

'Yes. I think our best course is to stay here until Guy comes back.' I sighed. I was not looking forward to his return.

HE CAME IN an hour later, his eyes widening with surprise at the sight of us sitting in his shop, Barak still dabbing his eyes with a cloth.

'What has happened?' Guy asked.

I told him. When I had finished, he sat down on a stool. He looked bereft.

'You should have come to me first. You should not have gone behind my back.' His voice trembled with anger.

'I did not feel you could see Piers clearly. And he is a thief, Guy.'

'And now he has gone.'

'I am sorry.'

There was a silence that lasted only a few moments, but felt like an hour. Then I said, 'There have been two more killings.' I told him about Lockley, and the note giving Goddard's address.

After a moment, Guy said, 'As there is nothing I can do for Lockley, I wish you luck in Hertfordshire.' He gave me a look that was stony, almost contemptuous. 'I will not see Piers hanged for stealing a little money, as the law prescribes.' He picked up the bag of coins from where I had put it on his table, slipping it into his robe. 'There, your evidence is gone. And now I would like you to leave, Matthew. I am visiting Adam in the morning.'

'Guy—'

'Go, Matthew, please.' His cold, angry tone struck me to the heart.

Barak and I left the shop, and we rode home in silence.

IN THE MORNING there was still no word from Harsnet. So I decided to go to the Bedlam. Guy would be there visiting Adam, and I wanted to talk to him.

I rode to Bishopsgate without incident. But as I passed through the gates into the Bedlam yard, I heard an unexpected sound: a woman screaming and sobbing in dreadful fear. For an awful moment I feared the killer had misdirected us again and the seventh killing was to be here, now. Then I saw that a woman was hammering and banging on the closed doors of the Bedlam building. As I rode closer, I saw that it was Ellen.

'Let me in, Master Shawms!' she was screaming. 'Please!'

I dismounted and hastily tied Genesis to the rail, then elbowed my way through the crowd. 'Ellen,' I said quietly, laying a hand on her shoulder.

She did not look round. She seemed to press herself more tightly against the door. 'Who is it?' she whispered.

'It is I, Master Shardlake. What on earth is the matter?'

'For pity's sake, Master Shardlake, make him let me in.' And with that her knees gave way and she slid down the door, sobbing wildly.

I banged on the door. 'Shawms!' I shouted. 'Open this door! What is happening?' From within the building I heard people shouting, and thought I heard Adam's voice among them.

A key turned and the door opened to reveal Shawms and the big keeper Gebons behind him. As soon as the door opened sufficiently, Ellen threw herself inside and stood there, breathing heavily. A gaggle of patients stood in the open door of the parlour, their expressions fearful.

'What are you doing to these people?' I demanded of Shawms.

'Ellen needed a lesson. Thanks to you she has taken over the welfare of Adam Kite and makes so bold as to tell me how he should be treated. Now she is moving on to the other patients, demanding that this drivelling old dolt be released into the care of her family.' He glared round at an old woman. 'As though her family wanted the trouble of her, any more than Ellen's family want her.' His voice rose. 'Have you not yet grasped what this place is, Master Shardlake? It is a rubbish heap, where people of wealth leave their mad relatives. A rubbish heap that generates gold for Warden Metwys.'

'Ellen is a member of your staff, even if she was a patient once. What in the devil's name have you done to her?'

Shawms laughed then, right in my face. 'Is that what she told you? Ellen is still a patient; she always will be. I have given her some of the duties of a keeper, for she is good with the patients. But sometimes she gets above herself, and I have to remind her who and what she is by putting her outside.'

He turned to Ellen, who was breathing heavily. 'That is her madness,' he continued brutally. 'She can't bear to go outside, says the world sways and rocks and will swallow her up. She's been like that ever since she was set on by a gang of youths down in Sussex where she comes from, and they made a woman of her before her time. Ain't that so, Ellen?'

Ellen clasped her hands in front of her. 'Yes, Master Shawms,' she said calmly. She looked from him to me, her long face filled with shame. 'So now, Master Shardlake, you know all about me.'

I felt great pity for the poor woman, but knew instinctively not to show it.

'It does not matter, Ellen,' I said quietly. 'Listen, poor Adam is distressed. Will you come with me and help him?'

She gave me a grateful look. 'Yes, of course,' she said, and began walking steadily down the corridor, feeling for her bunch of keys.

I turned to Shawms. 'I hope Adam is not too disturbed by this incident; I should have to report it to the court.'

He gave me a vicious look as I turned away.

I joined Ellen at the closed door to Adam's room. 'Ellen!' he cried from within. 'What have they done to you?'

'It's all right,' Ellen called. 'I am here.' She opened the door.

Adam was standing as near to the door as his chain would allow. His frantic expression turned to relief as Ellen entered. 'Are you all right?' he asked.

'Yes, Adam. Do not disturb yourself. Sit down.'

A stool had been brought into the room. As Adam hesitantly sat down, I realised that he had shown concern for someone else for once. Then he turned his wasted face to me, and said something I did not understand.

'My concern for Ellen was honourable, sir. Please say you saw that it was so. I was not sinning again. It was not like the wicked reverend's woman.' Then he put his head in his hands and began to cry.

And then the connection came to me. His vicar, Meaphon, was friends with Reverend Yarington. Timothy had described the boy who had visited the prostitute Abigail as tall and dark. Adam was tall and dark.

'Adam, does the name Abigail mean anything to you?'

At that the boy stared at me in horror. 'My sin is discovered,' he whispered. 'Oh, God, forgive me, do not strike me down.'

'Sir, what are you doing?' Ellen asked indignantly.

'Turning a key that must be turned,' I said. I knelt down beside Adam, making my voice calm. 'Adam, you came to Reverend Yarington's house once with a message from your own vicar, did you not?'

He looked at me with terrified eyes. 'Yes.'

'Abigail saw you and invited you in. She taught you things you had thought on but not experienced yet. Am I right?'

'How can you know that?' he whispered. 'You will not tell my parents?'

'No. I promise.'

'I was wax in her hands,' Adam said. 'Jesus, my shield, seemed powerless. She must have come from the devil to make me a sinner.'

'She was only a poor woman. Helpless herself, in the power of that hypocrite Yarington.'

'Yes. He is a hypocrite. I knew I should tell my parents. I turned to God for guidance but could feel nothing. Has He abandoned me?'

'I am no theologian, Adam. But one thing is for certain, you have not abandoned Him. Only sought to reach Him in the wrong way, perhaps.'

It was too much for the boy. He hid his face again and wept.

I turned to Ellen. 'I must leave now. The information Adam has given me is important. I know I leave him in good hands with you.'

Her face coloured. 'Do you mean that?'

'I do. If Dr Malton comes, please tell him what Adam said. And tell him . . . tell him I tried to see him.' I smiled at her. 'You are a good woman, Ellen. Do not let a bullying pig like Shawms make you think otherwise.'

I RODE HOME in thoughtful mood, reflecting that one aspect of the mystery was solved at least: the boy who had visited Yarington's house had been locked safely in the Bedlam all these weeks. It looked like the murderer was Goddard after all. But why had he sent us his address?

I was still deep in thought as I turned into Chancery Lane from the north. I was brought sharply to myself by a shout of 'Look out, there!' I saw a pedlar directly in front of Genesis, holding a three-wheeled cart full of trinkets. As I jerked the reins I glimpsed a ragged coat, and a filthy face framed by thick grey hair and a bushy beard.

'Ye'll have me over. Ye'll pay if ye break my goods!' he muttered over his shoulder as he hauled his cart out of the way.

I steadied Genesis and rode past Lincoln's Inn Gate to my house.

I went upstairs to change out of my riding clothes. On the way back to the kitchen I passed the parlour, where Tamasin was arranging some twigs dusted with early blossom in a vase. She wore an expression of pensive sadness.

She saw me and smiled. 'I thought these would make a pretty display. I took them from the garden; I hope you do not mind.'

'They will remind us that it is spring. Where is Jack?'

'He has gone over to Lincoln's Inn to see how Skelly is getting on alone.'

'I should go there.' I hesitated. I looked at her seriously. 'Tamasin, we may be nearly there. We have located the house of the man we think is behind all this, near Barnet. Sir Thomas Seymour has organised a party of men to go there and take him. We may have to go there tonight.'

'You have the murderer?' she asked.

'We are fairly sure who he is.'

'So Jack will be off adventuring again,' she said.

'Tamasin, he hates this. As I do, who brought him into it.'

'You are right,' she agreed. 'He fears this creature you are hunting.' She spread her arms wide in a despairing gesture. 'But I can give him no comfort. When I try to talk to him, he calls me a nag.' She sighed wearily.

'Tamasin—'

She raised a hand. 'No, sir. You mean well and I thank you. But I am talked out.' She curtsied and left the room.

When Barak returned from my chambers, he went to the parlour to eat some bread and cheese.

'Thanks for keeping an eye on the work,' I said.

He nodded. 'By the way, Orr says that pedlar who's taken to frequenting Chancery Lane is becoming a nuisance. He's called twice this last couple of days trying to sell trinkets, asking for one of the women of the house.'

I stared at him. 'Wait,' I said quietly. I was breathing hard with the thought that had come to my mind. 'This pedlar, is he a ragged greybeard?'

'Aye. Him that has been round here for days.'

'And carries his things in a three-wheeled barrow.'

'You don't think . . . But he's an old greybeard. And half the pedlars in London push three-wheeled carts.'

'But what a way to follow us, unnoticed. Barak, is it him?'

'He's in Hertfordshire.'

'He's concentrated our attention there. Fetch Orr,' I said. 'Then go and see if the pedlar's in sight. Don't let him see you.'

Barak rose from the table. He gave me a doubtful look, but hurried away. Orr appeared a minute later. 'What was that pedlar selling?' I asked.

'Cheap jewellery. Brushes and pans. I told him to be off.'

'Pedlars do not usually waste time on second calls if they have no luck the first time.'

'He asked for the woman of the house. Perhaps he thought he could wheedle a woman into buying something. When he called, he kept looking past me, into the house.'

Barak returned. 'He's coming down Chancery Lane from Aldgate. He'll be here in a minute.' He frowned. 'You're right, there's something odd. He's just pushing his cart down the street, not accosting passers-by.'

'I think he may be the killer,' I said quietly. 'What better way to go around unnoticed, follow people, listen to conversations, than pass yourself off as a ragged old pedlar whom people will notice only to avoid.'

Barak turned to Orr. 'Shall we try to take him now, we two?'

Orr nodded. 'He seems unarmed.'

'We must hurry, or he'll be past us and into the throng of Fleet Street.'

I stood up. 'I'm coming too.' I spoke with more bravado than I felt. 'I'll just fetch my sword.'

THE SUN WAS LOW in the sky, the house casting long shadows across Chancery Lane. From the gateway I saw that the pedlar had now passed my house, trundling his cart on down the gently sloping street. The three of us ran pell-mell after him. Lawyers and clerks passing by stopped and stared.

'We'll look silly if it's just some old pedlar,' Orr said.

As we ran up behind him, the pedlar heard us coming and turned, pulling a brake on one of the rear wheels of his cart. I caught another glimpse of a grey beard, wild hair, bright eyes in a dirty face. He turned to run.

Barak jumped him, grasping his ragged collar. The pedlar stayed upright and seized Barak's arm, preventing him from reaching his sword. Orr grabbed at the grey beard but it came off with a ripping sound. Then the man's knee came up between Barak's legs and Barak doubled over with a gasp. The pedlar jumped for his cart, thrust his hand in and pulled out a large sword. He stood at bay against the cart; Orr and I, swords drawn, had him pinned against it.

I tried to get a look at the pedlar's face. The bushy grey hair obscured his brow but something struck me as odd about the colour of his face. I realised that what I had taken for a dirty face was in fact caked with actor's make-up. Only the blue eyes, glittering with hatred, were real.

The pedlar made a sudden jump, striking out at me. More by luck than judgment I managed to parry the blow. Then Barak, face pale with pain, jumped to my side. He thrust at the pedlar's sword arm, but a sudden shout from the side of the road distracted him and he missed.

'Stop this melee!' Treasurer Rowland was yelling, disorienting us for a second. The pedlar took his chance and thrust his sword at Barak, catching him on the forearm and making him drop his sword. Then he jumped aside and ran at a man in the crowd, a law student who had dismounted from his horse to watch. The pedlar slashed at his cheek with his sword, then jumped into the horse's saddle. In seconds he was racing back up Chancery Lane towards Holborn. I turned wearily back to the scene around the cart.

Barak had received only a small flesh wound but the poor student was badly hurt. Treasurer Rowland ordered him taken back to Lincoln's Inn. Then he turned to me, furious, demanding to know why we had attacked a pedlar. Telling him it was the man who had killed Roger Elliard shut him up.

The little crowd of onlookers dispersed, and we were left with the cart. We looked through it but there was nothing there but trays of jewellery, some cloths and dusters and bottles of cleaning vinegar for silver.

'Big enough to hide a body,' Barak observed.

'Was it Goddard, sir?' Orr asked.

'With that false beard and the make-up on his face, who can say?'

'I saw no sign of a large mole,' Barak said. 'Surely it would be hard to hide.'

'Why was he here?' Orr asked.

'Perhaps to observe our comings and goings.' I thought a moment, then delved into the cart and pulled out the bottles of cleaning vinegar. One by one I emptied them into the bottom of the cart. The contents of the fourth made a hissing sound and began to sear the wood.

'Vitriol again,' I said. 'That is why he has been calling at the house. This was meant to be thrown at Tamasin or Joan.'

The three of us walked slowly home, leaving the cart where it was.

Joan was standing in the doorway. Her eyes widened at the sight of Barak's arm. 'What happened?' she asked, her voice trembling.

'The man who attacked Tamasin and me was outside,' I said. 'He got away.' I could not bear to tell her what might have happened had she, rather than Orr, opened the door to the pedlar. 'It's all right now.'

Barak leaned against the banister, his face pale as shock caught up with him. 'I'd have had him but for that old fool Rowland,' he said fiercely.

'Yes, I think you would.'

THE RIDER from Lambeth Palace called after midnight, when we had all gone to bed. Barak and I were told to go immediately to a conference with Archbishop Cranmer. We dressed quickly, fetched the horses and rode through the dark city to Whitehall Stairs, where a boat was waiting to ferry us across the Thames. Harsnet arrived outside Cranmer's office at the same time.

The archbishop was sitting behind his desk. Lord Hertford was not present but Sir Thomas Seymour was, a look of excitement on his face.

I told them of the incident with the pedlar.

'You could not see who he was?' Harsnet asked when I had finished.

'No. He was well disguised. His face was caked with make-up.'

Cranmer sat considering for a moment. Then he turned to Sir Thomas. 'Tell them the news from Hertfordshire,' he said.

'I found Kinesworth easily enough. The local magistrate knew all about the Goddard family. They lived in a manor house just outside the village. They were wealthy once, but Goddard's father was a drunk and lost all their lands when Goddard was still a boy. When he was old enough, Goddard went to Westminster Abbey to be a monk. The old woman lived on at the house alone until she died a few months ago and Goddard inherited it.'

I took a deep breath. 'Is he there now?'

'He comes and goes. He was seen riding out to London yesterday. We waited all day for him to come back, but smoke wasn't seen coming from the chimney of the house until well after nightfall.'

'So he could have been the pedlar on that timescale,' I said.

'Yes.'

'Then let us take him,' Sir Thomas said, his voice full of excitement.

Cranmer turned to him. 'How many men can you provide?'

'A dozen, my lord,' he answered confidently. I could see he was enjoying being the centre of attention. 'All strong young men.'

Cranmer nodded. 'I think it is time to end this matter now. I want you to go with Sir Thomas's party, Matthew. It seems that for the killer you are connected to his mission. That is all the clearer after the pedlar's attack.'

'Yes, Your Grace,' I said.

The archbishop turned to Seymour. 'This is not sport, Thomas,' he said firmly. 'If it goes wrong and the King finds out what we have been doing, it will not only be me who suffers. Curb your enthusiasm for adventure. And remember, Goddard must never be brought to trial.'

Sir Thomas flushed, but nodded. 'I understand, my lord.'

'Good. And thank you for what you have done so far.'

He turned to Barak, who was standing quietly by the door. 'I want you to help Sir Thomas organise his men into an armed party,' he said. 'You worked for Lord Cromwell; you have useful experience in such matters.'

'Yes, my lord.' Barak bowed.

The archbishop stood up. 'I pray you can end this horror,' he said.

Chapter 11

A little over an hour later, I sat on my horse outside my house. The sound of jangling harnesses approached from the direction of the Strand. A crowd of over a dozen young, strong-looking men, all wearing swords, rode quietly up to me. All were dressed in sober clothes, though I sensed an air of suppressed excitement. A tall man in his thirties was in the lead, Harsnet and Barak beside him. Sir Thomas was not there.

Harsnet introduced the tall man. 'Edgar Russell, Sir Thomas's steward.'

I nodded at the man, who bowed briefly in the saddle. I was glad to see that he had a serious, authoritative look about him.

'Where is Sir Thomas?' I asked.

Barak smiled. 'He's gone to fetch Dean Benson out of his bed, and bring him up to Hertfordshire to identify Goddard for certain, if we find him.'

'We must go now if we are to get there before dawn,' Russell said to me. 'Are you ready?'

I nodded. We rode through the dark and silent roads, no sound but the horses' hooves and the jingling of their harnesses, the cattle dim shapes in the meadows. It was monotonous, and once I almost dozed off in the saddle. It was still dark when Russell raised a hand for us to halt. We had come to a small country inn set back from the road.

'Magistrate Goodridge is inside,' Russell said, dismounting. 'Coroner, Master Shardlake, come inside. Someone will take your horses. You too, Barak,' he added with a smile. 'We need all the practical minds we can get.'

Inside was a long, low room set with tables. A fire burnt in a hearth, its warmth welcome after the long cold ride. A man of around sixty was sitting at one of the tables, a hand-drawn map before him. He rose to greet us, introducing himself as William Goodridge, the magistrate.

He bade us sit and, indicating the map, said, 'The house is a mile out of the village. There is lawn on all four sides, and beyond that, woodland.'

'The house looks big,' I said. 'How many rooms are there?'

'About a dozen, as I recall.'

'You are sure Goddard is still at the house now?' Harsnet asked.

'Oh, yes. The man I have watching sent a message half an hour ago saying there were lights at a window.'

Russell stood up. 'I hear horses. Somebody is coming.'

We all turned to the door as it opened, and Sir Thomas Seymour entered with four armed men. Dean Benson was with him as well, wrapped up against the cold in a heavy dark coat, looking miserable and afraid.

Sir Thomas smiled at the company. 'Well,' he said, 'we are all here now. The dean here took some persuading, but he came.'

He made a mock bow to the angry-looking Benson, and strode towards the map. The steward explained the layout of Goddard's house. Sir Thomas thought a moment, then turned to the company.

'Are you ready to storm this villain's citadel?' he asked.

'Yes, Sir Thomas!' The reply came in a chorus.

The magistrate called the innkeeper and asked him to prepare some breakfast. It was only bread and cheese but it was welcome. As we ate, a man came with a message that smoke was still coming from Goddard's chimney.

'All night?' Russell said. 'That's strange.'

'He's waiting for us,' I said quietly.

AT FIRST LIGHT we set off along the country lanes, arriving at length at a stretch of woodland. The old manor house was set in a little hollow in the middle. A plume of smoke rose from one of the tall brick chimneys. All the windows were shuttered. Russell whispered to his men to move through the wood as quietly as possible.

'What is Goddard doing in there?' Harsnet whispered.

'Whatever it is, we have him trapped now, surely,' Barak said.

We turned as Russell walked quietly towards us. 'We are ready to go in,' he said. 'Sir Thomas, me, Barak, Serjeant Shardlake and six others. Ten men. We'll rush the house. The rest of the men will stay in the woods, ready to catch him should he flee.' He looked around him.

'I will lead,' Sir Thomas said. He took a deep breath, then marched out of the trees towards the house, stepping carefully. We followed silently.

Sir Thomas reached the long grass that had once been lawn. Then we all jumped as a great tumult of sound erupted at his feet and a host of white shapes darted up from the grass. Sir Thomas let out a cry, and behind him came the whistling sound of swords being drawn from scabbards.

Then Barak laughed. 'It's geese,' he said. 'A flock of geese!'

Twenty angry birds flew away over the grass, honking angrily.

'Those geese were set to warn of intruders,' I said to Barak. 'He knows we are here now. We've lost surprise.'

Russell stepped out of the wood to join his master, waving to the rest of us, and we all loped through the grass and up to the front door.

'Kick it in,' Sir Thomas said brusquely, nodding to a large young man.

Before the man could launch a kick, Barak stepped forward quickly and grasped the handle. The door opened, smoothly, on well-oiled hinges.

'He's making it easy for us,' he said.

We gathered round the doorway, and Sir Thomas shouldered his way into the dim interior. We followed, our eyes darting around fearfully. We were in a large old entrance hall. On either side, two staircases ascended to a first-floor balcony. Behind each staircase a hallway led to further rooms beyond.

Russell rapped out orders. 'You two, up that staircase. You two, the other one. I'll take the left-hand doorway with Brown.'

'Master Shardlake and I will take the right-hand doorway,' Barak said.

'Very well. Master Harsnet, Sir Thomas, please be ready to help secure any rat that comes running out.'

Men began running to the steward's directions. I followed Barak towards the right-hand hallway. I saw that a door at the far end was half open and a dim red light flickered inside. Then a tinkling of breaking glass sounded, and we became aware of another sound within the room, a low continual hissing.

'What in God's name is that?' I whispered.

'I don't know.' Barak hesitated, then walked steadily on, his sword held before him. He reached the doorway and pushed the door open. We stared in.

The room was large, and on one wall a large fireplace was set, with a fire burning brightly. Straight ahead of us was an ornate, high-backed chair. A man was sitting in the chair, dressed in the black robe of a Benedictine monk, the hood raised over his head. The man stared straight at us. There was a large mole on one side of his nose, and his lips were drawn back into a terrible, triumphant smile. On the floor lay a smashed lamp: that must have been the tinkling sound we heard. The candle was still burning on the floor, on top of a thin trail of grey ash-like stuff. The ash led to a hissing, sparkling fire that was running quickly down a trail of dark powder to two large barrels under the window. I saw the shutters were not quite closed.

For once I reacted quicker than Barak, who seemed transfixed by the sight of the gunpowder trail. I grabbed his arm and shouted, 'Run!'

We fled the room, back down the corridor, shouting, 'Everybody get out, now! There's gunpowder. He's going to blow up the house!'

I heard footsteps running towards the door from all over the building. I followed Barak with huge strides, almost leaping.

Then I felt a hot, heavy impact at my back. It blew me off my feet as though I were a doll. Everything round me seemed to quiver, though strangely I heard no sound. My last thought before losing consciousness was, He did it, he made the earth quake.

WHEN I WOKE, my first terrible thought was that I was dead and had been sent to Hell, for all around me was smoke, lit from behind by fire. Then I saw white circular lights moving in the smoke. One approached and for a moment I feared to see a demon, but the shape resolved itself into Harsnet's face. He knelt beside me and I realised I was lying on damp grass.

'Stay still, Master Shardlake,' Harsnet said in soothing tones. 'Your back is burnt—not badly, but the village healing man has applied some lavender to it.' I became conscious then that my back hurt; at the same time I realised that Harsnet's voice sounded strangely muffled.

I sat up, shaking my head. A blanket half covered me and I pulled it round to cover my bare back, a movement that hurt it, making me wince.

'He had gunpowder,' I said, clutching Harsnet's arm. 'He lit the barrels—'

'Yes,' the coroner said gently. 'It is over. The back of the house has collapsed and the rest is burning fast. You saved our lives by calling out to us.'

'Did everyone get out?'

'Yes. But several were injured. One of Sir Thomas's men was thrown through the air and landed on his head. He is likely to die. A doctor has been sent for. You worried us, sir; you have been unconscious over an hour.'

I turned and saw Barak lying beside me, a blanket over his legs.

'Are you hurt?' I asked him.

'Came down with a bit of a bang. Think I've cracked a couple of ribs. The explosion blew my hose off. Your robe was blown to tatters too, and your doublet.' He spoke lightly, but I saw the horror in his eyes.

'It is all over,' Harsnet said quietly. 'He poured out the seventh vial, and made the earth shake. He killed himself doing it, probably thought he would be taken up to Heaven.' His mouth set. 'But now he is in Hell!'

'Why would Goddard kill himself, just at the culmination of his great scheme?' I asked. 'Surely if he thought it would bring about Armageddon he would want to see it.'

'Who knows what went on in his mind? I think he was possessed after all, Master Shardlake, and now the devil has gathered his soul.'

Harsnet's voice still sounded muffled. I hoped my ears had not been permanently damaged. I lay back on one elbow, exhausted.

'Would you like me to fetch you some water?' Harsnet asked.

'Please.' When he left me, I looked at the burning house as the last of the roof caved in. I turned to Barak. 'It's not over,' I said.

'But we saw him. That was Goddard, the mole on his nose. He set a trap. He had plenty of warning with the geese to set the fuse so it would blow us all to kingdom come.'

'But it didn't. We all got out,' I said. 'Did you see the window above those gunpowder barrels? The shutter was open slightly. There could have been someone else in there, who lit the fuse and got out.'

'But he was sitting there grinning at us. We saw him.'

'What if Goddard wasn't the killer? What if the seven vials are only a stage in some larger pageant? The next stage of which he can pursue untroubled if he is believed dead?'

Sir Thomas and Russell approached. Sir Thomas looked subdued.

'Well, Shardlake,' he said, 'here's a spectacular end to your hunt. You got out.' He looked at me accusingly. 'One of my men is likely to die.'

'I am sorry for it. But I am not sure Goddard was the killer,' I said. 'I think there was someone else in that room, who got away.' I turned to Russell. 'Did any of your men hear or see anything after the explosion?'

'Your brains are addled,' Sir Thomas said angrily.

But Russell nodded. 'Yes. Just afterwards one of my men saw something moving through the woods, said it looked like a man. But it was chaos there, everyone shocked by the explosion, animals panicking.'

'A deer,' Sir Thomas said. But from the look Russell gave me I could see he doubted too.

A HEADQUARTERS had been set up in the stables behind Goddard's house. I got Russell to help me there, then fetch the man who had seen something in the woods. He was another of Sir Thomas's young servants, keen and sharp.

'I was sure it was a man that darted past me,' he said. 'It was just a glimpse, a figure moving between the trees, but I'd swear it had two legs, not four.'

I was sitting on a bale of hay, Barak beside me. He looked at the young man and then at me. 'God help us. If not Goddard, then who is the killer?'

'I do not know.' I turned to see that Harsnet had entered the stables.

'It is over, Master Shardlake,' he said. 'Goddard ended it on his own terms but he did end it. Our duty now is to tell the archbishop.'

I looked at him. 'I know everyone would like it to be over. I wish I could believe that myself. But we cannot always believe what suits us.'

AN HOUR LATER, those of Sir Thomas's men who were uninjured were dismantling the pile of rubble that was all that remained of the rear wing. Part of the roof had collapsed straight down onto the interior of the house, and I stood watching as the slates were lifted. Beside me was a frowning Sir Thomas. Harsnet stood at a little distance, occasionally shaking his head. Beside him Dean Benson sat on a lump of brickwork. I looked at the lawn, where dazed figures wrapped in blankets still sat. A cart had arrived from Barnet and the more badly injured were being loaded onto it.

A shout from Russell made me turn round. Sir Thomas and Harsnet joined me in scrambling over the rubble. Russell was pointing at something by his feet. I saw that he had uncovered a severed arm wearing the tatters of a monk's robe. A moment later a man lifted a slate and jumped back with a cry. Underneath we saw a severed head, barely recognisable, for it was covered in thick dust. Sir Thomas, quite unaffected, took a handkerchief and began cleaning dust from the ghastly thing.

It was the man who had been sitting in the throne-like chair. I recognised the mole on the nose. Astoundingly, the head was still smiling and then, fighting a rush of nausea, I saw why. Tiny nails had been hammered in to hold the mouth open, run through the flesh into the jaw.

I looked up at Harsnet. 'That man was dead when we entered that room.'

Seymour bent and picked up the head with no more concern than if it had been a football. He carried it to where Dean Benson sat.

The cleric jumped up, his eyes wide with horror. 'Is that a . . .?'

'A head, yes.' He held it up. 'Whose?'

'That is Lancelot Goddard,' Benson said, and collapsed in a dead faint.

EARLY IN THE MORNING of the next day, Barak and I sat at breakfast. The journey back from Kinesworth had been uncomfortable for both of us. We had gone to bed early and slept uneasily. Blisters were rising on my back.

'How are your ribs?' I asked.

'Sore,' he replied with a grimace. 'But they're only bruised, not cracked.'

'Is Tamasin joining us for breakfast?'

'I don't know. I left her dressing.' He sighed. 'Sometimes I wonder if she thinks I get these knocks to spite her.'

'Are you still on poor terms?'

'Probably. When we got back, I told her I needed to sleep, but she wanted to know everything. I was too tired to talk,' he added. 'Too worried too.'

It was clear now that Goddard had been a victim, not the perpetrator, of the killings. The killer, whoever he was, was still on the loose.

'We're back to square one,' Barak said.

'And without any idea where he will strike next. One thing I am sure of. He will not end it now.'

'Do you think he will come after you?'

'I don't know. Unless Goddard had some involvement with the radical sects after he ceased to be a monk, which seems unlikely, he couldn't have been the intended seventh victim. But if I was, and was to die in that explosion, why bother setting up that display with Goddard in his seat? Why not just blow the house up with us all in it?' I sighed.

The door opened and Tamasin came in. She wore a plain dress and her blonde hair was unbound, falling to her shoulders. She looked between us with a hostile glance. 'You have both been in the wars, I see,' she said.

'Where is your coif?' Barak asked. 'Your hair is unbound like an unmarried woman.'

She ignored him and turned to me. 'Jack says you haven't caught him.'

'No,' I said. 'We have to go on searching,' I added quietly.

'He has killed eight people,' Barak said impatiently. 'Nine, if Sir Thomas's man who was injured in the explosion dies.'

Tamasin sat down and looked her husband in the eye, with an expression that was both angry and sad. 'It is not what you're doing now that makes me angry with you. It is what you've been like since our baby died.'

Barak looked at me, then back at her. 'You shouldn't be talking of this in front of someone else. Not that you haven't already, I know.'

'I talk in front of someone else because you won't *listen* when we talk alone.' Tamasin's voice rose to a shout. 'Do you ever think what it's been like for *me* since the baby died? Do you think a day passes without it all coming back to me, the day he was born. You weren't there, you were out drinking. Yes, that was when it started.'

'Tamasin—' Barak raised his voice but she raised hers higher.

'The pain, the awful pain, I never felt anything like it. Then the midwife telling me that the baby was twisted round in my womb, she couldn't bring him out alive and I would die unless she broke his little skull. You didn't hear that crack. It still sounds over and over in my head. Then she lifted him out and I saw he was dead . . .' Tears were rolling down her face now.

Barak had gone very pale. 'You never told me,' he said.

'I wanted to *spare* you!' she cried. 'Not that you spared me. Coming back drunk, always going on about your son, your poor son. My son too.'

'I didn't realise it had been like that,' Barak said.

'What in God's name did you think it was like?'

He swallowed. 'I've heard . . . that when a baby is twisted in the womb like that it can stop a woman having others. We—'

'I don't know if that's why there have been no others!' Tamasin shouted. 'Is that all you care about? Is that all you can say to me?'

'No, Tammy, I didn't mean—' Barak raised a hand. He should have taken her in his arms and comforted her, but he was too shocked by her outburst.

Tamasin stood up, turned round and left the room.

'Go to her,' I said. 'Go now.' But he just sat there, helpless, shocked.

'Poor Tamasin,' he whispered. At length he stood up and stepped to the door, but as he did so, the front door slammed.

Joan was in the hall. 'Tamasin's just gone out,' she said. 'I told her we weren't supposed to go out alone, but she just ignored me.'

Barak went past her. I followed him outside. We could see no sign of Tamasin. She had disappeared into the crowds.

TWO HOURS LATER, I was tying Genesis up outside the Bedlam. Barak had ridden off to see if Tamasin had gone to any of her friends from her days as a servant in Queen Catherine Howard's household. It seemed her outburst had shocked him into realising fully what his behaviour had done, and he was full of contrition. It was something he had to do alone, so I had ridden out to see Adam.

Hob Gebons let me in. He took me to Shawms's room, where the keeper produced a report to the court saying that Adam was eating, was kept secure, and received regular visits from his doctor.

'I'll see how Adam is today. If it is still as you say, I will approve the report,' I said to Shawms.

Gebons led me to Adam's cell. To my surprise, the boy was standing looking out of his window, into the back yard.

'Adam,' I said.

As soon as he saw me, he slid down the wall, bent over and began to pray. I went and joined him, kneeling with difficulty; it hurt my burnt back.

'Come on, Adam,' I said. 'You were not praying just now.' A thought struck me. 'Do you do this so you do not have to talk to people?'

He hesitated for a moment, then gave me a sideways look. 'Sometimes. People frighten me. They seek to hunt out my sins.' He hesitated. 'You did not tell my parents what . . . what I did with that Jezebel?'

'You mean the girl Abigail? No. I will say nothing, nor will Guy. We have a legal duty to keep your confidence. But your parents love you, Adam. I know your father wants you to go into the business with him one day.'

'I do not know. They say a son going into his father's trade can undo his reputation.' He hesitated, then added, 'And I do not want to be a stonemason, I do not like the work. That is another sin.'

'My father was a farmer, but I only ever wanted to be a lawyer. I do not think that was a sin. Does not God give us each our own callings?'

'He calls us to be saved.' Adam screwed his eyes shut. 'Father, look down on me, look down and save me, see my repentance . . .'

I rose slowly to my feet. I frowned. Something Adam said had rung a bell. Then I made the connection with what Timothy had said about visitors. I had spent so much time thinking about who the young man was who visited Abigail that I had missed the rest of what the boy had said. I found I was trembling. If I was right, I knew now who the killer was. It shocked me.

AN HOUR LATER I was knocking on Dorothy's door. I had stopped first at my house to question Timothy about Yarington, and although he could not give me the name I was looking for, he gave me a description. It was enough to send me hurrying round to Dorothy's.

Margaret the maid answered the door. 'Is Mistress Elliard in?' I asked.

'She has gone downstairs to have a word with Master Elliard's clerk about some payments due to his estate. Some clients have not paid because they know Master Elliard is dead. At least Master Bealknap has returned to his chambers. When he rediscovered his appetite, he was eating Mistress Elliard out of house and home.'

As I waited for Dorothy in the parlour, I realised it was days since I had seen her, since that almost-kiss. I feared she might be out of sorts with me, but when she entered the room, she only looked weary.

'Margaret tells me Bealknap is gone,' I said.

She nodded. 'I do not wish to be uncharitable, but that man is unbearable.'

'I feel responsible . . .' I shifted my position slightly, and a stab of pain went down my back. I winced.

'Matthew, what is the matter?' Dorothy stepped forward. 'Are you ill?'

'It is nothing. A slight burn.' I took a deep breath. 'We thought we had the killer, thought it was all over at last, but he escaped.'

'Will this never end?' she said quietly. 'Oh, I am sorry. You are tired, and hurt too. I am so selfish, caught up in my own troubles. Can you forgive me?'

'There is nothing to forgive.'

Dorothy had moved back to her favoured position, standing before the fire, the wooden frieze behind her. The light from the window caught the frieze, showing up the different colour of the poor repair.

'It is a shame that discoloured patch draws the eye so,' she said, shifting the conversation to mundane matters. 'The man who originally made it was such an expert. We contacted him again after that corner was damaged, but he was recently dead. His son came instead. He did a poor job.'

'The carpenter and his son. Do you . . . do you remember their names?'

She gave me a sharp look. 'Why does that matter?'

'One of the killer's other victims also had a carpenter come to repair a damaged screen. What was their name? The father and son?'

Dorothy went pale. 'Cantrell,' she said. 'Their name was Cantrell.'

Chapter 12

I ran back to my house to fetch Genesis, then rode faster than I had for years, down Fleet Street and past the Charing Cross. My burnt back throbbed and jolted with pain, but I ignored it. When I reached Whitehall Palace, I managed to convince the guards that my business was urgent.

Harsnet looked up as I entered his office. 'What has happened, Matthew?' he asked wearily. 'Not another killing?'

'No,' I said, and he looked relieved. 'But I think I know who the killer is.'

He stared at me. I told him about the works Cantrell and his father had done at Roger's house and Yarington's. His eyes widened, he leaned forward. When I had finished, he stood in thought.

'We should act now, Coroner,' I said.

'But Cantrell's eyes?' he said. 'He is half blind. We have seen him. And according to the guard there he never goes out.'

'What if his eyes weren't as bad as he pretended? Where better to hide than behind those great thick lenses? And he never lets the guard into the house. He could get out without his knowledge.'

'And he knew Lockley,' Harsnet said. 'And Goddard. And now, we know, Roger Elliard's and Reverend Yarington's houses. And he could have learned of people who had left the radical reformers' circles when he was with his father's group.' Harsnet picked up his coat. 'I will find two or three constables and we will go round there now.'

We walked quickly down to Westminster, and I waited impatiently in the busy square while Harsnet went to find the constables. At length he reappeared, with three sturdy young men carrying staffs and wearing swords.

We walked together to Dean's Yard. Leaving two of the constables to guard the front, Harsnet and I took the third and stepped into the noisome little lane that ran alongside the house. The constable pushed open the gate to Cantrell's yard. It was empty, the door to the little shed shut. I went with Harsnet to the rear window of the house and looked in. The parlour inside was empty. The constable meanwhile had entered the shed. He laughed. We joined him and saw Cantrell's guard sprawled on a heap of sacks. He was fast asleep, and the smell from him told that he was drunk. The constable kicked him. The man stirred, groaned and opened his eyes.

'Is this how you guard your ward?' Harsnet snapped.

The guard struggled to sit up. A dripping tap caught my eye, set in the side of a large barrel. I lifted the lid and saw that it was half full of beer.

'He made sure there was temptation in his way,' I said.

'Where is he?' Harsnet asked the wretched guard. 'Cantrell? Is he in?'

'I don't know,' the man mumbled. 'He makes me stay out here. He won't let me *in*, sir. That's the problem.'

Hasnet turned away. 'Come on, let's search the house.'

We wasted no ceremony. At a gesture from Harsnet the constable smashed the recently repaired window, and one after the other we stepped through into the miserable parlour. Inside, there was nothing but silence.

'Let's get those men in from the front,' I said.

The constables were sent to look through the house. I told them to disturb nothing. They returned minutes later to confirm the place was empty.

We turned to the door that led from the parlour to what Cantrell had said was his father's workshop. It was a stout oak door, firmly locked. It took two of the constables to break it down. Inside it was dark, the shutters drawn over the windows. We all hesitated for a moment on the threshold; then I stepped inside and opened the shutters, light spilling in.

There were three wooden chests against the wall. And I recognised the pedlar's cart. Cantrell had retrieved it. I went over and touched the handle.

I wondered whether the cart had belonged to Cantrell's father. Then a thought struck me. To get from Westminster up to Hertfordshire, Cantrell must have a horse. I called one of the constables over.

'Go and talk to the neighbours,' I said. 'Find out if any of them remembers Cantrell or his father having a horse.'

As the constable walked off, I lifted the lid of the nearest chest, dreading what might be within. It was a pile of disguising clothes, tattered robes and crowns of cloth. There were fake beards and wigs too—a whole wardrobe.

'Those must have cost money,' Harsnet said, glancing over.

The chest Harsnet had opened contained bottles and jars of herbs and drugs. I opened them carefully. One stoppered bottle contained a thick, bitter-smelling yellow liquid. I lifted it out. 'I think this is dwale.' I took another bottle, sniffed the contents carefully, then tipped a few drops on to the ground. The vitriol hissed and spat.

'There can be no doubt now,' Harsnet said.

I bent and opened the third chest. At the bottom, under some cloths, lay a large flat wooden case. I opened it, then stepped back with a gasp.

Inside the box, neatly laid out, were knives of different sizes, a little axe and even a small cleaver. Trays contained little hooks and pins, and pliers and tweezers of various sizes. The cleaver and some of the knives had blood on them, and a foul smell rose from the box.

'Goddard's surgical equipment,' I said.

Harsnet turned aside, his mouth twisting with disgust.

We went upstairs. There were two bedrooms. One, which had been stripped bare of all furniture except an old bed, I guessed had belonged to Cantrell's father. The other was his. There was an old truckle bed, another chest, old and scarred, and a table with a large copy of the Bible set on it.

Harsnet opened the Bible. 'Look at what he has done here,' he said.

I went over to him. He had opened the Testament at the Book of Revelation. The wide margins were filled with notes in red ink, in handwriting so tiny it was virtually illegible. The passages dealing with the consequences of the angels pouring out the seven vials of wrath were underlined.

I turned the pages, and stopped at the chapter on the Judgment of the Great Whore. 'Look at the underlinings here,' I said. 'Does this give us the clue to what he means to do next?'

Footsteps sounded on the stairs and the constable appeared. 'I spoke to an old woman downstairs,' he said. 'She said Cantrell's father had a horse.'

'Did she say what it looked like?'

He nodded. 'Brown, with a white triangle down its nose.'

I thanked him, and turned back to the Bible. I searched for what Cantrell might see here, what final enemy was to be destroyed. My mind tumbled and turned the words of the chapter. '*I will shew unto ye the judgment of the great whore . . . with whom the kings of the earth have committed fornica-tion . . .*' On to where the angel said she would explain her mystery to the saint: '*And the beast that was, and is not, even he is the eighth, and is of the seven, and goeth into perdition.*'

I thought, after the seven vials the next victim will be the eighth, the most important victim because, after her judgment, Armageddon comes at last. I thought furiously. Wouldn't his victim have to be a woman to symbolise the whore? Fornication with the kings of the earth. For Cantrell surely it would have to be a Protestant woman who had backslid. I thought, fornication, a king, the eighth. A woman who had not yet abandoned true religion but who would surely be seen to do so if she were to marry a religious conservative.

I stood up and turned to face Harsnet. I made myself speak steadily. 'I think . . .' I said, 'I think he means to kill Catherine Parr.'

I STOOD BEFORE Archbishop Cranmer's paper-strewn desk. The prelate stared at me intensely and I felt the force of the powerful mind behind those blue eyes. Both Seymour brothers were also looking at me. Harsnet and I had just finished telling them of our visit to Cantrell's house. We had gone immedi-ately to Lambeth Palace, and the Seymours had been summoned there.

'Then it seems Cantrell is the killer,' Cranmer said quietly. 'Have you left men at his house?'

'The three constables,' Harsnet replied. 'If he returns, they will take him.'

'But what if he does not?' Lord Hertford asked. As ever, he came straight to the point. 'What if he is even now pursuing his eighth victim?'

'I shall send a squad of men to Catherine Parr's house at once,' Sir Thomas said. 'To ride to her succour, ensure she is protected.'

'No.' Cranmer's voice was firm. 'What would the King think if he learned there was a mob of your men in her house?'

He called for his secretary and told him to fetch a dozen men from the palace guard, and order the barge to take a unit of men across the river.

The secretary looked confused. 'A dozen men, my lord? But that will leave the palace almost unguarded.'

'I don't care! Just do it!' It was the first time I had seen Cranmer truly lose his temper. 'And I want a fast rider sent now to Lady Latimer's house in Charterhouse Square. He is to say a gang of burglars has designs on the house. The steward is to lock all the doors and windows, and keep Lady Catherine safe until my guards arrive. Go now, do it!'

We donned our coats and hurried downstairs, through the Great Hall and out into the palace gardens. Barak was waiting there. I had sent a message home before riding to Lambeth, and he had ridden across. He had traced Tamasin to the house of one of her friends, but she had refused to see him. He was in a turmoil of anger and contrition.

There was a sound of hoofbeats and jingling harness, and a rider shot out of the palace gates. 'There goes the messenger,' Barak said.

A moment later, a dozen armed and helmeted men appeared round the corner of the house, led by a sergeant. He approached Harsnet.

'We're to go to Charterhouse Square, I'm told, sir.'

'Yes. Come, I will explain on the way to the landing stage.'

THE ARCHBISHOP'S secretary had done his work; the barge was waiting for us, and on the London side of the river we found a group of horses ready. We then rode fast and hard to the Charterhouse as dusk deepened to darkness. We stopped outside the Charterhouse Gate. A little way off, a group of beggars stood in the open doorway of the old abandoned chapel. They watched as the gate was opened and we rode into the Charterhouse precinct.

Sir Thomas's steward Russell emerged from the conduit house. He had been sent to oversee repairs to the lock mechanism, which had jammed when the watchman had tried to open the gates with Lockley down there. Seymour told his steward what had happened.

'I suggest sending three men of the archbishop's on foot to look around the area,' Sir Thomas said. 'If he is hanging around, we don't want to alarm him. Shardlake, Barak, you should stay out of the way for now. He knows you.'

His strategy made sense. Three of Cranmer's men were sent to reconnoitre. When they returned a few minutes later, they spoke quietly to Sir Thomas, who then hurried over to us with Russell following behind.

'Master Shardlake,' Sir Thomas said, 'you said Cantrell may have had a horse with a distinctive white mark on its face. Shaped like a triangle.'

'Yes. So his neighbour said. Otherwise it is all brown.'

'There is a horse answering that description tied up on the common behind the houses. No sign of an owner.'

Harsnet took a long, shuddering breath. 'It seems you were right, Matthew. I am sorry I doubted you.' He turned to Sir Thomas. 'The time for concealment is past. We must get to Catherine Parr's house now.'

We walked fast through the wooded square, emerging in front of the large houses on the eastern side. Lord Latimer's place was set back from the road in its own grounds. Lights shone at several of the windows. As we walked down the gravel path, the front door opened and a man emerged carrying a lantern. Lord Latimer's arms were stitched prominently on his doublet.

He approached Harsnet. 'Master Coroner?' he asked anxiously.

'Yes. Is all safe?'

He nodded. 'We've searched the house. There's no one here. We've told everyone there are robbers about.'

'He's around somewhere. I can feel it,' Barak muttered.

The steward looked at him sharply. 'I thought it was a gang of burglars.'

'It's one man we're after.' Harsnet looked into the steward's eyes. 'An assassin, a madman. Lady Catherine must be told she is in real danger.'

The man's eyes widened.

'Have you had any visitors today?' I asked.

'A messenger from the King came with a note for Lady Catherine.' The steward hesitated. 'She's been rather agitated since.'

'All right,' Harsnet said. 'Now go, tell her she must stay in her rooms. Two of you men, accompany him, guard her. I shall come to see her presently.'

Two men joined the steward and they ran back inside.

Harsnet turned to the others. 'I want six men patrolling the outside. Everyone else, inside with me.'

We entered a large hall with several doors leading off it. Harsnet led us through a door at the back, and down a flagged passage into a large kitchen. Half a deer was roasting on a range, a boy turning the spit. A group of frightened-looking servants sat round a large table.

'Where is the cook?' Harsnet asked.

A man in a stained apron stepped forward. 'I am, sir. Master Greaves.'

'What deliveries have there been today?'

He nodded at the spit. 'George brought that deer over from Smithfield. And the coalman came this morning.'

'Where do you get your coal?' I asked.

'Goodman Roberts, up at Smithfield. He's been delivering for years.'

The freckle-faced lad turning the spit looked up. 'He sent his new assistant this week,' he ventured. 'And last week. I let him in.'

I exchanged a glance with Barak. 'What was he like?' I asked the boy.

'I didn't really see his face, sir, it was so black with coal dust.'

'Was he tall or short?'

'Tall, sir, and thin. He took the coal down to the cellar in the hall.'

'Did you see him come out?'

'No. Master Greaves sent me to the larder to peel some turnips.'

'Did *anyone* see the coalman's boy leave?'

Heads were shaken round the table.

'Take us to the cellar,' Harsnet said.

The cook led the way back to the passage outside, halting before a wooden trap door set with an iron ring.

'What is down there exactly?' Harsnet asked.

'Flasks of wine and barrels of vegetables, and the coal. And there's another trap door there, leading down to the sewer passage.'

'Part of the Charterhouse system?'

'Yes, sir. After the water runs through our sewer it empties out into a stream that runs past the house. There's a large iron grille set into the wall where the water goes out. No one could get in or out that way.'

'I doubt he's down there,' Harsnet said. 'He'd be trapped. But we should do a thorough search.'

Torches were fetched, the hatch was opened and two of Cranmer's men climbed down to the cellar. They looked behind the barrels, thrust their swords into the pile of coal. Then they turned to the trap door. 'It's bolted on the outside,' one of them called out. 'There can't be anyone down there.'

'Look nonetheless.'

They opened the trap door; cold air and a filthy smell wafted up to us. They climbed down, and shortly after I heard the sound of booted feet on iron rungs again, and someone called, 'No one here!'

'Perhaps he got out of the house when Cranmer's messenger arrived and the search started,' Barak suggested. 'Knew something was up.'

Harsnet nodded gravely. 'If so, Lady Catherine will need to be watched for some while. You four men, search the house once again.'

We returned to the hall. 'I am going to see the steward again,' Harsnet said. He left Barak and me alone in the hallway.

'We might as well join the search,' I said, and started to climb the stairs.

We had just reached the top when there was a sudden yell from outside the house. 'Fire! Help! Fire!'

HARSNET RAN along the corridor towards us. He stared at me for a moment then we all ran to the nearest window, through which the glow of flames could be seen in the darkness. Across the lawn, a large wooden summerhouse was well ablaze, smoke drifting towards the house. Guards and servants ran to and fro, carrying buckets of water.

'He's trying to distract us,' I said urgently. 'Fetch the sergeant! Get those men back in the house!'

The coroner hesitated, then turned and ran down the stairs. Barak opened the window and leaned out. The summerhouse was blazing from end to end, but it was far enough from the house for the flames not to spread. As we watched, Harsnet ran outside, calling everyone back.

We hurried down the stairs. Through the open front door we saw guards running, the sergeant bawling at them to watch the doors and windows.

'This is chaos,' I said.

'Is he still outside, do you think?' Barak asked.

'He may have come back in after starting the fire.'

Barak did not answer. I turned to him. He raised a finger to his lips, pointing to the half-open door of a room behind us.

'There's an open window in there,' he whispered. 'I can feel a breeze.'

He drew his sword; I did the same with my dagger. Barak stepped back, waited a second, then kicked the door wide open. We lunged inside.

We were in a storeroom, stacked chairs and tables and a heap of large cushions lying against the walls. The room was empty, but one of the three windows giving onto the lawn was half open. I crossed to the window. In the moonlight I saw the summerhouse collapse in a great flurry of sparks. Then I heard, behind me, a metallic clatter and a thud.

I whirled round. Barak was lying senseless on the floor, his forehead red with blood, his sword beside him. Standing over him, the pile of cushions he had been lying under scattered around him, was Cantrell. He was carrying the piece of wood he had shown me at his house. He wore no glasses, but he did not squint or peer; there was little wrong with his vision.

I reached for my dagger, but Cantrell was quicker. In a single fluid movement he bent, picked up Barak's sword and thrust it at my throat.

'The Jew cannot help you.' Cantrell's voice was low, thick with gloating pleasure. 'Now I have you,' he said. 'I knew setting the summerhouse on fire would make everyone run about like ants!' He laughed, a childlike giggle that somehow chilled me to the bone.

'Catherine Parr is well guarded,' I said, trying to steady my breathing.

'I thought you would all think it had ended with Goddard, the pouring of the last vial.' He shook his head. 'But of course the devil knows Catherine Parr is the Great Whore that was foretold. The devil told you the truth, didn't he? She will be well guarded now.' He frowned, looking for a moment like a thwarted child, then smiled again. 'But the Lord has delivered you to me. Kneel down.' He released the pressure of the sword a little.

I hesitated, then knelt on the wooden floor. Cantrell pulled something from his pocket. A small glass vial, half filled with yellowish liquid. Still holding the sword to my throat, he unstoppered it. 'Drink this,' he said.

I looked at it fearfully. Dwale. The prelude to torture and death. 'You will never get us out of this room,' I said. 'The whole house is in uproar.'

'Drink it! Or I cut your throat and then the Jew's.' He pressed the sword to my neck. I felt a sharp pain, then blood trickling down my neck.

'All right!' I took the vial with a trembling hand. I thought, If I refuse and he kills me now, at least my death will be quick. But Barak would certainly die too. By drinking it I could live a little longer, and the instinct to do so is always powerful. I lifted it to my mouth. One gulp and it was gone. Immediately I felt strange, as though my body was enormously heavy. I tried to take a breath, but could not. Then everything slipped away.

I WOKE IN DARKNESS, to a cesspit smell that made me retch. My body felt thick and heavy. My wrists were bound in front of me, my ankles tied as well. I was propped up against a brick wall, my legs on a rough, slimy floor. There was a light to one side. I turned painfully towards it. A lantern with a fat candle in it illuminated a low, narrow brick passage. Cantrell sat cross-legged beside it, four feet or so away, looking at me with a brooding gaze.

'Where are we?' I asked. My mouth was dry, my voice came as a croak.

'In the sewer. Under the house.'

I looked round. There were long, narrow alcoves in the brickwork; they must connect to the lavatories above. Behind me, the passage stretched away into darkness. Ahead, I made out the shape of a large metal grille, a patch of moonlit sky beyond. The iron mesh was broken in a few places, metal spikes sticking out at odd angles. Beyond the grille I heard the sound of running water; it had to be the stream into which the sewer drained.

'I hid us under those cushions,' Cantrell said quietly, almost conversationally. He smiled. 'People came in, but they thought we were gone out of the window. I got you down here when the house was quiet.'

'And Barak?'

'Still hidden under the cushions. They'll find him.'

'Is he dead?'

Cantrell shrugged. 'I don't know. It doesn't matter.'

'Why am I still alive?' I ventured after a few minutes.

He frowned. 'I didn't complete the sequence.'

'I don't understand.'

He sighed, a long groaning sound. 'My head spins. Ever since God first spoke to me, so many messages, so many thoughts. God told me to set that fuse to give you time to escape, so you would think Goddard had done it all, but Goddard was not an apostate from true religion, so the prophecies were not fulfilled. *You* are the apostate the seventh vial must be poured out on; you have to die, still, in a great earthquake. For the prophecies to be fulfilled, for me to be able to kill the Great Whore. I see it now.' He looked at me. 'I knew you were the devil's man when you came to where I left Dr Gurney by the river. I marked your bent back, which is a sign of a twisted soul. I learned you were an apostate from true reform. And I thought, Yes, that is how a man possessed would look.'

I wondered with a shudder if he had rambled on like this to Tupholme, or Mistress Bunce, as they died in slow agony.

Cantrell reached into a pocket and pulled out a large, narrow pair of tweezers. He smiled. 'Don't think of rescue. They've no idea we are down here. After I hauled you down I used these to move the bolt back into position from below. There was just enough space; the hatch is a poor fit.'

He was silent for a while, then suddenly said, 'Goddard treated me badly. That hard tongue of his. He regretted it when I hammered nails into his jaw before I drugged him.'

I thought I caught a sound, back up the passage. I strained to hear. If they came quietly and took him by surprise, I might be saved. But it was nothing.

'The solicitor Felday said you knew Elliard,' Cantrell said at length.

'Yes. He was my friend. That was when I decided I would find you.'

'No, no. That was the devil.' Cantrell shook his head. 'Admit the truth,' he demanded. 'Say you are possessed by the devil. Say it.'

And then I heard it. Far away. A metallic clunk. A creak. A faint rushing sound. I understood and my heart sank. They were opening the doors up at the Charterhouse that held the water back. They knew we were down here, and they were going to drown us both like rats.

'Admit the devil is in you.' Cantrell's face was full of rage now. 'Come, admit it. I command you in Jesus' name.'

Then came a violent blast of cold air, and a roaring, crashing sound. Cantrell whirled round. In the light from his lantern I saw a wall of water rushing down on us. I thrust myself sideways, into an alcove. Cantrell had no time to make a sound before it sent him spinning away, arms outspread, as though he were flying.

THE VERY FORCE of the flood saved me, for I had rolled far enough into the alcove for the backwash to slam me up against the far end. I twisted amid the rush of water, thrust out my bound legs and made contact with a side wall, pressing my back into the other wall at the same time. The pain was excruciating but I knew I must not slip or I too would be swept away. The rushing water rose over my face. My hair streamed out as some nameless stinking thing slid past my nose. But I held on. My lungs burned and I felt my head swim. Is this the end? I thought. Does it end like this?

A great sucking sensation nearly dislodged me. Suddenly the water swirled down below my chest, then was gone with a last rushing boom.

I let myself tumble to the ground, shouting in agony as I landed on my shoulder, jarring it. I was a mass of pain, shivering with cold, wet through and stinking. I rolled out of the alcove. And then my heart leaped into my mouth as I saw him. He was sitting up against the grille, facing me.

I groaned. I was too weak to fight any more, even to think. But Cantrell stayed unmoving. I stared and stared through the gloom, and then I saw that he was impaled, a broken metal rod from the grille sticking right through his head. He must have been thrown against it by the full force of the flood. In his last seconds he must have realised that he had failed. I found it strange that I had felt no sense of his evil passing.

THREE DAYS LATER an unexpected visitor arrived at my house. I was still in bed, recovering from my ordeal, when a flustered Joan appeared to say that Lord Hertford himself had called. I told her to show him up.

Lord Hertford had always struck me before as a man of deadly seriousness, but today he was relaxed, giving me a friendly smile before sitting in the chair by my bed. I thought, Today he is the politician.

'I am sorry I must receive you here,' I said.

He raised a hand. 'I was sorry to hear of what you suffered in that sewer. We would never have got Cantrell had you not realised Goddard's killing was intended to mislead us. Catherine Parr would be dead by now.'

I sighed. 'I am sorry we could not get him sooner. Seven victims killed, and the solicitor, the innocent coalman and Thomas's man all dead.'

'Lady Catherine knows you saved her,' Lord Edward said quietly. 'She knows, and is grateful. She is a lady to remember favours a long time.'

'I am honoured.' Indeed I was, but at the same time apprehensive that someone else near the summit of the court had taken notice of me now. I looked again at Lord Hertford. He was smiling, he was happy.

'She would like to receive you herself to thank you, though I do not know when. She will have many calls on her time these next few months, for she has consented to marry the King. She has accepted that it is God's will.'

'The King's sixth marriage. Will she survive, do you think?'

'It will be as God ordains. The Parr family can look forward to high places at court now. And Archbishop Cranmer is out of danger.'

'He is?' I was glad to hear that at least.

'Yes. The King realised the accusations about his staff amounted to nothing. And Bishop Bonner's campaign against the godly men of London has likewise uncovered little that even he could call heresy. People are being released. The tide is starting to turn again in our favour.'

'What of Dean Benson?'

'Back at his post. We could not afford to make a scandal about the beggars' teeth now. Think of what might come out if we did.' He looked at me steadily for a moment. 'You have proved your worth, Master Shardlake. Would you work for me as once you did for Lord Cromwell?'

'Thank you, my lord, but all I want is a peaceful life. My work at the Court of Requests. I'm not fitted for a public life.'

He gave me a long, hard look, then nodded. 'Well,' he said, 'you have been through much. You need time to recuperate. But think on what I have said.'

'Coroner Harsnet would have drowned me,' I said. 'I thought he might visit me, but he has not.'

'I am sure he did not decide lightly to open those gates.'

'I am sure he decided it was God's will. How was he sure we were down there?' I asked curiously.

'The bolt in the hatch leading to the sewer had not been closed properly, though Cantrell thought it had. Harsnet could see someone had gone down there. But he knew that if he had sent his men down after you, Cantrell would surely have killed you before they reached him.'

'Harsnet must have known that letting that great flood go would kill both of us. It was sheer chance I managed to press myself into an alcove, and that the water level fell before I drowned.'

'The coroner felt it was necessary.'

'My lord, it is these necessary things those who work at Whitehall do that mean I will remain a lawyer.'

He got up, defeated for now. 'How is your man Barak?'

'He is all right. He was struck a nasty blow, but his head is thick.'

Poor Barak, I thought, as Lord Hertford's footsteps faded down the stairs.

We had returned from the Charterhouse to find Tamasin's things gone, a note for Barak. The old friend she had gone to when she left had been employed in the late Queen Catherine Howard's privy kitchen. Tamasin had been working with her when Barak and I met her in York two years before. Now the King was to marry Catherine Parr, a new queen's household was to be established and the chamberlain was looking for experienced servants. Tamasin had been offered a post; she had taken it, and the accommodation at Whitehall that went with it. She said she felt she and Barak needed time apart, and asked him not to contact her. He had been struck to the heart.

By THE END of the week I was up and about again, albeit still stiff and sore. I sent Barak to inform the Court of Requests that I could return to work the following Monday, and he came back with a sheaf of new cases. It was a pleasure to read them, to feel my old life returning.

On the Sunday before I went back to work I walked to Lincoln's Inn, where I had an invitation to visit Dorothy. Margaret opened the door and welcomed me in. Dorothy was in the parlour. The first thing I noticed was that the wooden frieze was gone, the wall bare.

Dorothy smiled at me, then came and took my hands. 'Matthew,' she said, 'I have been worried. You look tired, but thank God, not ill as I had feared.'

'No, I am tougher than people think. You got rid of the frieze?'

'I had it burnt in the kitchen yard. I watched while the flames took it. What made that creature kill all those innocent people?'

'It is a mystery. And perhaps it is better left so; it is no good thing to dwell on for too long.'

'I will thank you to the end of my days for what you did,' she said. 'I wanted Roger's murderer caught and punished and you have done that for me, and for him, at great cost.' She released my hands and stepped away.

'Matthew.' She spoke quietly. 'I told you a while ago that I did not know what my future would be. I am still uncertain. But I have decided to go and stay with Samuel in Bristol, for a month or two at least. Roger's affairs are pretty well settled, and now I need some time for reflection, some peace.'

'I shall miss you.'

'It will be only for a while,' Dorothy said. 'I will come again in June, to visit, and by then I shall have decided whether to stay in Bristol or come back to London.' She smiled. 'And now, Matthew, stay to dinner and let us talk of pleasant things, the old days before the world went mad.'

'I would like nothing better,' I said.

Epilogue
July 1543—three months later

The King and Catherine Parr were to be married that day, and in the larger London streets bonfires were being erected, together with spits for the roasting pigs that would be distributed later from the royal kitchens at Whitehall. As Barak and I walked along Cheapside, small boys ran up and down, bringing wood for the fires and hallooing excitedly at the prospect of the feast to come.

A month before, Lady Catherine had summoned me to the house in Charterhouse Square. She received me in a parlour hung with gorgeous tapestries, two ladies-in-waiting sewing by the window. She wore a dress of brown silk embossed with designs of flowers on its wide crimson sleeves, a necklace of rubies at her throat and a French hood set with pearls covering her auburn hair. She was tall, and her mouth and chin were too small to be pretty, yet she had tremendous presence.

I bowed deeply. 'My congratulations on your betrothal, my lady,' I said.

She nodded slightly in acknowledgement and I saw the stillness in her, the stillness of one who must stay controlled now to fulfil the role she had accepted on that great, terrible stage, the royal court.

'I know you saved my life, Master Shardlake,' she said in her rich voice. 'And suffered great risk and privation in the process.'

'I was glad to, my lady.'

She smiled, a smile of gentle warmth. 'I want you to know, Master Shardlake, that if ever you need a friend, or a favour, or anything that it will soon be in my power to grant, you have only to ask.'

In all my years on the fringes of the court no one had ever offered a favour without demanding something in return. 'Thank you, my lady,' I said. 'I shall remember your words with gladness in my heart.'

She smiled again and extended a delicate hand heavy with rings. I bent and kissed it.

'SIX WIVES the King's had now.' Barak's words dragged me from my reverie. 'We can't even get one between us.'

'Do not give up on Tamasin,' I said. 'I believe there is still hope there.'

'Don't see it.' Barak shook his head. 'But I'll keep trying.'

He had been several times to the kitchens at Whitehall Palace, to ask Tamasin to come back, begging her forgiveness. She had given it, but she would not come back to him, not yet at least, though she had promised she would remain loyal to her marriage vows.

As for me, the nature of my own disappointment was different, though it still bit deep. A few weeks ago, Dorothy had written a letter explaining that she had bought a small house in Bristol, near her son. Her letter ended:

> As for us, I realise what you have felt for me, the old feelings that per-haps were always there but that returned after Roger died. You behaved honourably, Matthew, and I believe your determination in hunting down Roger's killer was done for him as well as for me.
>
> Yet I know now that I will never marry again; the twenty years that Roger and I had together before that evil creature took him were, I know, blessed with a happiness that is rare among married couples. Any other marriage could only be a pale shadow, and that would be fair on nobody.
>
> Forgive me, and come and visit us.

I had not actually asked her to marry me, yet I would have, she knew that. I would not go to Bristol, not for a time at least; it would be too hard.

We passed the top of Bucklersbury, and I thought of Guy down at his shop. Our friendship was now restored, though I felt a new reserve in him sometimes. He was no longer angry with me for not going to see him before confronting Piers, but I wondered if he would ever trust me fully again.

'Any more subscriptions for the hospital?' Barak asked me.

'A few.'

'Have you tried asking Bealknap?'

We both laughed. Since my return to Lincoln's Inn, Bealknap had studiously avoided me. He was fully restored to health, but had not paid Guy's fees. He was too embarrassed to face me, yet he would look any sort of fool rather than part with some of his gold. Now, indeed, I pitied him.

We passed under Bishopsgate Bridge. 'Well, here we are,' Barak said dubiously. 'I don't know how you think a visit here is going to cheer us up.'

'Wait and see,' I said, as we rode under the Bedlam gate into the precinct of the hospital. We tied up the horses and I knocked at the door.

The big keeper Gebons opened the door, bowing to me.

'Are Goodman Kite and his wife here yet?' I asked.

'Aye, sir, they are. They are all in the parlour, with Ellen.'

'Come, then, Barak. This is what I wanted you to see.'

I led the way into the parlour. The scene there today could have come from any peaceful domestic home. Adam and his father sat at the table playing chess. Minnie Kite sat watching them, her face wearing a look of happy repose that I would not have believed possible four months ago. Beside her, Ellen sat knitting, a look of pride on her long, sensitive face.

'Well done, Adam.' Minnie laughed and clapped her hands as her son reached out and took her husband's king with a flourish.

As we entered, the company rose to greet us, but I bade them sit again.

'I have brought my assistant to see you, Adam,' I said. 'You may remember Master Barak from the court hearings.' Barak bowed to the company.

Adam glanced at Barak, and reddened slightly. 'I remember seeing you at court, sir,' he said. 'I was in a bad way then.'

'That you were.' Barak smiled, though he still looked uneasy.

Adam turned to me with a nervous smile. 'Master Shardlake, one day soon will you tell me more about life in the law?'

'I will, with pleasure.' On my last couple of visits, Adam had shown some interest in his legal position. It was a world away from that first appearance at court.

Daniel Kite stood. 'Come, son, shall we take a walk around the yard?'

'Yes, all right.' Adam got up, his mother close behind him.

We watched from the open front door as the little family walked slowly across the yard, talking quietly; Ellen stood a little behind us, afraid as ever to step too close to the world outside.

'Adam's parents care for him,' she said. 'They are not like those families that abandon their troublesome relatives here.' There was a note of bitterness in her voice; I looked at her and she forced a smile.

'This sudden interest of Adam's in the law is a new thing,' I said.

'Who knows, one day he may make a lawyer.'

'Aye. I will give him Barak's place, train him up. He will come cheaper.' Ellen laughed.

'Exploiting the mad, I call it,' Barak said. Then he turned to me. 'I ought to get over to the Old Barge. I have things to pack.'

'I will see you at Lincoln's Inn tomorrow morning.'

He bowed to Ellen and stepped outside. I sensed he was glad of the excuse to leave. He untied Sukey and rode away, raising his cap to the Kites as he passed them at the gate.

'Your assistant is moving house?' Ellen asked.

'Yes, he and his wife have separated. It is sad; he could not bear to stay in their old lodgings. He has taken a room near Lincoln's Inn. They may get back together in time; there is still a great bond between them. I hope so.'

'The papers requesting Adam's release go to the Court of Requests this week?' Ellen asked.

'Yes, on Thursday. If the judge agrees to the request, it will be forwarded to the Privy Council. I believe they will grant it.' I knew they would, for Cranmer had written to me, promising he would see the matter through.

'Is he ready?' Ellen asked. 'There are still times when I go into his room and find him kneeling on the floor, still times when he fears his damnation.'

'Guy believes it is time for him to leave, to *engage* with the world, as he puts it. Under continual care from his parents, of course, and Guy will visit him frequently. He cannot be certain Adam will not relapse, but he believes he will continue to make progress. I hope he is right,' I added quietly.

'I shall never see him again,' Ellen said bleakly. I turned to look at her. She had retreated a couple of steps away from the open door.

'That is sad,' I said. 'The Kites would be glad to have you visit him.'

'You know my situation, sir,' she said softly. 'Please do not press me.'

Shawms appeared from his office, gave us a dirty look as he passed by. When he had gone, Ellen said, 'Will you do something for me, sir?'

'Whatever I can, Ellen.'

'Will you come and visit me sometimes, when you have time? I love to hear what is happening in the outside world. I did not know the King was getting married again today until you told me.'

'I would rather you made some venture into the outside world, Ellen. Come, hold on to my arm. Will you not take just a few steps outside? Is it so hard?'

'Harder than you realise,' she said.

I looked at her. 'I will make a bargain with you, Ellen. I will come and see you, whenever I can, and tell you all the news. But I will always ask you to consider ways in which you may deal with your . . . difficulty, perhaps even overcome it.' I smiled. 'Is it a bargain?'

'You drive a hard deal, sir, like all lawyers.'

'I do. Will you agree to my terms?'

She gave a small, sad smile. 'I will. And thank you for your care.'

Just then, a great clamour of bells rang across the city. We looked out into the sunlit yard, listening to the joyful clamour. Out there, in a chapel in a palace, the King had finally married Catherine Parr.

C. J. SANSOM

Favourite place: Madrid
Winner: Best Historical Crime Novel Award 2005
Future plans: to write more books

RD: Why do you think there is so much interest in the Tudor period?

CJS: I think it's partly because the two long-reigning monarchs, Henry VIII and Elizabeth I, are such larger-than-life characters. One can't help being seduced by the drama of their lives. Also, so much was happening: economic upheavals, a changing class structure, the end of the medieval church, and all the amazing new things from America.

RD: Do you think the Tudors could teach us anything about life?

CJS: Actually, no. It was a time of religious fanaticism, growing social inequality and much cruelty. I think we have enough of those things today. But one habit that the Tudors had that we could certainly benefit from, especially in politics, is plain speaking.

RD: How do you set about researching your books?

CJS: I start with my own knowledge of the period then narrow it down to the particular focus I'm looking at—in the case of *Revelation*, the conflict between conservative and radical religious factions in London. I take notes from books and keep them in a folder to refresh my memory, although fortunately I seem to be able to retain quite a lot in my head. And the Internet is becoming more and more useful.

RD: Your novels really bring the sights, sounds and smells of the Tudor period to life. How do you achieve this?

CJS: My travels in the Third World have helped, because Tudor cities were similar in some ways. But a lot has to come from the imagination.

RD: You mix real historical figures such as Cranmer, Cromwell and Catherine Parr with fictional characters. Is that difficult to do?

CJS: I find it much easier to invent a fictional character than to portray a real one. Trying to imagine Thomas Cromwell and Catherine Parr was particularly interesting, whereas Archbishop Cranmer was difficult because he was such a complex man.

RD: Was the serial killer in your book a real person? Did you come across any others in the course of your research?

CJS: The character of the paedophile murderer was, unfortunately, real. He lived in fifteenth-century France. The other examples are fictitious. At one point I thought I had uncovered a medieval serial killer in fourteenth-century Liverpool, but this turned out to be a false lead. I do not know of any before Tudor times.

RD: Did you always want to be a writer and how did you get started?

CJS: I had wanted to be a writer since I was a child, but working full-time as a solicitor meant I could only dabble until the year 2000 when I took a year off work to have a real go at writing a publishable novel. I did not really expect to succeed.

RD: Do you miss anything about working in the legal profession?

CJS: Working with other people, and some of the interesting legal problems. But I can always invent some for Shardlake.

RD: Who are your favourite writers?

CJS: For thrillers—Ruth Rendell, P. D. James and Michael Connelly, and I will buy anything by Cormac McCarthy or Anne Tyler. I still love the first adult writer I read: H.G. Wells.

RD: How do you relax?

CJS: Reading books and watching films that have different subjects to those I write about. And watching *Lost* and *Judge Judy*.

RD: Your books have been phenomenally successful from the publication of the very first one, *Dissolution*. Were you taken by surprise by this?

CJS: I was simply astonished. It still hasn't sunk in properly.

HENRY'S LAST QUEEN

Catherine Parr (right), the last of Henry VIII's six wives, had been widowed twice before she married the king in 1543. While she might have been reluctant to take on the role of queen, as suggested in *Revelation*, Catherine seems to have made the most of the situation, using her position to promote the religious reform she came to believe in. She wrote her own book, *Prayers and Meditations*, printed in 1545, and her religious convictions greatly influenced her stepdaughter, the future Elizabeth I. After Henry's death in 1547, Catherine was able to marry her old love, Thomas Seymour, but her happiness was short-lived. She gave birth to her only child, Mary, in 1548, but died six days later.

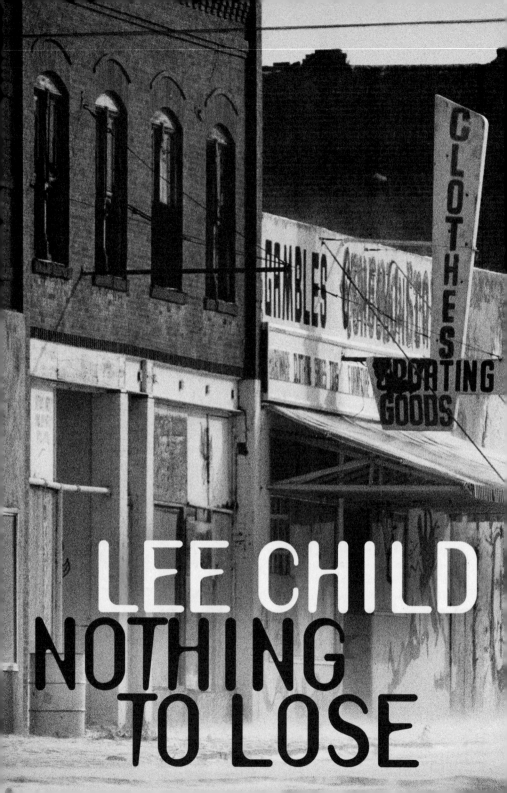

Jack Reacher's plan was to head directly to New Mexico, but he hitched a ride with an old guy and ended up in Hope—middle of nowhere, nothing but tens of thousands of flat, square miles and the distant Rocky Mountains ahead.

Might as well keep moving on down the dusty road to the next town, Despair. Nothing to lose, after all . . .

CHAPTER ONE

The sun was only half as hot as he had known sun to be, but it was hot enough to keep him confused and dizzy. He was very weak. He had not eaten for seventy-two hours, or taken water for forty-eight.

Not weak. He was dying, and he knew it.

The image in his mind showed things drifting away. A rowboat caught in a river current, straining against a rotted rope, pulling, tugging, breaking free. His viewpoint was that of a small boy in the boat, sitting low, staring back helplessly at the bank as the dock grew smaller.

Was he a boy or a man? He was old enough to vote and kill and die, which made him a man. He was too young to drink, even beer, which made him a boy. He had been called both. He had been called unhinged, disturbed, deranged, unbalanced, all of which he understood, except unhinged. Was he supposed to be *hinged*? Like a door? Maybe people were doors. Maybe things passed through them. He considered the question for a long moment and then he batted the air in frustration. He was babbling like a teenager in love with weed.

Which is exactly all he had been, a year and a half before.

He fell to his knees. The sand was only half as hot as he had known sand to be, but it was hot enough to ease his chill. He fell face down, exhausted, finally spent. He knew that if he closed his eyes he would never open them again. But he was tired. More tired than a man or a boy had ever been.

He closed his eyes.

THE LINE BETWEEN Hope and Despair was exactly that: a line, in the road, formed where one town's blacktop finished and the other's started. Hope's highway department had used thick, dark asphalt rolled smooth. Despair had a smaller budget. They had top-dressed a lumpy roadbed with hot tar and dumped grey gravel on it. Where the two surfaces met there was an inch-wide trench of no-man's-land filled with a black rubbery compound. An expansion joint. Jack Reacher stepped over it and kept on walking.

Hope and Despair were both in Colorado. Reacher was in Colorado because two days previously he had been in Kansas, and Colorado was next to Kansas. He had been in Calais, Maine, and had taken it into his head to cross the continent diagonally, all the way to San Diego in California. The Atlantic to the Pacific, cool and damp to hot and dry. He took buses where there were any and hitched rides where there weren't. He had arrived in Hope in a bottle-green Mercury Grand Marquis driven by a retired button salesman. He was on his way out of Hope on foot because that morning there had been no traffic heading west towards Despair.

He remembered that fact later, and wondered that he hadn't asked why.

In terms of his grand diagonal design, he was slightly off-course. He should have been angling directly southwest into New Mexico. But he wasn't a stickler for plans, the Grand Marquis had been a comfortable car and the old guy had been fixed on Hope because he had three grandchildren to see there, before heading onwards to Denver to see four more. And then in Hope he had looked at a map and seen Despair seventeen miles farther west and had been unable to resist the detour. Once or twice in his life he had made the same trip metaphorically. Now he figured he should make it for real, since the opportunity was right there.

The road between the two towns was a straight two-lane. It rose very gently as it headed west. The Rockies were visible up ahead, blue and massive and hazy. They looked very close. Then suddenly they didn't. Reacher breasted a slight rise, stopped dead and understood why one town was called Hope and the other Despair. Settlers struggling west 150 years before him would have stopped over in what came to be called Hope and would have seen their last great obstacle seemingly within touching distance. Then, after a day's or a week's repose, they would have moved on again and breasted the same slight rise, only to see that the Rockies' apparent proximity had been nothing more than a cruel twist of topography. From the top of the rise the great barrier seemed once again remote. A long month's hard trekking. Enough to drive the impatient from hope to despair.

Reacher stepped off Despair's gritty road and walked through crusted sandy earth to a table rock the size of a car. He levered himself up and lay down with his hands behind his head and stared up at the sky. It was pale blue and laced with long, high, feathery clouds. Back when he smoked he might have lit a cigarette to pass the time. But he didn't smoke any more. Smoking implied carrying a pack and a book of matches, and Reacher had long ago quit carrying things he didn't need. There was nothing in his pockets except paper money, an expired passport, an ATM card and a clip-together toothbrush. He owned the things in his pockets and the clothes on his back and the shoes on his feet. That was all.

He got to his feet and stood on tiptoe, high on the rock. Behind him to the east, eight or nine miles back, was a shallow bowl maybe ten miles in diameter, with the town of Hope roughly in its centre—maybe ten blocks by six of brick buildings and an outlying clutter of houses and barns. Ahead of him to the west were tens of thousands of flat square miles, completely empty except for the town of Despair, about eight or nine miles ahead. Despair looked larger than Hope. It was teardrop-shaped, with a conventional Plains downtown about twelve blocks square, and then a wider zone of activity beyond it, maybe industrial in nature. Despair looked less pleasant than Hope. For a brief moment Reacher considered backtracking, but he dismissed the thought. He hated turning back. Everyone's life needed an organising principle, and forward motion was Reacher's.

He climbed off the rock and rejoined the road. There was still no traffic. No chance of a ride. Reacher was a little puzzled, but mostly unconcerned. Many times in his life he had walked a lot more than seventeen miles at a stretch. He pulled his shirt loose on his shoulders and kept walking.

REACHER HAD SEEN movies about small-town America, in which the sets had been dressed to look more perfect than reality. This place was the exact opposite. Despair's main street looked like a designer and a whole team of grips had worked hard to make it dowdier and gloomier than it needed to be. Traffic was light. Sedans and pick-ups were moving slow and lazy. None of them was newer than three years old. There were few pedestrians.

Reacher made a random left turn and set about finding a diner. He passed a grocery store, a bar, a rooming house and a faded old hotel before he found an eatery. It took up the whole ground floor of a dull brick cube. The ceiling was high and the windows were floor-to-ceiling plate glass. The place might have been an automobile showroom in the past. The floor was tiled, the tables and chairs were plain brown wood, and the air smelt of boiled vegetables. There was a register station inside the door with a *Please Wait to be Seated* sign on a short brass pole with a heavy base. Same sign he

had seen everywhere, coast to coast. He figured there was a company somewhere turning them out by the million. He stood next to the register and
waited. There were eleven customers eating. One waitress. Not an unusual
ratio. The lone waitress would soon glance over at him and nod, as if to say,
I'll be right with you.

But she didn't. She glanced over, looked at him, then carried on with
what she was doing. Which wasn't much. She had all her eleven customers
pacified. She was stopping by tables and asking if everything was all right
and refilling coffee cups. Reacher turned and checked his reflection in the
door glass to see if he was committing a social outrage with the way he was
dressed. He wasn't. He was wearing dark grey trousers and a dark grey
shirt, both bought two days before in a janitorial surplus store in Kansas.
Janitorial supply stores were his latest discovery. Plain, strong, well-made
clothing at reasonable prices. His hair was short and tidy. He had shaved.

He turned back to wait.

Customers turned to look at him, appraised him quite openly, and then
looked away. The waitress made another slow circuit of the room, looking
everywhere except at him. He lost patience. He stepped past the sign and
moved into the room and sat down alone at a table for four. The waitress
watched him do it, and then she headed for the kitchen.

She didn't come out again.

Reacher sat and waited. The room was silent except for the clash of silverware on plates and the click of cups being lowered into saucers.

Nothing happened for close to ten minutes.

Then an old crew-cab pick-up truck slid to a stop on the kerb and four
guys climbed out. The shortest was probably an inch under six foot and the
lightest was maybe an ounce over 200 pounds. Two of them had broken
noses and none of them had all their teeth. They all looked pale and vaguely
unhealthy. And they all looked like trouble.

They grouped themselves into a tight little formation, paused a beat, and
came inside. They headed straight for Reacher's table. Three of them sat
down in the empty chairs, and the fourth stood at the head of the table.

'I don't want company,' Reacher said. 'I prefer to eat alone.'

The guy standing at the head of the table was the biggest of the four, by
maybe an inch and ten pounds. He said, 'You need to get going.'

'Going?'

'Out of here.'

'You want to tell me why?'

'We don't like strangers,' was the reply.

'Me neither,' Reacher said. 'But I need to eat. Otherwise I'll get all wasted and skinny like you four.'

'Funny man.'

'Just calling it like it is.' Reacher smiled, put his forearms on the table. He had thirty pounds and three inches on the big guy, and more than that on the other three. And he was willing to bet he had a little more experience and a little less inhibition than any one of them. But if it came to it, it was going to be his 250 pounds against their cumulative 900. Not great odds.

The guy who was standing said, 'We don't want you here. Leave now.'

'You want me to leave, I'll need to hear it from the owner.'

'We can arrange that.' The guy got up and headed for the kitchen. A long minute later he came back out with a man in a stained apron. The man walked up to Reacher's table and said, 'I want you to leave my restaurant.'

'Why?' Reacher asked.

'I don't need to explain myself.'

Reacher said, 'I'll leave when I've had a cup of coffee.'

'You'll leave now.'

'Black, no sugar.'

'I don't want trouble.'

'If I get a cup of coffee, I'll walk out of here. If I don't, these guys can try to throw me out, and you'll spend the rest of the day cleaning blood off the floor and all day tomorrow shopping for new chairs and tables.'

The guy in the apron said nothing.

Reacher said, 'Black, no sugar.'

The guy in the apron stood still for a moment and then headed back to the kitchen. A minute later the waitress came out with a single cup balanced on a saucer. She set it down in front of Reacher, hard enough to slop some of the contents out of the cup and into the saucer. 'Enjoy,' she said.

Reacher lifted the cup and wiped the base on his sleeve. Set the cup down on the table and emptied the saucer into it. Set the cup back on the saucer and squared it in front of him. Then he raised it again and took a sip.

Not bad, he thought. A decent commercial product, better than most diners. The cup was a porcelain monstrosity with a lip about three-eighths of an inch thick. It was cooling the drink too fast. Too wide, too shallow. Reacher believed a receptacle ought to serve its contents.

The four guys were still clustered all around. Reacher drank, slowly at first, and then faster as the coffee grew cold. He drained the cup and set it back on the saucer. Pushed it away, slowly. Then he moved his left arm fast and went for his pocket. The four guys jumped. Reacher came out with a dollar bill, flattened it and trapped it under the saucer.

'So let's go,' he said. He scraped his chair back and stood up. He pushed his chair in neatly and headed for the door. He sensed the four guys behind him. Heard their boots on the tiles.

Reacher pushed the door and stepped outside into the street. The air was cool, but the sun was out. He turned left and took four steps until he was clear of the parked pick-up. Then he stopped and turned back with the afternoon sun behind him. The four guys formed up in front of him, with the sun in their eyes. The guy that had stood at the head of the table said, 'Now you need to get out.'

Reacher said, 'I am out.'

'Out of town.'

'You going to tell me why?'

'We don't have to tell you why.' The guy on the end of the line pushed his cuffs above his elbows and took a step forward. Broken nose, missing teeth.

Reacher said, 'You're picking on the wrong man.'

'You think?'

Reacher nodded. 'I have to warn you. I promised my mother, a long time ago. She said I had to give folks a chance to walk away.'

'There are four of us. One of you.'

Reacher's hands were down by his sides, relaxed, gently curled. His feet were apart, securely planted. He folded the fingers of his left hand flat against his palm. Raised the hand, slowly. Brought it level with his shoulder, palm out. The four guys stared at it. The way his fingers were folded made them think he was hiding something. *But what?* He snapped his fingers open. *Nothing there.* In the same split second he moved sideways and heaved his right fist up like a convulsion and caught the guy that had stepped forwards with a colossal uppercut to the jaw. The man had been breathing through his mouth because of his broken nose and the massive impact snapped his jaw shut, lifted him off the ground and dumped him back down on the sidewalk. Unconscious before he got halfway there.

'Now there are only three of you,' Reacher said. 'You can still walk away.'

The guy that had been doing the talking said, 'You got lucky.'

Reacher nodded. 'Maybe you're right. Maybe one of you will stay on your feet long enough to get to me. The question is, which one will it be?'

Nobody spoke. Stalemate. Reacher thought through his next moves. A right-footed kick to the groin of the guy on his left, spin back with an elbow to the head for the guy in the middle, duck under the inevitable roundhouse swing incoming from the guy on the right, let him follow through, put an elbow in his kidney. Main difficulty would be limiting the damage. It was wiser to stay on the right side of the line, closer to brawling than homicide. In the distance beyond the three guys Reacher could see people going about their lawful business, cars and trucks driving slow on the streets.

Then he saw one particular car blow straight through a four-way junction and head in his direction. A Crown Victoria, white and gold, black push bars on the front, a light bar on the roof, antennas on the trunk lid. A shield on the door, with *DPD* scrolled across it. *Despair Police Department*. A heavyset cop in a tan jacket visible behind the glass.

'Behind you,' Reacher said. 'The cavalry is here.' But he didn't move. And he kept his eyes on the three guys.

The Crown Vic braked hard in the gutter. The door swung open. The driver took a riot gun from a holster between the seats. Climbed out. Pumped the gun and held it diagonally across his chest. He was a big guy. White, maybe forty. Black hair. A groove in his forehead from a Smokey the Bear hat that was presumably now resting on his passenger seat. He surveyed the scene. Not exactly rocket science, Reacher thought. Three guys surrounding a fourth? We're not exactly discussing the weather here.

The cop said, 'Back off now.' The three guys stepped back. The cop stepped forward. Now the three guys were behind the cop, who moved his gun. Pointed it straight at Reacher's chest.

'You're under arrest,' he said.

Reacher stood still and asked, 'On what charge?'

The cop said, 'I'm sure I'll think of something.' He swapped the gun into one hand and used the other to take the handcuffs out of the holder on his belt. One of the guys behind him stepped forward, took them from him and moved round behind Reacher's back.

'Put your arms behind you,' the cop said.

'Are these guys deputised?' Reacher asked.

'They're deputised,' the cop said. 'Including the one you just laid out.'

The guy behind him pulled Reacher's arms back and cuffed his wrists. The guy that had done all the talking opened the cruiser's rear door.

'Get in the car,' the cop said.

Reacher considered his options. Didn't take him long. He was handcuffed.

The cop's riot gun was a Mossberg. He respected the brand.

'In the car,' the cop said.

Reacher moved forwards and looped round the open door and jacked himself inside butt-first. The cop got back in the front. The suspension yielded to his weight. He reholstered the Mossberg.

THE POLICE STATION was in a brick building four blocks west and two blocks south of the restaurant. There was one other car there. Small town, small police department. The cops had the ground floor. The town court was upstairs. Reacher's trip to the booking desk was uneventful. He was uncuffed and gave up the stuff from his pockets and his shoelaces, then he was escorted down a winding staircase and put in a six-by-eight cell fronted by ancient ironwork that had been painted maybe fifty times.

'Lawyer?' he asked.

'You know any?' the desk guy asked back.

'The public defender will do.'

The cop nodded and locked the gate and walked away. Reacher lay down on the bed and closed his eyes. Welcome to Despair, he thought.

THE PUBLIC DEFENDER never showed. Reacher dozed for two hours and then the cop who had arrested him clattered downstairs and unlocked the cell.

'The judge is ready for you,' he said.

Reacher yawned. 'I haven't been charged with anything yet. I haven't seen a lawyer.'

'Take it up with the court,' the cop said. Reacher shrugged to himself and swung his feet to the floor. Walking was awkward without his shoelaces. On the stairs he had to hook his toes to stop his shoes falling off altogether. He shuffled past the booking desk and followed the cop up another flight to the courtroom. There was a centre aisle and four rows of spectator seating. Then a bullpen rail, a prosecution table and a defence table, a witness stand and a jury box and a judge's dais. All the furniture was pine, darkened by age and polish. There were flags behind the dais, Old Glory and something Reacher guessed was the state flag of Colorado.

The room was empty and smelt of dust. The cop pointed Reacher towards the defence table. Then a door in the back wall opened and a man in a cheap suit walked in. The cop jumped up and said, 'All rise.' Reacher stayed in his seat.

The man in the suit clumped up three steps and slid in behind the dais.

He was bulky, over sixty and had a full head of white hair. He picked up a pen, straightened a legal pad and looked at Reacher. 'Name?'

'I haven't been advised of my rights,' Reacher said.

'You haven't been charged with a crime,' the old guy said. 'This is an administrative matter. But I do need to ask you some questions. Name?'

The guy's manner was reasonably courteous, so Reacher shrugged and said, 'Jack Reacher. No middle initial.'

The guy wrote it down. 'Address?'

Reacher said, 'No fixed address.'

The guy wrote it down. Asked, 'Occupation?'

'None.'

'Purpose of your visit to Despair?'

'Tourism.'

'How do you propose to support yourself during your visit?'

'I didn't anticipate a major problem. This isn't exactly New York City.'

'Please answer the question.'

'I have a bank balance,' Reacher said.

'What was your last address?'

'An army post office box.'

'How long did you serve?'

'Thirteen years.'

'Until?'

'I mustered out ten years ago.'

'And you haven't had a permanent address since you left the army?'

'No, I haven't.'

The guy made a pronounced check mark against one of his lines. Two vertical scratches, two horizontal. 'Where did you stay last night?'

'In Hope,' Reacher said. 'In a motel.'

'And your bags are still there?'

'I don't have any bags.'

The guy made another check mark. 'You walked here?' he asked.

'I couldn't find a ride,' Reacher said.

'Why here?'

'Tourism,' Reacher said again.

The guy made another check mark. Then he skipped his pen down his list, slowly and methodically, fourteen answers, plus the check marks. He said, 'I'm sorry, but I find you to be in contravention of Despair's vagrancy ordinance. I'm afraid you'll have to leave.'

Reacher said, 'I'm not a vagrant.'

'Homeless for ten years, jobless for ten years, you beg rides or walk from place to place, what else would you call yourself?'

'Free,' Reacher said. 'And lucky.'

The judge nodded. 'I'm glad you see a silver lining. But this is a quiet, old-fashioned town, and we err on the side of caution. Itinerants have always been a problem. The officer will drive you to the town line.'

THE COP TOOK HIM downstairs again and gave him back his cash, his ATM card, his passport and his toothbrush. He handed over his shoelaces and waited while Reacher threaded them through the eyelets in his shoes and tied them. Then the cop put his hand on the butt of his gun and said, 'Car.' Reacher walked ahead of him, through the lobby, and stepped out of the street door. It was late in the day, late in the year, and it was getting dark. The cop moved to his cruiser. 'In the back,' he said.

Reacher heard a plane in the sky, far to the west. A single engine, climbing hard, small and lonely in the vastness. He pulled the car door and slid inside. The cop slammed the door and got in the front. He took off down the street, headed north. Six blocks to Main Street, Reacher thought. If he turns left, takes me west, maybe I'll let it go. But if he turns right, takes me back east to Hope, maybe I won't. He hated turning back.

At Main Street the cop came to a halt. He paused. Then he hit the gas and turned right. East. Back towards Hope.

The tyres rumbled over the rough road and pebbles spattered and skittered away to the shoulders. Twelve minutes later the car slowed and braked to a stop. The cop climbed out and opened Reacher's door.

'Out,' he said.

Reacher slid out and felt Despair's grit under his shoes.

The cop jerked his thumb to the east. 'That way,' he said.

Reacher stood still.

The cop took the gun off his belt. It was a Glock 9mm. 'Please,' he said. 'Just give me a reason.'

Reacher stepped forward, three paces. Saw the end of Despair's rough gravel and the start of Hope's smooth blacktop. He shrugged and stepped over the boundary. He faced east and listened as the car backed up, turned and crunched away across the stones.

When the sound was all gone in the distance he shrugged again and started walking back towards Hope.

CHAPTER TWO

Reacher had walked less than twenty yards when he saw the headlights. A big car, coming straight at him out of the gathering darkness. When it was 100 yards away he saw it was another cop car, another Crown Vic, painted black and white. It stopped short of him and a spotlight mounted on the windshield pillar lit up and played its beam up and down him twice. Then it clicked off again and the car crept forwards alongside him. The door had a gold shield painted on it, with *HPD* scrolled across the middle. *Hope Police Department*. The window buzzed down and a dome light came on inside. Reacher saw a woman cop at the wheel, short blonde hair backlit by the weak yellow bulb.

'Want a ride?' she asked.

'I'll walk,' Reacher said.

'It's five miles to town.'

'I walked out here, I can walk back.'

Reacher took three steps and heard the car's transmission go into reverse. Then the car came alongside him again, driving backwards, keeping pace as he walked. The woman said, 'Give yourself a break, Zeno.'

Reacher stopped. Said, 'You know who Zeno was?'

The car stopped. 'Zeno of Citium,' the woman said. 'The founder of Stoicism. I'm telling you to stop being so long-suffering.'

'Stoics have to be long-suffering. Stoicism is about the unquestioning acceptance of destinies.'

'Your destiny is to return to Hope. Doesn't matter to Zeno whether you walk or ride.'

'What are you anyway—a philosopher or a cop or a cab driver?'

'The Despair PD calls us when they're dumping someone at the line. As a courtesy.'

'This happens a lot?'

'More than you'd think.'

'Why do they do it?'

'Get in and I'll tell you, Reacher.'

'You know my name?'

'Despair PD passed it on. As a courtesy.'

Reacher shrugged again and put his hand on the rear door handle.

'Up front,' the woman said. 'I'm helping you, not arresting you.'

So Reacher looped round the trunk and opened the front passenger door. The seat was all hemmed in with radio consoles and a laptop terminal on a bracket. Not much leg room. The laptop screen showed a GPS map. A small arrow was blinking away at the far edge of a pink square labelled *Hope Township*. Next to it, Despair township was shaped like a blunt wedge. Its eastern border matched Hope's western limit exactly, then it spread wider. Its western line was twice as long as its eastern and bordered grey emptiness. Spurs off Interstates 70 and 25 clipped Despair's northwestern corner.

The woman cop buzzed her window back up, craned her neck and glanced behind her, then did a three-point turn across the road.

She was good looking and slightly built under a crisp tan shirt. Probably less than five foot six, probably less than 120 pounds, probably less than thirty-five years old. No jewellery, no wedding band. According to the badge pinned over her left breast, her name was Vaughan and she was a pretty good cop. She seemed to have won a bunch of awards and commendations.

He asked, 'Why did Despair run me out?'

The woman called Vaughan turned out the dome light. 'Look at yourself,' she said. 'What do you see?'

'Just a guy.'

'A blue-collar guy in work clothes, fit, strong and hungry.'

'I'm more green-collar than blue-,' Reacher said. 'I was in the army. Military cop.'

'When?'

'Ten years ago.'

'You working now?'

'No.'

'Well, then. You were a threat.'

'How?'

'West of downtown is the biggest metal-recycling plant in Colorado. There's nothing else in Despair's economy.'

'A company town,' Reacher said.

Vaughan nodded at the wheel. 'The guy that owns the plant owns every brick of every building. Half the population works for him full-time. The other half works for him part-time. The part-timers are insecure. They don't like people showing up, willing to work for less.'

'I wasn't willing to work at all.'

'You tell them that?'

'They didn't ask.'

'They wouldn't have believed you anyway. Standing around every morning waiting for a nod from the foreman does things to people. It's kind of feudal. The whole place is feudal. The money the owner pays out in wages comes right back at him, in rents. Mortgages, too. He owns the bank. No relief on Sundays, either. There's one church and he's the lay preacher.'

'So why don't people move on?'

'Some have. Those that haven't never will.'

Vaughan slowed. Hope's first built-up block was ahead in the distance. A mom-and-pop hardware store. That morning an old guy had been putting stepladders and wheelbarrows out on the sidewalk, building a display. Now the store was all closed up and dark.

He asked, 'How big is the Hope PD?'

Vaughan said, 'Me and two others and a watch commander.'

'You got sworn deputies?'

'Four of them. Why?'

'Are they armed?'

'No. In Colorado, deputies are civilian peace officers.'

'How many deputies does the Despair PD have?'

'Four, I think.'

'I met them.'

'And?'

'Theoretically, what would the Hope PD do if someone showed up and got in a dispute with one of your deputies and bust his jaw?'

'We'd throw that someone's sorry ass in jail, real quick.'

'Why?'

'You know why. Zero tolerance for assaults on officers. You'd have felt the same in the Military Police.'

'That's for damn sure.'

'So why did you ask?'

Reacher didn't answer directly. Instead he said, 'I'm not a Stoic, really. Zeno preached the passive acceptance of fate. I'm not like that. I don't like to be told where I can go and where I can't.'

Vaughan slowed some more and pulled in at the kerb. Put the transmission in Park and turned in her seat. 'My advice?' she said. 'Get over it and move on. Despair isn't worth it. Go get a meal at the diner. 'I'm sure you're hungry.'

Reacher nodded. 'Thanks for the ride,' he said.

AN HOUR LATER Reacher was still in the diner. He had eaten soup, steak, fries, beans and apple pie. Now he was drinking coffee. The diner had a bottom-less-cup policy and Reacher abused it mercilessly. It was a better brew than at the restaurant in Despair. The mug was still too thick at the rim, but closer to the ideal. The waitress came back every time he was ready for a refill. He left her a double tip, just in case the owner fired her for her generosity.

All the time he was thinking about Despair, and he was wondering why getting him out of town had been more important than busting him for the assault on the deputy.

It was dark when he left the diner. He walked three blocks to a grocery store where he bought three one-litre bottles of water, some chocolate-chip Powerbars and a roll of black garbage bags. The clerk at the register packed them all carefully into a paper sack and Reacher took his change and carried the sack four blocks to the same motel he had used the night before. He got the same room, at the end of the row. He went inside and put the sack on the night stand and lay down on the bed. He planned on a short rest. Until midnight. He didn't want to walk seventeen miles twice on the same day.

REACHER GOT OFF the bed at midnight and checked the window. No moon. He packed his purchases into one of the black garbage bags and slung it over his shoulder. Then he left the motel and headed west. The sidewalk ended twenty feet west of the hardware store. He stepped off the kerb onto the asphalt and built up a rhythm. Route-march speed, four miles an hour. Not difficult on the smooth flat surface.

Five miles later he stepped over the line between Hope and Despair. He got off the road immediately and looped fifty yards into the scrub north of the road. Near enough to retain a sense of direction, far enough to stay out of a driver's peripheral vision. It was an easy guess that the Despair PD would make the same assessment. He didn't want to blunder into a Despair cruiser. That event would have an altogether different conclusion from a pleasant ride with the pretty Officer Vaughan.

The night was cold. The ground was uneven. No chance of getting close to four miles an hour. He stumbled on. He had no flashlight. A light would be worse than climbing up on a rock and yelling, 'Here I am!'

A slow mile later the clock in his head told him it was a quarter to two in the morning. He heard an aero engine again, far away to the west. A single-engine plane, coming in to land. Maybe the same one he had heard take off, hours before. A Cessna or a Piper. He listened to it until he imagined it had touched down and taxied. Then he started walking again.

Four hours later he was level with the centre of downtown, 300 yards out in the scrub. The night was still cold. He drank water and ate a Powerbar. Then he studied the town. Darkness and stillness and the hidden glow from occasional lit windows. Farther in the distance he saw more lights. The residential areas, he guessed. Houses, apartment buildings, trailer parks.

Ten minutes later he saw headlight beams coming north. Two, three sets. Their light funnelled through the cross streets, paused at Main Street, and then swept west. More came after them. Soon every cross street was lit up bright by long processions of vehicles. Sedans, pick-ups and old-model SUVs all drove north to Main Street, then paused, jostled and swung west.

A company town. Six o'clock in the morning.

The people of Despair, going to work.

Reacher followed them on foot, 400 yards to the north. He stumbled on through the crusted scrub, tracking the road. A mile or more ahead, the horizon was lit up with an immense glow. Not dawn. That was going to happen behind him, to the east. The glow was from arc lighting, a huge rectangle of lights on poles surrounding some kind of massive arena. It looked to be about a mile long. Maybe half a mile wide. The biggest metal-recycling plant in Colorado, Vaughan had said.

Looks like the biggest in the world, Reacher thought.

In front of it, the long convoy of vehicles peeled off left and right and parked in neat rows on acres of beaten scrub. Their headlights shut down, one by one. Reacher watched men file inside, shuffling forwards in a long line, lunch pails in their hands. The gate was narrow, a personnel entrance. Reacher guessed the vehicle entrance was on the other side of the complex, convenient for the spurs off the I-70 and I-25 highways.

The last worker filed inside and the personnel gate closed. Reacher moved on, wheeling north and west in a wide circle, staying hidden. The sky was lightening, landscape features becoming visible. But the terrain was pitted with enough humps and dips to provide decent concealment.

The recycling plant was ringed by an endless solid wall welded out of metal plates painted white. The wall was topped with a continuous horizontal cylinder six feet in diameter. Impossible to climb. Like a supermax prison. His initial estimate of the size of the place had been conservative. It looked bigger than the town itself. Like a tail that wags a dog.

Work was starting inside. Reacher heard the groan of heavy machinery and the ringing sound of metal on metal. He moved round to the northwest corner, fifteen minutes' fast walk. The vehicle gate was visible now. A section of the west wall was standing open. A wide road ran from the horizon straight to it.

The road was a problem. If Reacher wanted to continue his progress, he would have to cross it somewhere. He would be exposed. But to whom, exactly? He guessed the Despair cops would stay in town east of the plant. And he didn't expect any roving surveillance teams out of the plant itself.

But that was exactly what he got.

Two white Chevy Tahoes came out of the vehicle gate. They drove fifty yards down the road and then plunged off it, one to the left and one to the right, onto beaten tracks of packed scrub created by endless previous excursions. The Tahoes had the word *Security* stencilled in black across their doors. They drove slowly, maybe twenty miles an hour, one clockwise, one counterclockwise, as if they intended to lap the plant all day long.

Reacher found a suitable rock and got down behind it. If the plant was a mile or more long and a half mile or more wide, then each circuit was about three and a half miles long. At twenty miles an hour, each circuit would take each truck a little more than ten minutes. With two trucks moving in opposite directions any one point would be free of surveillance for slightly more than five minutes. That was all.

Reacher hated turning back.

He struck out due west, staying in the dips and washes as far as possible. Ten minutes later the natural terrain gave way to where the land had been cleared and graded for the road. He crouched just east of the last available rock and watched for the Tahoes.

They came round much less often than he had predicted. The intervals were closer to ten minutes than five. Which was inexplicable, but good. What wasn't good was that the road itself was starting to get busy. The largest recycling plant in Colorado clearly needed input, and it clearly produced output: a lot of scrap and a lot of ingots. Shortly after seven o'clock in the morning a flat-bed semitrailer roared out of the gate and lumbered onto the road. It was laden with bright steel bars. It drove 100 yards and was passed by another flat-bed heading inwards. This one was loaded with crushed cars, dozens of them, layered like thin stripes. A container truck with Canadian plates left the plant and passed the semi. Then the counterclockwise Tahoe showed up, bounced across the roadbed and kept on going. Three minutes later its clockwise partner rotated in the opposite direction. Another semi left the plant and another headed in. It was like Times Square.

Inside the plant, giant gantry cranes were moving and cascades of welding sparks were showering everywhere. Smoke was rising and fierce blasts of heat from furnaces distorted the air. Reacher drank more water and waited for the Tahoes to pass one more time. Then he got up and walked across the road. He headed south, tracking the long side of the plant. The wall continued. It was maybe fourteen feet high, welded out of what looked like the roofs of old cars. The six-foot cylinder along the top looked to be assembled from the same material, moulded and welded together. Then the whole assembly had been sprayed glossy white.

It took Reacher twenty-six minutes to walk the length of the plant, which made it more than a mile long. At its far southwest corner he saw why the Tahoes were so slow. There was a second walled compound. Another huge rectangle of similar size. It was laid out along an axis running from the northeast to the southwest, not quite in line with the plant. Its northeastern corner was maybe fifty yards from the plant's southwestern corner. Tyre tracks showed that the Tahoes were lapping it too, passing and repassing through the fifty-yard bottleneck in a giant distorted figure of eight.

The second compound was walled with fieldstone, not metal. It was residential, with a screen of trees placed to block any view of industrial activity. There was a huge house, built out of wood in a chalet style, and there were outbuildings, including an oversized barn that was probably an aircraft hangar, because inside the whole length of the far wall was a wide, graded strip of dirt that could only be a runway.

Reacher stayed well away from the fifty-yard bottleneck. Too easy to be spotted there. Instead, he looped west again and aimed to circle the residential compound too, as if both enclosures were one giant obstacle.

BY NOON he was holed up way to the south, looking back at the recycling plant from the rear. The residential compound was closer, and to his left. Far beyond it to the northwest was a small grey smudge in the distance. A group of buildings, maybe five or six miles away. Maybe a gas station or a truck stop or a motel. Reacher narrowed his eyes and squinted, but he couldn't make out any detail. He turned back to the nearer sights. Nothing much was happening at the house. He saw the Tahoes circling and watched a continuous stream of trucks on the distant road. The plant belched smoke, flames and sparks. Its noise was softened by distance, but up close it must have been fearsome. The sun was high and the day was warm.

Reacher hunkered down and watched and listened until he got bored. Then he headed east, for a look at the far side of town.

By the middle of the afternoon he was level with where he had been at six o'clock in the morning, but maybe three miles due south of the settlement, looking at the backs of houses.

They were cheaply built, one-storey ranches with shingle siding and asphalt roofs. Some had garages, most had satellite dishes, tilted up and facing southwest like a regiment of expectant faces. It was a strange little suburb, miles from anywhere else, with empty vastness all around. Reacher suddenly understood that Despair had been built by people who had given up. They had come over the rise and seen the far horizon and had quit. And their descendants were still in town.

He ate his last Powerbar and drained the last of his water, then hacked a hole in the scrub with his heel and buried the wrappers, the empty bottles and his garbage bag. The noise coming from the distant plant was getting quieter. He guessed it was quitting time.

He dodged from rock to rock and got a little closer to the houses. The first cars and pick-up trucks straggled back close to twelve hours after they had left. A long day. They were heading east, towards darkness, so they had their headlights on. Their beams swung south down the cross streets, then they turned, variously left and right, and scattered towards driveways. Engines stopped and the beams died. Doors creaked open and slammed shut. Lights went on inside houses and the blue glow of televisions was visible behind windows. The sky was darkening.

Reacher moved closer. Saw men carrying empty lunch pails into kitchens. He saw hopeful boys with balls and mitts looking for a last game of catch. He saw some fathers agree and some refuse.

He saw the big guy who had blocked the end of the restaurant table. The senior deputy. He got out of the old listing crew-cab pick-up truck that Reacher had seen outside the restaurant. He clutched his stomach with both hands. He passed by his kitchen door and stumbled on into his yard. Then he bent from the waist and threw up in the dirt. He stayed doubled up for maybe twenty seconds and then straightened, shaking his head and spitting.

Reacher got within twenty yards and then the guy bent again and threw up for a second time. Reacher heard him gasp. Not in pain, but in annoyance and resignation.

'You OK?' Reacher called, out of the gloom.

The guy straightened up. 'Who's there?' he called.

Reacher said, 'Me.' He moved closer. Stepped into a bar of light coming from a neighbour's kitchen window.

The guy said, 'You.'

Reacher nodded. 'Me.'

'We threw you out.'

'Didn't take.'

The guy shrugged. 'I'm going inside. I didn't see you, OK?'

'How's your buddy? With the jaw? Teeth OK?'

'What do you care?'

'Calibration,' Reacher said. 'It's an art. Doing what you need to, no more, no less.'

'He had lousy teeth to start with. We all do.'

'Too bad,' Reacher said.

'I'm going inside,' the guy said again. 'I'm sick.'

'Bad food?'

The guy paused. Then he nodded. 'Must have been,' he said. 'Bad food.'

He headed for his house, slow and stumbling. Reacher watched him go, then turned and walked back into the shadows. Way to the west he heard an aero engine again, straining hard, climbing. The small plane, taking off once more. Seven o'clock in the evening.

Reacher loosened the neck of his shirt and set off east, back towards Hope. When the houses fell away he looped left into the dark towards where he figured the road must be. Eventually he saw a black stripe in the darkness. Indistinct, but different from the black plain that was the scrubland. He fixed its direction in his mind. Walking was difficult in the dark. He stumbled into bushes. He held his hands out in front of him to ward off table rocks. Twice he tripped on low, football-sized boulders and fell. The third time he tripped, it was not on a rock.

He sprawled forwards and some kind of a primitive instinct made him avoid landing right on top of the thing. He kicked his legs up and tucked his head in and rolled, ending up on his back. He lay still for a moment and then rolled onto his front and pushed himself to his knees. He opened his eyes wide and stared into blackness.

He shuffled forwards on both knees and one hand, with the other held low in front of him. A slow yard later it touched something.

Soft.

He spread his fingers. Clamped them loosely. Cloth. Probably worn cotton twill. Rubbed his fingertips and the ball of his thumb left and right. Squeezed. A leg. The size and heft of a human thigh was unmistakable. He skipped his hand three feet to the right and slid it up a back to a shoulder blade. Walked his fingers to a neck and an ear.

No pulse.

He shuffled closer on his knees and opened his eyes so wide the muscles in his face hurt. Too dark to see. Nothing to hear. He wasn't about to try tasting anything. That left smell and touch. Reacher had smelt more than his fair share of deceased organisms. This one wasn't particularly offensive. Stale sweat, no blood. No real information.

So, touch. Maybe an inch and a half or two inches of wiry hair, with a tendency to wave. Caucasian. Impossible to say what colour. The chin and the upper lip were rough with maybe four days of stubble. The cheeks and the throat were smoother. A young man, not much more than a boy.

The cheekbones were pronounced. The eyes were hard and dry, the facial skin was firm and shrunken. No fat anywhere. Starved and dehydrated, Reacher thought.

He found folds of cloth at the hip and the shoulder and rolled the body on its side. The way his hands were spaced told him it was maybe five-eight in height, and the weight was probably one-forty. The trousers were loose at the waist. No belt. The shoes were some kind of athletic sneakers.

Reacher wiped his hands on his own trousers and then started looking for a wound. He found nothing. No gashes, no gunshot wounds, no contusions, no broken bones. The hands were small and fairly delicate. No rings on the fingers. He checked the trouser pockets. No wallet, no coins, no keys, no phone. Nothing.

He sat back on his heels and stared up at the sky, willing a cloud to move and let some moonlight through. But the night stayed dark. He had been walking east, had fallen, had turned round. Therefore he was now facing west. He stood up, made a quarter-turn to his right. Now he was facing north. He started walking with small steps. He bent and swept his hands flat on the scrub and found four stones the size of baseballs. Straightened again and walked on. Five yards, ten, fifteen, twenty.

He found the road. The packed scrub gave way to the tarred pebbles. He butted three of his stones together and stacked the fourth on top, like a miniature mountain cairn. Then he stood up again, turned left and blundered on through the dark, east towards Hope.

CHAPTER THREE

The clock in his head said that it was midnight. Reacher had made good progress. Despair's cheap road crunched loudly under his feet but the hard level surface allowed him to speed up. He sensed the new blacktop ahead. He felt it coming. Then his left foot pushed off rough stones and his right landed on velvet-smooth asphalt.

He was back over the line.

He stood still for a second. Held his arms wide and looked up at the black sky. Then a spotlight clicked on and played over him.

A cop car. The beam died and a dome light came on inside the car and showed a small figure at the wheel.

Vaughan.

She was parked head-on, just waiting in the dark. Reacher walked towards her, put his hand on the handle of the passenger door, opened it and crammed himself into the space inside. The interior was full of soft radio chatter and the smell of perfume.

He asked, 'Are you free for dinner?'

She said, 'I don't eat with jerks.'

Reacher smiled at her and said nothing.

She asked, 'What were you doing?'

'Taking a stroll.'

'You're a stubborn man.'

Reacher nodded. 'I wanted to see Despair, and I did.'

'Was it worth it?'

'Not really.'

Vaughan started the motor and backed up a little, then turned across the width of the road. She got straightened up and accelerated.

'How did you know I was out here?' Reacher asked.

'Word was you'd left town heading west. I got suspicious. I'm working the graveyard shift, so I thought I'd play with this.' She leant forwards and tapped a black box mounted on the dash. 'Traffic camera and a hard disk recorder. It's got night vision.'

She moved her hand again and hit a key on the computer. The screen changed to a ghostly green wide-angle image of the scene ahead.

'I saw you half a mile away,' she said. 'A little green speck.' She tapped another key and spooled back through the time code and Reacher saw himself, a luminous sliver in the dark, getting bigger, coming closer.

'Very fancy,' he said.

Vaughan drove slow, about thirty miles an hour, as though she had more to say. She had one hand on the wheel, the other lay easy in her lap.

'Hungry?' she asked.

'Not really,' Reacher said.

'You should eat anyway. The diner will still be open.'

'I might go take a nap instead.'

'Go eat in the diner first.'

'Why? Are you on commission? Is the chef your brother?'

'Someone was asking about you. Some girl. She was asking if anyone had been thrown out of Despair more recently than her.'

'She was thrown out?'

'Four days ago.'

'They throw women out too?'

'Vagrancy isn't a gender-specific offence. I told her about you. Said if you were still in town you might be eating in the diner tonight. So I think she might come looking for you.'

'What does she want?'

'She wouldn't tell me,' Vaughan said. 'But my impression was her boyfriend is missing.'

REACHER GOT OUT of Vaughan's cruiser on First Street and walked down to Second. The diner was all lit up inside. Three booths were occupied. A guy on his own, a young woman on her own, two guys together. Maybe some Hope residents commuted big distances for work. Maybe they got back too late to face cooking at home.

The sidewalks close to the diner were deserted. No girls hanging around. No girls watching who was going in and coming out. Reacher went in and headed for a booth in the far corner where he could see the whole room at once. A waitress came over and gave him a napkin and silverware and a glass of iced water. She was young and could have been a college student. Maybe the diner stayed open all night to give people jobs, as well as meals. Maybe the owner felt some kind of a civic responsibility. Hope seemed to be that kind of a town.

The menu was a laminated card showing pictures of the food. The waitress came back and Reacher pointed to a grilled cheese sandwich and said, 'And coffee.' He settled back and watched the street through the windows. He figured that the girl who was looking for him might pass by once every fifteen or twenty minutes. It was what he would have done. Longer intervals might make her miss his visit. Most diner customers were in and out pretty fast.

But nobody passed by. The waitress came over with his sandwich and a mug of coffee. The coffee was fresh and the sandwich was OK.

After fifteen minutes he quit staring out at the sidewalk and started looking at the other customers inside the diner and realised she was already in there, waiting for him. The young woman, sitting three booths away.

Stupid, Reacher, he thought.

If their positions had been reversed he wouldn't have walked by every fifteen minutes. He would have come in out of the cold and sat down and waited for his mark to come to him. Like she had.

She was maybe nineteen, dirty blonde hair with streaks, wearing a short denim skirt and a white sweatshirt. Her features didn't add up all the way to beauty, but she had a kind of irresistible glowing good health that he had seen before in American girls. Her skin was perfect, honey-coloured. Her eyes were vivid blue.

She was the one he was waiting for. He knew that because as he watched her in his peripheral vision he could see she was sizing him up and deciding whether to approach. Deciding against, apparently.

Reacher didn't blame her. It was late at night and she was looking at an old guy twice her age, huge, dishevelled, somewhat dirty, and surrounded by an electric stay-away aura he had spent years cultivating.

So she was going to sit tight and wait him out. She was looking up, looking down, kneading her fingers, glancing suddenly in his direction as new thoughts came to her, and then glancing away again as she resolved them. Reacher gave it five more minutes and then fished in his pocket for cash. He left some bills on the table. Got up and headed for the door. At the last minute he changed direction and stepped over to the young woman's booth and slid in opposite her.

'My name is Reacher. I think you wanted to talk to me.'

The girl looked at him, opened her mouth and closed it again.

'A cop called Vaughan told me you were looking for someone who had been to Despair.'

'You're mistaken,' the girl said. 'It wasn't me.'

She wasn't a great liar.

Psychologists have figured out that the memory centre is located in the left brain, and the imagination engine in the right brain. Therefore people unconsciously glance to the left when they're remembering things, and to the right when they're making stuff up. This girl was glancing right so much she was in danger of getting whiplash.

'OK,' Reacher said. 'I apologise for disturbing you.'

But he didn't move. He stayed where he was, sitting easy. Up close the girl was prettier than she had looked from a distance. She had a dusting of freckles and a mobile, expressive mouth.

'Who are you?' she asked.

'Just a guy,' Reacher said. 'The judge in Despair called me a vagrant.'

She said, 'They called me a vagrant too.'

Her accent was unspecific. She wasn't from New York or Minnesota or the Deep South. Maybe somewhere in the Southwest.

'What's your name?' he asked her.

She glanced to her right again. 'Anne.'

Whatever her name was, it wasn't Anne.

The girl who wasn't Anne asked, 'Why did you go to Despair?'

'I liked the name. Why did you go there?'

She didn't answer.

He said, 'Anyway, it wasn't much of a place. I took a good look around.'

The girl went quiet, weighing her next question. She put her head on one side. 'Did you see any people?' she asked.

'Lots of people,' Reacher said.

'Did you see the airplane?'

'I heard one.'

'It belongs to the guy with the big house. Every night he takes off at seven and comes back at two in the morning.'

Reacher asked, 'How long were you there?'

'One day.'

'So how do you know the plane flies every night?'

She didn't answer.

'Maybe someone told you,' Reacher said.

No reply.

'No law against joyriding.'

'People don't joyride at night. There's nothing to see.'

'Good point.'

The girl was quiet. Then, 'When you went back, what people did you see?'

Reacher said, 'Why don't you just show me his picture?'

'Whose picture?'

'Your boyfriend's. He's missing. As in, you can't find him. That was Officer Vaughan's impression, anyway.'

'You trust cops?'

'Some of them.'

She said, 'Show me your wallet.'

'I don't have a wallet.'

'Prove it. Empty your pockets.'

Reacher nodded. He understood. The boyfriend is some kind of a fugitive. She needs to know I'm not an investigator. An investigator would have compromising ID in his wallet. He lifted his butt off the bench and dug out his cash, his old passport, his ATM card, his motel key. His toothbrush was in a plastic glass next to the sink in his room. The girl looked at his stuff and said, 'Thanks.'

He said, 'Now show me his picture.'

'He's not my boyfriend. He's my husband.' She hauled a grey messenger bag from the bench beside her into her lap and came out with a fat leather wallet. There was a plastic window on the outside with a California driver's licence behind it. Her picture was on it. She opened the billfold and eased out a snapshot. It showed the girl standing on a street with golden light and palm trees and a row of neat boutiques behind her. She was smiling, vibrant with love and happiness. She was in the arms of a guy about her age.

'This is your husband?' Reacher asked.

The girl said, 'Yes.'

Reacher squared the snapshot on the tabletop in front of him and asked, 'How old is this photo?'

'Recent.'

May I see your driver's licence?'

'Why?'

'Something I need to check.'

'I don't know.'

'I already know your name isn't Anne.'

The girl said nothing.

Reacher said, 'I'm not here to hurt you.'

She paused and then slid her wallet across the table. He glanced at her licence. Her name was Lucy Anderson.

'Lucy,' he said. 'I'm pleased to meet you.'

'I'm sorry about not telling you the truth.'

'Don't worry about it.'

Her licence said she was coming up to twenty years old. It said her address was an apartment on a street in LA. Her eyes were listed as blue, which was an understatement, and she was five foot eight inches tall.

Which made her husband at least six foot four. In the picture he looked to be well over 200 pounds. Not the guy Reacher had tripped over in the dark. Not even close. Way too big.

He slid the wallet back across the table.

Lucy Anderson asked, 'Did you see him?'

Reacher shook his head. 'No,' he said. 'I didn't. I'm sorry.'

'He has to be there somewhere.'

'What's he running from?'

She looked to the right. 'Why would he be running?'

'Just a wild guess,' Reacher said.

'Who are you?' she asked. 'And how did you know my name wasn't Anne?'

'A long time ago I was a cop. In the military. I still know things.'

Her skin whitened behind her freckles. She fumbled the photograph back into its slot, fastened the wallet and thrust it deep into her bag.

'You don't like cops, do you?' Reacher asked.

Lucy Anderson didn't answer. She slid off the bench sideways and stood up. She walked to the door and pushed out into the street. He watched her huddle into her sweatshirt and step away through the cold.

HE WAS IN BED before two o'clock in the morning. He set the alarm in his head for six thirty. He was tired, but he figured four and a half hours would be enough. He wanted time to shower before heading out for breakfast.

It was a cliché that cops stop in at diners for doughnuts before, during, and after every shift, but clichés were clichés only because they were so often true. Therefore Reacher slipped into the same back booth at five to seven in the morning and fully expected to see Officer Vaughan walk in inside the following ten minutes.

Which she did.

He saw her cruiser pull up and park outside. Saw her climb out onto the sidewalk. Saw her lock up and turn and head for the door. She came in and saw him, paused for a long moment and then slid in opposite him.

He asked, 'Coffee?'

'I don't drink coffee with jerks.'

'I'm not a jerk. I'm a citizen with a problem.'

'What kind of problem?'

'The girl found me.'

'And had you seen her boyfriend?'

'Her husband. But, no, I saw someone else.'

'Who?'

'Not saw, actually. It was pitch dark. I fell over him.'

'Who?'

'A dead guy.'

'Are you serious?'

'As a heart attack.'

'Why didn't you tell me last night?'

'I wanted time to think about it.'

'You're yanking my chain. There's what out there, a thousand square miles? And you just happen to trip over a dead guy in the dark?'

'I figure he was doing the same thing I was doing. Walking east from Despair, staying close enough to the road to be sure of his direction, far enough away to be safe. That put him in a pretty specific channel.'

Vaughan said nothing.

'But he didn't make it,' Reacher said. 'He died. He was Caucasian, by the feel of his hair. Maybe five foot eight, one-forty pounds. Young. Emaciated and dehydrated. No wounds.'

'What, you autopsied this guy? In the dark?'

'I felt around.'

'This is unbelievable.'

'It happened.'

'Where exactly?'

'Maybe four miles out of Despair.'

'You should call the Despair PD.'

'I wouldn't piss on the Despair PD if it was on fire.'

The waitress came over. Reacher ordered coffee and eggs. Vaughan ordered coffee. Reacher took that as a good sign. He waited until the waitress had bustled away and said, 'I want to go back and take a look, right now, in the daylight. You can drive me.'

'It's not my jurisdiction,' Vaughan said. 'I can't do it.'

'Unofficial. Off duty. Like a tourist.'

'Would you be able to find the place again?'

'I left a pile of stones on the side of the road.'

The waitress came back with the coffee and the eggs.

Vaughan said, 'I can't drive a Hope police cruiser in Despair.'

'So what else have you got?'

She was quiet for a long moment. Then she said, 'I have a truck.'

SHE MADE HIM WAIT on the sidewalk near the hardware store. The store was still closed. The window was full of tools. The aisle behind the door was piled high with the stuff that would soon be put out on the sidewalk.

Close to twenty minutes later, a blue Chevy pick-up, about fifteen years old, pulled up on the opposite kerb. Just a plain second-hand truck with a wheezy four-cylinder motor. Vaughan was wearing a red windbreaker and a khaki baseball cap. A good disguise. Reacher climbed in next to her.

There was no traffic, coming or going. Vaughan was holding the truck at a steady sixty. A mile a minute, probably close to its comfortable maximum. A hundred yards short of the line Vaughan said, 'We see anybody at all, you duck down.' Then the expansion joint thumped under the wheels and the tyres set up a harsh roar over Despair's sharp stones.

Seven minutes inside enemy territory, Vaughan started to slow.

'Watch the left shoulder,' Reacher said. 'Four stones, piled up.'

There was some trash on the shoulder. Not much, but enough to ensure that Reacher's small cairn was not going to stand out in glorious isolation like a beacon. Reacher twisted round in his seat. Nobody behind. Nobody ahead. Vaughan slowed some more.

'There,' Reacher said.

His cairn was thirty yards ahead on the left, a speck in the middle of nowhere. Vaughan passed it and turned a wide circle. She came back east and stopped level with the four stones. She put the transmission in park.

Reacher got out and stepped over the stones. In the dark the world had shrunk to an arm's length around him. Now it felt huge again. To the south the land ran all the way to the horizon, flat and essentially featureless. Vaughan stepped alongside him and he walked south with her, five paces, ten, fifteen. He stopped after twenty paces, stood on tiptoe, craned his neck and searched. He saw nothing. He turned 180 degrees and stared back at the road to make sure he hadn't drifted too far west or east. He hadn't.

'Well?' Vaughan called.

Reacher walked ten more yards east and started to trace a wide circle. A quarter of the way through it, he stopped. 'Look here.' He pointed at the ground. 'My footprints,' he said. 'From last night.'

They turned west and backtracked. Followed his footprints back towards Despair. Ten yards later they came to the head of a small diamond-shaped clearing. The clearing was empty.

'It's not here,' Vaughan said.

'But it was. This is the spot.'

The crusted sand was all churned up by multiple disturbances. There were dozens of footprints, facing in all directions. There were scrapes and slides and drag marks. Reacher crouched down and pointed at a depression in the centre of the clearing.

'This is where the boy gave it up,' he said. Then he pointed to a messed-up stony area four feet to the east. 'This is where I landed after I tripped over him. On these stones. I could show you the bruises, if you like.'

'Maybe later,' Vaughan said. 'We need to get going.'

Reacher pointed to four sharp impressions in the sand. Each one was a rectangle about two inches by three, at the corners of a larger rectangle.

'A stretcher,' he said. 'Folks came by and collected him. Maybe four or five of them, judging by the footprints.' He stood up and checked and pointed north and west. 'They came in that way, and carried him back out in the same direction, back to the road.'

'How did they find the body in the first place?'

'Buzzards,' Reacher said. 'It's the obvious way, on open ground.'

'So the proper authorities got him. Problem solved.'

Reacher gazed due west. 'I think there's more to it than that.'

VAUGHAN TOOK HER FOOT off the gas and slowed as they hit the edge of Hope. The hardware guy had his door open now and was piling his stuff on the sidewalk. He had some kind of a trick stepladder that could be put in about eight different positions. He had set it up like a painter's platform, good for reaching first-floor walls. Vaughan made a right on the next block and then a left, past the back of the diner. She pulled into a marked-off parking space outside a low brick building. The building could have been a suburban post office. But it wasn't. It was the Hope Police Department. It said so, in aluminium letters fixed to the brick. Vaughan shut off the engine and Reacher followed her down a path to the door. She unlocked it using a key from her bunch.

Inside, the place still looked like a post office. Dull, worn, institutional. There was a public enquiry counter and a space behind it with two desks. A watch commander's office in the corner, behind a solid door. Reacher asked, 'What happens next?'

'Always better to get out in front of a thing like this. You should call the State Police and volunteer information.'

'No.'

'Why not?'

'I was a soldier. I never volunteer for anything.'

'Well, I can't help you. Small departments like this don't work homicides. It's out of my hands. It was never *in* my hands.'

'The dead guy died of natural causes.'

'You sure? You felt around in the dark. They'll put that boy on a slab.'

'You could call,' Reacher said. 'You could call the State Police to find out what their thinking is.'

'They'll be calling us soon enough.'

'So let's get out in front, like you said.'

Vaughan stepped past the counter and headed for a desk that was clearly hers. Efficient and organised. There was an old-model computer front and centre and a console telephone next to it. She dialled the phone, asked for the duty desk and identified herself. She said, 'We have a missing persons enquiry. Male, Caucasian, approximately twenty years of age, five-eight, one-forty. We don't have a name.'

Then there was a pause. Reacher saw her yawn. She was tired. She had been working all night. She moved the phone a little way from her ear and he heard the faint tap of a keyboard in the distant state office. Denver maybe. Then a voice came back on and she clamped the phone tight.

Vaughan listened and said, 'Thank you.' Then she hung up. 'Despair didn't call it in.' She shook her head. 'They should have. An unexplained death out in open country, that's at least a matter for the coroner. Which means it would show up on the State Police system about a minute later.'

'So why didn't they call it in?'

'I don't know. But that's not our problem.'

Reacher thought of Lucy Anderson and the way she had wrung her hands in the diner. He looked across at Vaughan and said, 'It is our problem, kind of. The kid might have people worried about him.'

Vaughan nodded. Went back to her phone. She dialled and he heard a loud reply in her ear, 'Despair Police Department.' She ran through the same faked enquiry: missing person, Caucasian male, five-eight, one-forty. There was a short pause and then a short reply.

Vaughan hung up. 'Nothing to report,' she said.

Reacher sat down at the other desk and Vaughan moved stuff around on hers. She put her keyboard in line with her monitor and put her mouse in line with her keyboard and squared her phone behind it. Then she put pencils away in drawers and flicked at dust with the edge of her palm.

'Maybe the kid was local,' Reacher said. 'They knew who he was, so he wasn't a candidate for your missing persons inquiry.'

Vaughan shook her head. 'Any unexplained death has got to be reported to the coroner. In which case it would have showed up on the state system. Purely as a statistic. The State Police would have said, "Well, hey, we heard there was a dead guy in Despair this morning, maybe you should check it out."'

'But they didn't.'

'Because nothing has been called in from Despair. Which just doesn't add up. What the hell are they doing with the guy? There's no morgue over there. Not even any cold storage, as far as I know.'

'So they're doing something else with him,' Reacher said. 'Maybe they're covering something up.'

'You claim he died of natural causes.'

'He did,' Reacher said. 'From wandering through the scrub for days. Maybe because they ran him out of town, which might embarrass them.'

Vaughan shook her head again. 'They didn't run him out of town. We didn't get a call. And they always call us.'

'They never dump them to the west?'

'There's nothing there. It's unincorporated land.' She continued, 'Maybe there were no cops involved. Maybe someone else found him.'

'Civilians don't carry stretchers in their cars,' Reacher said.

Vaughan nodded vaguely. 'Start over,' she said. 'Who was this guy?'

'Caucasian male,' Reacher said.

'Not Hispanic? Not foreign?'

'I think Hispanics are Caucasians, technically. What I'm going on is his hair. He wasn't black. That's all I know for sure.'

'Olive-skinned or pale?'

'I couldn't see anything.'

'How did his skin feel? Olive skin feels different from pale skin. A little smoother and thicker.'

'Really?'

'I think so. Don't you?'

Reacher touched his cheek, under his eye. 'Hard to tell,' he said.

Vaughan got up and stepped across to Reacher's desk. 'Now compare. Try my face.' Reacher paused a beat.

'Purely for research purposes,' she said

He reached up and touched her cheek with the ball of his thumb. 'Texture was thicker than either of us. Smoothness somewhere between the two of us.'

'OK.' She touched her face. Then she leant down and touched his cheek with her hand. He felt a tiny jolt of voltage. She said, 'So he wasn't necessarily white, but he was younger than you. Less wrinkled and weather-beaten. Less of a mess. You should use a good moisturiser.'

'Thank you. I'll bear that in mind.'

'You said he was thin, wasted, in fact.'

'Noticeably. But he was probably wiry to begin with.'

'How long does it take for a wiry person to get wasted?'

'I don't know for sure. If you're moving around out of doors, burning energy, maybe two or three days.'

'That's a lot of wandering,' Vaughan said. 'We need to know why the good folks of Despair put in two or three days' sustained effort to keep him out.'

Reacher shook his head. 'Might be more useful to know why he was trying so hard to stay. He must have had a damn good reason.' He stopped abruptly, then he asked her, 'Can I borrow your truck?'

Vaughan said, 'No. You'll go back to Despair, you'll get arrested and I'll be implicated.'

'Suppose I don't go through Despair? I want to see what lies to the west. I'm guessing the dead guy didn't come through Hope. You would have seen him and remembered him. Likewise with the girl's missing husband.'

'It's a long loop,' Vaughan said. 'You have to go back practically all the way to Kansas.'

Reacher said, 'I'll pay for the gas.'

Vaughan sighed and slid her keys across the table. 'Go,' she said.

CHAPTER FOUR

The Chevy's seat didn't go very far back. Reacher ended up driving with his back upright and his knees splayed, like he was at the wheel of a tractor. The steering was vague and the brakes were soft. But it was better than walking. Reacher was done with walking, for a day or two at least.

A map in the door pocket confirmed what Vaughan had told him. He was going to have to drive east almost all the way back to the Kansas line, then north to I-70, then west again, then south on the same highway spur the metal trucks used. Total distance, close to 200 miles. And 200 miles back, if he obeyed Vaughan's injunction to keep her truck off Despair's roads.

Which he planned to. Probably.

The old truck's exhaust was leaking fumes, so he kept the windows cracked down an inch. At a steady sixty the wind whistled in, a mellifluous, high-pitched chord, underpinned by the bass growl of a bad bearing and the tenor burble of the tired old motor. The truck was a pleasant travelling companion on the state roads. On freeway I-70 it was less pleasant. Passing semis blew it all over the place. Reacher's wrists ached from holding it steady. He stopped once for gas and once for coffee, and both times he was happy to get a break.

The spur off I-70 was the same piece of road Reacher had observed leaving the plant at the other end: coarse blacktop, sand shoulders. Exactly four hours after leaving Hope he slowed and coasted to one side and came to a stop with two wheels in the sand. Traffic was light, limited to trucks of all types heading in and out of the recycling plant twenty miles ahead. They barrelled past and their bow waves rocked the old truck on its suspension.

Despair itself was invisible in the far distance, except for the hint of a smudge on the horizon. Five miles closer, but still fifteen miles away, was the group of low grey buildings Reacher had seen before, now on his right, a tiny indistinct blur. A gas station, maybe. Or a truck stop with a restaurant. Maybe it was the kind of place he could get a high-calorie meal.

Maybe it was the kind of place Lucy Anderson's husband and the unidentified dead guy might have had a high-calorie meal, on their way into Despair. Maybe someone would remember them.

Reacher bumped his right-hand wheels back onto the road and headed for the horizon. Twelve minutes later he stopped again, just short of a pole that held a small green sign: *Entering Despair, Pop. 2,691.* A hundred yards the wrong side of the line was the group of low buildings.

They weren't grey. That had been a trick of light and haze and distance. They were olive-green. Six low green buildings, identical metal prefabrications ringed by a razor-wire fence. The fence continued west to enclose a parking lot. The lot was filled with six Humvees, each of which had a quick-release machine-gun mount on top.

An army facility. More specifically, a military-police facility. More specifically still, a temporary encampment for a combat MP unit. Reacher recognised the format and the equipment mix.

Four guys were in the guard shack. Two came out. They were dressed in desert battle dress and were carrying M-16 rifles. They formed up side by side, executed a perfect left turn and jogged towards Reacher's truck, exactly in step, at exactly seven miles an hour, like they had been trained to. When they were thirty yards away they separated to split the target they were presenting. One guy headed for the sand and came up on Reacher's right. He stood off ten yards distant and swapped his rifle into the ready position. The other guy stayed on the blacktop and looped round and checked the truck's load bed. Then he came back and stood off six feet from Reacher's door and called out in a loud clear voice, 'Sir, please lower your window. Keep your hands where I can see them.'

Reacher put his hands high on the wheel and kept on staring left. The guy he was looking at was a specialist, young but with pronounced squint lines either side of his eyes. He was wearing glasses with thin black frames. The name tape on the right side of his vest said *Morgan*.

'At ease, Corporal,' Reacher said. 'Nothing to see here.'

The guy called Morgan said, 'Sir, that's a determination I'll need to make for myself.'

Reacher glanced ahead. Morgan's partner was still as a statue, the stock of his M-16 tucked tight into his shoulder. He was sighting with his right eye, aiming low at Reacher's front right-hand tyre.

Morgan said, 'Sir, you appear to me to be surveilling a restricted military installation.'

'Well, you're wrong. I'm lost,' Reacher said. 'I'm looking for Hope.'

Morgan took his left hand off his rifle and pointed straight ahead. 'That way, sir,' he said. 'Twenty-two miles to downtown Hope.'

Reacher nodded. Morgan was pointing southeast but hadn't taken his eyes off Reacher's hands. He was a good soldier. Experienced.

Morgan stepped in close to Reacher's fender again and a truck blew by. A New Jersey semi loaded with a closed forty-foot shipping container. Like a giant brick, doing sixty miles an hour. Noise, wind, a long tail of swirling dust. Morgan's trousers flattened against his legs, but he didn't blink.

He asked, 'Sir, do you have registration and insurance?'

'Glove compartment,' Reacher said, which was a pretty safe guess.

Morgan asked, 'Sir, may I see those documents?'

Reacher said, 'No.'

'Sir, now it seems to me that you're approaching a restricted installation in a stolen vehicle. Sir, I need you to show me those documents.'

Reacher shrugged and leant over and opened the glove compartment. Dug through ballpoint pens and packs of tissues and found a plastic wallet. He opened it, out of Morgan's sight. On the left was an insurance certificate, on the right a current registration. Both were made out to David Robert Vaughan, of Hope, Colorado. He waved the wallet in Morgan's direction.

Morgan said, 'Sir, thank you.'

Reacher put the wallet back in the glove compartment.

Morgan said, 'Sir, now it's time to be moving along.'

Which gave Reacher another problem. If he moved forward, he would be in Despair. If he U-turned, Morgan would wonder why he had abandoned Hope as a destination, and would be tempted to call in Vaughan's plate.

Reacher put the truck in gear and turned the wheel. 'Have a great day, Corporal,' he said, and hit the gas. A yard later he passed the green sign and temporarily increased Despair's population by one.

REACHER SAW all the same stuff he had seen the day before, but in reverse order. The plant's long end wall, welded metal, bright white paint, the sparks and the smoke coming from the activity inside, the moving cranes.

He saw the clockwise security Tahoe bouncing across the scrub in the distance far to his right. Its counterclockwise partner was much closer, coming on slow. It crossed the road right behind Reacher. He saw it slide past, huge in his mirror. He drove on and then the plant was behind him and downtown Despair was looming up on the right.

A mile ahead, a cop car pulled out of a side street. A Crown Vic, white and gold, a light bar on the roof. It nosed out and paused a beat and turned west. Straight towards Reacher.

Reacher cruised on. The sun was behind him, and therefore in the cop's eyes, which was a good thing. Reacher took his left hand off the wheel and put it against his forehead, like he was massaging his temple against a headache. He kept his speed steady and stared straight ahead.

The cop car shot past.

Reacher put his hand back on the wheel and checked his mirror.

The cop was braking hard. Not good.

Now he was pulling through a fast U-turn. Why?

Despair was a company town but its road had to be a public thorough-fare. Unfamiliar vehicles could not be rarities. Reacher checked the mirror again. The Crown Vic was accelerating after him. Nose high, tail squatting low. Maybe the security guy in the counterclockwise Tahoe had called it in.

Maybe he had seen Reacher's face and recognised it. Maybe the deputies from the family restaurant took turns as the security drivers.

Reacher drove on. He hit the first downtown block. Ten blocks ahead, a second Crown Vic pulled out. And stopped, dead across the road. Reacher braked hard and pulled a fast right into the chequerboard of downtown streets. A desperation move. He hit three four-way stops in succession and turned left, right, left without pausing or thinking. He figured the downtown area was about twelve blocks square, which meant there were about 288 distinct lengths of road between opportunities to turn off, which meant that if he kept moving, the chances of direct confrontation were pretty low.

But the chances of ever getting out of the maze were pretty low, too. As long as the second cop was blocking Main Street at its eastern end, then Hope was unavailable as a destination. And presumably the metal plant Tahoes were on duty to the west.

Reacher turned a random left, just to keep moving. The chase car flashed through the intersection, dead ahead, moving right. Reacher turned left on the same street and saw it in his mirror, moving away from him. Now he was heading west. He turned right and headed north to Main Street.

The second Crown Vic was still parked across the road, its light bar flashing red. It was nearly eighteen feet long. One of the last of America's full-size sedans. A big car, but at one end it left a gap of about four feet between the front of its hood and the kerb.

Vaughan's Chevy was close to six feet wide.

Reacher could get past the cop with two wheels up on the kerb. But then what? He would be faced with a twelve-mile high-speed chase, in a low-speed vehicle. No good.

He turned right again and headed back to the downtown maze. Saw the first Crown Vic flash past again, this time hunting east to west, three blocks away. He turned left and headed away from it, seeing the police station twice, and the bar, the rooming house and the faded old hotel that he had noticed before. He saw a storefront church. The only church in town, Vaughan had said, where the town's feudal boss was the preacher.

Reacher drove on. He would have liked to find a tyre bay, where he could get the old Chevy up on a hoist and out of sight, but he saw none.

He drove on, making random turns. He saw the first Crown Vic three more times, twice ahead of him and once behind him in his mirrors. The fourth time he saw it he was paused at a four-way junction. It came up at the exact same moment and paused in the mouth of the road directly to his right. Reacher and the cop were ten feet apart. The cop was the same guy that had arrested him. He looked over and smiled. Gestured *Go ahead*.

Reacher was a lousy driver, but he wasn't stupid. No way was he going to let the cop get behind him. He jammed the old Chevy into reverse and backed away. The cop turned, aiming to follow. Reacher waited until the guy was halfway through the manoeuvre and jammed the stick back into Drive and snaked past him. Then he hung a left and a right and a left again.

He drove on, endlessly. He passed the church and the old hotel for the third time each. Then the rooming house. Its door opened. In the corner of his eye he saw a guy step out. A young guy. Tall and blond and heavy. Blue eyes and a buzz cut and a dark tan. Reacher stamped on the brake and turned his head. But the guy was gone, moving fast, around the corner. In his mirror Reacher saw the chase car three blocks west. Turned left, turned right, drove more wide aimless circles.

He didn't see the young blond man again. But he saw the cop twice more. The guy was nosing around through distant intersections like he had all the time in the world. Which he did. The lone road was bottlenecked at both ends of town. He had Reacher trapped, and Reacher knew it.

Time to stand and fight.

REACHER PULLED to the kerb outside the restaurant and got out of Vaughan's truck. He took up a position leaning against one of the restaurant's floor-to-ceiling plate-glass windows. He chose to assume that however half-baked the Despair cops might be, they wouldn't risk shooting with bystanders in the line of fire. Behind him nine customers were eating late lunches.

Reacher unbuttoned his cuffs and folded them up. He flexed his hands and rolled his head in small circles to loosen his neck. Then he waited.

Two minutes and forty seconds later the Crown Vic came in from the west. It stopped and paused, like the guy was having trouble processing the information right in front of him. The truck, parked. The suspect, just standing there. Then the pause was over and the cop left his engine running and opened his door and slid out into the roadway. He took his Glock off his belt and held it straight out two-handed. 'Get in the car,' he called.

'Make me.'

'I'll shoot.'

'You won't.'

The guy went blank for a beat and then shifted his focus to the scene inside the restaurant. 'Get in the car,' he said again.

Reacher said, 'I'll take a pass on that.'

The cop paused. Then he shuffled back towards the driver's door. He kept his gun tight on Reacher and fumbled one-handed through the car window and grabbed up his microphone. He brought it to his mouth and clicked the button. Said, 'Bro, the restaurant, right now.' He clicked off again, tossed the microphone back on the seat and put both hands back on the gun.

The clock started ticking. Reacher couldn't afford for the second guy to arrive.

'Pussy,' Reacher called. 'A thing like this, you should have been able to handle it on your own.'

The cop's lips went tight and he stepped up out of the gutter onto the sidewalk, tracking with his gun, adjusting his aim.

Reacher kept his back against the glass and moved his right heel against the base of the wall. The cop stepped closer. The Glock's muzzle was within a foot of Reacher's throat.

Taking a gun from a man ready to use it was not always difficult. Taking one from a man who had already decided not to use it verged on the easy. The cop took his left hand off the gun and braced to grab Reacher by the collar. Reacher slid right, his back hard on the window and moved inside the cop's aim. He brought his left forearm up and over, fast, *one, two*, and clamped his hand right over the Glock and the cop's hand together. He squeezed hard and forced the gun away in one easy movement. He got it pointing at the floor and then, looking the cop in the eye and smiling briefly, he jerked forwards off his planted heel and delivered a colossal head butt direct to the bridge of the cop's nose.

The cop sagged back on rubber legs and Reacher kneed him in the groin. The guy went down more or less vertically but Reacher kept his hand twisted up and back so that the cop's own weight dislocated his elbow as he fell. He screamed and the Glock came free pretty easily after that.

Reacher scrambled round the Crown Vic's hood and hauled the door open. He tossed the Glock inside, slid in the seat and buckled the seat belt, then pulled it snug and tight. Reacher put the transmission in reverse and backed away from the Chevy. He spun the wheel and came back level with it, facing east. Waiting.

The second Crown Vic showed up within thirty seconds. It burst round a distant corner, fishtailed a little, then accelerated down the narrow street towards the restaurant, hard and fast and smooth.

When it was thirty yards away, Reacher stamped on the gas and smashed into it head-on. Sheet metal crumpled and hoods flew open. Glass burst and air bags exploded. Reacher was smashed forwards against his seat belt. Then the air bag collapsed and he was tossed back against the headrest. He pulled the Mossberg pump out of its between-the-seats holster, forced the door open against the crumpled fender and climbed out of the car.

The other guy hadn't been wearing his seat belt. He was lying sideways across the front seat with blood coming out of his nose and ears. Reacher was pretty sure both cars were undriveable but he made sure by racking the Mossberg twice and firing two booming shots into the tyres. Then he tossed the pump back through the first Crown Vic's window, walked over and climbed into Vaughan's Chevy. He backed away from all the wreckage. The waitress and the nine customers were all staring out through the restaurant windows. Two of them were fumbling for their cellphones.

Reacher smiled. Who are you going to call?

He turned the Chevy and headed north for Main Street, made another right and cruised east. He felt the roughness of Despair's road under his tyres as he kicked it up to sixty, but the roar was quieter than before. He was a little deaf from the air bags and the twin Mossberg blasts.

Twelve minutes later he bumped over the expansion joint and cruised into Hope.

CHAPTER FIVE

Reacher guessed Vaughan had got her head on the pillow a little after nine that morning, which was six hours ago. Eight hours' rest would take her to five o'clock. Or maybe she was already up. Some people slept worse in the daytime than the night. He decided to head for the diner. Either she would be there or he could leave her keys with the cashier.

She was there. Alone in the booth they had used before. She had an empty plate and a full coffee cup in front of her. She looked tired.

He locked the truck and went in and sat down opposite her. 'I have a confession to make.'

'You went to Despair. In my truck. I knew you would.'

'I had to.'

'Sure.'

'There's a new military base just inside the town line. Why would that be?'

Vaughan said, 'There are military bases all over.'

'This was a combat MP unit. Why would they put an MP unit out there?'

Vaughan said, 'I don't know why. The Pentagon doesn't explain itself to neighbourhood police departments.'

The waitress brought a cup for Reacher and filled it from a flask. Vaughan asked, 'What does a combat MP unit do exactly?'

Reacher took a sip of coffee. 'It guards things. Convoys or installations.'

'What's to defend in Despair?'

'Exactly,' Reacher said.

'And you're saying these MPs made you drive on through?'

'It was safer. They would have checked your plate if I hadn't.'

'Did you get through OK?'

'Your truck is fine. Although it's not exactly yours, is it?'

'What do you mean?'

'Who is David Robert Vaughan?'

She looked blank for a second. Then she said, 'You looked in the glove compartment. The registration.'

'A man with a gun wanted to see it.'

'Good reason.'

'So who is David Robert?'

Vaughan said, 'My husband.'

She turned her attention to her coffee.

Reacher said, 'I didn't know you were married.'

'That's because I didn't tell you,' she said.

They were silent for a long moment. Then Reacher said, 'I think I saw Lucy Anderson's husband today.'

'In Despair?'

'Coming out of the rooming house.'

'That's way off Main Street.'

'I was dodging roadblocks,' Reacher said. 'Long story.'

'But?'

'The Despair PD is temporarily understaffed,' Reacher explained.

'You took one of them out?'

'Both of them. And their cars.'

'You're completely unbelievable.'

'No, I'm a man with a rule. People leave me alone, I leave them alone. If they don't, I don't.'

'They'll come looking for you here,' Vaughan warned.

'No question. But not soon. They'll be hurting for a couple of days. Then they'll saddle up.'

REACHER LEFT VAUGHAN alone with her truck keys on the table in front of her and walked down to Third Street. He stopped at a pharmacy and bought shaving gear. Then he bought socks and underwear in an old-fashioned outfitters next to a supermarket. In the hardware store at the west end of First Street he found a rail of canvas work trousers and flannel shirts. Traditional American garments, made in China and Cambodia, respectively. He chose dark olive trousers and a mud-coloured checked shirt. He carried the stuff back to the motel, where he shaved and took a long shower, then dried off and dressed. He crammed all his old clothes in the trash. Better than doing laundry.

He stepped out and walked down the row of motel rooms. At each door he knocked and waited. Lucy Anderson couldn't be anywhere else. He hadn't seen any other overnight accommodation in town. A minute later she opened a door. She looked young and vulnerable. And wary and hostile.

He said, 'I'm pretty sure I saw your husband today. In Despair.'

Her face softened. 'Was he OK?'

'He looked fine to me.'

'What are you going to do about him?'

'What would you like me to do about him?'

Her face closed up again. 'You should leave him alone.'

'I am leaving him alone. I told you, I'm not a cop any more.'

'I don't believe you. You're a cop.'

The motel clerk stepped out of the office, forty feet to Reacher's left. She was a stout woman of about fifty. She saw Reacher and the girl and stopped walking and watched. Then she headed towards them. Reacher figured she was the nosy kind. He stepped back a pace.

Lucy turned her head and saw the clerk approach, then ducked back inside and slammed her door. Reacher turned away but knew he wasn't going to make it in time. The clerk was within calling distance.

'You should leave that girl alone,' she said. 'If you want to stay here.'

'I'm trying to help her.'

'You should investigate some real crimes.'

Reacher said, 'I'm not investigating any kind of crimes. I'm not a cop.'

The woman didn't answer.

Reacher asked, 'What real crimes?'

'Violations. At the metal plant in Despair. You should ask yourself why that plane flies every night.'

'I'm not an Environmental Protection Agency inspector. I'm not any kind of inspector.'

REACHER WAS HALFWAY back to his room when Vaughan's pick-up turned in off the street, moving fast. She braked hard and stopped with her radiator grille an inch from him. She leant out of the window and said, 'Get in.'

Reacher asked, 'Do I have a choice?'

'I'll use my gun and my cuffs if that's what it takes. Get in the car.'

The evidence was right there in the set of her jaw. So he climbed in. Vaughan waited until he closed his door behind him and then she said, 'We got a courtesy call. From Despair. They're coming for you.'

'They can't be. They can't even have woken up yet.'

'Their deputies are coming. All four of them.'

'So I hide in your car?'

'Damn straight.'

'You think I need protection?'

'My town needs protection. I don't want fighting in my streets.' She pulled a U-turn in the motel lot and headed back the way she had come.

Reacher said, 'I could leave town.'

'And go where?' Vaughan asked.

'Despair, obviously. I can't get in trouble there, can I? Their cops are still in the hospital and their deputies will be here until the plant opens up again at six tomorrow morning.'

Vaughan stayed quiet for a moment and then she said, 'There's another girl in town today. She came in with the supermarket delivery guy. He gave her a ride. She's like Lucy Anderson, but dark, not blonde. She's sitting staring west now like she's waiting for word from Despair.'

'From a boyfriend or a husband?'

'Possibly.'

'Possibly a dead boyfriend or husband, Caucasian, about twenty years old, five-eight and one-forty?'

'Possibly.'

'I should go there.'

Vaughan drove past the diner and kept on driving. Motion, just for the sake of it. Small yards, picket fences, mailboxes on poles that had settled to every angle except the truly vertical.

'I should go there,' Reacher said again.

Vaughan nodded. 'Wait until the deputies get here. You don't want to pass them on the road.'

FOR THE SECOND TIME that day, Vaughan gave up her pick-up truck and walked home to get her cruiser. Reacher drove the truck to a quiet side street and parked in the shadow of a tree and watched the traffic on First Street. The daylight was fading fast. The world was going grey and still.

At six thirty-two Reacher saw an old crew-cab pick-up truck flash through his field of vision. Moving smartly, from the Despair direction. A driver and three passengers inside. Big men.

The Despair deputies.

Reacher waited a beat and started the old Chevy's engine and moved off the kerb. He checked his mirror. The old crew-cab was 100 yards behind him, moving away in the opposite direction. The road ahead was empty. He forced the old truck up to sixty miles an hour. Five minutes later he thumped over the expansion joint and settled into a noisy cruise west.

Twelve miles later he turned left into Despair's downtown maze. First port of call was the rooming house. He parked at the kerb, killed the motor and wound the window down. Heard a single aero engine in the far distance, climbing hard. Seven o'clock. The Piper or Cessna, taking off again. *You should ask yourself why that plane flies every night*, the motel clerk had said.

Maybe I will, Reacher thought. One day.

He climbed out of the truck. The rooming house had a board on the wall next to the door: *Rooms to Rent*. Not the kind of place Reacher favoured. Such establishments implied residency for longer periods than he was interested in. Generally they rented by the week and had electric cooking rings in the rooms. Practically the same thing as setting up housekeeping.

He went up the stone steps and pushed the front door. It was open. Inside the air smelt of dust and cabbage. There were four interior doors, all dull green, all closed. In Reacher's experience the supervisor always chose a ground-floor room at the front, to monitor entrances and exits. Tenants had been known to sneak out just before final payment of long-overdue rent.

He opted for the door at the foot of the staircase. Better surveillance potential. He knocked and waited. A long moment later the door opened and revealed a thin man in a white shirt and a black tie. The guy was close to seventy years old and his shirt wasn't clean.

'Help you?' the old guy said.

'I'm looking for a friend of mine,' Reacher said. 'I heard he was staying here. Young guy, very big. Tanned, with short hair.'

'Nobody like that here.'

'What about another guy, shorter, wiry, about twenty?'

'No guys here at all, big or small.'

Reacher said, 'Can I see the rooms?'

'You think I'm lying?'

'I'm a suspicious person.'

'I should call the police.'

'Go right ahead.'

The old guy stepped away into the gloom and picked up a phone. Reacher crossed the hall and tried the opposite door. It was locked. He walked back and the old guy said, 'There was no answer at the police station.'

Reacher smiled. Despair was lawless. The way he liked it. 'So it's just you and me,' he said.

The old guy bowed to the inevitable. He took a worn brass key from his pocket and handed it over.

There were eleven guest rooms on the ground floor, four on the first and four on the second. All were identical. All empty. Each room had a narrow iron bed against one wall. The sheets had been washed so many times they were almost transparent. Near the ends of the beds were pine kitchen tables with two-ring electric cookers. Basic accommodation, for sure, but they were in good order. The floors were swept shiny. The beds were made tight.

Reacher stood in the doorway of each room before leaving it, smelling the air and listening for echoes of recent hasty departures. He found nothing and sensed nothing, eleven times over. So he headed back downstairs, returned the key and apologised to the old guy.

He drove Vaughan's old Chevy on down the street to the hotel. Paused for a moment in front of the storefront church. It had a painted sign running the whole width of the building: *Congregation of the End Times*. In one window it had a poster: *The Time is at Hand*. A quotation from the Book of Revelation. Chapter one, verse three. Reacher recognised it. The other window had a similar poster: *The End is Near*. Inside, the place was as gloomy as its exterior messages.

Reacher went outside, got back in the Chevy and drove to the hotel. He remembered the place from earlier daytime sightings as looking dowdy. By night it looked worse, like a city prison, in Prague, maybe, or Warsaw. Inside it had an empty and unappealing dining room on the left and a deserted bar on the right. Dead ahead was a deserted reception desk.

When searching a hotel the place to start is the register. Which over the years had become increasingly difficult. With computers there were all kinds of function keys to hit and passwords to discover. But Despair was behind the times. The register was a large square book bound in old red leather. According to the records the last room had been rented seven months previously, to a couple from California, who had stayed two nights.

Reacher left the hotel without a single soul having seen him and got back in the Chevy again. Next stop was two blocks over.

The town bar was a slice of the ground floor of yet another dull brick cube. One long narrow room. Low light. No music. All the customers were men. The after-work crowd. They were all tired, all grimy, all sipping beer.

Reacher stepped into the gloom, quietly. Every head turned and every pair of eyes came to rest on him. Stranger in the house. Reacher stood still and let them take a good look. A stranger for sure, but not the kind you want to mess with. Then he sat down on a stool and put his elbows on the bar. It was made of scarred mahogany that didn't match the walls, which were panelled with pine. There were framed mirrors all over the walls.

The bartender was a heavy man of about forty. He didn't look pleasant. Reacher raised his eyebrows and put a beckoning expression on his face and got no response at all.

A company town.

He swivelled his stool and faced the room. 'Listen up, guys,' he called. 'I'm not a metalworker and I'm not looking for a job. I'm just a guy passing through, looking for a beer.'

Sullen and hostile stares.

Reacher said, 'First guy to talk to me, I'll pay his tab for a week.'

No response.

Reacher turned back and looked the bartender in the eye and said, 'Sell me a beer or I'll start busting this place up.'

The bartender moved. But not towards his draught pumps. He picked up his telephone instead and dialled a long number. Reacher waited. The guy listened to a lot of ring tone and then started to say something. Then stopped and put the phone down again.

'Voicemail,' he said.

'Nobody home,' Reacher said. 'So it's just you and me. I'll take a Budweiser, no glass.'

The bartender decided not to be a hero. He shrugged and pulled a cold bottle out from under the bar. Opened it. Foam swelled out of the neck and ran down the side of the bottle. Reacher took a ten from his pocket and folded it lengthways so it wouldn't curl, and squared it in front of him.

'I'm looking for a big guy,' he said. 'Young. Maybe twenty.'

'Nobody like that here.'

'I saw him this afternoon. In town.'

'I can't help you.'

'What about another guy: same age, much smaller, maybe five-eight?'

'Didn't see him.'

Reacher took a long pull on his bottle. 'You ever work up at the plant?'

'Couple of years, way back.'

'And then?'

'He moved me here.'

'Who did?'

'Mr Thurman. He owns the plant.'

'And this bar too?'

'He owns everything.'

'Is that Mr Thurman's plane that flies every night?'

'Nobody else here owns a plane.'

'Where does he go?'

'I don't ask.'

Reacher drank a little more of his beer. The bartender stayed close. Reacher glanced at the mirrors. Checked reflections of reflections.

'You got a doctor in town?'

The bartender shook his head. 'There's a first-aid post at the plant.'

'With a vehicle?'

'An old ambulance. It's a big plant. It covers a big area.'

'Does the plant pay disability if there are accidents?'

'Mr Thurman looks after people if they get hurt on the job.'

Reacher nodded and went quiet again. Six minutes, he thought. I've been working on this beer for six minutes. Maybe ten more to go. He waited for the bartender to fill the silence, like he had to. Like he had been told to.

The guy said, 'A hundred years ago there were only five miles of paved road in the United States.'

Reacher said nothing.

The guy said, 'Then county roads got built, then state, then the Interstates. Towns got passed by. We were on the main road to Denver, once. People use I-70 now.'

Reacher said, 'Hence the closed-down motel and the feeling of isolation.'

'I guess.'

Eleven minutes, Reacher thought. Eight to go. Unless they're early.

Which they were.

Reacher looked to his right and saw two deputies step in through the fire door. He glanced in a mirror and saw the other two walk in the front.

FOUR DEPUTIES HEADING EAST to make a surprise arrest would not indicate their intention with a courtesy telephone call. Not in the real world. Therefore the courtesy call was a decoy, designed to flush Reacher westwards into safer territory. It was an invitation.

Which Reacher had accepted.

And the bartender had not called the station house. He had dialled too many digits. He had called a deputy's cell, and spoken just long enough to let the deputy know who he was, and therefore where Reacher was. Whereupon he had turned talkative and friendly, to keep Reacher sitting tight.

Which is why Reacher had not left the bar.

The big guy who had vomited the night before was one of the pair that had come in the front. With him was the guy Reacher had smacked outside the family restaurant. Neither one of them looked in great shape. The two who had come through the fire door looked large and healthy enough, but manageable. Four against one, no real cause for concern.

Then the situation changed.

Two guys stood up from the body of the room. They scraped their chairs back and stepped forwards. One lined up with the guys in the back, and one lined up with the guys in the front. They could have been the deputies' brothers. They looked the same and were built the same.

Reacher clamped his jaw and the beer in his stomach went sour. Six against one. Twelve hundred pounds against two-fifty. Rotten odds.

He took a last sip of Bud and set the bottle back on his napkin. Swivelled his stool and faced the room. He saw the other customers sidling backwards towards the far wall, hunkering down.

Both sets of three men took long paces forwards.

The big guy spoke, from six feet inside the front door. He said, 'You're in so much trouble you couldn't dig your way out with a steam shovel.'

Reacher said, 'You talking to me?'

'Damn straight I am.'

Reacher stayed on his stool, tensed up and ready, but not visibly so.

Outwardly he was still calm and relaxed. His brother Joe had been two years older, physically very similar, but temperamentally very different. Joe had eased into fights, reluctantly, slowly, rationally. Therefore he had been a frustrating opponent. Therefore his enemies had turned on Reacher, the younger brother. The first time, confronted with four baiting seven-year-olds, the five-year-old Reacher had felt a jolt of real fear. The fear had emerged as intense aggression. He had exploded into action and the fight was over. When his four assailants got out of the paediatric ward they had stayed well away from him for ever. Reacher had learned a valuable lesson. *Hit early, hit hard. Get your retaliation in first.*

He slipped forwards off his stool, turned, bent, grasped the iron stool, spun, and hurled it head-high as hard as he could at the three men at the back of the room. Before it hit he launched the other way and charged the new guy next to the guy with the damaged jaw. He led with his elbow and smashed it flat against the bridge of the guy's nose. The guy went down like a tree. Reacher jerked sideways and put the same elbow into the big guy's ear. Then he bounced away from the impact and backed into the guy with the bad jaw and buried the elbow deep in his gut. The guy folded forward. Reacher shoved him away and turned round fast.

The bar stool had connected. One of the deputies and the other new guy were sidelined for the moment. They were turned away, bent over, with the stool still rolling noisily at their feet.

The other deputy was untouched. He was launching forwards with a wild grimace on his face. Reacher danced two steps and took a left hook on the shoulder and put a straight right into the centre of the grimace. The guy stumbled back. Reacher's arms were clamped from behind in a bear hug. The big guy, presumably. Reacher snapped a reverse head butt that made solid contact. Not as good as a forward, but useful. Then he accelerated all the way backwards and crushed the breath out of the big guy against the wall. Reacher pulled his arms away and met the other deputy in the centre of the room. He dodged an incoming right and snapped a right of his own. It rocked the deputy enough to open him up for a colossal left to the throat.

One guy down for maybe a seven count, four down for maybe an eight count, the big guy still functional. Time to get serious.

The bartender had said: *Mr Thurman looks after people if they get hurt on the job.* Reacher thought: So let him. These guys are doing Thurman's bidding. Clearly nothing happens here except what Thurman wants.

The deputy in the centre of the room was rolling around on the floor and clutching his throat. Reacher kicked him in the ribs hard enough to break a couple, then he moved on to the two guys he had hit with the stool. One was crouched down, clutching his forearm. Reacher put the flat of his foot on his backside and drove him head-first into the wall. The other guy had maybe taken the edge of the seat in the chest. He was having trouble breathing. Reacher kicked his feet out from under him and then kicked him in the head. So far so good. Which puzzled Reacher, deep down. He was winning a six-on-one bar brawl and he had nothing to show for it except two bruised shoulders. It had gone way better than he could have hoped.

Then it started to go way worse.

The big guy put his hands in his trouser pockets and came out with two switchblades. He popped the first blade with a precision click, paused and popped the second. Reacher's stomach clenched. He hated knives. Guns can miss. Knives don't miss. The best defence against knives is distance.

Reacher clubbed a spectator out of his seat, grabbed the empty chair and held it out in front of him. He jabbed forwards like a fencer. The big guy brought his right hand up to shield his face and took the chair on the forearm. Reacher stepped back and jabbed again hard. Got one chair leg in the guy's solar plexus and another in his gut. The guy staggered one short step and then came back hard, arms swinging, the blades hissing through the air.

Reacher backed off. Shoved another spectator out of his seat, took hold of the empty chair and threw it high and hard. The big guy jerked his arms up and the chair bounced off his elbows. Reacher stepped in with the first chair, jabbed hard and caught the guy below the ribs, as 250 pounds punched through the blunt end of a chair leg into nothing but soft tissue.

The big guy dropped the knives and clamped his hands low down on his stomach then fell to his knees and puked blood. He tried to push himself upwards but he didn't make it. He collapsed sideways and curled into a ball.

Game over.

Reacher bent down and checked the pulse in the big guy's neck and found it weak and thready. He found a five-pointed star in the front pocket of the man's shirt. It was made of pewter and two lines were engraved in its centre: *Township of Despair, Police Deputy*. Reacher put it in his own shirt pocket. He found a bunch of keys and a thin wad of money. He kept the keys and left the cash. Then he looked around until he found the bartender.

'Call the plant,' Reacher said. 'Get the ambulance down here. Take care with the big guy. He doesn't look good.' Then he drained the last of his beer, set the bottle back down again and walked out into the night.

CHAPTER SIX

Reacher thumped back over the expansion joint at nine thirty in the evening and was outside the diner before nine thirty-five. He figured Vaughan might swing by there. That if he left her truck on the kerb she would see it and be reassured that he was OK. Or that her truck was OK.

He went inside to leave her keys and saw Lucy Anderson sitting alone in a booth. She was gazing into space and smiling. The first time he had seen her he had characterised her as not quite 100 per cent pretty. Now she looked pretty damn good. She looked like a completely different person.

She noticed him and looked over and smiled. It was a curious smile. There was contentment in it, but a little triumph, too. Like she had won a victory at his expense.

He handed Vaughan's keys to the cashier at the desk and the woman asked, 'Are you eating with us tonight?'

He thought about it. The adrenaline had drained away. He was hungry. No sustenance since breakfast, except for some empty calories from the bottle of Bud in the bar. So he said, 'Yes, I'm ready for dinner.'

He walked over and slid into Lucy Anderson's booth. She looked across the table at him and smiled the same smile all over again.

'What's changed?' he asked her.

'What do you think?'

'You heard from your husband.'

She smiled again. 'I sure did,' she said.

'He left Despair.'

'He sure did. Now you'll never get him.'

'I never wanted him.'

'Really,' she said, in the exaggerated and sarcastic way young people used the word. *How big an idiot do you think I am?*

'I'm not a cop,' Reacher said. 'I was once but I'm not any more.'

She didn't answer. He knew she wasn't convinced.

'I'm just a passing stranger, Lucy. I don't know anything.'

She smiled again. Happiness, triumph, victory.

Reacher asked, 'Where has your husband gone?'

'Like I'd tell you *that*.'

The waitress came by and Reacher asked her for coffee and steak. When she had gone away again he looked across at Lucy Anderson and said, 'There are others in the position you were in yesterday. There's a girl in town right now, just waiting.'

'I hope there are plenty of us.'

'I think maybe she's waiting in vain. I know that a boy died out there a day or two ago.'

Lucy Anderson shook her head. 'Not possible,' she said. 'None of us died. I would have heard.'

'Us?'

'People in our position.'

'Somebody died.'

'People die all the time.'

The waitress brought his coffee. He took a sip. It was OK. He looked at the girl again and said, 'Lucy, I wish you good luck, whatever the hell you're doing and wherever the hell you're going.'

'That's it? No more questions?'

'I'm just here to eat.'

He ate alone, because Lucy Anderson left before his steak arrived. He was through by ten thirty and headed back to the motel. He dropped by the office to pay for another night's stay. He always rented rooms one night at a time, even when he knew he was going to hang out in a place longer. It was a comforting ritual, intended to confirm his absolute freedom to move on.

He went back to his room and showered, but he was too restless to sleep. So he dressed again and went out and walked. On a whim he stopped at a phone booth and pulled the directory and looked up David Robert Vaughan. He was there in the book. Vaughan, D. R., with an address on Fifth Street.

Two blocks south. Perhaps he should take a look.

FIFTH STREET WAS a nice place to live, probably. Trees, yards, picket fences, mailboxes, small neat houses resting quietly in the moonlight. Vaughan's house had a large-size mailbox out front, mounted on a wooden post. The box had *Vaughan* written on both sides with stick-on italic letters. They had been carefully applied and were perfectly aligned. Rare, in Reacher's experience. To get seven letters each side level spoke of meticulous planning.

The house and the yard had been maintained to a high standard, too. The yard was covered with golden gravel, with neatly pruned shrubs and bushes pushing up through the stones. Reacher was no expert, but he could tell the difference between care and neglect. The house itself was a low, one-storey ranch maybe fifty years old. The siding and the roof tiles were not new, but they had been replaced within living memory and had weathered into pleasant maturity. No light inside, except a tiny green glow in one window. Probably the kitchen, probably a microwave clock.

Once upon a time Reacher had made his living storming darkened buildings. He had developed a sense, and his sense right then was that the Vaughans' house was empty. So where was David Robert?

Maybe they both worked nights. Some couples chose to coordinate their schedules that way. Maybe David Robert was a nurse or a doctor or worked night construction on the Interstates. Or maybe he was a long-haul trucker, or an actor or a musician, and was on the road for lengthy spells.

Reacher was no social animal, but right then he wanted to see people. It was not quite eleven thirty, yet no one was out and about. He walked back north to Second Street, glanced west and saw Vaughan's truck still parked where he had left it. The diner's lights were spilling out all over it. He figured the diner was the only place he was going to find any people.

He found three. The waitress, a middle-aged guy alone in a booth with a spread of tractor catalogues in front of him, and a frightened Hispanic girl alone in a booth with nothing.

Dark, not blonde, Vaughan had said.

She was tiny, and just eighteen or nineteen years old. Mid-brown skin and jet-black hair framed a face that had a high forehead and enormous eyes. The eyes were brown and looked like twin pools of terror and tragedy. Reacher guessed she had a pretty smile but didn't use it often. She was wearing a blue San Diego Padres baseball jacket with a blue T-shirt under it. There was nothing on the table in front of her.

Reacher stepped to the far side of the register where the waitress was standing. 'That girl,' he whispered. 'Didn't she order?'

'She has no money.'

'Ask her what she wants. I'll pay for it.'

He moved away to a different booth, where he could watch the girl without being obvious about it. He saw the waitress approach her, saw incomprehension in the girl's face, then doubt, then refusal. The waitress stepped over to Reacher's booth and whispered, 'She says she can't possibly accept.'

Reacher said, 'Go back and tell her there are no strings attached. Tell her I'm not hitting on her. Tell her I've been broke and hungry too.'

The waitress went back. This time the girl relented. She pointed to a couple of items on the menu. Then she turned in her seat and inclined her head in a courteous little nod, full of dignity, and went still again.

The waitress came straight back to Reacher and he asked for coffee. The waitress whispered, 'Her check is going to be nine-fifty. Yours will be a dollar and a half.' Reacher peeled a ten and three ones off the roll in his pocket and slid them across the table. The waitress picked them up and thanked him and asked, 'So when were you broke and hungry?'

'Never,' Reacher said.

'You made that up to make her feel better?'

'Sometimes people need convincing.'

'You're a nice guy,' the waitress said.

FROM A SAFE DISTANCE Reacher watched the Hispanic girl eat a tuna melt and drink a chocolate shake. Good choices: protein, fats, carbs, some sugar. If she ate like that every day she would weigh 200 pounds before she was thirty, but in dire need on the road it was wise to load up.

Reacher had seen plenty of people doing what the Hispanic girl was doing, in cafés and diners near bus depots and railroad stations. She was staying warm, saving energy, passing time. She was enduring.

Then she moved. She shifted sideways on her vinyl bench and stood up all in one smooth, delicate motion. She came to some kind of a decision and stepped towards Reacher's booth. She stood off about a yard and said, 'Thank you for my dinner.' Her voice matched her physique.

Reacher asked, 'You OK for breakfast tomorrow?'

She was still for a moment, then she shook her head.

'You OK at the motel?'

'That's why. I paid for three nights. It took all my money.'

'You have to eat.'

The girl said nothing. Reacher thought, Ten bucks a meal is thirty bucks a day, three days makes ninety, plus ten for contingencies or phone calls. He peeled five ATM-fresh twenties off his roll and fanned them on the table. The girl said, 'I can't take your money. I couldn't pay it back.'

'Pay it forwards instead. You know what that means?'

'I'm not sure.'

'Years from now you'll be in a diner somewhere and you'll see someone who needs a break. So you'll help them out.'

The girl nodded. 'I could do that.' She stepped closer and picked up the money. 'Thank you,' she said.

'Don't thank me. Thank whoever helped me way back.'

'Have you ever been to Despair?'

'Four times in the last two days.'

'Did you see anyone there?'

'I saw lots of people.'

She moved closer still and put her slim hips against the end of his table, then hoisted a cheap vinyl bag onto the laminate and rooted around in it. She came up with an envelope and pulled out a photograph.

'Did you see this man?' she asked.

It was a standard six-by-four. Glossy paper, no border. The green background was an expanse of grass and the foreground an expanse of T-shirt. The T-shirt was being worn by a thin guy of about nineteen or twenty.

Not thin, exactly. Lean and wiry.

He looked to be about five-eight. He looked to weigh about one-forty. He was Hispanic, but as much Mayan or Aztec as Spanish. He had shiny black hair and prominent cheekbones.

The girl asked, 'Did you see him?'

Reacher asked, 'What's your name?'

'*My* name? Maria.'

'What's his name?'

'Raphael Ramirez.'

'Is he your boyfriend?'

'Yes. Did you see him?'

Reacher looked again at Raphael Ramirez. Twenty years old. Five-eight, one-forty. The hair, the cheekbones. 'No,' he said. 'I didn't see him.'

THE GIRL LEFT the diner. Reacher watched her go and then he roused the waitress from the book she was reading and had her bring him more coffee.

'You'll never sleep,' she warned.

'How often does Officer Vaughan swing by during the night?' he asked.

The waitress smiled. 'At least once,' she said. She took the flask away and headed back to her book and left him with a steaming mug. He dipped his head and inhaled the smell. When he looked up again he saw Vaughan's cruiser glide by outside. She slowed, as if she was noting that her truck was back. But she didn't stop. She kept on going.

Reacher drank three more mugs of coffee. He read a ragged copy of the previous morning's newspaper all the way through and then jammed himself into the corner of his booth and dozed upright for an hour.

He left the diner at four o'clock in the morning.

You'll never sleep, the waitress had told him.

But not because of the coffee, he thought.

He got up and walked to the register and took Vaughan's truck keys off the counter. The waitress looked up but didn't speak.

Five minutes later Reacher thumped over the line and was back in Despair. He drove on. Main Street was deserted and silent. No cars, nobody on the sidewalks. The police station was dark. The rooming house was dark. The bar was closed up and shuttered. The hotel was just a blank façade with a dozen dark windows. The church was empty and silent.

Reacher headed on west. The metal plant was dark. The wall around it glowed ghostly white in the moonlight. The personnel gate was closed, the parking lot deserted. Reacher followed the wall and steered the truck left and right until its lights picked up the Tahoes' tracks. He followed their giant figure of eight round the plant and the residential compound. He stopped where the two loops met, in the throat between the plant's metal wall and the residential compound's fieldstone wall. He shut off his lights and turned off the engine. Then he rolled down the windows and waited.

HE HEARD THE PLANE at five past two in the morning. A single engine, far in the distance. He craned his neck and saw a light in the sky, way to the south. A small plane, on approach, buffeted by night-time thermals. Lights came on beyond the fieldstone wall. A dull, reflected strip. Reacher saw the plane jump left, correct right, line up with the lights. When it was 100 yards out, Reacher identified it as a Piper, probably a four-seater Cherokee.

It came in low, left-to-right across his windshield in a high-speed rush of light and air and sound. It cleared the fieldstone wall and dropped out of sight. A minute later the engine changed its note to a loud, angry buzzing. Reacher imagined the plane taxiing, bumping sharply over rough ground. Then he heard it shut down and stunned silence flooded in his windows.

The runway lights went off.

He saw and heard nothing more.

He waited ten minutes and then started the truck, backed up, turned and drove away on the blind side, with the bulk of the plant between him and the house. He bumped through the acres of empty parking, skirted the short end of the plant and joined the truck route. Four miles later he figured he'd gone far enough to be safe. He pulled to the shoulder and stopped. Turned his headlights off and slept.

AT SIX O'CLOCK in the morning he was back at the metal plant. The arena lights were already on and the place was lit up bright and blue, like day.

The parking lot was filling up fast. Reacher parked neatly between a sagging Chrysler sedan and a battered Ford pick-up. He slid out and locked up and put the keys in his pocket. Then joined a crowd of men shuffling their way towards the personnel gate. An uneasy feeling. Like entering a baseball stadium wearing the colours of the visiting team.

The gate was a double section of the metal wall, folded back on hinges. The path through it was beaten dusty by a million footsteps. There was no jostling, no impatience. The men needed to clock on, but clearly none of them wanted to. The line shuffled slowly forward, a yard, two, three.

The guy in front of Reacher stepped through the gate.

Reacher stepped through the gate.

Immediately inside there were more metal walls, head high, like cattle chutes, dividing the crowd left and right. The right-hand chute led to a holding pen where Reacher guessed the part-time workers would wait for the call. It was already a quarter full with men standing quiet and patient.

Reacher went left.

The left-hand chute narrowed down to four feet in width. It carried the line of shuffling men past an old-fashioned punch-clock centred in a giant slotted array of timecards. Each man pulled his card and offered it up to the machine, waited for the dull thump of the stamp and then put the card back.

Reacher walked straight past the machine. He followed the guy in front for thirty feet and then stepped out into the northeast corner of the arena. It was staggeringly huge. The total enclosed area must have been 300 acres.

Trucks and cranes were moving. Some of the cranes were bigger than anything Reacher had seen in a dockyard. Some of the trucks were as big as earth-moving machines. There were gigantic crushers set on enormous concrete plinths. There were piles of wrecked cars ten storeys high. The ground was soaked with oil and diesel and littered with curled metal swarf. Where it was dry it glittered. Steam, smoke and chemical smells drifted everywhere. Roaring and hammering rolled outwards in waves, beat against the metal perimeter and bounced back. Flames danced behind open furnace doors.

Like a vision of hell.

Some guys seemed to be heading for pre-assigned jobs, while others were milling in groups. Reacher skirted round behind them and followed the north wall, tiny and insignificant in the chaos. Way ahead of him the vehicle gate was opening. Five semitrailers were parked in a line, waiting to move out. On the road they would look huge and lumbering. Inside the plant they looked like toys. The two security Tahoes were parked side by side, tiny white dots in the vastness. Next to them was a stack of forty-foot shipping containers. They were piled five high. Each one looked tiny.

South of the vehicle gate was a long line of prefabricated metal offices. They were jacked up on short legs to make them level. At the left-hand end of the line two offices were painted white and had red crosses on their doors. The first-aid station. Next to it a white vehicle was parked. The ambulance. Next to the ambulance was a long line of fuel and chemical tanks. Beyond them a sinister platoon of men in black welding masks used cutting torches on a pile of twisted scrap. Blue flames threw hideous shadows. Reacher hugged the north wall and kept on moving. A quarter of the way along it he came across a pyramid of faded red oil drums. They were stacked ten high, stepped like a staircase. Reacher paused and glanced around, then levered himself up to the base of the tier. He climbed halfway up the stack and then turned to get an overview of the whole place.

What had looked like the south boundary was in fact an interior partition. Same height as the perimeter walls, same construction, with the sheer face and the horizontal cylinder. But it was only an internal division, with a closed gate. Beyond it the outer perimeter enclosed at least another 100 acres. Beyond the gate there were heavy cranes and high stacks of shipping containers, carefully placed to block a direct view of ground-level activity.

The internal gate had some kind of a control point in front of it. Reacher could make out two tiny figures stumping around in small circles, bored, their hands in their pockets. He lifted his gaze again beyond the partition. Cranes, screens, distant sparks. Other than that, nothing to see. He waited, watching the plant's internal traffic. Plenty of things were moving, but nothing was heading for the internal gate. It was going to stay closed.

He turned back and climbed down the oil-drum staircase. Stepped off to the rough ground. And then he saw the two men.

One was big and the other was a giant. The big guy was carrying a two-way radio and the giant was carrying a two-headed wrench as long as a baseball bat. The guy was easily six foot six and three-fifty pounds. He looked like he wouldn't need a wrench to take a wrecked car apart.

The guy with the radio asked, 'Who the hell are you?'

Reacher said, 'You first. Who are you?'

'I'm the plant foreman. Now, who are you?'

Reacher pulled the pewter star from his pocket and said, 'I'm with the PD. The new deputy. I'm familiarising myself with the community.'

'We didn't hear about any new deputies.'

'It was sudden.'

The guy raised his radio to his face and clicked a button and spoke low and fast. Names, codes, commands. Reacher didn't understand them, but he guessed the general drift. He glanced west and saw the Tahoes backing up and turning and getting set to head over.

The foreman said, 'Let's go visit the security office.'

Reacher stood still.

The foreman said, 'A new deputy should want to visit the security office. Establish liaison. If that's what you really are.'

Reacher didn't move. He glanced west again and saw the Tahoes halfway through their half-mile of approach. He glanced south and saw knots of men walking his way, the crew in the black welders' masks among them. Plenty of others were coming in from other directions, maybe 200 men with tools in their hands. Hammers, wrenches, cutting torches, foot-long cold chisels.

The foreman said, 'You can't fight them all.'

Reacher nodded. Four-on-one or even six-on-one might be survivable. But not 200-on-one. He said, 'So let's go. I can give you five minutes.'

The foreman said, 'You'll give us whatever we want.' He waved to the nearer Tahoe and it turned in close. The giant opened its rear door and Reacher climbed up into the back seat. The giant climbed in after him and crowded him against the far door panel. The foreman climbed in the front next to the driver and slammed his door and the vehicle took off, headed for the line of office buildings south of the vehicle gate. It drove through the middle of the approaching crowd and Reacher saw faces staring in at him.

The Tahoe stopped directly outside the security-office trailer at the north end of the array, closest to the vehicle gate. Next to it was a tangled pile of webbing straps, presumably once used to tie down junk on flat-bed trailers. Reacher spilt out of the car ahead of the giant and found himself at the bottom of a short set of wooden steps leading up to an office door. He went up them, pushed through the door and entered a plain metal prefabricated box. The foreman pointed Reacher towards a chair and then left again. The giant dragged a chair out of position and dumped himself down in it so that he was blocking the door. He put the wrench on the floor. Reacher sat on a wooden chair in a corner.

He waited twenty minutes, then the door opened and the giant scooted his chair out of the way. The foreman walked in again. 'Mr Thurman wants to see you,' he told Reacher. 'Follow me.'

Reacher followed the foreman out of the trailer and into the one next door. It was an identical metal box, but better appointed, with a carpet, leather armchairs and a mahogany desk. There were pictures on the walls, all of them prints of Jesus. On the corner of the desk was a Bible. Behind the desk was a man Reacher assumed was Mr Thurman. He was wearing a three-piece suit. He looked to be close on seventy years old, pink and plump and prosperous. He had white hair, worn moderately long, combed and teased into waves. He had a big, patient smile on his face. He could have been a game-show host, or a televangelist.

The foreman waited for a nod, then left again. Reacher sat down in an armchair and said, 'I'm Jack Reacher. You've got five minutes.'

The guy behind the desk said, 'I'm Jerry Thurman. I'm very pleased to meet you.'

Reacher said, 'Now you've got four minutes and fifty-six seconds.'

'Actually, sir, I've got as long as it takes.' Thurman's voice was soft and mellifluous. His cheeks quivered as he spoke. 'You've been making trouble in my town and now you're trespassing on my business premises.'

'Your fault,' Reacher said. 'If you hadn't sent those goons to the restaurant I would have eaten a quick lunch and moved on days ago. No reason to stay. You're not exactly running the Magic Kingdom here.'

'I don't aim to. This is an industrial enterprise.'

'So I noticed.'

'But you knew that days ago. I'm sure the people in Hope were quick to tell you all about us. Why poke around?'

'I'm an inquisitive person.'

'Evidently,' Thurman said. 'Which raised our suspicions a little. We have proprietary processes here that might be called industrial secrets.'

'I'm not interested in metal recycling.'

'We know that now,' he said. 'We made enquiries. You are what you claim to be. A passer-by who used to be in the army ten years ago.'

'That's me.'

'But you're persistent and you took a badge from a deputy in a fight.'

'Which he started. On your orders.'

'So we ask ourselves, why are you so keen to know what happens here?'

'And I ask myself, why are you so keen to hide it?'

Thurman shook his head. 'We're not hiding anything,' he said. 'And I'll prove it to you. I'll be your personal guide on a tour of the plant.'

He led Reacher outside and described the various functions carried out in the offices, which in order of appearance were Operations Management, Purchasing and Invoicing. He pointed out the first-aid post, and described its facilities and capabilities, and made a mildly pointed comment about the people Reacher had put in there.

They got into Thurman's Chevy Tahoe, which was painted black, not white, and Thurman drove. Reacher sat next to him. They headed away from the vehicle gate, moving slow. Then they moved on to the line of storage tanks and Thurman described their contents, which were gasoline and diesel and a liquid chemical called trichloroethylene, which was an essential metal degreaser, and oxygen and acetylene for the cutting torches.

Reacher was bored rigid after sixty seconds.

He tuned Thurman out and looked at things for himself. He got the general idea. Old stuff was broken up and melted down, and ingots were sold to factories, where new stuff was made, and eventually the new stuff became old stuff and showed up again.

Not rocket science.

Close to a mile later they arrived at the internal partition. Beyond the wall no more sparks were flying and no more smoke was rising. Activity seemed to have been abandoned. He asked, 'What happens back there?'

Thurman said, 'That's our junkyard. Stuff that's too far gone to work with goes in there. But our processes are highly developed. Not much defeats us any more.'

'Are you a chemist or a metallurgist or what?'

Thurman said, 'I'm a born-again Christian American and a businessman, in that order of importance. But I hire the best talent I can find. Our research and development is excellent.'

Reacher nodded and said nothing.

Thurman asked, 'Are you born-again?'

Reacher said, 'Once was enough for me.'

'I'm serious. You should think about it.'

'My father used to say, why be born-again, when you can just grow up?'

'Is he no longer with us?'

'He's in a hole in the ground in Arlington Cemetery.'

'Another veteran?'

'A Marine.'

'Thank you for his service.'

'Don't thank me. I had nothing to do with it.'

Thurman said, 'You should think about getting your life in order, you know, before it's too late. The Book of Revelation says the time is at hand. There are signs. And the possibility of precipitating events.' He said it primly and smugly, and with a degree of certainty, as if he had regular access to privileged insider information.

Reacher said nothing in reply. They drove on, past a small group of tired men wrestling with a mountain of tangled steel, then arrived at the mouth of the cattle chute leading to the personnel gate. Thurman stopped the truck, jiggled the stick into Park and sat back in his seat.

'Seen enough?' he asked.

'More than enough,' Reacher said.

'Then I'll bid you goodbye,' Thurman said. 'Our paths won't cross again.' He offered his hand and Reacher shook it. It felt soft and warm and boneless, like a balloon filled with water. Reacher opened his door and slid out, then walked back to the acres of parking.

Every window in Vaughan's truck was smashed.

CHAPTER SEVEN

It was a twenty-mile drive, cold and slow and very windy. Like riding a motorcycle without eye protection. Reacher's face was numb with cold and his eyes were watering as he entered Hope.

He passed the diner a little before nine o'clock in the morning. Vaughan's cruiser wasn't there. He drove south, crossed Third Street, and Fourth, and turned left on Fifth. He pulled up level with the mailbox with the perfectly aligned letters. Then he got out and put a palm on the Crown Vic's hood. It was still warm. He got back in the truck, backed up and swung the wheel, then bumped up onto Vaughan's driveway. He parked an inch from her garage door and slid out, then followed the path through the bushes to her door. He hooked her key ring on his finger and tapped the bell, briefly, just once. If she was awake, she would hear it. If she was asleep, it wouldn't disturb her.

She was awake.

The door opened and she peered out of the gloom. Her hair was wet from the shower and combed back. She was wearing an oversized white T-shirt.

She said, 'How did you find me?'

He said, 'Phone book.'

She saw the truck keys on his finger. He said, 'I have a confession.'

'What now?'

'Someone broke all the windows.'

She pushed past him and stepped outside. Turned to face the driveway. She studied the damage and said, 'Shit.' Then it seemed to dawn on her that she was out in the yard in her nightwear and she pushed back inside.

'Who?' she asked.

'One of a thousand suspects. I stopped by the metal plant.'

'You're an idiot.'

'I know. I'm sorry. I'll pay for the glass.' He slipped the keys off his finger and held them out. She didn't take them. Instead she said, 'You better come in.'

The kitchen seemed to be the heart of the home. The counters were tidy but there was enough disarray to make the room feel lived in. And there were what Reacher's mother had called 'touches': dried flowers, bottles of olive oil that would never be used, antique spoons. His mother had said such things gave a room personality. Reacher himself had been unsure how anything except a person could have personality, but over the years he had come to see what his mother had meant. And Vaughan's kitchen had personality. Her personality, he guessed.

It seemed to him that one mind had chosen everything and one pair of hands had done everything. There was no evidence of compromise or duelling tastes. In fact, there was no evidence of a second person. Reacher could see into the living room through an arch. There was a single armchair in there, a TV and some moving boxes still taped shut.

Vaughan said, 'Want coffee?'

'Always.'

Vaughan filled her machine with water. It was a big steel thing with CUISINART embossed on it in large letters. She spooned coffee into a gold basket and hit a switch. She said, 'Last night the deputies from Despair headed home after an hour.'

'They found me in the bar,' Reacher said. 'It was a trap.'

'And you fell for it.'

'They fell for it. I knew what they were doing.'

'How?'

'Because twenty years ago I used to deal with worse folks than you'll ever find in Despair.'

'What happened to the deputies?' Vaughan asked.

'They joined their full-time buddies in the infirmary.'

'All four of them?'

'All six of them. They added some on-site moral support.'

'You're a one-man crime wave. You've committed assault and battery on eight individuals and you've wrecked two police cars and you're still walking around.'

'That's the point,' Reacher said. 'I'm still walking around, but in Hope, not in Despair. All they ever want to do is keep people out of there. They're not interested in the law or justice. They came at me six against one and I walked away with two bruises. They're all weak and sick. The clerk at my motel figures they're breaking environmental laws. Maybe there's all kinds of poisons out there.'

'Is that what they're hiding?'

'Possibly,' Reacher said. 'But it's kind of odd that the victims would help to hide the problem.'

'People worry about their jobs,' Vaughan said. 'Especially in a company town. They don't have any alternatives.' She opened a cabinet and took out a mug. It was white, perfectly cylindrical, and made of fine bone china as thin as paper. She filled it from the machine and from the aroma Reacher knew it was going to be a great one. She glanced at the living room but placed the mug on the kitchen table instead. Reacher studied the boxes and the lone armchair in the living room and said, 'Just moved in?'

'A year and a half ago,' Vaughan said. 'I'm a little slow unpacking.'

'From where?'

'Third Street. David and I had a little cottage with an upstairs, but we decided we wanted a bungalow.'

Reacher asked, 'So where is David?'

'He's not here right now.'

'What does he do?'

'Not so much any more.' She sat in one of the chairs without the mug in front of it and tugged the hem of her T-shirt down. Her hair was drying and going wavy again. She was naked under the shirt and confident about it. Reacher was sure of that. He sat down opposite her.

She asked, 'What else?'

'A quarter of the plant is screened off. There's a secret area. I think Thurman's got a Pentagon contract to recycle military scrap, classified stuff. A Pentagon contract is the fastest way on earth to get rich these days.

And hence the MP unit down the road. Thurman is breaking up classified stuff back there and people would be interested in it.'

'So that's all? Legitimate government business?'

'No,' Reacher said. 'That's not all.' He took the first sip of his coffee. It was perfect. Hot, strong, smooth, and a great mug. 'There are at least two other things going on. At least two other factions in play, separate and probably unaware of each other. Like this morning, Thurman had me checked out. He saw that my paper trail went cold ten years ago and that therefore I was no obvious danger to him. So he played nice and gave me a guided tour. But meanwhile someone was busting your windows. The left hand doesn't know what the right is doing.'

'So what are the two other factions?'

'I have no idea. But Lucy Anderson's husband and the dead guy are involved somehow. Anderson's husband is another example of the left hand not knowing what the right is doing. They sheltered him and moved him on but threw his wife out of town. How much sense does that make?'

'I don't know.'

'When was the last time any normal person entered Despair and stayed?'

'I don't know,' Vaughan said.

'There was an entry in the hotel register from seven months ago.'

'That sounds about right.'

'And I met the new girl last night,' Reacher said. 'Sweet kid. Her name is Maria. I'm pretty sure the dead guy was her boyfriend. She showed me his picture. His name was Raphael Ramirez.'

'Did you tell her?'

'No. She asked me if I'd seen him. Truth is, I didn't. It was dark.'

'So she's still swinging in the wind?'

'I think she knows, deep down.'

'What happened to the body?'

'I don't think it ever left Despair. The only meat wagon and the only stretcher in Despair belong to the metal plant. And the metal plant has furnaces that could vaporise a corpse in five minutes flat.'

Vaughan went quiet, then got up and poured herself a glass of water. She stood against the counter and stared out of the window. The cotton material of her T-shirt was very slightly translucent. The light was all behind her and she looked spectacular. She asked, 'What else did Maria say?'

Reacher said, 'Nothing. I didn't ask her anything else.'

'Why not?'

'No point. The wives and the girlfriends aren't going to tell us anything. They've got a vested interest. Their husbands and their boyfriends aren't just hiding out in Despair. They're aiming to get help there. They're aiming to ride some kind of an underground railroad for fugitives. Despair is a way station, in and out. The women want to keep it secret.'

'What kind of fugitives?'

'I don't know what kind. But the Anderson guy was the right kind and Raphael Ramirez was the wrong kind.'

Vaughan stepped back to the table, took Reacher's mug from him and refilled it from the machine. Then she refilled her glass from the refrigerator and sat down. 'May I ask you a personal question?'

Reacher said, 'Feel free.'

'Why does this matter to you so much? Why do you care about what's happening in Despair? Bad stuff happens everywhere, all the time.'

'I'm curious, that's all.'

'That's no answer.'

'Maria,' Reacher said. 'She's the answer. She's a sweet kid. She's hurting.'

'Her boyfriend is a fugitive from the law. You said so yourself.'

'Ramirez looked like a harmless guy to me.'

'You can tell by looking at a photograph?'

'Sometimes. Would Maria hang out with a bad guy?'

'I haven't met her.'

'Would Lucy Anderson?'

Vaughan said nothing.

'And I don't like company towns,' Reacher said. 'I don't like feudal systems. I don't like smug, fat bosses lording it over people. And I don't like people so broken down that they put up with it.'

'You see something you don't like, you feel you have to tear it down?'

'Damn right I do. You got a problem with that?'

'No.' She took her free hand out of her lap and laid it on the table. Reacher wondered whether it was a gesture, conscious or subconscious. An appeal for a connection.

No wedding band. *He's not here right now.*

He put his own free hand on the table.

She asked, 'How do we know they were fugitives at all? Maybe they were undercover environmental activists, checking on the pollution. Maybe the Anderson guy fooled them and Ramirez didn't. It worries me, if they're using poisons over there. We share the same water table.'

'Thurman mentioned something called trichloroethylene. I don't know whether it's dangerous or not.'

'I'm going to check it out.'

'Why would the wife of an environmental activist be so scared of cops?'

'I don't know.'

'The Anderson guy was a guest. They gave him protection.'

'And Ramirez was left to die.'

'So why help one and keep the other out?'

'Because Ramirez was different in some way,' Vaughan said. She sipped her water. 'More dangerous to them.'

'Maybe I'm wrong,' Reacher said. 'Maybe they didn't try to keep him out. Maybe they never knew he was there. Maybe he needed to be there for some reason, but, when he knew he was failing, he tried to get back here and ran out of energy.'

Vaughan took her hand off the table. 'We need to talk to Maria.'

'She won't tell us anything.'

'We can try. We'll find her in the diner. Meet me there, later.'

'Later than what?'

'We both need to sleep.'

Reacher said, 'May I ask you a personal question?'

'Go ahead.'

'Is your husband in prison?'

Vaughan paused a beat, and then smiled, a little surprised, a little sad. 'No,' she said. 'He isn't.'

THE COFFEE DIDN'T KEEP Reacher awake at all. He took a long hot shower and climbed into bed. He was asleep within a minute.

He got out of bed at four o'clock and took another long hot shower. The motel soap was white and came in a small, paper-wrapped morsel and he used the whole bar. The shampoo smelt faintly of apples. He rinsed and stood under the water for a moment more. As he shut it off he heard someone knocking at his door. He wrapped a towel round his waist and padded across the room and opened up.

Vaughan.

She was in uniform. Her HPD cruiser was parked neatly behind her. She was staring in at him, openly curious. Not an unusual reaction. He had a dozen nicks and cuts, plus a dimpled .38 bullet hole in the left centre of his chest and a wicked spider's web of white lacerations on the right side of his abdomen, crisscrossed by seventy clumsy stitches done quick and dirty in a mobile army surgical hospital. Souvenirs of childhood mayhem, a psychopath with a small revolver and shrapnel from a bomb blast. All survivable. He had been a lucky man, and his luck was written all over his body.

Vaughan's gaze travelled upwards to his face.

'Bad news,' she said. 'I went to the library. Trichloroethylene is called TCE for short. It causes all kinds of cancer. Plus heart disease, liver disease, kidney disease. There was a case in Tennessee.'

'That's a long way from here.'

'This is serious, Reacher.'

He nodded. 'I know.'

'And we drink the ground water.' She went quiet.

He said, 'What else?'

'Maria is missing. I can't find her anywhere.'

Vaughan hung around in the open doorway and Reacher grabbed his clothes and dressed in the bathroom. He called out, 'Where did you look?'

'All over,' Vaughan called back. 'She's not here in the motel, she's not in the diner, she's not in the library, and there isn't anywhere else.'

'Did you speak to the motel clerk?'

'Not yet.'

'Then that's where we'll go first. She knows everything.'

THE CLERK IN THE MOTEL office had no useful information. Maria had left the hotel before seven o'clock that morning on foot, carrying only her bag. She hadn't come back. Vaughan asked her to open Maria's room. The clerk handed over her pass key immediately. No fuss about warrants.

Maria's room was identical to Reacher's, with only slightly more stuff in it. A pair of jeans hung in the closet. On the shelf above were one spare pair of pants, one bra and one clean T-shirt, all neatly folded together. On the floor of the closet was an empty blue suitcase, small, sad, battered.

On a shelf next to the bathroom basin were soaps, shampoos, lotions.

'Day trip,' Vaughan said. 'She's expecting to return.'

'Obviously,' Reacher said. 'She paid for three nights.'

'She went to Despair. To look for Ramirez.'

'That would be my guess.'

'But how? There's no bus or anything. There's never any traffic.'

'Maybe there was,' Reacher said. 'I came in with an old guy in a car. He was visiting family, and then he was moving on west to Denver. And if he was dumb enough to give me a ride, he'd have given Maria a ride for sure.'

'If he happened to leave this morning.'

'Let's find out.'

They returned the pass key and got into Vaughan's cruiser. She fired it up and they headed west to the hardware store. The sidewalk was piled high with ladders, buckets and wheelbarrows. The owner confirmed that he had been building the display early that morning. He had seen a small dark girl in a blue baseball jacket. She had been standing on the far sidewalk, looking east but clearly aiming to head west. A classic hitchhiker's pose. Then, just before eight o'clock, he had seen a bottle-green car heading west. He described the car as looking similar to Vaughan's cruiser.

'A Grand Marquis,' Reacher said. 'Same car. Same guy.'

The store owner had not seen the car stop, but the inference was clear.

'Is she in danger?' Vaughan asked.

'I don't know,' Reacher said. 'But she's probably not having the best day of her life.'

'We can't go to Despair in the Crown Vic.'

'So what else have you got?'

'Just the truck.'

'Got sunglasses? It's breezy, without the windshield.'

'Too late. I already had it towed. It's being fixed.'

Reacher said, 'Maria's domiciled in Hope. Now she's missing. The HPD should be entitled to head over to Despair in a car and make enquiries.'

'Domiciled? With one change of underwear?'

'What's the worst thing that can happen?'

Vaughan started to say something then shook her head and sighed.

THEY DROVE ELEVEN MILES into the setting sun with nothing to show for it except eyestrain. The twelfth mile was different. Way ahead in the glare Reacher saw vague smudges on the horizon: the first brick buildings.

Plus something else.

From a mile away it looked like a shadow, like a lone cloud blocking the sun and casting a random shape on the ground. He craned his neck and looked up. The sky was clear. Just the grey-blue of approaching evening.

Vaughan drove on.

Three-quarters of a mile out the shape grew. The sun blazed behind it and winked around its edges. It looked like a low, wide pile of something dark. From a half-mile out, it looked to be moving.

From a quarter-mile out, it was identifiable.

It was a crowd of people.

Vaughan slowed, instinctively. The crowd was perhaps 300 strong. Men, women and children. They were formed up in a rough triangle, facing east. Maybe six people at the front. Behind the six, twenty more. Behind the twenty, sixty more. Behind the sixty, a vast milling pool of people.

Vaughan stopped, fifty yards out.

The crowd compressed. People pushed inwards but they didn't link arms. They didn't link arms because they had weapons in their hands.

Baseball bats, pool cues, axe handles, broom handles, split firewood, carpenters' hammers. The people were rocking in place from foot to foot and jabbing their weapons up and down in the air. And they were chanting.

Reacher dropped his window an inch and heard the words 'Out! Out! Out!' He hit the switch again and the glass thumped back up.

Vaughan was pale. 'Unbelievable,' she said.

'Is this some weird Colorado tradition?' Reacher asked.

'I never saw it before. What are we going to do?'

Reacher watched, then said, 'Drive on and see what happens.'

Vaughan took her foot off the brake and the car crept forward.

The crowd surged forwards to meet it.

Vaughan stopped again, forty yards out.

They were ordinary people dressed in work shirts and faded sundresses and jeans jackets, but collectively they looked entirely primitive. Like a weird Stone Age tribe, threatened and defensive.

'Siren,' Reacher said. 'Use your siren.'

Vaughan lit it up. It was a modern synthesised unit, shatteringly loud, sequencing randomly from a basic *whoop-whoop-whoop* to a manic, hysterical digital cackling.

It had no effect. The crowd didn't flinch.

Reacher said, 'Can you get round them?'

She shook her head. 'We'd bog down on the scrub and they'd be all over us.'

She killed the siren.

The chanting grew louder. 'Out! Out! Out!'

They were close enough now to be seen clearly. Faces contorted with hate and rage, fear and anger. Reacher didn't like crowds. In Somalia and Bosnia he had seen what angry crowds could do. He said, quietly, 'Put the car in reverse and back up.'

Vaughan moved the lever and backed up. The crowd tracked the move.

Reacher stared ahead through the windshield. He sensed a change coming.

Vaughan asked, 'What do we do?'

Reacher didn't have time to answer. The change came. The chanting stopped. There was silence for a second. Then the six men at the front of the crowd raised their weapons high, shouted a command and charged.

The crowd streamed after them, yelling, stampeding, eyes wide, mouths open. They got within five feet. Then Vaughan stamped on the gas. The car shot backwards, the low gear whining loud, the rear tyres howling and making smoke. She got up to thirty miles an hour and then she flung the car into an emergency 180-degree turn, put the lever in drive and accelerated east. She didn't stop for five miles. She took most of the last mile to coast to a stop.

Vaughan slumped in her seat. 'We need the State Police,' she said. 'We've got mob rule back there and a missing woman. Whatever Ramirez was to those people, we can't assume they'll treat his girlfriend kindly.'

'We can't assume a thing,' Reacher said. 'We don't even know she's there.'

'So what do we do?'

'We verify. We call Denver.'

'What's in Denver?'

'The green car,' Reacher said. 'And the old guy who was driving it. If he left around eight this morning, he'll be there by now. We'll call him up, ask him if he gave Maria a ride and, if so, where exactly he let her out.'

'You know his name?'

'No.'

'Number?'

'No, but he was visiting three grandchildren in Hope. You need to get back to town and check with families that have three kids. Ask them if Grandpa just came by in his Grand Marquis. One of them will say yes. Then you'll get a number for his next stop.'

'What are you going to do?'

'I'm going back to Despair.'

HE GOT OUT of the car at five thirty-five, a little more than eight miles west of Hope, a little more than eight miles east of Despair. Right in the heart of no-man's-land. He watched Vaughan drive away and then started walking.

At seven o'clock he was a mile from where the crowd had gathered before, in Despair. He struck off the road into the scrub, south and west, at an angle, hustling, unwilling to slow down. The town ahead was dark and quiet. By seven thirty he was 600 yards out in the sand and he realised he hadn't heard the plane take off. No engine, no light in the sky. Why not?

By eight o'clock he was making his first approach. He was expected out of the east, therefore he was coming in from the southwest. Not a guarantee of safety, but better than a poke in the eye. Reacher figured competent individuals would be distributed all round the town, but not equally. In the dark, they would have to spread out, like a human perimeter. But they would stick fairly close together, each group in visual contact with the next. A circle a mile in diameter would barely enclose the town. It couldn't enclose the town and the plant together. Cover would be thin.

It wouldn't be a huge problem, Reacher thought.

He paused behind a rock, fifty yards from the back of a long line of workers' housing. Low, one-storey dwellings, well separated laterally, because desert land was cheap and septic systems didn't work with too much density. There were guards armed with clubs and bats in the gaps between the houses. Together they made a chain that went, armed guard, house, armed guard, house, armed guard, house, armed guard.

They thought the houses themselves were defensive elements.

They were wrong.

Reacher lined himself up behind a house that was entirely dark. He dropped to the ground and low-crawled straight for it. He budgeted five minutes. Fast enough to get the job done, slow enough to get it done safely. He stayed low all the way to the back stoop. Then he stood up and listened for a reaction, either outside the house or inside. Nothing.

He put his hand on the door handle and lifted. If a door squeaked, ninety-nine times in a hundred it was because it had dropped on its hinges. Upward pressure helped. He eased the door up and in and stepped into a dark and silent kitchen. A worn linoleum floor, the smell of fried food. Counters and cabinets, ghostly in the gloom. He moved through to the hallway. Smelt dirty carpet and worn furniture from a living room on his right. The front door was a plain hollow slab, with a rectangle of painted beading on it. He turned the handle and lifted. Eased it open, silently.

What if there was an axe handle or a bullet out there?

There was nothing out there. He was standing on a front stoop made of concrete. Ahead of him was a short path and a dark street. More houses on the other side. No guards between them. The guards were all behind him now, and they were all facing the wrong way.

Reacher headed due north, straight for the town centre. Once he saw a moving vehicle two streets away. He ducked behind a wooden fence and waited until the car had gone. Then he moved on, staying in the shadows.

The street with the police station in it had one street lamp burning. It cast a weak pool of yellow light. The police station itself was dark and the outer door was locked. Reacher took out the keys he had removed from the deputy in the bar. He looked at the lock and looked at the keys and selected a long brass item and tried it. The lock turned and the door swung open.

Like the town's hotel, the Despair PD was still in the pen-and-paper age. Arrest records were in a large black ledger on the booking desk. Reacher carried it to a window and tilted it so that it caught what little light was coming through. He flipped through the pages until he found his own entry, dated three days previously: *Reacher, J., male vagrant.*

The entry immediately before his own was three days older and said: *Anderson, L., female vagrant.*

He flipped back, looking for Lucy Anderson's husband. He didn't expect to find him, and he didn't. Lucy Anderson's husband had been helped, not hindered. Then he went looking for Ramirez. No trace. Therefore the guy hadn't escaped from custody. He had never been picked up at all.

He leafed backwards, patiently, a random three-month sample. Saw six names: Bridge, Churchill, White, King, Whitehouse, Andrews. Five male, one female, all vagrants, roughly one every two weeks.

He flipped ahead again, looking for Maria. She wasn't there. There was only one entry after his own. It was in new handwriting and said: *Rogers, G., male vagrant.* It had been made just seven hours earlier.

Reacher closed the book and walked to the head of the basement stairs. He felt his way down and opened the cell-block door. All the lights were burning. But all the cells were empty.

Reacher's next stop was out of town, which meant passing through the perimeter again, this time heading in the other direction. Easy to sneak up to the line, hard to walk away with a thousand eyes on his back. He didn't want to be the only thing moving, in front of a static audience. Better that the line moved, and broke over him like a wave over a rock.

He sorted through the bunch of keys, found the one he wanted, then he put the keys back in his pocket and moved back to the booking desk. He found what he wanted in the third drawer down: a quarter-full pack of Camel cigarettes and three books of matches.

He cleared a space on the floor under the desk and stood the arrest ledger in its centre, with the pages fanned out. He piled every scrap of paper he could find around it—memos, posters and old newspapers—and built a pyramid. He hid two matchbooks in it, with the covers bent back and the matches bent forward. Then he lit a Camel with a match from the third book. He smoked an inch, then folded the cigarette into the matchbook in a T-shape, nestled the assembly into the paper pyramid and walked away.

He left the street door open two inches, to set up a breeze.

Reacher headed south, to the big deputy's house. He knew where it was. He had seen it from the back, the first night, when the guy got home from work and threw up in the yard. It was a five-minute walk that took him ten, due to stealth and caution. The old crew-cab pick-up was parked in a parking space close by the kitchen.

The driver's door was unlocked. Reacher slid in behind the wheel. The seat was sagging and the upholstery smelt of sweat, grease and oil. Reacher pulled out the bunch of keys and found the car key. Plastic head, distinctive shape. He tried it, just to be sure. He put it in the ignition and turned two clicks. The wheel unlocked and the dials lit up. He turned it back again and climbed over the seats and lay down in the rear of the cab.

IT TOOK MORE than thirty minutes for the townspeople to realise their police station was on fire. By that time it was well ablaze. From his low position in the pick-up, Reacher saw leaping flames well before anyone reacted.

Then there was pandemonium.

Discipline broke down immediately. The perimeter collapsed inwards like a leaking balloon. Reacher lay still and people streamed past him, few and hesitant at first, then many and fast. They were running, looking at nothing except the bright glow ahead of them. The cross streets were suddenly crowded and the flow was all one way.

Reacher smiled. Like moths to a flame, he thought. Literally.

Then he scrambled over the seat backs and rotated the key. The engine turned over once and fired. He drove away slowly, with the lights off, heading to the northern end of the plant through the deserted scrubland. He saw headlights on the road coming away from the plant. Four moving vehicles. He bounced on over washboard undulations and jarred over rocks, until he saw the white gleam of the plant's metal wall in the darkness. He recalled the sheer fourteen-foot-high vertical plane, topped with a continuous horizontal cylinder six feet in diameter. It was a design derived from prison research. Reacher knew the theory. Stone or brick walls could be climbed, but six-foot cylinders were slick and flat and offered no grip at all.

So he drove on, through the empty acres of parking, hoping against hope that the personnel gate would be open and, if it wasn't, that the deputy's keys would unlock it. But it wasn't, and it didn't have a keyhole. It had a grey metal box set into the wall, with a ten-digit keypad.

Reacher returned to the pick-up and drove on, hoping that the vehicle gate on the west wall would be open. He guessed that the two white Tahoes had left in a hurry, with the ambulance and maybe a fire truck. And people in a hurry didn't always clean up after themselves. He slowed to a crawl. The vehicle gate was open. It was built like a double door. Each half cantilevered outwards and then swung through 100 degrees on a wheeled track. Both halves were standing wide open, creating a forty-foot gap in the wall.

Reacher parked the deputy's truck nose-out, blocking the gates' travel. He figured maybe it was motorised or on a time switch and, come what may, he wanted to keep it open.

He walked into the plant, glancing right at the line of offices and storage tanks. Beyond them, nearly a mile away, was the secret compound. He took half a step in its direction.

Then the lights came on.

There was an audible *whoomp* as electricity surged through cables and a split second later the whole place lit up brighter than day. A shattering sensation. Physical in its intensity. Reacher screwed his eyes shut and clamped his arms over his head.

As soon as he could, he opened his eyes again in a desperate hooded squint and saw Thurman walking towards him. He turned and saw the plant foreman heading in from a different direction. He turned again and saw the giant with the three-foot wrench blocking his path to the gate.

Thurman came close and took up a position alongside him, as if they were two old buddies standing together, surveying a happy scene. He said, 'I thought our paths were not going to cross again. Why are you here?'

Reacher paused a beat. Said, 'I'm thinking about leaving the state.' Which was permanently true. 'Before I go, I thought I'd drop by the infirmary and tell my former opponents no hard feelings.'

'There's only Underwood there at the moment,' Thurman said. 'The others are home now, on bed rest.'

'Which one is Underwood?'

'The senior deputy. You left him in a sorry state.'

'He was sick already.'

'You need to leave now,' Thurman said. 'I'm not joking.'

'You are,' Reacher said. 'You're a fat old man, telling me to leave. That's pretty funny.'

'I'm not alone here.'

Reacher turned and checked. The foreman was standing ten feet away. The giant was twenty feet away, holding the wrench.

Reacher said, 'You've got an office boy and a broken-down old jock with a big spanner. I'm not impressed.'

'They could do you considerable harm.'

'The first eight you sent didn't do much.'

Thurman said nothing.

Reacher said, 'I'm going to the infirmary now. You are, too. Your choice whether you walk there or I carry you there in a bucket.'

Thurman's shoulders slumped in an all-purpose sigh and shrug and he raised a palm to his two guys, like he was telling a couple of dogs to stay. Then he set off walking towards the line of cabins, Reacher at his side.

IT WAS A REAL sick bay. White walls, white linoleum floor, the smell of antiseptic. There were four hospital beds. One was occupied by the big deputy. Only he looked smaller than before. His hair looked thinner. His breathing was shallow and irregular. There was a medical chart clipped to the rail at the foot of his bed. Reacher scanned it. The guy had a whole lot of things wrong with him: fever, fatigue, weakness, breathlessness, headaches, rashes, blisters, sores, chronic vomiting, diarrhoea. Reacher dropped the chart back into position and asked, 'You have a doctor working here?'

Thurman said, 'A paramedic. We're doing the best we can.'

Reacher stepped alongside the bed. 'Can you talk?'

The big deputy rolled his head, tried to speak, but got hung up. He breathed hard and started again. 'The . . .' and then he blinked and started over, apparently with a new thought. He said, haltingly, 'You did this to me.'

'Not entirely,' Reacher said.

The guy rolled his head again, away and back, 'No, the . . .' and then he stopped again, fighting for breath.

Thurman grabbed Reacher's elbow. 'We need to leave. We're tiring him.'

'Did this guy work with TCE?'

Thurman paused a beat. 'What do you know about TCE?'

'A little. It's a poison.'

'It's a degreaser. It's a standard industrial product.'

'Whatever. Did this guy work with it?'

'No. And those that do are well protected.'

'So what's wrong with him?'

'Like he said, you did this to him.'

'You don't get symptoms like these from a fist fight.'

'I heard it was more than a fist fight.'

Reacher closed his eyes. Saw the bar again, the dim light, the tense silent people, the air thick with raised dust and the smell of fear and conflict. He opened his eyes again and said, 'He needs to be in a proper hospital.'

Thurman didn't answer. Reacher took a last look at the guy in the bed and then stepped away and walked out of the door, down the steps and back to the blazing arena. The foreman and the guy with the wrench stood where they had been before. Reacher heard Thurman close the infirmary door and clatter down the steps behind him.

Thurman asked, 'Are you leaving now, Mr Reacher?'

'Yes,' Reacher lied.

The guy with the wrench was looking beyond Reacher's shoulder, at Thurman, waiting for a sign, maybe hoping for a sign, slapping the free end of the wrench against his palm.

Thurman must have shaken his head because the guy just paused a beat and then stepped aside. Reacher walked on, back to the sick deputy's truck. It was where he had left it, with all its windows intact.

CHAPTER EIGHT

Vaughan was waiting 100 yards over the town line. She was parked on the left shoulder of the thick blacktop with her lights off. He slowed and held his arm out his window in a reassuring wave. She put her arm out of her own window, hand extended, an answering gesture. He coasted and came to a stop with his fingertips touching hers. To him the contact felt one-third like a mission-accomplished high-five, one-third like an expression of relief to be out of the lions' den again, and one-third just plain good. He didn't know what it felt like to her. She gave no indication. But she left her hand there a second longer than she needed to.

'Whose truck?' she asked.

'The senior deputy's. His name is Underwood.'

'Go and dump it back over the line,' Vaughan said. 'I'll drive you to town. We'll take a doughnut break.'

Reacher did as she said and left it there, keys in. Way behind him he could see a faint red glow on the horizon. Despair was still on fire. He didn't say anything about it. He just walked forwards and crossed the line again and climbed in next to Vaughan.

'You smell of cigarettes,' she said.

'I found one,' he said. 'I smoked a half-inch, for old times' sake.'

'They give you cancer.'

She took off east, one hand on the wheel and the other in her lap. 'I called Denver,' she said. 'About Maria. The old man picked her up. But he didn't let her out in Despair. She wanted to go to the MP base.'

THEY GOT TO THE DINER at twenty minutes past midnight. They didn't order doughnuts. Reacher ordered coffee and Vaughan ordered juice, a blend of three exotic fruits, none of which Reacher had ever encountered before.

'You're very healthy,' he said.

'I try.'

'Is your husband in the hospital? With cancer, from smoking?'

She shook her head. 'No,' she said. 'He isn't.'

Their drinks arrived and they sipped them in silence. Then Reacher asked, 'Did the old guy know why Maria wanted to go to the MPs?'

'She didn't tell him. But it's a weird destination, isn't it?'

'Very,' Reacher said. 'It's an active-service forward-operating base. Visitors wouldn't be permitted. Did the old guy actually see her get in?'

'Sure,' Vaughan said. 'He waited, like an old-fashioned gentleman.'

'Therefore a better question would be: If they let her in, what did they want from her?'

'Something to do with espionage?'

Reacher drained his mug. Shook his head. 'They're not worried about espionage. They're guarding the truck route. Which means they're worried about theft, of something heavy, too heavy for a regular car.'

'Something too heavy for a small plane, then?'

Reacher nodded. 'But the plane is involved somehow. There are three things going on over there. The military contract, plus something else, plus something else again.'

'OK,' Vaughan said. She moved the salt shaker, the pepper shaker and the sugar shaker to the centre of the table. 'Three things.'

Reacher moved the salt shaker to one side, immediately. 'The military contract is what it is. Nothing controversial. Nothing to worry about, except the possibility that someone might steal something heavy. And that's a problem for the MPs. No reason for the townspeople to get excited.'

'But?'

'But the townspeople *are* excited about something.'

'What something?'

'I have no clue.' He held up the sugar shaker, in his right hand. 'But it's the bigger of the two unknowns. Everyone is involved in it.' Then he held up the pepper shaker, in his left hand. 'This other thing is smaller. It involves a subset of the population. Everyone knows about the sugar, most *don't* know about the pepper, a few know about the sugar *and* the pepper.'

'So maybe Thurman's doing something and everyone is helping, but a few are also working on something else behind his back?'

Reacher nodded. 'And that something the few are working on involves these young guys. They either get through or they don't, depending on who they bump into first: the many sugar people or the few pepper people. And there's a new one now. Name of Rogers, just arrested, but I didn't see him.'

'Rogers? I've heard that name before.'

'Where?'

'I don't know.'

'Wherever, he was one of the unlucky ones.'

'The odds will always be against them.'

'Exactly.'

'Which was Ramirez's problem.'

'Ramirez didn't bump into anyone,' Reacher said. 'I checked the records. He was neither arrested nor helped.'

'Why? What made him different?'

'Great question,' Reacher said. 'What's the answer?'

REACHER GOT MORE COFFEE and Vaughan got more juice. The clock in Reacher's head hit one in the morning and the clock on the diner's wall followed it a minute later. Vaughan looked at her watch and said, 'I better get back in the saddle.'

Reacher said, 'OK.'

'Go get some sleep.'

'OK.'

'Will you come with me to Colorado Springs? I called a friend of a friend of David's. He knows a guy who works at the state lab. He told me to take some water in for testing. To find out how much TCE Thurman actually uses.'

'When?'

'Tomorrow, today, whatever it is now.'

'What time?'

'Leave at ten?'

'You still trying to keep me out of trouble? Even on your downtime?'

'I've given up on keeping you out of trouble, but I'd like your company.'

REACHER SHOWERED and was in bed by two o'clock in the morning. He slept dreamlessly and woke up at eight. He showered again and walked the length of the town to the hardware store. He went inside and found the racks of trousers and shirts and chose a new one of each.

He changed in his motel room, left his old stuff next to the trash can and walked to the office. The clerk was on her stool. Behind her shoulder, the hook for Maria's room had no key on it. The clerk saw him looking and said, 'She came back this morning, at about six.' She looked both ways and lowered her voice and said, 'In an armoured car. With a soldier.'

Reacher said, 'A Humvee?'

The woman nodded. 'The soldier didn't stay. Which I'm glad about. I couldn't permit that. She's too young to be fooling around with a soldier.'

Reacher paid his bill and walked back down the row, doing the maths. According to the old man's telephone testimony, he had let Maria out at the MP base around eight thirty the previous morning. She had arrived back in a Humvee at six. Therefore she had been held for twenty-one hours.

He stopped outside her door and knocked. A minute later she opened it.

'You OK?' he asked. She didn't look OK. She looked small and lost.

She didn't answer.

He said, 'You went to the MP base, asking about Raphael, but they couldn't help you?'

She didn't answer.

He said, 'Maybe I could. Or maybe the Hope PD could. You want to tell me what it's all about?'

'I can't tell you,' she said. 'I can't tell anyone.'

Simple as that. She couldn't tell anyone.

'OK,' Reacher said. 'Hang in there.'

He walked away, to the diner, and had breakfast.

AT FIVE TO TEN he was sitting in the plastic chair outside his door. Vaughan showed up at three minutes past the hour, in a plain black Crown Vic. An unmarked squad car, like a detective would drive. She stopped close to him and buzzed the window down. He said, 'Did you get promoted?'

'It's my watch commander's car. He took pity on me and loaned it. Since you got my truck smashed up.'

'Maria is back,' he said. 'The MPs brought her home early this morning.'

'Is she saying anything?'

'Not a word.' He got out of the chair, walked round the hood and slid in beside her. Vaughan was looking good. She was in old blue jeans and a white Oxford shirt, the neck open two buttons.

She said, 'You've changed.'

'In what way?'

'Your clothes, you idiot.'

'New this morning,' he said. 'From the hardware store.'

'What's the longest you ever wore a set of clothes?'

'Eight months,' Reacher said. 'Desert BDUs, during Gulf War One.'

'You were in the Gulf, the first time?'

'Beginning to end.'

Vaughan pulled out of the motel lot and headed north. It was an obvious cop car and the roads were empty and she averaged ninety most of the way to Colorado Springs, charging head-on towards the mountains. The air was clean and the view of Pikes Peak was spectacular.

The state water lab was in a stone government building. Water was a big deal all over Colorado. There wasn't much of it. Vaughan handed over her bottle and filled out a form, then a guy wrapped the form round the bottle, secured it with a rubber band and carried it away. He came back and told Vaughan that she would be notified of the results by phone, and to please let the lab know some figures for Despair's total TCE consumption.

'What are the symptoms,' Vaughan asked. 'If it's there already?'

The lab guy glanced at Reacher. 'Prostate cancer,' he said. 'Men go first.'

They got back in the car. Vaughan was distracted. Reacher wasn't sure why she had asked him to travel with her. They hadn't spoken much.

She pulled out and drove 100 yards down a tree-lined street, then stopped at a light at a T-junction. Left was west and right was east. The light turned green and she turned left.

'Where are we going?' Reacher asked her.

She didn't answer. She drove a mile between green hills and turned left through a grove of pines on a worn grey road that had no centre line. After another mile she slowed and made a right into a half-hidden driveway. She passed between two squat brick pillars. The bricks were brown and the mortar was yellow. Standard 1950s army issue. Twenty yards further on was a modern billboard: *Olympic TBI Center*. A second one said: *Authorised Personnel Only*. The drive ran straight for 100 yards to a group of low army buildings, long ago sold off. Reacher recognised the architecture.

They walked together to the main entrance. Three steps up, through the doors, onto the kind of mottled-green tiled floor Reacher had walked a thousand times before. Mid-fifties US Army, abandoned and run down. There was an oak hutch on the right, where once a busy sergeant would have sat. Now it was occupied by a mess of what looked like medical case notes and a civilian in a grey sweatshirt. He was a thin, sullen man of about forty, with unwashed black hair. He said, 'Hello, Mrs Vaughan.' Nothing more. No warmth in his voice. No enthusiasm.

Vaughan nodded but didn't reply. She walked to the end of the hall and turned into a large room. It was dirty and smelt of antiseptic and urine. It was completely empty, except for two men strapped into wheelchairs. Both men were young, both had open mouths and empty gazes. Both had shaved heads, misshapen skulls and wicked scars.

Reacher stood still. He looked at the guys in the wheelchairs. He was in a residential home. He looked at the dust and the dirt. He was in a dumping ground. He thought back to the initials on the billboard. TBI. Traumatic Brain Injury.

Vaughan had moved on into a corridor. Dust balls had collected against the skirting. Some were peppered with mouse droppings. He caught up with her, halfway along its length. 'Your husband had an accident?' he said.

'Not exactly,' she said.

'Then what?'

'Figure it out.'

Reacher stopped again. An old army building. Both men were young. 'War wounds,' he said. 'Your husband is military. He went to Iraq.'

Vaughan nodded. 'National Guard,' she said. 'His second tour. They didn't armour his Humvee. He was blown up in Ramadi.'

DAVID ROBERT VAUGHAN'S ROOM was a twelve-foot cube, painted dark green. It had a small sooty window. A narrow hospital bed was set to a forty-five degree slope. In it, under a tented sheet, was a compact, narrow-shouldered man. He had blond stubble on his chin and his cheeks. His blue eyes were wide open.

Part of his skull was missing.

A saucer-sized piece of bone wasn't there. It left a wide hole above his forehead and his brain was protruding. It swelled out like an inflated balloon, dark and purple and corrugated. It was draped with a thin man-made membrane like Cling Film.

Vaughan said, 'Hello, David. I've brought a friend to see you.'

No response. There never would be, Reacher guessed. The guy in the bed was completely inert. Not asleep, not awake. Not anything.

Vaughan bent and kissed her husband.

Then she stepped over to the cabinet and tugged an X-ray envelope out of a pile of file folders. She pulled a film out of the envelope and held it up against the light from the window. It was a composite image that showed her husband's head from four different directions.

'Iraq's signature injury,' Vaughan said. 'Blast damage to the human brain. Compression, decompression, shearing, impact with the wall of the skull. David got it all. His skull was shattered and they cut the worst of it away. They give them a plastic plate later, when the swelling goes down. But David's swelling never went down.'

She put the film back in the envelope and shuffled the envelope back into the pile. She pulled another one out. It was a chest film. White ribs, grey organs and small, bright pinpoints that looked like drops of liquid.

'That's why I don't wear my wedding band,' Vaughan said. 'He wanted to take it with him on a chain round his neck. The heat melted it and the blast drove it into his lungs.' She put the film back into the envelope and moved to the foot of the bed. 'He wore it for good luck,' she said.

Reacher asked, 'What was he?'

'Infantry, assigned to the First Armored Division.'

'And this was IED versus Humvee?'

She nodded. 'An improvised explosive device against a tin can. He might as well have been on foot in his bathrobe.'

'When was this?'

'Almost two years ago.'

The respirator hissed on.

'So you moved house,' Reacher said. 'You were thinking about a wheelchair. You bought a one-storey and took the door off the living room.'

She nodded. 'But he never woke up. What happened to David's head is a shearing injury. The very worst kind. His brain stem is OK but the rest of his brain doesn't even know it's there. This is all he will ever be. He can't move and he can't see and he can't hear and he can't think.'

Reacher said nothing.

Vaughan moved to the head of the bed and laid her hand on her husband's cheek, very gently, very tenderly. Said, 'Will you shave David?'

'Don't the orderlies do that?'

'They should, but they don't. And I like him to look decent. It seems like the least I can do.'

She took a grocery bag out of the green metal cabinet. It held shaving gel, a half-used pack of disposable razors, soap, a flannel. Reacher found a bathroom across the hall and stepped back and forth with the wet flannel, soaping the guy's face. He smoothed blue gel over his chin and cheeks and lathered it with his fingertips and then set about using the razor. A completely instinctive sequence of actions when applied to himself became awkward on a third party.

While he worked with the razor, Vaughan cleaned the room. She had a second bag in the cabinet that held cloths, sprays and a dustpan and brush. She went through the whole twelve-foot cube very thoroughly. Reacher finished up and Vaughan stopped a minute later and stood back and looked.

'Good work,' she said.

'You too. Although you shouldn't have to do that yourself.'

'I know.'

They repacked the grocery bags and put them away in the cabinet. Reacher asked, 'How long were you married?'

'We're still married.'

'I'm sorry. How long?'

'Twelve years. Eight together, then he spent two in Iraq, and the last two have been like this.'

'What are you going to do?'

'I don't know. People say I should move on. Accept destiny, like Zeno. But then I think, first they do this to him, and now I should divorce him? What do you think I should do?'

'I think you should take a walk,' Reacher said. 'Right now. Alone. Walking by yourself is always good. Get some fresh air. See some trees. I'll bring the car and pick you up before you hit the four-lane.'

'What are you going to do?'

'I'll find some way to pass the time.'

VAUGHAN SAID GOODBYE to her husband and they walked out. She kept on going. Reacher waited until she was small in the distance, then headed back to the entrance. He crossed to the hutch and asked, 'Who's in charge here?'

The guy in the sweatshirt said, 'I am, I guess. I'm the shift supervisor.'

Reacher asked, 'How many patients here?'

'Seventeen,' the guy said.

'You run this place according to a manual?'

'Sure. It's a bureaucracy, like everywhere.'

'You want to show me the part in the manual where it says it's OK to keep the rooms dirty and have mouse shit in the corridors?'

The guy blinked and swallowed and said, 'There's no point *cleaning*, man. They wouldn't *know*. This is the vegetable patch.'

'Wrong answer,' Reacher said. 'This is not the vegetable patch. This is a veterans' clinic. And David Robert Vaughan is my brother.'

'Really?'

'All veterans are my brothers.'

'He's brain dead, man.'

'Are you?'

'No.'

'Then listen up. And listen very carefully. The people here deserve your best, and I'm damn sure their relatives deserve it.'

'Who are you, anyway?'

'I'm a concerned citizen,' Reacher said. 'I could call the newspapers or the TV. I could get you fired. But I don't do stuff like that. I offer personal choices instead. You want to know what your choice is?'

'What?'

'Do what I tell you or become patient number eighteen.'

The guy went pale.

Some officers of Reacher's acquaintance yelled. He had always found it more effective to speak low and quiet, enunciating clearly as if to an idiot child. Calm, patient voice, huge physique. It had worked then and it was working now. The guy in the sweatshirt was swallowing hard.

Reacher said. 'Your patients served their country with honour and distinction, so you're going to get off your skinny ass and you're going to organise your people and you're going to get this place cleaned up. Starting right now. I'm going to come back, maybe tomorrow, maybe next month, and if I can't see my face in the floor I'm going to turn you upside-down and use you like a mop. Then I'm going to kick your ass so hard your colon is going to get tangled up in your teeth. Are we clear?'

The guy paused and shuffled and blinked. Then he said, 'OK.'

'With a cheery smile,' Reacher said.

The guy forced a smile.

'Bigger,' Reacher said.

The guy forced dry lips over dry teeth.

'That's good,' Reacher said. 'And every time Mrs Vaughan comes by you're going to stand up and welcome her warmly and her husband's room is going to be sparkling, and her husband is going to be shaved. You've got sixty seconds to get started, or I'll break your arm.'

The guy made a phone call, then used a walkie-talkie and fifty seconds later there were four guys in the hall. They had buckets and mops and a minute after that the buckets were full of water. Reacher left them to it. He walked back to the car and set off in pursuit of Vaughan.

He caught up with her a mile down the road. She slid in next to him and he drove on, retracing their route through the pines, through the hills. She said, 'Thank you for coming.'

'No problem,' he said.

'You know why I wanted you to come?'

'Yes. You wanted someone to understand why you live like you live and do what you do.'

'And?'

'You wanted someone to understand why it's OK to do what you're going to do next.'

'Which is what?'

'Which is entirely up to you. And either way is good with me.'

She said, 'I lied to you before.'

He said, 'I know.'

'Do you?'

He nodded at the wheel. 'You knew about Thurman's military contract. And the MP base. The Pentagon told you all about them. And you didn't want to talk about it, which means that it's not just any old military scrap getting recycled there.'

'Isn't it?'

Reacher shook his head. 'It's combat wrecks from Iraq. Thurman's place is a specialist operation. Secret, miles from nowhere.'

'I'm sorry.'

'Don't be. I understand.'

'There are blown-up Humvees there,' she said. 'They're like monuments to me. Like shrines. To the people who died. Or nearly died.'

They drove on, across the low slopes of the mountains. Reacher said, 'It doesn't explain Thurman's taste for secrecy. And it doesn't explain the MPs, either. What's to steal? A Humvee is a car, basically.'

Vaughan said nothing.

Reacher said, 'And it doesn't explain the plane. And nothing explains all these young guys.'

'So you're going to stick around?'

He nodded at the wheel. 'For a spell,' he said. 'Because I think something is about to happen. That crowd impressed me. I think they were all stirred up because they're heading for the end of something.'

VAUGHAN SAT QUIET and Reacher drove all the way back to Hope. He bypassed Despair and came in from the east, the long way round. They hit town at five in the afternoon. Reacher pulled off First Street and headed down to Third, to the motel. Vaughan looked at him enquiringly. Reacher said, 'Something I should have done before.'

They went in together. The nosy clerk was at the counter. Behind her, three keys were missing from their hooks. Reacher's own, for room twelve, plus Maria's, room eight, plus one for the occupant of room four.

'Tell me about the woman in room four.'

The clerk looked at him and paused a second. 'She's from California,' she said. 'She's been here five days. She paid cash for a week. Young. Maybe twenty-five, twenty-six.'

'What's her name?'

'Mrs Rogers.'

Back in the car, Vaughan said, 'Another one. But her husband wasn't arrested until yesterday, though she's been here five whole days.'

Reacher said, 'My guess is they were on the road together up till five days ago. He found the right people in Despair and went into hiding. She came directly here to wait it out. Then he got flushed out by the mass mobilisation yesterday, bumped into the wrong people and got picked up.'

'So where is he now?'

'He wasn't in a cell. So maybe he got back with the right people again.'

Vaughan said, 'I knew I had heard the name. His wife came in with the supermarket delivery guy. He drives in from Topeka, Kansas, every few days. He gave her a ride. He mentioned it to me. He told me her name.'

'Maria came in the same way. That's how I knew about her.'

'How did Lucy Anderson come in?' Reacher asked.

Vaughan paused. 'I don't know. The Despair police dumped her at the line.'

'So she came in from the west. Which raises a question, doesn't it?' Reacher said. 'Maria came in from the east, from Kansas, but she asked the old guy in the green car to let her out at the MP base west of Despair. How did she even know it was there?'

'Maybe Lucy Anderson told her. She would have seen it.'

'I don't think they talked at all.'

'Then maybe Ramirez told her about it,' Vaughan suggested. 'He came in from the west and saw it.'

'But why would it be a topic of conversation with his girlfriend?'

'I don't know.'

Reacher asked, 'Is your watch commander a nice guy?'

'Why?'

'Because we need to borrow his car again.'

'When?'

'Later tonight.'

'Later than what?'

'Than whatever—But first we're going shopping.'

They got to the hardware store just as it was closing. The old guy in the brown coat was clearing his sidewalk display. Reacher went in and bought a slim flashlight and two batteries and a two-foot wrecking bar from the old guy's wife. Then he went back out and bought the trick stepladder that opened to eight different positions. It was light, made of aluminium and it folded into a neat package. He put it into the Crown Vic's rear seat.

CHAPTER NINE

Vaughan invited him over for dinner, at eight o'clock. She was very formal about it. She said she needed the intervening hours to prepare. Reacher spent the time in his room. He took a nap and then he shaved, showered and cleaned his teeth. And dressed. He put on his trousers and his shirt, raked his fingers through his hair and checked the result in the mirror. His appearance was what it was. Some people liked it, some didn't.

He walked two blocks from Third to Fifth, then turned east. He walked through the plantings and shrubs and touched the bell.

Vaughan got there in nine seconds flat. She was in a black knee-length sleeveless A-line dress, and black low-heel shoes, like ballet slippers. She was freshly showered. She looked young and full of energy.

The kitchen was full of candlelight and two appetisers were standing on the counter. She said, 'The main course isn't ready. I screwed up the timing. It's something I haven't made for a while.'

'Three years,' Reacher said.

'Longer,' she said.

'You look great,' he said. 'The prettiest view in Colorado.'

'Better than Pikes Peak?'

'Considerably.'

She said, 'You look good, too. You clean up well.'

'I try my best.'

She asked, 'Should we be doing this?'

He said, 'I think so.'

'Is it fair to David?'

'David never came back. He never lived here. He doesn't know.'

'I want to see your scar again.'

'Because you're wishing David had come back with one, instead of what he got?'

'I guess.'

Reacher said, 'We were both lucky. I know soldiers. They fear grotesque wounds. That's all. Amputations, mutilations, burns. I'm lucky because I didn't get one, and David is lucky because he doesn't know he did.'

Vaughan said nothing.

Reacher said, 'And we're both lucky because we both met you.'

Vaughan said, 'Show me the scar.'

Reacher unbuttoned his shirt and slipped it off. Vaughan hesitated a second and then touched the ridged skin, very gently. Her fingertips were cool and smooth. They burnt him, like electricity.

'What was it?' she asked.

'A truck bomb in Beirut.'

'Shrapnel?'

'Part of a man who was standing closer.'

'That's awful.' She put her hand flat against the scar and then slid it round his back. She did the same with her other hand. She hugged his waist and then she raised her head and he bent down and kissed her. Her eyes were closed. He cradled her head with one hand and put the other low on her back. A long, long kiss.

She came up for air.

'It's OK to do this?' she asked him.

'I think so,' he said.

'Because you're moving on.'

'Two days,' he told her. 'Three, max.'

'No complications,' she said. 'Not like it might be permanent.'

'I can't do permanent,' he said.

He bent and kissed her again. Moved his hand and caught the tag of her zip and pulled it down. She was naked under the dress. He scooped her up and carried her down the hallway, to where he imagined the bedrooms must be. Two rooms. One smelt unused, one smelt like her. He carried her in and put her down and her dress slipped from her shoulders.

AFTERWARDS, THEY ATE. Pork cooked with apples and spices and brown sugar and white wine. For dessert, they went back to bed. At midnight, they showered together. Then they dressed. At one o'clock, they went out.

Vaughan drove. She insisted on it. It was her watch commander's car. Reacher was happy to let her. She was a better driver than him.

'Won't they be there again?' Vaughan asked.

'Possible,' he said. 'But I doubt it. They got all pumped up yesterday and thought they'd got rid of us. They don't have the stamina to do it all again.'

There was thick cloud in the sky. No moon. No stars. Pitch black. Perfect. They thumped over the line and a mile later Reacher said, 'It's time to be stealthy. Turn all the lights off.'

Vaughan clicked the headlights off and the world went dark. She braked hard. 'I can't see anything,' she said.

'Use the night vision,' he said. 'Watch the computer screen, not the windshield. It's how tank drivers do it.'

She tapped keys and the laptop screen lit up and then stabilised into a pale green picture of the landscape ahead. Green scrub on either side, vivid boulders, a bright ribbon of road spearing into the distance. She took her foot off the brake and crawled forward, staring at the thermal image.

'It's killing me not to glance ahead,' she said. 'It's so automatic.'

'This is good,' Reacher said. 'Stay slow.' He figured that at twenty or thirty there would be almost no engine noise. He leant left and put his head on her shoulder and watched the screen. A tiny flare of heat on the horizon showed where the embers of the police station were still warm.

Reacher glanced ahead through the windshield a couple of times, but there was nothing to see. He recalled walking back to Hope, stepping over the line, not seeing Vaughan's cruiser. But she had seen him. *I saw you half a mile away*, she had said. *A little green speck.*

He stared at the screen, watching for little green specks. Two miles. Four. Still nothing ahead. Six miles. Eight.

'We must be getting close,' she whispered.

He nodded, on her shoulder.

The screen showed background glow from the downtown blocks. Then there were window-sized patches of brighter colour, heat leaking from roofs with imperfect insulation. But there were no little green specks. Not dead ahead, anyway. The camera's fixed angle was useless against the cross streets. Reacher stared sideways into the darkness as they rolled past each opening. Saw nothing. Vaughan was holding her breath, her foot feather-light on the pedal. The car journeyed onwards, a little faster than walking, a lot slower than running.

Two green specks stepped out ahead.

They were maybe a quarter of a mile away, at the west end of Main Street. Two figures, emerging from a cross street. A foot patrol. Vaughan braked gently and came to a stop. Six blocks behind her, six ahead.

'Can they see us?' she whispered.

Reacher said, 'We can't see them, they can't see us. Law of physics.'

The screen lit up with a white flare. Cone-shaped. Moving. Sweeping.

'Searchlight,' Reacher said.

'They'll see us.'

'We're too far away. And I think they're shining it west.'

Then they weren't. The screen showed the beam turning through a complete circle. Its light lit up the night mist like fog.

They waited two minutes, then three, then five.

The green specks moved from the centre of the screen to the left-hand edge. Slow, blurred, a ghost trail of luminescence following behind them. Then they disappeared into a cross street. The green stabilised.

'Foot patrol,' Reacher said. 'Maybe worried about fires.'

'Fires?' Vaughan said.

'Their police station burnt down last night.'

'Did you have something to do with that?'

'Everything,' Reacher said. 'We should get going. Let's get past them while their backs are turned.'

Vaughan feathered the gas and the car rolled forward. One block. Two.

'Faster,' Reacher said.

Vaughan speeded up. Twenty miles an hour. Thirty. She gripped the wheel and held her breath and stared at the laptop screen. Ten seconds later they were through the town and in open country on the other side.

Four minutes after that, they were approaching the metal plant. The thermal image showed the sky above the plant to be lurid with heat. It was coming off the dormant furnaces and crucibles in waves as big as solar flares. The metal wall was warm and showed up as a continuous horizontal band of green. It was much brighter at the southern end. Much hotter around the secret compound. It glowed like crazy on the screen.

'Some junk yard,' Reacher said.

'They've been working hard in there,' Vaughan said. 'Unfortunately.'

The acres of parking seemed to be empty. The personnel gate was closed.

Vaughan said, 'No sentries?'

Reacher said, 'They trust the wall. As they should. It's a great wall.'

They drove on, slow and dark and silent, past the lot, past the north end of the plant, onto the truck route. The Tahoes' beaten tracks showed up on the screen, almost imperceptibly lighter than the surrounding scrub. Compacted dirt, therefore no ventilation, therefore slightly slower to cool at the end of the day. Reacher pointed and Vaughan turned the wheel so that they were following the ghostly green image of the Tahoes' ruts counterclockwise, all the way around the metal plant to the place where Reacher had decided to break in.

The white metal wall was blazing hot in the south and cooler in the north. Vaughan stopped a quarter of the way along its northern stretch. Then she pulled a tight left and bounced out of the ruts and nosed slowly head-on towards the wall and stopped with her front bumper almost touching it. The base of the windshield was about five feet down and two feet out from the cylinder's maximum bulge.

Reacher got out and dragged the stepladder from the rear seat. He laid it on the ground, unfolded it and adjusted it into an upside-down L-shape. Then he estimated by eye and relaxed the angle a little beyond ninety degrees and locked all the joints. He lifted it high. He jammed the feet in the gutter at the base of the Crown Vic's windshield, where the hood's lip overlapped the wipers. He let it fall forwards gently and it hit the wall with a soft metallic noise. The long leg of the L came to rest almost vertical. The short leg lay on top of the cylinder, almost horizontal.

'Back up about a foot,' he whispered.

Vaughan moved the car and the base of the ladder pulled outwards to a kinder angle and the top fell forwards by a corresponding degree and ended up perfectly flat.

Vaughan shut the engine down. The laptop screen turned itself off and they were forced back to the visible spectrum, which didn't contain anything very visible. Just darkness. She carried the flashlight and Reacher took the wrecking bar from the trunk. He levered himself up onto the hood, stepped forwards to the base of the windshield and started to climb the ladder. He carried the wrecking bar in his left hand and gripped the upper rungs with his right. The aluminium squirmed against the steel and set up a weird harmonic in the hollows of the wall. He crawled along the short horizontal leg of the L on his hands and knees. He shuffled off sideways and lay like a starfish on the cylinder's top surface. The white paint was shiny and slick enough to be dangerous. He raised his head and looked around.

He was six feet from where he wanted to be.

The pyramid of old oil drums was barely visible in the dark, two yards to the west. Its top tier was about eight feet south and eighteen inches down from the top of the wall. He swam forwards and grabbed the ladder again. It shifted sideways towards him. He called down, 'Get on the bottom rung.'

The ladder straightened under Vaughan's weight. He hauled himself towards it and clambered over it, then turned round and lay down again on the other side. Now he was where he wanted to be. He called, 'Come on up.'

He saw the ladder flex and sway and bounce a little and the strange harmonic keening started up again. Then Vaughan's head came into view. She made it over the angle and climbed off and lay down in the place he had just vacated. He handed her the wrecking bar and hauled the ladder up sideways, awkwardly, crossing and uncrossing his hands until he had the thing approximately balanced on top of the curve. He glanced right, into the arena, and tugged the ladder a little closer to him and then fed it down on the other side of the wall until the feet of the short leg of the L came to rest on an oil drum two tiers down from the top. The long leg sloped gently between wall and pyramid, like a bridge.

'I love hardware stores,' he said.

'I love solid ground,' Vaughan said.

He took the wrecking bar back from her and stretched forwards and got both hands on the ladder rails. He jerked downwards, hard, to make sure it was seated tight. Then he supported all his weight with his arms, like he was chinning a bar, and let his legs slide off the cylinder. He kicked and struggled until he was lying lengthways on the ladder. Then he got his feet on the rungs and climbed down backwards. He stepped off onto the oil drum, held the ladder steady and called up to Vaughan, 'Your turn.'

She came down the same way he had, backwards.

They clambered down the pyramid and off onto the sticky dirt, then covered the quarter-mile to the vehicle gate in less than five minutes.

The white Tahoes were parked close together near one end of it and there was a line of five flat-bed semis near the other. Four, facing outwards, were loaded with steel bars. Product, ready to go. The fifth was facing inwards. It was loaded with a closed shipping container with the words *China Lines* stencilled on it. Scrap, incoming. Reacher glanced at it, passed it by and headed towards the offices. Vaughan walked with him. Reacher stopped outside the second white-painted infirmary unit.

'Underwood might talk, without Thurman here,' he said.

'The door might be locked.'

But the door wasn't locked. And the sick deputy wasn't talking. The sick deputy was dead.

He was still tucked tight under the sheet, but he had taken his last breath some hours previously. That was clear. And maybe he had taken it alone. He looked untended. His eyes were clouded and open. His hair was thin and messy, like he had been tossing on the pillow.

'TCE?' Vaughan said.

'Possible,' Reacher said.

We're doing the best we can, Thurman had said.

Bastard, Reacher thought.

'This could happen in Hope,' Vaughan said. 'We need the data for Colorado Springs. For the lab.'

'That's why we're here,' Reacher said.

They stood by the bedside for a moment longer, then they backed out, headed down the steps and on up the line to the office marked *Purchasing*. The door was secured with a padlock through a hasp, but the screws securing the hasp to the jamb yielded to the weight of the wrecking bar. There were three desks inside the room, three phones and a wall of filing cabinets.

'Where do we start?' Vaughan whispered.

'Try T for TCE.'

The T drawers were crammed with papers. But none of the papers referred to trichloroethylene. Everything was filed according to supplier name. Tri-State had renewed a fire insurance policy eight months previously, Thomas was a telecommunications company that had supplied four new cellphones three months previously, Tomkins had put tyres on two front-loaders six months ago, and Tribune had delivered binding wire. All essential activity for the metal plant's operation, no doubt, but none of it chemical in nature.

'I'll start at A,' Vaughan said.

'And I'll start at Z,' Reacher said. 'I'll see you at M or N, if not before.'

Vaughan was faster than Reacher. She had the flashlight. He had to rely on stray beams spilling his way. He started to worry about the dawn. It wasn't far away. He was opening the last of the S drawers when Vaughan said, 'Got it.' She had the first of the K drawers open. 'Kearny Chemical of New Jersey,' she said. 'TCE purchases going back seven years.'

She lifted the file out of the drawer and riffled through the papers.

'Take the whole thing,' Reacher said.

Vaughan jammed the file under her arm and pushed the drawer shut with her hip. Reacher opened the door and they stepped out into the dark. Reacher used the flashlight and found the fallen screws and pushed them back into their holes with his thumb. They held loosely and made the lock look untouched. Then he followed Vaughan as she retraced their steps. They dodged round the China Lines container together and headed into open space.

Reacher stopped again. Turned round. 'Flashlight,' he said.

Vaughan gave up the flashlight and Reacher switched it on and played the beam across the side of the container. It was forty feet long, dirty white, with a vertical row of Chinese characters stencilled low in one corner.

Plus a word, hand-written in capitals, in chalk: *CARS*.

Reacher stepped closer. The container had a double door, secured in the usual way with four foot-long levers that drove four sturdy bolts which ran the whole height of the container and socketed home in the box sections top and bottom. Three of the levers were merely slotted into their brackets, but the fourth was secured with a padlock and guaranteed by a plastic tag.

Reacher said, 'This is an incoming delivery. I want to see what's inside.'

'There are cars inside. Every junk yard has cars.'

He nodded in the dark. 'I've seen them come in from neighbouring states on open flat-beds. Not locked in closed containers.'

Vaughan was quiet for a beat. 'You think this is army stuff from Iraq?'

'It's possible.'

'I don't want to see. It might be Humvees if it's from Iraq. And we need to get going. It's late. Or early.'

'I'll be quick,' he said. 'Don't watch, if you don't want to.'

He held the flashlight in his teeth and stretched up tall, then jammed the tongue of the wrecking bar through the padlock's hoop. He jerked down.

No result. He tried again. *One, two, jerk.* Nothing.

He thought about finding some chain and hooking a Tahoe up to it. But the chain would break before the padlock. He let the frustration build. Then he jammed the wrecking bar home for a third try. *One. Two.* On *three* he jerked downwards with all the force in his frame. His whole 250 pounds of bodyweight reinforced the blow. The padlock broke.

He ended up sprawled in the dirt. Curved fragments of metal hit him on the head and the shoulder. The wrecking bar clanged off the ledge and caught him on the foot. He didn't care. He climbed back up and broke the tag and smacked the levers out of their slots and opened the doors. He switched on the flashlight and took a look inside.

Cars. There were four of them. Strange makes. Dusty, sandblasted, pastel colours. They were opened like cans, ripped, peeled, twisted. They had holes through their sheet metal the size of telephone poles. The licence plates were covered with neat Arabic numbers.

Reacher turned in the doorway and called into the darkness, 'No Humvees.' He leant down and took Vaughan's hand and pulled her up. She followed the flashlight beam as he played it around.

'From Iraq?' she asked.

He nodded. 'Civilian vehicles.'

'Why bring them here?'

'I don't know. Just look at the damage.'

'What did it?'

'Cannon fire, maybe. Some kind of big shells.'

'Artillery versus sedans?' Vaughan said. 'That's kind of extreme.'

'You bet it is,' Reacher said. 'What the hell is going on over there?'

THEY CLOSED THE CONTAINER and hiked the quarter-mile back to the oil-drum pyramid and scaled the wall in the opposite direction. Out, not in. It was just as difficult. They stepped off onto the Crown Vic's hood and slid back to solid ground. Reacher folded the ladder and packed it in the rear seat. Vaughan put the Kearny Chemical file in the trunk, under the mat.

They drove west to the truck route. Four miles past the MP base Reacher told Vaughan to pull over.

'We're going to sleep for a while and then watch the traffic,' he said. 'I'm working on a theory. But I can't tell you yet. I might be wrong.'

WHEN THE FIRST RAYS of the morning sun hit the left-hand corner of the windshield, Reacher woke up. Vaughan stayed asleep.

The first truck to pass them was heading east towards Despair. A flat-bed semi with Nevada plates, loaded with a tangle of rusted-out junk—washing machines, tumble driers, bicycle frames. Ten minutes later a second flat-bed blew by, heaped with wrecked cars. Its tyres whined loud and Vaughan woke up. She glanced ahead at it and asked, 'How's your theory doing?'

Reacher said, 'Nothing to support it yet. But also nothing to disprove it.'

'Good morning.'

'To you, too.'

Next was a semi coming west, out of Despair. The bed was loaded with steel bars: a dense, heavy load. Black smoke was pouring from the stack.

'One of the four we saw last night,' Vaughan said.

Reacher nodded. 'The other three will be right behind it. The business day has started.'

The second and third of the outgoing semis appeared on the horizon. Before the fourth showed up another incoming truck blasted by. A container truck. A blue China Lines container on it. New Jersey plates.

Vaughan said, 'Combat wrecks.'

Reacher nodded and said nothing. The truck disappeared in the morning haze and the fourth outgoing load passed it. Then the world went quiet again. Reacher turned to watch the western horizon a mile away, where a small shape wobbled in the haze. A box truck, far away, tan-coloured.

He said, 'Pay attention, now.'

The truck took a minute to cover the mile and then it roared past. It had no logo on it. No writing of any kind. It had Canadian plates, from Ontario.

'Prediction,' Reacher said. 'We're going to see that truck heading out again within about ninety minutes.'

'Why wouldn't we? It'll unload and go home.'

'Unload what?'

'Whatever is in it. Scrap metal, perhaps?'

'From Ontario?' Reacher shrugged. 'That's a long way. Especially if you consider that Canada has steel mills of its own. Why haul it all out here?'

'OK. So what was in that truck?' Vaughan asked.

'My guess is nothing at all.'

Reacher kept his focus on the eastern horizon and the clock in his head while plenty more trucks passed in both directions. Vaughan got out and brought the captured file from under the mat in the trunk. She took the papers out and started with the oldest page first. It was a purchase order for 5,000 gallons of trichloroethylene. The second-oldest page was identical. As was the third. The fourth fell into the following calendar year.

Vaughan said, 'Fifteen thousand gallons in the first year. Is that a lot?'

'I don't know,' Reacher said. 'We'll have to let the state lab be the judge.'

The second year of orders came out the same. Then the third year jumped way up, to five separate orders for a total of 25,000 gallons. The fourth and fifth years held steady, but the sixth year jumped again: 30,000 gallons. Iraq, getting worse: a 20 per cent increase. And the current year looked set to exceed even that. There were already six orders in, and the year still had a whole quarter to run. Then Vaughan paused and looked at the six pages again. 'No,' she said. 'One of these pages is different.'

Reacher asked, 'Different how?'

'One of the orders isn't for trichloroethylene. And it isn't in gallons. It's for something called trinitrotoluene. Thurman bought twenty tons of it.'

'When?'

'Three months ago. Maybe it's another kind of degreaser.'

'It isn't. Trichloroethylene is TCE. Trinitrotoluene is TNT.'

'Thurman bought twenty tons of dynamite? Why?'

'TNT isn't dynamite, it's a specific chemical compound. A yellow solid. Much more stable. It melts easily and pours. That's how they get it into bombs and shaped charges. It's a reagent: carbon, hydrogen, nitrogen and oxygen. Some complicated formula, lots of sixes and threes and twos.'

'OK, but why did he buy it?'

'I don't know.'

Vaughan riffled back through the pages she had already examined. 'Whatever, he never bought any before,' she said. 'It's new.'

Reacher glanced ahead through the windshield. Saw the tan box truck heading back towards them. He took the red bubble light off the dash and held it in his hand. 'Stand by,' he said. 'We're going to stop that truck.'

'We can't,' Vaughan said. 'We don't have jurisdiction here.'

'The driver doesn't know that. He's Canadian.'

VAUGHAN WAITED for the truck to pass, then pulled out onto the road. Reacher opened his window and clamped the bubble light on the roof. Vaughan hit a switch and the light started flashing. She hit another switch and her siren quacked twice.

Nothing happened for ten long seconds, then the driver braked hard and aimed for a spot where the shoulder was wide. Vaughan skipped past and tucked in again and the two vehicles came to a stop, nose-to-tail.

She said, 'A search would be illegal.'

Reacher said, 'I know. Just tell the guy to sit tight, five minutes. We're going to take a photograph.'

Vaughan got out and cop-walked to the driver's window. She spoke for a moment, then walked back. Reacher said, 'Back up on the other shoulder, at right angles. We need to see the whole truck, side-on with the camera.'

Vaughan reversed across the blacktop and came to rest on the opposite shoulder, with the front of her car pointed dead-centre at the side of the truck. She hit laptop keys and the screen lit up with a picture of the truck.

Reacher said, 'We need to see the thermal image.'

Vaughan toggled keys until the road surface and the background scrub showed up as a baseline grey. The hood of the truck glowed warm, with a bright centre where the engine was. The exhaust pipe was a vivid line, with green gases shimmering out of the end in clouds. The cab was warm, a generalised green block with a slight highlight where the driver was sitting.

The box body was cold at the rear but got warmer three-quarters of the way forward. A section five feet long directly behind the cab was glowing.

Reacher stuck his arm out of the window, waved the driver on and peeled the bubble light off the roof. The truck lurched as the gears caught and it pulled across the rumble strip, then it lumbered away in the traffic lane.

Vaughan asked, 'What did we just see?'

'A truck on its way to Canada.'

'Is this part of your theory?'

'Pretty much all of it.'

'Want to tell me about it?'

'When it's across the border. I don't want to put you in a difficult position.'

They turned round and drove west. First stop was a coffee shop, for a late breakfast. Second stop was a Holiday Inn, where they rented a beige room and showered and made love and went to sleep. They woke up at four in the afternoon, made love then showered again. At five thirty, after a light dinner, they were on the road again, heading back towards Despair.

CHAPTER TEN

Vaughan drove. The setting sun was behind her, bright in her mirror. The truck route was busy in both directions. The metal plant ahead was still sucking stuff in and spitting it out again. Reacher watched the licence plates. He saw representatives from all of Colorado's neighbouring states, plus a container truck from New Jersey, heading outwards, presumably empty.

He thought, Licence plates.

He said, 'I was in the Gulf. I told you that, right?'

Vaughan nodded. 'You wore the same BDUs every day for eight months. A delightful image.'

'We spent most of the time in Saudi and Kuwait, of course. But there were a few covert trips into Iraq. I remember their licence plates being silver. The ones we saw last night were off-white.'

'You think those weren't Iraqi cars?'

'I think Iran uses off-white plates.'

'We're fighting in Iran and nobody knows?'

'We were fighting in Cambodia and nobody knew. But I think it's more likely there's a bunch of Iranians heading west to Iraq to join in the fun every day. Like commuting to a job. Maybe we're stopping them at the border crossings. With artillery.'

They passed the MP base just before six fifteen. Neat, quiet, six parked Humvees, four guards in the shack. All in order and recently resupplied.

For what?

They slowed for the last five miles and tried to time it right. Traffic had died away to nothing. The plant was closed. Presumably the last stragglers were heading home. Vaughan made the left onto Despair's old road and then found the Tahoes' ruts in the gathering gloom and followed them through the throat of the figure of eight and round to the back of the residential compound.

She parked there and went to pull the key, but Reacher put his hand on her wrist and said, 'I have to do this part alone.'

Vaughan said, 'Why?'

'Because this has to be face to face, and the whole deal here is that you're permanent and I'm not. Wait on the road. Any hassle, take off for home and I'll make my own way back.'

He left the ladder and the wrecking bar and the flashlight where they were, in the car. But he took the captured switchblades with him. He put one in each pocket, just in case.

Then he hiked the fifty yards through the scrub and climbed the field-stone wall surrounding Thurman's residential compound.

IT WAS STILL LIGHT enough to see the house and outbuildings. There was a three-car garage at the end of a straight quarter-mile driveway that led to an ornamental iron gate in the wall. The house itself was built of oiled boards and had numerous peaked gables. It was magnificent. Reacher located the Piper's hangar inside a big barn. He could smell the plane. Cold metal, oil, unburned hydrocarbons from the tanks. He leant against the hangar's wall, on the blind side, away from the house. The clock in his head showed one minute before seven in the evening.

He heard footsteps at one minute past. Long strides, a heavy tread. The big guy from the plant, hustling. Lights came on in the barn. A rectangle of glare that spilt forward, shadowed with wings and propeller blades.

Then more footsteps. Slower. A shorter stride. An older man, overweight.

Reacher took a breath and stepped round the corner of the barn into the light. The big guy was standing behind the Piper's wing, just waiting. Thurman was on the path leading from the house. He was dressed in a suit and was carrying a small, plain cardboard box. He was carrying it reverentially, out in front of his body. He stopped dead on the path. Reacher watched him try to find something to say, and then watched him give up. So he filled the silence himself. He said, 'Good evening, folks.'

Thurman said, 'You're trespassing. You need to leave now.'

'I'll leave when I've seen what's in that box. I'm curious about what part of Uncle Sam's property you're smuggling out of here every night.'

The big guy from the plant squeezed round the tip of the Piper's wing. He asked his boss, 'You want me to throw him out?'

Reacher saw Thurman thinking about his answer. There was debate in his face, like he was playing a game and thinking eight moves ahead.

Thurman said, 'No, let him stay.'

Reacher said, 'What's in the box?'

Thurman said, 'Not Uncle Sam's property. God's property.'

'God brings you metal?'

'Not metal.' Thurman stood still for a second. Then he stepped round his underling, still carrying the box two-handed out in front of him, like a wise man bearing a gift. He knelt and laid it at Reacher's feet, then stood up and backed away again. Reacher looked down. The box might be booby-trapped, or he might get hit on the head while he crouched down next to it. But he felt either thing was unlikely.

He knelt next to the box. Unlaced the crisscrossed flaps. Raised them. The box held crumpled newspaper, with a small plastic jar nested in it. A sample jar, for urine or other bodily fluids. Reacher had seen many of them.

The jar was a quarter full with black powder, coarser than talc.

Reacher asked, 'What is it?'

Thurman said, 'Ash.'

'From where?'

'Fly with me tonight and find out. I have nothing to hide. And I don't mind proving my innocence, over and over and over again, if I have to.'

The big guy helped Thurman up onto the wing and watched as he folded himself in through the small door. Then he passed the box up. Thurman took it and laid it on the rear seat. Reacher made it into the copilot's seat, slammed the door and squirmed around until he was as comfortable as he was ever going to get, then buckled his harness. Beside him, Thurman buckled his and hit a bunch of switches. Dials lit up and pumps whirred and the whole airframe tensed and hummed. Then Thurman hit the starter button and the plane lurched forward, out of the hangar and down the taxiway.

At the north end of the runway the Piper went light, the nose lifted and the far horizon slid away as the plane clawed its way into the night sky.

Reacher was dumped forwards in his seat against his harness straps. He looked over at the dash and saw the altimeter reading 2,000 feet. He watched the compass. It was holding steady on south and east. He consulted his mental maps again and figured they were going to exit Colorado just left of the state's bottom right-hand corner. He thought about Vaughan. She would be wondering why he hadn't come back over the wall.

Thurman said, 'You broke into a container last night. You saw the cars.'

Reacher said, 'Did I?'

'It's a fair guess.'

'Why do they bring them to you?'

'There are some things any government feels it politic to conceal.'

'What do you do with them?'

'The same thing we do with all wrecks. We recycle them. Steel is a wonderful thing, Mr Reacher. Recycling is where the action is.'

There was nothing but darkness below, relieved occasionally by tiny clusters of yellow light: hamlets, farms, gas stations.

Reacher asked, 'How is Underwood doing? The deputy?'

Thurman paused a moment. Then he said, 'He passed on.'

'Did you call the coroner?'

'No need. He was old, he got sick, he died.'

'He was about forty.'

'A good Christian has nothing to fear in death, Mr Reacher. One door closes, another opens.'

The plane flew steadily through the dark, south of southeast. Thurman leant back, his gut between him and the stick, his hands held low. The engine held fast on a mid-range roar and the whole plane shivered with vibration and bucked occasionally on rough air. Reacher closed his eyes. Flight time to the state line would be about seventy or eighty minutes.

They flew on and the air got steadily worse. Reacher opened his eyes. Downdraughts dropped them into troughs like a stone. Then updraughts hurled them back up again. They were sideswiped by gusts of wind like a pinball caught between bumpers. Reacher opened his eyes. There was no storm outside, just roiling evening thermals coming up off the plains.

Thurman asked, 'Are you afraid of flying?'

'Flying is fine,' Reacher said. 'Crashing is another story.'

Thurman started jerking the stick and hammering the rudder. At first Reacher thought they were seeking smoother air. Then he realised Thurman was deliberately making things worse. He was diving where the down-draughts were sucking and climbing with the updraughts. The plane was hammering all over the sky.

Thurman said, 'This is why you need to get your life in order. The end could come at any time. Maybe sooner than you expect.'

Reacher said nothing. He closed his eyes again.

Dead on an hour and a quarter total elapsed time Thurman hit a couple of switches, fired up his radio and clamped a headset over his ears. Reacher opened his eyes. The headset had a microphone on a boom that came off the left-hand earpiece. Thurman flicked it with his fingernail and said, 'It's me, on approach.' Reacher heard a muffled, crackling reply and saw lights come on below. Red and white runway lights, he assumed. Thurman started a long slow descent. The plane jerked and dropped and levelled and dropped again. Twin lines of red and white drew closer. Then the wheels touched down and bounced once and settled back. Thurman cut the power and the plane rolled to a stop. Reacher could see the vague outlines of brick buildings in the middle distance and a vehicle approaching. A Humvee.

A soldier.

REACHER OPENED the Piper's door and climbed out to the wing. Thurman passed him the cardboard box and he took it one-handed and slid down to the tarmac. A soldier stepped forward, snapped to attention. He threw a salute and stood there like a ceremonial detail, expectantly. Thurman climbed down behind Reacher and took the box from him. The soldier, a private first class, stepped forwards again. Thurman bowed slightly and offered the box. The soldier bowed, took the box, then turned on his heel and slow-marched back to the Humvee. Thurman followed him and Reacher followed Thurman.

The PFC stowed the box in the Humvee's load bed and then climbed in the front. Reacher and Thurman got in the back. The soldier drove them towards a building that stood alone in a patch of lawn. Lights were on in two ground-floor windows. The Humvee parked and the soldier retrieved the box from the load bed and slow-marched it into the building. A minute later he came back out again without it.

Thurman said, 'Job done, for tonight, at least.'

Reacher asked, 'What was in the jar?'

'People,' Thurman said. 'We scrape them off the metal, all that's left of them. Soot, baked onto steel. We put the day's gleanings into jars. It's as close as we can get to a proper burial.'

'Where are we?'

'Fort Shaw, Oklahoma. They deal with recovered remains here. They're associated with the identification laboratory in Hawaii.'

'You come here every night?'

'As often as necessary. Which is most nights, sadly.'

'What happens now?'

'They give me dinner and fuel my plane.'

The PFC climbed back into the front seat and the Humvee turned round and drove 100 yards to the main cluster of buildings. It parked by a side door with a sign that said it led to the Officers' Club.

Thurman turned to Reacher and said, 'I won't ask you to join me for dinner. They'll have just one place set and it would embarrass them.'

Reacher nodded. He knew how to find food on post. 'I'll be OK.'

The PFC in the front of the Humvee craned round. 'Sir, chow in the mess until ten, if you're interested.'

'Thanks, soldier,' Reacher said.

Thurman climbed out and disappeared through the Officers' Club door. Reacher remained in the sharp night air as the Humvee drove away, then he made his way back to the stand-alone building. He went in the front door and found himself in a small square hallway with doors on either side. He tried the left-hand door. An administrative office, nobody in it. He tried the right-hand door and found a medic with the rank of captain at a desk, with Thurman's jar in front of him. The guy was young for a captain, but medics got promoted fast.

'Help you?' the guy said.

'I flew in with Thurman. I was curious about his jar. Is it what he says it is?'

'Are you authorised to know?'

'I used to be. I was an MP. I did some forensic medicine with Nash Newman, who was probably your boss back when you were a second lieutenant. He may be retired now.'

The guy nodded. 'I heard of him. He is retired now. '

'So are there people in the jar?'

The guy nodded again. 'Oxides of potassium, sodium, iron, calcium, maybe a little magnesium. Consistent with burnt human flesh and bone.'

'What do you do with it?'

'Nothing,' the guy said. 'There's no DNA in it. It's soot, basically. But Thurman's a sentimental old guy. We can't turn him away. So we stage a little ceremony and accept whatever he brings. Then we move it off our desks onto Hawaii's. I imagine they stick it in a closet and forget about it.'

'I'm sure they do. Does Thurman tell you where it comes from?'

'Iraq, obviously.'

Reacher asked, 'You got a phone I could use?'

The guy pointed to a console on his desk. 'Help yourself,' he said.

Reacher dialled 411 upside-down and got the number for David Robert Vaughan, Fifth Street, Hope, Colorado. He said the number once under his breath to memorise it and then dialled it.

No answer.

He put the phone back in its cradle and asked, 'Where's the mess?'

'Follow your nose,' the medic said. Which was good advice. Reacher walked back to the main cluster and circled it until he smelt the aroma of fried food coming out of a powerful extraction vent. The mess kitchen.

Reacher went inside and got in line, picked up a cheeseburger the size of a softball, plus fries, plus beans, plus a mug of coffee. All in all, probably better than the limp piece of grilled fish the officers were getting.

He took more coffee and sat in an armchair and read the papers. He figured the PFC would come for him when Thurman was ready. If they took off just after midnight, and had ninety minutes in the air, that should get them back to Despair by two, which seemed to be the usual schedule.

The mess kitchen closed. Reacher finished the papers and dozed. The PFC never showed. At twelve ten in the morning Reacher woke up and heard the Piper's engine. By the time he made it outside the little white plane was lifting off. He stood and watched it disappear into the darkness.

Reacher was ninety minutes' flying time from where he needed to be, in the middle of the night, in the middle of nowhere.

THE HUMVEE CAME BACK from the flight line and the PFC got out and nodded to Reacher like nothing was wrong. Reacher said, 'I was supposed to be on that plane.'

The soldier said, 'No, sir. Mr Thurman told me you had a one-way ticket. He told me you were heading south from here, on business of your own.'

Reacher checked the map in his head. There were no highways in the Oklahoma panhandles. None at all. Just a thin red tracery of state four-lanes and county two-lanes. He looked at the soldier. 'You want to drive me out to a road?'

'Which road?'

'Any road that gets traffic more than once an hour. And Thurman wasn't entirely frank with you. I need to go north.'

'The 287 goes all the way up to I-70. It's about two hundred miles.'

The PFC let him out at twelve forty-five and it was quarter past one in the morning before he saw his first northbound vehicle, a Ford F150 that didn't even slow down. Ten minutes later an old Chevy Blazer did the same thing. Hitchhiking had become more difficult. Reacher blamed the movies. They made people scared of strangers.

At ten to two a dark Toyota pick-up at least slowed and took a look before passing by, which was progress of a sort. Then at a quarter past two an old Suburban hove into view, a plain utilitarian vehicle such as plain utilitarian people drive. The best hope so far.

Reacher stepped off the shoulder and cocked his thumb.

The Suburban's headlights came on. It slowed. The guy behind the wheel wanted a chance to look over his potential passenger.

A decision was made. The truck rolled forwards and stopped again. The window came down. The driver was a fat, red-faced man. He was clinging to the wheel like he would fall out of his seat if he didn't. He said, 'Where are you headed?' His voice was slurred.

Reacher said, 'I'm trying to get to a place called Hope, Colorado.'

'Never heard of it. Are you drunk?'

Reacher said, 'No.'

The guy said, 'Well, I am. A lot. So you drive to wherever, let me sleep it off, and then point me towards Denver, OK?'

Reacher said, 'Deal.'

The guy heaved himself over into the passenger seat, collapsed its back and went straight to sleep. According to the smell of his breath he had been drinking bourbon all evening.

The Suburban was old and worn and grimy. The motor had a lot of weight to haul and it didn't want to go much faster than sixty miles an hour. There was a cellphone on the centre console. Reacher switched it on. The phone showed no service. The middle of nowhere.

The road narrowed from four lanes to two. Five miles ahead Reacher cold see a pair of red taillights. Moving north a little slower than the Suburban. The speed differential was maybe five miles an hour, which meant it took sixty whole minutes to close the gap. The lights were on a U-Haul truck, cruising at about fifty-five. He pulled out and tried to pass, but the Suburban bogged down at about sixty-two, which would have put Reacher on the wrong side of the road for a long, long time. Maybe for ever. So he eased off and tucked in behind the truck, checked the phone again.

Still no signal. They were in the middle of the Comanche National Grassland. Like being way out to sea. The closest cell tower was probably in Lamar, which was about an hour ahead.

Reacher followed the wallowing U-Haul truck for sixty solid minutes, then Lamar loomed up ahead. Low dark buildings, a tall water tower, a lit-up gas station. Reacher checked the Suburban's gauge. Half full. But a thirsty motor and many miles to go. He followed the truck to the pumps.

The guy from the U-Haul was youngish, well-built, with long hair. He was wearing a tight, black, short-sleeved shirt with a clerical collar. Some kind of a minister of religion. Probably played a guitar. He poked a credit card into a slot on the pump and pulled it out again. Reacher used his ATM card and did the same. The pump started up and he selected regular unleaded and watched in horror as the numbers flicked around.

He got out of the gas station ahead of the U-Haul and headed north as fast as the old Suburban would go. The drunk guy was leaking alcohol through his pores. Reacher cracked a window. The night air kept him awake and the whistle masked the man's snoring. It was four thirty in the morning. ETA in Hope around dawn.

Then the Suburban's engine blew.

The motor lost power and a hot wet smell came in through the vents. There was a muffled thump under the hood, the motor died and the Suburban slowed rapidly. Reacher steered to the shoulder and stopped.

Blown head gaskets. A week in the garage. Not good.

The drunk guy slept on.

Half a mile south Reacher could see the U-Haul's lights coming his way. He leant over the sleeping guy and found a pen and an old service invoice in the glove compartment. He turned the invoice over and wrote: *You need a new car. I borrowed your cellphone. Will mail it back.* He signed the note: *Your hitchhiker.* He took the Suburban's registration for the guy's address and folded it into his pocket. Then he ran fifty feet south and stepped into the traffic lane and waved his arms above his head. The truck slowed and came to rest a yard in front of Reacher. The window came down.

'Need help?' the driver asked. He smiled, wide and wholesome. 'Dumb question, I guess.'

'I need a ride,' Reacher said. 'The engine blew.'

'Want me to take a look?'

Reacher said, 'No.' He didn't want the minister to see the drunk guy. 'No point, believe me. I'll have to send a tow truck.'

'I'm headed north to Yuma. You're welcome to join me.'

Reacher nodded. The Yuma road crossed the Hope road about two hours ahead. He would need a third ride, for the final western leg. His ETA was now about ten in the morning, with luck. He said, 'Thanks.'

THE U-HAUL SMELT of warm exhaust fumes, hot oil and plastic, but the seat was reasonably comfortable. Reacher had to fight to stay awake. He wanted to be good company. He asked, 'What are you hauling?'

The guy in the collar said, 'Used furniture. Donations. Our church runs a mission in Yuma.'

'Do you play the guitar?'

The guy smiled again. 'We try to be inclusive.'

'Where I'm going, there's an End Times Church. What do you know about them?'

'Have you read the Book of Revelation?'

Reacher said, 'I've heard of it.'

The minister said, 'Its correct title is the Revelation to Saint John the Divine. It was written either in Ancient Hebrew or Aramaic, then translated into Koine Greek and then translated into Latin, and then into Elizabethan English, copied by hand many times, with opportunities for error and confusion at every single stage. Now it reads like a bad acid trip.'

'What does it say?'

'Broadly, the righteous ascend to heaven, the unholy are left on earth and are visited by various colourful plagues and disasters, Christ returns to battle the Antichrist in an Armageddon scenario and no one ends up happy.'

'When is all this supposed to happen?'

'It's perpetually imminent, apparently.'

Reacher thought back to Thurman's smug little speech in the metal plant. *There are signs*, he had said. *And the possibility of precipitating events.*

Reacher asked, 'What would be the trigger?'

The minister shrugged. 'There's something about a red calf being born in the Holy Land. End Times enthusiasts comb through ranches, looking for cattle a little more auburn than usual. They ship pairs to Israel, hoping they'll breed a perfect redhead. They want to get things started. Because they're awfully sure they're among the righteous.'

'That's it? Red calves?'

'Most enthusiasts believe that a major war in the Middle East is absolutely necessary, which is why they've been so unhappy about Iraq. Apparently what's happening there isn't bad enough for them.'

There was no more conversation after that, either theological or secular. The Hope road arrived exactly two hours into the trip. Reacher got out and waved the truck away and then he walked into the dark empty vastness. Predawn was happening way to the east, over Kansas. Colorado was still pitch black. There was no cellphone signal.

No traffic, either.

Not for the first twenty minutes. Then a lone car came north, but it didn't turn off. An SUV came south, and slowed, but it turned east, away from Hope. Reacher turned his collar up and crossed his arms over his chest and trapped his hands under his biceps for warmth. Cloudy diffused streaks of pink and purple lit up the far horizon. A new day. Maybe a good day. Maybe a bad day. Maybe the last day. *The End is Near*, Thurman's church had promised. Maybe a meteorite the size of a moon was hurtling closer.

Or maybe not.

Reacher saw headlights in the east. When the vehicle was 300 yards away he saw that it was a big rigid panel van with a refrigerator unit mounted on top. Fresh food delivery. Food drivers usually didn't like to stop. They had schedules to keep.

Reacher raised his hand high, thumb extended. *I need a ride.* Then he raised both arms and waved. The distress semaphore. I *really* need a ride.

The driver looked down. The truck kept on moving.

Then it slowed. The air brakes hissed loud, the springs squealed and the truck came to a stop. The window came down and the driver peered out. He said, 'It's going to rain.'

Reacher said, 'That's the least of my problems. I'm headed for Hope and my car broke down.'

The guy at the wheel said, 'My first stop is Hope.'

Reacher said, 'You're the supermarket guy. From Topeka.'

'So quit stalling and climb aboard.'

Dawn chased the truck west. The world lit up cloudy and pale gold and the supermarket guy killed his headlights and sat back and relaxed. Reacher asked him if he often carried passengers and he said that about one morning in five he found someone looking for a ride. Reacher said he had met a couple of women who might have ridden with him.

'Tourists,' the guy said.

'More than that,' Reacher said.

'How much do you know?'

'All of it.'

'How?'

'I figured it out.'

The guy nodded at the wheel. 'Wives and girlfriends,' he said. 'Looking to be close by while their husbands and boyfriends pass through the state.'

'Understandable,' Reacher said. 'It's a tense time for them.'

'And?'

'And nothing. Not my business.'

Reacher checked his borrowed cellphone again. No signal. There was nothing on the radio, either. The supermarket guy hit a button that scanned the whole AM spectrum, and he came up with nothing. Just static.

CHAPTER ELEVEN

Reacher made it to Hope just before ten in the morning. He got out on First Street, walked down to Fifth and turned east. The old blue Chevy pick-up was in Vaughan's driveway. It had glass in its windows again. He walked to the door and rang the bell. He stood on the step for thirty long seconds and then the door opened.

Vaughan looked out at him and said, 'Hello.' She looked still and calm.

Reacher said, 'I tried to call you twice. Where were you?'

'Here and there. You'd better come in.'

She led him through the hall. The kitchen looked just the same as before: neat, clean, decorated, three chairs at the table. There was a glass of water on the counter and coffee in the machine.

Reacher said, 'I'm sorry I didn't get right back.'

'Don't apologise to me.'

'What's wrong?'

'You want coffee?'

'After you tell me what's wrong.'

'OK. We shouldn't have done what we did the night before last.'

'Which part?'

'You know which part. I started to feel bad about it. So when you didn't come back with the plane I switched off my phone and my radio and drove out to see David and tell him all about it.'

'In the middle of the night?'

Vaughan shrugged. 'They let me in. They treated me very well, actually.'

'And what did David say?'

'That's cruel.'

Reacher shook his head. 'It isn't cruel. It's a simple question.'

'What's your point?'

'That David no longer exists. Not as you knew him. And that you've got a choice to make. There have been tens of thousands of men in David's position over more than a century. And therefore there have been tens of thousands of women in your position. Those women all made a choice.'

Vaughan said nothing. She took a fine china mug from a cupboard, filled it with coffee from the machine. She handed the mug to Reacher and asked, 'What was in Thurman's little box?'

'You saw the box?'

'I was over the wall ten seconds after you. I saw the whole thing. *Fly with me tonight* . . . He ditched you somewhere, didn't he?'

Reacher nodded. 'Oklahoma. An army base.'

'What was in the box?'

'Soot,' Reacher said. 'People, after a fire. They scrape it off the metal.'

Vaughan sat down at her table. Reacher sat opposite her. 'But you can breathe easy,' he said. 'There are no wrecked Humvees at the plant. Humvees don't burn like that. Tanks do. No way out of a burning tank. Soot is all that's left.'

'I see.'

'In less than four years a bunch of ragtag terrorists have figured out how to take out battle tanks belonging to the US Army. No wonder the Pentagon ships the wrecks in sealed containers to a secret location.'

Vaughan got up, walked over to her counter and picked up her glass of water. She emptied it in the sink and refilled it from a bottle in her refrigerator. Took a sip. 'What does Thurman do with the wrecked tanks?'

'He recycles the steel.'

'Why would the Pentagon deploy MPs to guard recycled steel?'

'The MPs are there to guard something else.'

'Like what?'

'A main battle tank's armour includes a thick layer of depleted uranium. It's a by-product from enriching natural uranium for nuclear reactors. It's toxic and radioactive. That's what the MPs are there for. It's the kind of thing you want to keep track of. Terrorists could steal it and break it up into small jagged pieces and pack them into an explosive device. It would make a perfect dirty bomb.'

Vaughan said, 'They're cutting it up at the plant. That must make dust and fragments and vapour. No wonder everyone looks sick.'

Reacher nodded. 'The deputy died from it,' he said. 'He told me so. From his deathbed he said, "The", and then he stopped. But then he said, "You did this to me." I thought he was accusing me, but he was pausing for breath. He was actually saying, "The U did this to me." He was using the chemical symbol for uranium. "The uranium did this to me."'

Vaughan said, 'The air at the plant must be thick with it.'

Reacher nodded. 'Remember the way the wall glowed? On the infrared camera? It wasn't hot. It was radioactive.'

Vaughan sipped her bottled water and stared into space. 'They send cars to Despair, too. We saw them. In the container. From Iraq or Iran.'

Reacher nodded. 'The plant in Despair is about uranium recycling. But depleted uranium, DU, isn't just for armour. They make shells out of it, too. Those cars were hit with depleted uranium. They're tainted, so they have to be processed appropriately. And they have to be hidden away because we're using DU shells against civilian vehicles.'

'What the hell is happening over there?'

Reacher said, 'Your guess is as good as mine.'

Vaughan sipped more water. 'Tell me what you know about dirty bombs.'

'A dirty bomb uses contaminated metal, not just nails or ball bearings, for extra shrapnel,' Reacher said. 'It's usually radioactive waste and it's packed around the explosive charge. If a dirty bomb goes off in a city, the city will be abandoned.'

'How much uranium would the terrorists need to steal?'

'The more the merrier.'

Vaughan said, 'I think they're already stealing it. That truck we photographed? The front of the load compartment was glowing just like the wall.'

Reacher shook his head. 'No. I think that was something else entirely.'

REACHER SAID, 'Will you walk to town with me. To the motel?'

Vaughan hesitated. 'I don't know if I want to be seen with you. Especially at the motel. People are talking.'

'I'll be gone tomorrow. So let them talk for one more day.'

'Tomorrow?'

'Maybe earlier. I might need to stick around to make a phone call. Apart from that, I'm done here.'

'Who do you need to call?'

'Just a number. I don't think anyone will answer.'

'What's at the motel?'

'I'm guessing we'll find room four is empty.'

They walked together through the damp, late-morning air to the motel. They bypassed the office and headed down to room four, where a maid's cart stood outside. The bed was stripped and the closets were empty.

Vaughan said, 'Mrs Rogers has gone.'

Reacher nodded and they backtracked to the office. The clerk was on her stool behind the counter and room four's key was back on its hook.

Reacher glanced at the phone and asked, 'Did Mrs Rogers get a call?'

The clerk nodded. 'Six o'clock last night. She seemed very happy. She checked out and called a cab to take her to Burlington.'

'What's Burlington?'

'Mostly the airport bus to Denver.'

Reacher nodded. 'Thanks for your help.'

They walked to the diner. The place was practically empty. Too late for breakfast, too early for lunch. Reacher slid into the booth that Lucy Anderson had used the night he had met her. Vaughan sat across from him. The waitress delivered iced water and silverware and they ordered coffee.

'What exactly is going on?' Vaughan asked.

'All those young guys,' Reacher said. 'What did they have in common? They were young, they were guys and the only white one we saw had a hell of a tan.'

'So?'

Reacher said, 'I sat right here with Lucy Anderson. She was cautious and a little wary,' Reacher said. 'But when I said I had been a cop, she panicked. I put two and two together and figured her husband was a fugitive. The more she thought about it, the more worried she got. She was very hostile the next day.'

'Figures.'

'Then I caught a glimpse of her husband in Despair and went back to check the rooming house where he was staying. It was empty, but it was very clean.'

'Is that important?'

'Crucial,' Reacher said.

The waitress came over with two mugs, two spoons and a flask full of fresh coffee. She poured and walked away. Reacher took a sip.

'But I was misremembering all along. I didn't tell Lucy Anderson that I had been a cop,' he said. 'I told her I had been a *military* cop. That's why she panicked. And that's why the rooming house was so clean. The people passing through it were all soldiers. Lucy thought I was tracking them.'

Vaughan said, 'Deserters.'

Reacher nodded. 'That's why the Anderson guy had such a great tan. He had been in Iraq. But he didn't want to go back.'

'The truck was from Canada and they're offering asylum up there.'

Reacher nodded. 'Like a taxi service. The glow on the camera wasn't stolen uranium. It was a guy in a hidden compartment. Body heat, like the driver. The shade of green was the same.'

Vaughan sat still and quiet for a long time. The waitress came back and refilled Reacher's mug twice. Vaughan didn't touch hers.

Reacher said, 'Some kind of an antiwar activist group must be running an escape line. Maybe local service families are involved. They send guys up here with legitimate metal deliveries, and then their Canadian friends take them north over the border. There was a couple at the Despair hotel seven months ago. A buck gets ten they were the organisers, recruiting sympathisers. And the sympathisers busted your truck's windows. They thought I was getting too nosy and they were trying to move me on.'

Vaughan pushed her glass out of the way. 'You knew about this yesterday,' she said. 'You waited until that truck was over the border before you told me. Why?'

'I wanted Rogers to get away.'

'For God's sake, Reacher, you were a military cop. You hunted deserters.'

Reacher said nothing.

'They had a duty,' Vaughan said. 'David *did* his duty. They should do theirs, and you should do yours.'

'Duty is a transaction, Vaughan. It's a two-way street. We owe them, they owe us. And what they owe us is a solemn promise to risk our lives and limbs only if there's a damn good reason. That's all gone now. Now it's all about political vanity and electioneering.'

'You served thirteen years and you support deserters?'

'I understand their decision. Precisely because I served those thirteen years. I had the good times. I wish they could have had them too.'

'People don't want to hear that their loved ones died for no good reason.'

'I know. But that doesn't change the truth.'

'I hate you.'

'No, you don't,' Reacher said. 'You hate the politicians, and the commanders, and the voters and the Pentagon.' Then he said, 'And you hate that David didn't go AWOL after his first tour.'

Vaughan turned and faced the street. Closed her eyes. She stayed like that for a long time. Then she spoke. Just a whisper. She said, 'I asked him to. I begged him. I said we could start again anywhere he wanted, anywhere in the world. But he wouldn't agree. Stupid, stupid man.'

Reacher moved to sit beside her and held her while she cried. She crushed her face into his chest. She cried for her shattered life and her broken dreams. Finally she lifted her head. 'Why didn't Raphael Ramirez make it?'

Reacher said quietly, 'Ramirez was different. One phone call from your desk will explain it. We might as well go there and make it. Maria has waited long enough.'

Vaughan said, 'One call to who?'

'The MPs west of Despair. Ask them to fax Ramirez's file. Tell them you know they know who he is.'

ELEVEN MINUTES after Vaughan finished her call, Hope Police Department's fax machine sucked up a blank page and fed it back out with writing on it.

Raphael Ramirez had been a private in the Marine Corps. At the age of eighteen he had been deployed to Iraq. At the age of nineteen he had served a second deployment. At the age of twenty he had gone AWOL ahead of a third deployment. He had been arrested five days later in Los Angeles.

Reacher and Vaughan walked back to the motel, where they found Maria. She answered the door tentatively, as if she was certain that all news would be bad, and there was nothing in Reacher's face to change her mind. He and Vaughan led her outside and sat her in the plastic chair outside her room. Reacher took room nine's chair and Vaughan took room seven's.

Reacher said, 'Raphael was a Marine.'

Maria nodded. Said nothing.

Reacher said, 'He had been to Iraq twice. He didn't want to go back a third time. So nearly four weeks ago he went on the run. Did he call you?'

'He called most days.'

'What happened in Iraq?'

'He saw things. He said the people we were supposed to be helping were killing us, and we were killing the people we were supposed to be helping. It was driving him crazy.'

'So he ran. And he called most days. But then he didn't call, for two or three days. Right?'

'He lost his cellphone. Then he got a new phone and he called to say he had found some people. They were going to get him to Canada through Despair. He said I should come here and wait for his call.'

Reacher said, 'It wasn't exactly like that, Maria. Raphael was arrested in LA. The Marines caught up with him. He didn't lose his phone. He was in jail for two or three days.'

'He didn't tell me that.'

'He wasn't allowed to.'

'Did he break out again?'

Reacher shook his head. 'My guess is he made a deal. The Marine Corps offered him a choice. Five years in Leavenworth, or go undercover to bust the escape line to Canada. Names, addresses, routes, all that kind of stuff. He agreed and they turned him loose. The MPs found out what was going on and they were told to stonewall you.'

'So where is Raphael now? Why doesn't he call?'

Reacher said, 'Marines have a code. Did Raphael tell you about it?'

Maria said, 'Unit, corps, God, country.'

Reacher nodded. 'Raphael's primary loyalty was to his unit, a handful of guys just like him.'

'I don't understand.'

'I think he agreed to the deal but couldn't carry it through. He couldn't betray guys just like him. I think he rode up to Despair but didn't call in to the Marines. I think he stayed on the edge of town until he got thirsty and hungry. He started hallucinating and decided to walk to Hope and find you.'

'So where is he?'

'He didn't make it, Maria. He collapsed halfway. He died.'

For the second time in an hour Reacher watched a woman cry. Vaughan held her and Reacher said, 'He was a good man, Maria. He was just a kid who couldn't take any more. And in the end he didn't betray what he believed in.' He said those things over and over again, in different orders, and with different emphases, but they didn't help.

REACHER AND VAUGHAN walked to the diner, where Reacher ate for the first time since the burger he had scored in the Fort Shaw mess the night before. He topped up his caffeine level with four mugs of coffee and when he had finished he said, 'There's one more thing on my mind.'

CHAPTER TWELVE

Three miles before Despair they slowed and bumped down off the road and started a long loop to the north. It was slow-going across the open land. Occasionally they found dry washes and followed them through looping meanders at a higher speed. Then it was back to picking their way around table rocks bigger than the Chevy itself.

Vaughan asked, 'What exactly is on your mind?'

'I like to be able to explain things to myself,' Reacher said.

'What can't you explain?'

'The way they were so desperate to keep people out. Everyone in town is involved. The first day I showed up, even the waitress in the restaurant knew exactly what to do. Why would they go to those lengths?'

'They're playing ball with the Pentagon.'

'The Pentagon wouldn't ask for that. They trust walls and distance and geography, not people.'

'Maybe Thurman asked the people himself.'

'I'm sure he did. But why?'

They hit the truck route two miles west of the plant and bumped up onto the blacktop. Three minutes after that, they arrived at the MP base.

Two guys came out of the guard shack immediately. One was Morgan, the bespectacled specialist with the squint lines. Vaughan introduced herself by name, and as an officer with the Hope PD. Morgan saluted her, in a way Reacher knew meant the MPs had run her plate the first time around. They had found out what her husband had been, and what he was now.

Five minutes later they were face to face across a desk with a one-striper called Connor. He was a small, lean man, maybe twenty-six. He had been to Iraq. He asked, 'Is this an official visit from the Hope PD?'

Vaughan said, 'Yes. Mr Reacher is a civilian advisor.'

'So how can I help?'

Reacher said, 'Long story short, we know about the DU salvage at Thurman's plant.'

Connor said, 'That bothers me a little.'

'It bothers us a little too. Homeland Security rules require us to be told.'

'It's classified,' Connor said.

Reacher nodded. 'We understand that. But we think we're entitled to know when and how the scrap DU gets transported out and what route is used. How long ago did the first convoy leave?'

'It didn't. The first convoy will happen about two years from now.'

Reacher said, 'So right now they're stockpiling the stuff at the plant?'

Connor nodded. 'The steel moves out, the DU stays.'

'You like that?'

'What's not to like?'

'The guy is sitting on a mountain of dangerous stuff.'

'And? What could he possibly do with it?'

REACHER AND VAUGHAN got back in the truck and Vaughan asked, 'Why does it matter that Thurman is stockpiling depleted uranium?'

Reacher said, 'I don't like the combination. He's got twenty tons of radioactive waste and twenty tons of TNT. He's an End Times enthusiast. I spoke to a minister last night. He said that End Times people can't wait to get things started. Thurman himself said there might be precipitating events on the way. These people are fanatics. They seem to think they can nudge things along. They're trying to breed red cows in Israel.'

'How would that help?'

'Don't ask me. Another requirement seems to be a major war in the Middle East.'

'We've already got one.'

'Not major enough.'

Vaughan was quiet for a moment. 'Iran is working with uranium. They're boasting about it.'

'There you go,' Reacher said. 'What would happen next?'

'We'd attack Iran. Iran would attack Israel. Israel would retaliate.'

'Precipitating events,' Reacher said.

'That's insane.'

'We have an End Times nutcase with twenty tons of TNT and twenty tons of DU and four Iranian cars and a limitless supply of shipping containers, some of which were last seen in the Middle East.'

Vaughan said, 'But no judge in America would sign off on a search warrant. Not with what we've got. It's just a crazy theory.'

Reacher said, 'I'm not looking for a search warrant. I'm waiting for dark.'

'It's going to rain.'

'Probably.'

'We're not going to sit here until dark, in the rain.'

'No, we're not. We're going to rest up at the Holiday Inn.'

The same room was not available, but they got one just like it. Indistinguishable. They did all the same things in it. Showered, went to bed, made love.

Afterwards she said that David had been better in bed. Reacher wasn't offended. She needed to believe it. And it was probably true.

The rain started after an hour. It was heavy. It drummed on the hotel's roof and sheeted against the window. A cosy feeling, in Reacher's opinion. He liked being in bed, listening to rain.

DARKNESS CAME three hours later. With it came doubts from Vaughan. As they pulled on their clothes, she said, 'If you're serious about this, you should call the State Police. Or the FBI.'

Reacher said, 'I would have to give my name. I don't like to do that.'

'You're not a one-man justice department.'

Outside the hotel it was still raining.

'What's on your mind?'

'I don't want you to go there. Because of the radiation.'

'It won't hurt me.'

'OK. *I* don't want to go there. I might want children one day.'

That's progress, Reacher thought. He said, 'It's the dust that's the problem. And this rain will damp it down. And you don't have to come in. Just drive me there.'

They left thirty minutes later. Traffic was slow. The roads were running with water, like rivers. Vaughan put her wipers on high. They batted back and forth, furiously. She found the turn east and took it. Within minutes the old Chevy was the only car on the road.

'This is good,' Reacher said. 'We'll have the place to ourselves.'

Up ahead they saw a horizontal sliver of blue light. The plant, lit up. Close up, the glow was smaller because only the farthest quarter was illuminated. The secret compound.

Vaughan said, 'Well, they're working.'

'Good,' Reacher said. 'Maybe they left the gates open.'

They hadn't.

'OK,' Reacher said. 'Same place as before.'

The Tahoes' beaten ruts were soft and full of water. The Chevy spun its wheels and fishtailed and clawed its way forward. Vaughan found the place and backed in, leaving the tailgate under the curve of the metal cylinder.

Reacher was soaked to the skin even before he got his stuff out of the load bed. He knelt in the mud beside the truck and adjusted the ladder to the L-shape that had worked before. He put the flashlight in one pocket and hooked the crook of the wrecking bar in the other. Then he started up the ladder. He made it over the angle of the L and stopped. The cylinder was slick with running water. Manoeuvring had been hard before. Now it was going to be very difficult. It was fourteen feet to the ground. Without the ladder on the inside it wasn't clear how he would ever get out again.

He thought, I'll worry about that later.

He nudged himself forwards and rolled over onto his stomach as he slid.

The wrecking bar thumped and banged and then ninety degrees past top dead centre he was free-falling through empty air.

He hit the ground a whole lot later than he thought he would. But there was no physical damage. He got to his feet, found the wrecking bar he'd dropped and set off walking towards the inner compound.

Its gate was open.

An invitation. A trap, almost certainly. Like moths to a flame. Reacher slogged onwards. Within ten paces his shoes were carrying pounds of sticky mud and water was running into his eyes. Ahead he could make out the white security Tahoes, parked to the left of the main vehicle gate. He walked past the security office, Thurman's office and the Operations office and stopped outside Purchasing. He climbed the steps and used his fingernails to pull the screws out of the padlock hasp. The door sagged open.

He headed straight for the row of filing cabinets and pulled the Thomas file. The cellphone supplier. Clipped to the back of the original purchase order were the contracts, the fees, the rebates, the makes, the models. And the numbers. He tore off the sheet with the numbers and folded it into his trouser pocket. Then he headed back out into the rain.

One mile and forty minutes later he was approaching the inner gate.

It was still open. Light spilt out in a solid bar the width of the opening. Reacher walked in, fast and casual. No alternative. He was as lit up and vulnerable as a stripper on a stage. He was up to his ankles in water. Ahead on the left was a pile of shipping containers, stacked in an open V, point outwards. To their right and thirty feet farther away was a second V. He aimed for the gap between them. Stepped through, and found himself alone in an arena within an arena within an arena. An area of maybe thirty acres. Apart from cranes and gantries and crushers, and backhoes and bulldozers, and carts and dollies and trailers, there were two items of interest.

The first was a mountain of wrecked main battle tanks. It looked like an elephants' graveyard. Bent gun barrels reared up, like giant tusks or ribs. Turret assemblies were dumped and stacked haphazardly, peeled open like cans. There were traces of desert camouflage paint, but most of the metal was scorched dull black. Reacher felt he could hear men still screaming under it. He turned away.

The second item of interest was 100 yards east.

An eighteen-wheel semi truck. Ready to roll. A tractor, a trailer, a shabby blue forty-foot China Lines container on the trailer. The tractor was huge, with an air filter the size of an oil drum, twin chrome smokestacks and a forest of antennas. The container was clamped tight to the trailer. It had a double door, secured with four foot-long levers, all in the closed position. There were no padlocks. No tags.

Reacher put the wrecking bar in one hand, pulled himself up with the other and got a precarious, slippery foothold on the container's bottom ledge. Put his free hand on the nearest lever and pushed it up.

It wouldn't move. It was welded to its bracket. An inch-long worm of metal had been melted into the gap. The three other levers were the same. And the doors had been welded to each other. Reacher jammed the wrecking bar into the space between two welds and pushed hard.

Impossible. Like trying to lift a car with a nail file.

He climbed down and looked again at the trailer clamps. They were turned tight. And welded. He dropped the wrecking bar and walked back towards the inner gates. They were 200 yards away.

And they were closing, moving slowly, but smoothly.

Reacher started forwards involuntarily, and then stopped. Four figures walked in through the closing gap. On the right was Thurman. On the left was the giant with the wrench. In the middle was the plant foreman. He was pushing Vaughan in front of him. She was stumbling, as if every few paces she was getting a shove in the back.

They met in the centre of the hidden space. Thurman and his men stopped and stopped and stood still five feet short of an imaginary line that ran between the pile of wrecked tanks and the eighteen-wheeler. Reacher stopped five feet on the other side. Vaughan kept on going, picking her way through the mud and made it to Reacher's side. She put a hand on his arm and turned.

Two against three.

Thurman called, 'What are you doing here?'

Reacher said, 'I'm looking around. What's in the truck?'

Thurman said, 'My tolerance for you is exhausted.'

'What's in the truck?'

Thurman breathed in, breathed out. He said, 'There are gifts in the truck. Clothes, blankets, medical supplies, prosthetic limbs, dried and powdered foodstuffs, purified water, antibiotics, vitamins. They were bought with tithes from the people of Despair.'

'Who are the gifts for?'

'For refugees and displaced persons in Afghanistan. Jesus said, "Whatever you wish that men would do to you, do so to them. Love your enemies and pray for those who persecute you, so that you may be sons of your Father who is in heaven."'

Reacher said, 'Where are the cars from Iran?'

'The what?'

'The cars from Iran.'

Thurman said, 'Melted down and shipped out.'

'You bought twenty tons of TNT from Kearny Chemical. Where is it?'

Thurman smiled. 'Oh, that,' he said. 'It was a mistake. A coding error. A new girl in the office was one number off, on Kearny's order form. We got TNT instead of TCE. We sent it back on the same truck.'

'Where is the uranium? You pulled twenty tons of depleted uranium out of these tanks.'

'You're standing on it,' Thurman said. 'It's buried in the ground.'

Reacher said nothing. He glanced right, at the eighteen-wheeler. Left, at the backhoe. Down, at the ground. The rain splashed in puddles all around.

'Satisfied?' Thurman asked.

Reacher said, 'I might be. After I've made a phone call.'

'What phone call?'

'I think you know.'

Thurman said, 'This is not the time for phone calls.'

Reacher said, 'Not the place, either. I'll wait until I get back to Hope.'

Thurman glanced at the gate. 'Turn out your pockets,' he said.

'Worried about those numbers? Maybe I memorised them.'

'Turn out your pockets.'

'Make me.'

Thurman went still. Then he stepped back, abruptly, and raised his right arm. The big guy slapped the wrench in and out of his palm. Both guys moved a step closer. The foreman was on Reacher's right and the big guy was on his left. Both of them close, but not within touching distance.

Reacher said, 'We don't have to do this. We could walk out of here friends.'

The foreman said, 'I don't think so.'

'Then you won't walk out of here at all.'

'Big talk.'

Reacher said nothing.

The foreman glanced across at the big guy. He said, 'Let's do it.'

Get your retaliation in first.

He feinted left, towards the giant. The big guy rocked back, surprised. Reacher planted his heel very carefully in the mud and jerked the other way.

He smashed the foreman in the stomach with his elbow. A 500-pound colli-sion. Behind the stomach lies the coeliac plexus, the largest autonomic nerve centre in the abdominal cavity. A heavy blow can shut the whole thing down. Result, great pain. Consequence, a fall to the ground.

The foreman fell face first into a foot-wide rut filled with water. Reacher kicked him in the side to roll him out of it. He didn't want the guy to drown. Thurman had backed off. The big guy was crouched eight feet away.

Reacher backed off.

The big guy followed. Reacher stopped.

The big guy swung. Reacher stepped back.

Thirty acres. Reacher wasn't fast and he wasn't nimble but he had nat-ural stamina. The big guy was breathing hard and every missed swing was jacking his fury. Reacher kept on moving and stopping and dodging. Eventually the big guy learned. After a dozen fruitless swings he recog-nised that his tactics were futile. He sent the wrench spinning away into the marshy ground and got ready to charge. Reacher smiled. Because by then the damage was done. The guy was going to lose. He didn't know it. But Reacher knew it.

And Thurman knew it.

Thurman was hurrying back towards the gate. Hurrying, but slowly. An old man. Reacher called, 'Vaughan, don't let him leave. He has to stay here.' He saw her move in the corner of his eye.

The giant launched himself. A crazed lunge, across fifteen feet of dis-tance, 350 pounds, coming on like a train. His boots churned in the liquid mud. No traction. Reacher feinted left and stepped right and tripped him. The man splashed down in the water and slid a full yard. He struggled to get up, his hands and knees scrabbling in the mud.

Fifty feet north, Vaughan had hold of Thurman's collar. He was trying to get free. Reacher lined up and kicked the giant in the head, like he was punting a football, instep against ear. The impact pin-wheeled the guy's body a whole two feet and dropped him back in the mud.

The giant lay still.

The foreman lay still.

Game over.

Reacher checked his hands for broken bones and found none. He stood still, got his breathing under control and glanced north through the light. Thurman had broken free of Vaughan's grasp and was heading for the gate again. Reacher set off in their direction. Paused to collect the giant wrench from where it had fallen. He hefted it up and carried it on his shoulder like an axe. He caught Vaughan ten yards from the gate, passed her and clamped a hand on Thurman's shoulder, pressing downwards. The old guy folded up and went down on his knees. Reacher moved on to the gate. He found the little grey box. Saw the keypad. Swung the wrench and smashed it to splinters. Hit it again. And again. Wires tore and ruptured.

Thurman was still on his knees. He said, 'What are you doing? Now we can't get out of here.'

'Wrong,' Reacher said. 'You can't, but we can.'

'How?'

'Wait and see.'

Reacher trudged through the mud and rolled Thurman's men into what medics called the recovery position. On their sides, necks at a natural angle, one leg straight and the other knee drawn up. No danger of choking. Then Reacher and Vaughan fought their way across to the eighteen-wheeler.

Vaughan said, 'You really think this is a bomb?'

Reacher said, 'Don't you?'

'What if you're wrong?'

'What if I'm right?'

'How much damage could it do?'

'Twenty tons of TNT, twenty tons of shrapnel. It won't be pretty.'

'How do we get out of here? You can't climb the wall.'

'But you can,' Reacher said.

THEY TALKED for five fast minutes about what to do and how to do it. Knives, welds, the average size and thickness of a car's roof panel, canvas straps, Tahoes, low-range gearing. Thurman was pacing aimlessly 100 yards away. They left him there and headed through the mud to the wall. They picked a spot ten feet left of the gate. Reacher took the two switchblades out of his pocket and handed them to Vaughan. Then he stood with his back to the wall, directly underneath the maximum radius of the horizontal cylinder above. He bent down and curled his left palm and made a stirrup. Facing him, Vaughan put her right foot into it. He took her weight and she balanced with her wrists on his shoulders, straightened her leg and boosted herself up. He cupped his right hand under her left foot. She stood upright in his palms.

'I'm ready,' Vaughan said.

Reacher lifted. Vaughan was about five foot four. Arms raised, she could probably stretch to just shy of seven feet. Their total height was nearly fifteen feet, and the wall was only fourteen feet high.

Vaughan was wobbling and struggling to balance. Reacher felt her weight shift, equalising. He boosted her sharply upwards, used her momentary weightlessness to shift his hands flat under her shoes, stepped forwards half a pace, and locked his arms straight.

She fell forwards and met the bulge of the cylinder with the flats of her forearms. 'I'm there,' she said.

He felt her reach up and straighten her arms. He heard the first switchblade pop open. He heard her stab downwards with the knife. The wall clanged and boomed.

'Won't go through,' she called.

'Harder,' he called back.

She stabbed again. No boom. Just a little metallic clatter.

'The blade broke,' she called. 'The metal is too thick.'

'It's not. It's from an old Buick, probably. It's aluminium foil. And that's a good Japanese blade. Hit it hard. Who do you hate?'

'The guy that killed David.'

'He's inside the wall. His heart is the other side of the metal.'

He heard the second switchblade open. Then a convulsive jerk through her legs and another dull boom through the metal.

A different boom.

'It's in,' she called. 'All the way.'

He felt her take her weight on the wooden handle.

'It's slicing through,' she called.

'It'll stop when it hits a weld.'

He felt it stabilise a second later. Called, 'Ready?'

'On three,' she called. 'One, two, *three.*'

She jerked herself upwards and he helped as much as he could, fingertips and tiptoes, and then her weight was gone. He walked away to get a better angle and saw her lying longitudinally on top of the cylinder, legs spread, both hands wrapped tight round the knife handle. She rested like that for a second, then shifted her weight and slid down the far side of the bulge, still holding tight to the knife handle. Her weight started pulling the blade through the metal. It would jam again at the next weld, which he figured was maybe five feet down, allowing for the size of a typical car's roof panel. She would be hanging off the wall at full stretch with about four feet of clear air under the soles of her shoes.

A survivable fall. Probably.

He waited what seemed like a long time, and then he heard two hard thumps on the outside of the wall. He closed his eyes and smiled. Their agreed signal. Out, on her feet, no broken bones.

'Impressive,' Thurman said, from ten yards away.

Reacher turned. The old guy was still hatless.

'But your friend can't open the gate. She doesn't have the combination.'

'Have faith, Mr Thurman. A few minutes from now you're going to see me ascend.'

Reacher took up station six feet from the wall and a yard left of where Vaughan had gone over. Thurman backed off and watched.

Three minutes passed. Then four. Then without warning a long canvas strap snaked up and over the wall and the free end landed four feet to Reacher's right. The kind of thing used for tying down scrap cars to a flatbed trailer. Vaughan had driven Thurman's Tahoe up to the security office, had found a strap of the right length in the pile near the door and had weighted its end by tying it around a scrap of pipe. He pictured her after the drive back, twenty feet away through the metal, swinging the strap like a cowgirl with a rope, building momentum, letting it go, watching it sail over.

Reacher grabbed the strap, freed the pipe and retied the end into a generous two-foot loop. He wrapped the canvas round his right hand and walked towards the wall. Kicked it twice and backed off a step, put his foot in the loop and waited. He pictured Vaughan securing the other end to the trailer hitch on Thurman's Tahoe, climbing into the driver's seat, selecting four-wheel drive for maximum traction across the mud, selecting the low-range transfer case for delicate throttle control. He had been insistent about that. He didn't want his arms torn off at the shoulders when she hit the gas.

He waited. Then the strap went tight above him and started to quiver. The canvas round his hand wrapped tight, stretched a little. Then he felt serious pressure under his foot and he lifted slowly, smoothly into the air.

'Goodbye, Thurman,' he said. 'Looks like it's you that's getting left behind this time.'

When his hips hit the maximum curve of the cylinder, he unwrapped his hand and hung on. He let the loop round his foot pull his legs up sideways and then he kicked free of it and came to rest spread-eagled on his stomach along the top of the wall. He jerked his hips and sent his legs down the far side, pushed off and fell, two long seconds. He hit the ground on his back

NOTHING TO LOSE | 451

and knocked the wind out of himself. He rolled over and forced some air into his lungs, then got to his feet. He unhooked the strap from the Tahoe's trailer hitch, then he climbed into the passenger seat and slammed the door.

'Thanks,' he said.

'Where to now?' Vaughan asked.

'The hotel in Despair. The first phone call is one that you get to make.'

THEY ABANDONED Thurman's Tahoe next to where Vaughan's old Chevy was waiting. They transferred between vehicles and three miles later they were in downtown Despair. It was still raining. The hotel door was not locked. Inside, the place looked just the same. The empty dining room, the deserted bar, the register on the desk. The large square leather book, easy to swivel around, easy to read. Reacher put his fingertip under the last registered guests, the couple from California, from seven months previously. He tilted the book so that Vaughan had a clear view of their names and addresses.

'Call them in,' he said. 'And if they're helping the deserters, do whatever your conscience tells you to.'

'If?'

'I think they might be into something else.'

Vaughan made the call from her cell and they waited for the call back. Vaughan said, 'Gifts are a perfectly plausible explanation. Churches send foreign aid all the time. Why are you so convinced?'

'The container was welded to the trailer. And that's not how containers get shipped. They get lifted off and put on boats. By cranes. The welding suggests they don't mean for that container to leave the country.'

Vaughan's phone rang. A three-minute wait. The upside of all the Homeland Security hoopla. Agencies talked, computers were linked. She answered and listened, four long minutes. Then she thanked her caller and clicked off.

'Can't rule out the AWOL involvement,' she said. 'They're listed as activists. And activists can be into all kinds of things.'

'What kind of activists?'

'They run something called the Church of the Apocalypse in LA.'

'The Apocalypse is a part of the End Times story,' Reacher said. 'Maybe they came here to recruit Thurman. Maybe they recognised his special potential.'

Vaughan said nothing.

'Four more phone calls,' Reacher said. 'That's all it's going to take.'

THEY DROVE WEST and parked on a kerb at the edge of town. Three miles away, they could see the plant's lights, faint and blue, blurred by the rain on the windshield, a sepulchral glow in the middle of nowhere. Reacher took the cellphone he had borrowed out of his pocket. Then he took out the sheet of paper from the purchasing office. The new cellphone numbers. The paper was wet and soggy and he had to peel apart the folds very carefully.

'Ready?' he asked.

Vaughan said, 'I don't understand.'

He dialled the third number down. Heard a ring tone in his ear, twice, four times, six times, eight. Then the call was answered.

The big guy, from the plant.

Reacher said, 'How are you? Been awake long?'

The guy said, 'Go to hell.'

Reacher clicked off and dialled the second number on the list. It rang eight times and the plant foreman answered.

Reacher said, 'Sorry, wrong number.'

He clicked off.

Vaughan asked, 'What exactly are you doing?'

'How did the insurgents hurt David?'

'With a roadside bomb.'

'Detonated how?'

'Remotely, I assume.'

Reacher nodded. 'By radio, from the nearest ridge line. But if Thurman *has* built a bomb, he'll probably want a lot more distance than that. Which would take a very powerful radio. My guess is he'll use one built by Verizon or T-Mobile.'

'A cellphone?'

Reacher nodded again. 'The phone companies are proud of the fact that you can call anywhere from anywhere.'

'And the number is on that list?'

'It would make sense,' Reacher said. 'Three months ago, Thurman ordered twenty tons of TNT and four new cellphones. My guess is he kept one phone for himself and gave two to his inner circle, so they could have secure communications. The fourth phone is buried in the heart of that container, with the ringer wired to a primer circuit.'

'And you're going to call that number?'

Reacher said, 'Soon.'

He dialled the first number on the list. It rang, and Thurman answered, fast and impatient, like he had been waiting for the call. 'You guys over the wall yet? Or are you still in there?'

Thurman said, 'We're still in here. Why are you calling us?'

'You starting to see a pattern?'

'The other phone was Underwood's. He's dead, so he won't answer. So there's no point calling it.'

Reacher said, 'OK.' He clicked off and laid the phone on the Chevy's dash. Stared out through the windshield.

Vaughan said, 'You can't do this. It would be murder.'

Reacher said, '*Live by the sword, die by the sword*. Thurman should know that quotation better than anyone. It's from the Bible. Matthew, chapter twenty-six verse fifty-two. I'm sick of people who claim to live by the scriptures, cherry-picking the parts they find convenient.'

'You could be completely wrong about him.'

'Then there's no problem. Gifts don't explode. We have nothing to lose.'

'But you might be right.'

'In which case Thurman's no better than whoever blew up David's Humvee. Worse, even. David was a combatant. Thurman is going to have that thing driven to a city somewhere. With children and old people all around. He's going to put thousands more people in your situation.'

Vaughan said nothing.

'And for what?' Reacher said. 'For some stupid, deluded fantasy.' He entered the final number into his phone and held it out to Vaughan. 'Your choice,' he said. 'Green button to make the call. Red button to cancel it.'

Vaughan didn't move. Then she took her hand off the wheel. Held her index finger out straight. She held it still, close to the phone.

She pressed the green button.

NOTHING HAPPENED. Not at first.

Reacher wasn't surprised. He knew a little about cellphone technology.

Maybe at this point a ring tone starts up in your earpiece. But it means nothing. It's there to reassure you. You're not even close to connected. The circuit is complete and the tone in your ear morphs from phoney to real and the target phone starts its urgent ringing an average of seven seconds later.

Vaughan took her finger back and stared forwards out of the windshield.

'Nothing,' she said.

Reacher said, 'Wait.'

They stared into the distance. The blue arena lights hung and shimmered in the wet air, pale and misty.

Six seconds. Seven.

The silent horizon lit up with an immense white flash that filled the windshield and bloomed instantly higher and wider. The rain all around turned to steam as the air superheated and jets of white vapour speared up and out in every direction like 100,000 rockets had launched simultaneously. The vapour was followed by black soot a mile high and a mile wide. It rolled and tore and folded back on itself as white-hot shrapnel was flung through it at more than 15,000 miles an hour.

The sound arrived three seconds after the light. First a crisp deafening *crump* and then a banshee screaming from the shrapnel in the air and an otherworldly pelting sound as a million blasted fragments fell back to earth. After ten long seconds there was just the patient rain on the Chevy's roof.

VAUGHAN CALLED OUT the whole of the Hope PD. All four deputies, her brother officer and her watch commander. The state cops showed up next. They confirmed that the MPs had the road blocked to the west.

Dawn came and the rain finally stopped. The sky turned hard blue and the air turned crystal clear. Every detail was visible: the mountains, their rocky outcrops, their pine forests. Reacher borrowed a pair of binoculars from Vaughan's watch commander and climbed to the second floor of the last building to the west. He struggled with a jammed window, crouched down and put his elbows on the sill, focusing into the distance.

Not much to see.

The white metal wall was gone. The plant was mostly a black smoking pit. Thurman's residential compound had been obliterated.

Reacher came downstairs to find federal agencies had arrived. Gossip was flowing. Air-force radar in Colorado Springs had detected metal 15,000 feet up. The rain was seen as a mercy. DU dust was believed to be strongly hygroscopic. Nothing bad would drift. Nevertheless, the site was gong to be fenced off for ever, on a three-mile radius.

No hard information was volunteered by the townsfolk. No hard questions were asked by the agencies. The words on everyone's lips were, 'An accident at the plant.' If the agencies had doubts, they knew better than to voice them. State officials arrived with contingency plans. Food and water was trucked in. Buses were to be laid on for job searches in neighbouring towns. Special welfare would be provided for the next six months.

By the middle of the afternoon Reacher and Vaughan had nothing more to do. They set off down the road to Hope and went to Vaughan's house, where they showered and dressed again.

Reacher took the borrowed phone out of his pocket and dropped it on the bed. Followed it with the registration from the old Suburban's glove box. Asked Vaughan to mail both things back, with no return address on the package. She said, 'That sounds like the start of a farewell speech.'

'It is,' Reacher said. 'And the middle, and the end.'

They hugged, a little formally, like two strangers who shared many secrets.

Reacher got a ride easily. A stream of vehicles was heading east, emergency workers, journalists, men in suits in plain sedans. Reacher rode with a post-hole digger from Kansas who had signed up to dig some of the 16,000 holes necessary for the hurricane fence sealing off the site. The guy was cheerful. He was looking at months of steady work.

Reacher got out in Sharon Springs, where there was a good road south. He figured San Diego was about 1,000 miles away, or more, if he followed some detours.

LEE CHILD

Born: 1954, Coventry
Homes: Manhattan, South of France
Website: www.jackreacher.co.uk

It is often said that opportunity springs from adversity, and it was certainly the case for Lee Child. His writing career began in 1995 when, at the age of forty, he lost his job at Granada Television in Manchester after eighteen years with the company. He had a family to support and a mortgage to pay, but even so he was determined not to go back into corporate life. Instead, he decided to try his chances as a novelist. 'I'd been a thriller reader for years,' he says. 'And I started thinking, "I could do one of these." I went into it with a fury that was a perfect balance of creativity and financial necessity. With hindsight, it does seem a rather crazy and incredibly risky thing to have done, but I saw it as the best option I had.'

It was a gamble that paid off extraordinarily well. Child's first novel, *Killing Floor*, introducing the nomadic Jack Reacher, achieved resounding international success and, with *Nothing to Lose* being the twelfth book in the series, the Reacher brand continues to go from strength to strength. An earlier Reacher adventure, *One Shot*, has recently been optioned for filming by Tom Cruise's production company.

So what or who inspired this former transmission controller to write as he does? Child recalls his childhood love of Enid Blyton, whose books were 'primers on mystery fiction'. He also claims that his familiarity with American dialogue comes from his career in television and many years of watching American TV shows. He made the decision to make Reacher an American partly to appeal to the US market, but also because he was attracted to the States, where he now lives for part of the year.

Child says he enjoys America's vast open spaces, and 'the recklessness of it all', so it is perhaps no surprise that Jack Reacher is a free spirit, with a desire to roam that is fulfilled in his many adventures. It may be that this attitude is at the root of his popularity, for, as Child says, the fact that Jack Reacher is 'unencumbered by mortgages and responsibilities seems to be a fantasy that appeals to men especially.' However, to the author's surprise, Reacher has also proved popular with female readers, despite the fact that Reacher's own attitude to women has become less engaged. In the earlier novels, he has a girlfriend, Jodie, but in recent books his romances are more fleeting and he frequently moves on without a backward glance.

Even though Lee Child left his life in the UK behind some years ago now, he says he still has a fondness for Britain and sometimes feels a nostalgia for little things, such as Marmite and the BBC, and 'the way it stays light so late in May and June'. Although America has turned him into something of a baseball fan, he remains devoted to Aston Villa and tries to catch as many of their football games as he can on TV or the Internet.

Child produces one Reacher novel a year and likes to write between September and March, usually for five or six hours a day. He has homes in New York and the South of France, but leaves them to write. When he's in France, he goes to an office in a fourteenth-century building close by, whereas in New York he takes the lift to an apartment on the twenty-seventh floor of the block where he lives, overlooking the Empire State Building. Child says that what satisfies him most about writing best sellers is that 'I can make good money without hurting anyone', together with the knowledge that 'just occasionally, books touch lives'.

A TOWN LIKE DESPAIR

Company towns in America were first created in the 19th and early 20th century by employers—often factory or mine owners—who wanted to provide their workers with a decent place to live. In return for a home with good amenities, the employer/landlord would expect rent and years of loyal service. Some bosses, however, were much like the modern-day Thurman in *Nothing to Lose,* and had little or no concern for their employees' welfare.

One famous company town is Hershey, founded by Milton S. Hershey in 1905 to give all workers at his chocolate factory (right) a good standard of housing. A genuine philanthropist, Hershey built a community centre, theatre and sports arena for his workforce, but always insisted that the factory and its product should remain the focus of the town.

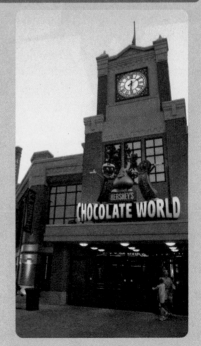

PATRICIA WOOD

LOTTERY

Life, like the dictionary,
can be learned one word at a time.
That's what thirty-one-year-old
Perry L. Crandall's grandmother's
always taught him, so he's working his
way patiently through its 852 pages.
He may be a little slow but, thanks to
Gram's down-to-earth wisdom, he knows
how to get by in simple style.
Then comes the $12 million lottery win
that turns Perry's life upside down . . .

Prologue

My name is Perry L. Crandall and I am not retarded. Gram always told me the L stood for Lucky. 'Mister Perry Lucky Crandall, quit your bellyaching!' she would scold. 'You got two good eyes, two good legs, and you're honest as the day is long.' She always called me lucky and honest.

Being *honest* means you don't know any better.

My cousin-brother John called me lucky too, but he always snickered hard after he said it. 'You sure are a lucky bastard. No high-pressure job, no mortgage and no worries. Yeah, you're lucky all right.' Then he would look at his wife and laugh harder. He is a lawyer.

John said lawyers get people out of trouble. Gram said lawyers get people into trouble. She ought to know. It was a lawyer who gave her the crappy advice on what to do after Gramp died.

I am thirty-two years old and I am not retarded. You have to have an IQ number less than 75 to be retarded. I read that in *Reader's Digest*. I am not. Mine is 76.

'You have two good ears, Perry. Two! Count 'em!' Gram would hold my chin and cheeks between her fingers so tight that my lips would feel like a fish. She stopped doing that because of evil arthritis. Arthritis is when you have to eat Aleve or Bayer and rub Bengay. 'You're lucky,' she said. 'No evil arthritis for you. You're a lucky, lucky boy.'

I am lucky. I know this because I am not retarded.

I know this because I have two good arms.

And I know this because I won twelve million dollars in the Washington State Lottery.

1

I write things down so I do not forget.
'Writing helps you remember. It helps you think, Perry, and that's a good thing,' Gram said.
'You're just a little slow.' That's what my old teacher Miss Elk said.
The other kids had different names for me. *Moron. Idiot. Retard.* Miss Elk told them to be nice. She said I was not any of those things.

'Don't you pay any attention to them, Perry,' Gram told me when I cried. 'Those other kids are just too goddamned fast. If you want to remember, you write it down in your notebook. I'm old. I have to write things down,' she said. 'People treat you the same when you're old as when you're slow.'

Slow means you get to a place later than fast people.

Gram had me do a word a day in the dictionary since I was little.

'One word, Perry. That's the goddamned key. One word at a time.'

Goddamned is an adjective, like 'I'll be goddamned!' Gram will be reading something in the newspaper and it will just come out all by itself. Out of the blue. 'Goddamn.' Or sometimes 'Goddamned.' Or even, 'Goddamn it.'

At ten, I was still in the A's. Gram and I sat down and added it up. Our dictionary has 75,000 words and 852 pages. If I did one word a day, it would take me 205 years to finish. At three words, it would take 68 years. I wrote this all down. It is true because calculators do not lie and we used a calculator. Gram said we needed to pick up the pace.

That is when we got our subscription to *Reader's Digest*. We bought it from a girl who needed money for her school band to go to Florida.

'This is better than chocolate bars!' Gram was excited when the first one came. 'Word Power! Here you go, Perry!'

It was the February issue and had hearts on the cover. We saved every copy that came in the mail. I remember I was on the word *auditor*. An auditor is a listener. It says so in the dictionary and in *Reader's Digest* Word Power. Answer D. A listener. I decided right then to be an auditor.

We picked up the pace and by the time I turned thirty-one, I was on page 337. Gram was right. That day my words were *herd, herder, herdsman, here, hereabouts* and *hereafter*. *Hereafter* means future.

'You have to think of your future!' Gram warns each time I deposit my cheque in the bank. Half in chequing and half in savings. For my future. 'It is important to think of your future, Perry,' she tells me. 'Remember that!'

My best friend, Keith, agrees with everything Gram says. 'That L. It sure does stand for Lucky, Per.' Keith drinks beer wrapped in a brown paper sack and calls me Per for short. He works with Gary and me at Holsted's Marine Supply. I have worked for Gary Holsted since I was sixteen years old.

Keith is older and bigger than me. I do not call him fat because that would not be nice. I can always tell how old people are by the songs they like. For example, Gary and Keith like The Beatles, so they are both older than me. Gram likes songs you never hear any more, like 'Hungry for Love' by Patsy Cline and 'Always' by somebody else who is dead. If the songs you like are all by dead people, then you are really old.

Before Holsted's, I learned reading, writing and math from Gram and boat stuff from Gramp. After he died, I had to get a job for money. I remember everything Gramp showed me about boats and sailing. Our family used to own the boat yard next to Holsted's.

'It's a complicated situation.' Whenever Gram says this, her eyes get all hard and dark like two black olives.

Just before he died, Gramp took out a loan for a hoist for the yard.

A *loan* is when someone gives you money then takes collateral and advantage. After that, you drop dead of a stroke by the hand of God.

A hoist lifts boats up in the air and costs as much as a boat yard.

That is what the bank said.

GRAM SAYS I have to be careful. 'You're suggestible, Perry.'

'What's *suggestible*?' I ask.

'It means you do whatever people ask you to do.'

'But I'm supposed to.' I get in trouble if I do not do what Gram says.

'No. There are people you listen to, and others you don't. You have to be able to tell the difference.' Gram slaps the kitchen table hard with her hand.

'Like who?' I ask.

We make a list.

'For example, a policeman.' Gram draws numbers on the paper. 'He's number one on the list.'

'I always have to do what Ray says.' I already know this. That is the law. Officer Ray Mallory has a crew cut and wears sunglasses even when it rains.

Gram is number two on our list. I do everything she says. I do not ever do what Chuck at church says because he is a jerk. A jerk is someone you cannot trust, so Chuck is not on our list. Gary Holsted is number three, because he is my boss.

Keith helps us with the list.

'Keith, you should be on the list.' I want to make him number three.

'I don't need to be on any list, Per,' he says. Per sounds like pear. Keith is not on the list because he is my friend. A *friend* is someone who calls you something for short like Per for Perry. You never have to do what friends say, but you want to, because you are friends.

We add and subtract people from our list all the time. Sister Mary Margaret used to be number five, but Gram took her off because she tried to collect money from us. 'That goddamned church has enough money! It doesn't need ours!' Gram was mad and used a pink eraser to rub out Sister Mary Margaret's name. When Sister is nice to us at bingo, we put her back on the list.

On nice days, I ride my bike down the hill to Holsted's. On rainy days, I take the bus. It takes ten minutes and stops right in front of our house in Everett, Washington.

Everett stinks. When I ask why, everybody says something different.

'It's because all of us fart at the same time.' Keith laughs, then lifts one cheek and lets one go.

'Don't be smart!' Gram always cautioned about being smart. 'It's because of the paper mills.' She smacks Keith in the head with her paper for farting.

I am lucky to live with Gram. I have been with Gram since I was a baby. I am the youngest. There is John, my oldest cousin-brother. He looks just like me except he is taller, has jagged teeth, a grey-brown moustache and gets married a lot. David is next oldest and looks just like John except he is shorter, thinner and has blue eyes. He is married to Elaine. Gram calls her different names like *That Woman* and *HER*. David is an MBA.

'MBA! It means *Must Be Arrogant*, Perry. You remember that! Marrying *The Ice Queen* is his comeuppance.' Gram cackles like a witch on Halloween when she says this. She is good at witch laughs.

Gram says *comeuppance* means you get what you deserve.

John is a lawyer. David's wife Elaine is a lawyer. My mother Louise married my father who was a lawyer, but I think he is dead.

'Money runs through your mother's hands like water. You remember that, Perry. Marrying a lawyer is as bad as being one! You remember that too!' Gram warns. 'Not one of them goes on our list!'

I call my mother Louise. She likes it better than Mother. Sometimes I cannot tell who she is because I do not see her very often and her hair is always different. It gets longer or shorter and changes colour.

'Everybody in our family is either a lawyer or married to one,' I tell Gram, 'except for you and me.'

'That's a good thing, Perry,' she says. 'It's a goddamned good thing.'

MONDAY, I WORK all day at Holsted's Marine Supply. I unload big trucks, put away orders and carry packages out to cars, trucks and SUVs. I mop the floor, clean the two front windows and empty all the trash cans. I also file papers in the back office because you just need to know the alphabet for that. I am very good at the alphabet. Keith does the cash register, and when Gary goes home, Keith lets me ring up customers.

It takes me longer to learn something but, when I do, I learn it good. This year I learned how to use the air machine. It is called a compressor and blows up inner tubes and fenders. Those are squishy things on boats that need to be blown up. I am very good at blowing up fenders.

'Yeah, Per, you're a real good worker.' Keith tells me this all the time.

I watch the store so he can take a nap. He needs naps at least two or four times a day. I don't take naps at all. Keith can sleep standing up. That is so cool. Sometimes he snores. He has a bushy grey beard and two scars. One is from a bar fight.

'What's a bar fight?' I asked him.

'See, Per, um . . . a bar fight is when . . . uh it's when a guy says "fuck you", and then you say "fuck you", and then you fight.'

Keith says the F-word more than anybody else I know. I do not say the F-word. Gram does not let me. 'Only morons and jackasses talk dirty, Perry! Morons, jackasses and Keith.' Gram likes Keith even though he talks dirty.

On Tuesday, I have my special sandwich at Gilly's next to the marina. They have pretend crab, which I like. After I buy my sandwich, I go to the Marina Handy Mart down the street. I buy a Coke Slurpee, five Lotto tickets, one PayDay candy bar, a bag of Hershey's Kisses and the *National Enquirer.* The paper is for Gram. She gets it for the crossword puzzle.

I like talking to Cherry who works at the counter at Marina Handy Mart. She is pretty, funny, and her name rhymes with mine. That is what Gram says. 'Cherry and Perry! Get it? You're both *errys*!'

'Only Lotto?' Cherry likes MegaBucks because you can win more money, but Gram and I are stick-in-the-muds. 'No sense changing,' Gram says. 'Lotto's good enough for us.' Gram likes the fact that Lotto comes out like a cash register receipt and you get more numbers for your money. We always bought lottery tickets, right from the beginning. It was cool then because you got shiny green tickets. The first person who won was a nurse. A million dollars. Gram said it was the Lord rewarding a selfless profession. She was very disappointed to read in the paper, years later, that the nurse lost all that money.

'How do you lose a million dollars?' Gram shakes her head. 'What if we won? Just think of it. We could do anything we want! We could go to Hawaii, where it's not so goddamned cold!' She pulls her sweater tight over her shoulders. Gram is always cold.

'We can do anything we want right now,' I say. That is true. If we save our money and decide, we can do whatever we want.

'Don't be smart.' Gram frowns at me, but I laugh.

It is fun thinking about winning the lottery.

At seven o'clock Tuesday nights, we go to bingo at St Augustine's Catholic Church. We are not Catholic, but we like the nuns and bingo. We like Sister Mary Joan because she is nice all the time. We only like Sister Mary Margaret when she is on our list.

'How are you doing, Perry?' They are friendly and do not treat me like I am retarded. I am not retarded, but some people treat me like I am. The nuns are always very interested in how I am doing.

'What's your numbers, sonny?' Chuck the bingo helper says this each time he walks behind me. My name is not Sonny. Chuck shoves my chair and jabs me in the back. My markers slide off the numbers on my card whenever he pushes me.

'Leave him alone!' Gram says.

'Woman, you got eyes in the back of your head,' Chuck says.

I laugh. Gram's eyes are right where they are supposed to be.

Chuck is the only one at bingo who treats me like I am retarded.

'Ignore him, Perry! He's a jerk!' Gram says.

Saturday is the busiest day at Holsted's. Everybody needs lots of boat stuff on weekends, like rope, metal parts and beer. They have to buy the beer from Marina Handy Mart. Holsted's does not sell beer. Our floor is grey tile and gets very dirty from wet and muddy feet. The parking lot is gravel and has puddles. Most people do not clean their shoes off on the mat before they walk into the store. That is so rude.

I work until six thirty on Saturday. Gary leaves early. Keith and I close up. He gives me a ride home then stays for spaghetti night. We have our weekly cribbage contest. Gram makes the tomato sauce in the big pan. It has to simmer for two hours. It is the only thing she cooks now. Keith and Gram play first, while I boil the noodles. The loser sets the table while I play the winner.

Keith thinks he has to coach me. 'Throw two away. Come on, Per! Sometime today!' he complains, but I take my time. When I play cards with Keith, he gets antsy. *Antsy* is when you think everybody else is too slow. Most people are antsy. I always win at cribbage. You only have to know numbers like what makes fifteen and how to add up to thirty-one. The rest is luck. And I am lucky.

On Sunday morning, Gram and I eat cinnamon rolls, read the paper and check our Lotto numbers. This is my very favourite time because we pretend to win the lottery.

'This is it! I can feel it in my bones.' Gram can feel a lot in her bones.

'Oh-two. Oh-five. One-four. Two-four. Three-two. Four-four.' I read them off to Gram. She says *nope* after each number that is wrong and *yep* for each right number. We check all ten numbers twice. That is like getting more chances to win. That is so cool.

We have another game we play. It is lottery list. The *What would be the first thing you'd buy if you won the lottery*? game. We play with Keith.

'A new TV!' That would be me.

'Hawaii!' That would be Gram.

'Cable!' That would be me too. I really like Animal Planet.

'Fix up *Diamond Girl.*' That would be Keith. *Diamond Girl* is his sailboat.

'A year's supply of tequila.' That would be Keith again. I am surprised he does not say beer too, or maybe Mexican babes. He talks about Mexican babes all the time. They are close to Texas in Mexico. That is a country.

'Fix Yo's heater.' That is Gram. She is always cold. Yo is Keith's truck.

The end of the game is when one person can't think of anything else they would buy. It is always Gram. She says she is fortunate.

'I'm fortunate I own my own house, damned fortunate I have you to help with expenses, and goddamned fortunate your grandpa worked his ass off then had the courtesy to drop dead without lingering.' *Lingering* is a word that means costing a lot of money to die. She says she hopes she does not linger. She is damned fortunate and I am lucky.

Gram says we make a good pair.

FALL IS MY FAVOURITE time of year, *Reader's Digest* is my favourite book and my favourite candies are Hershey's Kisses. I like to wear flannel jackets, I bounce when I'm happy and my bike is blue with red spray paint.

'Hey, Gram!' I yelled when I found it laying in our side yard all splattered. It looked like it was bleeding. 'What happened to my bike?'

'Some asshole decided to be a moron, that's what,' Gram said. After that, she made me lock it up in our garage every night.

I like to ride my bike to work so I can pretend I am flying or sailing. Boats are my favourite thing besides riding my bike. 'Sailing and riding a bike are like flying because of air and physics,' Gramp told me. He taught me how to sail boats, and Keith teaches me how to fix them. Keith and I earn extra cash by working on other people's boats.

'Smoother, Perry, you missed a spot.' Keith has to inspect my work. We are sanding teak on a boat that is supported on jacks high in the air. It is hauled out at the boat yard. The foreman carries a clipboard and tells us to hurry. 'We don't have all day!' he yells. I think that is funny because we do.

We painted the bottom of this boat yesterday and have to finish a light sand on its rail today. *Light sand* means working hard and sweating. The wooden parts of boats need to be sanded and varnished. It is hard work, but cool to see how beautiful they look when they are done.

'We bring them back from the dead, Per!' Keith says. 'They'd be dumped or sunk. We are defenders of a lost art. Look at those new boats, Per. No character! Not one piece of teak. What a waste.' *A lost art* means we are the only ones doing the work. *No character* means easy to take care of.

When this boat goes into the water, it will be moved into a slip. The owner says he is going to put the varnish on himself and save money.

'That's what they all say, Per!' Keith chortles. 'Twenty minutes into the job, he'll be back here bellyaching about it being too hard on his knees, and you and I will have another thousand bucks under the table.'

The first time I heard *under the table*, I thought it meant hide. I had to ask Keith for sure.

'It means we get to keep all the money ourselves instead of giving some of it to the government.'

'You mean cheat?' I do not want to go to jail.

'No. It's OK, Per. We don't owe them a dime! They didn't do any of the work, did they? They didn't help us one bit. Just don't tell anybody, OK?'

Keith and I make a lot of money under the table sanding and varnishing for people who are too lazy to do it themselves.

EVERY MORNING I get up, go to the bathroom, shave, and comb my hair. I wear jeans and a flannel shirt with an undershirt. Gram says only low-class people go without undershirts. I definitely like undershirts. Everett is too cold to be naked under a shirt any time of the year.

I am a good cook. I make oatmeal and other stuff too, like macaroni and cheese, and toasted tuna sandwiches. Gram used to do all the cooking, but now she sits at the kitchen table, works on her crossword puzzle and tells me what to do. She likes me to *stretch*. That means try new things.

'Don't get in a rut, Perry. Stretch yourself. Do something new,' she says. She always tells me to read instructions carefully.

'What's braising?' I ask. Cookbooks are like dictionaries. They use hard words.

'Cook in liquid,' Gram says.

'Why don't they just say that then?' I complain.

'Don't be smart!' Gram does not even have to look up from her puzzle.

Oatmeal is easy now. It used to be difficult. Gram says life is difficult. 'Life is tough, Perry. It's full of rude surprises and obstacles to overcome. Sometimes misfortune just smashes you upside the head. It's difficult. Most things in life are difficult.'

While I eat my breakfast, I do my words and write.

Gram buys me big black books from the school supply aisle at Kmart. I remember the first one I got.

'What's this?' I asked. 'It has nothing inside.' The pages were blank.

'It's a journal. A scrapbook for words. You have to do the writing.' Gram poked her skinny finger deep into my shoulder. 'It will help you remember, develop your mind.' Gram jabbed her finger again and it hurt.

'Oww!' I yelped.

'Quit your bellyaching! Now, write!' Gram said.

So that is what I do. I write. I do my words. I think. And I listen. I am an auditor.

HOLSTED'S MARINE SUPPLY is a two-storey white warehouse between the big commercial harbour and the brand-new Everett Marina. We sit right next door to Carroll's Boatyard. People come into Holsted's to buy things like lines, which are ropes, and hatches, and fenders. Whatever they need. We have a lot of stuff packed into shelves and hanging up on walls. I have worked here longer than anybody, except for Gary.

I am good at inflating fenders. It is my newest job and I have to concentrate. My hair gets in my eyes and I have to push it back. I need a haircut.

A fat man with a cigar looks over my shoulder. I can see two spots of dark wet on his blue shirt under his armpits. I am afraid his ash will drop on me and sizzle a hole through my skin. Burns hurt and they leave a scar.

'You sure you know how to do that?' The man chews on his cigar. I think that is a very stupid question, but people ask stupid questions all the time. They ask Keith, 'Can I tie up here?' in front of the post labelled NO MOORING. They ask Gary, 'Can I fish here?' by the marker NO FISHING.

Most people do not read. I read all the time.

The man asks me again if I know what I am doing. 'Hey! I'm talking to you!' he says.

'Yes, I know what I'm doing.' It is the only answer I can give. When I talk, I talk slow. This worries people.

'Hey, is he OK?' The man looks at Gary. Being OK is very important.

'Yes!' Gary and I say this at the same time. This seems to worry the man even more. When people watch me, I go slower because it makes me nervous. All I have to do is hold the fender from moving, but the man stands very close. I smell his smoky breath. When I finish, I hand him his fender.

'Here you go, sir.' It is important to be polite to customers so they will come back and spend more money.

The man chews his cigar, looks at his watch, squeezes his fender and talks to Gary, all at the same time. 'I need to get to the San Juans . . . Three weeks' vacation . . . Can we speed this up?' he asks.

Vacations are when you stop being in a hurry to go to work and start being in a hurry to go someplace else.

'My idiot son threw a fender off the stern and it wasn't tied on. You'd think he was retarded! Oh, sorry.' The man looks at me.

Retarded. Idiot. These are words I know. They mean foolish or stupid. I am not foolish. I am not stupid. I am not retarded. I am slow. Gram says we are all idiots really, and that idiot comes from the Greek word *idios.*

'It means private citizen, Perry, a loner, someone just concerned with himself!' Gram says. 'That pretty much sums up everybody I know.'

She first told me this the day I came home from school crying. Somebody called me an idiot.

'Teasing is a cross we all bear,' Gram said. 'It will make you a better person. Name-calling just proves the other guy is ignorant. Who called you that?' When she found out it was my teacher she said, 'I could just spit nails!' I remember I laughed at *spit nails*, and cried because I wanted my old teacher, Miss Elk.

It was my last day of school. I was thirteen years old. I never went back. Gram taught me herself then. I learned more from Gram than anyone else in the world.

2

Gram died on Tuesday, August 12. She did not linger, she just did not wake up. Gram said in an emergency to call the number 911 on the phone. It was our drill and we practised.

'What do you do if I don't talk to you in the morning or can't wake up?' she would ask.

'Call nine-one-one,' I would say.

'What do you do if I am lying on the floor and don't move?'

'Call nine-one-one,' I would answer.

That morning she did not wake up or talk. Her face was white and her cheek was cold when I touched it. I called 911. When the paramedics came, they covered Gram up in a cloth and took her away. I called Holsted's first.

'Gary? Gram died and I can't come into work today.' I was crying so hard that Gary had to ask me three times what happened. It is very important to let Gary know anytime I cannot come to work.

Gram's address book sits right by the phone. It is blue and has mountains on it. She put every number we ever needed inside. The back cover has our family emergency phone number list. *Emergency* means something bad has happened or something you did not expect.

The top number is my mother, Louise Crandall. She makes me nervous because she waves her hands around and does not ever look at me. The last time I saw her was when Gramp died. No one answers, so I leave a message. I hate that because machines go too fast. I just say 'Call Gram', but get confused because Gram is dead.

I am scared of calling because I do not know these people, not like I know Keith and Gary. My cousin-brother John is number two, but there is no answer, not even a recorder. Number three is my other cousin-brother, David. He answers on the second ring.

'David, this is Perry L. Crandall.' It is important to identify yourself on the phone. After I told him about Gram, he swore.

'Oh, hell!' That is what he said.

David comes to pick me up in his car and we go to get John and Louise. They say we are going to an arrangement place. Everybody talks except for me. I become a problem.

What are we going to do about Perry? I hear them ask.

It's going to be a real problem now without Gram, they say.

I am it. I am a problem.

They thought Gram took care of me, but I was the one who took care of her. That is what she said. 'We make a good pair. Just the two of us. I don't know what I would do if I didn't have you to take care of me, Perry.' She said this every single day since Gramp died.

They say things behind my back. They think I do not understand what their words mean, but I am an auditor and I hear them clearly. Louise, John and David are making arrangements. *Arrangements* are something nobody wants to do, and cost money nobody wants to spend.

In the arrangement place, I sit alone against the wall and wait. I can see what they are doing from my chair. I have two good eyes. I hear them talk. I have two good ears. Gram told me she wanted to be buried next to Gramp at Marysville Memorial Park. We made plans to buy the plot, but it cost over two thousand dollars, and we had to fix the roof instead.

Louise and John are talking to a man dressed in black. The badge on his chest says FUNERAL DIRECTOR and below that it says STEVEN. He looks like an actor, all sad, and talks low like it was his Gram. I thought he must have known her. His face looks so glum.

'Hey, Steven, did you know my Gram?' I say. His face turns red.

'Don't be stupid, Perry,' John says.

She had money set aside for a funeral. We don't have to use it all. But we don't want anybody to think we aren't doing what we should.

Didn't Grandma say not to make a fuss?

Don't worry, Mom. You'll get something out of this. We won't spend it all.

'Eight hundred bucks to cremate. What about an urn? Jesus! This brass one is over a hundred!' John's voice is squeaky.

David pulls my hand and I get up. We walk around the room looking at dead-people stuff, like caskets and vases.

'This wood box is pretty. She would like that,' I say. It is square and glossy. The tag says it is made of walnut.

'It's called an urn. It's for ashes. You're probably the only one who knows what Gram would like.' David speaks very soft and looks at me. He does not scare me as much as John and Louise.

'We should buy this box,' I say.

The others stop talking and look at me.

'Yeah. Well. You're not paying for it,' John says.

'I can. I can pay for it.' My voice comes out much louder than I want. I have $517 in my chequing account and payday is next week. My cheque-book is in my pocket. I do not tell them about my savings account. Gram said not to. 'Perry, your savings account is your own goddamn business! Don't you say a thing! Ever! It's for your future,' Gram warned. 'Our family's a bunch of vultures and don't you forget it!'

Vultures are animals, but they can be people too.

Gram is dead now. I keep forgetting this and start to worry. I know this because I reach up to my forehead with my fingers and feel wrinkles. Gram called them worry lines. I worry because none of these people are on my list. I do not have to do what they say, but I am afraid not to.

'Put your chequebook away. You're going to need all your money to live on, Perry,' David says. He is the only one besides me who looks sad.

Louise sits in a chair, putting on more red lipstick and using a tiny little mirror. Her hair is now whitish-gold.

'Too bad about Grandma, Perry,' she says, and blots her lips on a tissue.

Gram. Her name is Gram, but I do not tell Louise this. It is something she should know.

They keep talking. That is OK.

We need to decide about Perry. What's he going to do?

Well, he can't live with us and Mom's not exactly known for her care and feeding of children.

Isn't he on disability? Doesn't he get cheques?

I thought he worked.

Well, his employer should be the one to take care of him. They should be responsible. We shouldn't have to take care of him.

I chose the most beautiful box for Gram while my cousin-brothers argued. I chose the one I knew she would like. And wrote the cheque to Steven.

Later that night, when I am home alone, I look at Gram's picture and wonder where she is.

I remember asking questions when Gramp passed away. 'Where do we go when we die, Gram?'

She grabbed me tight to her chest and said, 'We go into wind and rain. We turn into the sea and the fog. That's where we go, Perry. Each time it rains, think of Gramp. Each time the wind blows he will be there, and when I die, I'll be there too.'

I think that is true. I hear drips on the roof as it starts to rain. I think of Gram. And I wait for the wind to blow.

GRAM'S MEMORIAL SERVICE was held at Sullivan Park on Silver Lake. It was *most appropriate*, John said. That meant it was close to where everyone had to get to that day and it was free. All of the family came, except for my mother Louise and David's wife, Elaine.

My cousin-brothers come by an hour early to pick me up. While I talk to David, John takes a lady carrying a pink poodle around to look at Gram's house. They walk across the lawn and stare into the front window, but do not go inside. I am glad because it is a mess. Gram and I have a lot of crap.

'Who is she?' I ask David.

'John's new wife, CeCe,' he says.

'What does she do? Is she a lawyer?' Almost everybody in my family is a lawyer.

'No, she shops.' David gives a short laugh.

There's nothing of any value. The property is a gold mine though.

How long are we staying? I have a hair appointment.

Only as long as we have to. Twenty minutes max.

Even though it is not winter, the park is wet. Rain falls out of the sky. My cousin-brothers stand together. John's wife CeCe sits in his car with her poodle. She does not want it to get wet. I never knew dogs could be pink. David says it is dyed, but it looks alive to me. It even barked once.

The minister shakes my hand and says he is very sorry for my loss. He tells me Gram is in a much better place. What a crock, I think. Gram would have wanted to be at our house. At our place. *Crock* means untrue or a lie. It can also mean a pot you cook beans in.

I am happy because I get to take Gram home with me in her box.

'You can put her up in the mountains,' David says to me.

Gram would not want to be in a park or in the mountains. She wanted to be next to Gramp at Marysville Memorial Park. I do not tell them this. They do not seem to care where Gram wants to be. They all talk above my head in the parking lot, before David drives me home.

How is he going to live? What provisions did Gram make for Perry?

There's no will. It will be up to us.

But John, she said—

David! Shut up about it. There IS NO WILL. You think Grandma trusted lawyers after what happened? The estate will be split between us!

I listen to John and David. Gram always told me she was concerned about what would happen to me when she was gone. 'You're so goddamned suggestible,' she said. 'Suggestible and honest! A terrible combination!

They'll take advantage of you.' She would shake her head and click her tongue. *Advantage* means up to no good. That was why she would not put any of them on our list.

John drives behind us all the way to Gram's house and follows us to the door. CeCe stays in the car and complains through the open window.

I'm going to be late! You have to wrap this up!

David and John go from room to room looking for papers. We have to find papers. I help.

Here we go. Christ! Hardly anything in the accounts. What did they live on? Social Security . . . Perry's job . . . What does he do, anyway?

Christ, David, I don't know! Here it is. The title. Thank God THAT wasn't mortgaged. He's on the title to the house. Jesus! What'd she do that for?

We could sell it and invest the proceeds for him. We'll need to have him sign a Power of Attorney. Elaine can take care of it.

Elaine! That bitch. Just because you listen to her doesn't mean I have to! Besides, it should be split between all of us. It's only fair.

BLAH! BLAH! A car horn blares and John opens the front door.

'We have to leave now!' CeCe screams. She is very loud.

'You coming over to the house, David?' John says.

'Yeah. I'll drop by later with Elaine. She wants to be there.'

'It's a *Family* Meeting, David. Elaine doesn't *need* to be there.'

'Yeah, well, I'll let you tell her that,' David mutters, and turns to me. 'Don't worry, we'll take care of you,' he says, and pats me on the shoulder.

I say 'OK', and go back inside.

WHEN A PERSON DIES, their body goes away, but their voice stays. I hear Gram every day. *Be careful, Perry*, she says. *Don't be smart*, she warns.

I would rather have her with me.

My family says they will be over to dispose of the assets. *Assets* are things that can be used to pay debts. They are also an advantage, the dictionary says. This is most likely what Gram meant when she told me John, David and Louise would take advantage.

Louise comes by first. Her hair is now red and matches her lipstick.

'I just wanted a couple of things to remind me of Grandma.' She holds a Kleenex to her face, but her eyes are not wet. Louise takes Gram's jewellery box and the mother-of-pearl brush and mirror set. She sets these things carefully in the front seat of her car. When she comes back inside, she goes straight to the dining room and opens the china cabinet.

'Is this real or fake?' Louise picks up all of Gram's things, and turns them over in her hands. The china. The crystal. 'I'll have to take these with me. Find me a box, Perry. I'll have them all appraised.'

John comes next. He brings his own boxes.

'Where's the boat model?' he asks. 'That's an original. I'd like to have that. What about the watercolours? I thought Gramp had a Winslow Homer. How about those signed prints? Do you know where they are?'

I have trouble answering all his questions.

I help him wrap Gramp's model so it does not get scratched. John's eyes are dry. As dry as mine are wet. I have to wipe my nose on my sleeve.

'For Christ's sake, use a handkerchief and stop sniffing.' John's eyes move from side to side. Looking. I do not know what he is looking for. I hope he finds it and leaves. He fills all his boxes and I help carry them to his car. When his car rolls out of the driveway, he does not wave goodbye.

I sweep the kitchen and put the dishes that Louise did not take back into the cupboard. A car horn honks outside. It is David.

'You are last, David.' I say this as he walks through the door.

David looks around. 'God, this takes me back.' He walks slowly from room to room. 'Where's Gramp's boat model? Did you know I helped with that? I did the masts and cut the sails.' When he sees my face, he says, 'John took it, didn't he? What about the watercolours? Who took the china?'

'We could not find Homer,' I tell him, 'but John took the signed prints and the model. He said it might be worth a lot of money,' I say.

David shakes his head. 'Jesus!' he says, and turns away. 'I should have gotten here sooner. What's left? Nothing but a bunch of crap!' He kicks a box. I jump. 'One lousy point! Did you know that?' He looks at me.

'What?' I ask.

'The bar exam,' he says. 'I missed it by one point. I failed it twice. That's why I got my MBA. One point.' He shakes his head. 'Mom and John never let me forget it. Neither does Elaine. Elaine passed on her first try. She's brilliant. Really brilliant.'

He does not look like he thinks she is brilliant. He sounds sad.

David walks into the living room, to Gram's bedroom, and back again. I follow behind. He opens drawers and cupboards.

'Isn't there anything left? Elaine wondered about the jewellery?'

'Louise took the jewellery, but the coin collection is still here,' I tell him. I just remembered this. Neither John nor Louise asked about it.

'Well, that's something,' he says. 'That might satisfy her.' He smiles slowly. 'Did you know I sorted all Gramp's pennies and dimes when I was little? I used to bring Gramp all my change from my lunch money at school. He'd look through it and pick out the ones he wanted.'

I listen to David talk. I am not afraid of him, but I still hear Gram say, *Careful.* 'David is weak,' Gram used to say. 'More like his father than John is. He's a weak man. Exactly like your father. That's why they married the same kind of woman. The kind that wears the pants and spends the money.'

I help carry the coin collection out to his BMW. David gives me a hard hug around the shoulders and leaves whistling.

I call Holsted's to leave a message for Keith. He does not have a phone on his boat. I will need help to empty the house before it is sold. There is a lot of stuff to clear out and pack. Gram's housedresses and aprons. Her shoes. I set one dress aside to keep. The yellow one with green stripes. It smells like Gram. I love that dress. She always wore it to bingo.

Keith is my friend and gives me a hand when it is time to move.

'Why are you selling the house?' Keith asks this for the eighth or twelfth time. I have lost count. 'I sure don't understand your family,' he says over and over. 'That wife of your brother's. What's her name? Elaine? She's a bitch on wheels!'

I looked at Elaine's feet the last time I saw her and I did not see any roller skates. I think he has her mixed up with someone else.

'They say it's for the best. It will be better for my future.'

'Better for them, maybe.' Keith is what Gram used to call cynical. *Cynical* means you are honest in a nasty way.

Keith has a 1982 Toyota truck that has rust spots and is painted with grey primer. He calls his truck Yo because the To and Ta are rubbed off the tailgate. Yo carries five loads to the dump. 'A hell of a crap hauler!' Keith says, and slaps Yo's dashboard with his hand.

It took Keith and me two weeks to finish because we could only work on the house after getting off work at Holsted's. We had to hurry, because John said the house would close soon. That did not mean the doors would shut, it meant I would have to move out.

'You'll have to find somewhere else to live.' John told me this.

He got mad when I called him to let him know we needed more time.

'Come on, Perry. How much time does it take to get rid of all that garbage?' John yelled. 'Christ! Just use a backhoe!' and he laughed over the phone. I did not know what was funny about a backhoe.

'What's a backhoe?' I asked Keith. 'Is that like a tractor?'

He got pissed. 'The shits!' he said. 'The money-grubbers!'

Keith asked why he wasn't invited to Gram's funeral.

'John said it was just for the family,' I said. 'Gary wasn't invited either.' I feel bad about that.

'Your family is a bunch of *fucks*. You hear me, Per?'

I start to cry again.

'Don't worry, Per. You'll get through this. Everybody does,' he says, and pats my back. 'Life goes on, Per. It surely does go on.'

Keith and I pile old crossword puzzle books in boxes for the dump. I take one to keep. Gram's handwriting is like a spider's web, all wavy and thin. I like to look at it and think of her doing the crosswords.

'Why'd you let them take all the valuable things?' Keith is my friend. Friends are people who get mad when they think someone does something unfair to you. He does not understand.

'I got all the things I wanted,' I tell him. 'The melamine dishes decorated with anchors and flags that Gram and Gramp used to have on their boat, the free silverware from when we bought groceries at QFC.'

I also have my clothes, four shoe boxes of Gram's papers and pictures, and two large boxes of stuff marked SAVE. I can keep all the dictionaries and crossword puzzle books I want. I find three thesauruses. I do not know what a thesaurus is. I have to look it up in the dictionary.

'Sounds like a frigging dinosaur.' Keith does not care about words.

'It means treasure. A book of words,' I say. 'Gram always said words are the key to life. She would want me to keep these.' *Treasure.* I like that.

I am responsible for Gram's house until it is sold. I mow the lawn and wash the windows until they shine. I vacuum the living room carpet, scrub the kitchen floor tiles and hose off the driveway. Keith helps me.

John said we would not get much money for Gram's house. We did escrow. I think it has something to do with birds. John told me there would be a lot of paperwork, but I had to go to work at Holsted's.

'We can handle it for you. Sign here.' He gave me a paper. It gave him my Power to the house so he could write my name thirty-two times. Escrow is when you have to write your name thirty-two times. That is what he said.

Keith takes me back to Gram's house for the last time. John hands me an envelope with a $500 cheque inside marked HOUSE SALE. I will put $250 in my chequing account and $250 in my savings account. Spend half and save half, Gram always said. I would rather have had Gram and our house than $500. It does not seem like much money for a house.

'That's it!' John smiles over my head. Elaine stands behind him, next to David, and Louise stands on the other side. I hand David the key to Gram's house. Elaine grabs it out of his hand and John grabs it out of hers.

They make me sweat and my armpits smell. Gram always said she knew when they were up to something.

'They have that look!' she would say.

'What look?' I always asked.

'Don't be smart,' Gram would say. Her lips would stretch tight and her brown eyes would squint.

They have that look now, I hear her say inside my ear.

I HAVE NO PLACE to live so Gary lets me move into the apartment right above Holsted's where Otis the security guard used to stay, before he stole money out of the cash register and was arrested.

'This will work fine, Perry. You need a place to live and I need someone to live over the store at night,' Gary said.

To get to my apartment I have to climb up a long outside stairway right above Holsted's main entry. My front door opens into a large space. Half is the kitchen and half is the living room. The kitchen side has a stove, refrigerator and counter.

'The sink leaks so you have to keep a bucket underneath,' Gary warns.

I have four cupboards. I put my cans and cereal in the top ones and keep dishes in the bottom ones. The living room is neat because it has a big picture window that has a view of the parking lot and marina. I can look down and see who comes into Holsted's. That is so cool.

A long wall across from the door fits Gram's couch perfectly. My table and chairs sit next to the window. I put Gram's double bed in the bedroom. Gram's old white nightstand is on one side with my clock radio on top.

There is a short hall off the living room with a washer and drier at the end, a bathroom on one side and my bedroom door on the other. I have a toilet, sink and shower, but no tub. That is OK. I do not like bathtubs because that is where they put murdered people on TV.

Keith helped me carry all of my furniture up to my apartment. He only said the F-word twice and the S-word once when he pinched his finger between the doorframe and the sofa.

Keith's twenty-seven-foot Catalina sailboat *Diamond Girl* is moored in the first slip on C dock. 'She's named after the best song in the world,' that's what Keith says. He first heard it the day he left Vietnam. He calls it Nam.

I can see his boat from my window and when he sees me he waves. I like to visit Keith, but I do not want to bother him. I would like to live on a twenty-seven-foot Catalina. That would be so cool.

I have Gram's ashes with me. Her wooden urn stays on the bottom shelf of my bedside table. It is like us being together again, but she does not talk out loud. She is only in my head now.

My life is different with Gram gone. I do not go to bingo any more on Tuesdays. I have no one to play with because Keith does not like bingo. I only asked him to go once.

'You want to go to bingo, Keith?'

'Stick needles in my eye, Per! Go inside a Catholic church? Not on your life!' That is what Keith says when he really does not want to do something.

On Sunday morning, I wake up early, walk to Marina Handy Mart and get a paper and box of powdered-sugar doughnuts or cinnamon rolls. It gives me a chance to see Cherry. When I get home, I sit upstairs and watch out my window until Keith wakes up. If he wants me to come over, he will wave. Then we will sit together in his cockpit and eat cinnamon rolls or doughnuts. It does not matter if it is cold or raining. I feed seagulls pieces of my doughnut, which makes Keith mad.

'Jesus, Per! Don't encourage the little shits!' He throws empty beer cans at them, but never hits any because aluminium beer cans are too light. They end up in the water and he has to get a net with a long handle and scoop them up out of the Sound so the harbourmaster doesn't get pissed off.

I do not have to share the Sunday paper, because Keith is not interested in the newspaper except for sports. That makes me sad because I like to share. It takes me all week to read the paper. Gram used to say I got my money's worth. Getting your money's worth is funny. I mean, you mostly get something for money, except maybe when you sell a house.

Cherry works the register at Marina Handy Mart. She has a pretty smile and a beautiful face. I like to take my time and visit on Sundays. It is hard not to stare.

'I'm sorry about your Gram,' she says, and plays with the silver ball on her tongue. Cherry looks sorry. I hear her click the stud against her teeth.

'Give me five Lotto tickets and a Slurpee, please.' I set a bag of Hershey's Kisses on the counter. I do not pick up the *Enquirer.*

'Don't you want the paper?' Cherry's hair is very colourful. It is green and blue stripes with brown.

'No.' My throat is tight and my eyes fill with water like from sad movies.

'You can do the puzzle, you know. It might make you feel better,' she says. Her eyes are dark brown like a seal except they are not wet.

'OK, then.' I have a hard time getting words out of my mouth.

'Cherry is a very nice girl,' Gram would say. 'Even though she has earrings all over her face and tattoos up her butt!'

I do not think Cherry has tattoos up her butt. She has a flower on her shoulder, a cat on one arm and a chain thing around her ankle. Cherry told me the only one that hurt was the one on her foot. That is because it was on bone.

'The ones that hurt are close to the bone,' she says.

Being without Gram is close to the bone, I think. I want to stay and talk to Cherry, but I do not know what to say, so I leave.

I check my lottery tickets on Sunday. When no numbers match, I throw the tickets into the trash. I work on the crossword for six days straight. I get three answers, but it is harder without Gram. Crossword puzzles are difficult when there is no one to help. Most things in life are difficult, Gram used to say. Everything is harder without Gram.

I still have to do my wash on Wednesdays, but it is only my clothes and not Gram's. I only have two small loads. I used to do four loads. I would have sheets, towels, Gram's underwear and her pyjamas. Those are the whites. My shirts, jeans and Gram's dresses are the darks. Gram said it was important to have the dark clothes and the white ones separate so they do not run or change colours. Thinking of this makes me sad, so I have to cry again.

I stayed in my pyjamas and put all my other clothes into the washer. I dumped soap in, turned the dial and closed the lid. At Gram's house on days off, I always cleaned the bathroom and Gram did the kitchen floor. Now I have to do all the chores. It takes a long time.

I am scrubbing the toilet bowl with a brush when I hear BANG! CRASH! CRASH! I run into the hall. There is soapy water all over the floor. I slip and fall on my butt. It hurts. I crawl on my hands and knees and have to use all my clean towels to mop it up. The washer is still leaking and I turn it off quick so it does not explode and kill me.

It is a very bad day.

My pyjama bottoms are soaked. I must have made a lot of noise because Keith and Gary come running upstairs and bang on my door. I am embarrassed, all dripping wet, but I open the door and tell them what happened.

'My clothes are dirty. The washer is broken. There's water all over the floor. I have nothing to wear. Gram is dead and there's no one to help me.'

I cannot stop crying and get the hiccups. Gary goes into my kitchen and brings me back a glass of water. He makes me sit on the couch and hands me a paper towel to wipe my face. Paper towels are rough and they hurt. It is better to use toilet paper, but I do not tell him that. It would hurt his feelings.

'Have you had anything to eat?' Keith asks. He looks around at the mess in my apartment. I am ashamed. My elbow throbs and my knee prickles.

'No,' I tell him. That is the truth. I forgot to buy my cereal.

Keith is my friend. He goes down to his boat and brings me back a Snickers bar and a sweatshirt and pair of jeans. Gary finds Gramp's old belt in my drawer. Keith's pants are too big for me. They drag on the floor, but I do not care. He helps throw my wet laundry in the back of Yo and drives me to Nick's Laundromat. He keeps me company and we eat Cheetos while my laundry washes and dries. He even helps me fold everything.

'You let me know when you need help like this. You hear, Per?' Keith tells me it's going to take a while for me to adjust. 'Gary and I will be here to help you. Call us. OK?'

Adjust means that you have to change because things are different. When things are different, even though you do not like them, you have to adjust.

Gary ordered a new washer-drier from Sears and had them take the old one away. The new one is tall and white. The drier is on top and the washer part is on the bottom. It is a Kenmore and I know how to make it work.

'Hey, Keith! Can I wash your clothes? I can wash your clothes.' This is my first good idea since Gram died.

'Yeah, that would be great, Per. Thanks!' He gives me a pat on the back.

Now we are both happy. I guess I needed to wash more than just my own clothes to not be so sad. Gary gives me all the rags and towels from Holsted's to clean too. I have lots of clothes to wash now.

Life goes on. Gram's voice is in my ear.

I LEAN AGAINST the Handy Mart counter and spread my things out so Cherry can ring them up. I like to take my time when Cherry is working.

'No PayDay?' she asks. Cherry remembers everything I buy.

'No. I have to watch my pennies now,' I say. That is what Gram always said. *Watching your pennies* means you cannot spend too much on extra things like PayDay candy bars and big bags of Hershey's Kisses.

The utility company sent me the last electric bill from the house. It was $216.94. John mailed it and wrote a letter saying that it was my responsibility because Gram and I were the last ones who lived there. It took almost half my cheque from Holsted's.

The bill from Gram's ambulance ride was $1,198.32. They told me to send what I could, so I talked to Gary. He helped me figure it out. I mail them a cheque for $56.28 each month. This means I can run out of money before my next cheque if I am not careful.

'What do David and John say? Can't they give you a hand?' Gary asked.

'It is my responsibility,' I say.

'Use some of your savings, Perry. You have savings, don't you?' he asks.

'Gram said it's for my future.' I cannot use it for bills.

'Your future is now!' I can tell Gary does not understand Gram's rules. She was ahead of him on my list. Even dead, she comes first. It is very important to have rules and save for the future.

I like to buy the *Enquirer* now because it reminds me of Gram, and that is important. It is only seventy-five cents. I buy a tuna sandwich from Marina Handy Mart because it is cheaper than Gilly's fake crab. I buy five Lotto tickets because Gram would want me to. I buy a much smaller bag of Hershey's Kisses. I save them as treats and eat them only when I miss Gram too much. I have to make them last a long time because there are lots of times I miss her, like on bingo nights.

Cherry puts everything in a plastic bag for me. Her fingernails are interesting. They have little pictures of animals on them.

'I do them myself with a kit from the drugstore. You like them?' Cherry wriggles them in front of me. 'So where's your friend, Keith?' she asks.

'At work.' I know he will be by later for beer. Cherry knows this too, but she always asks where he is. I try to think of something else to say. 'Your fingers are cool. Is it hard to do?'

'Nah, it's easy. You just paste them on. Well, tell Keith hi from me. OK?'

The door whooshes shut as I leave to go back to work.

Sunday morning, I go to Marina Handy Mart and buy the paper. It is heavy and full of ads. I like to read the ads. They are interesting and I learn a lot, like the Toyota Prius can get fifty-five miles to the gallon or 650 miles between fill-ups and there is a company that makes address labels with any picture you want on them. Stuff like that. I also bought a box of powdered-sugar doughnuts, which I like better than cinnamon rolls.

I eat my doughnuts, read my paper and watch for Keith to move around on his boat. I have to watch carefully. I cannot visit him unless he waves.

He waves today so I come down.

It is cool, but there is no wind. Keith sits on a blanket in his cockpit and holds a full glass in his hand.

'What are you drinking?' I ask. It looks red. Like blood.

'The hair of the dog that bit me, Per!' he says.

'What?' I ask. I do not see any hair in his drink and Keith does not look like he has a dog bite. There is no bandage on him that I can see.

'It's just tomato juice and vodka. Healthy, Per,' he says. 'Vegetables and cereal! Nothing healthier for breakfast! Especially if you have a hangover.'

A hangover is when you drink too much alcohol all at once. Keith is almost always hung over. He gives me plain juice without the vodka. Gram never allowed me to drink vodka or any kind of alcohol.

'Cherry says hi,' I say.

'She's working today?' Keith sounds surprised.

'No, that was Wednesday, I think.' I feel bad I did not remember to tell him.

'Thanks for nothing.' Keith uses mad words, but laughs at the same time.

We sit on the rocking boat together. *Diamond Girl* has white fibreglass with dark blue trim. There is grey dirt smudged on the gelcoat. 'I could wax and polish her for you.' And I rub a spot with my sleeve. 'Keith, you want me to clean your decks with a hose and scrubbing brush?' I ask. It is important to help your friends.

'Yeah sure,' he says. 'We'll get around to it one day.'

It is quiet. I can hear waves plop against *Diamond Girl.*

'Anyone ever tell you you're a peaceful guy?' Keith leans back. His eyes are squinting even though it is cloudy. 'You're like having a cat that talks. Company that doesn't take a lot of energy to maintain.'

'No one ever says peaceful. They call me retarded and other stuff,' I say.

'Smack 'em the next time they call you that,' Keith says.

I cannot punch. I am not a fighter.

'OK,' I say, and throw another piece of doughnut to the seagulls when I see Keith close his eyes.

WINNING TICKET SOLD

That is the Monday-morning headline. I am happy for that person, but Keith and I have to paint underneath a boat. Bottom paint is very thick and we have to stir it with a paddle attached to an electric drill. That is Keith's job. Opening the lid is mine. I use a hammer and a screwdriver.

SPLAT! The lid flies off and splashes blue boat paint all over my shirt.

'Shit!' I put my hand over my mouth. I did not mean to say that. It just flew out past my tongue. I hear Gram in my head. *Wash that mouth out with soap!*

'Perry, I'm surprised at you.' Keith only uses Perry when I have done something wrong. He will say, 'Perry, you threw away the invoice,' or 'Perry, you put the label gun in the wrong drawer.'

Painting boat bottoms is hard work because we have to use a roller and hold our arms up high. My shirt is dirty and stiff with paint when I get home. I am sad because it is my favourite shirt and used to be Gramp's. It even has his name on the front pocket. *George Crandall.* I put it in the washer right away but the paint does not come out. I decide to keep it anyway, and say out loud, 'This will be my paint shirt.' I try to use Gram's voice.

Gram never threw anything away. I decide that I am just like her, and hang Gramp's shirt back up in my closet.

WINNER HAS NOT COME FORWARD TO CLAIM 12 MILL PRIZE

The Tuesday headline is still on the front page, but higher. Gary has the paper on his desk. I read the story while I wait for him to call the guy to fix our air compressor. It broke after I inflated six fenders in a row. WHOOOSH! And then nothing. Gary calls Fritz Dias on the phone and has him come by. Fritz repairs all our machines.

'What you do, Perry? You broke it? How you do that?' Fritz says, and laughs. He is from Spain or Africa or maybe Germany and very smart about machines. He smiles all the time and has a gold tooth. That is so cool, I think.

'Just the diaphragm. Here, see?' He spreads the parts to the compressor all over the floor. 'You press the button and here, see this? That moves and then over here, see this valve and this hose? The air comes out here.'

He talks to me like a real person while he takes it apart. He never treats me like I am retarded. I help by handing him his tools.

'You're a great helper, Perry,' he says.

WINNING TICKET COMES FROM EVERETT MARINA HANDY MART

Wednesday's headline is right in the top middle. I have the day off and go downstairs to pick up Keith's dirty laundry. Keith is working in the back office. The newspaper is lying on the counter. Nobody is looking at it, so I borrow the front page and read the story while I cook my oatmeal. It is all about the Marina Handy Mart and there is an interview with the manager. I wonder if Cherry knows the person who won. I can walk over to Handy Mart later and maybe buy a sandwich and talk to her. She will be famous because she works there and they sold the ticket. That is so cool.

I have all my Wednesday chores to do. My oatmeal is too hot to eat, so I start the washer before breakfast. I hear the CHUG CHUG CHUG of the machine as I pour milk and sprinkle sugar. It is like having company. Keith's jeans are in the first load along with two of my shirts.

The Sunday paper is on my company TV tray and my cereal bowl is on my regular one. I pick up the front page.

The Lotto numbers are in a line at the bottom.

I do not have to check mine because someone else has already won. I wonder why they have not picked up their money yet. If I won, I would get my money right away. I miss Gram. She would read the numbers and I would check them. I take a bite of oatmeal, then get up and find my sack. I pull out my Lotto ticket. I go back to the sofa and make believe Gram is next to me.

'Gram, you want to read the numbers?' I ask.

'OK,' I say. I pretend I am her.

'Here they are.' I set them in front of me on the TV tray. 'Hey, Gram! We have the first number right! OK, here we go. Oh-nine.'

I try to make my voice like Gram's. '*Yep.*'

'One-oh.'

'*Yep.*'

'One-nine.'

'*Yep.*'

'Three-two.'

'*Yep.*'

'Four-four.'

'*Yep.*'

'Four-seven.'

'*Yep.*'

'Oh! Oh! Gram! We got all the numbers!' The spit goes out of my mouth. All the numbers are there. I read them twice. I read them again just to make sure. It was me all along. I am the winner. I am lucky!

I jump up so high my cereal bowl flips off my tray. I can hear my feet hit the floor as I dance up and down. Oatmeal splashes all over and I slip.

'Holy cow!' I yell. It is OK to say cow. Cow is not a bad word.

Goddamn! I hear Gram say. *Goddamn!*

Twelve million dollars, I hear her say.

How much is that?

I sit back down on the sofa and bounce.

Perry, it is important to think at times like these. I hear Gram's voice in my head. *Think.*

What do you do when you have the numbers? How long do I have before

they give my money away? I turn my ticket over. There are instructions on
the back: 'Claim prizes in excess of $600 at the lottery office in Olympia.'

What is excess? I step in more oatmeal. Gram's dictionary is on the floor.
Excess. *More than. Surplus.* I know $12 million is way more than $600.

I need to go to the office in Olympia. My armpits are wet and I am hot.
I open my window to cool off. I do not know where to go in Olympia. I do
not even know where Olympia is.

Who should I talk to? Who should I call? I see Gram's blue phone book
with the list of emergency numbers. I wonder if this is a family emergency.
Maybe John knows. He is smart. I dial his number.

'John, can you take me to Olympia?'

'Perry! Why the hell are you calling me? It's the middle of the week, for
Christ's sake! I'm busy! I'm at work. Find someone else to take you to
Olympia.' He hangs up before I can explain.

When I call David, his answering machine comes on. I drop the phone. It
is hard to leave a message. His machine goes too fast. I do not have Louise's
phone number. I decide to bother Keith at Holsted's.

'Keith, I have to go to Olympia. It's really important. Can you take me?'

Keith does not sound at all bothered. 'Yeah, no problem, Per. Yo will
need some gas, but sure, I can take you.' Keith is my friend. A friend is
someone who does what you want without asking why.

I count twenty-three ones in my wallet. I hope gas is not more than twenty-
three dollars. Hey, I am rich, I think. I sing in my head and then out loud.

'I am rich. I am rich. I am rich,' and bounce on the couch.

3

'I told Holsted it was an emergency.' Keith calls Gary by his last name
when he is in a good mood. He turns on the radio to the oldies station.

Keith used to be a hippie, then an army guy, then a ferry captain. Now
he is a drunk. That is what he says. Gram used to call him a philosopher.

'That's a five-dollar word to describe someone who doesn't have a red
cent,' Keith told her. Gram just laughed at him. She liked Keith.

We head south down the freeway. Keith drives extremely fast. I feel for
my lottery ticket through my shirt pocket. It is still there.

'Why do you need to go to Olympia?' he asks.

When I tell him he swerves into the other lane.

'Holy fucking shit! You're fucking kidding me! Are you sure? Holy fuck!' His hands are shaking on the wheel. 'You need some help on this. Shit!' He gets very quiet.

I have my wallet out and lay ten one-dollar bills on the seat. 'For the gas. I hope it is enough,' I say.

That is all it takes to make him go off again. 'Jesus! Shit!'

Keith's grey hair is long, greasy and tied in a ponytail. I think he looks like Willie Nelson from the back. From the front, he looks like an old fat white guy, but I do not tell him this. It would not be nice.

'Where do we have to go?' His hands squeeze the wheel like a sponge.

'PO box two-one-six-seven Olympia.' I read this slowly off the ticket.

'That's only a box number. We need the address. We'll have to ask someone when we get to Olympia.'

It takes three hours in traffic, plus we do not know exactly where we need to go. We stop at the Pancake House when we finally get to Olympia.

'Everybody knows where the lottery office is! It's just a few blocks over!' Pamela, the cashier, says. We order something to drink. She flutters her eyes at Keith and gives us free refills on our coffee. We are both grinning. 'Did you win or something?' she asks.

Keith gets quiet and looks at me. I stop bouncing. We push our lips straight.

'No, we just need to find out where it is, just in case,' Keith says.

'Yeah, in case,' I add.

I do not finish my third cup of coffee because it can make you pee and I do not know if the lottery office has a bathroom.

The building we want is eight blocks away. The outside is made of concrete painted light green. There is only a small sign above the door. I am surprised that it is not big and fancy, as they have all that money. The people at the lottery office are friendly and smile. They make me a giant cardboard cheque and take my picture while I hold it.

'Won't this be cool to hang up on my wall?' I ask Keith.

'Yeah, it'll be cool all right,' he agrees.

I get a copy of the picture right there from an instant camera. I am smiling, but my hair hangs over my eyes. I need a haircut. My ears stick out and my eyes look dark, like Gram's. I think I look pretty good, but Keith pushes my hair off my forehead and says I look goofy. I laugh. Keith is my friend.

Keith pulls my arm, bends down, whispers in my ear. 'You got to get some good financial advice, and not from those brothers of yours!'

'They like me to call them cousins.' I feel important. Everybody is looking at me.

'Trust me, after this they'll be your fucking blood brothers.' Keith's eyes are narrow and he has white spit in the corner of his mouth. He looks like that cool jungle guy hunting on Animal Planet. That was when Gram and I could still afford cable and had a TV that worked. This gives me an idea.

'Hey,' I say. 'I can get Animal Planet now.' This makes me excited. 'Hey!' I think of something else. I have a lot of good ideas today. 'I can get a TV!'

Margery from the lottery office wants to talk with me. 'Do you have family?' she asks. 'I mean someone who helps you.'

I know what she really means. She thinks I am retarded. She thinks I cannot take care of myself. I hate that, and it upsets me.

'Hey, he's not retarded if that's what you're getting at!' Keith yells.

I am glad Keith yelled because my words get jumbled and thick in my throat. I stop being angry and get embarrassed. I feel better when Margery apologises. She leads us into another office when a bunch of people with cameras and microphones crowd into the main room.

First, they ask to see my ticket and a man checks all the numbers. Next, I have to sign the back of the ticket with my address and phone number. Then I show my Washington State Picture ID and Social Security card. I have to fill out lots of paperwork so that Uncle Sam gets his share. I do not have an Uncle Sam. People just say that when they mean taxes. Taxes are something you have to pay even though you do not want to. Finally, the lottery people ask me what I want to do. They tell me I can get my money once a year for twenty-five years or all at once. If I take my money all at once, I only get half.

Keith stands behind me full of advice. 'Don't take the lump sum!' He hisses like a snake. 'It's a rip-off, Per. If you take it all you'd only get six mill, plus all the taxes! You'd only end up with three mill at the end.'

Three million dollars sounds good to me, but Keith says payments are the way to go. Winning the lottery is very complicated.

'You can take sixty days to decide,' Margery says.

I tell her I do not need sixty days, I can decide right now. 'I want the payments like Keith says so I can buy a TV,' I tell her.

Margery looks like she does not think a TV is a good idea. She squeezes her lips tight like Gram used to as she gives me papers to sign. She tells me the amount I will get each year, but I am so excited I forget. Margery tells me to wait while they put a smaller cheque into an envelope.

Keith remembers for me. 'Nearly four hundred fucking thousand dollars a year for twenty-five years! You need to think about what you'll do when you quit working at Holsted's,' Keith says. 'You can travel. Do whatever you want.'

That makes me sad. 'I don't want to quit my job. I like working at Holsted's!' I say.

Maybe there is a rule when you win the lottery you have to give your job away to someone who needs it. I hope not.

Margery leads Keith and me out through a hidden door in the back, but all the men with cameras see us leave the parking lot. As we drive back home, they follow us in blue and silver cars. Keith is a great driver. We double back, make two very exciting turns and run a red light. It is like a movie when guys are in a car getting away with money from a bank.

We would have escaped like those guys, except Keith forgets we need gas. We run out just after Tacoma. The reporters from the newspapers and magazines are very nice. They give us a ride to the gas station and talk to me while Keith puts gas in an orange can.

What are you going to do with the money?

How will this change your life?

Do you plan to give any to charity, to your family, to the church?

The questions come so fast all I can do is smile and nod.

Keith yells, 'Don't say anything, Per! They can turn what you say around until you don't recognise it. No! Don't let them take pictures!'

Keith is a good boxer. He misses one reporter, but catches another full in the face and gives him a bloody nose. They don't seem to mind and take us back to Yo anyway. When we get there, a policeman is writing a ticket.

'When's the last time you registered your truck?' he asks Keith.

I feel bad I got him into trouble. I wrote him a cheque for five hundred dollars right there.

'It's a loan,' Keith said. 'I consider it only a loan. I'll pay you back.'

A loan to a friend means you don't have to pay it back. I know this.

'That's OK,' I say. And we get into Yo and drive away.

THE SUN IS RED, orange, or maybe yellow, and bounces through the sky when I look at it through Yo's back window. It is Yo bouncing, but I pretend it is the sun. I like to bounce.

It takes only two hours for us to get home from Olympia. I look out Yo's window at the sun and think about being rich.

I am rich. That is so cool.

When we get back to my apartment, we stomp up the stairs together and Keith helps me nail my big cheque on the wall. We use long brass tacks and one of my heavy black dress shoes.

'Hey, someone's running up the stairs,' Keith says.

It is Gary. 'What the hell are you guys doing up here? Sounds like a herd of elephants!' Gary's office is right underneath my living room.

'Hey Gary, guess what? I won the lottery,' I say.

He smiles at me. 'That's very funny, Perry.'

Then he stops speaking and his eyes get big. He walks over and touches the cheque nailed to the wall. His face turns white. I have to help him sit down on my chair by the door.

'Shit! You're kidding, right? You have to get some financial advice. Is that the only cheque they gave you? Did they give you a smaller one? They did, didn't they? You'd better put it right in the bank. Shit! We have to take him to the bank, Keith!' Gary looks sick. Maybe he has indigestion.

'You need a Tums, Gary? I got a Tums.' I always carried them for Gram. 'You want Pepto-Bismol? I got Pepto-Bismol.' I have everything.

The cheque that Margery gave me is folded up tight in my wallet. Gary puts his head between his knees and takes deep breaths. Keith has to help me fill out my deposit slip there are so many zeros. I write big, but very neatly. I have to make the zeros skinny so all of them fit inside the lines.

Gary refuses to ride in Yo, so we ride to Everett Federal in his Jeep Cherokee. Keith and Gary are in the front and I sit by myself in the back. I feel important like I am a sports guy just like Tiger Woods, except I am not brown and I do not know how to play golf.

They know me at my bank. Every second Tuesday I deposit my cheque from Holsted's. Judy, the teller, always smiles and gives me a red-and-white-striped mint along with my receipt. A receipt is a piece of paper that says the bank has your money. Gary gets a parking place right in front, which is very lucky. I watch cars circling around and around trying to find an empty space. Of course, if we had Yo, we could park in Handicapped because Yo is a disabled vehicle. That is what Keith says.

The lobby of my bank is crowded, but we do not have to stand in line. Gary whispers to a teller and we cut to the front. A lady whose chest tag says NORMA leads us through a door into a big room with a brown leather couch. I am too nervous to bounce. We wait only a few minutes for Mr Jordan. He is the president of the bank and I am just a little bit afraid.

He is tall and has a huge stomach and curly blond hair. He shakes my hand. 'Well, Mr Crandall.' Mr Jordan sits down in his chair and leans back. He makes a steeple with his fingers and says, 'Well . . .' over and over.

I sit in a chair across, and Keith and Gary are on either side of me. They are like bodyguards from that movie with the gangsters. This is so cool. The bank president talks about what the bank can do with all my money.

'We have some excellent and fiscally responsible ideas that would be to your benefit. I can recommend that you—' he says, but does not get to finish because Keith stands up.

'He's not interested,' Keith interrupts.

He tells Mr Jordan that I am considering my options. I like the sound of that. I decide to say I am considering my options, if anybody else asks me about what I am going to do with my money. It sounds really smart.

I deposit half of my money into my chequing account and the other half into my savings account. That is what I do. Gram told me always to use half and save half. I get one hundred dollars cash in ones, fives and tens from the teller. This makes me feel rich. I have never had that much money at once. Mr Jordan does not quite look as happy when I leave as when I came.

Keith will not tell me what to do. 'It's your call, Per. You'll have plenty other people telling you what you should do with the money.' He shakes his head. 'Better you than me. I'd just spend it on booze and Mexican babes.'

On the way back to my apartment, we swing by Gilly's and pick up sandwiches for everybody at the store. Keith runs into Marina Handy Mart for beer. Gary does not even frown. All of it is my treat. It makes me feel good that I get to buy beer and sandwiches for everybody.

'This is the best feeling in the world!' I tell them.

KEITH DRINKS BEER while I straighten my bank papers on the kitchen counter.

I will need a desk, I decide. Rich people have desks. I chew on a sandwich, sit at my kitchen table and do my words. I am careful not to spill crab and mayonnaise on my dictionary.

Then I remember I have to finish my laundry. I look over at Keith. He is stretched out sideways on Gram's couch and his eyes are closed. My couch now. When John sat on it at Gram's he said it smelt like cat pee, but it does not. It smells like Gram. That is why I like it. Keith snorts. I cannot decide whether he has passed out or is just taking a nap. It can be hard to tell sometimes. Seven beer cans are scattered on the floor. Seven is nothing for Keith. I have seen him drink more. I get up, and move clothes from the washer to the drier.

While it rumbles I make a list of what I can buy with my lottery money:

1. Big flat-screen (twenty-seven inches) TV
2. Cable with Animal Planet
3. New jacket (green) with hood

That is as far as I get. My phone rings. I try to grab it fast before it wakes Keith, but he does not stir. He keeps snoring on the couch. It makes it hard to hear. I put the receiver to my head and cover my other ear.

It is John. I am surprised. I hear the sound of traffic behind his voice.

'I'm in Everett. Where do you live?' He never asked where my apartment was when I moved.

'My place is above the store,' I tell him.

'Where's the store?' He has never come to see me at Holsted's. I tell him it is next door to Gramp's boat yard. He hangs up on me.

My phone rings again right away.

'Oh darling! I just saw the news on the television! Lucky, lucky boy! How is my precious?' I do not know who this is. I do not recognise the voice.

'Miss Elk?' It might be Miss Elk.

'No! Silly! It's your mother! When can I come see you? Tomorrow?'

She has never called me on the phone before. Gram said she was allergic to consideration. 'Only her own feelings, Perry. That's all she ever cares about. She's allergic to anyone else's. I don't know what my son was thinking,' Gram said. Louise hangs up only after I promise to write her a cheque.

My phone rings again. It is my other cousin-brother, David.

'Where are you?' I hear David's wife Elaine in the background. *You'd better get over there now!*

'Home,' I say.

'I'm coming right over.' David does not know where I live either.

After I tell him, he hangs up.

My drier buzzes, so I fold the clothes and put Keith's in a separate pile. I go get my Sears catalogue and page through to see what kind of televisions they have. I do not find flat screens, but my catalogue is five years old.

After our TV broke, Gram and I would take the bus to Kmart and watch the new televisions. We would pretend to choose which one to buy. I wish I won the lottery when she was alive. She would really love having a TV again. I do not have time to think about that any more because there is a banging on my door so loud my teeth rattle.

'It's me. John!' I recognise his growling shout. 'Open up!' John calls out through the door. I count to five then turn the knob. John sounds angry, but the kind of angry that he does not want me to know about.

I hear Gram say *Be careful* in my head.

'Well, my brother is quite the lucky one.' John's smile reminds me of the piranha I saw on Discovery Channel, all pokey with teeth. 'You need to pack a suitcase. On the other hand, don't bother. We'll get you new clothes. Yours smell like that old couch.'

This surprises me. He has never offered to buy me anything. Gram said when a person offers to do something it is usually to their advantage. I wait.

'We have the spare room all set up, you can stay with CeCe and me. You can't stay here. People are going to descend on you like a swarm of flies.'

When Gram died, John's spare room was torn up. I am happy for him it is fixed now.

'I'm OK.' I stop speaking when I see John's face move. His eyebrows go down and his lips get small like they used to when Gram told him she would not lend him money.

'Who's he?' John points to Keith asleep on the couch.

'My friend, Keith.' I tell him.

'See, they're after you already! You've got to be careful,' John warns.

I am uncomfortable. My neck itches. I do not know why John is here. He has never come for a visit before.

My knocker rattles again. John pushes past me to open the door. It is David.

'I can't believe you won the lottery!' David smiles and tries to shake my hand, but John steps in front, blocking him.

'Don't you mean *we*?' John smiles so wide his teeth and gums show.

'No, I mean Perry, you moron!' David pushes him away.

'Who are you calling a moron, you pipsqueak?' John says.

They are both so loud Keith wakes up. 'What the hell!' His eyes look like bottle caps, all round and white around the edges. Keith rolls off the couch onto the floor. That had to hurt. I do not have carpet on my floor, only brown linoleum tile. I am afraid that David and John will fight each other.

'Go away,' I say. When they do not listen, I sit down on the couch. There is more room now that Keith has fallen off.

I'm surprised that wife of yours let you out of her sight. As long as you're here, make yourself useful. Tell Perry he needs to come with me.

Why you? Just what are you planning? David's chin juts out.

John's teeth are bared. He looks like his wife's dog, Gigi, except he is bigger and does not have curly pink hair. *We need to decide what to do. Take charge of this situation.* He chin wiggles and he is frowning like a Halloween pumpkin.

I laugh. John scowls at me and David scowls at John. Keith is crawling around on the floor trying to wake up.

'What's so funny, Perry?' John yells.

'He's just nervous. He's not responsible. Someone has to take care of him, watch out for him,' David says. 'Elaine says he can stay with us.'

'*Elaine says! Elaine says!*' John makes his voice high like a girl's. 'Is that all you can say? Perry needs to stay with me and CeCe!'

I did not need to be taken care of when Gram died. But now I do.

'I think you both have worn out your welcome.' When Keith gets to his feet, he looks fierce. Like the Hulk, only he is not green and his shirt is not ripped.

John and David end up going out the door very fast. Keith's foot is right behind them. He is a good boxer even without his hands. Keith slams the door so hard the window shudders.

'I can sue you for assault!' I hear John shout as his feet make loud tromps down the stairs. *Sue* means that you will get back at someone when they do something you do not like. Sue is also a girl's name.

'Over my dead body, assholes! You two don't fool me!' Keith yells through the door. 'No siree, Bob! I'm not fooled!'

Not being fooled is what everybody says when they are.

GRAM STARTED a baby book, my first book, when I was born. It had my picture from the hospital when I looked like a monkey.

'All babies look like monkeys, Perry, every single one,' Gram said.

'Do monkey babies look like humans to monkeys?'

'Don't be smart!' Gram said.

I learned to print my name with Gram's help when I was six. Gram helped me write in my baby book. Inside we put pictures of me and Gram and Gramp. When I was seven my book was full and Gram bought another.

Now I have to buy my own books. I keep my words and ideas in them. And pictures. I like to put pictures in. I have lots of ideas and lots of books.

I came to live with Gram when I was just a baby. I like to read my first book again from the very beginning, whenever I miss Gram.

Sat up by himself—ten months.

Walked—two years.

First word Ga! for Gramp—two and a half years. George was so proud.

George was my Gramp. I like to know that he was proud of me.

There are other things inside my book. Letters in Gram's handwriting stamped with RETURN TO SENDER on the envelope.

Dear Louise,
    Gramp and I have no problem keeping Perry, but you have to be a part of his life. All boys need their mothers . . .

G.J.,
    We need to hear from you. We need to know why . . .

G.J. is my father. That is what Gram said. I think his name was George too. But he was called G.J. His name is only letters.

'He's your father, but he's no son of mine,' Gram would say.

Gram said she and Gramp needed me so Louise lent me to them. They liked me so much they kept me for good. That is cool.

There is a picture of me as a baby crawling. Gram's handwriting is underneath. *Perry loves his Gramp and follows him around like a puppy.* I laugh. I like to think of myself as a puppy. There is another one of me in our boat, with a red hat and matching mittens. Gram's words are above. *Perry went sailing with Gramp. He's picked it up real fast and is learning to work the tiller.*

Gram wrote all the things I could do. *Perry is reading words now. That teacher doesn't know what she is talking about. He reads signs and we do the crossword together. I tell him which square to put the words in and he does a real good job.*

Doing things faster, better and bigger is important to people.

'It's like a goddamn contest!' Gram said this when I had trouble reading and writing in school. My teachers would invite all the parents to meetings and Gram would come. She would bring my papers home and we would work together to make them better. She told me about how mad she got during those school meetings. The teachers would call me names.

Maybe Downs, but he doesn't look it.

You have to accept the fact that Perry is retarded . . . mildly retarded.

'It's like they're talking about a goddamn cheese, Perry! Mild shmild my ass!' Gram said. 'It's just a bunch of names! Perry, you're just slow and that's not a bad thing. You'll still end up at the same place. People like names. It makes them feel superior,' Gram said.

Superior is when someone thinks they are better than you only they are not.

IT'S HARD TO KNOW *who to trust,* Keith says. He is talking to Gary. *How much do you know about those brothers of his, anyway?* He takes a long drag of his cigarette. I eat Hershey's Kisses while Gary and Keith talk.

John's a lawyer and David has some kind of accounting business. The wives are a couple of gold-diggers. That's all Gram would say. Gary does not smoke. He coughs and tells me to open my window. It is late fall and I am cold, but I open the window anyway. He is number three on my list.

Then we have to keep our eyes open and make sure they don't try anything underhanded. I don't trust lawyers further than I can kick them in the ass. Keith blows smoke up into the air.

I can't imagine they'd try anything overtly illegal. Besides, they have money of their own. Why would they try to get Perry's? Gary says.

You're fucking naive, Gary. Those kind, they never have enough money. I think we should get Per his own lawyer.

I think we should ask Perry. It's up to him. Gary turns to look at me. 'Perry, what do you want to do?' he asks.

'Let's go get my TV. I haven't bought a TV yet.'

'Yeah, we'll get your TV.' Keith squashes his cigarette out in my sink. I hope he will clean it up, but it looks like he won't. He paces in a circle. 'When those brothers of yours call you, tell them you don't need their help.' He puts another cigarette between his lips. I watch him hunt through his pockets.

'I don't need their help,' I say.

'That's right!' Keith bends down and uses my stove for a light.

'Hey, Keith, that is dangerous. You can blow your face up like that!' I sound just like Gram. Gram knew all the ways a person could get hurt.

Gary says I should invest the money for my future. *Invest* means you give other people your money.

'There are things you can buy called mutual funds that invest in a lot of different businesses and you earn dividends or interest. For example, what kind of businesses are you interested in?' Gary asks.

'Stores where you buy things for boats,' I tell him. 'Like your store, Gary.' I get a really good idea. 'How about I invest in your store?' I ask.

Gary shakes his head. 'No, Perry, I'm not looking for a partner. I mean, I'd like to expand. But a partner? I don't think so.'

Keith stands up and puts his cigarette out in his empty beer can. *Why not?* he asks. *Why not let him invest in your store?*

Jeez! I don't know. I never thought about it. I don't know if the business could support another person. The competition is getting tough.

No, Gary, think about it. It's a good plan. He likes it here.

They are talking about me now. I want to remind them that I am still here listening, but I do not. Gary's head is slick and shiny. He used to have more hair. It was brown, the same colour as mine. He takes it from the side and combs it up over the bald place, but it does not stay. He tells me his head is too hot for hair, but I think it is from him worrying. Worries just tumble in your head and can push hair out from the inside. This is what I believe.

You should think about it seriously, says Keith. *I mean it. Look at all the improvements you could make. There's a hell of an opportunity here, Gary. The Everett waterfront is going to take off soon. You need to be able to take advantage when the time comes.*

There is that word again. *Advantage.*

Talk about investments makes me think. I could be a businessman. I could be an investor in Holsted's Marine Supply. Investor. That sounds so cool. I am excited. Way too excited to even bounce. I think about how much I like my apartment. I can look at the boats out my window. It does not have a yard, but that is OK because I definitely do not like mowing grass or pulling weeds. I would need a yard if I got a dog, unless I walked it every day, but then I could get a cat. Cats don't need yards.

At least think about it, Gary, OK? Keith asks.

I'll think about it. As he goes out the door, he asks, 'You guys coming?'

Keith said, 'Nope, we got a TV to buy. We'll be in later.'

THE MAN at the TV store has a name tag that says PATRICK PERRY.

'Hey my name's Perry L. Crandall. We have the same name,' I say.

'Welcome to Top Electronics. How can I help you?' He looks at Keith.

'My friend here needs a TV. You probably should be talking to him.'

Patrick shows us a small white television in the corner. 'This is our least expensive model. It's good value.'

I walk over to the big flat screens. 'I need a bigger one. How about this?' I point to one hanging on the wall. 'I have plenty of money,' I say.

Patrick smiles and winks at Keith. 'I'm sure you do,' he says.

'How about this one?' Keith touches the biggest plasma screen in the store. Patrick looks confused. 'It's over a thousand.'

Keith points to me and says, 'I see you haven't met my friend, Perry Crandall. You know, *the* Perry L. Crandall? *The lottery winner*?'

'You want a stand with that?' Patrick talks to me directly.

For £1,883.45 I buy a twenty-seven-inch plasma TV. For $300 I get a stand to put it on.

'We got a sale on stereos. You want a stereo? A DVD player?' Patrick looks like he is dizzy.

He sits down on a console when I say, 'Sure!'

I have to write three cheques because I keep finding things to buy. Patrick says he will have his helpers take everything out to Yo when we are finished.

'Thank you very much, Mr Crandall.' He shakes my hand hard.

'Hey, Keith, I don't have any music except for Gramp's records.' I remember this when we walk past a music store. I have no idea what to buy.

Keith helps. 'You got to have the Doobie Brothers, and here, Per, some Eagles, The Beatles . . .' He collects an armful. 'Oh, and Jimmy Buffett!'

I walk over to the movie section and pick out ten right away. I set them down on the counter so I can go get more. The lady at the counter frowns.

'This is ridiculous. You're going to have to put all these back! You've got over five hundred dollars worth of stuff here!' She glares at me.

'Here's the number for Mr Jordan at the bank. He'll tell you Perry's cheque is good.' Keith is smiling like he is enjoying causing a scene.

The cashier is on the phone to my bank when her manager comes out from the back room. He stops when he sees me and holds out his hand.

'Hey, aren't you the guy who just won the lottery? Perry Crandall?' He turns to the lady at the register. 'His picture is in today's paper. He just won twelve million dollars in the lottery! Jesus! How lucky can you get!'

Other people crowd around. I start to feel uncomfortable. One man taps my shoulder, for luck, he says. The cashier introduces herself as Shirley.

The manager gives me two free movies he thinks I might like. I give Shirley a CD of The Smashing Pumpkins to say thank you.

She smiles and says, 'Come back again anytime.'

She likes me now, even though she does not know me.

Everybody at the mall was nice and none of them even knew me.

4

Miss Elk was my best teacher. I was ten years old when I went to her special class. She was the best special teacher I ever had. *Special* means very good or better. Or it can mean a class that you go to at school. She liked me so much she kept me for two years. She taught me to read better and I loved her. I told her I would marry her when I got older. She laughed and said she was already married. It ended up being a good thing. She would have been way too old for me, Gram said.

School can be a scary place. I remember I wanted to go like all the other kids. You got to ride on a bus. It was yellow. The big boys in the back would punch me in the head as they got off the bus. Anytime they passed me, they shoved, pushed and took my papers or called me retard. They did not know my class was special.

I always wondered why. 'Why are people mean?' I would ask Gram. 'Why do they call me names?'

Gram could not answer me. 'I just don't know, Perry. People can be cruel.'

'Everybody belongs to the world. Everybody has a right to be here,' Miss Elk said. I like that. Everybody belongs.

The end of my second year with Miss Elk I found out I liked to read. It was strange. One minute it was hard and the next it was fun. Gram was impressed and wanted me to stay with Miss Elk all the time, but the principal said no. Then they took me out of Miss Elk's class.

My next teacher made me sit by myself in a regular class.

'This is Perry, everyone. He is special. He will be joining our class. He will be sitting back here with Mrs Kennedy. Perry? Have a seat.'

'Can't I sit over there with the other kids?'

She told me no. She said to be quiet and sit down.

I had something called pull-out. When the class got too fast for me, I was pulled out so I would not slow the other kids down. Mrs Kennedy helped me two times a week. The other times I just sat.

The teacher sent notes home.

He is a disruption.

He is negatively influencing the classroom environment.

'Can I sit with the other kids?' I asked.

'No! I have had enough! You are disruptive and disrespectful!' I only stuck my tongue out once. Maybe twice. I was bored.

My teacher complained to the principal. 'I simply cannot teach a student this cognitively challenged.' She meant retarded.

I was thirteen. I was too tall to stay in elementary school, so Gram took me home. She did not want me to go to junior high. The school sent us letters. Gram wrote on them in felt pen. *NO LONGER AT THIS ADDRESS.*

I missed riding the bus to school, but Gram showed me how to ride the Everett city bus to Gramp's boat yard. I would go there after my lessons with Gram. Gramp and I would come home together in time for dinner. We would have chicken or meat loaf or tuna casserole. Those were good times. Gram did not have the evil arthritis and Gramp was not dead.

After Gramp died, we had a problem. It had to do with money.

'We lost the boat yard,' Gram would say, and then she would throw a dish or plate. It was good that we had melamine. The boat yard had to be sold. Gary Holsted and Gram talked at our house and then I worked for him at Holsted's Marine Supply right next door to our old boat yard.

'He's the only friend we have, Perry,' Gram would say. And she would not say anything more. Just like when I would ask her about my father.

'Never you mind, Perry. Never you mind,' and her lips would disappear.

I GET A LOT of mail. Six or twenty letters a day, sometimes more. I never got much mail before, but I get mail now.

Dear Lottery Winner . . .

To the Lucky Lottery Winner . . .

To Mr Perry Crandall, Lottery Winner . . .

I make a big pile on my counter because I do not know what to do with them all. Gram said that if someone you do not know sends you something, it is probably a bad thing. Some of the letters have lots of tiny print that is hard to read. Others tell me sad stories. There is one about a kid with cancer. Another one is about dying orphans in Africa and Kentucky.

There are people standing outside my door. Some of them I know, like my teacher Miss Elk from school. She wants to shake my hand and ask me to donate to her new school. That is cool.

'How much do you want?' I ask.

'How much can you give?' she asks.

I write her a cheque for five hundred dollars. That is all the zeros that I can fit in the line without Keith's help.

'Hey! Perry! Long time no see!'

I do not know this man. 'Who are you?' I ask him.

'Kenny! Kenny Brandt! Don't you remember me? We were buddies growing up! I lived down the street from you in the yellow house. Remember?' His blond hair is thin on top and he is shorter and skinnier than me. He could be my ex-neighbour Kenny but I have not seen him for a long time and do not recognise him. 'So you got anything to spare for old times' sake? I lost my job. My wife left me. I could use a few bucks.'

'I'm sorry,' I say. Having no job is hard, but I have a good idea. 'Hey! I know! You can talk to Gary. He could find you a job.' I go to get a pen out of my drawer. 'Here is Gary's phone number. Call him, OK?'

Kenny looks down at the piece of paper and then at me.

'Screw you, asshole! I need money, not a frigging number!' He throws the paper at me and stomps out the door, slamming it behind him.

When Keith and Gary come upstairs, they chase everybody away. Gary says we need a security guard to keep intruders out. I laugh. These people are not intruders. They knocked first and I opened my door and let them in.

My family calls me all the time now.

Nobody shouts, except for John and sometimes Elaine. Keith says they will never leave me alone now.

'Bloodsuckers! Vultures! Hyenas!' Keith's face is all red and blotched. 'Listen, Perry, this is important. Are you listening?' I have to listen because Keith's mouth is in front of my face. His breath smells like dog poop and beer. I do not tell him this. It definitely would not be nice.

'Yeah.' I am an auditor. I listen.

'Your brothers are up to no good,' Gary says.

'Ha! That's what Gram always told me.'

'Perry, you have to promise me not to fill out or sign anything anybody sends you. *Anything!* Do you understand?' Gary sounds worried.

'Yeah.' I have to think about that for a minute. 'What about cheques?' I ask. 'I have to sign my cheques.'

'Don't sign any *papers*. Do not write your name for them. I think your brothers plan to take advantage of you. They want your money,' Keith says.

'They can have some.' That is a good idea. 'Hey, Keith, I could give them some. Wouldn't that be OK?'

'*No!* No, Perry. Listen. They want all of it. They will not be satisfied.'

Gary says I need a plan. 'You have a tremendous opportunity to help people and have a great future for yourself, but you have to be careful. Please let Keith or me know if someone wants something from you again. OK?'

Gary is nice and has known me for a long time.

'What's all this?' Gary starts looking through papers on my counter. 'Holy crap! Have you been sending these people money?' he asks. He holds up a letter from a Girl Scout leader.

'They want to go on a trip to Canada,' I explain. 'It's educational.'

'Per, these people are ripping you off! You've got to stop this! They'll only send you more of these!' Keith waves a letter in the air.

Gary agrees. 'Keith is right. Look here. See this? If you deposited the cheque from this company, you would give up an interest in the rest of your lottery winnings for ever. You could lose it all. You have to be careful.'

Gram says careful too, deep inside my head. *Careful.*

They are right. I have not been thinking clearly. It is very important to think, Gram said.

'You can't be giving everybody money. It's not a good idea,' Keith says.

'OK,' I say. That seems to make them both feel better.

'Just watch out for any of their funny business, Per. Let Gary and me help you with your mail,' Keith says.

Funny business is something bad and not at all funny.

I MISS GRAM. I still do everything the same in the morning. I get up, go to the bathroom, use my electric razor and comb my hair. I put on jeans with my flannel shirt and an undershirt underneath. I put on my socks and slip on my boat shoes. I cook my oatmeal and do my words while I eat.

I have been rich for almost a month.

I have good friends. I am lucky, just like Gram said. Keith is my best friend and then Gary. I have known them both the longest. They were my friends before. I have new friends now. Like in Holsted's when I am working. People I do not even know come in just to talk to me.

Are you that guy who won the lottery?

Hey guys, it's him!

How many tickets did you buy?

Did you have the computer pick or did you have your own lucky numbers?

I am famous now and people listen to what I have to say. They do not interrupt. They do not say I am slow. Before I won the lottery, people would always ask for Keith to help them instead of me. That is stupid because I am the one who knows where everything is. I unload the boxes and put things away on the shelves. Keith always had to ask me. 'Hey, Perry, where'd we put the snatch blocks?' He would be looking in the wrong aisle. 'Hey, Perry, do you know where the teak cleaner is?' It would be right in front of him. Before I won the lottery, people did not want to talk to me. Now they do.

Keith laughs and says our customers will buy whatever I suggest. 'That guy just bought two pairs of Sperrys. He probably doesn't even have a boat. He just decided to buy the shoes from you, Per,' he says.

'He told me he just wanted to wash his driveway. I told him you do not slip in the wet when you wear boat shoes. He thought that was a good idea.'

Every day, more people come in to see me. They smile and ask me questions about the lottery. They talk to me like they want to be friends and then we talk about boats. I know a lot about boats. People have a hard time finding things they want. They tell me this. I just listen. They come into Holsted's to find out about the lottery and leave with what they need for their boat.

We sell out of all the T-shirts that say HOLSTED'S MARINE SUPPLY. I fill out another catalogue order form. 'Hey, Gary, look, we can put anything on the back we want.' I point to a blank space on the order form.

'Go for it, Per. What do you want to put?' Gary is filling out time sheets.

Keith comes over. 'People are buying all sorts of crap now, Per. If you hand it to them, they're buying it. Put whatever you want.'

'Can I put my name?'

'Sure. Why not?'

Keith sets out more pens that say HOLSTED'S FOR YOUR BOATING NEEDS. We used to give them away, but I accidentally dumped them into a box that was marked two dollars and we sold every one.

I order more pens and key chains with floats. If we order a lot, we can get it in three days. I also order T-shirts that say HOLSTED'S MARINE SUPPLY on one side and PERRY L. CRANDALL WORKS HERE on the other. That is so cool. I always wanted my name on a shirt.

'This seems like a big order, but OK.' Gary initials my order form. It is the first one I have ever filled out.

Even though I won the lottery, I unpack all the boxes that come in on Saturday. It is my job.

The box of key chains is huge. There are 500 of them. I take the key chains out and put them into a box next to the pens. They all say HOLSTED'S MARINE SUPPLY. I make a sign: *Matching pen and key chain. Get both for five dollars.* The number five is a good number. Most people have five-dollar bills and it is easier to add up. Tons of people came in that morning and everything was gone by Sunday afternoon.

Gary laughs. 'Per, I don't know about you. I think maybe you were holding out on us before.'

I laugh with him and feel happy that he called me Per.

When Keith hands Gary another order form on Monday, he passes it over to me. 'This is your job now,' he says.

We sell out of T-shirts again. The white pens and floating key chains now have HOLSTED'S MARINE SUPPLY, HOME OF PERRY L. CRANDALL LOTTERY WINNER printed on the side in bright green letters.

'Don't look at me!' Keith says to Gary as he unfolds more invoices. 'Ask Perry. He seems to know what people want.'

They want my name on stuff. I laugh again. It is so easy. I just ask the customers what they want. They always tell me.

'What would you like to see in our store?' I say, and carry a yellow pad and write down everything they tell me.

'It's wonderful what you're doing,' they say to Gary before they walk out of the store. 'Just wonderful.'

'What am I doing?' Gary looks at Keith and shrugs.

Keith winks at me. 'You've turned Per into a businessman, Gary. All he had to do was win the lottery and now he's a businessman.'

That is what I want to be most of all. A businessman.

ON WEDNESDAY MORNING, John comes over to my apartment.

'I tried to call. Your phone is busy. It must be off the hook,' he says.

'No, that was Franklin. He says I can call him Frank,' I explain.

'Frank? Who the hell's Frank?' he asks.

'I don't know. He says he's a friend of Elaine's,' I say.

Frank says he is my friend too, but I have never seen him.

'What does he want?' John asks.

'To help me with the money. To give me advice.'

'You don't need a stranger's help, Perry. That's what David and I are here for,' he says.

Everybody wants to help me with the money.

John's grey coat is wet from the rain and drips all over my floor.

'We're just trying to help you. You need to keep us in the loop,' he says.

I do not know what *in the loop* means.

'Where's your fat friend, Keith?' He peels off his black gloves.

'He's not fat. Those are stomach muscles. And he had to go to the vet hospital,' I say. Keith is a vet, which is not like a dog doctor. It has to do with the army, and Vietnam.

'Where's your boss?'

'He's downstairs working the register.'

'Where's your bank statement? I'd like to help with your accounting, check your numbers.' John is already shuffling through papers on my kitchen counter. He holds something up. 'Are these all your papers?'

'It's not nice to look at other people's stuff,' I say, but he ignores me.

'What happened? You seem to have spent a great deal of money already. What's going on, Perry?' His voice gets louder, then he suddenly stops and takes a deep breath. 'I'm just trying to watch out for you. To help you. We're all concerned about you.' He is speaking softly, like he is singing.

Maybe he really wants to help me now.

I try to think. I rock back and forth on the sofa. It is almost time for *Judge Judy.* I already missed *Gilligan's Island.* I wonder when he will leave.

'Perry, what have you done?' John brings a kitchen chair over and plops down. He puts a hand on my shoulder.

'Investments,' I tell him. Gram told me not to tell them about my savings account, so I do not. I put my savings-account papers in Gram and Gramp's cardboard box. I do not leave them out for anyone to see. They are private.

'CeCe and I would really like you to come over for a visit, spend the night,' he says.

'Why?' I ask. Keith told me to ask why, if John or David or Louise wanted me to go somewhere.

'Well, Perry, we'd all like to get to know you better. Spend some time together. Plus it's time for a Family Meeting.'

When someone invites you to their house, you say yes so you do not hurt their feelings. Hurting people's feelings is rude. I go with John to his house. I do not have a suitcase, so John stuffs my clothes into a pillowcase. That is definitely not cool because when I unpack they will be all wrinkled.

I try to tell him, but he says, 'Don't worry about it, Perry.'

But I do. I am the one who has to fold them.

He tells me to hurry, but I have to write a note to Keith. I leave it on the table. It says, GONE TO JOHN'S HOUSE. Keith and I were going to get pizza and watch a DVD tonight. He can always watch a DVD without me. I have to lock the door to my apartment so no one will go inside and steal my TV. It is good that Keith has his own key.

John lives in a big white house in Bellevue. It takes an hour to get there. His front yard has green bushes with red flowers. There is a hot tub on the redwood deck behind the house and a tall stone wall around the back yard. He shows me around as he tells me the rules. I am not allowed to use the hot tub. I am not allowed to go outside. I am not allowed in the living room. There are many *not alloweds* at his house. John tells me to sit at the table and he goes to use his phone. I hear him from the kitchen.

We're having another Family Meeting tonight. Perry will be here.

I'm sure we can get him to sign. I don't think he'll be any problem at all. He's very suggestible.

Eight o'clock tonight. Everybody needs to be there.

After he hangs up, he says, 'I've got to go back to work. You have to amuse yourself until CeCe and I get home.'

When people tell you to amuse yourself, it means you are bothering them.

JOHN'S FIRST WIFE was Lenore and his second wife was Grace. I do not know who three and four were. Number five is CeCe. She used to be his receptionist. John does not have any children. Neither does David.

Gram always told me that was good. 'Get them both out of the gene pool! That's what I say.' The gene pool is something you want other people out of.

I sit on the sofa in the family room with CeCe's poodle, Gigi, and watch Animal Planet. If you do not scratch her just right, Gigi will bite you. She bit me twice already. You can get rabies from dogs if they are frothing at the mouth. I look carefully at Gigi's spit. It does not look like froth. I love dogs even when they bite.

I decide to channel hop. That is when you click the remote and go from channel 03 to channel 099 and back again. Gigi likes it when I channel hop and growls at all the commercials.

I hope I do not have to stay long. I need to go to work tomorrow. I want to go home right after the Family Meeting.

I am by myself for the rest of the day. It is rude to leave guests alone in your house. John did not say I could open any cupboards, so I do not eat lunch. It is also rude not to feed your guests. No one gets home until after eight. I have not had dinner and I am hungry.

I am happy but a little nervous when everyone arrives. My mouth is dry. My stomach grumbles loud.

'So, Perry, how's it going?' David's wife, Elaine, asks. She has never wanted to know how it was going before. I do not know how to answer.

'It is going fine,' I finally say. She hugs me so tight it hurts.

'I hope you know we are going to a lot of trouble to help you,' she whispers in my ear. David pats me on the back and I cough.

John and CeCe are already sitting at the dining room table. There are crackers and weird yellow mush in a bowl. CeCe says it is hummus. It tastes like nut pudding. I do not like it and eat crackers naked. I want a glass of water, but no one offers me anything and it is not polite to ask. They all have wineglasses. I never drink wine. Gram would not let me.

I think we should initiate guardianship proceedings immediately.

John, we've gone over this before. I told you it's problematic.

Says who?

John, Elaine's firm specialises in these issues.

And we should listen to you because? Oh. That's right, David. You didn't actually PASS the bar.

You always bring that up!

Stop it all of you. We have decisions to make.

Be careful. He's L-I-S-E-N-I-N-G. CeCe says this, but it is stupid because I am a very good speller and she is not.

Great! Where'd you find her, John? She's worse than your last one.

Shut up, Elaine!

It is after nine when Louise comes through the front door. I do not know who she is at first because her hair is now black.

'Louise.' 'Darling.' 'Mother.' John and Elaine talk at the same time, but Louise ignores them and hugs me. She smells like old flowers.

'Oh honey! Such a lucky boy! Boy! Now, what are we going to do with all that lovely money?' She does not touch my face but kisses something in the air next to me.

'All the money that's left anyway,' John says. He has papers in his hand. 'If you've blown this much in a month, Perry, nothing will be left in a year.'

I am mad because that is my private stuff. It is not nice to take someone's private stuff.

Elaine puts a hand on his arm. 'Shhhh. You'll scare him,' she says. 'You have to be gentle.' Her eyes move like the lizards' eyes at Pets R Us. She is much scarier than either John or David.

'It's OK, Perry. It's your money.' David puts his hand on my shoulder.

'Now, that's the stupidest thing I've heard you say tonight, David.' Elaine rolls her eyes. 'Perry needs to have us be in charge of his finances. A simple general Power of Attorney, Perry, and your problems will be over.'

John tells me, 'I consider this everybody's money. You're wasting it. We're a family. Families share money. Don't you want to share? What could you possibly have spent it on?'

Be careful. Gram's voice.

'Investments,' I say again. 'Stuff. A TV.' I already told him once. I am getting even madder. They think I am stupid. I can see it in their faces.

'What investments?' They all ask this at the same time. They do not wait for my answer and start to talk among themselves all at once.

That does it. He needs protection! We need to declare him incompetent!

Guardianship is problematic. I keep telling you this! The court blocks use of the funds and requires regular reporting. It won't meet our needs.

We have to figure out another way. We have to gain his trust, get to know him so we know the best way to go about this. It shouldn't be that difficult. He's very suggestible. Very, very suggestible . . .

We need to decide how to invest the money when we do get it into a trust.

When we cash it out and sell the annuity I think it should go right into mutual funds. It's more liquid.

I disagree. We need to pick some stocks. I've got a guy at Hawthorne Group who's sharp, a real hotshot.

I think real estate. The market is hot right now.

CeCe, forget real estate, you don't know what you're talking about.

Look, we'll have to get going on this. I have obligations . . .

What's the matter, John? Dipping into the till again, are we?

You're a real bitch, Elaine. You know that?

Stop it, you two! We should split it up between all of us, but I should get more! I'm his mother.

No. It should be split evenly. It's only fair.

We're just thinking of Perry's future. Our future.

They are boring, so I decide to leave and go into the other room. No one notices, or if they do they say nothing. Animal Planet is not on, so I take a shower, put on my pyjamas and get into bed. The room is strange. The sounds are strange. I am uncomfortable and want to go home.

WHEN I WAKE UP, it is morning. I wonder if John has oatmeal in his kitchen. I decide to ask him when I hear him moving around. He sounds grumpy and talks to me through his bedroom door.

'What! What do you want, Perry?'

'Do you have oatmeal, John? I eat oatmeal for breakfast. Can I have some breakfast?' I am embarrassed to ask, but I did not get dinner and I do not want to starve to death. People can die when they do not eat enough food.

'I don't know, Perry. Look for yourself! I don't have time right now. I have to leave. Fix yourself some eggs or something. Watch TV in the family room. Let Gigi out in the back yard to do her stuff, but make sure she comes right back inside. Wipe her feet with a towel so she doesn't get the carpet dirty. CeCe and I have to go. We'll be back this afternoon.'

After they leave, I am lonely and bored. I wish Keith would come over. Ten minutes later, I hear banging at the front of the house. I do not know what I should do. It is not nice to answer other people's doors.

'Hey, Per!'

When I recognise Keith's voice, I am happy and open the door. I am still in my pyjamas. 'How did you get here? This is like magic, Keith! I was just thinking that I wish you were here, and you appeared. That is so cool,' I say.

'Sorry, Per, I had a few beers last night or I would have been here sooner.

I didn't see your note until this morning. I found John's address in the blue book by your phone. *No problemo.*' Keith walks into the living room and looks around. 'I waited until I saw your brother and his wife getting into their car in the driveway. You ready to go?'

'Yeah, I'm ready to go,' I say. 'Just let me put on my clothes.'

Keith tracks mud all over the white living room carpet.

'Hey Keith, you got mud all over your boots. John will get mad.' I hope he takes them off, but he just sits on the white sofa, picks the dirt clumps stuck to his soles and flicks them off onto the glass coffee table.

'So this is where that brother of yours lives.' He stands up. 'Holsted was worried when you didn't come home. Of course, I knew the *son of a bitch* would come back. Holsted is so naive.'

'Do you want some breakfast? I can make eggs,' I offer. I am hungry and hope we can eat before we leave.

'Sure,' he says, then, 'No. I'll make the eggs and you get dressed. Make sure you pack up everything you want to take home.' On his way to the kitchen, Keith opens the cupboard over the bar. He starts pulling out bottles. 'Courvoisier. Ahhhh. Cognac. Oh yeah! That's a good one.' He talks to himself. 'I'll take this . . .' Then to me, 'Hurry up, Per! We don't have all day.'

I put on my underwear, pull on my jeans and button my shirt. When I walk into the kitchen, I smell something burning. The kitchen is empty. Smoke is pouring from a frying pan on the stove. There are four eggs burned hard to the bottom of a pan. I dump them into the disposal and get another pan. I am cooking more eggs when Keith comes back.

'I found these in the office,' he says. 'Look at all these credit card bills! See? They're all maxed out. For such a fancy house your brother seems to owe a shitload of money. What's this? Hey, look here! He's being sued! Misappropriation of funds. Sweet Jesus!'

'It's not nice to snoop.' I set two plates out and butter toast.

Keith sits down at the table. 'What did you do with them last night?'

'We had a Family Meeting.'

'What about?'

'Stuff. Investments. Money. They want me to be responsible.'

'Interesting. Here's a big one that defers payment. It says John expects to come into a pile of money soon.' Keith reads while he shovels eggs and toast into his mouth. 'Did either of your brothers ask for a loan?'

'No. A loan is when you borrow money and have to pay it back. They all just wanted cheques. They do not want to pay me back,' I say.

'The money-grubbing creeps. When is John getting home?' Keith asks.

'He said this afternoon but I don't know. Why?'

'Because I want to sit in his hot tub. I have a bad back.' He stands up.

'I'm not allowed.' I start to worry. We have made a huge mess in John's house. Gigi is howling in the other room and there is a wet spot on the rug. I was supposed to let her out in the back yard to poop and pee. I forgot.

'Yeah? Well, they didn't say anything about me.' Keith goes out onto the deck and flips a switch that causes bubbles to spring up from the bottom of the tub. He peels off his shirt and drops his pants. I hope John's neighbours are not looking over the fence.

My hands shake and my stomach is achy. I need a Tums. My heart is pounding so loud I hear it in my ears. I pace from room to room. I forget about Gigi until I notice she did a poop on the carpet. I try to pick it up with a paper towel, but I drop one piece and it rolls under the sofa.

'Keith!' I do not want to be here when John and CeCe get home.

I hear Keith in the hot tub singing. '*Sure do shine . . . glad I love ya . . . glad you're mine . . .* Watch some TV, Per! I'll be done in a minute,' he hollers.

'I am too upset to watch TV, Keith! We'll get in trouble!'

I hear Gigi scratching and whining in the office. Long gouges line the bottom of the door. She must have gotten in there while Keith was snooping. Gigi bites my ankle, but I have thick socks on. I pick her up by the collar and throw her too hard into the bathroom. She hits the wall as I slam the door.

'Sorry!' I tell her, but she does not sound like she forgives me. Her growls and barks echo off the tiles.

When I come back to the deck Keith is out of the hot tub.

'Hot damn! That felt good.'

There are pieces of burnt egg in the sink and dishes all over the table. There is a giant yellow puddle bright like the sun on the white tile in the hall. Gigi must have peed there too. I open the cupboard below the sink, grab a garbage bag, run into the spare room and stuff my clothes inside.

'Keith!' I yell again. 'We have to go!'

He is back in John's office, sitting at the desk, reading more papers.

'Shit, what's all this?' He pages through a long yellow tablet. *Mutual funds. Financial services. Guardianship* . . . I think they're up to something. It looks like your family is researching how to invest a whole pile of money. They want to create a family trust, it says here.'

'We have to go, Keith.' I am scared that John will come back and catch us snooping. My stomach is queasy. I look for a Tums in my jeans pocket.

There are two tablets left. I unwrap one quickly and pop it into my mouth.

Keith picks up some other papers and stuffs them into his shirt.

My hands are sweating. I am in so much trouble. 'Hurry!' I cry.

I swing my bag of clothes over my back. I walk out the door. Keith follows behind carrying a sack of bottles.

'Hey Keith, isn't that stealing?' I ask.

Keith pulls the door shut behind us with one hand.

'Nah. I'll ask him next time he comes over to your place,' he says.

'OK,' I say, and we drive home.

5

Gary and Keith are hard-talking. It is like they are fighting but not mad. Gary thinks everything will be fine and calls Keith cynical and overexcited. Keith paces the small back office, three steps each way. We are both supposed to be unpacking boxes. Instead, I hang outside the door and eavesdrop. That is like being an auditor without permission.

John is telling creditors he expects to get cash soon and look at this! Keith waves papers in Gary's face. *What if he tries to get guardianship?*

How can he do that? The courts would have to declare Perry incompetent and he's obviously not. Gary sits up.

Gary, don't be naive! They're lawyers! They'll figure out a way!

When they see me standing there they stop talking.

'Per, you've got to be careful around that family of yours!' Keith says.

'Yeah, Per. Keith's right. You've got to be careful,' Gary echoes.

'OK,' I say, but they do not look convinced.

Keith pulls a tiny stool over and sits down across from Gary. His bottom hangs over each side like a big W. 'Gary, we have to do something.'

'OK. I'll talk to my lawyer about bringing Per in as an investor. Maybe there's something we can do to protect him from that family of his.'

'Oh boy!' I say, and bounce against the doorway.

'No promises, Per. We'll run the numbers, and then see what the lawyer says,' Gary warns.

I hope the numbers will be good.

Keith leans back, farts and falls off his stool.

KEITH AND I decide to take Friday afternoon off. It is cold even though the sky is blue. So cold it gets in your head and nose even with the sun out. We are on *Diamond Girl*. The sky is so bright I can see it in the water. I can also see huge sea anemones attached to the dock. They look like big white dinosaur flowers. They are really animals, Gramp told me.

Keith turns the key and pushes a button to start his engine.

BROOOM! Brooom! Brooom! Brooom! Clunk. He tries again.

BROOOM! Brooom! Brooom! Brooom! Clunk. He says the F-word.

BROOOM! BROOOM! BROOOM! The engine starts. It sputters, pings and sounds sick to me, but Keith laughs like he has just heard a good joke.

He tells me to toss him the aft lines. I know all about lines. I do not need to be told. I help boats into the fuel dock all the time. I stretch out on the bow as we head out into the Sound past the spit.

The engine quits. CONK! Keith says the F-word again.

Diamond Girl is a sloop, which means she only has one mast. She has two sails. The one in front is called a jib, or foresail. You can even call it a jenny. That is also a girl's name. Keith starts to unwind the jib from the forestay.

'Why are you pulling the sheet? There's no wind,' I say. A sheet is a piece of rope that is attached to a sail and not something on a bed. Keith pulling the sheet is not a great idea. The sail just hangs off the stay.

'Shit!' Keith cannot see to steer with the sail hanging down like that.

'Hey Keith, I'll get the oar.' I try to be helpful.

He says the F-word again and growls while he furls the sail back up. Keith tells me he hates the guys to see us scull back. It is embarrassing. It insults a sailor to scull, Keith says.

The water is flat and calm. That means it will be easier to get back, because there will be little current. We go faster with me sculling than we did with the engine. Keith smokes a cigarette while I work the oar.

'I need to get my tank scrubbed. I must have dirty fuel.' Keith says this each time his engine quits.

'Why don't you get it repaired?' I ask this each time too.

'Money, Per, it costs money.'

'Oh.' Then I get one of my good ideas. 'Hey, Keith, I have money now. Let's get the engine fixed.'

'No, Per, that's not necessary.'

People say it is not necessary when they really want to do something but think it may be a problem. It is not a problem for me. I get excited because it means we can go out on more sailing trips. It also means we might not have to scull any more and embarrass Keith. Fixing up *Diamond Girl* was on Keith's lottery list, so it must be a good idea.

It takes two hours to get back to the slip. I jump off the bow, tie the line to the cleat and catch the aft line. Gram used to say that sometimes I could be stubborn. I feel this is one of those times.

Lots of people do inboard engine repair in the harbour. My favourite is Marty. Mr Martin really, but everyone calls him Marty. He is sixty-seven years old. I know this because he calls Gary on the phone at least twice a week. 'Holsted! I need Racor filters. Put it on my account!' He always expects me to bring them. 'I'm sixty-seven years old with a bum hip!' he complains. 'I can't walk down the dock every time I need a damn filter!' His shop is at the far end of the pier.

He laughs when I ask him to fix Keith's engine.

'That'll be the day. What's he gonna use for money?' Marty asks.

'I'll pay for it. I want us to go out farther, maybe to Whidbey Island or all the way around Camano.'

'That'll be a job.' He grinds his cigarette out on the dock and gets up. Then he puffs, huffs and limps after me over to Keith's boat.

'OK, Keith, turn her over.' Marty steps onto *Diamond Girl*. She sinks like a dog with a sore back. That's what Gram used to say. Marty weighs a lot.

I hear Keith mutter. Marty and Keith always growl at each other. It is hard to tell if they like each other. They bum cigarettes from each other and argue all the time. I do not need to be there. Keith and Marty do not notice when I walk away.

I decide to go to Marina Handy Mart and visit Cherry.

I THINK ABOUT CHERRY a lot. Keith calls her a plus-sized girl with giant tits, and laughs. Gary says she has too many tattoos and earrings. I think she is neat, and beautiful, and smart.

'Hey, Cherry.' The bell tinkles when I walk through the door.

'Hey, Perry. How you doing?' Cherry is reading a magazine.

I want to say something that will make her laugh, but I cannot think of one thing, so I decide to buy a Coke.

'What are you reading?' I ask, and set my drink on the counter.

'*People*. It's a good one this week. Hey, you should be in it. They do stuff about lottery winners.' Cherry rings up my soda. 'You're the first person I ever knew who won anything. I don't even buy MegaBucks any more.'

'Why not?' Cherry always plays MegaBucks.

'Well, Perry, just think about it for a moment,' she says. 'What are the odds? A million or more to one, right? What are the odds that I win, and I have a friend who wins? That's practically impossible! You just saved me a pile of money. There's no point to playing any more. No way I'd win now!'

'I'm sorry.' Because of me, my friends have no chance at winning the lottery. I feel sad for them. I look at Cherry's face. She has black lipstick today and it matches her eyelashes.

'Where's your nose ring?' I can think of nothing else to say. I am sweating under my pits. Maybe I forgot deodorant. I quickly lift up my arm and smell when Cherry bends down to put her magazine under the counter.

'At home. Sometimes I don't feel like wearing it. I have my tongue one in, though.' And she sticks it out to show me. 'My dad hates them.'

Cherry's mouth shuts and makes a deep frown as she hands me my change. I try to think of something else to say as I pop open my Coke.

'I don't have a dad. I mean, I think my dad's dead,' I say.

'You're lucky,' Cherry says. 'I wish mine was dead.'

I just nod, smile and hope I do not look too goofy.

Shouts echo in the parking lot outside. Three guys stomp into the store. Their heavy sweatshirts hang down their arms. They look like motorcycle men, except they do not have helmets or bikes.

'Hey! Anybody here?' The man that says this has a scraggly beard and huge dirty hands.

'You got any beer in this dump?' The one next to him spits a long brown stream of liquid onto the tile floor. They all have greasy blond hair. They scare me. I put my change in my pocket and turn to leave.

The man with the beard grabs me by the arm as I walk past and lifts me up. 'Do I know you?' he says.

His fingers tighten on my arm and my Coke drips on his sneakers.

'Shit! You dumped Coke on my shoes! Tell me you're sorry, you little screw-up! You hear me?' He lifts me higher up off the floor. My shoulder is twisting. My arm burns. My soda can flips out of my numb hand, bounces across the tiles and splashes over the legs of the two other men. They yell and dance backwards into the aisle.

'I'm sorry! I'm really sorry.' I am. I am very sorry and I am very scared. My heart is beating. Thump THUMP THUMP thump. When the man hears my voice, he smiles so wide I see his grey teeth. It is not a nice smile at all.

'Well, well, well, we have a little retard here.'

His two friends come closer. One of them starts laughing deep and slow.

'LEAVE HIM ALONE, ASSHOLES!'

I did not know Cherry could holler that loud. I am impressed. The baseball bat she hits the man with is aluminium.

'I called the POLICE, and if you don't get your sorry butts out of this store, I'm shooting you guys with THIS!' She waves a spray can in her other hand. 'IN FACT! I think it's a good idea to use this NOW!' And she did.

Something comes out of the can with a *whoosh!* The man lets go of my arm and drops me. I fall to the floor next to the cereal shelf. I can feel tears run down my face from the spray. I throw up again and again.

I hear thumps as Cherry smacks the men over and over with the bat. THWACK! THUNK! Sirens start soft and get louder.

Cherry told me afterwards there is a special button for the police under the counter at all Handy Marts.

The police tell Cherry it was dangerous to do what she did.

'They could have been armed. You did a very foolish thing.' Officer Mallory looks at my arm, but he talks to Cherry. She sits behind the counter answering their questions.

All three men sit on the floor with handcuffs around their ankles and wrists and wait to go to jail. They have something called outstanding warrants. An *outstanding warrant* means the police are looking for you.

The other officer writes my name on the police form, then looks at my face. 'Hey, aren't you the guy who won the lottery? You are, aren't you!'

'That's right!' Officer Mallory hoots at the three men sitting on the floor. 'You idiots just assaulted Perry L. Crandall. He's a millionaire. He'll have your sorry asses in jail for ever!' He is still laughing as he helps his partner load the men into a big police van in the Handy Mart parking lot.

'You need to go to the emergency room.' Cherry's face is all shiny and her make-up runs down her cheeks from her sweat. She looks like a raccoon. 'Let me call Keith for you,' she says.

When Keith peels into the parking lot with Yo, Cherry hangs the CLOSED sign on the door and locks the store. She rides with us to the hospital and pats my shoulder the whole way. I do not tell her that makes it hurt worse.

Keith and Cherry talk while I get my X-ray. It is so cool. They have a big machine that takes a picture of inside my arm. I do not have a broken bone, but the doctor gives me a sling anyway, which is cool. He tells me it is a bad sprain and that I am lucky. I know this. I know I am lucky.

'That's what the L stands for,' I try to say after the doctor gives me a shot. But it comes out like '*Thash wash the ell shtanns foorr.*'

After we pick up my pain pills at the pharmacy, Keith drives us to Denny's. We have an early dinner together. I lean back against the booth while Keith and Cherry talk.

'I can't believe I did what I did. I know it was stupid.' Cherry says.

'We all do stupid things, but really, what else were you gonna do? You're quite a gal.' Keith takes two pills out of my bottle and swallows them with his beer. He lifts Cherry's hair out of her face. 'You've got beautiful eyes. Anybody ever tell you that you have beautiful eyes?'

'It's just so bizarre I can defend Perry, but I can't defend myself against my dad. Way he looks when he drinks, the yelling, and when he gets angry he smacks me around.'

'You tell me when that happens! Day or night, you let me know! Nobody deserves that shit! Nobody! You hear me?' Keith's words are mad, but they come out soft. Like a hug. My eyes are closed but I feel Cherry's smile and it makes me warm. Their voices murmur and surround me like a blanket.

I love Cherry. She saved my life.

LOTTERY WINNER ASSAULTED AT MARINA HANDY MART

That was the headline in the paper. The next part made me really upset.

RETARDED MAN ATTACKED BY THUGS: THREE ARRESTED

'I am not retarded,' I tell Keith. 'I am not retarded, I'm slow. My number is seventy-six. They lied. Can I sue?'

I am embarrassed. I hope Cherry does not see the paper. Gary listens to us talk from the back office. The door is open.

'If people sue other people each time somebody lies or makes a mistake we won't get any work done at all. You can make the paper print a retraction, but it'll just make a mountain out of a molehill,' Gary says. He is practical. I bet he wouldn't be so practical if he was the one called retarded.

Whenever Gary says one thing, Keith does just the opposite.

'I think Per has a point. Hey, Per, gimme that article! What's the phone number of the paper anyway?' Keith walks over to the phone.

He must know how I feel. He is my friend.

'I'd like to talk to the reporter who wrote the piece on the lottery winner.' I restock the shelves. I can only use my good arm. My other one is in a sling and hurts. I take my pills only at night to help me sleep. They are almost gone because I am sharing them with Keith.

'Yeah. This is a friend of Perry Crandall and, yeah, I'll hold.' Keith has to lean on the counter and all the customers have to go around him. Gary comes out from the back office to ring up.

'Keith, we need that phone. Don't tie it up,' Gary warns.

'No I don't want to email!' Keith ignores him. 'Who do I need to talk to? Well, put her on!'

I buy everybody lunch on the days I work. It is so cool. I mean, when a person can buy lunch for everybody, every day, it makes that person feel rich inside no matter how much money they have.

'How you feeling, Perry?' Cherry talks to me when I pick up drinks. The Gilly's guy is making our sandwiches. I have to go back and pick them up.

'Fine. I'm feeling fine.' There are at least twenty people in Marina Handy Mart all shaking Cherry's hand and patting her on the back. She does not really have time to talk to me. Her hair is one more colour than usual. Orange or maroon maybe. She is so beautiful, I just stare.

When I get back to the store, Keith hands me a piece of paper with the name *Marleen Rafters*. There is a phone number written underneath.

'She's a reporter. She's going to do a story on us.' Keith looks excited.

'What kind of a story?' I hand him his sandwich.

Keith does not look me in the eye and takes a big bite. He talks with his mouth full. 'You know, having money, being famous and all.'

It sounds like Keith would like to be famous. I know how it is being famous now. I tell him that being famous is not all it's cracked up to be.

'Be careful, Keith. It's not what you think it is. It can be embarrassing.'

Keith does not look like he believes me. 'Don't you want your picture in the paper?' he asks. Tuna pieces hang off his beard.

'Yeah, I guess. I don't know.' I am confused. That is different from having my name on T-shirts, pens and key chains. People would know my face. I try to explain it to him. 'It's just that, before, people didn't like me when they didn't know me. Then other people decided they didn't like me even when they did know me. Now people like me and they don't even know me at all. Sometimes they haven't ever met me and they like me.' I am thinking about all the letters I get now. All the letters that people write asking me for things. 'It is the same thing, only the opposite of before,' I say.

It is hard to put into words. It is complicated. That means your feelings have many parts to them, but Keith seems to understand. A smile slowly comes across his face.

'You're wise, Per,' he says finally. 'Fucking wise.'

'For a slow guy, you mean,' I correct him. 'F-word wise for a slow guy.'

JOHN AND DAVID come to visit Wednesday on my day off. I am doing laundry so I do not hear them knock. They walk right in. That is so rude.

'We need to talk. We saw the papers. This is exactly what we were telling you about. You need protection.' John is pacing. He talks softly but his fingers are bunched into tight fists.

'How's your arm?' David asks. He does not scare me as much as John does.

There is a short, heavy man with black hair with them carrying a six-pack of Coke and a bag of potato chips. He hands me a can of Coke and offers me chips. I sit down on my couch. David stands in front of me. John paces. The stranger sits next to me.

'This is our friend, Mike Dinelli,' David says. 'He will be coming around to check on you. He's here for your protection.'

Mike grabs my hand and shakes it hard up and down. He is strong. His brown eyes look all shiny like chocolate pudding in the can, which I like because it is fast. You just have to pop the top off and use a spoon.

'How you doing, Perry? Good to meet you,' he says.

'Hello, Mike,' I say.

'I'll be coming around to chat with you from time to time, Perry. See how you're doing. Make sure you're all right.'

'We worry that you may be attacked again,' David says.

'You need to start depending on us more,' John says.

They start to talk among themselves.

Did you get the police record of the assault?

Why do we need that?

For evidence. To prove incompetence.

Can you leave that alone, John? Didn't you listen to Elaine? We're wasting time even thinking about it.

Listen to her and be pussy-whipped the way you are? No, thanks!

ENOUGH! Get a grip and stop bickering. It won't get you anywhere and you don't need to frighten your brother. Am I making myself clear?

Mike rises, walks up to John, grabs his arm and twists. John drops to his knees. David backs up. It is very interesting.

Now, you assured me he would sign by now. It is obvious to me you don't have the influence you think you do. It's time for me to get involved. Do what I say, and stop wasting time arguing. If this doesn't work out you are going to have much more to worry about than each other. Capisce?

I do not know that word.

Capisce?

Mike says this again and releases John's arm. He sits back down next to me. John and David close their mouths and nod their heads.

Mike turns to me and smiles. 'Perry. I'm a financial adviser. Do you know what that is?' He leans back. 'Nice couch,' he says, and pats the back. 'This afghan looks homemade. It's nice work. I have an aunt that crochets like this. Did your Gram make it?'

Mike is cool. He likes Gram's couch. He also likes Hershey's Kisses. We sit and talk while David and John look out my window and hiss at each other. They sound like hoses.

When they leave, I go back downstairs.

'Who were your visitors?' Gary's head lifts up.

'Probably those brothers of his again,' Keith snorts. 'Am I right, Per?'

'No, there was also a guy named Mike,' I say.

Gary and Keith sit with me in the back office.

'You're so suggestible, Perry.' Gary says this just like Gram used to.

'Damn right!' Keith pounds the desk with his fist. He comes over to me and says, 'You have to *not* talk with your brothers unless one of us is around!' He holds my cheeks together just like Gram. 'Just be careful, OK?'

'OK,' I say, and laugh because he still has a hold of my face and it is hard talking through fish lips.

Gary hands me a piece of paper at the same time Keith lets go of me.

'Here, Per, I wrote down your new phone number. It's unlisted.'

'I don't want a new number. I like my old one. It's got only twos, threes and eights.' I am upset. It takes me a long time to not forget my numbers.

'Complete strangers are calling collect and you're accepting the charges! The bill last month was over eight hundred dollars! It goes to the company. I *had* to change it and pay extra to have it unlisted.'

'This is such a gyp! Those people said they knew me!'

I put the paper in my pocket and go back to work unpacking boxes. Taking advantage is something other people do a lot of, I grumble to myself.

THERE IS A LOT of unpacking to do, and it gives me ideas for where to put things on the shelves so they are easier to find. This cheers me up.

'We need to put the covers and short lines by the fenders. It makes it easier,' I say to Keith.

I make a little place and organise fender covers by colour and size. I look for a piece of cardboard and some coloured markers to make a sign.

DON'T FORGET! I write big letters. *DO YOU HAVE LINES?* And then underneath, *DO YOU HAVE COVERS? YOUR FENDERS LAST LONGER IF YOU DO.* This is true. Gramp told me. I tack up my sign with duct tape.

I hear Gary complaining three days later. 'Where'd all the lines and fender covers go? I can't find any more in the back.'

The fender covers are all gone. Sold. Two customers told me it reminded them they needed new lines too, and thanked me.

'We sold out,' I say to Gary. He looks at my signs and then at me.

'This is a really good idea.' He sounds surprised. 'How about we order some more?'

'I already did.' I have good ideas. Gary and Keith both say so.

During lunch, I have some more ideas.

'People like to eat and drink when they buy things,' I announce.

'How do you figure?' Gary usually eats his lunch at his desk. Sandy, his wife, tries to make him eat healthy and fixes him salads in plastic bowls. 'That's fucking rabbit food, Gary. Eat like a real man!' Keith says, and buys him a Gilly's BLT, then threatens to tattle on him after he eats it.

I was too busy to go buy our sandwiches. I gave Keith a fifty-dollar bill and he went to Marina Handy Mart and then to Gilly's. He was gone for a long time. He brought me back a fake crab sandwich.

'At the grocery store customers buy stuff and walk around eating it and then they have cups in their cars and McDonald's and stuff. People eat all the time.' I say this to Gary while I eat.

'He's got a point.' Keith pulls open a beer and it makes a *pop* sound.

Running a store is easy. You just have to get things people want to buy. You have to listen. It helps if you are an auditor. People tell you what they want all the time. *Do you have Perrier?* That is what all the ladies ask as their husbands or boyfriends look at boat stuff. Or, *Do you sell lattes?*

After lunch, I take pieces of my sandwich and feed the birds. Nobody likes it when I do this. I do not know why. Birds have to eat too, especially seagulls. I watch them fight with each other over my sandwich.

'Rats with wings, Perry! You shouldn't feed them.' I didn't hear Marty come up behind me and I jump. 'You can tell Keith his engine is fixed. You want to take him my bill?'

'I get the bill. It goes to me,' I tell him.

'OK. Well, I replaced all the filters. I scrubbed the tank and practically had to rebuild the whole thing. The guts were all screwed up.' Marty always calls the inside of an engine the guts. He hands me a paper with Keith's name at the top and a list of all the parts he used for Keith's engine.

I pull my chequebook out of my back pocket and write Marty a cheque for $1,103.73 for parts and labour. He has to help me.

I walk back to the store and give Keith the copy of Marty's bill. It is marked *paid* in Marty's cramped handwriting.

'Shit! You didn't need to spend all that money! He ripped you off!' Keith checks everything on the invoice. 'I probably needed the filters, but holy fuck! He charged us extra for our own gaskets. Look!' Keith is always happiest when he can yell and complain about something. He looks almost cheerful and gives me a slap on the back. That is his way of saying thank you.

'Keith, let's sail to Kingston or up to Anacortes or somewhere.' I want to go on a sailing trip.

'It's pretty cold now, but yeah, when the weather clears we'll go up to Whidbey and anchor out.'

I was so excited about fixing *Diamond Girl* that I made him take Yo up to Ron's gas station at the corner to repair the heater and get a tune-up. Gram always told me that it was important to show people that you appreciate them. Keith always took us places in Yo. It was only fair.

'It's the first time Yo has been worked on since I bought him.' Keith sounds amazed. Like he won a prize.

When I show Keith the final bill from Ron's, he gets all upset again. He jumps up and down then rips the invoice up into tiny pieces. They scatter all over the floor.

'You going to sweep those up?' Gary looks disapproving.

I run to get the broom and dustpan.

'Shit! Five hundred dollars for a fucking tune-up!' Keith's face is purple.

'It's OK, Keith,' I say while I sweep the pieces up and put them in the trash. 'I'm doing this for Gram! It was something she always wanted to do for you,' I say. 'It was on her lottery list.'

Keith would take her to the doctor whenever she needed to go. We could ask him to take us to Costco for TP and paper towels. Those things are very hard to carry on the bus because they are so big. We both always appreciated the rides, even though Gram would complain about Yo's heater. 'If we won the lottery, I'd fix that goddamn heater!' Gram would promise Keith.

Gram would be happy that Yo's heater is fixed. She was always cold.

'Hey, let's go to Hawaii!' I say. 'Let's take Gram to Hawaii.'

'What?' Keith sits up straight.

'It was on Gram's lottery list. Gram wanted to go somewhere warm.'

Keith looks dizzy and says, 'Gram is dead, Per.'

'I know that, but I think Gram would still like to go to Hawaii. The three of us could go together,' I say.

'You mean like spread her ashes?' Keith smiles when he says this.

'You spread mayonnaise and you spread peanut butter. It does not make sense to spread ashes,' I tell him.

'You sprinkle them,' he says.

'Like sugar on cereal? Like my oatmeal?'

'No! You throw them in the air off a mountain or toss them into the ocean. When I die, I want my ashes spread out into the Sound,' Keith says. 'Then the water will just take me away. I'd go all over the world and it wouldn't cost me a dime!'

'I don't think Gram would want to be floating around in the water even in Hawaii. I never ever saw her in a bathing suit.'

'So Waikiki, huh? Let's check it out.' He grabs the phone book.

WE FLY FIRST-CLASS.

First-class is when you pay a lot of money to cut in line. It is very cool. People mutter and stare when we go ahead of them. Nobody believes we are first-class. The seats are bigger, which is a good thing for Keith. We also get real silverware and free drinks.

The stewardess lady checks our tickets so often that Keith asks her if she has a problem with us. Then he smiles and says, 'I don't think you've met my friend, Perry L. Crandall.' He introduces me. 'You might have seen him in the newspaper when he WON THE WASHINGTON STATE LOTTERY?' He says this very loud and looks around.

Boy, people were interested. The nice man sitting across talks to us both and gives me his card. He sells insurance. The stewardess stops checking our tickets and instead gives us packages of mixed nuts and cookies, as many as we want. They act like they like me.

Then I remember. These people like me because I won the lottery.

The stewardess hands me a tiny plastic pin.

'Look! Airplane wings, Keith!' I think they are totally cool.

'Do you want a pair?' The stewardess hands Keith a package too.

'Do you think she thinks I'm retarded?' I whisper in Keith's ear. 'Are these just for kids?'

'Nah, Per. She gave me a pair too. She doesn't think that.'

That would have spoilt the whole trip for me, but it is OK. Keith says so.

When we land in Hawaii, my ears pop like going down a big hill. I notice two things right away. One is that it is very hot when we get off the plane. The other thing is that all the signs have words with lots of aaas, eees, iiis and ooos. Those are vowels. I am so excited I laugh. 'Ha!'

'What's the matter?' Keith is sweating like a pig. Of course, I never saw a real pig except at the petting zoo at Woodland Park. If one did sweat, it would look like Keith. All pink and dripping.

'I am really happy, Keith.'

'That's why I like you, Per. That and you have money now.' And he laughs back at me.

Riding the cab is exciting. The driver opens the car door even though he knows we probably can. Hawaii is just like Everett except that it has palm trees, is warmer, and everybody says 'Aloha'. Our hotel is right on the beach. I can hear the ocean roar, like a machine.

I am so happy I start to bounce. 'Hey! I have an idea! Let's buy swimsuits!'

'Shorts, Per, we just need shorts,' but Keith follows me into a gift shop anyway. There is one in the lobby of our hotel. A lobby is a place where they keep anything you might need to buy, like coconut bras, hula girl lamps or towels with dolphins.

I absolutely do not understand the lady in the store.

'I thought you said we were in America,' I whisper to Keith. The language is probably Hawaiian, with all those extra vowels.

'We *are* in America, Per. It's called an accent,' Keith whispers back.

Accents are when people speak and they don't sound like you.

The ocean in Hawaii is wonderful. I never saw anything like it. So blue and warm like a bath. I stand waist-deep in the water.

'Hey, you can float on your back!' I point at Keith. His stomach is like a giant ball.

'Go ahead! You can too!' he says.

'I can't swim. I don't want to drown.'

Keith is my friend and tries to teach me to dog paddle. I sink, flip over and then float on my back. 'Hey, look at me! I can float! This is so cool! Hawaii sure is great!'

'You will be swimming for real before we go home. I swear!' Keith says.

People say 'I swear' when they are not sure that they can do something, but they want to convince you they will.

We stay in the water until dinnertime. Nobody cares that we drip water and sand all the way back to our hotel room.

We can do anything we want. That is so cool.

THE BRIGHTEST SUN in the world comes up in Hawaii. Part of our balcony faces the ocean and the other part faces a big rock called Diamond Head. It used to be a volcano, but it was shut off or something. I think they should turn it back on. That would be exciting. I imagine yelling at Keith. 'Hey, Keith! Volcano! You better run!'

Down in the lobby they have papers that tell all the things tourists can do in Hawaii. All the papers are very colourful and have interesting things to read. We get pages and pages of stuff and take them up to our room. I look at pictures of boats and dolphins.

Gram's box is on the dresser. It is turned so she can see through the sliding glass door out to the ocean.

'OK, Per. So where you going to scatter her ashes?' Keith moves Gram an inch over so she has a better view.

'What do you mean *scatter*?' I ask.

'You know. Like we talked about. Spread. Sprinkle,' Keith says.

'Nowhere. I don't want to scatter Gram in Hawaii, just give her a little visit.'

'Don't you want to leave even any of her ashes here?'

'Keith, that would be gross! She needs to be kept together!' I can feel myself getting a teeny bit upset. I miss Gram. I do not want to leave even a little piece of her in Hawaii.

'OK. OK. I get it. Just a little trip. Don't get all wound up.'

Keith always tells me not to get wound up. I never tell him not to drink, pick his nose or fart.

Keith asks the valet guy at the front of the hotel, 'My buddy and I are here for a few days. What should we do?'

'Go on the *Arizona* Memorial Tour,' he says.

He puts us on a bus and we take a motorboat ride across the water.

'Hey Keith! Look! Fish!' I scream.

'Shhhhhh! Don't yell,' he hisses.

I notice everybody on the boat is quiet.

Arizona is a dead ship from a war that makes everybody sad.

'Hey, Keith! Look at this stuff.' There are lots of names of people who died in a war and a tiny church room with blue-and-yellow-glass windows. The lady next to me looks like Gram except she is shorter and has kind of fuzzy hair. Her skin is dark brown. Gram's was white or maybe grey.

'Hi. I'm Perry. What's your name? You look like my Gram,' I say.

'I'm Myrtle. Is your Gram here?' She looks around.

'No, she's back in the hotel room. She's dead,' I tell her.

Myrtle raises her eyebrows and her mouth falls open. She looks better after I tell her Gram is just ashes in a box now.

Myrtle calls me unique. *Unique* means you are not like other people in a good way. It is not like *different*, which means you are not like other people in a bad way.

We talk about war.

'I think war is bad. People get killed. That is my opinion.' Gram always told me to tell people it is only my opinion. 'Remember everybody doesn't think the same,' Gram would say.

'Yeah, war is bad all right.' Myrtle has to wipe wet out of her eyes.

Blue, shiny pieces of oil bubble up from the wreck. They look like puddles in the rain when cars drive through them after the sun comes out.

'Keith, you were in a war, right?' I ask Keith during the bus ride back.

'Yeah.' He has wet in his eyes too.

'What's it like?' I ask.

He leans his head back against the seat. 'You don't want to know,' he says.

'Yeah, Keith. Yeah I do.'

He turns to me and his voice is thunder. 'No, Perry, *you don't.*'

I sit and think. And I think it is Keith who doesn't want to know.

I LEARN THREE THINGS in Hawaii. One, that people like me because I won the lottery. Two, that you can do things you want to do even if you're dead. And three, if I want Cherry to be my girlfriend I will have to buy her presents. I learn that last thing at the airport.

We are waiting to get on the airplane and Keith and I are looking at all the cool things for sale, like coconuts you can mail and shark jaws. I see a girl. She has blonde hair, not coloured like Cherry's, but she has earrings in her face and tattoos just like Cherry.

'Hey, that looks like Cherry,' I tell Keith.

'Look at the guy with her. He's old enough to be her fucking grandfather,' Keith growls.

The Cherry-girl is trying on bracelets and smiling.

'Sometimes that's the only way a guy can get a girlfriend,' Keith tells me.

I get an idea. 'Do you think Cherry would like this?' I show him a necklace.

'Sure, yeah. Girls like that kind of shit.'

I buy Cherry the necklace and a box of chocolate-covered macadamia nuts. Keith buys a box of pens that—when you click them on—make a hula girl naked. That is cool.

I am way too tired to bounce on the plane. I feel like I have used up all my fun for the rest of my life. I think about this the whole trip back. That all of us are given so much fun in life, kind of like brains. Some people save theirs until they are old and some people use it all up at the beginning of their lives. I'm using my fun up in the middle. That is so cool.

I have been back two days and I have not seen Cherry. I go to get a Slurpee, but she has the day off. I have to buy another Slurpee the next day.

'Hey, Cherry, I'm back from HAWAII!' My sunburn is peeling off my forehead. Keith said everybody would think I either went on vacation or had a grungy skin disease. I hope Cherry does not think I have a disease. 'I went on vacation and got you something.'

She smiles when she sees the chocolate. She smiles even bigger when she sees the necklace. I help her put it on right there in the store.

'Awesome! Thanks.' She has to bend down next to the metal wall of the refrigerator to see how the necklace looks around her neck. She could have asked me. I would have told her she looked beautiful.

Cherry grabs me by the neck, pulls my head over and gives me a big smacking kiss on my cheek.

Keith was right. Presents are a good way to get a girlfriend.

When I get home, I have to sit on Gram's couch and bounce I am so happy.

6

Mike Dinelli comes into the store on Thursdays to make sure I am all right. On Thursday afternoon, Gary plays golf and Keith goes to Pacific Marine Supply for our orders.

John calls to see if Mike has come by and asks for a cheque.

David calls to see if John has called and asks for a cheque.

Elaine calls to see if David or John has called and tells me to send her a cheque.

Louise just calls and asks for a cheque.

Mike brings me lunch. He always brings me a giant bag of Hershey's Kisses. It is so cool that I do not need to buy them any more.

I can't go out to eat lunch with Mike because I have to watch the store. He says we can just stand and talk. 'We need to get to know each other,

Perry. I'm a friend of John and David's and want to be your friend too.'

'OK,' I say.

He is a protector and wants my Power. He brings a piece of paper each time he comes.

You need to sign this paper.

Can you write your name here on this line?

It's important that you sign. This will protect you.

I do not want to give my Power away when I am working at Holsted's. I am too busy. We can get a lot of people on Thursdays. I look through catalogues to find stuff for the store.

'So, Mr Crandall,' Mike says, and laughs.

'Perry. Call me Perry,' I say. This is our joke. I told him when people call me Mr Crandall it makes me feel like I am in trouble, and so he teases me. This is a good tease. I like it when I have jokes with people.

'My company has a specific plan for lottery winners who have selected the annuity option. It allows access to the money now instead of waiting for the yearly payments. Both your brothers think it would be a wise investment for you.' Mike looks hungry.

'Do you want to buy a cookie or some coffee?' I ask.

Now that Holsted's has a corner for drinks and snacks, all the fishermen come in. They sit in chairs, drink coffee and talk with each other. Gary complains that they never buy stuff, but I know they do.

'It's a good deal for you, Perry. You could invest the cash and earn a lot more.' Mike's voice stays very low. He keeps looking at the door like he expects it to open.

'How much money would you give me?'

'Well, we take the rest of your payments and you would get four million cash right now.' Mike talks fast, and his pink gums show.

'But I won twelve million.' Four for twelve does not sound fair.

'If you do it any other way you will have enormous tax consequences. This way, since you could invest all your money at once, it's really to your advantage. Your brothers think it's the best plan.'

When he says that word *advantage*, it makes me think of Gram. Gram would tell me, 'Whenever anyone ever says *it's to your advantage*, Perry? It is to theirs. You remember that.'

'Well, it would be unfair of me to take advantage of you just because I won the lottery. You probably ought to invest your money for yourself,' I say. He is my friend. You do not take advantage of your friends.

Gram would be proud of me. Mike does not look happy. In fact, he looks like he needs a Tums.

'Hey, Mike. You need a Tums?' I ask. I worry. Mike is my friend and I do not want my friends to be sick.

This is always when Mike stops talking. When he sighs loud and when he leaves. He looks like he has worries.

'Marleen Rafters called this morning,' Keith says. 'She'll be out at three. We can take off work early and talk to her on *Diamond Girl*.'

'Marleen?' I do not know a Marleen.

'She's that reporter,' Keith says. 'Remember? She's doing a story on us.'

Now I know why he is wearing a tie and clean pants.

Gary is not upset about us taking extra time off for our interview. 'Advertising, Keith!' he says. 'Make sure you talk about the store and make sure they get the address right in the paper. Here. Give her a Holsted's Marine Supply pen and key chain.'

Marleen is tall, has a deep gravelly voice and wears jeans with a flannel shirt. She has heavy black boots that she removes in order to come onto *Diamond Girl*. No one is supposed to wear boots on boats because they make black marks on the fibreglass. Marleen looks a lot like Keith. Her hair is the same grey-brown pulled back into a ponytail just like his.

'Hi, Perry. I'm Marleen. That's Arleen with an M.' She shakes my hand.

I laugh. 'Ha! I'm Perry with a P!' I say. 'Hey, I've seen you on TV!'

'You probably have. I do features on the news.' Marleen smiles at me.

I whisper to Keith, 'A TV star. Cool!'

Keith looks disappointed and whispers back, 'A dyke, Per! Just my luck!'

A dyke is both something to keep back water and a girl who likes other girls instead of boys. Marleen is nice. She talks to me.

'People take advantage and jump to conclusions, I see . . .' and her voice trails off like the end of a song. She says *I see* sixteen times. I know because I keep track. Then she asks the wrong thing.

'So do people treat you differently when they find out you're retarded?'

I do not say a word at first. If I were a cartoon, I would have steam shooting out of my ears.

'I don't know. Do they?' Spit drops fly out my mouth. I am really mad.

'Well . . .' Marleen looks at Keith. 'Did I say something wrong?'

'Bingo!' Keith says. He pinches out his cigarette and tosses the end overboard. 'Per's not retarded. He's slow. That's different than retarded.'

'What's your number?' I ask Marleen. My hands are shaking.

She looks confused. 'You mean my phone number? What do you mean?'

'No. Your number. My number is seventy-six. I am not retarded.'

'I don't know my number,' she says.

'Ha!' I say. 'Then how do you know you're not retarded?'

'I'm not.'

'How do you know?'

'I just know I'm not.' She looks at Keith like she expects him to help.

'Hey, don't look at me. He's got a point. I have no idea what my number is. Shit! I let myself be drafted. I could very well be retarded.' Keith bends down to light another smoke.

Marleen writes down everything I say and some other things that I don't. I look over her shoulder at her notebook.

Keith knows I am still mad and mouths *I'm sorry.*

PEOPLE WOULD ASK Gram questions.

Didn't his mother know?

Didn't she get tested?

Couldn't she terminate?

Gram would get angry. 'So you'd kill him just because he's slow?'

My first IQ number test was not good. It came out a bad number and both Gram and Gramp were upset. Gram asked me about it and I told her. First, I was scared. I thought I was in trouble. And second I had to pee really bad. I was worried that I would wet my pants. I could not concentrate. *Concentrate* means do your best job. I could not do my best job.

'You're slow, Perry! There's not a goddamned thing wrong with you that time won't fix.' Gram tried to make my teacher give me the number test again, but she said no.

The IQ score will not change appreciably from one test to another. There's a range of about ten per cent.

Gram was mad. 'You mean his test could be ten points higher?'

'That is unlikely.' People say this when they are wrong and they don't want to argue any more.

It was different with my next teacher, Miss Elk. She helped me take a new number test. She told me I could be anything I wanted. I stayed after school and practised doing tests until I was not scared. I tried hard to do my best job. My number came out 76. It was a good number, Gram said. The best number, and she and Gramp cheered.

We were happy, but the school did not care. They said the second test did not count.

I told this to Keith when he asked. We talked about lots of things. About school. About what I like to eat. About sailing. He is my friend. Friends want to know all about you.

'Gram was a good teacher. She didn't mind that I was slow, but lots of people do.' I name each one. 'First, there is the bus driver. He gets cranky if you do not have the right change. Then there is the grocery store lady at check-out in the fifteen-things-or-less line.' I take deep breaths because it is hard to talk about being slow. 'If you are in that line and lose track of how many things you have, people think you are retarded, they stare at you and say mean things. If you have twenty things and go in the fifteen-things-or-less line and you are in a suit and talking on your cellphone, then you are just rude. That is OK. It is better to be rude than retarded,' I tell him.

I explain things to Keith that he did not know. He did not know there are many numbers that mean retarded. Retarded is lower than 70 or it can be lower than 75.

But it is not 76. It is never 76.

I LIKE THE WALK to Marina Handy Mart. It calms me down. I can think. Sometimes I hum. There is a sidewalk the whole way and it is close to the water. I sometimes go there to get Chef Boyardee ravioli for dinner. Ravioli are little meat pieces in dough covered with spaghetti sauce. They taste good, are easy to fix and are better than SpaghettiOs.

When I walk in the Marina Handy Mart door, the bell tinkles.

'Hey, Cherry!' I call.

Cherry can make anybody feel better. She is so pretty. I want to ask her if she is my girlfriend today, but I stop when I see her. Something is very wrong. She is slumped behind the cash counter crying. I can tell because her eyes are red and there is snot hanging from her nose ring. She has a Kleenex and is blowing, which is good.

'Hey, Perry.' When she wipes her face, I can see she has purple and blue all around one eye and a long scrape on her cheek.

'Cherry. Wow! Did you get in an accident?'

'No. Well. Yeah. Yeah, I guess you could say that.' She blows her nose again, and she starts crying hard.

'Please don't cry, Cherry.' I pat her hand. Boyfriends help girlfriends when they are in trouble, but I do not know what to do.

I decide to buy lunch sandwiches from Marina Handy Mart instead of Gilly's so I can talk to Cherry longer. Cherry walks with me to the back and helps me find the right sandwiches. They have tuna, which is OK. I like tuna. When I am done choosing sandwiches Cherry looks a little happier. She touches my hand when she gives me back my change.

'Thanks, Perry,' she says. 'Thanks a lot.'

I walk back to work and wonder what kind of accident she had.

Keith is standing talking to a customer when I carry the lunches into the back room. The man's voice is loud and flat. I stand by the door. I want to tell Keith about his sandwich, but I do not want to interrupt. It is not polite.

'So you know him?' the man says.

'Yeah, we've known each other for a long time.' Keith waves me over.

The man looks over at me. He has silver hair and big feet. 'It must be nice to have a friend who's a millionaire,' he says.

I get it. They are talking about me. I am embarrassed.

'Here, meet Perry Crandall. Perry, this is Ernie. Ernie, Perry.' Keith puts a hand on my shoulder.

'Nice to meet you, Ernie.' I hold out my hand.

Ernie looks from Keith to me. 'Interesting. So . . . are you sharing your winnings with your family and friends?'

'Yeah, sure,' I say. Sharing is a good idea and it is a nice thing to do.

Keith sweeps the air with his hand. 'Hey, he does what he wants.'

'I bet he does. Lucky you.' Ernie gives a sharp barking laugh.

'Hot damn!' says Keith after Ernie has left. 'Not only do people get excited to meet a lottery winner, they get excited to meet the friend of one. And jealous too.' He follows me into the back room to get his sandwich.

That is another thing. People are jealous of the lottery.

When I take a bite of my sandwich I remember to tell Keith something.

'Cherry has a black eye and scratched cheek,' I say.

'What? How?' Keith sits straight up.

'An accident,' I answer.

'Shit! God *damn* him!' Keith growls. He shoves his sandwich in the trash and grabs his jacket. 'I'll be back!' He sounds like Terminator. That is cool.

WHEN A DAD beats up his daughter, he does not necessarily go to jail. But when a guy beats a dad up for beating up his daughter, they both go to jail. It is very confusing. A person only gets to make one phone call when they are arrested. I learned this from Keith. He was able to make one right away because Officer Ray Mallory recognised him at the station. Keith calls me.

'I need to be bailed out. You need to pick me up. Yo's over at Marina Handy Mart,' Keith says.

'I do not have a driver's licence,' I tell him.

'I know that. Cherry should be on her way. I need five hundred bucks. Bring your chequebook.'

Bail can be what you do to water that gets in your boat or it can be money to get out of jail. After I hang up the phone, there is a knock at my door.

It is Cherry carrying a backpack. 'Perry. We have to get Keith out of jail.' She is panting from running up my stairs.

'I know. He called me,' I tell her.

Cherry's shirt is ripped on the bottom and her jeans drag on the floor. Her stomach hangs over her belt. It looks soft and white. There is a gold ring hooked through her bellybutton. She is so beautiful I can only stare into her eyes. They are brown, red and wet.

'I can drive. We can take Yo. Keith threw his keys to me just before the cops took him.' Cherry sniffs and wipes her eyes with her sleeve. I think she should use a Kleenex because her black make-up is all over her shirt.

'I need someplace to stay,' she says. 'I can't go back home now.' She takes a breath like it is hard for her to talk. 'I could only think of you or Keith. I have no one else I can ask.' Her face is pointed down like she is sad, or like she expects me to say no.

'Yes,' I say. 'Yes, you can stay here.' Why would anyone say no, I wonder. I could never say no to Cherry. 'Let's go get Keith.'

When Cherry hears me say this, she drops her backpack on my floor and smiles. Her eyes are still wet, but her smile is so beautiful I cannot speak.

Cherry talks to me all the way to the police station.

'I had just gotten off. I had an early shift. I left right after you bought your sandwiches. My dad was already home from work. I didn't expect him that early and I told him that if he touched me again I would call the police. For real this time. He thought I was kidding. He screamed at me and slapped me so hard he gave me a bloody nose. I ran into the bedroom, grabbed the phone and dialled nine-one-one. And then Keith just blew through our front door like the Hulk, fists flying! It was so awesome. He punched my dad in the face, threw him into the wall and knocked him out. He was amazing.' Cherry sighs. 'I was so bummed because I had already made my call. It was the first time I ever called the cops when he beat me. They took both Keith *and* my dad in.'

'I wish I had been there.' It would have been very exciting.

Cherry and I both like Hulk comics. We like Slurpees and PayDays too.

Officer Mallory recognises Cherry and me. He told me that they don't usually take cheques, but they know mine is good. That is so cool.

Keith is very glad to see us. He has only one tiny cut over his eye, a bump on his lip and a bloody shirt.

'Hey, thanks, Per.' Keith slaps me on the back. He says thank you ten more times. Cherry hugs Keith and says thank you about twenty times. I do not slap anybody on the back. I just pay Keith's fine. Keith stuffs a bunch of papers in his pocket and we walk out to Yo. He slides into the driver's seat and I squeeze next to Cherry by the passenger door. Nobody talks much on the way home. Cherry just sniffs every once in a while.

We stand in the parking lot in front of Holsted's looking at each other and then Keith tells us good night. He strolls to his boat. Cherry follows me upstairs to my front door. She keeps looking back at Keith as we climb the steps, but he does not turn around.

I give her a tour of my place.

'You can sleep in my bed and I can sleep on Gram's couch. Here is my bathroom and a clean towel.' I have never had a guest before.

When I show her my TV, I can tell she is impressed.

'Oh, wow! That's awesome!' And she runs her hand over the top just like I do when I can't believe I finally have a TV.

I let Cherry take a shower first. She comes out wearing pink sweatpants and a fleece shirt, and sits down on Gram's sofa. I take my turn in the bathroom. When I come out in my pyjamas and robe, Cherry is standing at the window looking out. Keith is sitting in his cockpit smoking a cigarette. *Diamond Girl* is very still in the water. I can see her hull reflected in the smooth black surface. I am feeling strange as I stand next to Cherry. Kind of excited, nervous, bouncy. I grab the blanket Gram made, wrap it around my middle and lie down on the couch. I squeeze my eyelids shut tight. I do not know what else to do. Cherry walks into the bedroom.

As she passes me, she says, 'Night, Perry,' and 'Thanks.' I hear the door shut and try to go to sleep. It takes me a long, long time.

I really, really like Cherry.

'SO YOU HAVE a room-mate now.' That is what Gary says. Then he always asks, 'How's it working out?'

I say fine, but it is not just me, it is Keith. We both have a room-mate. It is like we share Cherry. She spends a lot of time on *Diamond Girl*. Cherry and

Keith talk and smoke in his cockpit. She tells me that since I do not smoke it's not fair for them to puff away in my apartment.

Keith and I eat good dinners now. Keith eats with us every night. Cherry cooks Hamburger Helper, chilli, Chicken Tenders, and makes us both eat salads. She cleans my bathroom and mops my floor. It is so cool. I do not have to do anything. She even washes all our clothes on Wednesdays. She folds my clothes and everything. I only have to set the table. I tell Cherry I can cook, but she says she has to earn her keep. She still works at Marina Handy Mart, but I do not let her pay rent.

She is a hard worker like me. Sometimes she answers my phone.

'Who's Elaine?' she asks me.

'My cousin-brother David's wife.'

'She left a message for you. Says she has papers for you to sign. What a bitch! She called me a slut on the phone. She doesn't even know me!'

When Keith and Cherry are on *Diamond Girl*, I go into my bedroom. Cherry has her things neatly folded in my dresser. We share, but I only go into the bedroom to look at Gram and Gramp's boxes. When I miss them, I can bring them back by looking at pictures and sorting through their things.

It is almost dinnertime and I hear my front door open.

'Perry? Are you here?' It is Cherry's voice. It always sounds like she is singing. I love her voice. 'You want roni-cheese for dinner? I bought hot dogs too!' she calls out.

She walks into the room before I have time to take my mess off the bed.

'Perry? What are all these?'

'Gram and Gramp's stuff. It is mine now.'

'Cool,' she says. 'You're so lucky. I don't have anything like this. I have nothing from my family.'

She sits on the edge of the bed and looks at my memory things. I get Gramp's record player out and put on one of Gramp's records.

'This one is Sousa. Army guys march to this,' I tell her.

We both kick our feet in time to the music.

'What's this?' she asks, and unfolds a piece of paper. 'It looks like a list.'

I take it from her hand. It has all the names of the people I am supposed to listen to: Gary, Officer Ray Mallory, firemen.

I have not looked at this list for a long time. I have not needed it. It is like I can decide who to listen to on my own now.

'Nothing. It is nothing,' I say.

I fold it back up and put it into Gram's box.

MY FIRST CHRISTMAS after the lottery was cool-sad. Cool because Christmas is magic, but sad because Gram was not there to share it. Gram and I loved Christmas decorations.

'Hey, Cherry! Keith and I are going to drive around tonight and look at Christmas lights. You want to come?' I do not know why, but my armpits get all wet and my stomach is lumpy like when I eat too many nachos with cheese and peppers or whenever I visit Cherry at Marina Handy Mart. Her black eye is gone and she wears shiny blue glitter on her eyelashes.

'Sure. Yeah. That sounds fun.' Cherry looks like she means it.

I want to yell *yippee* and bounce, but I wait until I get back to Holsted's.

We put more oil in Yo, because he leaks, and drive all the way to Seattle. Pretend snow fluffs down and it is perfect. Gram called snow that didn't stick *pretend snow*. 'All of the advantages of snow, but none of the problems,' Gram said. 'No getting stuck in the road, no slipping, no messing up bus schedules. And it still makes it feel like Christmas.'

Cherry squishes me next to the door, which makes me hot, cold and bouncy. She sits in the middle. Cherry does not seem to bother Keith like I do when I bounce or talk too much or sit too close. He puts an arm around her and takes it off only when he has to shift gears.

When we get to the neighbourhood with all the decorations, the snow is sticking on the ground and Yo slides as we turn a corner. There are a lot of other people that have the exact same idea of looking at Christmas lights. We end up in the middle of a long line of cars and have to go slowly.

The houses all have coloured lights that flash and move.

'I love the blue lights. Look at that one!' Cherry points out to the left.

'Look over there!' I point to the other side where someone put a giant plastic Snoopy in a sled on their porch.

Poor Keith has to look back and forth each time one of us gets excited. He eventually just stares straight ahead, bites his lip and tries not to rear-end the car in front. When we come to the end, Cherry and I are hungry so Keith stops at Dick's Drive-In for milk shakes and French fries.

'What's your favourite part of Christmas, Keith?' Cherry asks.

'When it's over.' Keith looks grumpy.

'Why are you so irked? It's Christmas.' She pokes him with a fry.

I want to tell Cherry to stop asking questions. They are the same questions Gram used to ask. Keith does the same thing to Cherry that he did to Gram. He pulls out his wallet, opens it up and flips out a picture.

'See this? Her name's April. She used to be my wife. And the baby? My son, Jason. It was taken more than thirty years ago. She married my ex-best buddy, Roger. Last time I saw her was the day I shipped out to Nam.' Keith's eyes squeeze shut, then open again. 'December the 24th, 1971. I signed both divorce and adoption papers at the same time, hiding under a table in the mess tent while Charlie mortared the hell out my company. I thought I was gonna die anyway. What did it matter? Those fucking lawyers take advantage of a grunt's fear of death. They're a bunch of money-grubbing bastards. I even had to pay for the privilege of losing my wife and son to that back-stabbing asshole. So, no.' He puts his picture away. 'Christmas is a real drag.'

Cherry is quiet and I am sad now.

I know tonight Keith will drink. He will start with beer. Afterwards he will look for the bottles he took from John's house. I know he keeps them in the galley of his boat. The next day he will be hung over, and he will not drink for days. Then something will remind him, and he will start all over again.

It is after eleven when we get back to Everett. Keith parks Yo in the hand-icapped space.

'Hey! You can't park there,' Cherry says. She does not know our rules.

'It's for disabled trucks too. Yo qualifies. He leaks enough oil to be anaemic.' Keith glares at her, and then he looks back down at his feet like he is sorry for snapping.

'Hey, Cherry, you coming?' I ask, and start walking up my stairs.

She looks down and kicks her foot in the gravel. 'I think I'll hang out on Keith's boat for a while if it's OK with you, Perry. Just leave the door unlocked for me.' Cherry lifts her head, stares at Keith and smiles.

He stares back and his face completely changes. He smiles back at her real slow. They do not say a word. They just stare at each other.

'You guys OK?' I ask.

They do not answer me.

'Cherry?' I say again.

Keith's eyes get wide like he is just waking up. 'I'll take care of her, Per, don't you worry. You go on up to bed.'

'OK.' I am tired. I need to go to bed.

I take a shower, get into my pyjamas and stand in front of my window looking out at the falling snow. I put Hershey's Kisses into my mouth one by one and stare outside. The lights at the pier make the dock look like a Christmas card. It is not good to eat a lot of candy before you go to bed, so I put my bag away, go into the bathroom and brush my teeth.

When I come back to the window, I can see a yellow glow through the portholes on Keith's boat. I see them flicker and flash, then go dark. After a while, I notice *Diamond Girl* moving. She is rocking hard back and forth. Back and forth. Back and forth. I watch until she stops moving and floats gently on the water. It is quiet. I yawn and go to bed.

CHRISTMAS IS A TIME for giving. It was hard to decide what to buy Louise, David and John. *Fruit baskets*. Gram told me in my head. *Send them big fancy baskets of fruit*. I appreciated Gram helping me out.

I sent them cheques too. I had to send Louise's fruit basket to John's house because I do not have her real address. She has a PO, which is a sort of a box. You cannot send flowers to a PO. I think it is too small for a fruit basket. Louise comes by Holsted's three days before Christmas to ask for another cheque. I hide in the back room and peek out through the crack in the door. Her hair is brown with yellow stripes now. She still scares me.

Keith tells her to wait and goes over to where I am hiding. 'You want me to kick her skinny little ass outside?' he hisses.

'No.' I hiss back. We both sound like snakes.

I kneel on the floor and write another cheque.

'Shit! You don't have to give her money each time she comes,' Keith says.

He doesn't understand. I give her money to go away. Not to make her come.

'Is she gone?' I whisper through the door.

'Yeah, she's gone,' Keith says.

We spend Christmas Eve with Gary's family. Gary's wife Sandy is funny and blonde and his daughters Kelly and Meagan know me from when they come into the store. Kelly is the older one and Meagan is the younger. Their house smells like turkey and pumpkin pie. My stomach is grumbling.

Keith brings in the presents from Yo and sets them under the tree. It takes him five trips. He is on his best behaviour and only says the S-word twice.

Meagan and Kelly look impressed with all the earrings on Cherry's face and the colours of her hair.

'I took out my silver stud because it's Christmas,' she says, and sticks out her tongue to show them the hole. They both stare into her mouth and then she leads them into the bathroom so she can show them the ring in her navel.

Cherry has on a red top with sparkles and a long skirt. She is so beautiful. I am bouncing because I bought her a present that I think she will really like. If she likes it a lot she might be my girlfriend.

There is a real tree in the living room. It has lights with red, green, blue, white and yellow bulbs. They move and sparkle. Sandy gives us all special cardboard glasses, and when we put them on they make the lights turn into bells and angels and stars. I keep mine on even when I unwrap my presents. I am like a movie star. I get shirts, a giant box of Hershey's Kisses, a Game Boy, which is cool, but I do not know how to work it, and lots of other stuff.

Cherry unwraps her present from me first. Diamond earrings that I bought her from Zales. She is so happy she screams and runs into the bathroom.

'I think she likes them,' Sandy whispers to me. I think so too.

Gram always said the most happiness you can collect is when you give things to people you love. I have a lot of happiness in my heart as I watch everybody else open presents I bought for them.

On the way home Cherry talks about her mother. 'When I was little, before my mom and dad started drinking, we had a tree, and my aunts, uncles and cousins would visit. After they separated, it just wasn't the same.' Cherry looks sad as she says this.

'Gram and I had a fake tree. We put it up the day after Thanksgiving and took it down New Year's Day,' I say. 'It was all silver. Remember, Keith? It was in the first load we took to the dump.'

After everyone goes to bed, I lay stockings for Cherry and Keith in front of the TV. It is like a pretend fireplace. I am very good at stockings. First, you buy candy and oranges because they last the longest. Then you buy little stuff like pens, tiny flashlights and soap samples. I do good stockings.

I sleep on the couch and Keith and Cherry sleep in the bedroom. The thumping noise only keeps me up a little while. I am very tired. The next thing I know, Cherry is poking me in the ribs to get up.

'Santa came last night!' she sings.

And oh boy! Did he! Santa, which was most likely both Cherry and Keith, brought me my own laptop computer. Another stocking with my name on it was right next to theirs. I got a hat, new socks with sailboats on them and a whistle that I blew until Keith yelled, 'Shut the fuck up, Per!'

That's OK.

Cherry showed me how to use my computer and I wrote down all the directions. She said she would give me computer lessons every day as part of her present. Christmas is always a good day. But this Christmas was double wonderful. Keith and Cherry went back to *Diamond Girl* after dinner for a smoke. I sat up until late playing with my computer. Before I went to sleep, I heard Gram's voice.

Merry Christmas, Perry, she said.

Merry Christmas, Gram, I said back.

7

My words today are *pass*, *passable* and *passage*. I type them into my new computer. I started my new book in Word. I like that. *Word*. That pretty much tells you what it is. Word for my words.

Pass. The first definition I read makes me sad. It means die. To pass on. I have to shut down my computer so I can think about Gram again.

The lottery reminds me of Gram. When we bought tickets she would say, 'You know, Perry, life's all just one big goddamned lottery. Some of us have brains, some of us don't. Some people draw cancer. Others win car accidents and plane crashes. It's just a lottery. A goddamned lottery.'

I did not win the brains lottery, but I won the other kind.

January is cold and wet in Everett. I send more cheques to my cousin-brothers. They still want my Power. Soon it will be February. It will still be grey, but that is the heart month.

I wonder what kind of Valentine's Day present Cherry would like. I think she might be my girlfriend now. She wears her diamond earrings all the time. Maybe I should buy her chocolate. Girls like chocolate.

Keith and Cherry fight sometimes when he watches basketball on my TV and then has a few beers like eight or twelve. I have to count the cans.

'You need to stop drinking this shit!' Cherry screams very loud. She is as feisty as Keith.

Keith yells back. 'It's none of your fucking business and I'll fucking drink if I fucking want to!' Then Cherry cries and Keith hugs her and tells her she's his *Diamond Girl*. He whispers in her ear and pets her hair, and they kiss and make up, which is cool.

Sometimes I get embarrassed when they argue in front of me.

'Perry, it's no big deal. It just means we're a family and families fight in front of each other. They fight, then kiss and make up.' Cherry rubs my hand.

Families are cool. I used to have a family with Gram and Gramp and now I have a family with Keith and Cherry. We are also a family with Gary and Sandy. We have spaghetti nights together on Saturday, just like with Gram. I told Gary about our spaghetti nights when I thanked him for Christmas.

'I really miss those spaghetti nights. Keith, Gram and I played cribbage, and I used to beat them both,' I said.

'Having spaghetti night sounds like a good plan,' Gary said. 'Maybe you can beat Keith on a regular basis in cribbage, but I don't think you can beat me in Scrabble, and for sure not Sandy,' he teased.

Sandy's tomato sauce is almost as good as Gram's. When we do not play cribbage or Scrabble we play Crazy Eights, or Monopoly. Keith is good at Monopoly and beats us all. I am still best at cribbage, but I am getting pretty good at Scrabble too because of all my words. I did not know there was a game for words. I think I might end up liking Scrabble best.

KEITH AND I have a meeting with Gary and then we go to his lawyer's office. Gary's lawyer is Tom Tilton.

'Hey, Mr Tilton, my cousin-brother's a lawyer,' I say.

'Call me Tom, Perry. Would you prefer to use him?' Tom asks.

'No!' Both Gary and Keith say this at the same time and so loud I have to put my hands over my ears.

They do business talk, but I listen carefully. I am an auditor.

What can we do to protect Perry from his brothers?

How does Perry feel about all this?

He's wanted to be a part of Holsted's for a while.

What kind of partnership do you recommend?

I listen closely. It is hard to understand, but I try.

I write Holsted's Marine Supply a very big cheque with many zeros. Keith has to help me fit them in. I am now an investor. I have lots of papers to take home and keep. It makes me a businessman. I spent a lot of the money in my chequing account. Over half. But I still have my savings account. I do not touch that. It is for my future.

'He's protected, right?' Keith looks over my shoulder. 'Let me read that, Per, before you sign.' Keith is my friend. So is Gary.

I have lots of protection now. I have Keith. I have Gary.

And I have Mike Dinelli.

John comes with Mike sometimes. I hear them talk.

We need more time. We can convince him. We just need a bit more time.

Time is something you're running out of. My partners need some guarantees that the money will be replaced. They are getting impatient.

Mike sounds hungry when he talks like that. Doing business must make people hungry, I decide. Even Gary, Keith and I are hungry after we do our business. We go to Gary's house and order pizza and eat ice cream.

It is like a party except we do not have balloons or cake.

Gary holds a glass of wine in his hand and leans against his sofa. 'So, Per, I'm curious, what else do you think we need to do at the store?'

I make myself think hard. I am an official businessman now.

Sandy and Cherry are in the kitchen fixing ice cream. They yell at us, asking whether we want chocolate or strawberry. It distracts me.

'I am still thinking,' I say.

I think better when it is quiet, but this is good practice for me. Businessmen need to be able to think even when they are distracted.

'Sailing books and cards, a place that you can learn to do boat stuff,' I say. 'Fishing stuff. Magazines. Things with boats on them and people who know a lot about sailing.'

Gary nods. He was always nice to me before, but now he listens. I am not faster, but it is like people think I am. Money has made the slow part of me not so important.

Keith treats me the same. He still yells at me and slaps me on the back. He still gets cranky, like when I bug him about calling April and Jason.

'Maybe they want to hear from you. Know where you are.' I said this to him yesterday.

He just shook his head. 'No they don't, it's too late. You don't know what you're talking about, Per,' he said. 'Shut the fuck up!'

I WORRY ABOUT KEITH, especially when he drinks. So does Cherry. I worry like Gram did. 'I worry about Keith,' Gram would say, but when I asked her what she meant, she would only say, 'I just worry.'

There was one time we went to watch the fireworks over the harbour. Keith invited Gram and me to sit in the cockpit of *Diamond Girl* and watch Fourth of July celebrations. Keith was OK the first ten minutes, and then he looked sweaty and started clenching his fists. Green and red sparkly aerials scattered and faded across the black sky. I could not take my eyes off the glitter above my head. Loud explosions and bangs. One right after another.

Keith started going crazy in a quiet way. Gram noticed it first. I was still looking up. My eyes on the sky. When I finally looked down, Gram was holding Keith. He was sobbing and crying into her chest.

'They were kids,' he cried. 'Just tiny babies. Women and babies. The bastards just blew them up like they were nothing!'

When the fireworks were finished, Gram and I sat on the rocking boat until Keith fell asleep. We had to take the bus back home.

I asked Gram later what happened.

She did not answer right away, but shook her head and pressed her lips together. 'That goddamned war,' she finally said. 'It destroyed him. Vietnam ruined Keith.' She said this over and over.

I was confused. 'Vietnam is a country,' I said. 'How did it ruin Keith?'

'That war. That goddamned war,' she answered, then she turned away and walked out of the room.

BOYFRIENDS GIVE GIRLFRIENDS presents on Valentine's Day. I give Cherry a card, chocolates and a gold bracelet with her name on it in red stones. I went to Zales again. They were nice. They like me because I spend money.

Cherry has the day off and comes downstairs to eat lunch with us.

'Ohhhh, I *love* it, Per!' She kisses me on the cheek three times and hands me a card and a box. I unwrap it. It is a giant box of Hershey's Kisses.

The card says *Happy Valentine's Day, Love, Cherry*. She loves me. She wrote it down. That means it is true. My mouth is dry and my heart is beating fast. Cherry must be my girlfriend now.

She gives me a hug and says, 'At least someone around here remembers Valentine's Day.' She sticks her tongue out at Keith, but he ignores her.

'I'm taking Sandy out tonight. You guys want to baby-sit?' Gary asks.

'Cherry won't be able to. She'll be busy tonight,' Keith says quickly.

His voice has something in it I have never heard before. I see two red spots form on Cherry's cheeks.

I am disappointed Cherry will not be baby-sitting. 'I'll do it,' I tell Gary.

'I'll bring you home with me and then run you back when we're done,' he says. 'We shouldn't be too late.'

I wish I could talk to Cherry about being my girlfriend before I leave, but she and Keith are in a corner of the store with their heads together. I see Keith take one of Cherry's hands and bring it up to his lips.

THREE HOURS LATER, Gary drives me home, tells me about their dinner and dance, and asks me about Keith and Cherry.

'So what's up with Cherry and Keith? Sandy thinks there's something there.' He pulls up in front of the store. 'What do you think?'

I do not know what he means. 'I don't know,' I say. 'We're all friends. We're a family. I do not know what is there.' And I tell him good night.

Yo is nowhere in the parking lot and *Diamond Girl* is dark and still. I take a shower and throw myself down on my couch. I am all TVed out after Kelly and Meagan, and fall asleep on my stomach with my arms under my face.

The night glows. The moon is out. Music wakes me.

'*Diamond girl . . . sure do shine . . .*'

My eyes open. The sound is coming from the parking lot. I get up. I tiptoe to the window and look out. It is dark. The stars are brilliant. They are reflecting in the water. Yo is in the parking lot and the driver's door is open.

'*Glad I love ya ... Glad you're mine.*'

Music comes out of Yo. Keith and Cherry are dancing close together. Keith is wearing a suit. I have never seen him in one and he does not look fat. Cherry's dress is long and sparkly and drags on the ground. Keith takes one hand and closes it around Cherry's hair. He brings her head close to his and kisses her hard. They kiss for a long, long time. I watch them turn and walk slowly all the way down the dock, weaving to the boat, arm in arm.

Dancing. They look like Sandy and Gary. Like a couple.

And then I get it. Cherry is Keith's girlfriend. Not mine. And I start to cry.

The next morning Yo's battery is dead.

MY LIST is two pages long and I show it to Keith.

'What's this?' he asks.

'The lottery list. See, I marked off TV, trip to Hawaii and fix *Diamond Girl* and Yo. Remember our game we played with Gram?'

'What's this next thing?' He squints. Keith needs glasses so he can read.

'The plot at Marysville Memorial Park. I want to buy the plot next to Gramp so Gram can be with him.'

Keith tells me he thinks this is a good idea and that he will drive me to Marysville in Yo. Cherry comes with us. She says she thinks she knows where it is. She does not.

We have an easy time finding Marysville but a hard time finding the cemetery. I know where it is, but I do not know how to get there. Keith does not know where it is and does not know how to get there. Cherry does not know where it is, but thinks she knows how to get there.

We stop at an IHOP restaurant to look through their phone book. Then we have to eat pancakes. We also stop at the Chevron station in Marysville to ask and at Katy's Bakery to get doughnuts. There is a Shell gas station at a stoplight, so we ask again. This time Cherry writes down what they say.

Marysville Memorial Park is green and wet, maybe because they just watered the lawn with sprinklers. The office has lots of wood panelling.

'Can I help you?' A tall white-haired man in a black suit walks out from behind a counter. He must be the cemetery man.

'We want to buy the plot next to George Crandall.' Keith knows exactly what to ask. We tell him Gram died last August and I start to cry. Cemetery man looks a little confused until I put Gram's box on the counter.

The cemetery man's name is Leo. That means lion.

It is going to cost more than $2,600, Leo says. I can buy the plot next to Gramp, but I still need a vault for Gram's urn. That is a little marble house for dead people. It was very interesting. There are lots of other charges too.

'Do you want a graveside service?' Leo asks.

I look at Keith. 'What do you think, Keith?' I ask.

'We can do our own,' Cherry tells Leo. Then to me hard in my ear, 'They charge you for that, you know. They charge for everything.'

We need someone to dig the hole for the vault and someone to bury it plus any engraving we want on the headstone. After Leo adds it all up, I write out the cheque. They take Gram and I say goodbye. I am sad because it was nice to have her at home, but I know she will be happier to be buried finally next to Gramp. I cry again and even Keith looks teary. Cherry hugs us both—first me, then Keith. We have to write down what we want engraved.

Keith prints: *DOROTHEA MARIE KESSLER CRANDALL.*

'Anything else?' he asks. 'How about dates?'

'OK,' I say, and write down the years.

'What about a saying?' Leo asks.

This is getting complicated. 'What do you mean?' I ask.

'You know, like *Rest in Peace*. That sort of thing,' Cherry offers.

I know she is just trying to be helpful. 'Gram never rested,' I tell her.

'Was there a poem or a Bible verse she liked?' Leo asks.

I try to think of something, but Gram was never one for Bible verses.

'What about *She will be missed* or *We loved her dearly*?' When Leo says this all three of us start to cry and he has to open another box of Kleenex.

Then I get an idea. When I write the words down, Keith laughs.

Leo frowns. 'Are you sure?' he asks. When we tell him yes, he takes our filled-out paper and says everything will be ready in twenty days.

Three weeks later Keith, Cherry and I drive back to Marysville Memorial Park and we have our very own little private service.

Gram and Gramp are together now. The large red granite headstone reads GEORGE HENRY CRANDALL on one side and DOROTHEA MARIE KESSLER CRANDALL on the other, with all the dates below. And underneath in the middle?

DON'T BE SMART.

Gram would like that.

'WE NEED TO TALK.' John is on the phone. David, Louise, Elaine, John and Mike call me each week. They ask about a cheque, about signing papers, about my Power, about selling the lottery payments, about investing. When I think it might be them, I sometimes let the answering machine get it.

My family makes me uncomfortable when they call. They ask how I am, but before I can answer, they ask about the money.

'How you doing, Perry?' John does not wait for me to talk and asks, 'Have you thought any more about cashing in the lottery payments and investing in—' I hear something that sounds like *trustmutualdividendsandinvestintaxshelterannuities*. It does not mean anything to me.

'What do you need, John?' Even though I ask, I know what it will be about.

'Things are coming to a head here. We're running out of time. Everybody's worried about you. Do you have a will, Perry?' John speaks extra slow like he thinks I do not understand American.

'A will? I don't think so. Why?'

'We think you need one. Mike says you're a real businessman. He says you need a will to be a businessman.'

I like it when people call me a businessman. 'Mike is smart. A will sounds cool.'

'Look, Perry, Mom's not doing too well with her investments. I have some pressing financial obligations. David has money problems of his own. We were all hoping you'd help us out. After all, we're family. We want you to sell your lottery annuity. Invest in the family trust. Share your winnings. It would be the fair thing to do. I mean, we would if it were us.'

I hear Gram snort in my head. *Likely story.*

'Perry, it will be so much better when you finally let all of us help you. There are legal ways of decreasing the tax bite. It's ludicrous that you haven't taken advantage of our expertise before. For instance, when we create the trust, we can manage it for you. You wouldn't have to do a thing. We will do all the work. You'll see. You won't regret it. You hear me?'

I hear Gram in my head again. *Careful.*

I do not say a word. I do not have to. John does all the talking. He always does. One minute he and David want to help me invest my lottery money, and the next they want to split it between us. It is very confusing.

When I hang up, it is pouring. I can see wet drops on my window. I used to call rainy days sad days. 'The sky is crying,' I would tell Gram. 'The sky is crying for Gramp.' It is crying now for both of them.

I go into the bedroom for Gramp's music. *Ride of the Valkyries*, the cover says. There are horses and someone with a beard on the cover. I remove the disk, place it on the turntable, click the on switch and set the needle on the record. I pretend I am in a movie and shut my eyes.

I am in a boat. I hear trumpets and they sound like waves. Like wind. I am sailing. Standing at the bow of *Diamond Girl*. I taste pretend salt on my lips. I feel the lurch and crash of the hull against the water.

I play Gramp's music and walk into the living room to look out my window. The water is a colour I do not know. Maybe grey or green. Keith's blue tarp is over his cockpit. I see lights through the ports. They shine like candles inside of a pumpkin. I know Cherry is in there with him and wish they would ask me down for a visit tonight.

Cherry is Keith's girlfriend and Keith is my friend. I know this now.

I miss Gram. I want Cherry. My throat is full of sadness. My heart hurts. I listen for Gram's voice, but she is somewhere else. Maybe with Gramp. I lean my forehead against the cold window and think about what I should do.

As spring gets closer, we have more days that Gramp would call sail days. Mild, but breezy. Cherry has never sailed, and now that *Diamond Girl*'s engine has been fixed, Keith says maybe we should all go to Whidbey Island for the weekend.

'Oh yeah!' I am excited. 'Yeah, Keith, let's go.'

Gary gives Keith a brand-new VHF handheld radio. After we put in the batteries, Keith lets me try it out. It is so cool.

'Everett Marina. Everett Marina. This is *Diamond Girl* requesting outbound clearance. Over.' The radio crackles and pops.

Roger that, Diamond Girl! You're clear outbound. Over and out.

It is nearly two in the afternoon when we leave the slip. The sun sparkles on the water. *Diamond Girl*'s motor goes PUTT. PUTT. PUTT. Keith steers out towards Whidbey and I wrap and stow the lines.

'How'd you know how to do that, Per?' Cherry watches me from the cockpit. 'I'm a tiny bit afraid of being out in the water in a boat. They sink, don't they? Boats do? You guys know I can't swim, right?' she asks.

'That's OK,' I say. 'I can't swim either, Cherry.' I pull Keith's life jackets out. 'See, we have these. This will keep you from drowning. You can wear one if you want.'

'Yeah, I think I will.' She takes one from me and I help her put it on. I have to lengthen the strap that goes around her waist. I accidentally touch her boob but she does not seem to notice. Touching is OK if it is an accident.

Keith points *Diamond Girl* straight into the brisk breeze and shifts into neutral. I pull hard on the sheet. Sailing is something I know how to do. When the sail is raised, I tie off to the cleat on deck and quickly sit down.

'Watch your head, Cherry!' I yell as the boom shifts. The wind is at our beam and *Diamond Girl* heels to one side. Cherry's eyes get large and she grips the side of the cockpit.

We are flying. We are free. We are sailing. The wind hits my face and I open my mouth to taste the salty air. Cherry watches me and does the same.

We fly for hours. Gramp is with me in my head. So is Gram. I close my eyes and decide if I have to die, I would die right now. I am that happy.

Keith knows a small bay around the corner from the Whidbey Marina. The sun lowers in the sky. We need to anchor before it gets dark. We coast along the shoreline, then tack back and forth. The waves push us along.

'Here,' Keith says, and stops the motor. I help him drop and set the anchor. We are not far from the beach. *Diamond Girl* does not draw much water. It is only about twenty feet deep.

It slowly gets dark. Cherry opens cans of chilli and heats them on the propane stove. We eat bread with no butter with chilli on paper plates. We do not want to wash dishes. Cherry mixes hot cocoa and we munch oatmeal cookies. The breeze dies down. The water is glassy smooth. Car lights move and flash from shore. We watch them while we talk and doze.

'They wish they were us,' Cherry says sleepily and leans against Keith.

I wrap a blanket around my shoulders and stretch out on the other side of the cockpit. This is where I always sleep on *Diamond Girl*.

Keith goes below and comes back up with a guitar. I am surprised because I did not know Keith could play any instrument. He strums and sings to us. His voice is clear and deep.

Sailing . . . take me away . . .

Cherry snuggles against him while he plays and I see her look up, take one finger and brush his beard. He turns and sings into her ear. I can tell he likes Cherry and she likes him.

I wish Cherry liked me better than Keith but I do not think she does. Even though I bought her presents, she likes Keith best. Even though I am rich, she likes Keith best. He is poor, and rude, and crude, like Gram would say. But Cherry still likes him best.

It is hard.

Keith sings to me. To us. I can listen to him for ever, but I fall asleep with him singing in my ear. I am asleep. And *Diamond Girl* rocks.

GRAM HARDLY EVER talked about my father. I thought he was dead.

Then I heard John and David talking. They came to visit after Mike Dinelli left on Thursday. They always come when Gary and Keith are not at Holsted's.

Mike suggested Perry needs a will. He pointed out that Mom would get all the money if Perry died now.

You think he'll die?

Anything can happen.

What exactly do you mean by that?

Don't be naive, David. You probably believe in the Easter Bunny, Santa Claus and that Dad actually sends Mom money each month from his stash in the Cayman Islands.

They said my father was alive. I had no idea.

David said the Cayman Islands were like Hawaii. All sunny.

I had no idea my father was lying in the sun in the Cayman Islands after stealing a bunch of his client's money. No idea at all. I wonder why he stole money. I wonder why he left and I wonder why I never knew.

I ask Gary and Keith if they knew the answer to all my whys.

Gary sighs. 'It's time you knew, Perry.' And he tells me about my father. 'It went on for years. He sucked them dry. When he got in trouble, your Gramp took a loan out against his business for the bail so your dad wouldn't have to go to jail before the trial. When he skipped town, they lost the money.' Gary looks up at the ceiling. I look up too, but there is nothing there.

'Your Gramp mortgaged everything to buy the hoist for the yard. It was his last chance to turn it all around. When things got tough, he just needed a break, a loan to tide him over. Those bastard grandsons of his never got back to him. Wouldn't return his calls. Then it was too late. He lost it all,' Gary says. 'Everything he worked for his whole life was gone.'

Keith listened to the story without interrupting. Then he clears his throat and says, 'I wouldn't be surprised if they tried the same crap on Perry.'

'No,' I say. 'They just want my Power.'

'Shit!' Gary leaps to his feet. He does not say the S-word very often. Keith says enough bad words for everybody.

Power of Attorney? Could they be that stupid? That underhanded?

Gary dials the phone. 'Tom? I need to talk with you now!'

Gary and Keith say things I do not understand, but I listen. I am an auditor.

What did your lawyer say?

With a Power of Attorney, they could sell his lottery annuity. Embezzle all his money legally. Shit! What are we going to do?

We have to watch out. Make sure they don't get him to sign anything.

'Aren't you upset about all this?' Keith asks me. 'Aren't you worried about what your brothers are doing? About what your father did?'

I can tell he wants to help.

'Cousin-brothers. They are my cousin-brothers, and no I'm not upset,' I say. 'I am sad. I am sad for Gram and Gramp. I am sad for everybody. I wonder why Gram didn't want me to know. It was only money.'

And I walk back upstairs.

It was only money, I think, as I lie on my couch.

THE WAREHOUSE on the other side of Carroll's Boatyard is for sale. Gary wants to buy it and I want to be a businessman. It is a good idea, so I decide to spend more of my chequing account money on investing in Holsted's. I do not touch my savings. We meet with Gary's lawyer Tom Tilton again. Keith comes with me. He helps me with my business.

'Make sure this is on the up-and-up,' he says.

Up-and-up means fair. It means right. It means no one will take advantage. Keith's shirt is tucked in and his hair is clean and combed. His ponytail is neatly tied. His beard is trimmed. I notice he has new shoes.

'You look nice, Keith,' I say. He does. He looks real good. He is trying not to drink, which I think is a good thing. He now goes to AA meetings at the Veterans' Hospital every Saturday morning at nine.

Everyone starts to talk at once. I listen. I am an auditor.

Is there a way we can protect Perry?

It's a lot of money for him to handle.

He's doing great so far.

But those brothers of his are up to something. I know it.

This is boring. I start to think up ideas.

'Hey!' I say. 'I need a will! Can I do a will?'

'You want a will?' Tom looks surprised. He wears a shiny blue tie that sparkles and long hair like a rock star, but he does not have a guitar.

The lawyer takes out papers and helps me make a will.

'I can help you make a will. Who would you like for your beneficiary?'

'My what?'

'Who do you want to leave your money to when you die?'

'When I die? Am I going to die?' I look at Keith after I say this. I am worried. 'Do you die right after you make a will?'

'No, Per. A will is when you get to decide what happens to your money, just in case you die.' Keith speaks calmly. He knows I do not want to die.

Gary says, 'It's just a precaution really, but as a businessman, it's important to take care of these things. It's a pretty good idea. What made you decide to make a will?'

'John did,' I say. 'Mike did too. They wanted me to come to his office and make one.'

Keith and Gary look at each other.

Why in the world would they suggest a will?

His mother would get all the money, not the brothers, unless Per specified otherwise.

But he'd have to die before they'd get it.

Holy shit, do you think they'd risk it?

'I'll tell you what,' Keith says. 'We'll both make wills.'

'So who do you want to have all your money after you die? You're in business now. You have assets. It shows financial responsibility when you make sure things are taken care of after you die.' Tom talks fast like a machine gun in a movie.

'But I'll be dead,' I tell him.

'What about your loved ones?'

I have to think. Then I get a good idea. 'I want to leave all my money to Keith, Cherry and you, Gary.'

'What about your family?' the lawyer asks.

'They already have lots of money. That's what Gram always told me. That's why she gave everything of hers to me. She even gave me the house.'

'She left the house to you? I thought it went to your brothers.' Gary has wrinkles on his forehead.

'No, I gave John my Power and he signed thirty-two times. It was escrow. That's how I got five hundred dollars.'

Keith starts fuming. 'Gary, what did I tell you?'

Keith! Sit down! You're like a bull in a china shop!

Gary, I fucking told you that you were naive and you said not to worry! Stop. Just stop. Tom?

We have a saying at our firm that successful small swindles always precede big ones. I can't say there was anything illegal. It certainly sounds immoral, but being immoral is not against the law.

'What about my will?' I ask. They are boring when they talk to each other and not to me. It is rude to ignore your friends.

'I tell you what, Perry. It's not a good idea to exclude relatives. You

should leave them something or it's possible your will could be contested.'
He tells me *contested* means they wouldn't have to do what I wanted.

'I've got an idea,' Keith says, and starts laughing. 'How about this?' and
he tells us his plan.

I think it is a good idea. The lawyer asks me if I am sure.

'Yes, I am sure!' I say this in my shouting voice.

Keith has a very good idea. If I die, my mother gets $5,000 and Gramp's
record player, David gets $5,000 and my twenty-seven-inch flat-screen TV,
and John gets $5,000 and the best thing of all, Gram's couch.

Gary laughs and says, 'If anything will guarantee Per's safety, that will.'

When we finish, Keith and I get copies of our wills. I feel like a good
businessman because I have many papers to take back to my apartment.

While Gary finishes talking to the lawyer, Keith goes to the bathroom to
take a leak and I take out my calculator and do my adding. My bank statement for this month is in my pocket. I will have my next lottery cheque in
October. I get interest from my savings account, plus my regular cheque from
Holsted's. I will get an even bigger salary now because I am partner. I told
Gary that I do not need as much as him because I am not married and I do not
have two children, a wife and a mortgage, but he said we are partners and
partners have to share. He said Holsted's is doing well. That is so cool.

I still do not talk about my savings account. Gram said not to. My chequing
account does not have as many zeros now, after my last investment in
Holsted's, but it is still a lot of money. That's OK. I am a businessman.

At Holsted's Gary tells everyone I am a new partner. He announces that
we will be expanding. He promotes Keith to manager. Keith's first job is to
hire more employees. He brings in Charles from Pacific Marine Supply and
tells me he already hired another employee.

The next day I see who it is. Cherry stands at the computer register. She
only has earrings in her ears, and her long-sleeved shirt covers her tattoos.

'This is the same machine I worked with at Marina Handy Mart,' she says.

Cherry is wonderful with the customers, especially the ones who do not
know what they want. Instead of making them feel stupid, the way Keith
and Gary do, she helps them figure out what they need. Usually that means
they buy more than they actually want because they are so grateful to her.

Soon she will not let Keith or Gary help customers.

'Only Perry and I should work the register. You and Keith do not have
good people skills,' she lectures.

Cherry is the one who takes my picture and sends it into the *Everett*

Herald business column PEOPLE ON THE MOVE. 'Holsted's Marine Supply adds a partner,' it says above my photo. It has my name underneath, how long I have worked at Holsted's and says that I won the Washington State Lottery.

Cherry is very smart. It is good advertising.

WE ARE DOING BUSINESS for our new warehouse. It is big enough to store boats during the winter and we get the keys today. It is called closing. I think that is funny. I mean, we get the keys. Shouldn't they call it opening?

Gary's lawyer is talking. I do not understand what he is saying.

'What language is he speaking?' I whisper to Keith.

'Bullshit!' he whispers back. 'He's talking Bullshit with a capital B. All lawyers learn it at school.'

I am bored. I kick my feet against the chair until Keith looks at me and puts a finger to his lips. I look around the room and listen. I am an auditor.

I sent copies of Perry's will to John, David and Louise as you suggested. I told them I thought it was in Perry's best interest that they had this information. They were rather surprised, as you predicted.

Jeez! Did they say anything?

Not to me.

I did not hear from my cousin-brothers for two days. David called first.

'Perry, we heard about your will. We just wanted you to guard your assets. That's all. Hell! I was only trying to protect you. Make sure you made the right decisions.'

I can make my own decisions, I think, but I sent him a cheque. I have to make each cheque amount smaller so I do not run out of money in my account and make the bank mad at me.

John called next.

'Don't worry, Perry, we'll always be there for you. Christ! We were all just concerned.' He breathes hard through the phone.

I mailed him and CeCe each a cheque.

When people are concerned, they want cheques.

Everybody wants cheques.

I BUG KEITH again and make him mad. I do not mean to, I just can't understand why he doesn't want to meet his son, Jason. See what he looks like. He could take a vacation and go. I would if I found out I had a son.

'Cherry and I can watch *Diamond Girl*,' I say. 'Friends do jobs for each other like watch their stuff while they are gone. Don't you want to see him?'

Cherry looks worried. I can tell because she has wrinkles in her forehead. We sit in the cockpit. It is drizzling. It always rains in Everett.

'Don't be so freaking stupid! How many fucking times do I have to tell you? No. I. Do. Not. Want. To. See. Him. I was stupid. I was an ass. I signed my rights away. So leave it the fuck alone!'

'Don't talk to him like that!' Cherry speaks loud when she is mad. Her face is all red. She puts a hand on Keith's chest, but he pulls it off.

'Don't you start with me, woman!' Keith jumps out of the cockpit and marches down the dock. We can hear his feet pound all the way to Yo.

Diamond Girl rocks with the force of his leaving, like she wants to follow. We hear the roar of Yo's engine and the spatter of gravel in the parking lot. Cherry is shaking and her eyes are wet. She touches my hand.

'Don't worry, Per, he doesn't mean it. Really.' Then she starts to cry and I hold her.

'I know,' I say as I pat her back, 'I know.' My feelings are hurt and my throat is thick. Keith is my friend. I am unhappy. I hope he comes back.

'He's trying to stop drinking, you know,' Cherry says. She wipes her eyes on her shirt and sniffs. 'He is trying to stop.'

'That's good,' I tell Cherry. 'Gram always wanted him to stop. Keith always said he didn't have a reason to.'

'He'll have a reason to now. He'll stop now, because he'll have a reason.' Cherry sounds sure of herself and smiles while she rubs her belly.

My stomach flips. She is so pretty. I pat her hand. I am relieved. It worries me when Keith gets upset and mad. I do not like it.

We sit together in the cockpit. It feels like spring and the weather is warm.

'Perry?' Cherry licks her lips like she is nervous. 'Umm. Do you like working at Holsted's?' she asks. It does not sound like that is what she really wanted to ask me. She looks over at the parking lot like she is willing Keith to come back.

'I love it. It's the best job in the world,' I say. I try to think of something else to say. 'How about you, Cherry? Do you like Holsted's?'

'Yeah, I like it a lot,' she says. 'I love it actually. It's the best job I ever had.'

It is quiet and the water laps against *Diamond Girl*. I wonder how long Keith will be gone.

'What's that?' Cherry points to a bird.

'A baby gull. They are brown instead of white. You want to feed it?'

Cherry goes below and brings up a package of crackers. We spend an hour breaking them up into pieces and tossing them into the air for the birds, and the water for the fish. We laugh and talk about birds, fish and boats.

Keith is gone a long, long time. It is dusk. We hear Yo's engine whine in the parking lot and then go silent. When he climbs into the cockpit, his shirt is wet. He is breathing hard like he has been running.

'I'm sorry, Per.' He grips my shoulder. 'I'm so sorry.' He hugs me hard.

'I'm sorry, hon. Forgive me?' He wraps Cherry in his arms and kisses her so long I have to look away. Cherry whispers something in his ear and he whispers back. They hold each other tight and turn into one giant person. I do not see where Keith starts and Cherry ends. They do not notice me leave.

When I look down out of my window later on, they are leaning against each other sitting in *Diamond Girl*'s cockpit. I stand there and watch the sun go behind the mountains.

I am an auditor, but there is nothing to hear except the beating of my heart. Now I am a watcher, I think, as I stand and stare out. Half of the sun shines, half is behind the jagged peaks. It sinks until just an edge is left.

What's the matter, Perry? I hear Gram's voice. She is here with me. Like when I would come home crying from school.

What's the matter, Perry? I hear her voice. And I talk to Gram.

I tell her how much I love Cherry and I cry.

8

'There's been a terrible accident.' Gary's face is serious. His voice is flat. 'I have to go.'

'Who?' I ask. 'Who is it?'

When a person dies in an accident, they have to be identified. They have to be identified, just in case it's not them. In case it is someone else.

'Who?' I ask.

Gary looks down at the floor and says nothing. I see the tiny muscle in his jaw move and jump. I know. I think I know. I ask Gram in my heart to please make it someone else. Please not make it Keith.

'Officer Mallory thinks it might be Keith,' Gary whispers softy. And he turns and walks out the door.

I put away boxes while I wait. Box after box. They are brown. I peel the tape carefully. I do not want it to rip. To tear. *Please, Gram.*

Cherry is in the employee bathroom. She has to pee again.

Keith teased Cherry, this morning, before he left for his AA meeting. 'Woman, you spend a lot of time in that bathroom. Are you ever coming out?' Keith rattled the knob. 'I'm leaving now. Give me a kiss goodbye.'

'I'll kiss you when you get back!' Cherry yelled through the door.

I cannot say anything. Gary told me not to until he was sure. I open box after box. Carefully. I do not tear the tape. I wish on the tape. If it does not rip, then Keith is fine. Keith is OK.

I hear Gary's Jeep before I see him. He walks through the door. His face has no colour. His voice is low and scratchy like when you walk on gravel.

When he tells us what happened Cherry's mouth falls open, but nothing comes out. She gets smaller and smaller until she is gone. I am crying so hard my eyes are shut tight, but I make no sound. I hear nothing. Just a roar. A roar of sad.

Hitting a tree at fifty miles an hour is not a good thing. Keith was not even drinking. He came around a corner. There was a lady and two kids in the road. Their car was stopped and the hood was up. He had to hit them or a tree. He and Yo hit the tree hard. That is what the lady told Officer Mallory.

And that is what Gary told us when he got back from the morgue.

A morgue is a cold place they keep dead people.

'I want to see him! I didn't kiss him goodbye. I want to kiss him goodbye!' Cherry wails.

'God, no, Cherry, please,' Gary says, and holds her shoulders.

'I have to, Gary. Please? Take me? Please?'

Gary takes us both to see Keith. We have to sit on a hard brown bench. The walls are green. We wait. The man asks us if we are sure.

'Are you sure you want to do this?' He is kind. I see that in his eyes. I want to say no, I am not sure, but Cherry says yes.

The man unzips the bag that Keith is in. He looks like he is asleep. We can only see part of his face. The rest is covered by a sheet. His beard has small bits of glass in it that sparkle under the light. They are pieces from Yo's shattered windshield, the man says. There is a small purple bruise above Keith's brow and his skin looks empty like there is no one inside.

I hear a shudder. I feel it vibrate through me as Cherry bends down to kiss Keith's cheek. I hold Cherry tight with my arm and with my other hand brush Keith's hair off his forehead like he used to do to me. 'Your fucking hair's in your eyes, Per,' he used to say. 'You look goofy, Per.'

'You don't look goofy, Keith.' I say. 'You don't.' And my voice cracks.

I have never heard a sound like the one that Cherry is making. It is like her soul flying out. I shut my eyes tight because they are wet again.

It is harder than Gramp. Harder than Gram. Harder than anything. When I open my eyes, Cherry is being sick on the floor. She cannot stand and Gary helps me carry her back to the car.

We go to Everett General Hospital emergency room. The same place I got my arm fixed after I got beat up.

'Please? Can't you do anything for her? Give her something?' Gary asks the doctor.

They give Cherry a shot and a bottle of sadness pills. I did not know you could get pills for sadness.

When we get back to the apartment, we lay Cherry down on the bed. Gary takes off her shoes, and covers her with Gram's blanket. I stand and watch her lying there. My heart is breaking. I feel it breaking like Yo's windshield.

'Stay with her, OK? I'll get Sandy.' Gary hugs me and goes downstairs. I hear his Jeep drive away. I am alone with Cherry.

I do not know what to do or say.

I drop to my knees next to the bed. There are black streaks of mascara over Cherry's cheeks. Her eyes are open but her breathing is deep and slow.

I hold her head in my hands. I pat it like Keith did, over and over. Her eyes turn to me. They ask a question with no words. They ask a question that I am unable to answer.

I can only say, 'I'm sorry, Cherry.'

But her eyes just stare into space. They just stare.

DIAMOND GIRL'S ENGINE starts on the first try. BROOM! BROOM! I feel it shaking under my feet. I have watched Keith take her out so often I know I can do it myself.

I have no trouble casting off the lines. Gary's family stands by helplessly and I tell them what to do. Where to sit. Cherry is beside me.

I hear Keith's voice.

I could do it blindfolded.

I could do it with my head up my ass.

'That boy is crude and rude!' Gram always said. She would laugh. She loved Keith and I loved Keith too.

Six people on *Diamond Girl* are as much as she can handle. Gary brought three brand-new life jackets from the store so we would have enough.

We head out towards Whidbey Island. The sky is so blue it looks like it is painted on. Like Cherry's eye shadow. There is one big cloud shaped like a flower. I like that. A flower for Keith. Puget Sound is green and shiny.

Diamond Girl cuts through the water.

I am doing Keith's job. It is up to me. Steering. That is what he used to do. When I think of this, tears come and I cannot see clearly. Cherry puts her arms around me. I give the tiller to Gary, and he guides Keith's boat.

We go out into the strait, and head into the current, until we feel it is the right place. The perfect place. A place Keith would want to be. 'Spread my ashes out in the Sound,' he told me. 'I want to travel the world for free.'

When we toss Keith's ashes out into the water, the seagulls swoop and flap overhead. They think we are giving them food, but it is only Keith.

We have to laugh because Keith would have roared and yelled, 'Fuck you, birds!' He never liked seagulls.

'Fuck you, birds!' We all call out.

It is the first time I have ever said that word.

I will not say it ever again.

Keith's ashes fall with a clump onto the water like little pieces of gravel. Some of his dust flies back into my eyes and makes me tear up. Cherry cannot look at all and hides her face until we tell her he is all gone.

A seal pops up next to *Diamond Girl*, he swims around and around and follows us all the way back to the slip. I think it is Keith telling us he is OK. The seal hangs around *Diamond Girl* for hours. We feed it fish that we steal from Marty's bait pail and sit on *Diamond Girl* until it is dark and talk. We do not want to leave. It is like the last time we are with Keith.

Gary's family leaves together and we watch them from *Diamond Girl*'s cockpit as they drive away. When they are gone, Cherry gives me a sadness pill and tells me about her dad. I swallow it dry and it sticks in my throat.

Cherry leans against me. Her head is on my chest. I stroke her hair.

'I just turned eighteen. He can't touch me now,' she says. 'Nobody can.'

'You look a lot older. I thought you were twenty.' I wish I knew she had a birthday. I would have given her a present.

'Thank you, Per,' she says, and looks pleased even though she is crying.

We both take another pill, and wait for our sadness to go away.

'My dad is such an asshole.' She talks about her family and about Keith. 'Keith beat the crap out of him for me,' she says, and starts to cry harder. Her tears drip down my arm. 'We were gonna be married. He wanted to marry me. I loved him, Perry. I really did,' she sobs.

We do not want to leave the cockpit. We do not want to stop talking about Keith.

'I will never stop loving him,' she tells me. She says that she wants to die. 'He was the best thing that ever happened to me and he loved me back. I know he did,' she cries.

'*You* were the best thing that ever happened to him,' I tell her.

We take another pill each.

They do not work.

And we cry.

AFTER WE RUN OUT of the sadness pills, I wake up at the same time each night. The clock flashes two-zero-one. My heart hurts when I breath and my eyes are wet. Whenever I wake up, I remember Keith is dead.

I see a shadow in the room. Cherry is standing by the window staring. I get up and grab her hands. They are like ice. Her face is dry. Her breath comes in sharp pants like a dog. I lead her back to bed. She lies on her back, but her eyes are open. When I know she will stay put, I go back to Gram's couch, wrap Gram's afghan around myself and shiver like I have a fever.

When the alarm goes off in the morning, Cherry is still in bed.

'Get up, Cherry. You need to get up,' I tell her.

Her eyes are wide. They do not blink.

'We've got to go to work. You have to get up, Cherry. Please?' I ask.

She does not move.

I thought we were getting better. I thought our sadness was leaving us. On Wednesday, we even cleaned the apartment. Cherry scrubbed the kitchen and I scoured the bathroom shower. After we finished, I started the washing machine while Cherry went into the bedroom to gather up our dirty clothes.

She did not come back.

I found her sitting on the floor with Keith's jeans held to her breast.

'We have to keep these, Perry. Don't wash these, OK?' I could hardly understand her words she was sobbing so hard.

She spent the rest of the day in bed.

She sleeps later and later each morning. Today she is not even talking, and I have to help her get dressed. She has not eaten in two days.

I fix oatmeal, set a bowl in front of her and give her a spoon. 'Come on, Cherry, you have to eat,' I tell her, 'or you will get sick.'

She lifts the spoon and slides the cereal into her mouth. I am glad because I did not want to feed her. That would be spooky. As if she were a big baby.

By the time we get downstairs to the store, we are an hour late. Charles, the newest guy, is at the register, so I decide to have Cherry help me unpack boxes. Boxes are good. You do not have to think to unpack them. First you slice them with the cutter, second you pry open the cardboard and third you lift the stuff out. I do not think. It feels good not to think.

Gary brings Sandy and the girls in to help. We need a lot of help at the store without Keith.

I have to set the alarm extra early each morning so there is time to help Cherry get dressed. I cannot sleep because I need to be ready to put her back to bed when she gets up in the night to stare at *Diamond Girl* through the window. I am so tired, and so sad, there is an ocean of hurt in my heart.

My eyes open. It is late. There is a voice. Keith's voice.

Take care of her, Per. Take care . . .

I see the moon shining over the floor. Cherry is not at the window, but I hear a noise. It is coming from the kitchen.

I get up. It might be a burglar. The bedroom door is open and I look inside. Cherry's bed is empty. I walk into the kitchen.

When I see what she is doing, I feel fear at first. But I am like the Hulk. I become strong.

'No!' I shout. 'Don't,' I tell her. 'Please?'

She is holding a knife to her wrist. It presses into the skin and starts to make a cut. I grab her arm, and pry the handle from her fingers. There is one small drip of blood that trickles down her arm. It is bright red. I lead her into the bathroom and put a Band-Aid over her wound. My hands shake as I smooth it over her skin.

'Don't do this, Cherry. Keith would not want you to,' I say, and brush the hair off her neck. I smooth the tears off her cheek. 'I don't want you to.'

I do not know what else to say.

I lead her back into the bedroom, lie down next to her and hold her in my arms until her eyes close and she falls asleep.

WE GET LESS SAD even without the pills. We get less sad because *life goes on*, as Keith always said. As Gram said.

Cherry gets up on her own now without my help. She fixes us both oatmeal for breakfast and talks to me. She tells me she is pregnant.

'I'm having Keith's baby,' she says.

She needs my help. It is not too late for Keith to be a father. I want to be a father for Keith. I never even imagined that I would help Keith be a father.

Cherry wants me to know that she does not want to take advantage of me. 'I don't know if I'll ever love anybody again, Per. I'm sorry, but I don't know what to do or where to go,' she says.

Cherry also wants me to know that she still loves Keith best even though he is dead. I say I understand, because I do. I love Keith best too. Sometimes friends have to take care of friend stuff. This is one of those times. I still hurt. I still feel guilty for liking Cherry. But I am excited too. It is one last thing I can do for Keith. A big favour. The biggest favour.

Cherry said she never had a boyfriend before Keith. 'I'm fat and ugly, Perry,' she says. 'People would stare at me when I ate. My aunt would tell me to lose weight. My cousins would call me fatty.'

I definitely do not think she is fat or ugly. It is mean what people say. 'Kids at school would call me retard.' I do not like to tell anybody this, especially Cherry. I am afraid she will think it is true.

'I am not fat and you are not retarded. We are us!' she says, and gives me a kiss and a hug. That is so cool.

Cherry quit smoking and eats only vegetarian pizza. We order half Meat Eaters for me and half vegetarian for her. That's what she calls me now, a Meat Eater.

We talk about names.

'We will call him Baby Keith,' I say. It will be another Keith.

'What if it's a girl?' she asks.

'It won't. I am positive.' I am sure of this.

It will be Baby Keith, I hear Gram say.

Gary helps us fix up the apartment. While Gary and I paint, Cherry stays on *Diamond Girl* so the smells will not hurt the baby. We make the nursery in a corner of the bedroom. We order a crib from Sears, and when it comes, Sandy and Gary help us put it together.

'Starting over,' Gary says. 'A new beginning. A new life.'

Our apartment looks cool. We have Gram's couch, my TV and a coffee table from Kmart. We bought a brand-new bed. I found sailboat bedspreads in the catalogue and ordered them for the store. I got an extra one for us.

We sold all the spreads that I ordered in one week. Gary just laughs. He tells me to order anything I want for Holsted's.

Cherry is smart. She has us study the business news every night and shows me how to go online and find message groups from sailors.

'See here, Per? Sailors from all over the world go online and talk. They tell people smart enough to listen what they need. Those smart people are us.' She has me take notes. 'It's a way to find out what new stuff boaters want. We have to be proactive.' *Proactive* is another word Cherry learned from the business news. *Proactive* means taking charge. She tells Gary that she is making us a website so boaters can order from us anywhere direct.

We always stand at the window each night and watch. It is a habit now. We look out at the water, at the reflection of the lights and at *Diamond Girl*. I hold Cherry close. My arms fit around her stomach. It is getting bigger because of the baby.

Cherry will talk about Keith at these times and cry.

'I wish I had told him about the baby,' she says this over and over.

I do not say anything and the voices come.

He knew, Gram says. *Tell her he knew.*

I knew, Keith says. *Tell her.*

Truth is many things. Sometimes truth is what we want or maybe what we have. It may be what we choose to believe. Sometimes it is something real, something genuine. Sometimes you know the truth when you speak it. I am slow, but I know this.

'He knew, Cherry. He knew you were having his baby,' I say.

I feel her sink. I feel her sag. It may be the truth or it may be a very good lie that turns into the truth. I do not know.

'How do you know?' she breathes into my chest.

The answer comes out of my heart and I know exactly what to say.

'He told me. He told me he could tell.' When I say this, I know it is true, and I believe it myself.

Cherry cries. Big gulping sobs. She cannot stand and I hold her up.

I reach my arms around her tight and I do not let her go.

IT IS LATE at night. Our lights are off. We are ready to go to sleep. The rain plops against the door like tiny knocks. We are watching *Diamond Girl* outside. Pretending Keith is there, tying her up in the rain.

'He's putting on another line. The wind's blowing hard. If he doesn't tighten her up, she may pull loose. See him there?'

'Where?' Cherry will ask.

'Right there. See?' I will point. 'He's waving.' And we will wave back.

It is a game we play.

Tonight Cherry is silent. She does not wave at the pretend Keith. Instead her arm crawls around my waist and she pulls me tight. I pat her hand and she hugs me even closer. Her other hand rubs my belly and moves down.

My stomach clenches and drops like I am on a roller-coaster ride.

My head is all mixed up with thinking. I am happy Cherry is with me, but I am sad Keith is not. My privates are getting hard. Cherry takes my hand and puts it on her boob. My head gets dizzy and I am spinning.

She takes both my hands and leads me walking backwards into the bedroom. Her steps are sure and even. Mine are not. I jerk forward and she catches me. Her bare hand touches my privates. I am shaking and sweating. I am scared, but I am not so scared that I want her to stop.

Keith and I talked about man things. He told me about privates and what they do. We sat in his cockpit while he drank beer and I drank Coke. He told me all about the hot Mexican babes he knew in San Antonio. 'Hot, Per. Hot! Beautiful and smart. Whoa, Momma!' he said.

Gram would have washed both our mouths out with soap if she had heard us. I asked Keith questions.

'But how do you know when to do it and what to do?' I asked him.

He told me all about it, and then said, 'All you have to do is let nature take its course.'

'Does nature feel good?' I asked.

'Yeah, Per,' he said, and closed his eyes. 'Nature feels real good.'

I wish I had paid more attention. I wish I could remember everything he said, but there is nothing in my head but wind and waves.

She takes off my shirt. She unbuttons my pants.

She pulls me down on top of her. Cherry is soft and moves against me. When she does this I find out it is true. Every bit of it.

All you have to do is let nature take its course. Just like Keith said.

And nature feels real good.

I HAVE BEEN RICH for almost a year.

When my cousin-brothers found out about Keith they started calling even more, but I did not answer. I had to think by myself. And then I knew.

I knew what to do.

My words today are *share*, *shareholder*, *sharer* and *shark*. *Share* means you give part of your things to other people and a shark has teeth and bites.

I dial David's number first, then I dial John's. I say it is time for another Family Meeting. I call the Family Meeting this time. It is my decision. I am like the Hulk. I have Power.

Both my cousin-brothers come to the apartment to pick me up. John's hand is on my shoulder pushing me a little, as I walk down the stairs. David gets into the front seat of a long black car and I sit in the back with John.

Mike Dinelli is at the wheel.

It's about time, he says. *It's almost too late for you, John. My associates have been discussing the increasing likelihood of some unfortunate accident befalling you.*

We drive away in short spurts. I can hear gravel hit the side of the building. I see Gary running out of Holsted's, but Mike goes fast out of the parking lot. I crane my neck around to see Gary through the back window.

He is waving and yelling. 'Stop! Come back! *Stop!*'

Don't worry, Gary, I think. I know what I am doing.

We drive to John's office. It is in a tall building that stretches to the sky.

I have never seen John's office. There are pictures on the wall.

'What are those?' I ask David. It looks like when I was little and could not colour in the lines.

'Abstract art, Perry. They're valuable. John is a collector,' he whispers.

I laugh. 'Ha! I think they look like mistakes.'

We step into a room with a big brown table. When John sits down in one of the chairs, the leather makes a sound like a fart and I think of Keith. I think he would understand what I am doing.

I will give my family the lottery money. I am a businessman. I have my salary from Holsted's. I have my savings account. I do not need the next lottery cheque. I will sign papers so my family gets the rest of the money. I will not give them my Power. I am the Hulk and the Hulk is not fooled.

It is important for me to sign papers, John says. *Crucial*, Mike says. That means bigger than important. I sit at the table. My family surrounds me. They look like jackals. I know what jackals are because I watch Animal Planet. They all have pointy teeth. Just like the sharks, I think.

It is for the family. It is only fair.

David owes money to creditors.

John owes money to Mike's company.

Louise needs to be maintained. She is very expensive.

Mike Dinelli is a good friend. He has to clean some money for his firm.

I do not need to do Power, I tell them. I will sell the rest of my lottery payments to Mike. I do not tell them about my savings account.

Families are important. Even Gram said that. If you can help your family, then you do it. I sign my name fifteen times. *Perry L. Crandall*. Mike hands me each paper to sign. The pen is heavy and silver. The ink is black.

'What's the L stand for Perry?' Mike asks.

'Lucky,' I say. 'The L stands for Lucky.'

He does not laugh. He does not even smile.

I tell them the money can go into the family trust. Managed by the trustee. They cannot agree on a trustee.

Not you, John! Not on your life! Do you think we're idiots? You drained your client's accounts. How can we be sure you won't do the same with us?

Well, not you, Elaine! I won't go for that!

Not Mom. She doesn't have a clue.

David.

Yes. David. He can be the trustee. He's too stupid to try anything.

Such a nice sentiment for a wife, Elaine.

I hear John and Elaine still arguing in the background as I sign more papers. They talk about putting money in the trust. Taking money from a laundry. Mike is using all the money from the lottery and giving them other, different, dirty money. I do not care about that.

Keith and Gram are quiet in my head. They know I can make this decision. It is mine to make. This is my good idea. I am very calm. My hands are not shaking and I hold them out in front of me. They are good hands I think.

I don't believe it! We didn't even need the Power of Attorney.

He signed. He just signed it away.

My troubles are over. I'll get a cheque to you tomorrow or the next day, Mike, after this cash is deposited.

Are you OK with this, Perry? Are you OK?

Shut up, David.

It isn't right. We need to give him something. We should have had him wait until he got the next payment.

David, give it a rest! It's over! If you feel guilty, give him part of your share. If Elaine will let you. Ha! Ha!

After all the papers are signed, the money is gone and I am free. They do not need me any more. Louise and John are arguing with Mike. Elaine is sitting at the table with a calculator, smiling.

David is the only one who hugs me goodbye. 'You take care of yourself, Per,' he says, and pats me on the back.

It is the first time he has ever called me Per. That is so cool. He walks me downstairs and calls me a cab. The taxi takes me back to my apartment.

I walk upstairs, stand by my window and watch *Diamond Girl* bounce against the dock. She looks lonely.

Life goes on. It is Keith's voice. It is what he used to say.

And now I hear Gram. *You're a lucky boy, Perry L. Crandall*, I hear her say. *That L stands for Lucky!* I know she is right. And I know two other things.

I am not retarded.

And if you can give people what they want, you should. It is good to give people what they want. This is a great day. No one in my family will bother me any more. They have what they want. And so do I.

I hear footsteps on the stairs. Cherry comes through the door.

I open my arms wide and she walks right into them.

'Are you OK?' I hear her ask. She has wrinkles on her forehead and I kiss them away.

I say nothing. I am so OK, I cannot speak.

Our door swings open again and it is Gary. He did not knock before he walked in, which is rude, but he is my friend, so I do not tell him this.

'Are you all right?' he asks. 'What did they want?'

'The money,' I finally say. 'They just wanted the money.'

He has wrinkles on his forehead too, but he does not need to worry. There is no reason for wrinkles.

'It's OK now,' I say. This is true. It is OK. It is.

I HAVE AN *INTERVIEW* on TV. That means they ask you questions. After Gary found out about what happened, he called Marleen. He suggested she might do a special story on lottery winners. Her bosses, the television guys, thought it was a good idea.

Before the programme starts, Marleen gives me a hug. 'I'm sorry about your friend Keith,' she says.

'I am too,' I say. 'He would have really liked to be on TV. He always wanted to be famous.'

A man named Roy clips a microphone to my neck. 'When that green light comes on, there'll be over a million people watching you,' he says.

That is so cool. There are six of us sitting onstage with Marleen. She wears a blue suit, high heels and dark red lipstick. She looks totally different.

Marleen looks into the camera. 'Investors want to buy the annuities from the lottery winners. Organised crime uses lottery winnings to launder money.'

She sounds like she has just figured this all out, but I know it is written on a card in front of her. That is such a gyp. I always thought they had to memorise the stuff they say, but they do not. If I had known it was all written down for them, I would have tried to be a TV guy.

She turns to me. 'So, Perry. Is all of your lottery money gone? Is there anything left after you sold your lottery annuity? Did your family take it all?'

'Yeah, I guess. It was a trust. They said it was a trust for investments.' I tried to remember all the words they used, but I cannot.

I do not tell her about my savings account.

Marleen moves to the lady sitting next to me. Her name is Lucille. She won $20 million. Her money is all gone.

'I said I was going to share it with my family. I didn't realise they could sue me for it if I said that. I sold my annuity and divided it up, but that wasn't enough. They came back for more. I still owe taxes.' She starts crying. Marleen hands her a Kleenex and she blows her nose hard.

Other people lost their money even faster then Lucille did. Five months. Eight months. A year.

All the people are sad. They won money and they are sad.

We lost everything, they say. *We had millions, and we lost it.*

'So you're worse off now, after the lottery,' Marleen says.

'No,' I say. 'I'm not.' But nobody listens. Nobody hears what I have to say. I am a partner in Holsted's. And I have Cherry.

I do not have Keith, Gram or Gramp. That is hard, but like Gram always said, life is tough. *Most things in life are difficult*, Gram says in my head.

Marleen asks again about my family. She says that my family took all my money. I tell her that they did not take it. I gave it to them.

'You gave it to them? Why?' Her mouth is open.

'Because they asked, and because they were my family,' I say. 'Because people should get what they want.' Then I say something that she does not understand. Nobody does. 'Because I didn't need it,' I say.

'What? Why?' Marleen's eyes are all squinty. That distracts me. It is hard to explain to someone who will not understand.

Gram used to say I was suggestible. I may have been. Maybe I still am. But letting my family have the rest of the money was fair because they seemed to need it and I did not.

When I get back to the apartment, Cherry says I looked real good on TV. That is so cool.

'HOW ABOUT the name Holsted and Crandall Marine Supply, Perry? How does that sound?' Gary asks me.

'I think it sounds fine. I think it sounds pretty good,' I say.

We are partners, Gary said. We are a family. He says I have good ideas, like the time I told him to have a coffee place. People like to drink coffee when they shop. We make a lot of money from people buying cookies, brownies and coffee. We sell fancy takeout picnic lunches for boat people.

We have a fishing corner that is bigger now. I tell Gary about a retired friend of Marty's, named Rick, who sits on the dock every day. He knows a lot about fishing. He talks to people in our store about how to catch fish. He teaches fishing the same way big hardware stores show people how to lay tiles. I know this because Gram and I watched at Home Depot one weekend when we wanted to fix our bathroom. I tell Gary this is what we need to do.

'So, what? We need to have workshops each weekend?'

'No,' I say. 'People work all week. We need to be different. We need to call them playshops.'

'You're brilliant, Per,' Gary says. 'You make a really good partner.'

We have playshops on caulking teak decks and filling in bungholes. We have them on patching fibreglass and sail repair. We have them on anything that a person might need to do on a boat. Cherry organises the playshops. She is a good people person. Our playshops are a success. Success is doing well when everyone thought you would not. I am a success.

EVERETT CHAMBER OF COMMERCE TO HOLD BANQUET
HONOURING LOCAL BUSINESSES

The Chamber of Commerce is a bunch of businesspeople that give each other awards. Holsted's is getting an award for having big ideas. Cherry will wear her new dress. It is long and red. Her stomach is huge. She will have Keith's baby any day now. She likes red. You can only see one small tattoo when she puts it on. Her hair is brown now and very short. I get mine cut and buy a new suit. Gary helps pick it out.

'Navy blue, Per. That's your colour.'

I look like a businessman. I look like Perry L. Crandall.

A banquet is a big dinner. They give you fancy hot food and real napkins. My collar is tight around my neck and makes it hard to swallow my dinner. I am not used to suits. They make me walk funny. Gary has to make a speech, and Mr Jordan from Everett Federal bank introduces him.

'I'd like to present this year's Business Vision Award to Holsted and Crandall Marine Supply.'

When Gary stands up, he grabs me by the elbow and drags me up to the front of the room with him. White faces stare up at me. It is quiet.

'I'd like to thank you all. Winning this award is a great honour. The person responsible is standing right next to me,' Gary says. 'My partner,

Perry L. Crandall.' He pushes me in front of the microphone and whispers, 'It's OK, Per. Just talk to them like you talk to me. Go ahead.'

I have to say some words to a lot of people I do not know. I am so scared, I think I might wet my pants. I do not know what to say. All I see are faces. Then I hear them. I hear Gram. I hear Keith. Telling me what to do. But they are saying words I already know. And I am not scared any more. I do not need them to tell me what to say.

'My name is Perry L. Crandall and I am not retarded.' I say this and take a deep breath. 'My Gram always said the L in my name stands for Lucky. It does. I am lucky.' Some faces laugh because they know about the lottery, but that is not the luck I am talking about.

'I am lucky to be a businessman and I am lucky to have a family. I am lucky because I am a good worker. Being a good worker is very important. I learned how to work hard from my Gramp. I learned how to try hard and do words from my Gram, and I learned all about love from my friend, Keith.' Some of the faces are smiling. Some of these faces knew Keith, some knew Gram and some knew my Gramp.

'They would be happy that people get to know me now. They would be happy that after people get to know me, they decide maybe they like me, or maybe they don't. But that's OK. They get to know me. I am a businessman. That is so cool. Thank you.'

The people stand up and clap. They clap for a long, long time. Mr Jordan hands Gary a wood thing to hang on our wall. It has both our names on it.

My picture is in the business section of the Sunday paper. I think I look goofy. Cherry tells me no.

'It's a great picture, Perry. I'm cutting it out. We'll put it in your book.'

THE MONEY IS ALL GONE.

That is what the newspaper said when they printed the interview story. It is also what Louise said in the letter she wrote to ask me for more money. She wrote me saying she saw my picture in the Sunday paper and asked me to sell my share of Holsted's. I said no. It is what I decided.

Gram said no in my head. Keith is there with her. He said no. And Cherry is beside me and helped me write the letter answering Louise.

'*NO WAY!*' she wrote in giant letters on the outside of the envelope.

And then she went into labour.

Labour is when you work really hard to have a baby. I am glad he did not hear all the bad language she used, because he was still inside. It took him fourteen hours to decide to come out. He is a thinker. Like me.

Baby Keith was born the next day at noon. I was the second person to hold him besides the nurse. Her name was Carol. She was dressed in blue. Keith Perry George Crandall. Eight pounds and seven ounces.

He was huge. Keith would have been proud that he had the biggest baby in the hospital that week. I was hoping they gave a prize but they did not. That is such a gyp.

A WEEK LATER, we are reading the paper and looking for Baby Keith's name. He is listed on the back page under birth announcements. The front page has a photo of my cousin-brother John. Cherry is the one who found it.

'Perry, look at this! It's your brother John. It says he's in protective custody. He's turning state's evidence for some money-laundering scam!'

Cherry says *protective custody* means John is in jail. She says it means there are bad people out there that want to hurt him. The newspaper says that his brother David has disappeared.

'What happened, Cherry?' I ask her. 'Read me the rest.'

'It says here that David Crandall is wanted for questioning. They think he's left the country with the proceeds of the trust.' She laughs. 'Like his father! He ran off. Vamoosed! He ditched that bitch of a wife of his, grabbed all the money and dug out. Elaine, John and Louise are left holding the bag. David took it all! Ha! Good for him!'

Holding the bag means somebody took what was inside and you have nothing. Except for a bag. 'I wonder where he is,' I say.

'The Caymans. South America. He's probably with your father spending all the money.' And she laughs again.

Baby Keith sucks on her boob. That is so cool. I did not know boobs gave out baby food.

Two months later, a postcard comes in the mail addressed to me. There is a beautiful picture of a white beach with palm trees. The postmark is from the country named after a nut. It is not signed but I think it is from David.

It's just like you said on TV, Per. Everybody should get what they want. Take care and God bless.

'I don't think you have to worry about any of them any more,' Gary says.

But I do not worry.

Gary says Holsted and Crandall is our future and we cannot sell it.

'If someone ever asks you to sell, they are trying to take advantage of you, because they think you're retarded. They're making a big mistake.' He laughs. 'You're definitely not retarded, but you know what, Perry? It wouldn't make a damn bit of difference. You're still one hell of a businessman.'

We are going to open another store in Anacortes next fall. It is another place with lots of boats and people who need boat stuff, just like Everett.

Gary asked my advice and I told him. It was my idea.

'Lots of boats stop in Anacortes on their way to the San Juan Islands. Those boaters always forget something. We should have a store there,' I say.

'That's what I mean, Per, one hell of a businessman,' Gary says.

Epilogue

Wolfgang Amadeus Mozart said, 'Neither a lofty degree of intelligence nor imagination nor both together go to the making of genius. Love, love, love, that is the soul of genius.'

This was written inside the card Cherry got me for my birthday. It was tied to the collar of a brown puppy.

'He's chocolate Lab and something else. The lady didn't know what,' Cherry told me.

I was so excited I bounced, and my puppy did too. Just like me.

'Everybody should get what they want,' Cherry said, and kissed my bouncing chin. 'Especially you.'

A dog! He licks my face and follows me around. I named him Bounce because that is what we both do when we are happy. He knows his name and I already taught him to sit. He is very smart. He comes when I whistle and asks to go outside when he has to poop and pee. I take him for walks and do not even need a leash. That is so cool. Even Gary likes that we have Bounce. He says dogs are good for security.

The card Cherry gave me sits on my desk at work. I read it every day. I do not understand the first part, but I understand the second. *Love.* It is something that cannot be taken. I think that is true. I keep the card to remind me that I have what I want. I have always had what I wanted. Love. When I was young, I had Gramp and Gram. When I got older, I had Gary and Keith. And now I have Cherry and Baby Keith. And Bounce.

Baby Keith will be one year old next week.

I play with him every morning when I help change and feed him. He started eating real food like us. He only has four teeth. Cherry says he will get more soon, but I am not sure. I never saw a baby grow up before.

Whenever Baby Keith cries, he stops right away when I pick him up. That is so cool. He started walking at nine months. That is fast for a baby, Cherry says. If he falls down or is hungry, he will stop crying just for me.

'He loves you, Per.' Cherry will watch us and smile. 'Like me,' she says.

Baby Keith says, 'Da. Da.' He grabs my hand and puts it in his mouth.

'He's beautiful,' I say, and my fingers brush his cheek.

Baby Keith comes into Holsted and Crandall's every day. He is quiet and looks around with wide brown eyes. I know what he is doing. He is studying for the time he will work at our store. I help him walk around and give him boxes to push and cardboard to tear.

Cherry and I are married now. I thought about this for many months.

First, I heard Gram's voice. *Are you going to marry her, Perry? Are you?*

Then Keith's voice. *Marry her, Per.*

'Should we get married?' I ask.

'Why?' she asks me. 'What difference would it make?' Then she kisses me and says, 'But I will if you want to.'

That is a good answer, I think. People should get what they want.

'I want to, Cherry,' I say. 'Baby Keith needs a mother and father with the same last name so when he goes to school nobody will tease.' This is very important for Baby Keith, I tell her.

She takes my hand and says, 'You're right, Per. You're absolutely right.'

We get married on *Diamond Girl* and have something called a honeymoon. It is a tiny trip that you take after you get married.

We do not go far. We sleep on *Diamond Girl*. She stays tied to the dock. The water laps against the hull and Baby Keith sleeps between us. Bounce stays up in the cockpit. He is too big for down below now. He grew fast because his paws were too big for his body.

Diamond Girl is mine. Keith left her to me. I scrub her gelcoat and wax and polish her sides like I always wanted to do for Keith. I do it for us now, for Cherry and me. She shines now like a real diamond.

I would rather have Keith alive, but a sailboat is cool. I also got $75,000 from Keith's life insurance policy from Holsted's. It will be for Baby Keith's education. He will go to college. He is smart, and not at all slow.

Cherry and I invest together.

'More than a quarter of a million dollars in the savings account now.' That is what Cherry says. 'That's a lot of money.' Then she looks at me and smiles. 'But it's only money, isn't it? It doesn't really matter. It is us that matter. That's just for our future.' She says that just like Gram. But she knows it is not just for mine. It is for hers too, and Baby Keith's. We are a family.

I am teaching Cherry how to sail. Out on Puget Sound the waves are green. The sky is blue with grey clouds over Whidbey Island. It is warm and there is just enough wind. Baby Keith is asleep, wrapped in his life jacket and harness. He lies sideways on the floor of the cockpit. Bounce sits next to me looking for seagulls. He is a good seagull finder.

'No, Bounce,' I tell him. 'Quiet,' I whisper. 'You will wake Baby Keith.' And he looks at me and does what I say. That is so cool.

I am very careful with Cherry and Baby Keith. Sometimes I worry.

'Am I too slow?' I ask Cherry. 'Am I too slow for people?'

But she only smiles. 'You are fast enough for me,' she says.

We watch seals dive and swim and think of Keith. Cherry puts her hand in the water and we talk about him. And remember. Then she blows me a kiss and laughs. It is good to hear her laugh.

I turn *Diamond Girl* around and teach Cherry how to work the tiller.

'Push! The other way!' I say. 'You can do it!'

She pushes. 'It's the opposite of what you think,' Cherry says. 'Not like a car. It's the opposite.' She tries again. 'Like a lot of things,' she tells me. 'Like money. Like love. The opposite of what you think.'

I still do my words every day. I am up to the U's because sometimes I have time only for two words. I am very busy. I have lots to do, like work at Holsted and Crandall's, play with Baby Keith and walk Bounce every day. I buy blank books for Baby Keith, just like the ones Gram got for me. I tape pictures on each page and write things down just like Gram. I still get imitation crab sandwiches at Gilly's and I buy Slurpees at Marina Handy Mart. My family has Saturday spaghetti nights with Gary's family.

My name is Perry L. Crandall and I am not retarded.

I am a businessman. I have Bounce. I have Baby Keith. And I have Cherry. Gram was right about my name. The L does stand for Lucky.

This is true.

PATRICIA WOOD

Former careers: teacher; US Army WAC
Place of residence: Hawaii
Blog: pkwood.blogspot.com

RD: What inspired you to write *Lottery*?
PW: The idea came to me through an intermingling of many circumstances: a former brother-in-law had Down syndrome so I knew a little about what it's like to appear to others to be 'slow'; I have taught students with mental challenges; and my father once won the Washington State Lottery.

RD: Did the win change his life, and was it for better or worse?
PW: It did change his life, and not entirely for the better. At times it was difficult for him to know who his friends were, and it greatly altered the dynamics in our extended family. A lottery win often comes to define a person and the luck can bring about guilt.

RD: Where did you grow up and what do you remember about it?
PW: I grew up in Seattle and on San Juan, a small island in Puget Sound off the coast of Washington State. As a child, I spent hours along the shore, and the pungent smell of seaweed permeates my memories and instantly takes me back to my youth.

RD: You served for a time in the Women's Army Corps. Did you enjoy that part of your life, and how long did it last?
PW: I joined the army when I was studying to become a nurse but couldn't afford to stay at college. I was on active duty for just over two years in the early 70s. It was a unique experience—I was caught between the Vietnam conflict and the peace movement—and I have created some of my most compelling and authentic characters from that time, eg Keith in *Lottery*.

RD: How did you meet your current husband, and which of you first came up with the idea of living on a boat?
PW: I met Gordon when I was teaching riding for the University of Washington. He became interested in my competitive riding and I became interested in his fascination with sailing. So it was a mutual decision, really. He lived aboard a 27-foot sloop while he was at college and is still an avid sailor. I, too, have always lived near the sea.

RD: When did you move to Hawaii and was it a hard decision?
PW: My husband is from Hawaii, but it was I who had an irresistible urge to move here after my very first trip to the island of Oahu. As soon as I stepped off the plane and

smelled the fragrant plumeria, I knew I had to move to Hawaii. Luckily, Gordon was happy to move back home, too.

RD: What's it like living on a boat, as you do?

PW: It's an experience unlike any other. The accommodations on board *Orion* are compact and she requires us to be alert to both the weather and her inner workings. The gusty trade winds push her hard against her lines and sea turtles and fish surround her. I go to sleep to the sound of lapping water and am prepared to go up on deck at a moment's notice to tighten a flapping halyard. It is not for everyone, but it is for us.

RD: And what do you enjoy most about Hawaii?

PW: The climate and environment—the warmth, the sun, the sapphire ocean and caressing breezes. There is a unique ambiance in the tropics. We also have a wide diversity of cultures and ethnicities here. But what do I truly love most? The fact I do not have to shovel any snow off my sidewalk in the winter.

RD: You've wanted to write since you were very young, yet *Lottery* is your first published novel; what made you start work on it when you did?

PW: At fifty I took stock of my life and decided that if I wanted to be a novelist I'd better start now. Once I started writing, I couldn't stop. I like to think being an author gives one permission to be a wee bit schizophrenic, and I hear the characters talking to me in my head. When Perry first spoke, it was out of the blue: 'My name is Perry L. Crandall and I am not retarded.' And then, bit-by-bit, he told me his whole story.

RD: Can you sum the book up in a single phrase?

PW: I think it's a statement of our times, about how we marginalise people, how we value money and intelligence, and how we sometimes don't value heart.

RD: Have you ever been afraid when sailing, riding or doing other sports?

PW: I am a risk taker. I have fear but it is a fear of not trying. Of not taking chances and living one of those 'lives of quiet desperation'. But I only take risks over which I have control: for example, after over a hundred scuba dives, and with the work I have done in marine science, I have no fear of sharks because I know about them.

RD: And if you had to describe yourself in three words?

PW: Nonconforming Renaissance Woman.

RD: If you could keep one thing for eternity—a possession, a memory, perhaps—what would it be?

PW: To always remember each time love came into my life.

RD: What, to you, is the key to a happy and fulfilled existence?

PW: To not take no for an answer. Be persistent, focused, and have fun.

RD: Are there things you still want to achieve in your life?

PW: Yes, many. I want to write more books. Travel. Learn about other places and people. Teach writing.